Praise for
Charlaine Harris
and her Anthony Award–winning
Sookie Stackhouse novels

"It's the kind of book you look forward to reading before you go to bed, thinking you're only going to read one chapter, and then you end up reading seven." —Alan Ball on *Dead Until Dark*

"Vivid, subtle, and funny in her portrayal of southern life."
—*Entertainment Weekly*

"Charlaine Harris has vividly imagined telepathic barmaid Sookie Stackhouse and her small-town Louisiana milieu, where humans, vampires, shapeshifters, and other sentient critters live . . . Her mash-up of genres is delightful, taking elements from mysteries, horror stories, and romances." —*Milwaukee Journal Sentinel*

"Blending action, romance, and comedy, Harris has created a fully functioning world so very close to our own, except, of course, for the vamps and other supernatural creatures."
—*The Toronto Star*

"[An] entertaining series . . . It['s] easy to understand why these oddly charming books have become so popular."
—*The New Orleans Times-Picayune*

"[A] light, fun series." —*Los Angeles Times*

"It's a bit hard to imagine having vampires and werewolves lurking around every corner, but Harris has a way of making the reader buy it hook, line, and sinker." —*The Monroe (LA) News-Star*

"I love the imaginative, creative world of Charlaine Harris!"
—Christine Feehan, #1 *New York Times* bestselling author of
Ruthless Game

W9-BUL-141

continued . . .

DEAD IN THE FAMILY

"Another delicious installment of Charlaine Harris's southern vampire mysteries . . . Harris treasures the everyday routines of small-town family life, burnishing little moments until they glow."
—*Los Angeles Times*

"What sucked me in? Definitely the book's oddly charming, often funny mix of the mundane and the absurd. And the chills and thrills in boudoirs and various locales around the South aren't too bad, either."
—*The Seattle Times*

"A light and entertaining world . . . engaging."
—*Phillyist*

"Old friends abound, characters deepen, and you'll hope the next book is not too far away. This series is very much alive and kicking despite all the death in the titles."
—*SFRevu*

"A well-told, enjoyable story with some definite twists. Fans of the series will definitely want to read about Sookie's latest adventure."
—*Vampire Genre*

"A perfectly rendered narrative . . . one of the most powerful and thematically coherent novels in the series . . . with incredible emotional poignancy and thematic cogency."
—*Dear Author*

"It's almost like a newer take on the Southern Grotesque genre that we love so dearly—this time only with vampires."
—*Seatlest*

DEAD AND GONE

"Harris's creation offers a magical and mysterious twist on traditional vampire stories."
—*Houston Chronicle*

FROM DEAD TO WORSE

"The series continues to be inventive and funny, with an engaging, smart, and sexy heroine."
—*The Denver Post*

ALL TOGETHER DEAD

"Charlaine Harris's talent is a marvelous thing . . . Both new and old characters continue to charm us as they develop. Reading just one of the books will addict you."
—*The Eternal Night*

DEFINITELY DEAD

"A grand blend of mystery-cum-fantasy with dollops of romance and humor."
—*Library Journal*

DEAD AS A DOORNAIL

"[A] delightful southern vampire detective series."
—*The Denver Post*

DEAD TO THE WORLD

"A supernatural battle to rival anything in Harry Potter . . . wacky humor and [a] giddy breakneck pace."
—*The Dallas Morning News*

CLUB DEAD

"Charlaine Harris delivers both horror and humor as seen from the unique perspective of rural America."
—Tanya Huff, author of *The Truth of Valor*

LIVING DEAD IN DALLAS

"A genre mix refreshingly free of the expected tropes."   —*Locus*

DEAD UNTIL DARK
One of *Locus* Magazine's Best Books of the Year

"Highly original, extraordinarily riveting, erotic, and exotic . . . Harris weaves storytelling magic in a tale of vampires and small-town Louisiana."   —Lynn Hightower, author of *When Secrets Die*

DEAD IN
THE FAMILY

Charlaine Harris

ACE BOOKS, NEW YORK

THE BERKLEY PUBLISHING GROUP
Published by the Penguin Group
Penguin Group (USA) Inc.
375 Hudson Street, New York, New York 10014, USA
Penguin Group (Canada), 90 Eglinton Avenue East, Suite 700, Toronto, Ontario M4P 2Y3, Canada
(a division of Pearson Penguin Canada Inc.)
Penguin Books Ltd., 80 Strand, London WC2R 0RL, England
Penguin Books Ireland, 25 St. Stephen's Green, Dublin 2, Ireland (a division of Penguin Books Ltd.)
Penguin Group (Australia), 250 Camberwell Road, Camberwell, Victoria 3124, Australia
(a division of Pearson Australia Group Pty. Ltd.)
Penguin Books India Pvt. Ltd., 11 Community Centre, Panchsheel Park, New Delhi—110 017, India
Penguin Group (NZ), 67 Apollo Drive, Rosedale, North Shore 0632, New Zealand
(a division of Pearson New Zealand Ltd.)
Penguin Books (South Africa) (Pty.) Ltd., 24 Sturdee Avenue, Rosebank, Johannesburg 2196,
South Africa

Penguin Books Ltd., Registered Offices: 80 Strand, London WC2R 0RL, England

This is a work of fiction. Names, characters, places, and incidents either are the product of the author's imagination or are used fictitiously, and any resemblance to actual persons, living or dead, business establishments, events, or locales is entirely coincidental. The publisher does not have any control over and does not assume any responsibility for author or third-party websites or their content.

DEAD IN THE FAMILY

An Ace Book / published by arrangement with Charlaine Harris, Inc.

PRINTING HISTORY
Ace hardcover edition / May 2010
Ace mass-market edition / April 2011

Copyright © 2010 by Charlaine Harris, Inc.
Excerpt from *Dead Reckoning* copyright © by Charlaine Harris, Inc.
Cover art by Lisa Desimini.
Cover design by Judith Lagerman.
Interior text design by Kristin del Rosario.

ISBN: 978-0-441-02015-7

ACE
Ace Books are published by The Berkley Publishing Group,
a division of Penguin Group (USA) Inc.,
375 Hudson Street, New York, New York 10014.
ACE and the "A" design are trademarks of Penguin Group (USA) Inc.

PRINTED IN THE UNITED STATES OF AMERICA

10 9 8 7 6 5 4 3 2 1

This book is dedicated to our son Patrick,
who has not only met our hopes, dreams,
and expectations for him,
but exceeded them.

ACKNOWLEDGMENTS

I am only the first step in the creation of this book. Many other people helped in different capacities along the way: Anastasia Luettecke, who taught me about Roman names; Dr. Ed Uthman, who helps me with medical stuff; Victoria and Debi, my continuity mavens; Toni L. P. Kelner and Dana Cameron, whose gentle comments after their first reading keep me from committing many an error; Paula Woldan, whose help and friendship keep me going; Lisa Desimini, the cover artist; Jodi Rosoff, my wonderful publicist; Ginjer Buchanan, my long-suffering editor; and my Mod Squad: Michele, Victoria, Kerri, MariCarmen, and Lindsay (current), and Debi, Beverly, and Katie (retired).

DEAD IN
THE FAMILY

MARCH
THE FIRST WEEK

"I feel bad that I'm leaving you like this," *Amelia said. Her* eyes were puffy and red. They'd been that way, off and on, ever since Tray Dawson's funeral.

"You have to do what you have to do," I said, giving her a very bright smile. I could read the guilt and shame and ever-present grief roiling around Amelia's mind in a ball of darkness. "I'm lots better," I reassured her. I could hear myself babbling cheerfully along, but I couldn't seem to stop. "I'm walking okay, and the holes are all filled in. See how much better?" I pulled down my jeans waistband to show her a spot that had been bitten out. The teeth marks were hardly perceptible, though the skin wasn't quite smooth and was visibly paler than the surrounding flesh. If I hadn't had a huge dose of vampire blood, the scar would've looked like a shark had bitten me.

Amelia glanced down and hastily away, as if she couldn't bear to see the evidence of the attack. "It's just that Octavia keeps e-mailing me and telling me I need to come home and accept my judgment from the witches' council, or what's left of it," she said in a rush. "And I need to check all the repairs to my house. And since there are a few tourists again, and people returning and rebuilding, the magic store's reopened. I can work there part-time. Plus, as much as I love you and I love living here, since Tray died . . ."

"Believe me, I understand." We'd gone over this a few times.

"It's not that I blame you," Amelia said, trying to catch my eyes.

She really didn't blame me. Since I could read her mind, I knew she was telling me the truth.

Even *I* didn't totally blame myself, somewhat to my surprise.

It was true that Tray Dawson, Amelia's lover and a Were, had been killed while he'd been acting as my bodyguard. It was true that I'd requested a bodyguard from the Were pack nearest me because they owed me a favor and my life needed guarding. However, I'd been present at the death of Tray Dawson at the hands of a sword-wielding fairy, and I knew who was responsible.

So I didn't feel guilty, exactly. But I felt heartsick about losing Tray, on top of all the other horrors. My cousin Claudine, a full-blooded fairy, had also died in the Fae War, and since she'd been my real, true fairy godmother, I missed her in a lot of ways. And she'd been pregnant.

I had a lot of pain and regret of all kinds, physical and mental. While Amelia carried an armful of clothes downstairs, I stood in her bedroom, gathering myself. Then I braced my shoulders and lifted a box of bathroom odds and ends. I descended the stairs carefully and slowly, and I made my way out to her car. She turned from depositing the clothes across the boxes already stowed in her trunk. "You shouldn't be doing that!" she said, all anxious concern. "You're not healed yet."

"I'm fine."

"Not hardly. You always jump when someone comes into the room and surprises you, and I can tell your wrists hurt," she said. She grabbed the box and slid it into the backseat. "You still favor that left leg, and you still ache when it rains. Despite all that vamp blood."

"The jumpiness'll get better. As time passes, it won't be so fresh and at the front of my mind," I told Amelia. (If telepathy had taught me anything, it was that people could bury the most serious and painful of memories, if you gave them enough time and distraction.) "The blood is not just any vampire's. It's Eric's blood. It's strong stuff. And my wrists are a lot better." I didn't mention that the nerves were jumping around in them like hot snakes just at this moment, a result of their having been tied together tightly for several hours. Dr. Ludwig, physician to the supernatural, had told me the nerves—and the wrists—would be back to normal, eventually.

"Yeah, speaking of the blood . . ." Amelia took a deep breath and steeled herself to say something she knew I wouldn't like. Since I heard it before she actually voiced it, I was able to brace myself. "Had you thought about . . . Sookie, you didn't ask me, but I think you better not have any more of Eric's blood. I mean, I know he's your man, but you got to think about the consequences. Sometimes people get flipped by accident. It's not like it's a math equation."

Though I appreciated Amelia's concern, she'd trespassed into private territory. "We don't swap," I said. *Much.* "He

just has a sip from me at, you know . . . the happy moment."
These days Eric was having a lot more happy moments than
I was, sadly. I kept hoping the bedroom magic would return;
if any male could perform sexual healing, that male would
be Eric.

Amelia smiled, which was what I'd been aiming for. "At
least . . ." She turned away without finishing the sentence,
but she was thinking, *At least you feel like having sex.*

I didn't so much feel like having sex as I felt like I ought to
keep trying to enjoy it, but I definitely didn't want to discuss
that. My ability to cast aside control, which is the key to good
sex, had been pinched out of existence during the torture. I'd
been absolutely helpless. I could only hope that I'd recover in
that area, too. I knew Eric could feel my lack of completion.
He'd asked me several times if I was sure I wanted to engage
in sex. Nearly every time, I said yes, operating on the bicycle
theory. Yes, I'd fallen off. But I was always willing to try to
ride it again.

"So, how's the relationship doing?" she said. "Aside from
the whoopee." Every last thing was in Amelia's car. She was
stalling, dreading the moment when she actually got into her
car and drove away.

It was only pride that was keeping me from bawling all
over her.

"I think we're getting along pretty well," I said with a
great effort at sounding cheerful. "I'm still not sure what
I feel as opposed to what the bond is making me feel." It
was kind of nice to be able to talk about my supernatural
connection to Eric, as well as my regular old man-woman
attraction. Even before my injuries during the Fae War, Eric
and I had established what the vampires called a blood bond,

since we'd exchanged blood several times. I could sense Eric's general location and his mood, and he could feel the same things about me. He was always faintly present in the back of my mind—sort of like turning on a fan or an air filter to provide a little buzz of noise that would help you get to sleep. (It was good for me that Eric slept all day, because I could be by myself at least part of the time. Maybe he felt the same way after I went to bed at night?) It wasn't like I heard voices in my head or anything—at least no more than usual. But if I felt happy, I had to check to make sure it was me and not Eric who felt happy. Likewise for anger; Eric was big on anger, controlled and carefully banked anger, especially lately. Maybe he was getting that from me. I was pretty full of anger myself these days.

I'd forgotten all about Amelia. I'd stepped right into my own trough of depression.

She snapped me out of it. "That's just a big fat excuse," she said tartly. "Come on, Sookie. You love him, or you don't. Don't keep putting off thinking about it by blaming everything on your bond. Wah, wah, wah. If you hate the bond so much, why haven't you explored how you can get free of it?" She took in the expression on my face, and the irritation faded out of her own. "Do you want me to ask Octavia?" she asked in a milder voice. "If anyone would know, she would."

"Yes, I'd like to find out," I said, after a moment. I took a deep breath. "You're right, I guess. I've been so depressed I've put off making any decisions, or acting on the ones I've already made. Eric's one of a kind. But I find him . . . a little overwhelming." He was a strong personality, and he was used to being the big fish in the pond. He also knew he had infinite time ahead of him.

I did not.

He hadn't brought that up yet, but sooner or later, he would.

"Overwhelming or not, I love him," I continued. I'd never said it out loud. "And I guess that's the bottom line."

"I guess it is." Amelia tried to smile at me, but it was a woeful attempt. "Listen, you keep that up, the self-knowledge thing." She stood for a moment, her expression frozen into the half smile. "Well, Sook, I better get on the road. My dad's expecting me. He'll be all up in my business the minute I get back to New Orleans."

Amelia's dad was rich, powerful, and had no belief in Amelia's power at all. He was very wrong not to respect her witchcraft. Amelia had been born with the potential for the power in her, as every true witch is. Once Amelia had some more training and discipline, she was going to be really scary—scary on purpose, rather than because of the drastic nature of her mistakes. I hoped her mentor, Octavia, had a program in place to develop and train Amelia's talent.

After I waved Amelia down the driveway, the broad smile dropped from my face. I sat on the porch steps and cried. It didn't take much for me to be in tears these days, and my friend's departure was just the trigger now. There was so much to weep about.

My sister-in-law, Crystal, had been murdered. My brother's friend Mel had been executed. Tray and Claudine and Clancy the vampire had been killed in the line of duty. Since both Crystal and Claudine had been pregnant, that added two more deaths to the list.

Probably that should have made me long for peace above all else. But instead of turning into the Bon Temps Gandhi, in my heart I held the knowledge that there were plenty of people I wanted dead. I wasn't directly responsible for most of the deaths that were scattered in my wake, but I was haunted by the feeling that none of them would have happened if it weren't for me. In my darkest moments—and this was one of them—I wondered if my life was worth the price that had been paid for it.

MARCH
THE END OF THE FIRST WEEK

My cousin Claude was sitting on the front porch when I got up on a cloudy, brisk morning a few days after Amelia's departure. Claude wasn't as skilled at masking his presence as my great-grandfather Niall was. Because Claude was fae, I couldn't read his mind—but I could tell his mind was there, if that isn't too obscure a way to put it. I carried my coffee out to the porch, though the air was nippy, because drinking that first cup on the porch had been one of my favorite things to do before I . . . before the Fae War.

I hadn't seen my cousin in weeks. I hadn't seen him during the Fae War, and he hadn't contacted me since the death of Claudine.

I'd brought an extra mug for Claude, and I handed it to him. He accepted it silently. I'd considered the possibility he might throw it in my face. His unexpected presence had knocked me off course. I had no idea what to expect. The breeze lifted his long black hair, tossed it around like rippling ebony ribbons. His caramel eyes were red-rimmed.

"How did she die?" he said.

I sat on the top step. "I didn't see it," I said, hunching over my knees. "We were in that old building Dr. Ludwig was using as a hospital. I think Claudine was trying to stop the other fairies from coming down the corridor to get into the room where I was holed up with Bill and Eric and Tray." I looked over at Claude to make sure he knew the place, and he nodded. "I'm pretty sure that it was Breandan who killed her, because one of her knitting needles was stuck in his shoulder when he busted into our room."

Breandan, my great-grandfather's enemy, had also been a prince of the fae. Breandan had believed that humans and the fae should not consort. He'd believed that to the point of fanaticism. He'd wanted the fae to completely abstain from their forays into the human world, despite the fae's large financial stake in mundane commerce and the products it had produced . . . products that helped them blend into the modern world. Breandan had especially hated the occasional taking of human lovers, a fae indulgence, and he'd hated the children born as a result of such liaisons. He'd wanted the fae separate, walled away into their own world, consorting only with their own kind.

Oddly enough, that's what my great-grandfather had decided to do after defeating the fairy who believed in this apartheid policy. After all the bloodshed, Niall concluded that peace among the fae and safety for humans could be reached only if the fae blocked themselves into their world. Breandan had achieved his ends by his own death. In my worst moments, I thought that Niall's final decision had made the whole war unnecessary.

"She was defending you," Claude said, pulling me back into the moment. There was nothing in his voice. Not blame, not anger, not a question.

"Yeah." That had been part of her job, defending me, by Niall's orders.

I took a long sip of coffee. Claude's sat untouched on the arm of the porch swing. Maybe Claude was wondering if he should kill me. Claudine had been his last surviving sibling.

"You knew about the pregnancy," he said finally.

"She told me right before she was killed." I put down my mug and wrapped my arms around my knees. I waited for the blow to fall. At first I didn't mind all that much, which was even more horrible.

Claude said, "I understand Neave and Lochlan had hold of you. Is that why you're limping?" The change of subject caught me off guard.

"Yeah," I said. "They had me for a couple of hours. Niall and Bill Compton killed them. Just so you know—it was Bill who killed Breandan, with my grandmother's iron trowel." Though the trowel had been in my family's toolshed for decades, I associated it with Gran.

Claude sat, beautiful and unreadable, for a long time. He never looked at me directly nor drank his coffee. When he'd reached some inner conclusion, he rose and left, walking down the driveway toward Hummingbird Road. I don't know where his car was parked. For all I knew, he'd walked all the way from Monroe, or flown over on a magic carpet. I went into the house, sank to my knees right inside the door, and cried. My hands were shaking. My wrists ached.

The whole time we'd been talking, I'd been waiting for him to make his move.

I realized I wanted to live.

MARCH
THE SECOND WEEK

*JB said, "Raise your arm all the way up, Sookie!" His hand-*some face was creased with concentration. Holding the five-pound weight, I slowly lifted my left arm. Geez Louise, it hurt. Same with the right.

"Okay, now the legs," JB said, when my arms were shaking with strain. JB wasn't a licensed physical therapist, but he was a personal trainer, so he'd had practical experience helping people get over various injuries. Maybe he'd never faced an assortment like mine, since I'd been bitten, cut, and tortured. But I hadn't had to explain the details to JB, and he wouldn't notice that my injuries were far from typical of those incurred in a car accident. I didn't want any speculation going around Bon Temps about my physical problems—so I made the occasional visits to Dr. Amy Ludwig, who looked suspiciously like a hobbit, and I enlisted the help of JB du Rone, who was a good trainer but dumb as a box of rocks.

JB's wife, my friend Tara, was sitting on one of the weight

benches. She was reading *What to Expect When You're Expecting*. Tara, almost five months pregnant, was determined to be the best mother she could possibly be. Since JB was willing but not bright, Tara was assuming the role of Most Responsible Parent. She'd earned her high school spending money as a babysitter, which gave her some experience in child care. She was frowning as she turned the pages, a look familiar to me from our school years.

"Have you picked a doctor yet?" I said, after I'd finished my leg lifts. My quads were screaming, particularly the damaged one in my left leg. We were in the gym where JB worked, and it was after hours, because I wasn't a member. JB's boss had okayed the temporary arrangement to keep JB happy. JB was a huge asset to the gym; since he'd started working, new female clients had increased by a noticeable percentage.

"I think so," said Tara. "There were four choices in this area, and we interviewed all of them. I've had my first appointment with Dr. Dinwiddie, here in Clarice. I know it's a little hospital, but I'm not high risk, and it's so close."

Clarice was just a few miles from Bon Temps, where we all lived. You could get from my house to the gym in less than twenty minutes.

"I hear good things about him," I said, the pain in my quads making stuff start to slide around inside my head. My forehead broke out in a clammy sweat. I was used to thinking of myself as a fit woman, and mostly I'd been a happy one. There were days now when it was all I could do to get out of bed and get in to work.

"Sook," JB said, "look at the weight on here." He was grinning at me.

For the first time, I registered that I'd done ten extensions with ten more pounds than I'd been using.

I smiled back at him. It didn't last long, but I knew I'd done something good.

"Maybe you'll babysit for us sometime," Tara said. "We'll teach the baby to call you Aunt Sookie."

I'd be a courtesy aunt. I'd get to take care of a baby. They trusted me. I found myself planning on a future.

MARCH
THE SAME WEEK

I spent the next night with Eric. As I did at least three or four times a week, I woke up panting, filled with terror, completely at sea. I held on to him as if the storm would sweep me away unless he was my anchor. I was already crying when I woke. It wasn't the first time this had happened, but this time he wept with me, bloody tears that streaked the whiteness of his face in a startling way.

"Don't," I begged him. I had been trying so hard to act like my old self when I was with him. Of course, he knew differently. Tonight I could feel his resolve. Eric had something to say to me, and he was going to tell me whether I wanted to listen or not.

"I could feel your fear and your pain that night," he said, in a choked voice. "But I couldn't come to you."

Finally, he was telling me something I had been waiting to learn.

"Why not?" I said, trying very hard to keep my voice

level. This may seem incredible, but I had been in such shaky condition I hadn't dared to ask him.

"Victor wouldn't let me leave," he said. Victor Madden was Eric's boss; he'd been appointed by Felipe de Castro, King of Nevada, to oversee the conquered kingdom of Louisiana.

My initial reaction to Eric's explanation was bitter disappointment. I'd heard this story before. *A vampire more powerful than me made me do it:* Bill's excuse for going back to his maker, Lorena, revisited. "Sure," I said. I turned over and lay with my back to him. I felt the cold, creeping misery of disillusionment. I decided to pull my clothes on, to drive back to Bon Temps, as soon as I gathered the energy. The tension, the frustration, the rage in Eric was sapping me.

"Victor's people chained me with silver," Eric said behind me. "It burned me everywhere."

"Literally." I tried not to sound as skeptical as I felt.

"Yes, literally. I knew something was happening with you. Victor was at Fangtasia that night, as if he knew ahead of time he should be there. When Bill called to tell me you'd been taken, I managed to call Niall before three of Victor's people chained me to the wall. When I—protested—Victor said he couldn't *allow* me to take sides in the Fae War. He said that no matter what happened to you, I couldn't get involved."

Rage made Eric fall silent for a long moment. It poured through me like a burning, icy stream. He resumed his story in a choked voice.

"Pam was also seized and isolated by Victor's people, though they didn't chain her." Pam was Eric's second-in-command. "Since Bill was in Bon Temps, he was able to ignore Victor's phone messages. Niall met Bill at your house to track you. Bill had heard of Lochlan and Neave. We all had. We knew time would run out for you." I still had my back to Eric, but I was listening to more than his voice. Grief, anger, desperation.

"How did you get out of the chains?" I asked the dark.

"I reminded Victor that Felipe had promised you protection, promised it to you *personally*. Victor pretended not to believe me." I could feel the bed move as Eric threw himself back against the pillows. "Some of the vampires were strong and honorable enough to remember they were pledged to Felipe, not Victor. Though they wouldn't defy Victor to his face, behind his back they let Pam call our new king. When she had Felipe on the line, she explained to him that you and I had married. Then she demanded Victor take the telephone and talk to Felipe. Victor didn't dare to refuse. Felipe ordered Victor to let me go." A few months ago, Felipe de Castro had become the king of Nevada, Louisiana, *and* Arkansas. He was powerful, old, and very crafty. And he owed me big-time.

"Did Felipe punish Victor?" Hope springs eternal.

"There's the rub," Eric said. Somewhere along the line, my Viking honey had read Shakespeare. "Victor claimed he'd temporarily forgotten our marriage." Even if I sometimes tried to forget it myself, that made me angry. Victor had been sitting right there in Eric's office when I'd handed the ceremonial knife to Eric—in complete ignorance that my action constituted a marriage, vampire-style. I might have been ignorant, but Victor certainly wasn't. "Victor told our king that I was lying in an attempt to save my human lover from the fae. He said vampire lives must not be lost in the rescue of a human. He told Felipe that he hadn't believed Pam and me when we'd told him Felipe had promised you protection after you saved him from Sigebert."

I rolled over to face Eric, and the bit of moonlight coming

in the window painted him in shades of dark and silver. In my brief experience of the powerful vampire who'd maneuvered himself into a position of great power, Felipe was absolutely no fool. "Incredible. Why didn't Felipe kill Victor?" I asked.

"I've given that a lot of thought, of course. I think Felipe has to pretend he believes Victor. I think Felipe realizes that in making Victor his lieutenant in charge of the whole state of Louisiana, he has inflated Victor's ambitions to the point of indecency."

It was possible to look at Eric objectively, I discovered, while I was thinking over what he'd said. My trust had gotten me burned in the past, and I wasn't going to get too close to the fire this time without careful consideration. It was one thing to enjoy laughing with Eric or to look forward to the times when we twined together in the dark. It was another thing to trust him with more fragile emotions. I was really not into trust right now.

"You were upset when you came to the hospital," I said indirectly. When I'd wakened in the old factory Dr. Ludwig was using as a field hospital, my injuries had been so painful I'd thought dying might prove easier than living. Bill, who had saved me, had been poisoned with a bite from Neave's silver teeth. His survival had been up in the air. The mortally wounded Tray Dawson, Amelia's werewolf lover, had hung on long enough to die by the sword when Breandan's forces stormed the hospital.

"While you were with Neave and Lochlan, I suffered with you," he said, meeting my eyes directly. "I hurt with you. I bled with you—not only because we're bonded, but because of the love I have for you."

I raised a skeptical eyebrow. I couldn't help it, though I could feel that he meant what he was saying. I was just willing to believe that Eric would have come to my help much faster, if he could have. I was willing to believe that he'd heard the echo of the horror of my time with the fae torturers.

But my pain and blood and terror had been my own. He might have felt them, but from a separate place. "I believe you would have been there if you could have," I said, knowing my voice was too calm. "I really do believe that. I know you would have killed them." Eric leaned over on one elbow, and his big hand pressed my face to his chest.

I couldn't deny that I felt better since he'd brought himself to tell me. Yet I didn't feel as much better as I'd hoped, though now I knew why he hadn't come when I'd been screaming for him. I could even understand why it had taken so long for him to tell me. Helplessness was a state Eric didn't often encounter. Eric was supernatural, and he was incredibly strong, and he was a great fighter. But he was not a superhero, and he couldn't overcome several determined members of his own race. And I realized he'd given me a lot of blood when he himself was healing from the silver chains.

Finally, something inside me relaxed at the logic of his story. I believed him in my heart, not just in my head.

A red tear fell on my bare shoulder and coursed down. I swept it up on my finger, putting my finger to his lips— offering his pain back to him. I had plenty of my own.

"I think we need to kill Victor," I said, and his eyes met mine.

I'd finally succeeded in surprising Eric.

MARCH
THE THIRD WEEK

"So," my brother said. "As you can tell, me and Michele are still seeing each other." He was standing with his back to me, turning the steaks on the grill. I was sitting in a folding chair, looking out over the large pond and its dock. It was a beautiful evening, cool and brisk. I was actually content to sit there and watch him work; I was enjoying being with Jason. Michele was in the house making a salad. I could hear her singing Travis Tritt.

"I'm glad," I said, and I was sincere. It was the first time I'd been in a private setting with my brother in months. Jason had been through his own bad time. His estranged wife and their unborn child had died horribly. He'd discovered his best male friend had been in love with him, sick in love. But as I watched him grilling, listened to his girlfriend singing inside the house, I understood that Jason was a great survivor. Here my brother was, dating again, pleased at the prospect of eating steak and the mashed potato casserole I'd brought and the salad Michele was making. I had to admire Jason's determination to find pleasure in his life. My brother was not a very good role model in a lot of ways, but I could hardly point fingers.

"Michele is a good woman," I said out loud.

She was, too—though maybe not in the way our gran would have used the term. Michele Schubert was absolutely out-front about everything. You couldn't shame her, because she wouldn't do something she wouldn't own up to. Operating on the same principle of full disclosure, if Michele had a grievance with you, you knew about it. She worked in the Ford dealership's repair shop as a scheduler and clerk. It was a tribute to her efficiency that she still worked for her former father-in-law. (In fact, he'd been known to say he liked her a tad better than he liked his son, some days.)

Michele came out on the deck. She was wearing the jeans and Ford-logo polo shirt she wore to work, and her dark hair was twisted in a knot on her head. Michele liked heavy eye makeup, big purses, and high heels. She was barefoot now. "Hey, Sookie, you like ranch dressing?" she asked. "Or we got some honey mustard."

"Ranch will be fine," I said. "You need any help?"

"Nope, I'm good." Michele's cell phone went off. "Dammit, it's Pop Schubert again. That man can't find his ass with both hands."

She went back in the house, the phone to her ear.

"I worry, though, about putting her in danger," Jason said in the diffident voice he used when he was asking my opinion about something supernatural. "I mean . . . that fairy, Dermot, the one that looks like me. Do you know if he's still around?"

He'd turned to face me. He was leaning against the railing of the deck he'd added to the house my mom and dad had built when they were expecting Jason. Mom and Dad hadn't gotten to enjoy it for much more than a decade. They'd died when I was seven, and when Jason had gotten old enough to live on his own (in his estimation), he'd moved out of Gran's and into this house. It had seen many a wild party for two or three years, but he'd become steadier. Tonight it was very clear to me that his recent losses had sobered him further.

I took a swallow from my bottle. I wasn't much of a drinker—I saw too much overindulgence at work—but it had been impossible to turn down a cold beer on this bright evening. "I wish I knew where Dermot was, too," I said. Dermot was the fraternal twin of our half-fairy grandfather Fintan. "Niall sealed himself into Faery with all the other fairies who wanted to join him, and I'm keeping my fingers crossed that Dermot's in Faery with him. Claude stayed here. I saw him a couple of weeks ago." Niall was our great-grandfather. Claude was his grandson from Niall's marriage to another full fae.

"Claude, the male stripper."

"The owner of a strip club, who strips himself on ladies' night," I corrected. "Our cousin models for romance covers, too."

"Yeah, I bet the girls faint when he walks by. Michele's got a book with him on the cover in some genie costume. He must love every minute of it." Jason definitely sounded envious.

"I bet he does. You know, he's a pain in the butt," I said, and laughed, surprising myself.

"You see him much?"

"Just the once, since I got hurt. But when I picked up the mail yesterday, he'd sent me some free coupons for ladies' night at Hooligans."

"You think you'll ever take him up on it?"

"Not yet. Maybe when I'm . . . in a better mood."

"You think Eric would mind you seeing another guy naked?" Jason was trying to show me how much he'd changed by his casual reference to my relationship with a vampire. Well, give my brother points for "willing."

"I'm not sure," I said. "But I wouldn't watch other guys take off their clothes without letting Eric know about it ahead of time. Give him a chance to put in his two cents. Would you tell Michele you were going to a club to watch women strip?"

Jason laughed. "I'd at least mention it, just to hear what she'd say." He put the steaks on a platter and gestured to the sliding glass doors. "We're ready," he said, and I pulled the door open for him. I'd set the table earlier, and now I poured the tea. Michele had put the salad and the hot potato casserole on the table, and she got some A-1 steak sauce from the pantry. Jason loved his A-1. With the big barbecuing fork, Jason put one steak on each plate. In a couple of minutes, we were all eating. It was kind of homey, the three of us.

"Calvin came into the dealership today," Michele said. "He's thinking of trading in his old pickup." Calvin Norris was a good man with a good job. He was in his forties, and he carried a lot of responsibility on his shoulders. He was my brother's leader, the dominant male in the werepanther community centered in the little settlement of Hotshot.

"He still dating Tanya?" I asked. Tanya Grissom worked at Norcross, same as Calvin, but she sometimes filled in at Merlotte's when one of the other waitresses couldn't work.

"Yeah, she's living with him," Jason said. "They fight pretty often, but I think she's staying."

Calvin Norris, leader of the werepanthers, did his best not

to get involved in vampire affairs. He'd had a lot on his plate since the Weres had come out. He'd declared that he was two-natured the next day in the break room at work. Now that the word had gotten around, it had only earned Calvin more respect. He had a good reputation in the Bon Temps area, even if most of the people who lived out in Hotshot were regarded with some suspicion since the community was so isolated and peculiar.

"How come you didn't come out when Calvin did?" I asked. That was a thought I'd never heard in Jason's head.

My brother looked thoughtful, an expression that sat a little oddly on him. "I guess I just ain't ready to answer a lot of questions," he said. "It's a personal thing, the change. Michele knows, and that's all that's important."

Michele smiled at him. "I'm real proud of Jason," she said, and that was enough. "He manned up when he turned panther. Wasn't like he could help it. He's making the best of it. No whining. He'll tell people about it when he's ready."

Jason and Michele were just startling me all over the place. "I haven't ever said anything to anyone," I assured him.

"I never thought you would. Calvin says Eric is like a chief vampire," Jason said, hopping into a different topic.

I don't talk about vampire politics at any length with nonvamps. Just not a good idea. But Jason and Michele had shared with me, and I wanted to share a little back. "Eric's got some power. But he's got a new boss, and things are touchy."

"You want to talk about that?" I could tell Jason was uncertain about hearing whatever I chose to tell them, but he was trying hard to be a good brother.

"I better not," I said, and saw his relief. Even Michele was glad to turn back to her steak. "But apart from dealing with other vampires, Eric and I are doing okay. There's always some give and take in relationships, right?" Though Jason had had scores of relationships over the years, he'd learned about give and take only recently.

"I been talking to Hoyt again," Jason said, and I understood the pertinence. Hoyt, Jason's shadow for years, had dropped off my brother's radar for a while. Hoyt's fiancée, Holly, who worked at Merlotte's with me, wasn't a big Jason fan. I was surprised Jason had his best buddy back, and I was even more surprised Holly had consented to this renewal.

"I've changed a lot, Sookie," my brother said, as if (for once) he'd been reading *my* mind. "I want to be a good friend to Hoyt. I want to be a good boyfriend to Michele." He looked at Michele seriously, putting his hand over hers. "And I want to be a better brother. We're all we got left. Except for the fairy relations, and I'd just as soon forget about them." He looked down at his plate, embarrassed. "I can't hardly believe that Gran cheated on Grandpa."

"I had an idea about that," I said. I'd been struggling with the same disbelief. "Gran really wanted children, and that wasn't going to happen for her and Grandpa. I was thinking maybe she was enchanted by Fintan. Fairies can mess with your mind, like the vamps can. And you know how beautiful they are."

"Claudine sure was. And I guess if you're a woman, Claude looks pretty good."

"Claudine really toned it down since she was passing for human." Claudine, Claude's triplet, had been a stunning six-foot-tall beauty.

Jason said, "Grandpa wasn't any picture in the looks department."

"Yeah, I know." We looked at each other, silently acknowledging the power of physical attraction. Then we said, simultaneously, "But *Gran*?" And we couldn't help but laugh. Michele tried hard to keep a straight face, but finally she couldn't help grinning at us. It was hard enough thinking about your parents having sex, but your grandparents? Totally wrong.

"Now that I'm thinking about Gran, I've been meaning to ask you if I could have that table she put up in the attic," Jason said. "The piecrust table that used to sit by the armchair in the living room?"

"Sure, swing by and pick it up sometime," I said. "It's probably sitting right where you put it the day she asked you to take it up to the attic."

I left soon after with my almost-empty casserole dish, some leftover steak, and a cheerful heart.

I certainly hadn't thought having dinner with my brother and his girlfriend was any big deal, but when I got home that night I slept all the way through until morning, for the first time in weeks.

MARCH
THE FOURTH WEEK

"There," said Sam. I had to strain to hear him. Someone had put Jace Everett's "Bad Things" on, and just about everyone in the bar was singing along. "You've smiled three times tonight."

"You counting my facial expressions?" I put down my tray and gave him a look. Sam, my boss and friend, is a true shapeshifter; he can change into anything warm-blooded, I guess. I haven't asked him about lizards and snakes and bugs.

"Well, it's good to see that smile again," he said. He rearranged some bottles on the shelf, just to look busy. "I missed it."

"It's good to feel like smiling," I told him. "I like the haircut, by the way."

Sam ran a self-conscious hand across his head. His hair was short, and it hugged his scalp like a red gold cap. "Summer's coming up. I thought it might feel good."

"Probably will."

"You already started sunbathing?" My tan was famous.

"Oh, yeah." In fact, I'd started extra early this spring. The first day I'd put on my swimsuit, all hell had broken loose. I'd killed a fairy. But that was *past*. I'd lain out yesterday, and not a thing had happened. Though I confess I hadn't taken the radio outside, because I'd wanted to be sure I could hear if something was sneaking up on me. But nothing had. In fact, I'd had a remarkably peaceful hour lying in the sun, watching a butterfly waft by every now and then. One of my great-great-grandmother's rosebushes was blooming, and the scent had healed something inside me. "The sun just makes me feel real good," I said. I suddenly remembered that the fae had told me that I came from sky fairies, instead of water fairies. I didn't know anything about that, but I wondered if my love of the sun was a genetic thing.

Antoine called, "Order up!" and I hurried over to fetch the plates.

Antoine had settled in at Merlotte's, and we all hoped he'd stick with the cooking job. Tonight he was moving around the small kitchen like he had eight arms. Merlotte's menu was the most basic—hamburgers, chicken strips, a salad with chicken strips cut up on it, chili fries, French-fried pickles— but Antoine had mastered it with amazing speed. Now in his fifties, Antoine had gotten out of New Orleans after staying in the Superdome during Katrina. I respected Antoine for his positive attitude and his determination to start over after losing everything. He was also good to D'Eriq, who helped him with food prep and bused the tables. D'Eriq was sweet but slow.

Holly was working that night, and in between hustling drinks and plates she stood by Hoyt Fortenberry, her fiancé, who was perched on a barstool. Hoyt's mom had proven to be only too glad to keep Holly's little boy on the evenings Hoyt wanted to spend time with Holly. It was hard to look at Holly and recognize her as the sullen Goth Wiccan she'd been in one phase of her life. Her hair was its natural dark brown and had grown to nearly shoulder length, her makeup was light, and she smiled all the time. Hoyt, my brother's best friend again since they'd mended their differences, seemed like a stronger man now that he had Holly to brace him up.

I glanced over at Sam, who'd just answered his cell phone. Sam was spending a lot of time on that phone these days, and I suspected he was seeing someone, too. I could find out if I looked in his head long enough (though the two-natured are harder to read than simple basic humans), but I tried hard to stay out of Sam's thoughts. It's just rude to rummage around inside the ideas of people you care about. Sam was smiling while he talked, and it was good to see him looking—at least temporarily—carefree.

"You see Vampire Bill much?" Sam asked when I was helping him close up an hour later.

"No. I haven't seen him in a long time," I said. "I wonder if Bill's dodging me. I went by his house a couple of times and left him a six-pack of TrueBlood and a thank-you note for all he did when he came to rescue me, but he never called me or came over."

"He was in a couple of nights ago when you were off. I think you ought to pay him a visit," Sam said. "I'm not saying any more."

MARCH
THE END OF THE FOURTH WEEK

On a beautiful night later that week, I was rummaging in my closet for my biggest flashlight. Sam's suggestion that I needed to see Bill had been nagging at me, so after I got home from work, I resolved to take a walk across the cemetery to Bill's house.

Sweet Home Cemetery is the oldest cemetery in Renard Parish. There isn't much room left for the dead, so there's one of those new "burial parks" with flat headstones on the south side of town. I hate it. Even if the ground is uneven and the trees are all grown up and some of the fences around the plots are falling down, to say nothing of the earliest headstones, I love Sweet Home. Jason and I had played there as kids, whenever we could escape Gran's attention.

The route through the memorials and trees to Bill's house was second nature, from the time he'd been my very first boyfriend. The frogs and bugs were just starting up their summer singing. The racket would only build with the hotter weather. I remembered D'Eriq asking me wasn't I scared, living by a graveyard, and I smiled to myself. I wasn't afraid of the dead lying in the ground. The walking and talking dead were *much* more dangerous. I'd cut a rose to lay on my grandmother's grave. I felt sure she knew I was there and thinking of her.

There was a dim light on at the old Compton house, which had been built about the same time my house had been. I rang the doorbell. Unless Bill was out in the woods roaming around, I was sure he was home since his car was there. But I had to wait some time until the creaking door swung open.

He switched on the porch light, and I tried not to gasp. He looked awful.

Bill had gotten infected with silver poisoning during the Fae War, thanks to the silver teeth of Neave. He'd had massive amounts of blood then—and since—from his fellow vampires, but I observed with some unease that his skin was still gray instead of white. His step was faltering, and his head hung a little forward like an old man's.

"Sookie, come in," he said. Even his voice didn't seem as strong as it had been.

Though his words were polite, I couldn't tell how he really felt about my visit. I can't read vampire minds, one of the reasons I'd initially been so attracted to Bill. You can imagine how intoxicating silence is after nonstop unwanted sharing.

"Bill," I said, trying to sound less shocked than I felt. "Are you feeling better? This poison in your system . . . Is it going away?"

I could swear he sighed. He gestured me to precede him into the living room. The lamps were off. Bill had lit candles. I counted eight. I wondered what he'd been doing, sitting alone in the flickering light. Listening to music? He loved his CDs, particularly Bach. Feeling distinctly worried, I sat on the couch, while Bill took his favorite chair across the low coffee table. He was as handsome as ever, but his face lacked animation. He was clearly suffering. Now I knew why Sam had wanted me to visit.

"You are well?" he asked.

"I'm much better," I said carefully. He'd seen the worst they'd done to me.

"The scars, the . . . mutilation?"

"The scars are there, but they're much fainter than I ever expected they'd be. The missing bits have filled in. I kind of have a dimple in this thigh," I said, tapping my left knee. "But I had plenty of thigh to spare." I tried to smile, but truthfully, I was too concerned to manage it. "Are you getting better?" I asked again, hesitantly.

"I'm not worse," he said. He shrugged, a minimal lift of the shoulders.

"What's with the apathy?" I said.

"I don't seem to want anything any longer," Bill told me, after a lengthy pause. "I'm not interested in my computer anymore. I'm not inclined to work on the incoming additions and subtractions to my database. Eric sends Felicia over to package up the orders and send them out. She gives me some blood while she's here." Felicia was the bartender at Fangtasia. She hadn't been a vampire that long.

Could vampires suffer from depression? Or was the silver poisoning responsible?

"Isn't there anyone who can help you? I mean, help you heal?"

He smiled in a sardonic sort of way. "My creator," he said. "If I could drink from Lorena, I would have healed completely by now."

"Well, that sucks." I couldn't let him know that bothered me, but *ouch*. I'd killed Lorena. I shook the feeling off. She'd needed killing, and it was over and done with. "Did she make any other vampires?"

Bill looked slightly less apathetic. "Yes, she did. She has another living child."

"Well, would that help? Getting blood from that vamp?"

"I don't know. It might. But I won't . . . I can't reach out to her."

"You don't know if it would help or not? You-all need a Handy Hints rule book or something."

"Yes," he said, as if he'd never heard of such an idea. "Yes, we do indeed."

I wasn't going to ask Bill why he was reluctant to contact someone who could help him. Bill was a stubborn and persistent man, and I wasn't going to be able to persuade him otherwise since he'd made up his mind. We sat in silence for a moment.

"Do you love Eric?" Bill said, all of a sudden. His deep brown eyes were fixed on me with the total attention that had played a large part in attracting me to him when we'd met.

Was everyone I knew fixated on my relationship with the sheriff of Area Five? "Yes," I said steadily. "I do love him."

"Does he say he loves you?"

"Yes." I didn't look away.

"I wish he would die, some nights," Bill said.

We were being really honest tonight. "There's a lot of that going around. There are a couple of people I wouldn't miss myself," I admitted. "I think about that when I'm grieving over the people I've cared about who've passed, like Claudine and Gran and Tray." And they were just at the top of the list. "So I guess I know how you feel. But I—please don't wish bad stuff on Eric." I'd lost about as much as I could stand to lose in the way of important people in my life.

"Who do you want dead, Sookie?" There was a spark of curiosity in his eyes.

"I'm not about to tell you." I gave him a weak smile. "You might try to make it happen for me. Like you did with Uncle Bartlett." When I'd discovered Bill had killed my grandmother's brother, who'd molested me—that's when I should have cut and run. Wouldn't my life have been different? But it was too late now.

"You've changed," he said.

"Sure, I have. I thought I was going to die for a couple of hours. I hurt like I've never hurt before. And Neave and Lochlan enjoyed it so much. That snapped something inside me. When you and Niall killed them, it was like an answer to the biggest prayer I'd ever prayed. I'm supposed to be a Christian, but most days I don't feel like I can even presume to say that about myself any longer. I have a lot of mad left over. When I can't sleep, I think about the other people who didn't care how much pain and trouble they caused me. And I think about how good I'd feel if they died."

That I could tell Bill about this awful secret part of me was a measure of how close I'd been to him.

"I love you," he said. "Nothing you do or say will change that. If you asked me to bury a body for you—or to make a body—I would do it without a qualm."

"We've got some bad history between us, Bill, but you'll always have a special place in my heart." I cringed inside when I heard the hackneyed phrase coming from my own mouth. But sometimes clichés are true; this was the truth. "I hardly feel worthy of being cared about that strongly," I admitted.

He managed a smile. "As to your being worthy, I don't think falling in love has much to do with the worth of the object of love. But I'd dispute your assessment. I think you're a fine woman, and I think you always try to be the best person you can be. No one could be . . . carefree and sunny . . . after coming as close to death as you did."

I rose to leave. Sam had wanted me to see Bill, to understand his situation, and I'd done that. When Bill got up to see me to the door, I noticed he didn't have the lightning speed he'd once had. "You're going to live, right?" I asked him, suddenly frightened.

"I think so," he said, as if it didn't make any difference one way or another. "But just in case, give me a kiss."

I put one arm around his neck, the arm that wasn't burdened with the flashlight, and I let him put his lips against mine. The feeling of him, the smell of him, triggered a lot of memories. For what seemed like a very long time, we stood pressed together, but instead of growing excited, I grew calmer. I was oddly conscious of my breathing—slow and steady, almost like the respiration of someone sleeping.

I could see that Bill looked better when I stepped away. My eyebrows flew up.

"Your fairy blood helps me," he said.

"I'm just an eighth fairy. And you didn't take any."

"Proximity," he said briefly. "The touch of skin on skin." His lips quirked up in a smile. "If we made love, I would be much closer to being healed."

Bullshit, I thought. But I can't say that cool voice didn't make something leap south of my navel, in a momentary twinge of lust. "Bill, that's not gonna happen," I said. "But you should think about tracking down that other vampire child of Lorena's."

"Yes," he said. "Maybe." His dark eyes were curiously luminous; that might have been an effect of the poisoning, or it might have been the candlelight. I knew he wouldn't make an effort to reach out to Lorena's other get. Whatever spark my visit had raised in him was already dying out.

Feeling sad, concerned, and also just a tiny smidge pleased—you can't tell me it's not flattering to be loved so much, because it is—I went home through the graveyard. I patted Bill's tombstone by habit. As I walked carefully over the uneven ground, I thought about Bill, naturally enough. He'd been a Confederate soldier. He'd survived the war only to succumb to a vampire after his return home to his wife and children, a tragic end to a hard life.

I was glad all over again that I'd killed Lorena.

Here's something I didn't like about myself: I realized I didn't feel bad when I killed a vampire. Something inside me kept insisting they were dead already, and that the first death had been the one that was most important. When I'd killed a human I'd loathed, my reaction had been much more intense.

Then I thought, *You'd think I'd be glad that I was avoiding some pain instead of thinking I should feel worse about taking out Lorena.* I hated trying to figure out what was best morally, because so often that didn't jibe with my gut reaction.

The bottom line of all this self-examination was that I'd killed Lorena, who could have cured Bill. Bill had gotten wounded when he came to my rescue. Clearly, I had a responsibility. I'd try to figure out what to do.

By the time I realized I'd been alone in the dark and should have been mortally afraid (at least according to D'Eriq), I was walking into my well-lit backyard. Maybe worrying about my spiritual life was a welcome distraction from reliving physical torture. Or maybe I felt better because

I'd done someone a good turn; I'd hugged Bill, and that had made him feel better. When I went to bed that night, I was able to lie on my side in my favorite position instead of tossing and turning, and I slept with no dreams—at least, none that I could remember in the morning.

For the next week, I enjoyed untroubled sleep, and as a result I began to feel much more like my former self. It was gradual, but perceptible. I hadn't thought of a way to help Bill, but I bought him a new CD (Beethoven) and put it where he'd find it when he got out of his daytime hiding place. Another day I sent him an e-card. Just so he knew I was thinking about him.

Each time I saw Eric, I felt a little more cheerful. And finally, I had my very own orgasm, a moment so explosive it was like I'd been saving up for a holiday.

"You . . . Are you all right?" Eric asked. His blue eyes looked down at me, and he was half-smiling, as if he wasn't sure whether he should be clapping or calling an ambulance.

"I am very, very all right," I whispered. Grammar be damned. "I'm so all right I might slide off the bed and lie in a puddle on the floor."

His smile became more secure. "So that was good for you? Better than it's been?"

"You knew that . . . ?"

He cocked an eyebrow.

"Well, of course you knew. I just . . . had some issues that had to work themselves out."

"I knew it couldn't be my lovemaking, wife of mine," Eric said, and though the words were cocky, his expression was definitely on the relieved side.

"Don't call me your wife. You know our so-called marriage is just strategy. To get back to your previous statement.

A-one lovemaking, Eric." I had to give credit where credit was due. "The no-orgasm problem was in my head. Now I've self-corrected."

"You are bullshitting me, Sookie," he murmured. "But I'll show you some A-one lovemaking. Because I think you can come again."

As it turned out, I could.

Chapter 1
APRIL

I love spring for all the obvious reasons. I love the flowers blooming (which happens early here in Louisiana); I love the birds twittering; I love the squirrels scampering across my yard.

I love the sound of werewolves howling in the distance.

No, just kidding. But the late, lamented Tray Dawson had once told me that spring is the favorite season of werewolves. There's more prey, so the hunt is over quickly, leaving more time to eat and play. Since I'd been thinking about Weres, it wasn't such a surprise to hear from one.

On that sunny morning in the middle of April, I was sitting on my front porch with my second cup of coffee and a magazine, still wearing my sleep pants and my Superwoman T-shirt, when the Shreveport packleader called me on my cell phone.

"Huh," I said, when I recognized the number. I flipped the phone open. "Hello," I said cautiously.

"Sookie," said Alcide Herveaux. I hadn't seen Alcide in months. Alcide had ascended to the position of packleader the year before in a single evening of mayhem. "How are you?"

"Right as rain," I said, nearly meaning it. "Happy as a clam. Fit as a fiddle." I watched a rabbit hop across the clover and grass twenty feet away. Spring.

"You're still dating Eric? He the reason for the good mood?"

Everyone wanted to know. "I'm still dating Eric. That sure helps keep me happy." Actually, as Eric kept telling me, "dating" was a misleading term. Though I didn't think of myself as married since I'd simply handed him a ceremonial knife (Eric had used my ignorance as part of his master strategy), the vampires did. A vampire-human marriage isn't exactly like a "love, honor, and obey" human pairing, but Eric had expected the marriage would earn me some perks in the vampire world. Since then, things had gone pretty well, vampire-wise. Aside from the huge glitch of Victor not letting Eric come to my aid when I was dying, that is—Victor, who really needed to die.

I turned my thoughts away from this dark direction with the determination of long practice. See? That was better. Now I was hopping out of bed every day with (almost) my old vigor. I'd even gone to church the past Sunday. Positive! "What's happening, Alcide?" I asked.

"I got a favor to ask," Alcide said, not entirely to my surprise.

"What can I do for you?"

"Can we use your land for our full-moon run tomorrow night?"

I made myself pause to think about his request rather than

automatically saying yes. I'm learning through experience. I had the open land the Weres needed; that wasn't the issue. I still own twenty-odd acres around my house, though my grandmother had sold off most of the original farm when she was faced with the financial burden of raising my brother and me. Though Sweet Home Cemetery took a chunk out of the land between my place and Bill's, there'd be enough room— especially if Bill didn't mind allowing access to his land as well. I remembered the pack had been here once before.

I turned the idea around to look at it from all angles. I couldn't see any obvious downside. "You're welcome to come," I said. "I think you should check with Bill Compton, too." Bill hadn't responded to any of my little gestures of concern.

Vampires and werewolves are not inclined to be buddies, but Alcide is a practical man. "I'll call Bill tonight, then," he said. "You got his number?"

I gave it to him. "Why are you-all not going to your place, Alcide?" I asked, out of sheer curiosity. He'd told me in casual conversation that the Long Tooth pack celebrated the full moon at the Herveaux farm south of Shreveport. Most of the Herveaux land was left in timber for the pack hunts.

"Ham called today to tell me there's a small party of oneys camping by the stream." "Oneys," the one-natured, is what the two-natured Weres call regular humans. I knew Hamilton Bond by sight. His farm was adjacent to the Herveaux place, and Ham farmed a few acres for Alcide. The Bond family had belonged to the Long Tooth pack as long as the Herveauxes.

"Did they have your permission to camp there?" I asked.

"They told Ham my dad always gave them permission to fish there in the spring, so they didn't think to ask me. It might be true. I don't remember them, though."

"Even if they're telling the truth, that's pretty rude. They should have called you," I said. "They should have asked you if it was convenient for you. You want me to talk to them? I can find out if they're lying." Jackson Herveaux, Alcide's late dad, hadn't seemed like the kind of man who'd casually allow people to use his land on a regular basis.

"No thanks, Sookie. I hate to ask you for another favor. You're a friend of the pack. We're supposed to watch out for you, not you for us."

"Don't worry about it. Y'all can come out here. And if you want me to shake hands with these supposed buddies of your dad's, I can do that." I was curious about their appearance on the Herveaux farm so close to the full moon. Curious and suspicious.

Alcide told me he'd think about the fishermen situation, and thanked me about six times for saying yes.

"No big deal," I said, and hoped I was telling the truth. Eventually, Alcide felt he'd thanked me enough, and we hung up.

I went inside with my coffee cup. I didn't know I was smiling until I looked in the living room mirror. I admitted to myself I was looking forward to the wolves' arrival. It would be pleasant to feel I wasn't alone in the middle of the woods. Pathetic, huh?

Though our few evenings together were good, Eric was still spending a *lot* of time on vampire business. I was getting a little tired of it. Well, not a little. If you're the boss, you should be able to get some time off, right? That's one of the perks of being a boss.

But something was up with the vampires; I was unhappily familiar with the signs. By now, the new regime should have been firmly in place, and Eric should have thoroughly established his new role in the scheme of things. Victor Madden should have been fully occupied down in New Orleans with the running of the kingdom, since he was Felipe's representative in Louisiana. Eric should have been left to run Area Five in his own efficient way.

But Eric's blue eyes got all glittery and steely when Victor's name came up. Mine probably did, too. As things stood now, Victor had power over Eric, and there wasn't much we could do about that.

I'd asked Eric if he thought Victor might claim dissatisfaction with Eric's performance in Area Five, a terrifying possibility.

"I'm keeping paperwork to prove differently," Eric said. "And I'm keeping it in several places." The lives of all Eric's people, and maybe my life, depended on Eric planting his feet firmly in the new regime. I knew so much rested on Eric's making his position impregnable, and I knew I shouldn't whine. It's not always easy to make yourself feel the way you ought to feel.

All in all, some howling around the house would be a nice change. At least it would be something new and different.

When I went to work that day, I told Sam about Alcide's phone call. True shapeshifters are rare. Since there aren't any others in this area, Sam occasionally spends time with others who have two forms. "Hey, why don't you come out to the house, too?" I suggested. "You could turn into a wolf, right, since you're a pure shifter? And then you'd blend right in."

Sam leaned back in his old swivel chair, glad to have an excuse to stop filling in forms. Sam, who is thirty, is three years older than me.

"I've been dating someone in the pack, so it might be fun," he said, considering the idea. But he shook his head after a moment. "That would be like going to an NAACP meeting in blackface. Being an imitation in front of the real thing. That's why I've never gone out with the panthers, though Calvin's told me I'd be welcome."

"Oh," I said, feeling embarrassed. "I didn't think of that. I'm sorry." I did wonder who he was dating, but there again, not my business.

"Ah, don't worry about it."

"I've known you for years, and I should know more about you," I said. "Your culture, that is."

"My own *family* is still learning. You know more than they do."

Sam had come out when the Weres had. His mother had come out the same night. His family had had a rough time handling the revelation. In fact, Sam's stepfather had shot Sam's mother, and now they were getting divorced—no big surprise there.

"Is your brother's wedding back on?" I said.

"Craig and Deidra are going to counseling. Her parents were pretty upset that she was marrying into a family with people like me and Mom in it. They don't understand that any kids Craig and Deidra have simply can't turn into animals. It's only the firstborn of a pure shifter couple." He shrugged. "I think they'll pull through, though. I'm just waiting for them to set a new date. You still willing to go with me?"

"Sure," I said, though I had an uneasy twitch when I pictured myself telling Eric I was going out of state with another man. At the time I'd promised Sam I'd go, the situation between Eric and me hadn't gelled into a relationship.

"You're assuming taking a Were as your date would be offensive to Deidra's family?"

"Truth be told," Sam said, "the Great Reveal in Wright didn't go over as well for the two-natured as it did in Bon Temps."

I knew from the local news that Bon Temps had been lucky. Its citizens had simply blinked when the Weres and the other two-natured announced their existence, taking a page from the vampire book. "Just let me know what happens," I said. "And come out to my place tomorrow if you change your mind about having a run with the pack."

"Packmaster didn't invite me," Sam said, smiling.

"Landowner did."

We didn't talk about it any more the rest of my shift, so I figured Sam would find something else to do for his moon time. The monthly change actually runs for three nights—three nights when all the two-natured, if they can, take to the woods (or the streets) in their animal form. Most of the twoeys—those born with their condition—can change at other times, but the moon time . . . that's special to all of them, including those who'd come to their extra nature by being bitten. There's a drug you can take, I hear, that can suppress your change; Weres in the military, among others, have to use it. But they all hate to do that, and I understand they're really no fun to be around on those nights.

Fortunately for me, the next day was one of my days off that week. If I'd had to come home from the bar late at night, the short distance from the car into the house might have been a little nerve-racking with the wolves on the loose. I'm not sure how much of their human consciousness remains when the Weres change, and not all of Alcide's pack members are personal friends of mine. Since I'd be at home, the prospect of hosting the Weres was more or less carefree. When company's coming to hunt in your woods, there's no preparation to be done. You don't have to cook or clean house.

However, having outside company was good motivation to complete some yard chores. Since it was another beautiful day, I put on one of my bikinis, pulled on sneakers and gloves, and set to work. Sticks and leaves and pinecones all went in the burn barrel, along with some hedge clippings. I made sure all the yard tools were put away in the shed, which I locked. I wound up the hose I'd used to water the potted plants I'd arranged around the back steps. I checked the clamp on the lid on the big garbage can. I'd bought the can specifically to keep the raccoons out of the trash, but a wolf might get interested, too.

I passed a pleasant afternoon, puttering around in the sun, singing off-key whenever the spirit moved me.

Right at dusk, the cars started arriving. I went to the window. I noticed the Weres had been considerate enough to carpool; there were several people in each vehicle. Even so, my driveway would be blocked until morning. *Lucky I planned to stay at home,* I thought. I knew some of the pack members, and I recognized a few of the others by sight. Hamilton Bond, who'd grown up with Alcide, pulled up and sat in his truck, talking on his cell phone. My eyes were drawn to a skinny, vivid young woman who favored flashy fashions, the kind I thought of as MTV clothes. I'd first noticed her in the Hair of the Dog bar in Shreveport, and she'd been assigned the task of executing injured enemies after Alcide's pack had won the Were war; I thought her name was Jannalynn. I also recognized two women who'd been members of the attacking pack; they'd surrendered at the end of the fight. Now they'd joined their former enemies. A young man had surrendered, too, but he could have been any one of a dozen moving restlessly around my yard.

Finally, Alcide arrived in his familiar truck. There were two other people sitting in the cab.

Alcide himself is tall and husky, as Weres tend to be. He's an attractive man. He's got black hair and green eyes, and of course, he's very strong. Alcide is usually well mannered and considerate—but he has his tough side, for sure. I'd heard rumors through Sam and Jason that since he'd ascended to packleader, that tough side had been getting a workout. I noticed that Jannalynn made a special effort to be at the truck door when Alcide emerged.

The woman who slid out after him was in her late twenties, and she had some good solid hips on her. She wore her brown hair slicked back into a little knob, and her camo tank top let me know she was muscular and fit. At the moment, Camo was looking around the front yard like she was the tax assessor. The man who got out the other door was a little older and a lot harder.

Sometimes, even if you're not telepathic, you can tell by looking at a man that he's had a rough life. This man had. The way he moved told me he was on the alert for trouble. Interesting.

I watched him, because he needed watching. He had shoulder-length dark brown hair that flared around his head in a cloud of corkscrews. I found myself eyeing it enviously. I'd always wished I could get my hair to do that.

After I'd gotten over my hair envy, I noticed that his skin was the brown of mocha ice cream. Though he wasn't as tall as Alcide, he had thick shoulders on an aggressively muscled body.

If I'd had a "Bad to the Bone" alert on the brick path up to the front porch, it would have gone off just after Corkscrew set his foot on it. "Danger, Will Robinson," I said out loud. I'd never seen Camo or Corkscrew before. Hamilton Bond got out of his truck and came over to join the little group, but he didn't come up the porch steps to stand beside Alcide, Corkscrew, and Camo. Ham held back. Jannalynn joined him. The Long Tooth pack appeared to be both expanding its ranks and rearranging its pecking order.

When I answered the knock on the door, I had my hostess smile in place. The bikini would have been sending the wrong message (*Yum, yum, available!*), so I'd pulled on some cutoff jeans and a Fangtasia T-shirt. I pushed open the screen door. "Alcide!" I said, truly glad to see him. We gave each other a brief hug. He felt awfully warm, since all my recent hugging experiences had been with the less-than-room-temperature Eric. I felt a sort of emotional ripple and realized that though Camo was smiling at me, our embrace hadn't been a welcome sight to her. "Hamilton!" I said. I nodded at him since he wasn't within hugging distance.

"Sookie," Alcide said, "some new members for you to meet. This is Annabelle Bannister."

I'd never met anyone who looked less like an "Annabelle" than this woman. I shook hands with her, of course, and told her I was pleased to meet her.

"You know Ham, and you've met Jannalynn, too, I think?" Alcide said, inclining his head back.

I nodded at the two at the foot of the steps.

"And this is Basim al Saud, my new second," Alcide said. It was pronounced "bah-SEEM," and Alcide trotted the name out like he introduced Arabic people to me all the time. Okeydokey. "Hi-dee-do, Basim," I said. I held out my hand.

One of the meanings of "second," I knew, was the person who scares the shit out of everyone, and Basim seemed well qualified for the job. Somewhat reluctantly, he extended his own hand to mine. I shook it, wondering what I'd get from him. Weres are often very hard to read because of their dual nature. Sure enough, I didn't get specific thoughts: only a confused blur of mistrust and aggression and lust.

Funny, that was pretty much what I was getting from the misnamed Annabelle. "How long have you been in Shreveport?" I asked politely. I glanced from Annabelle to Basim to include them both in the question.

"Six months," Annabelle said. "I transferred from the Elk Killer pack in South Dakota." So she was in the Air Force. She'd been stationed in South Dakota and then reassigned to Barksdale Air Force Base in Bossier City, adjacent to Shreveport.

"I've been here two months," Basim said. "I'm learning to like it." Though he looked exotic, he had only the faintest trace of an accent, and his English was much more precise than mine. Going strictly by the haircut, he was definitely not in the armed services.

"Basim left his old pack in Houston," Alcide said easily, "and we're glad he's become one of us." "We" didn't include Ham Bond. I might not be able to read Ham's mind as clearly as if he were human, but he was no big Basim fan. Neither was Jannalynn, who seemed to regard Basim with both lust and resentment. There was lots of lust going around the pack this evening. Looking at Basim and Alcide, that wasn't too hard to understand.

"You have a good time here tonight, Basim, Annabelle," I said, before turning to Alcide. "Alcide, my property extends maybe an acre beyond the stream to the east, about five acres south to the dirt track that leads to the oil well, and north around the back of the cemetery."

The packleader nodded. "I called Bill last night, and he's okay with us spilling over into his woods. He's not going to be at home until dawn, so we won't be bothering him. What about you, Sookie? Are you going into Shreveport tonight, or staying home?"

"I'll be here. If you need me for anything, just come to the door." I smiled at all of them.

Annabelle thought, *Not effing likely, Blondie.*

"But you might need the phone," I said to her, and she jumped. "Or some first aid. After all, Annabelle, you never know what you're going to meet up with." Though I'd started out smiling, there was no smile on my face by the time I finished.

People should make an effort to be polite.

"Thanks again for the use of your land. We'll be heading into the woods," Alcide said quickly. The dark was falling steadily, and I could see the other Weres drifting into the cover of the trees. One of the women threw back her head and yipped. Basim's eyes were rounder and more golden already.

"Have a good night," I said, as I stepped back and latched the screen door. The three Weres started down the front steps. Alcide's voice drifted back. He was saying, "I *told* you she was telepathic," to Annabelle as they went across the driveway into the woods, trailed by Ham. Jannalynn suddenly started running for the tree line, she was so anxious to change. But it was Basim who glanced back at me as I pushed the wooden door shut. It was the kind of look you get from the animals in the zoo.

And then it was full dark.

The Weres were a bit of a disappointment. They didn't

make as much noise as I'd thought they would. I stayed in the house, of course, all locked up, and I pulled my curtains closed, which wasn't my normal habit. After all, I lived in the middle of the woods. I watched a little television, and I read some. Somewhat later, while I was brushing my teeth, I heard howling. I thought it came from far off, probably near the eastern edge of my property.

Early the next morning, just as dawn was breaking, I woke up because I heard car engines. The Weres were taking their departure. I almost turned over to go back to sleep, but I realized I had to get up and pay a trip to the bathroom. After I took care of that, I was a little more awake. I padded down the hall to the living room and peeked through a gap in the front curtains. Out of the tree line came Ham Bond, a bit worse for wear. He was talking to Alcide. Their trucks were the only remaining vehicles. Annabelle appeared a moment after.

As I looked at the early morning light falling across the dewy grass, the three Weres walked across the lawn slowly, clothed as they had been the night before, but carrying their shoes. They looked exhausted but happy. Their clothes weren't bloody, but their faces and arms were speckled. They'd had a successful hunt. I had a *Bambi* twinge, but I suppressed it. This was little different from going up in a blind with a rifle.

A few seconds later Basim emerged from the woods. In the slanted light, he looked like a woodland creature, his wild hair full of bits of leaf and twig. There was something ancient about Basim al Saud. I had to wonder how he'd become a werewolf in wolfless Arabia. As I watched, Basim turned away from the other three and came to my front porch. He knocked, low and firm.

I counted to ten and opened the door. I tried not to stare at the blood. You could tell he'd washed his face in the stream, but he'd missed his neck.

"Miss Stackhouse, good morning," Basim said courteously. "Alcide says I should tell you that other creatures have been passing through your property."

I could feel the pucker between my eyes as I frowned. "What kind, Basim?"

"At least one was a fairy," he said. "Possibly more than one fairy, but one for sure."

That was incredible for about six reasons. "Are these tracks . . . or traces . . . fresh? Or a few weeks old?"

"Very fresh," he said. "And the scent of vampire is strong, too. That's a bad mixture."

"That's unpleasant news, but something I needed to know. Thanks for telling me."

"And there's a body."

I stared at him, willing my face to stillness. I have a lot of practice at not showing what I'm thinking; any telepath has to be good at that. "How old a body?" I asked, when I was sure I had my voice under control.

"Around a year and a half, maybe a little less." Basim wasn't making a big deal about finding a body. He was strictly letting me know it was there. "It's quite far back, buried very deeply."

I didn't say anything. Geez Louise, must be Debbie Pelt. Since Eric had recovered his memory of that night, that's one thing I'd never asked him: where he'd buried her body after I'd killed her.

Basim's dark eyes examined me with great attention. "Alcide wants you to call if you need help or advice," he said finally.

"Tell Alcide I appreciate the offer. And thanks again for letting me know."

He nodded, and then he was halfway back to the truck, where Annabelle sat with her head resting on Alcide's shoulder.

I raised my hand to them as Alcide started the truck, and I shut my door firmly as they left.

I had a lot to think about.

Chapter 2

I went back to the kitchen, looking forward to my coffee and a slice of the applesauce bread Halleigh Bellefleur had dropped off at the bar the day before. She was a nice young woman, and I was real glad she and Andy were expecting a baby. I'd heard that Andy's grandmother, ancient Mrs. Caroline Bellefleur, was beside herself with delight, and I didn't doubt it for a moment. I tried to think about good things, like Halleigh's baby, Tara's pregnancy, and the last night I'd spent with Eric; but the disturbing news Basim had told me gnawed at me all morning.

Of all the ideas I had, calling the Renard Parish's sheriff's office was the one that got almost zero brain time. There was no way I could tell them why I was worried. The Weres were out, and there was nothing illegal about letting them hunt on my land. But I couldn't picture myself telling Sheriff Dearborn that a Were had told me fairies had been crossing my property.

Here's the thing. As far as I'd known until this moment, all the fairies except my cousin Claude had been barred from the human world. At least, all the fairies in America. I'd never wondered about those in other countries, and now I closed my eyes and winced at my own stupidity. My great-grandfather Niall had closed all the portals between the fae world and ours. At least, that was what he'd told me he was going to do. And I'd assumed they were all gone, except for Claude, who'd lived among humans as long as I'd known him. So how come there'd been a fairy tromping through my woods?

And who could I ask for advice on the situation? I couldn't just sit on my hands and do nothing. My great-grandfather had been looking for the self-loathing half-human renegade Dermot until the moment he closed the portal. I needed to face the possibility that Dermot, who was simply insane, had been left in the human world. However it had come about, I had to believe that fae proximity to my house couldn't be a good thing. I needed to talk to someone about this.

I might confide in Eric, since he was my lover, or in Sam, because he was my friend, or even in Bill, because his land shared a boundary with mine and he would also be concerned. Or I could talk to Claude, see if he'd give me any insight into the situation. I sat at the table with my coffee and my hunk of applesauce bread, too distracted to read or turn on the radio to catch the news. I finished one cup of coffee and started another. I showered, in an automatic sort of way, and made my bed and did all my usual morning tasks.

Finally, I sat down at the computer I'd brought home from my cousin Hadley's New Orleans apartment, and I checked my e-mail. I'm not methodical about doing this. I know very few people who might send me e-mail, and I simply haven't gotten into the habit of looking at my computer every day.

I had several messages. I didn't recognize the return address on the first one. I moved the mouse to click on it.

A knock at the back door made me jump like a frog.

I pushed back my chair. After a second's hesitation, I got the shotgun from the closet in the front room. Then I went to the back door and peeked through the new peephole. "Speak of the devil," I muttered.

This day was just full of surprises, and it wasn't even ten o'clock.

I put down the shotgun and opened the door. "Claude," I said. "Come in. You want a drink? I've got Coke and coffee and orange juice."

I noticed that Claude had the strap of a big tote bag slung over his shoulder. From its solid appearance, the bag was jammed with clothes. I didn't remember inviting him to a slumber party.

He came in, looking serious and somehow unhappy. Claude had been in the house before, but not often, and he looked around at my kitchen. The kitchen happened to be new because the old kitchen had burned down, so I had shiny appliances and everything still looked squared away and level.

"Sookie, I can't stay in our house by myself any longer. Can I bunk with you for a while, Cousin?"

I tried to pick my jaw up off the floor before he noticed how shocked I was—first, that Claude had confessed he needed help; second, that he confessed it to me; and third, that Claude would stay in the same house with me when he normally thought of me as about on the same level as a beetle. I'm a human and I'm a woman, so I've got two strikes against me as far as Claude's concerned. Plus, of course, there was the whole issue of Claudine dying in my defense.

"Claude," I said, trying to sound only sympathetic, "have a seat. What's wrong?" I glanced at the shotgun, unaccountably glad it was within reach.

Claude gave it only a casual glance. After a moment, he put down his bag and simply stood there, as if he couldn't figure out what to do next.

It seemed surreal to be in my kitchen alone with my fairy cousin. Though he had apparently made the choice to continue living among humans, he was far from warm and fuzzy about them. Claude, albeit physically beautiful, was an indiscriminate jerk, as far as I'd observed. But he'd gotten his ears surgically altered to look human, so he wouldn't have to expend his energy perpetuating a human appearance. And as far as I knew, Claude's sexual connections had always been with human males.

"You're still living in the house you shared with your sisters?" It was a prosaic three-bedroom ranch in Monroe.

"Yes."

Okay. I was looking for a little expansion on the theme here. "The bars aren't keeping you occupied?" Between owning and operating two strip clubs—Hooligans and a new place he'd just taken over—and performing at Hooligans at least once a week, I'd imagined Claude to be both busy and well-to-do. Since he was handsome to the nth degree, he made a lot of money in tips, and the occasional modeling job boosted his income. Claude could make even the most staid grandmother drool. Being in the same room with someone so gorgeous gave women a contact high . . . until he opened his mouth. Plus, he no longer had to share the club income with his sister.

"I'm busy. And I don't lack for money. But without the company of my own kind . . . I feel I'm starving."

"Are you *serious?*" I said without thinking, and then I could have kicked myself. But Claude needing me (or anyone, for that matter) seemed so unlikely. His request to stay with me was wholly unexpected and unwelcome.

But my gran chided me mentally. I was looking at a member of my family, one of the few still living and/or accessible to me. My relationship with my great-grandfather Niall had ended when he'd retreated into Faery and pulled the door shut behind him. Though Jason and I had mended our fences, my brother very much led his own life. My mom, my dad, and my grandmother were dead, my aunt Linda and my cousin Hadley were dead, and I rarely saw Hadley's little son.

I had depressed the hell out of myself in the space of a minute.

"Do I have enough fairy in me to be any help to you?" That was all I could think of to say.

"Yes," he said very simply. "I already feel better." This seemed a weird echo of my conversation with Bill. Claude halfway smiled. If Claude looked incredible when he was unhappy, he looked divine when he smiled. "Since you've been in the company of fairies, it's accentuated your streak of fairy essence. By the way, I have a letter for you."

"Who from?"

"Niall."

"How's that possible? I understood the fae world was shut off now."

"He has his ways," Claude said evasively. "He's the only prince now, and very powerful."

He has his ways. "Humph," I said. "Okay, let's see it."

Claude pulled an envelope out of his overnight bag. It was buff-colored and sealed with a blue blob of wax. In the wax was imprinted a bird, its wings spread in flight.

"So there's a fairy mailbox," I said. "And you can send and receive letters?"

"This letter, anyway."

Fae were very good at evasion. I huffed out a breath of exasperation.

I got a knife and slid it under the seal. The paper I extracted from the envelope had a very curious texture.

"Dearest great-granddaughter," it began. "There are things I didn't get to say to you and many things I didn't get to do for you before my plans collapsed in the war."

Okay.

"This letter is written on the skin of one of the water sprites who drowned your parents."

"Ick!" I cried, and dropped the letter on the kitchen table.

Claude was by my side in a flash. "What's wrong?" he asked, looking around the kitchen as if he expected to see a troll pop up.

"This is skin! Skin!"

"What else would Niall write on?" He looked genuinely taken aback.

"Ewww!" Even to myself, I sounded a little too girly-girly. But honestly . . . skin?

"It's clean," Claude said, clearly hoping that would solve my problem. "It's been processed."

I gritted my teeth and reached down for my great-grandfather's letter. I took a deep, steadying breath. Actually, the . . . material hardly smelled at all. Smothering a desire to put on oven mitts, I made myself focus on reading.

"Before I left your world, I made sure one of my human agents talked to several people who can help you evade the scrutiny of the human government. When I sold the pharmaceutical company we owned, I used much of my profit to ensure your freedom."

I blinked, because my eyes were tearing up a little. He might not be a typical great-grandfather, but by golly, he'd done something wonderful for me.

"He's bribed some government officials to call off the FBI? Is that what he's done?"

"I have no idea," Claude said, shrugging. "He wrote me, too, to let me know that I had an extra three hundred thousand dollars in my bank account. Also, Claudine hadn't made a will, since she didn't . . ."

Expect to die. She had expected to raise a child with a fairy lover I'd never met. Claude shook himself and said in a cracked voice, "Niall produced a human body and a will, so I don't have to wait years to prove her death. She left me almost everything. She said this to our father, Dillon, when she appeared to him as part of her death ritual."

Fairies told their relatives they had passed, after they'd translated to spirit form. I wondered why Claudine had appeared to Dillon instead of to her brother, and I asked Claude, phrasing it as tactfully as I could.

"The next oldest receives the vision," Claude said stiffly. "Our sister, Claudette, appeared to me, since I was older than her by a minute. Claudine made her death ritual to our father, since she was older than I."

"So she told your dad she wanted you to have her share of the clubs?" It was pretty lucky for Claude that Claudine had let someone else know about her wishes. I wondered what happened if the oldest fae in the line was the one who was doing the dying. I'd save that question for later.

"Yes. Her share of the house. Her car. Though I already had one." For some reason, Claude was looking self-conscious. And guilty. Why on earth would he look guilty?

"How do you ride in it?" I asked, sidetracked. "Since fairies have such issues with iron?"

"I wear the invisible gloves over exposed skin," he said. "I put them on after every shower. And I've built up a little more tolerance with every decade of living in the human world."

I returned to the letter. "There may be more I can do for you. I will let you know. Claudine left you a gift."

"Oh, Claudine left me something, too? What?" I looked up at Claude, who didn't look exactly pleased. I think he hadn't known the contents of the letter for certain. If Niall hadn't revealed Claudine's legacy, Claude might not have. Fairies don't lie, but they don't always tell all the truth, either.

"She left you the money in her bank account," he said, resigned. "It contains her wages from the department store and her share of the income from the clubs."

"Aw . . . that was so nice of her." I blinked a couple of times. I tried not to touch my savings account, and my checking account wasn't too healthy because I'd missed a lot of work recently. Plus, my tips had suffered because I'd been so down. Smiling waitresses make more than sad waitresses.

I could sure use a few hundred dollars. Maybe I could buy

some new clothes, and I really needed a new toilet in the hall bathroom. "How do you do a transfer like that?"

"You'll get a check from Mr. Cataliades. He is handling the estate."

Mr. Cataliades—if he had a first name, I'd never heard it—was a lawyer, and he was also (mostly) a demon. He handled the human legal affairs of many supernaturals in Louisiana. I felt subtly better when Claude said his name, because I knew Mr. Cataliades had no bone to pick with me.

Well, I had to make up my mind about Claude's housemate proposal.

"Let me make a phone call," I said, and pointed to the coffeepot. "If you need some more, I can make some. Are you hungry?"

Claude shook his head.

"Then after I call Amelia, you and I need to have a little chitchat."

I went to the phone in my bedroom. Amelia was an earlier riser than me, because my job kept me up late. She answered her cell phone on the second ring. "Sookie," she said, and she didn't sound as gloomy as I'd anticipated. "What's up?"

I couldn't think of any casual way to lead into my question. "My cousin would like to stay here for a while," I said. "He could use the bedroom across from mine, but if he stays upstairs, we'd each have a little more privacy. If you're coming back anytime soon, of course he'll go on and put his stuff in the downstairs bedroom. I just didn't want you to come back to find someone sleeping in your bed."

There was a long silence. I braced myself.

"Sookie," she said, "I love you. You know that. And I loved living with you. It was a godsend to have somewhere to go after that thing with Bob. But right now I'm stuck in New

Orleans for a while. I'm just . . . in the middle of a lot of stuff."

I'd expected this, but it was still a tough moment. I hadn't really expected her to come back. I'd hoped she'd heal faster in New Orleans—and it was true she hadn't mentioned Tray. It sounded like more than grieving was going on. "You're okay?"

"I am," she said. "And I've been training with Octavia some more." Octavia, her mentor in witchcraft, had returned to New Orleans with her long-lost love. "Also, I finally got . . . judged. I've got to pay a penalty for—you know—the thing with Bob."

"The thing with Bob" was Amelia's way of referring to accidentally turning her lover into a cat. Octavia had returned Bob to his human form, but naturally Bob hadn't been happy with Amelia, and neither had Octavia. Though Amelia had been training in her craft, clearly transformational magic had been beyond her skills.

"So, they're not going to whip you or anything, right?" I asked, trying to sound as if I were joking. "After all, it's not like he died." Just lost a big chunk of his life and missed Katrina entirely, including being able to inform his family that he'd survived.

"Some of them would whip me if they could. But that's not how we witches roll." Amelia tried to laugh, but it wasn't convincing. "As a penalty, I've got to do, like, community service."

"Like picking up litter or tutoring kids?"

"Well . . . mixing potions and making up bags of common ingredients so they're ready to hand. Working extra hours in the magic store, and killing chickens for rituals every now and then. Doing a lot of legwork. Without pay."

"*That* sucks," I said, because money is almost always a touchy subject with me. Amelia had grown up rich, but I had not. If someone deprives me of income, I get pissed off. I had a fleeting moment of wondering how much Claudine's bank account might have had in it, and I blessed her for thinking of me.

"Yeah, well, Katrina wiped the New Orleans covens out. We lost some members who'll never come back, so we don't get their contributions anymore, and I never use my dad's money for the coven."

"So, the bottom line?" I said.

"I've gotta stay down here. I don't know if I'll ever make it back to Bon Temps. And I'm really sorry about that, because I really liked living with you."

"Same here." I took a deep breath, determined not to sound forlorn. "What about your stuff? Not that there's that much here, but still."

"I'll leave it there for now. I've got everything here I need, and the rest is yours to use as you see fit till I can make arrangements to get it."

We talked a bit more, but we'd said everything important. I forgot to ask her if Octavia had found a way to dissolve Eric's blood bond with me. Possibly I wasn't very interested in an answer. I hung up, feeling both sad and glad: glad that Amelia was working off her debt to her coven and that she was happier than she'd been in Bon Temps after Tray's death, and sad because I understood she didn't expect to return. After a moment of silent farewell to her, I went to the kitchen to tell Claude that the upstairs was all his.

After I'd absorbed his gratified smile, I moved on to another issue. I didn't know how to approach my question, so finally I simply asked him. "Have you been out in my woods back of the house?"

His face went absolutely blank.

"Why would I do that?" he said.

"I didn't ask for your motivation. I asked if you had been there." I know evasion when I hear it.

"No," he said.

"That's bad news."

"Why?"

"Because the Weres tell me a fairy's been back there very recently." I kept my eyes fixed on his. "And if it's not you, who could it be?"

"There aren't many fairies left," Claude said.

Again, evasion. "If there are other fairies that didn't make it in before the portal was shut, you could hang around with them," I said. "You wouldn't need to stay with me, with my little dash of fairy blood. Yet here you are. And somewhere in my woods is yet another fairy." I eyed his expression. "I don't see you excited about tracking down whoever it is. What's the deal? Why don't you dash out there, find the fairy, do some bonding, and be happy?"

Claude looked down. "The last portal to close was in your woods," he said. "Possibly it's not completely shut. And I know Dermot, your great-uncle, was on the outside. If Dermot is the fairy the Weres sensed, he wouldn't be glad to see me."

I thought he would have more to say, but he stopped right there.

That was plenty of bad news, and another whopping dollop of dodging the issue. I was still dubious about his goals, but Claude was family, and I had precious little family left. "All right," I said, opening a kitchen drawer where I stowed odds and ends. "Here's a key. We'll see how this pans out. I have to go to work this afternoon, by the way. And we have to have a talk. You know that I've got a boyfriend, right?" I was already feeling kind of embarrassed.

"Who are you seeing?" Claude asked, with a sort of professional interest.

"Ah, well . . . Eric Northman."

Claude whistled. He looked both admiring and cautious. "Does Eric spend the night? I need to know if he's going to jump me." Claude looked as though that wouldn't be totally unwelcome. But the pertinent issue was that fairies are really intoxicating to vampires, like catnip to cats. Eric would have a hard time restraining himself from biting if Claude was close to him.

"That would probably end badly for you," I said. "But I think, with a little care, we can get around it." Eric seldom spent the night at my house because he liked to be back in Shreveport before dawn. He had so much work to get through every night that he'd found it was better for him to wake up in Shreveport. I do have a hidden place where a vampire can stay in relative safety, but it's not exactly deluxe, not like Eric's house.

I was a little more concerned about the possibility of Claude bringing strange men back to my house. I didn't want to encounter someone I didn't know when I was on my way to the kitchen in my nightie. Amelia had had a couple of overnight guests, but they'd been people I knew. I took a deep breath, hoping what I was about to say wouldn't come out homophobic. "Claude, it's not that I don't want you to have a good time," I said, wishing this conversation were over and done with. I admired Claude's unblushing acceptance of the fact that I had a sex life, and I only wished I could match that nonchalance.

"If I want to have sex with someone you don't know, I'll take him to my house in Monroe," Claude said, with a wicked little smile. He could be perceptive when he chose, I noted. "Or I'll let you know ahead of time. That okay?"

"Sure," I said, surprised at Claude's easy compliance. But he'd said all the right words. I relaxed some as I showed Claude where strategic kitchen stuff was, gave him some tips on the washer and the dryer, and told him the hall bathroom was all his. Then I led him upstairs. Amelia had worked hard on making one of the little bedrooms pretty, and she'd decorated the other one as a sitting room. She'd taken her laptop with her, but the TV was still there. I checked to make sure that the bed was made up with clean linens and the closet was mostly clear of Amelia's clothing. I pointed out the door to the walk-in attic, in case he needed to store anything. Claude pulled it open and took a step inside. He looked around at the shadowy, crowded space. Generations of Stackhouses had stored things they thought they might need someday, and I admit it was a little on the cluttered and chaotic side.

"You need to go through this," he said. "Do you even know what's up here?"

"Family debris," I said, looking in with some dismay. I'd just never worked up the heart to tackle it since Gran died.

"I'll help you," Claude declared. "That will be my payment to you for my room."

I opened my mouth to point out that Amelia had given me cash, but then I reflected, again, that he was family. "That would be great," I said. "Though I don't know if I'm up to it yet." My wrists had been aching this morning, though they were definitely better than they'd been. "And there are some other jobs around the house that are beyond me, if you wouldn't mind giving a hand."

He bowed. "I would be delighted," he said.

This was a different side of Claude from the one I'd come to know and disparage.

Grief and loneliness seemed to have woken something in the beautiful fairy; he appeared to have come to the realization that he had to show a little kindness to other people if he wanted to receive kindness in return. Claude seemed to understand that he needed others, especially now that his sisters were gone.

I was a little more at ease with our arrangement by the time I left for work. I'd listened to Claude moving around upstairs for a while, and then he'd come down with an armful of hair-care products to arrange in the bathroom. I'd already put out clean towels for him. He seemed satisfied with the bathroom, which was very old-fashioned. But then Claude had been alive in a time before indoor plumbing, so maybe he saw it from a different perspective. Truthfully, hearing someone else in the house had relaxed something deep inside me, a tension I hadn't even known I felt.

"Hey, Sam," I said. He was behind the bar when I came out of the back room, where I'd left my purse and put on an apron. Merlotte's wasn't very busy. Holly, as always, was talking to her Hoyt, who was dawdling over his supper. With her Merlotte's T-shirt, Holly was wearing pink and green plaid shorts instead of the regulation black.

"Looking good, Holly," I called, and she gave me a radiant smile. While Hoyt beamed, Holly held out her hand to show off a brand-new ring.

I let out a shriek and hugged her. "Oh, this is so great!" I said. "Holly, it's so pretty! So, have you picked a date yet?"

"It'll be in the fall, probably," Holly said. "Hoyt has to work long hours through the spring and summer. That's his busy time, so we figured maybe October or November."

"Sookie," Hoyt said, his voice dropping and his face growing solemn. "Now that Jason and I have mended our fences, I'm going to ask him to be my best man."

I glanced very quickly over to Holly, who'd never been a big Jason fan. She was still smiling, and if I could detect the reservations she had, Hoyt couldn't.

I said, "He'll be thrilled."

I had to hustle off to make the rounds of my tables, but I smiled while I worked. I wondered if they'd have the ceremony after dark. Then Eric could go with me. That would be great! That would transform me from "poor Sookie who hasn't even ever been engaged" to "Sookie who brought the gorgeous guy to the wedding." Then I thought of a contingency plan. If the wedding was a daytime wedding, I could get *Claude* to go with me! He looked exactly like a romance cover model. He'd *been* a romance cover model. (Ever read *The Lady and the Stableboy*, or *Lord Darlington's Naughty Marriage*? Woo-hoo!)

I was unhappily aware that I was thinking about the wedding strictly in terms of my own feelings . . . but there's nothing more forlorn than being an old maid at a wedding. I realize that it's silly to feel like you're on the shelf at twenty-seven. But I had missed some prime time, and I was increasingly conscious of that fact. So many of my high school friends had gotten married (some more than once), and some of them were pregnant—like Tara, who was coming through the door in an oversized T-shirt.

I gave a wave to let her know I'd come talk to her when I could, and I got an iced tea for Dr. Linda Tonnesen and a Michelob for Jesse Wayne Cummins.

"What's up, Tara?" I bent over to give her a neck hug. She had plunked herself down at a table.

"I need some caffeine-free Diet Coke," she said. "And I need a cheeseburger. With lots of French-fried pickles." She looked ferocious.

"Sure," I said. "I'll get the Coke and put in your order right now."

When I returned, she drank the whole glass. "I'll be sorry in five minutes because I'll have to go to the bathroom," she said. "All I do is pee and eat." Tara had big rings under her eyes, and her complexion was not at its best. Where was the glow of pregnancy that I'd heard so much about?

"How much longer do you have to go?"

"Three months, a week, and three days."

"Dr. Dinwiddie gave you a due date!"

"JB just can't *believe* how big I'm getting," Tara said, with an eye roll.

"He said that? In those words?"

"Yep. Yes. He did."

"Geez Louise. That boy needs a lesson or two in rephrasing."

"I'd settle for him keeping his mouth shut entirely."

Tara had married JB knowing brains weren't his strong suit, and she was reaping the result, but I *so* wanted them to be happy. I couldn't be all, "You made your bed, now you gotta lie in it."

"He loves you," I said, trying to sound soothing. "He's just . . ."

"JB," she said. She shrugged and summoned up a smile.

Then Antoine called that my order was up, and the avid expression on Tara's face told me that she was more focused on the food than on her husband's tactlessness. She returned to Tara's Togs a happier and fuller woman.

As soon as it was dark, I called Eric on my cell while I was in the ladies' room. I hated to sneak off on Sam's time to call my boyfriend, but I needed the support. Now that I had his cell number, I didn't have to call Fangtasia, which was both bad and good. I'd never known who was going to answer the phone, and I'm not a universal favorite among Eric's vampires. On the other hand, I missed talking to Pam, Eric's second-in-command. Pam and I are actually almost friends.

"I am here, my lover," Eric said. It was hard not to shiver when I heard his voice, but the atmosphere of the ladies' room in Merlotte's was not at all conducive to lust.

"Well, I'm here, too, obviously. Listen, I really need to talk to you," I said. "Some things have come up."

"You're worried."

"Yes. With good reason."

"I have a meeting in thirty minutes with Victor," Eric said. "You know how tense that's likely to be."

"I do know. And I'm sorry to pester you with my problems. But you're my boyfriend, and part of being a good boyfriend is listening."

"Your boyfriend," he said. "That sounds . . . strange. I am so *not* a boy."

"Foof, Eric!" I was exasperated. "I don't want to stand here in the bathroom trying to talk terminology! What's the bottom line? Are you going to have free time later or not?"

He laughed. "Yes, for you. Can you drive over here? Wait, I'll send Pam for you. She'll be at your house at one o'clock, all right?"

I might have to hurry to get home by then, but it was

doable. "Okay. And warn Pam that . . . Well, tell her not to get carried away by anything, hear?"

"Oh, certainly, I'll be glad to pass that very specific message along," Eric said. He hung up. Not big on saying goodbye, like most vampires.

This was going to be a very long day.

Chapter 3

Luckily for me, all the customers cleared out early, and I was able to get my closing work done in record time. I called, "Good night!" over my shoulder and hared out the back door to my car. When I parked behind the house, I noticed Claude's car wasn't there. So he was probably still in Monroe, which simplified matters. I hurried to change clothes and freshen my makeup, and just as I put on some lipstick, Pam knocked at the back door.

Pam was looking especially Pammish tonight. Her blond hair was absolutely straight and shining, her pale blue suit looked like a vintage gem, and she was wearing hose with seams up the back, which she turned around to show me.

"Wow," I said, which was the only possible response. "You're looking great." She put my red skirt and red and white blouse to shame.

"Yes," she said with considerable satisfaction. "I am. Ah . . ." She became utterly still. "Do I smell fairy?"

"You do, but there's not one here now, so just rein it in. My cousin Claude was here today. He's going to be bunking with me for a while."

"Claude, the mouthwateringly beautiful asshole?" Claude's fame preceded him. "Yes, that Claude."

"Why? Why is he staying with you?"

"He's lonely," I said.

"Do you really believe that?" Pam's pale brows were arched incredulously.

"Well . . . yes, I do." Why else would Claude want to stay at my house, which was not convenient to his job? He certainly didn't want to get in my pants, and he hadn't asked to borrow money.

"This is some fairy intrigue," Pam said. "You were a fool to be taken in."

Nobody likes being called a fool. Pam had stepped over the line, but then "tact" was not her middle name. "Pam, that's enough," I said. I must have sounded serious, because she stared at me for all of fifteen seconds.

"I've offended you," she said, though not as if the idea gave her pain.

"Yeah, you have. Claude's missing his sisters. There aren't any fairies left for him to intrigue with since Niall closed the portal, or doors, or whatever the heck he closed. I'm the closest Claude's got to his kind—which is pretty pitiful, since I just have a dab of fairy in me."

"Let's go," Pam said. "Eric will be waiting."

Changing the subject when she had nothing left to say was another of Pam's characteristics. I had to smile and shake my head. "How'd the meeting with Victor go?" I asked.

"It would be a good thing if Victor met with an unfortunate accident."

"You really mean that?"

"No. I really wish someone would kill him."

"Me, too." Our eyes met, and she gave me a brisk nod. We were in synch on the Victor issue.

"I suspect his every statement," she said. "I question his every decision. I think he's out to take Eric's position. He doesn't want to be the king's emissary any longer. He wants to carve out his own territory."

I pictured a fur-clad Victor paddling a canoe down the Red River with an Indian maiden sitting stoically behind him. I laughed. As we got into Pam's car, she looked at me darkly.

"I don't understand you," she said. "I really don't." We went out to Hummingbird Road and turned north.

"Why would being a sheriff in Louisiana be a step above being the emissary of Felipe, who has a rich kingdom?" I asked very seriously, to make up my lost ground.

"'Better to reign in hell than serve in heaven,'" Pam said. I knew she was quoting someone, but I didn't have a clue who it was.

"Louisiana is hell? *Las Vegas* is heaven?" I could almost believe some cosmopolitan vampire would consider Louisiana as less than desirable as a permanent residence, but Las Vegas—divine? I didn't think so.

"I'm just saying." Pam shrugged. "It's time for Victor to get out from under Felipe's thumb. They've been together a long time. Victor is ambitious."

"That's true. What do you think Victor's strategy is? How do you think he plans to dislodge Eric?"

"He'll try to discredit him," Pam said, without pausing a beat. She'd really been thinking about this. "If Victor can't do that, he'll try to kill Eric—but he won't do it directly, in combat."

"He's scared of fighting Eric?"

"Yes," Pam said, smiling. "I do believe he is." We'd reached the interstate and were on our way west to Shreveport. "If he challenged Eric, it would be Eric's right to send me in first. I would so love to fight Victor." Her fangs gleamed briefly in the dashboard light.

"Does Victor have a second? Wouldn't he send that second in?"

Pam cocked her head to one side. She seemed to be thinking about it as she passed a semi. "His second is Bruno Brazell. He was with Victor the night Eric surrendered to Nevada," she said. "Short beard, an earring? If Eric allowed me to fight for him, Victor might send in Bruno. He's impressive, I grant you. But I would kill him in five minutes or less. You can put money on that."

Pam, who had been a Victorian middle-class young lady with a secret wild streak, had been liberated by becoming a vampire. I had never asked Eric why he'd chosen Pam for the change, but I was convinced it was because Eric had detected her inner ferocity.

On an impulse, I said, "Pam? Do you ever wonder what would have happened to you if you hadn't met up with Eric?"

There was a long silence, or at least it seemed long to me. I wondered if she was angry or sad about her lost chance for a husband and children. I wondered if she was looking back with longing on her sexual relationship with her maker, Eric, which (like most vampire-vampire relationships) hadn't lasted long, but had surely been very intense.

Finally, just when I was going to apologize for asking, Pam said, "I think I was born for this." The faint light from the dashboard illuminated her perfectly symmetrical face. "I would have been a dismal wife, a terrible mother. The part of me that has taken to slashing the throats of my enemies would have surfaced if I'd remained human. I wouldn't have killed anyone, I suppose, because that wasn't on my list of things *I could do*, when I was human. But I would have made my family very miserable; you can be sure of that."

"You're a great vampire," I said, since I couldn't think of anything else to say.

She nodded. "Yes. I am."

We didn't speak again until we reached Eric's house. Oddly enough, he'd bought a place in a gated community with a strict building code. Eric liked the daytime security of the gate and the guard. And he liked the fieldstone house. There weren't too many basements in Shreveport, because the water level was too high, but Eric's house was on a slope. Originally, its downstairs was a walk-in from the back patio. Eric had had that door pulled out and the wall made solid, so he had a great place to sleep.

Until we'd become blood bonded, I'd never been to Eric's house.

Sometimes it was exciting being so closely yoked with Eric, and sometimes it made me feel trapped. Though I could scarcely believe it, the sex was even better now that I'd recovered, at least in large part, from the attack. At this moment, I felt like every molecule in my body was humming because I was near him.

Pam had a garage-door opener, and she pressed it now. The door swung up to reveal Eric's car. Other than the gleaming Corvette, the garage was spotless: no lawn chairs, no bags of grass seed or half-empty paint cans. No stepladder, or coveralls, or hunting boots. Eric didn't need any of those accoutrements. The neighborhood had lawns, pretty lawns, with rigidly planted and mulched flower beds—but a lawn-care service trimmed every blade of grass there, pruned every bush, raked every leaf.

Pam got a kick out of closing the garage door once we were inside. The kitchen door was locked, and she used a key so we could pass from the garage into the kitchen. A kitchen is largely useless to a vampire, though a little refrigerator is necessary for the synthetic blood, and a microwave is handy to heat it to room temperature. Eric had bought a coffeemaker for me, and he kept some food in the freezer for whatever human was in the house. Lately, that human had been me.

"Eric!" I called, when we came through the door. Pam and I took off our shoes, which was one of Eric's house rules.

"Oh, go get your greeting over with!" Pam said, when I looked at her. "I've got some TrueBlood and some Life Support to put away."

I passed from the sterile kitchen into the living room. The kitchen colors were bland, but the living room echoed Eric's personality. Though it wasn't often reflected in his clothing, Eric harbored a love of deep colors. The first time I'd been to his house, the living room had surprised the hell out of me. The walls were a sapphire blue, the crown molding and base-boards a pure, gleaming white. The furniture was an eclectic collection of pieces that had appealed to him, all upholstered in jewel tones, some intricately patterned—deep red, blue, the yellow of citrine, the greens of jade and emerald, the gold of topaz. Since Eric is a big man, all the pieces were big: heavy, sturdy, and strewn with pillows.

Eric came out of the doorway to his home office. When I saw him, every hormone I had stood to attention. He's very tall, his hair is long and golden, and his eyes are so blue the color practically pops out of the whiteness of his face, a face that is bold and masculine. There's nothing epicene about Eric. He wears jeans and T-shirts, mostly, but I've seen him in a suit. *GQ* missed a good thing when Eric decided his talents lay in building a business empire rather than modeling. Tonight he was shirtless, sparse dark gold hair trailing down to the waist of his jeans and gleaming against his pallor.

"Jump," Eric said, holding out his hands and smiling. I laughed. I took a running start, and leaped. Eric caught me, his hands clamped around my waist. He lifted me up until my head touched the ceiling. Then he lowered me for a kiss. I wrapped my legs around his torso, my arms around his neck. We were lost in each other for a long moment.

Pam said, "Back to earth, monkey girl. Time is passing."

I noted that she was blaming me and not Eric. I pulled away and gave him a special smile.

"Come, sit, and tell me what's wrong," he said. "Do you want Pam to know, too?"

"Yes," I said. I figured he'd tell her anyway.

The two vampires sat at opposite ends of the dark red couch, and I sat across from them on the gold and red love seat. In front of the couch was a very large square coffee table with inlaid woodwork on the top and elaborately carved legs. The table was scattered with things Eric had been enjoying recently: the manuscript of a book about the Vikings that he'd been asked to endorse, a heavy jade cigarette lighter (though he didn't smoke), and a beautiful silver bowl with a deep blue enamel interior. I always found his selections interesting. My own house was kind of . . . cumulative. In fact, I hadn't picked out anything in it but the kitchen cabinets and appliances—but my house was the history of my family. Eric's house was the history of Eric.

I brushed a finger across the inlaid wood. "Day before yesterday," I began, "I got a call from Alcide Herveaux."

I wasn't imagining that the two vampires had a reaction to my news. It was minute (most vampires aren't given to extravagant expressions), but it was definitely there. Eric leaned forward, inviting me to continue my account. I did, telling them that I'd also met some of the new additions to the Long Tooth pack, including Basim and Annabelle.

"I've seen this Basim," Pam said. I looked at her with some surprise. "He came to Fangtasia one night with another Were, another new one . . . that Annabelle, the brown-haired woman. She's Alcide's new . . . squeeze."

Though I'd suspected as much, it was still a little astonishing to me. "She must have hidden assets," I said, before I thought.

Eric raised an eyebrow. "Not what you thought Alcide would pick, my lover?"

"I liked Maria-Star," I said. Like so many other people I'd met in the past two years, Alcide's previous girlfriend had met an awful end. I'd grieved for her.

"But before that, he had long associated with Debbie Pelt," Eric said, and I had to struggle to control my face. "You can see that Alcide's catholic in his pleasures," Eric continued. "He carried the torch for you, didn't he?" Eric's slight accent made the outmoded phrase sound exotic. "From a true bitch, to a startling talent, to a sweet photographer, to a tough girl who doesn't mind visiting a vampire bar. Alcide has very variable taste in women."

That was true. I'd never put it together before.

"He sent Annabelle and Basim to the club for a purpose. Have you been reading the newspapers lately?" Pam asked.

"No," I said. "I've been enjoying *not* reading the papers."

"Congress is thinking of passing a bill requiring all the werewolves and shifters to register. Legislation and issues regarding them would then fall under the Bureau of Vampire Affairs, as laws and lawsuits pertaining to us, the undead, do now." Pam was looking very grim.

I almost said, "But that's not *right*!" Then I understood how that would sound—as if I thought it was okay to require the vampires to register, but Weres and shifters shouldn't have to. Thank God I didn't open my mouth.

"Not too surprisingly, the Weres are furious about this. In fact, Alcide has told me himself that he thinks the government has sent people to spy on his pack, the idea being that they would then give some kind of secret report to the people in Congress who are considering this bill. He doesn't believe it's only his pack that's being singled out. Alcide has good sense." Eric sounded approving. "But he believes he's being watched."

Now I understood why Alcide had been so concerned about the people camping on his land. He'd suspected they weren't what they appeared to be.

"It would be awful to think your own government was spying on you," I said. "Especially after you'd been thinking of yourself as a regular citizen your entire life." The enormity of the impact of this piece of legislation was still sinking in. Instead of being a respected and wealthy citizen in Shreveport, Alcide (and the other members of his pack) would become like . . . illegal aliens. "Where would they have to register? Could the kids still go to school with all the other children? What about the men and women at Barksdale Air Force Base? After all these years! Do you think the bill really has a chance of passing?"

Pam said, "The Weres believe it does. Maybe it's paranoia. Maybe they've heard something through the members of Congress who are two-natured. Maybe they know something we don't know. Alcide sent this Annabelle and Basim al Saud to tell me they might be in the same boat with us soon. They wanted to know about the area representative for the BVA, what kind of woman she is, how they could deal with her."

"Who is the rep?" I asked. I felt ignorant and ill-informed. Obviously I should have known this, since I was intimately involved with a vampire.

"Katherine Boudreaux," Pam said. "She likes women somewhat more than men, like I do." Pam grinned a toothy grin. "She also loves dogs. She has a steady lover, Sallie, who shares her house. Katherine is not interested in having a side affair, and she is unbribable."

"You've tried, I take it."

"I tried to interest her sexually. Bobby Burnham tried the bribe." Bobby was Eric's daytime man. We disliked each other intensely.

I took a deep breath. "Well, I'm real glad to know all this, but my real problem came after the Weres used my land."

Eric and Pam were looking at me sharply and with great attention, all of a sudden. "You let the Weres use your property for their monthly run?"

"Well, yeah. Hamilton Bond said there were people camping out on the Herveaux land, and now that I've heard what Alcide's told you—and I'm wondering why he didn't tell me all this—I can see why he didn't want to have a run on his own land. I guess he thought the campers were government agents. What would the new agency be called?" I asked. It wouldn't be BVA, would it? If the BVA was still only "representing" vampires.

Pam shrugged. "The legislation going through Congress proposes it be called the Bureau of Vampire and Supernatural Affairs."

"Get back to your issues, my lover," Eric said.

"Okeydokey. Well, when they were leaving, Basim came to the front door and told me he'd smelled at least one fairy and some other vampire traveling through my land. And my cousin Claude says he wasn't the fairy."

There was a moment of silence.

"Interesting," Eric said.

"Very odd," Pam said.

Eric ran his fingers over the manuscript on the coffee table as if it could tell him who'd been traipsing around my property. "I don't know the credentials of this Basim, except that he was thrown out of the pack in Houston and Alcide took him in. I don't know why he was expelled. I expect it was for some disruption. We'll check on what Basim told you." He turned to Pam. "That new girl, Heidi, says she's a tracker."

"You got a new vamp?" I asked.

"This is one sent us by Victor." Eric's mouth was set in a grim line. "Even from New Orleans, supposedly, Victor is running the state with a tight hand. He sent Sandy, who was supposed to be the liaison, back to Nevada. I suspect Victor thought he didn't have enough control over her."

"How can he get New Orleans up and running if he travels around the state as much as Sandy did?"

"I'm assuming he's leaving Bruno Brazell in charge," Pam said. "I think Bruno pretends Victor is in New Orleans, even when Victor isn't. The rest of Victor's people don't know where he is half the time. Since he killed off all the New Orleans vampires he could find, we've had to rely on the information of our one spy who survived the massacre."

Of course I wanted to veer off and discuss the spy—who would be that brave and reckless, to spy for Eric in the bailiwick of his enemy? But I had to stick to the main subject, which was the sneakiness of Louisiana's new regent head honcho. "So Victor likes to be in the trenches," I said, and Eric and Pam looked at me blankly. Older vampires don't always have a complete grasp of the vernacular. "He likes to see for himself and do for himself, rather than rely on the chain of command," I explained.

"Yes," Pam said. "And the chain of command can be quite heavy and literal, under Victor."

"Pam and I were talking about Victor on the drive over here. I wonder why Felipe de Castro chose Victor to be his representative in Louisiana." Victor had actually seemed okay the two times I'd met him face-to-face, which only went to show that you can't judge a vampire by his good manners and his smile.

"There are two schools of thought about that," Eric said, stretching his long legs out in front of him. I had a flash of how those long legs looked spread wide on crumpled sheets, and I forced my mind back to the current subject of discussion.

Eric gave me a fangy smile (he knew what I was feeling) before he continued. "One is that Felipe wants Victor as far away as he can get him. I believe that Felipe feels that if he gives Victor a big chunk of red meat, he won't be tempted to try to snatch the whole steak."

"While others of us," Pam said, "think that Felipe simply appointed Victor because Victor is very efficient. That Victor's devotion to Felipe is possibly sincere."

"If the first theory is correct," Eric said, "there isn't perfect trust between Felipe and Victor."

"If the second theory is correct," Pam said, "and we act against Victor, Felipe will kill us all."

"I'm getting your drift," I said, looking from First Theory (shirtless with blue jeans) to Second Theory (cute vintage suit). "I hate to sound really selfish, but the first thought that popped into my mind is this. Since Victor wouldn't let you come to help me when I needed you—and incidentally I know that I owe you big-time, Pam—that means Victor's not honoring the promise, huh? Felipe promised me that he would extend his protection to me, which he ought to have, because I saved his life, right?"

There was a significant pause while Eric and Pam considered my question.

"I think Victor will do his best not to openly cause you harm, until and if he decides to try to become king in his own right," Pam said. "If Victor decides to make a grab for the kingship, all promises made by Felipe are so many words without meaning." Eric nodded in agreement.

"That's just great." I probably sounded petulant and selfish, because that was the way I felt.

"This is all assuming we don't find a way to kill him first," Pam said quietly. And we were all silent for a long moment. There was something that creeped me out, no matter how much I agreed that Victor should die, about the three of us talking about murdering him.

"And you think this Heidi, who's supposed to be such a great tracker, is here in Shreveport to be Victor's eyes and ears?" I said briskly, trying to throw off the chill that had fallen on me.

"Yes," said Pam. "Unless she's here to be Felipe's eyes and ears, so Felipe can keep track of what Victor is doing in Louisiana." She had that ominous look on her face, the one that said she was going to get her vampire game on. You did not want Pam to look that way when your name entered the conversation. If I were Heidi, I would take care to keep my nose clean.

"Heidi," which conjured up braids and full skirts in my imagination, seemed like a very perky name for a vampire.

"So what should I do about the Long Tooth pack's warning?" I said, to bring the discussion back to the original problem. "You're going to send Heidi to my place to try to track the fairy? I have to tell you something else. Basim scented a body, not a fresh one, buried very deep at the back of my property."

"Oh," Eric said. "Whoops." Eric turned to Pam. "Give us some alone time."

She nodded and went out through the kitchen. I heard the back door shut.

Eric said, "I'm sorry, my lover. Unless you've buried someone else on your property and kept it from me, that body is Debbie Pelt's."

That was what I'd been afraid of. "Is the car back there, too?"

"No, the car is sunk in a pond about ten miles south of your place."

That was a relief. "Well, at least it was a werewolf who found it," I said. "I guess we don't have to worry about it, unless Alcide can identify her scent. They won't go digging the body up. It's none of their doings." Debbie had been

Alcide's ex-girlfriend when I'd had the misfortune to meet her. I don't want to drag out the story, but she'd tried to kill me first. It took me a while, but I'm over the angst of her death. Eric had been with me that night, but he hadn't been in his right mind. And that's yet another story.

"Come here," Eric said. His face held my very favorite expression, and I was doubly glad to see it because I didn't want to think too much about Debbie Pelt.

"Hmmm. What will you give me if I do?" I gave him a questioning eye.

"I think you know very well what I will give you. I think you love me to give it to you."

"So . . . you don't enjoy it at all?"

Before I could blink he was on his knees in front of me, pushing my legs apart, leaning in to kiss me. "I think you know how I feel," he said, in a whisper. "We are bonded. Can you believe I'm not thinking of you while I work? When my eyes open, I think of you, of every part of you." His fingers got busy, and I gasped. This was direct, even for Eric. "Do you love me?" he asked, his eyes fixing mine.

This was a little difficult to answer, especially considering what his fingers were doing. "I love being with you, whether we're having sex or not. Oh, God, do that again! I love your body. I love what we do together. You make me laugh, and I love that. I like to watch you do anything." I kissed him, long and lingeringly. "I like to watch you get dressed. I like to watch you undress. I like to watch your hands when you're doing this to me. *Oh!*" I shuddered all over with pleasure. When I'd had a moment of recovery, I murmured, "If I asked you the same question, what would your answer be?"

"I would say exactly the same thing," Eric said. "And I think that means I love you. If this is not true love, it's as close as anyone gets. Can you see what you've done to me?" He didn't really have to point. It was pretty damn obvious.

"That looks painful. Would you like me to nurse it?" I asked, in the coolest voice I could manage.

In reply, he simply growled. We switched places in an instant. I knelt in front of Eric, and his hands rested on my head, stroking. Eric was a sizable guy, and this was a part of our sex life that I'd had to work on. But I thought I was getting pretty good at it, and he seemed to agree. His hands tightened in my hair after a minute or two, and I made a little noise of protest. He let go and gripped the couch instead. He growled, deep in his throat. "Faster," he said. "Now, now!" He shut his eyes and his head fell back, his hands opening and closing spasmodically. I loved having that power over him; that was another thing I loved. Suddenly, he said something in an ancient language, and his back arched, and I moved with increased purpose, swallowing down everything he gave me.

And all this with most of our clothes on. "Was that enough love for you?" he asked, his voice slow and dreamy.

I climbed into his lap and wound my arms around his neck for an interlude of cuddling. Now that I had recovered my pleasure in sex, I felt limp as a dishrag after a session with Eric; but this was my favorite part, though it made me feel very "women's magazine" to admit it.

As we sat holding each other, Eric told me about a conversation he'd had with a fangbanger at the bar, and we laughed about it. I told him about how torn up Hummingbird Road was while the parish was patching it. I suppose this is the kind of thing you talk about with someone you love; you figure they'll care about trivial topics, since those things are important to you.

Unfortunately, I knew that Eric had more business to get

through that night, so I told him I'd go back to Bon Temps with Pam. Sometimes I stayed at his place, reading while he worked. It's not easy to arrange alone time with a leader and businessman who's awake only during the hours of darkness.

He gave me a kiss to remember him by. "I'll send Heidi to you, probably night after next," he said. "She'll verify what Basim says he smelled in the woods. Let me know if you hear from Alcide."

When Pam and I left Eric's house, it had started raining. The rain put a little chill in the air, and I turned the heat on low in Pam's car. It wouldn't make any difference to her. We drove for a while in silence, each lost in our own thoughts. I watched the windshield wipers fan back and forth.

Pam said, "You didn't tell Eric about the fairy staying with you."

"Oh, gosh!" I put my hand over my eyes. "No, I didn't. There was so much else to talk about, I completely forgot."

"You realize Eric won't like another man living in the same house with his woman."

"Another man who is my cousin and also gay."

"But very beautiful and a stripper." Pam glanced over at me. She was smiling. Pam's smiles are somewhat disconcerting.

"You can strip all you want to—if you don't like the person you're looking at while you're naked, it's not going to happen," I said tartly.

"I kind of understand that sentence," she said, after a moment. "But still, having such an attractive man in the same house . . . It's not good, Sookie."

"You're kidding me, right? Claude is *gay*. Not only does he like men, he likes men with beard stubble and oil stains on their blue jeans."

"What does that mean?" Pam said.

"That means he likes blue-collar guys who work with their hands. Or their fists."

"Oh. Interesting." Pam still had an air of disapproval. She hesitated for a moment, then said, "Eric hasn't had anyone like you in a long, long time, Sookie. I think he's levelheaded enough to keep on course, but you have to consider his responsibilities. This is a perilous time for the few of us in his original crew remaining since Sophie-Anne met her final death. We Shreveport vampires doubly belong to Eric, since he's the only surviving sheriff from the old regime. If Eric goes down, we all go down. If Victor succeeds in discrediting Eric or somehow eating into his base here in Shreveport, we'll all die."

I hadn't put the situation to myself in terms that dire. Eric hadn't spelled it out to me, either. "It's that bad?" I said, feeling numb.

"He is male enough to want to look strong in front of you, Sookie. Truly, Eric's a great vampire, and very practical. But he isn't practical nowadays—not when it comes to you."

"Are you saying you don't think Eric and I should see each other anymore?" I asked her directly. Though generally I was very glad that vampire minds were closed to me, sometimes I found it frustrating. I was used to knowing more than I wanted to know about how people were thinking and feeling, rather than wondering if I was right.

"No, not exactly." Pam looked thoughtful. "I would hate to see him unhappy. And you, too," she added, as an afterthought. "But if he's worried about you, he won't react the same as he would—as he should . . ."

"If I weren't in the picture."

Pam didn't say anything for a while. Then she said, "I

think the only reason Victor hasn't abducted you to hold you over Eric is because Eric married you. Victor's still trying to cover his ass by doing everything by the book. He isn't ready to rebel against Felipe openly. He'll still try to show justification for whatever he does. He's walking on thin ice with Felipe right now because he almost let you get killed."

"Maybe Felipe will do the job for us," I said.

Pam looked thoughtful. "That would be ideal," she said. "But we'll have to wait for it. Felipe's not going to do anything rash when it comes to killing a lieutenant of his. That would make his other lieutenants uneasy and uncertain."

I shook my head. "That's too bad. I don't think it would bother Felipe very much at all to kill Victor."

"And it would bother you, Sookie?"

"Yes. It would bother me." Though not as much as it ought to.

"So if you could do it in a rush of rage when Victor was attacking you, that would be far preferable to planning a way to kill him when he couldn't fight back effectively?"

Okay, put like that my attitude didn't make much sense. I could see that if you were willing to kill someone, planning to kill someone, wishing someone would die, quibbling about the circumstances was ridiculous.

"It shouldn't make a difference," I said quietly. "But it does. Victor has to go, though."

"You've changed," Pam said, after a little silence. She didn't sound surprised or horrified or disgusted. For that matter, she didn't sound happy. It was more as though she'd realized I'd altered my hairstyle.

"Yes," I said. We watched the rain pour down some more.

Suddenly, Pam said, "Look!" There was a sleek white car parked on the shoulder of the interstate. I didn't understand why Pam was so agitated until I noticed that the man leaning against the car had his arms crossed over his chest in an attitude of total nonchalance, despite the rain.

As we drew abreast of the car, a Lexus, the figure waved a languid hand at us. We were being flagged down.

"Shit," Pam said. "That's Bruno Brazell. We have to stop." She pulled over to the shoulder and stopped in front of the car. "And Corinna," she said, sounding bitter. I glanced in the side mirror to see that a woman had gotten out of the Lexus.

"They're here to kill us," Pam said quietly. "I can't kill them both. You have to help."

"They're going to try to kill us?" I was really, really scared.

"That's the only reason I can think of that Victor would send two people on a one-person errand," she said. She sounded calm. Pam was obviously thinking much faster than I was. "Showtime! If the peace can be kept, we need to keep it, at least for now. Here." She pressed something into my hand. "Take it out of the sheath. It's a silver dagger."

I remembered Bill's gray skin and the slow way he moved after silver poisoning. I shuddered, but I was angry with myself for my squeamishness. I slid the dagger from the leather sheath.

"We have to get out, huh?" I said. I tried to smile. "Okay, showtime."

"Sookie, be brave and ruthless," Pam said, and she opened her door and disappeared from sight. I sent a last waft of love toward Eric by way of good-bye while I was sticking the dagger through my skirt's waistband at the back. I got out of the car into the pelting darkness, holding my hands out to show they were empty.

I was drenched in seconds. I shoved my hair behind my ears so it wouldn't hang in my eyes. Though the Lexus's headlights were on, it was very dark. The only other light came from oncoming headlights from both sides of the interstate, and the brightly lit truck stop a mile away. Otherwise, we were nowhere, an anonymous stretch of divided interstate with woods on either side. The vampires could see a lot better than I could. But I knew where everyone was because I cast out that other sense of mine and felt for their brains. Vampires register as holes to me, almost black spots in the atmosphere. It's negative tracking.

No one spoke, and the only noise was the pelting of the rain drumming on the cars. I couldn't hear an oncoming vehicle. "Hi, Bruno," I called, and I sounded perky in a crazy way. "Who's your buddy?"

I walked over to him. Across the median, a car whizzed by going west. If the driver caught a glimpse of us, it probably looked as though two Good Samaritans had stopped to help some people with car trouble. Humans see what they want to see . . . what they expect to see.

Now that I was closer to Bruno, I could tell that his short brown hair was plastered to his head. I'd seen Bruno only once before, and he was wearing the same serious expression on his face that he'd worn the night he'd been standing in my front yard ready to move in and burn down my house with me in it. Bruno was a serious kind of guy in the same way I'm a perky kind of woman. It was a fallback position.

"Hello, Miss Stackhouse," Bruno said. He wasn't any taller than me, but he was a burly man. The vampire Pam had called Corinna loomed up on Bruno's right. Corinna was— had been—African-American, and the water was dripping off the tips of her intricately braided hair. The beads worked into the braids clicked together, a sound I could just pick up under the drumming of the rain. She was thin and tall, and she'd added to her height with three-inch heels. Though she was wearing a dress that had probably been very expensive, her whole ensemble had suffered by the drenching it had taken. She looked like a very elegant drowned rat.

Since I was almost out of my head with alarm anyway, I started laughing.

"You got a flat tire or something, Bruno?" I asked. "I can't imagine what else you'd be doing out here in the middle of nowhere in the pouring rain."

"I was waiting for you, bitch."

I wasn't sure where Pam was, and I couldn't spare the brainpower to search for her. "Language, Bruno! I don't think you know me well enough to call me that. I guess you-all have someone watching Eric's house."

"We do. When we saw you two leaving together, it seemed like a good time to take care of a few things."

Corinna still hadn't spoken, but she was looking around her warily, and I realized she didn't know where Pam had gone. I grinned. "For the life of me, I don't know why you're doing all this. It seems like Victor should be glad to have someone as smart as Eric working for him. Why can't he appreciate that?" *And leave us alone.*

Bruno took a step closer to me. The light was too poor for me to make out his eye color, but I could tell he was still looking serious. I thought it was strange when Bruno took the time to answer me, but anything that bought us more time was good. "Eric is a great vampire. But Eric will never bow to Victor, not really. And he's accumulating his own power at a pace that makes Victor anxious. He's got you, for one thing. Your great-grandfather may have sealed himself away, but who's to say he won't come back? And Eric can use your stupid ability whenever he chooses. Victor doesn't want

Eric to have that advantage." And then Bruno had his hands around my neck. He'd moved so quickly I couldn't possibly react, and I knew vaguely over the pounding in my ears that there was a sudden and violent commotion going on to my left. I reached behind me to pull the knife, but we were suddenly down in the tall, wet grass at the edge of the shoulder, and I kicked my leg up and over, and pushed, trying to get on top. I kind of overdid it, because we began rolling down into the drainage ditch. That was a pity, because it was filling with water. Bruno couldn't drown, but I sure could. Wrenching my shoulder with the force of my effort, I yanked the knife out of my skirt when I rotated to the top, and as we rolled yet again I saw dark spots in front of my eyes. I knew this was my last chance. I stabbed Bruno up under his ribs.

And I killed him.

Chapter 4

Pam yanked Bruno's body off me and rolled him all the way down into the water coursing through the ditch. She helped me up.

"Where were you?" I croaked.

"Disposing of Corinna," literal-minded Pam said. She pointed to the body lying by the white car. Fortunately, the corpse was on the side of the car concealed from the view of the rare passerby. In the poor light it was hard to be sure, but I believed Corinna was already beginning to flake away. I'd never seen a dead vampire in the rain before.

"I thought Bruno was such a great fighter. How come *you* didn't take him on?"

"I gave you the knife," Pam said, giving a good imitation of surprise. "He didn't have a knife."

"Right." I coughed and, boy, did that hurt my throat. "So what do we do now?"

"We're getting out of here," Pam said. "We're going to

hope that no one noticed my car. I think only three cars passed since we pulled over. With the rain and poor visibility, if the drivers were human, we have a very good chance that none of them will remember seeing us."

By then we were back in Pam's car. "Wouldn't it be better if we moved the Lexus?" I said, wheezing out the words.

"What a good idea," Pam said, patting me on the head. "Do you think you can drive it?"

"Where to?"

Pam thought for a moment, which was good, because I needed the recovery time. I was soaked through and shivering, and I felt awful.

"Won't Victor know what's happened?" I asked. I couldn't seem to stop asking questions.

"Maybe. He wasn't brave enough to do this himself, so he has to take the consequences. He's lost his two best people, and he has nothing to show for it." Pam was enjoying the hell out of that.

"I think we get out of here right now. Before some more of his people come to check, or whatever." I sure wasn't up for fighting again.

"It's you who keeps asking questions. I think Eric will be here soon; I'd better call him to tell him to stay away," Pam said. She looked faintly worried.

"Why?" I would have loved to have Eric appear to take charge of this situation, frankly.

"If someone is watching his house, and he leaps into his car and drives in this direction to come rescue you, it'll be a pretty clear indication that we're responsible for what happened to Bruno and Corinna," Pam said, clearly exasperated. "Use your brain, Sookie!"

"My brain is all soggy," I said, and if I sounded a little

testy, I don't think that's any big, amazing thing. But Pam was already hitting a speed-dial number on her cell. I could hear Eric yelling when he answered the phone.

Pam said, "Shut up and I'll explain. Of course, she lives." There was silence.

Pam summed up the situation in a few pithy phrases, and she concluded with, "Go somewhere it's reasonable to be going in a hurry. Back to the bar in answer to some crisis. To the all-night dry cleaners to pick up your suits. To the store to pick up some TrueBlood. Don't lead them here."

After a squawk or two, Eric apparently saw the sense in what Pam was saying. I couldn't hear his voice clearly, though he was still talking to her.

"Her throat will be bruised," Pam said impatiently. "Yes, she killed Bruno herself. All right, I'll tell her." Pam turned to me. "He's proud of you," she said with some disgust.

"Pam gave me the knife," I croaked. I knew he could hear me.

"But it was Sookie's idea to move the car," Pam said, with the air of someone who's going to be fair if it kills her. "I'm trying to think of where to put it. The truck stops will have security cameras. I think we'll leave it on the shoulder well past the Bon Temps exit."

That's what we did. Pam had some towels in her trunk, and I put them down on the seat of Bruno's car. Pam poked around in his ashes to retrieve the Lexus key, and after looking over the instrument panel, I figured I could drive it. I followed Pam for forty minutes, staring longingly at the Bon Temps sign as we sped past it. I pulled over to the shoulder right after Pam did. Following Pam's instructions, I left the key in the car, wiped off the steering wheel with the towels (which were damp from their contact with me), and then scuttled to Pam's car and climbed in. It was still raining, by the way.

Then we had to return to my house. By then I was aching in every joint and a little sick to my stomach. Finally, finally, we pulled up to my back door. To my amazement, Pam leaned over to give me a hug. "You did very well," she said. "You did what had to be done." For once, she didn't look as if she were secretly laughing at me.

"I hope this all turns out to be worth it," I said, sounding as gloomy and exhausted as I felt.

"We're still alive, so it was worth it," Pam said.

I couldn't argue with that, though something within me wanted to.

I climbed out of her car and trudged across the dripping backyard. The rain had finally stopped.

Claude opened the back door as I reached it. He had opened his mouth to say something, but when he took in my condition, he closed it again. He shut the door behind me, and I heard him lock it.

"I'm going to shower," I said, "and then I'm going to bed. Good night, Claude."

"Good night, Sookie," he said, very quietly, and then he shut up. I appreciated that more than I could say.

*When I got into work the next day at eleven, Sam was dust-*ing all the bottles behind the bar.

"Good morning," he said, staring at me. "You look like hell warmed over."

"Thanks, Sam. Good to know I'm looking my best."

Sam turned red. "Sorry, Sookie. You always look good. I was just thinking . . ."

"About the big circles under my eyes?" I pulled down the skin of my cheeks, making a hideous face for his benefit. "I was real late getting in last night." *I had to kill someone and move his car.* "I had to go over to Shreveport to see Eric."

"Business or pleasure?" And he ducked his head, clearly not believing he'd said that, either. "I'm sorry, Sookie. My mom would say I got up on the tactless side of the bed today."

I gave him a half hug. "Don't worry. Every day is like that for me. And I have to apologize to you. I'm sorry I've been so ignorant about the legal trouble facing shifters and Weres right now." It was definitely time for me to look at the big picture.

"You had some good reasons to concentrate on yourself the past few weeks," Sam said. "I don't know that I could have recovered the way you have. I'm real proud of you."

I didn't know what to say. I looked down at the bar, reached for a cloth to polish away a ring. "If you need me to start a petition or call my state representative, you just say the word," I told him. "No one should make you register anywhere. You're an American. Born and bred."

"That's the way I look at it. It's not like I'm any different from the way I've always been. The only difference is that now people know about it. How did the pack run go?"

I'd almost forgotten about it. "They seemed to have a good time, far as I can tell," I said cautiously. "I met Annabelle and the new guy, Basim. Why is Alcide beefing up the ranks? Have you heard anything about what's been happening in the Long Tooth pack?"

"Well, I told you I'd been dating one of them," he said, looking away at the bottles behind the bar as if he were trying to spot one that was still dusty. If this conversation continued in the same vein, the whole bar would be spanking clean.

"Who would that be?" Since this was the second time he'd mentioned it, I figured it was okay for me to ask.

His fascination with the bottles was transferred to the cash register. "Ah, Jannalynn. Jannalynn Hopper."

"Oh," I said, in a neutral way. I was trying to give myself a little time to make my face bland and receptive.

"She was there the night we fought the pack that was trying to take over. She, ah . . . took care of the wounded enemies."

That was an extreme euphemism. She'd cracked their skulls with her clenched fists. Trying to prove that it wasn't National Tactless Day at *my* house, I said, "Oh, yes. The, ah, very slim girl. The young one."

"She's not as young as she looks," Sam said, bypassing the obvious fact that her age was not the first issue one could have with Jannalynn.

"Okeydokey. How old is she?"

"Twenty. One."

"Oh, well, she's quite a girl," I said solemnly. I forced a smile to my lips. "Seriously, Sam, I'm not judging your choice." Not much. "Jannalynn's really, really . . . She's dynamic."

"Thanks," he said, his face clearing. "She gave me a call after we fought in the pack war. She's into lions." Sam had changed into a lion that night, the better to fight. He'd made a magnificent king of beasts.

"So, how long have you two been dating?"

"We've been talking for a while, but we went out for the first time maybe three weeks ago."

"Well, that's great," I said. I made myself relax and smile

more naturally. "You sure you don't need a note from her mom?"

Sam threw the dust cloth at me. I grabbed it and threw it back.

"Can you two quit playing? I got to talk to Sam," Tanya said. She'd come in without my hearing her.

She's never going to be my best friend, but she's a good worker and she's willing to come in two evenings a week after she gets off her day job at Norcross. "You want me to leave?" I asked.

"No, that's okay."

"Sorry, Tanya. What do you need?" Sam asked, smiling.

"I need you to change my name on my paychecks," Tanya said.

"You changed your name?" I must have been extra slow that day. But Sam would have said it if I hadn't; he looked just as blank.

"Yeah, me and Calvin went to a courthouse across the state line in Arkansas and got married," she said. "I'm Tanya Norris now."

Sam and I both stared at Tanya in a moment of silent astonishment.

"Congratulations!" I said heartily. "I know you'll be real happy." I wasn't so sure about Calvin being happy, but at least I managed to say something nice.

Sam chimed in, too, with all the right things. Tanya showed us her wedding ring, a broad gold band, and after going into the kitchen to show it to Antoine and D'Eriq, she left as abruptly as she'd arrived to drive back to work at Norcross. She'd mentioned they'd registered at Target and Wal-Mart for the few things they needed, so Sam dashed into his office and picked out a wall clock to give them from all the

Merlotte's employees. He put a jar out by the bar for our contributions, and I dropped in a ten.

By that time, people were coming in for lunch, and I had to get busy. "I never did get around to asking you some questions," I said to Sam. "Maybe before I leave work?"

"Sure, Sook," he said, and began filling glasses with iced tea. It was a warm day.

After I'd served drinks and food for about an hour, I was surprised to see Claude coming through the door. Even in rumpled clothes he'd obviously picked up off the floor to pull on, he looked breathtakingly gorgeous. He'd pulled his hair back into a messy ponytail . . . and it didn't detract.

It was almost enough to make you hate him, really.

Claude slouched over to me as if he were in Merlotte's every day . . . and as if his kind and tactful moment last night had never been. "The water heater's not working," he said.

"Hi, Claude. Good to see you," I said. "Did you sleep well? I'm so glad. I slept well, too. I guess you better do something about the water heater, huh? If you want to shower and wash your clothes. Remember me asking you to help me out by handling some things I can't? You could call Hank Clearwater. He's come out to the house before."

"I can go have a look," a voice said. I turned to see Terry Bellefleur standing behind me. Terry is a Vietnam War vet, and he's got some awful scars—both the kind you can see and the kind you can't. He'd been very young when he'd gone to war. He'd been very old when he returned. His auburn hair was graying, but it was still thick, and long enough to braid. I'd always gotten along real well with Terry, who could do just about anything around the yard or in the house, by way of repairs.

"I would sure appreciate it," I said. "But I don't want to

take advantage, Terry." He'd always been kind to me. He'd cleared away the debris of my burned kitchen so the builders could start working on the new one, and I'd had to insist he take a fair wage for it.

"No problem," he muttered, his eyes on his old work boots. Terry survived on a monthly government check and on several odd jobs. For example, he came into Merlotte's either very late at night or early in the morning to clean the tables and the bathrooms, and to mop the floors. He always said keeping busy kept him fit, and it was true that Terry was still built.

"I'm Claude Crane, Sookie's cousin." Claude held out his hand to Terry.

Terry muttered his own name and took Claude's hand. His eyes came up to meet Claude's. Terry's eyes were unexpectedly beautiful, a rich golden brown and heavily lashed. I'd never noticed before. I realized I'd never thought about Terry as a *man* before.

After the handshake, Terry looked startled. When he was faced with something out of his normal path, usually Terry reacted badly; the only question was of degree. But at the moment, Terry seemed more puzzled than frightened or angry.

"Ah, did you want me to come look at it now?" Terry asked. "I have a couple of hours free."

"That would be wonderful," Claude said. "I want my shower, and I want a hot one." He smiled at Terry.

"Dude, I'm not gay," Terry said, and the expression on Claude's face was priceless. I'd never seen Claude nonplussed before.

"Thanks, Terry, I'd sure appreciate it," I said briskly. "Claude's got a key, and he'll let you in. If you have to buy some parts, just give me the receipts. You know I'm good for it." I might have to transfer some money from my savings to my checking, but I still had what I thought of as my "vampire money" safely stashed at the bank. And Mr. Cataliades would be sending me poor Claudine's money, too. Something relaxed inside me every time I thought about that bit of money. I'd been balanced on the fine edge of poverty so many times that I was used to it, and the knowledge of that money I'd be able to sock in the bank was a huge relief to me.

Terry nodded and then went out the back door to get his pickup. I speared Claude with a scowl. "That man is very fragile," I said. "He had a bad war. Just remember that."

Claude's face was slightly flushed. "I'll remember," he said. "I've been in wars myself." He gave me another quick graze on the cheek, to show me he'd recovered from the blow to his pride. I could feel the envy of every woman in the bar beating against me. "I'll be gone to Monroe by the time you get home, I suppose. Thanks, Cousin."

Sam came to stand beside me as Claude went out the door. "Elvis has left the building," he said dryly.

"No, I haven't seen him in a while," I said, definitely on auto-mouth. Then I shook myself. "Sorry, Sam. Claude's one of a kind, isn't he?"

"I haven't seen Claudine in a while. She's a lot of fun," Sam said. "Claude seems to be . . . more typical of the general run of fairies." There was a question in his voice.

"We won't be seeing Claudine anymore," I said. "As far as I know, we won't be seeing any fairies but Claude. The doors are shut. However that works. Though I understand there's still one or two lurking around my house."

"There's a lot you haven't told me," he said.

"We need to catch up," I agreed.

"What about this evening? After you get off? Terry's supposed to come back and do some repairs that have piled up around here, but Kennedy is scheduled to take the bar." Sam looked a little worried. "I hope Claude doesn't make another pass at Terry. Claude's ego is as big as a barn, and Terry's so . . . You never know how he's going to take stuff."

"Terry's a grown man," I reminded Sam. Of course, I was trying to reassure myself. "They both are."

"Claude isn't a man at all," Sam said. "Though he's a *male*."

It was a huge relief when I noticed Terry'd returned an hour later. He seemed absolutely normal, not flustered, angry, or anything else.

I had always tried to keep out of Terry's head, because it could be a very frightening place. Terry did well as long as he kept his focus on one thing at a time. He thought about his dogs a lot. He'd kept one of the puppies from his bitch's last litter, and he was training the youngster. (In fact, if ever a dog was taught to read, Terry would be the man who'd done it.)

After he'd worked on a loose doorknob in Sam's office, Terry sat at one of my tables and ordered a salad and some sweet tea. After I took his order, Terry silently handed me a receipt. He'd had to get a new element for the water heater. "It's all fixed now," he said. "Your cousin was able to get his hot shower."

"Thanks, Terry," I said. "I'm going to give you something for your time and labor."

"Not a problem," Terry said. "Your cousin took care of that." He turned his attention to his magazine. He'd brought a copy of *Louisiana Hunting and Fishing* to read while he waited for his food.

I wrote Terry a check for the element and gave it to him

when I brought his food. He nodded and slipped it in his pocket. Since Terry's schedule meant he wasn't always available to fill in, Sam had hired another bartender so he could have some regular evenings off. The new bartender, who'd been at work for a couple of weeks, was really pretty in a supersized way. Kennedy Keyes was five-eleven, easy; taller than Sam, for sure. She had the kind of good looks you associate with traditional beauty queens: shoulder-length chestnut hair with discreet blond highlights, wide brown eyes, a white and even smile that was an orthodontist's wet dream. Her skin was perfect, her back straight, and she'd graduated from Southern Arkansas University with a degree in psychology.

She'd also done time.

Sam had asked her if she wanted a job when she'd drifted in for lunch the day after she'd gotten out of jail. She hadn't even asked what she'd be doing before she'd said yes. He'd given her a basic bartender's guide, and she'd studied every spare moment until she'd mastered an amazing number of drinks.

"Sookie!" she said, as if we'd been best friends since childhood. That was Kennedy's way. "How you doing?"

"Good, thank you. Yourself?"

"Happy as a clam." She bent to check the number of sodas in the glass-fronted refrigerator behind the bar. "We need us some A&W," she said.

"Coming right up." I got the keys from Sam, then went back to the stockroom to find a case of root beer. I got two six-packs.

"I didn't mean you to get that. I coulda gotten them!" Kennedy smiled at me. Her smile was kind of perpetual. "I appreciate it."

"No problem."

"Do I look any smaller, Sookie?" she said hopefully. She half turned to show me her butt and looked at me over her own shoulder.

Kennedy's issue didn't seem to be that she had been in jail, but that she had put on weight in jail. The food had been crappy, she'd told me, and it had been high on the carbohydrate count. "But I'm an emotional eater," she'd said, as if that were a terrible thing. "And I was real emotional in jail." Ever since she'd gotten back to Bon Temps, she'd been anxious to return to her beauty queen measurements.

She was still beautiful. There was just more of her to look good.

"You're gorgeous, as always," I said. I looked around for Danny Prideaux. Sam had asked Danny to come in when Kennedy was working at night. This arrangement was supposed to last for a month, until Sam was sure people wouldn't take advantage of Kennedy.

"You know," she said, interpreting my glance, "I can handle myself."

Everyone in Bon Temps knew that Kennedy could handle herself, and that was the problem. Her reputation might constitute a challenge to certain men (certain men who were assholes). "I know you can," I said mildly. Danny Prideaux was insurance.

And there he came through the door. He was taller than Kennedy by a couple of inches, and he was of some racial mixture that I hadn't figured out. Danny had deep olive skin, short brown hair, and a broad face. He'd been out of the army for a month, and he hadn't yet settled into a career of any sort. He worked part-time at the home builders' supply store. He was willing enough to be a bouncer for a few nights a week, especially since he got to look at Kennedy the whole time.

Sam drifted out of his office to say good night and brief Kennedy on a customer whose check had bounced, and then he and I went out the back door together. "Let's go to Crawdad Diner," he suggested. That sounded good to me. It was an old restaurant just off the square around the courthouse. Like all the businesses in the area around the square, the oldest part of Bon Temps, the diner had a history. The original owners had been Perdita and Crawdad Jones, who'd opened the restaurant in the forties. When Perdita had retired, she'd sold the business to Charlsie Tooten's husband, Ralph, who'd quit his job at the chicken processing plant to take over. Their deal was that Perdita would give Ralph all her recipes if he'd agree to keep the name Crawdad Diner. When Ralph's arthritis had forced him to retire, he'd sold Crawdad Diner to Pinkie Arnett with the same condition. So generations of Bon Temps diners were ensured of getting the best bread pudding in the state, and the heirs of Perdita and Crawdad Jones were able to point with pride.

I told Sam this bit of local history after we'd ordered country-fried steak with green beans and rice.

"Thank God Pinkie got the bread pudding recipe, and when the green tomatoes are in season, I want to come in every other night to have 'em fried," Sam said. "How's living with your cousin?" He squeezed his lemon slice into his tea.

"I hardly know yet. He just moved in some stuff, and we haven't had a lot of overlap."

"Have you seen him strip?" Sam laughed. "I mean, professionally? I sure couldn't do that on a stage with people watching."

Physically, there sure wouldn't be anything stopping him. I'd seen Sam naked when he changed from a shifter form into human. Yum. "No, I always planned on going with Amelia, but since she went back to New Orleans I haven't been in a strip-club kind of mood. You should ask Claude for a job on your nights off," I said, grinning.

"Oh, sure," he said sarcastically, but he looked pleased.

We talked about Amelia's departure for a while, and then I asked Sam about his family in Texas. "My mom's divorce came through," he said. "Of course, my stepdad's been in jail since he shot her, so she hasn't seen him in months. At this point, I'm guessing the main difference to her is going to be financial. She's getting my dad's military pension, but she doesn't know if her job at the school will be waiting for her or not when the summer's over. They hired a substitute for the rest of the school year after she got shot, and they're waffling over having Mom back."

Before she'd gotten shot, Sam's mom had been the receptionist/secretary at an elementary school. Not everyone was calm about having a woman who turned into an animal working in the same office as them, though Sam's mom was the same woman she'd been before. I was baffled by this attitude.

The waitress brought our plates and a basket of rolls. I sighed with anticipated pleasure. This was much nicer than cooking for myself.

"Any news on Craig's wedding?" I asked, when I could yank myself away from my country-fried steak.

"They finished couples counseling," he said with a shrug. "Now her parents want them to have genetics counseling, whatever that is."

"That's nuts."

"Some people just think anything different is bad," Sam said as he buttered his second roll. "And it's not like Craig could change." As the firstborn of a pure shifter couple, only Sam felt the call of the moon.

"I'm sorry." I shook my head. "I know the situation's hard on everyone in your family."

He nodded. "My sister Mindy's gotten over it pretty well. She let me play with the kids the last time I saw them, and I'm going to try to get over to Texas for the Fourth of July. Her town has a big fireworks display, and the whole family goes. I think I'd enjoy it."

I smiled. They were lucky to have Sam in their family—that was what I thought. "Your sister must be pretty smart," I said. I took a big bite of country-fried steak with milk gravy. It was blissful.

He laughed. "Listen, while we're talking family," he said. "You ready to tell me how you're really doing? You told me about your great-grandfather and what happened. How are your injuries? I don't want to sound like I expect you to tell me everything that goes on in your life. But you know I care."

I did a little hesitating myself. But it felt right to tell Sam, so I tried to give him a nutshell account of the past week. "And JB has been helping me with some physical therapy," I added.

"You're walking like nothing happened, unless you get tired," he observed.

"There's a couple of bad patches on my left upper thigh where the flesh actually . . . Okay, not going there." I looked down at my napkin for a minute or two. "It grew back. Mostly. There's a kind of dimple. I have a few scars, but they're not terrible. Eric doesn't seem to mind." In fact, he had a scar or two from his human life, though they hardly showed against the whiteness of his skin.

"Are you, ah, coping okay with it?"

"I have nightmares sometimes," I confessed. "And I have some panic moments. But let's not talk about it anymore." I smiled at him, my brightest smile. "Look at us after all these years, Sam. I'm living with a fairy, I've got a vampire boy-friend, you're dating a werewolf who cracks skulls. Would we ever have thought we'd say this, the first day I came to work at Merlotte's?"

Sam leaned forward and briefly put his hand over mine, and just then Pinkie herself came by the table to ask us how we'd liked the food. I pointed to my nearly empty plate. "I think you can tell we did," I said, smiling at her. She grinned back. Pinkie was a big woman who clearly enjoyed her own cooking. Some new customers came in, and she went off to seat them.

Sam took his hand back and began working on his food again. "I wish . . ." Sam began, and then he closed his mouth. He ran a hand through his red gold hair. Since he'd had it trimmed so short, it had looked tamer than usual until he tousled it. He laid his fork down, and I noticed he'd managed to dispose of almost all his food, too.

"What do you wish?" I asked. Most people, I'd be scared to ask them to complete that sentence. But Sam and I had been friends for years.

"I wish that you would find happiness with someone else," he said. "I know, I know. It's none of my business. Eric does seem to really care about you, and you deserve that."

"He does," I said. "He's what I've got, and I'd be real ungrateful if I weren't happy with that. We love each other." I shrugged, in a self-deprecating way. I was uncomfortable with the turn of the conversation.

Sam nodded, though a wry twist to the corner of his mouth told me, without even hearing his thoughts, that Sam didn't think Eric was such an object of worth. I was glad I couldn't hear all his thoughts clearly. I thought Jannalynn was equally inappropriate for Sam. He didn't need a ferocious, anything-for-the-packmaster kind of woman. He needed to be with someone who thought he was the greatest man around.

But I didn't say anything.

You can't say I'm not tactful.

It was dreadfully tempting to tell Sam what had happened the night before. But I just couldn't. I didn't want to involve Sam in vampire shit any more than he already was, which was very little. No one needed stuff like that. Of course, I'd worried all day about the fallout from those events.

My cell phone rang while Sam was paying his half of the bill. I glanced at it. Pam was calling. My heart leaped into my throat. I stepped outside the diner.

"What's up?" I asked, sounding just as anxious as I really was.

"Hello to you, too."

"Pam, what happened?" I wasn't in the mood for playfulness.

"Bruno and Corinna didn't show up in New Orleans for work today," Pam said solemnly. "Victor didn't call here, because, of course, there was no good reason for them to come up here."

"Did they find the car?"

"Not yet. I'm sure the highway-patrol officers have put a sticker on it today, asking the owners to come and remove it. That's what they do, I've observed."

"Yes. That's what they do."

"No bodies will appear. Especially since after the downpour of last night, there won't be a trace." Pam sounded smug about that. "No blame can attach to us."

I stood there, phone to my ear, on an empty sidewalk in my little town, the streetlight only a few feet away. I'd seldom felt more alone. "I wish it had been Victor," I said, from the bottom of my heart.

"You want to kill someone else?" Pam sounded mildly surprised.

"No, I want it to be over. I want everything to be okay. I don't want any more killing at all." Sam came out of the restaurant behind me and heard the distress in my voice. I felt his hand on my shoulder. "I have to go, Pam. Keep me posted."

I shut the phone and turned to face Sam. He was looking troubled, and the light streaming from overhead cast deep shadows on his face.

"You're in trouble," he said.

I could only keep silent.

"I know you can't talk about it, but if you ever feel like you have to, you know where I am," he said.

"You, too," I said, because I figured with a girlfriend like Jannalynn, Sam might be in almost as bad a position as I was.

Chapter 5

The phone rang while I was in the shower Friday morning.
Since I had an answering machine, I ignored it. As I was
reaching out for my towel with my eyes shut, I felt it being
thrust into my hand. With a gasp, I opened my eyes to see
Claude standing there in his altogether.

"Phone's for you," he said, handing me the portable phone
from the kitchen. He left.

I put it to my ear automatically. "Hello?" I said weakly.
I didn't know what to think about first: me seeing Claude
naked, Claude seeing me naked, or the whole fact that we
were related and naked in the same room.

"Sookie? You sound funny," said a faintly familiar male
voice.

"Oh, I just got a surprise," I said. "I'm so sorry. . . . Who
is this?"

He laughed, and it was a warm and friendly sound. "This
is Remy Savoy, Hunter's dad," he said.

Remy had been married to my cousin Hadley, who was now dead. Their son, Hunter, and I had a connection, a connection that we needed to explore. I'd been meaning to call Remy to set up a playdate for me and Hunter, and I chided myself now for putting it off. "I hope you're calling to tell me that I can see Hunter this weekend," I said. "I've got to work Sunday afternoon, but I have Saturday off. Tomorrow, that is."

"That's great! I was going to ask if I could bring him over this evening, and maybe he could spend the night."

That was a lot of time to spend with a kid I didn't know; more important, a kid who didn't know me. "Remy, do you have special plans or something?"

"Yeah. My dad's sister died yesterday, and they've set the funeral for tomorrow morning at ten. But the visitation is tonight. I hate to take Hunter to the visitation and the funeral . . . especially considering, you know, his . . . problem. It might be pretty hard on him. You know how it is. . . . I can't ever be sure what he'll say."

"I understand." And I did. A preschool telepath is tough to be around. My parents would have appreciated Remy's predicament. "How old is Hunter now?"

"Five, just had a birthday. I was worried about the party, but we got through that okay."

I took a deep breath. I'd told him I'd help out with Hunter's problem. "Okay, I can keep him overnight."

"Thanks. I mean, *really* thanks. I'll bring him over when I get off work today. That okay? We'll be there about five thirty?"

I would get off work between five and six, depending on my replacement being on time and how full my tables were. I gave Remy my cell number. "If I'm not home, call my cell. I'll be back here as soon as I can. What does he like to eat?"

We talked about Hunter's routine for a few minutes, and then I hung up. By then, I was dry, but my hair was hanging in damp rattails. After a few minutes with the blow-dryer, I set off to talk to Claude once I was securely dressed in my work clothes.

"Claude!" I yelled from the bottom of the stairs.

"Yes?" He sounded totally unconcerned.

"Come down here!"

He appeared at the head of the stairs, his hairbrush in his hand. "Yes, Cousin?"

"Claude, the answering machine would have picked up the phone call. Please don't come in my room without knocking, and especially don't come in my bathroom without knocking!" I would definitely employ the door lock from now on. I didn't think I'd ever used it before.

"Are you a prude?" He seemed genuinely curious.

"No!" But after a second, I said, "But maybe compared to you, yes! I like my privacy. I get to decide who sees me naked. Do you get my point?"

"Yes. Objectively speaking, you have beautiful points."

I thought the top of my head would pop off. "I didn't expect this when I told you that you could stay with me. You like men."

"Oh, yes, I definitely prefer men. But I can appreciate beauty. I *have* visited the other side of the fence."

"I probably wouldn't have let you stay here if I'd known that," I said.

Claude shrugged, as if to say, "Wasn't I smart to keep it from you, then?"

"Listen," I said, and then stopped, because I was rattled. No matter what the circumstances, seeing Claude naked . . . Well, your first reaction wouldn't be rage, either. "I'm going to tell you a few things, and I want you to take me seriously."

He waited, brush in hand, looking only politely attentive.

"Number one. I have a boyfriend, and he's a vampire, and I'm not interested in cheating on him, and that includes seeing other guys naked . . . in my bathroom," I tacked on hastily, thinking of twoeys of all sorts. "If you can't respect that, you need to leave, and you'll just have to cry all the way home. Number two. I'm having company tonight, a little kid I'm babysitting, and you better act appropriate around him. You picking up what I'm laying down?"

"No nudity, be nice to the human kid."

"Right."

"Is the child yours?"

"If he were mine, I'd be raising him, you can bet your money. He's Hadley's. She was my cousin, the daughter of my aunt Linda. She was the, ah, the girlfriend of Sophie-Anne. You know, the former queen? And she became a vampire, eventually. This little boy, Hunter, is the son Hadley had before all that happened to her. His dad's bringing him by." Was Claude related to Hadley? Yes, of course, and therefore to Hunter. I pointed that out.

"I like children," Claude told me. "I'll behave. And I'm sorry to have upset you." He gave a stab at sounding contrite.

"Funny, you don't look sorry. At all."

"I'm crying inside," he said, smiling a wicked smile.

"Oh, for goodness' sake," I said, turning away to complete my bathroom routine alone and unobserved.

I'd calmed down by the time I got to work. *After all,* I thought, *Claude has probably seen a gazillion people naked in his time.* Most supes didn't think nudity was any big deal. The fact that Claude and I were distantly related—my great-grandfather was his grandfather—wouldn't make any difference to him; in fact, it wouldn't make any difference to most of the supes. *So,* I told myself stoutly, *no big deal.* When I hit a slow time at work, I called Eric's cell and left a message to tell him I was expecting to babysit a child that night. "If you can come over, great, but I wanted you to know ahead of time that someone else will be here," I told the voice mail. Hunter would make a pretty effective chaperone. Then I thought about my new upstairs roomer. "Plus, I kind of forgot to tell you something the other night, and probably you aren't going to like it much. Also, I miss you." There was a beep. My message time was up. Well . . . good. There was no telling what I would've said next.

The tracker, Heidi, was supposed to arrive in Bon Temps tonight. It seemed like a year since Eric had decided to send her over to check my land. I felt a little concerned when I thought of her arrival. Would Remy think Hunter attending the funeral was so bad, if he knew who else was dropping by my house? Was I being irresponsible? Was I putting the child at risk?

No, it was paranoid to think so. Heidi was coming to scout around in my woods.

I had thrown off my niggling worry by the time I was preparing to leave Merlotte's. Kennedy had arrived to work for Sam again because he'd made plans to take the Were girl, Jannalynn, to the casinos in Shreveport and out to dinner. I hoped she was real good to Sam, because he deserved it.

Kennedy was contorting herself in front of the mirror behind the bar, trying to discern a weight loss. I looked down at my own thighs. Jannalynn was really, really slim. In fact, I'd call her skinny. God had been generous with me in the bosom department, but Jannalynn was the possessor of little apricotlike boobs she showed off by wearing bustiers and tank tops with no bra. She gave herself some attitude (and altitude) by wearing fantastic footwear. I was wearing Keds. I sighed.

"Have a nice night!" Kennedy told me brightly, and I straightened my shoulders, smiled, and wiggled my fingers good-bye. Most people thought Kennedy's big smile and good manners had to be put on. But I knew Kennedy was sincere. She'd been trained by her pageant-queen mom to keep a smile on her face and a good word on her lips. I had to hand it to her; Danny Prideaux didn't faze Kennedy at all, and I felt like he'd make most girls pretty nervous. Danny, who'd been brought up to expect the world to beat him down so he better throw the first punch, lifted a finger to me to second Kennedy's farewell. He had a Coke in front of him, because Danny didn't drink on duty. He seemed content to play Mario Kart on his Nintendo DS, or to simply sit at the bar and watch Kennedy work.

On the other hand, lots of men would be nervous about working with Kennedy since she'd served time for manslaughter. Some women would be, too. But I had no problem with her. I was glad Sam had stepped up for her. It's not that I approve of murder—but some people just beg to be killed, don't they? After all I'd been through, I was forced to simply admit to myself that I felt that way.

I got home about five minutes before Remy arrived with Hunter. I'd had just enough time to pull off my work clothes, toss them in the hamper, and put on a pair of shorts and a T-shirt before Remy knocked at the front door.

I looked through the peephole before I opened the door, on the theory that it's better to be safe than sorry.

"Hey, Remy!" I said. He was in his early thirties, a quietly good-looking man with thick light brown hair. He was wearing clothes suitable for an evening visitation at a funeral home: khakis, a white-and-brown-striped broadcloth shirt, polished loafers. He'd looked more comfortable in the flannel and jeans he'd been wearing the first time I'd met him. I looked down at his son. Hunter had grown since I'd seen him last. He had dark hair and eyes like his mother, Hadley, but it was too early to say who he'd favor when he grew up.

I squatted down and said, *Hi, Hunter.* I didn't say anything out loud, but I smiled at him.

He'd almost forgotten. His face lit up. *Aunt Sookie!* he said. Pleasure ran through his head, pleasure and excitement. "I have a new truck," he said out loud, and I laughed.

"You gonna show it to me? Come on in, you two, and let's get you settled."

"Thanks, Sookie," Remy said.

"Do I look like my mama, Dad?" Hunter asked.

"Why?" Remy was startled.

"That's what Aunt Sookie says."

Remy was used to little shocks like this by now, and he knew it would only get worse. "Yes, you look like your mom, and she was good-looking," Remy told him. "You're a lucky young man, Son."

"I don't want to look like a girl," Hunter said doubtfully.

You don't. "Not a bit," I said. "Hunter, your room is right here." I indicated the open doorway. "I used to sleep in this room when I was a kid," I said.

Hunter looked around, alert and cautious. But the low twin bed with its white bedspread and the old furniture and the worn rug by the bed were all homey and unthreatening. "Where will you be?" he asked.

"Right here, across the hall," I told him, opening the door to my room. "You just call out, and I'll come a-running.

Or you can come climb in the bed with me, if you get scared in the night."

Remy stood, watching his son absorb all this. I didn't know how often the little boy had spent the night away from his dad; not too often, from the thoughts I was picking up from the boy's head.

"The bathroom's the next door down from your room, see?" I pointed in. He looked into the old-fashioned room with his mouth hanging open.

"I know it looks different from your bathroom at home," I said, answering his thoughts. "This is an old house, Hunter." The claw-foot tub and the black-and-white tiles were not what you saw in the rental houses and apartments Remy and Hunter had lived in since Katrina.

"What's upstairs?" Hunter asked.

"Well, a cousin of mine is staying up there. He's not home right now, and he comes in so late you may not even see him. His name is Claude."

Can I go up there and look around?

Maybe tomorrow we'll go up together. I'll show you the rooms you can go into and the rooms that Claude is using.

I glanced up to see that Remy was looking from Hunter to me, and he didn't know whether to be relieved or worried that I could talk to his son in a way he could not.

"Remy, it's okay," I said. "I grew up, and it got easier. I know this is going to be tough, but at least Hunter is a bright boy with a sound body. His little problem is just . . . less straightforward than most other kids'."

"That's a good way to look at it." But Remy's worry didn't diminish.

"You want a drink?" I said, not sure what to do with Remy now. Hunter had asked me silently if he could unpack his bag, and I'd told him——the same way——that unpacking was fine with me. He'd already unloaded a little backpack full of toys onto the bedroom floor.

"No, thank you. I got to get going."

It was unpleasant to realize that I spooked Remy in the same way his son spooked other people. Remy might need my help, and I could tell he thought I was a pretty woman, but I could also see that I gave him the creeps. "Is the visitation in Red Ditch?" I asked. That was the town where Remy and Hunter lived. It was about an hour and a quarter's drive southeast from Bon Temps.

"No, in Homer. So this is kind of on the way. If you run into any problems, just call my cell and I can come pick him up on the way home. Otherwise, I'll stay the night in Homer, go to the funeral at ten tomorrow, stay for the lunch at my cousin's home afterward, and pick Hunter up later in the afternoon, if that suits you."

"We'll be fine," I said, which was sheer bravado on my part. I hadn't taken care of kids since I'd sat with my friend Arlene's young 'uns, way back when. I didn't want to think about that; friendships that end bitterly are always sad. Those kids probably hated me now. "I've got videos we can watch, and a puzzle or two, and even some coloring books."

"Where?" Hunter asked, looking around like he expected to see a Toys "R" Us.

"You say good-bye to your daddy, and we'll go looking for them," I told him.

"Bye, Dad," Hunter said, waving a casual hand at Remy.

Remy looked nonplussed. "Want to give me a hug, champ?"

Hunter held up his arms, and Remy picked him up and swung him around.

Hunter giggled. Remy smiled over the child's shoulder.

"That's my boy," he said. "Be good for your aunt Sookie. Don't forget your manners. I'll see you tomorrow." He put Hunter down.

"Okay," Hunter said, quite matter-of-factly.

Remy had been expecting a big fuss, since he'd never been away from the boy for so long. He glanced at me, then shook his head with a smile. He was laughing at himself, which I thought was a good reaction.

I wondered how long Hunter's calm acceptance would last. Hunter looked up at me. "I'll be okay," he said, and I realized he was reading my mind and interpreting my thought in his own way. Though I'd had this experience before, it had been filtered through an adult's sensibility, and we'd had the fun of experimenting with combining our telepathy to see what happened. Hunter wasn't filtering and rearranging my thoughts as someone older would.

After hugging his son again, Remy left reluctantly. Hunter and I found the coloring books. It turned out that Hunter liked to color more than anything else in the world. I settled him at the table in the kitchen and turned my attention to supper preparation. I could have cooked a meal from scratch, but I figured something that required little attention would be best the first time he stayed with me. *You like Hamburger Helper?* I asked silently. He looked up, and I showed him the box.

I like that, Hunter said, recognizing the picture. He seemed to turn all his attention back to the turtle and butterfly scene he was coloring. The turtle was green and brown, approved turtle colors, but Hunter had gone to town on the butterfly. It was magenta, yellow, blue, and emerald green . . . and he hadn't finished it yet. I noted that staying in the lines was not Hunter's main goal. Which was okay.

Kristen used to make Hamburger Helper, he told me. Kristen had been Remy's girlfriend. Remy had told me he and Kristen had broken up over her inability to accept Hunter's special gift. Not so surprisingly, Kristen had come to believe Hunter was creepy. Adults had thought I was a weird kid, too. Though I understood that now, at the time it had been painful. *She was scared of me,* Hunter said, and he looked up for a second. I could understand that look.

She just didn't understand, I said. *There aren't many people like us. Am I the only other one?*

No. I know one other, a guy. He's a grown-up. He lives in Texas. Is he okay?

I wasn't sure what Hunter meant by "okay" until I looked at his thoughts a little longer. The little boy was thinking of his dad and some other men he admired—men who had jobs and wives or girlfriends, men who worked. Regular men.

Yes, I answered. *He found a way to make a living with it. He works for vampires. You can't hear vampires.*

I never met one. Really?

The doorbell rang. "I'll be back in a minute," I told Hunter, and I walked swiftly to the front door. I used the peephole. My caller was a young vampire female—presumably Heidi, the tracker. My cell phone rang. I fished it out of my pocket.

"Heidi should be there," Pam said. "Has she come to the door?"

"Brown ponytail, blue eyes, tall?"

"Yes. You can let her in."

This was all very timely.

I had the door open in a second. "Hi. Come in," I said. "I'm Sookie Stackhouse." I stood aside. I didn't offer to shake hands; vampires don't do that.

Heidi nodded to me and stepped into the house, darting quick looks around her, as if openly examining her surroundings were rude. Hunter came running into the living room, skidding to a stop as he saw Heidi. She was tall and bony, and possibly a mute. However, now Hunter could test my words.

"Heidi, this is my friend Hunter," I said, and waited for Hunter's reaction.

He was fascinated. He was trying to read her thoughts, as hard as he could. He was delighted with the result, with her silence.

Heidi squatted. "Hunter, you're a fine boy," she said, to my relief. Her voice had an accent I associated with Minnesota. "Are you going to be staying with Sookie for long?" Her smile revealed teeth that were a little longer and sharper than the general run of humans', and I thought Hunter might be scared. But he eyed her with genuine fascination.

Did you come to eat supper with us? he asked Heidi.

Out loud, please, Hunter, I said. *She's different from humans, but she's not like us, either. Remember?*

He glanced at me as if he were afraid that I was angry. I smiled at him and nodded.

"You gonna eat supper with us, Miss Heidi?"

"No, thank you, Hunter. I'm here to go back in the woods and look for something we're missing. I won't disturb you any longer. My boss asked me to introduce myself to you, and then go about my work." Heidi stood, smiling down at the little boy.

Suddenly, I saw a pitfall right in front of me. I was an idiot. But how could I help the boy if I didn't educate him? *Don't let her know you can hear things, Hunter,* I told the child. He looked up at me, his eyes amazingly like my cousin Hadley's. He looked a little scared.

Heidi was glancing from Hunter to me, obviously feeling that something was going on that she couldn't discern.

"Heidi, I hope you find something back there," I said briskly. "Let me know before you leave, please." Not only did I want to know if she found anything, but I wanted to know when she was off the property.

"This should take no more than two hours," she said.

"I'm sorry I didn't tell you, 'Welcome to Louisiana,'" I told her. "I hope you didn't mind too much, moving here from Las Vegas."

"Can I go back to color?" Hunter asked.

"Sure, honey," I said. "I'll be there in a minute."

"I gotta go potty," Hunter called, and I heard the bathroom door close.

Heidi said, "My son was his age when I was turned."

Her statement was so abrupt, her voice so flat, that it took me a moment to absorb what she'd told me.

"I'm so sorry," I said, and I meant it.

She shrugged. "It was twenty years ago. He's grown now. He's a drug addict in Reno." Her voice still sounded flat and emotionless, as if she were talking about the son of a stranger.

Very cautiously, I said, "Do you go see him?"

"Yes," she said. "I go to see him. At least I did before my former—employer—sent me here."

I didn't know what to say, but she was still standing there, so I ventured another question. "Do you let him see you?"

"Yes, sometimes. I called an ambulance one time when I saw he'd overdosed. Another night, I saved him from a vamp-blood addict who was going to kill him."

A herd of thoughts thundered through my head, and they were all unpleasant. Did he know the vampire watching him was his mother? What if he OD'd in the daytime, when she was dead to the world? How would she feel if she wasn't there the night his luck finally ran out? She couldn't always be on hand. Could it be he'd become an addict because his mother kept popping up when she should be dead?

"In the old days," I said, because I had to say something, "vampires' makers left the area with the new vamps as soon as they were turned, to keep them away from their kin, who'd recognize them." Eric and Bill and Pam had all told me that.

"I left Las Vegas for over a decade, but I returned," Heidi said. "My maker needed me there. Being part of the world isn't as great for all of us as it is for our leaders. I think Victor sent me to work for Eric in Louisiana to get me away from my son. I wasn't any use to them, they said, as long as Charlie's troubles were distracting me. But then again, my skill in tracking was only discovered when I was finding the man who sold bad drugs to Charlie."

She smiled a little, and I knew what kind of end that man had met. Heidi was spooky in the extreme.

"Now, I'll be going to the back of your property to see what I can find. I'll let you know when I'm through." Once she'd walked out the front door, she vanished into the woods so swiftly that by the time I went to the back of the house to look out, she'd melted into the trees.

I've had a lot of strange conversations, and I've had some heart-wrenching conversations—but my talk with Heidi had been both. Fortunately, I had a couple of minutes to recover while I served our plates and monitored Hunter's hand washing.

I was glad to discover that the boy expected to say a prayer before he ate, and we bowed our heads together. He enjoyed his Hamburger Helper and green beans and strawberries. While we ate, Hunter told me all about his father, by way of table conversation. I was sure Remy would be horrified if he could hear the tell-all approach Hunter took. It was all I could do not to laugh. I guess the discussion would have seemed strange to anyone else, because half of it was mind-to-mind and half of it was spoken.

Without any reminder from me, Hunter took his plate from the table to the sink. I held my breath until he slid it onto the counter carefully. "Do you have a dog?" he asked, looking around as if one might materialize. "We always give our scraps to the dog." I remembered the little black dog I'd seen running around the backyard of Remy's little house in Red Ditch.

No, I don't, I told him.

You've got a friend that turns into a dog? he said, his eyes big with astonishment.

"Yes, I do," I said. "He's a good friend." I hadn't counted on Hunter picking that up. This was very tricky.

"My dad says I'm smart," Hunter said, looking rather doubtful.

"Sure you are," I told him. "I know it's hard being different, because I'm different, too. But I grew up to be okay."

You sound kind of worried, though, Hunter said.

I agreed with Remy. Hunter was a smart little boy.

I am. It was hard for me, growing up, because no one understood why I was different. People won't believe you. I sat down in a chair by the table and pulled Hunter onto my lap. I was worried this was too much touching for him, but he seemed glad to sit there. *People don't want to know that someone can hear what they're thinking. They don't have any privacy when people like us are around.*

Hunter didn't exactly get "privacy," so we talked about the concept for a while. Maybe that was over the head of most five-year-olds—but Hunter wasn't the average kid.

So is the thing out in the woods giving you privacy? Hunter asked me.

What? I knew I'd reacted with too much anxiety and dismay when Hunter looked upset, too. *Don't worry about it, honey,* I said. *No, he's no problem.*

Hunter looked reassured enough for me to feel that it was time to change the subject. His attention was wandering, so I let him scramble down. He began playing with the Duplos he'd brought in his backpack, transporting them from the bedroom to the kitchen with his dump truck. I thought of getting him some Legos for a belated birthday present, but I'd check with Remy first, get his okay. I listened in to Hunter while I was doing the dishes.

I found out that he was as interested in his anatomy as most five-year-olds are, and that he thought it was funny that he got to stand up when he peed and I had to sit down, and that he hadn't liked Kristen because she didn't really like him. *She pretended to,* he told me, exactly as if he'd known when I was listening in to him.

I'd been standing at the sink with my back to Hunter, but it didn't make any difference in our conversation, which was another strange feeling.

Can you tell when I'm listening to your head? I asked, surprised.

Yeah, it tickles, Hunter told me.

Was that because he was so young? Would it have "tickled" in my head, too, if I'd met another telepath when I was that age? Or was Hunter unique among telepaths?

"Was that lady who came to the door dead?" Hunter said. He'd jumped up and run around the table to stand by my side while I dried the skillet.

"Yes," I said. "She's a vampire."

"Will she bite?"

"She won't bite you or me," I said. "I guess sometimes she bites people if they tell her that's okay." Boy, I was worried about this conversation. It was like talking about religion with a child without knowing the parents' preferences. "I think you said you'd never met a vampire before?"

"No, ma'am," he said. I started to tell Hunter he didn't have to call me "ma'am," but then I stopped. The better manners he had, the easier this world would be for him. "I never met anything like that man in the woods, either."

This time he had my undivided attention, and I tried hard not to let him read my alarm. Just as I was about to ask him careful questions, I heard the screen door to the back porch open, and then footsteps across the boards. A light knock at the back door told me that Heidi had returned from scouting in the woods, but I looked out the little window in the door to be sure. Yep, it was the vampire.

"I'm through," she said, when I opened the door. "I'll be on my way."

I noticed Hunter didn't run to the door as he had last time. He was behind me, though; I could feel his brain buzzing. He was not exactly scared, but anxious, as most children are about the unknown. But he was definitely pleased that he couldn't hear her. I'd been pleased when I found out vampire brains were silent to me, too.

"Heidi, did you learn anything?" I said hesitantly. Some of this might not be appropriate for Hunter to hear.

"The fae tracks in your woods are fresh and heavy. There are two scents. They crisscross." She inhaled, with apparent delight. "I love the smell of fae in the night. Better than gardenias."

Since I'd already assumed she'd detect the fae Basim had

reported smelling, this wasn't a big revelation. But Heidi said there were definitely two fae. That was bad news. It confirmed what Hunter had said, too.

"What else did you find?" I stepped back a little, so she could see Hunter was behind me and tailor her remarks accordingly.

"Neither of them is the fairy I smell here in your house." Not good news. "Of course, I smelled many werewolves. I also smell a vampire—I think Bill Compton, though I've only met him once. There's an old c-o-r-p-s-e. And a brand-new c-o-r-p-s-e buried due east from your house, in a clearing by the stream. The clearing is in a stand of wild plums."

None of this was reassuring. The old c-o-r-p-s-e, well, I'd expected that, and I knew who it was. (I spared a moment to wish Eric hadn't buried Debbie on my property.) And if Bill was the vampire walking through the woods, that was all right . . . though it did make me worry that he was just roaming around brooding all night instead of trying to build a new life for himself.

The new corpse was a real problem. Basim hadn't said anything about that. Had someone buried a body on my property in the last two nights, or had Basim simply left it off his list for some reason? I was staring at Heidi while I thought, and she finally raised her eyebrows. "Okay, thanks," I said. "I appreciate your taking the time."

"Take care of the little one," she said, and then she was across the back porch and out the door. I didn't hear her walk around the house to her car, but I didn't expect to. Vampires can be mighty quiet. I did hear her engine start up, and she drove away.

Since I knew my thoughts might worry Hunter, I forced myself to think of other things, which was harder than it sounds. I wouldn't have to do it long; I could tell my little visitor was getting tired. He put up the expected fuss about going to bed, but he didn't protest as much when I told him he could take a long bath first in the fascinating claw-foot tub. While Hunter splashed and played and made noises, I stayed in the bathroom, looking through a magazine. I made sure he actually cleaned himself in between sinking boats and racing ducks.

I decided we'd skip washing his hair. I figured that would be an ordeal, and Remy hadn't given me any instructions one way or another on hair washing. I pulled the plug. Hunter really enjoyed the gurgle of the water as it went down the drain. He rescued the ducks before they could drown, which made him a hero. "I am the king of the ducks, Aunt Sookie," he crowed.

"They need a king," I said. I knew how stupid ducks were. Gran had kept some for a while. I supervised Hunter's towel usage and helped him get his pajamas on. I reminded him to use the toilet again, and then he brushed his teeth, not very thoroughly.

Forty-five minutes later, after a story or two, Hunter was in bed. At his request, I left the light in the hall on, and his door was ajar an inch or two.

I found I was exhausted and in no mood to puzzle over Heidi's revelation. I wasn't used to tending to a child, though Hunter had been easy to care for, especially for a little guy who was staying with a woman he didn't know well. I hoped he'd enjoyed talking to me brain-to-brain. I also hoped Heidi hadn't spooked him too much.

I hadn't let myself focus on her macabre little biography, but now that Hunter was asleep, I found myself thinking about her story. It was an awful pity that she'd had to return to Nevada during her son's lifetime. In fact, she now probably looked the same age as her son, Charlie. What had happened to the boy's father? Why had her maker required her return? When she'd first been turned, vampires hadn't yet shown themselves to America and the rest of the world. Secrecy had been paramount. I had to agree with Heidi. Coming out of the coffin hadn't solved all the vamps' problems, and it had created quite a few new ones.

I would almost rather not have known about the sadness Heidi carried around with her. Naturally, since I was my grandmother's product, such a wish made me feel guilty. Shouldn't we always be ready to listen to the sad stories of others? If they want to tell them, aren't we obliged to listen? Now I felt I had a relationship with Heidi, based on her misery. Is that a real relationship? Was there something sympathetic about me that she liked, something that called this story forth? Or did she routinely tell new acquaintances about her son, Charlie? I could hardly believe that. I figured Hunter's presence had triggered her confidences.

I knew (though I didn't want to admit it to myself) that if Heidi remained so distracted by the issue of her junkie son, one night he'd get a visit from someone ruthless. After that, she'd be able to focus her whole attention on the wishes of her employer. I shivered.

Though I didn't think Victor would hesitate a second to do such a thing, I wondered, *Would—or could—Eric?*

If I could even ask myself that, I knew the answer was yes.

On the other hand, Charlie made a great hostage to ensure Heidi's good behavior. As in: "If you don't spy on Eric, we'll pay Charlie a visit." But if that ever changed . . .

All this Heidi meditation was by way of dodging the more

immediate issue. Who was the fresh corpse in my woods, and who had planted it there?

If Hunter hadn't been there, I would've picked up the phone to call Eric. I would've asked him to bring a shovel and come to help me dig a body up. That was what a boyfriend should do, right? But I couldn't leave Hunter alone in the house, and I would've felt terrible if I'd asked Eric to go out in the woods by himself, even though I knew he wouldn't think anything about it. In fact, probably he'd have sent Pam. I sighed. I couldn't seem to get rid of one problem without acquiring another.

Chapter 6

At six in the morning, Hunter climbed onto my bed. "Aunt Sookie!" he said, in what he probably thought was a whisper. Just this once, his using our mind-to-mind communication would have been better. But naturally, he decided to talk out loud.

"Uh-huh?" This had to be a bad dream.

"I had a funny dream last night," Hunter told me.

"Uh?" Maybe a dream within a dream.

"This tall man came in my room."

"Did?"

"He had long hair like a lady."

I pushed up on my elbows and looked at Hunter, who didn't seem frightened. "Yeah?" I said, which was at least borderline coherent. "What color?"

"Yellow," Hunter said, after a little thought. I suddenly realized that most five-year-olds might be a little shaky on the identification of colors.

Uh-oh. "So what did he do?" I asked. I struggled to sit all the way up. The sky outside was just getting lighter.

"He just looked at me, and he smiled," Hunter said. "Then he went in the closet."

"Wow," I said inadequately. I couldn't be sure (until dark, that is), but it sounded very much as though Eric was in the secret hiding place in my closet and dead for the day.

"I gotta go pee," Hunter said, and slid off my bed to scamper into my bathroom. I heard him flush a minute later, and then he washed his hands—or at least, he turned on the water for a second. I collapsed back onto my pillows, thinking sadly of the hours of sleep I was doomed to lose. By sheer force of will, I got out of bed in my blue nightgown and threw on a robe. I stepped into my slippers, and after Hunter exited my bathroom, I entered it.

A couple of minutes later we were in my kitchen with the lights on. I went directly to the coffeepot, and I found a note propped on it. I recognized the handwriting immediately, and the endorphins flooded my system. Instead of being incredulous that I was up and moving so ungodly early, I felt happy that I was sharing this time with my little cousin. The note, which had been written on one of the pads I keep around for grocery lists, said, "My lover, I came in too close to dawn to wake you, though I was tempted. Your house is full of strange men. A fairy upstairs and a little child downstairs—but as long as there's not one in my lady's chamber, I can stand it. I need to talk to you when I rise." It was signed, in a large scrawl, "ERIC."

I put the note aside, trying not to worry about Eric's urgent need to talk to me. I started the coffee to perking, and then I pulled out the griddle and plugged it in. "I hope you like pancakes," I told Hunter, and his face lit up. He put his orange juice cup down on the table with a happy bang, and juice slopped over the edge. Just as I was about to give him a long look, he jumped up and fetched a paper towel. He took care of the spill with more vigor than attention to detail, but I appreciated the gesture.

"I love pancakes," he said. "You can make 'em? They don't come out of the freezer?"

I hid a smile. "Nope. I can make 'em." It took about five minutes to mix up a batch, and by then the griddle was hot. I put on some bacon first, and Hunter's expression was ecstatic. "I don't like it floppy," he said, and I promised him it would be crisp. That was the way I liked it, too.

"That smells wonderful, Cousin," said Claude. He was standing in the doorway, his arms spread wide, looking as good as anyone can look that early in the morning. He was wearing a maroon University of Louisiana at Monroe T-shirt and some black workout shorts.

"Who are you?" Hunter asked.

"I'm Sookie's cousin Claude."

He has long hair like a lady, too, Hunter said.

He's a man, though, just like the other man. "Claude, this is another cousin of mine, Hunter," I said. "Remember, I told you he was coming to visit?"

"His mother was—" Claude began, and I shook my head at him.

Claude might have been about to say any number of things. He might have said, "the bisexual" or "the one the albino, Waldo, killed in the cemetery in New Orleans." These would both have been true, and Hunter needed to hear neither of them.

"So we're all cousins," I said. "Were you hinting around that you wanted to eat some breakfast with us, Claude?"

"Yes, I was," he said gracefully, pouring himself some coffee from the pot without asking me. "If there's enough for me, too. This young man looks like he could eat a lot of pancakes."

Hunter was delighted with this idea, and he and Claude began topping each other on the number of pancakes they could consume. I was surprised that Claude was so at ease with Hunter, though the fact that he was charming the child effortlessly was no surprise to me. Claude was a professional at charming.

"Do you live here in Bon Temps, Hunter?" Claude was asking.

"No," said Hunter, laughing at the absurdity of such an idea. "I live with my daddy."

Okay, that was enough sharing. I didn't want anyone supernatural knowing about Hunter, understanding what made him special.

"Claude, would you get out the syrup and the molasses?" I said. "It's in the pantry over there."

Claude located the pantry and brought out the Log Cabin and the Brer Rabbit. He even opened both bottles so Hunter could smell them and pick which one he wanted on his pancakes. I got the pancakes on the griddle and made some more coffee, pulling some plates out of the cabinets and showing Hunter where the forks and knives were so he could set the table.

We were a strange little family grouping: two telepaths and a fairy. During our breakfast conversation, I had to keep each male from knowing what the other was, and that was a real challenge. Hunter told me silently that Claude must be a vampire, because he couldn't hear Claude's thoughts, and I had to tell Hunter that there were some other people we couldn't hear, too. I pointed out that Claude couldn't be a vampire because it was daytime, and vampires couldn't come out in the daytime.

"There's a vampire in the closet," Hunter told Claude. "He can't come out in the daytime."

"Which closet would that be?" Claude asked Hunter.

"The one in my room. You want to come see?"

"Hunter," I said, "the last thing any vampire wants is to be disturbed in the daytime. I'd leave him alone."

"Your Eric?" Claude asked. He was excited by the idea of Eric being in the house. Damn.

"Yes," I said. "You know better than to go in there, right? I mean, I don't have to get tough with you, right?"

He smiled at me. "You, tough with me?" he said, mockingly. "Ha. I'm fae. I am stronger than any human."

I started to say, "So how come I survived the war between the fae and so many fairies didn't?" Thank God I didn't. The minute after, I knew how good it was that I'd choked on those words, because I could see by Claude's face that he remembered who'd died all too well. I missed Claudine, too, and I told him so.

"You're sad," Hunter said accurately. And he was picking up on all this, which shouldn't be thought of in his hearing.

"Yes, we're remembering his sister," I said. "She died and we miss her."

"Like my mom," he said. "What's a fay?"

"Yes, like your mom." Sort of. Only in the sense that they were both dead. "And a fae is a special person, but we're not going to talk about that right now."

It didn't take a telepath to pick up on Claude's interest and curiosity, and when he sauntered back down the hall to use the bathroom, I followed him. Sure enough, Claude's steps slowed and stopped at the open door to the bedroom Hunter had used.

"Keep right on walking," I said.

"I can't take a peek? He'll never know. I've heard how handsome he is. Just a peek?"

"No," I said, knowing I'd better stay in sight of that door until Claude was out of the house. Just a peek, my round rosy ass.

"What about your ass, Aunt Sookie?"

"Oops! Sorry, Hunter. I said a bad word." Didn't want Claude to know I'd only thought it. I heard him laughing as he shut the bathroom door.

Claude stayed in the bathroom so long that I had to let Hunter brush his teeth in mine. After I heard the squeak of the stairs and the sound of the television overhead, I was able to relax. I helped Hunter get dressed, and then I got dressed myself and put on some makeup under Hunter's unwavering attention to the process. Evidently, Kristen had never let Hunter watch what he considered to be a fascinating procedure.

"You should come to live with us, Aunt Sookie," he said.

Thanks, Hunter, but I like to live here. I have a job.

You can get another one.

"It wouldn't be the same. This is my house, and I love it here. I don't want to leave."

There was a knock on the front door. Could Remy be arriving this early to collect Hunter?

But it was another surprise altogether, an unpleasant one. Special Agent Tom Lattesta stood on the front porch.

Hunter, naturally, had run to the door as fast as he could. Don't all kids? He hadn't thought it was his dad, because he didn't know exactly when Remy was supposed to show up. He just liked to find out who was visiting.

"Hunter," I said, picking him up, "this is an FBI agent. His name is Tom Lattesta. Can you remember that?"

Hunter looked doubtful. He tried a couple of times to say the unfamiliar name and finally got it right.

"Good job, Hunter!" Lattesta said. He was trying to be friendly, but he wasn't good with kids and he sounded fake. "Ms. Stackhouse, can I come in for a minute?" I looked behind him. No one else. I thought they always traveled in pairs.

"I guess so," I said, without enthusiasm. I didn't explain who Hunter was, because it was none of Lattesta's business, though I could tell he was curious. He'd also noticed there was another car parked outside.

"Claude," I called up the stairs. "The FBI is here." It's good to inform unexpected company that someone else is in the house with you.

The television fell silent, and Claude came gliding down the stairs. Now he was wearing a golden brown silk T-shirt and khakis, and he looked like a poster for a wet dream. Even Lattesta's heterosexual orientation wasn't proof against a surge of startled admiration. "Agent Lattesta, my cousin Claude Crane," I said, trying not to smile.

Hunter and Claude and I sat on the couch while Lattesta took the La-Z-Boy. I didn't offer him anything to drink.

"How's Agent Weiss?" I asked. The New Orleans–based agent had brought Lattesta, based in Rhodes, out to my house last time, and in the course of many terrible events, she'd been shot.

"She's back at work," Lattesta said. "Still on a desk job. Mr. Crane, I don't believe I've met you before?"

No one forgot Claude. Of course, my cousin knew that very well. "You haven't had the pleasure," he told the FBI man.

Lattesta spent a moment trying to figure that out before

he smiled. "Right," he said. "Listen, Ms. Stackhouse, I came up here today to tell you that you're no longer a subject for investigation."

I was stunned with the relief that swept over me. I exchanged glances with Claude. God bless my great-grandfather. I wondered how much he'd spent, how many strings he'd pulled, to make this come true.

"How come?" I asked. "Not that I'm going to miss it, you understand, but I have to wonder what's changed."

"You seem to know people who are powerful," Lattesta said, with an unexpected depth of bitterness. "Someone in our government doesn't want your name to come up in public."

"And you flew all the way to Louisiana to tell me that," I said, putting enough disbelief into my voice to let him know I thought that was bullshit.

"No, I flew all the way down here to go to a hearing about the shooting."

Okay. That made more sense. "And you didn't have my phone number? To call me? You had to come here to tell me you weren't going to investigate me, in person?"

"There's something wrong about you," he said, and the façade was gone. It was a relief. Now his outside matched his inside. "Sara Weiss has undergone some kind of . . . spiritual upheaval since she met you. She goes to séances. She's reading books about the paranormal. Her husband is worried about her. The bureau is worried about her. Her boss is having doubts about putting her back out in the field."

"I'm sorry to hear that. But I don't see that there's anything I can do about it." I thought for a minute, while Tom Lattesta stared at me with angry eyes. He was thinking angry thoughts, too. "Even if I went to her and told her that I can't do what she thinks I can do, it wouldn't help. She believes what she believes. I am what I am."

"So you admit it."

Even though I didn't want the FBI noticing me, that hurt, oddly enough. I wondered if Lattesta was taping our conversation.

"Admit *what*?" I asked. I was genuinely curious to hear what he'd say. The first time he'd been on my doorstep, he'd been a believer. He'd thought I was his key to a quick rise in the bureau.

"Admit you're not even a human being."

Aha. He really believed that. I disgusted and repelled him. I had more insight into what Sam was feeling.

"I've been watching you, Ms. Stackhouse. I've been called off, but if I can tie you in to any investigation that will lead back to you, I'll do it. You're *wrong*. I'm leaving now, and I hope you—" He didn't get a chance to finish.

"Don't think bad things about my aunt Sookie," Hunter said furiously. "You're a *bad man*."

I couldn't have put it better myself, but I wished for Hunter's own sake that he had kept his mouth shut. Lattesta turned white as a sheet.

Claude laughed. "He's scared of you," he told Hunter. Claude thought it was a great joke, and I had a feeling he'd known what Hunter was all along.

I thought Lattesta's grudge might constitute a real danger to me.

"Thanks for coming to give me the good news, Special Agent Lattesta," I said, in as mild a voice as I could manage. "You have a safe drive back to Baton Rouge, or New Orleans, or wherever you flew in."

Lattesta was on his feet and out the door before I could say another word, and I handed Hunter to Claude and followed him. Lattesta was down the steps and at his car, fumbling around in his pocket, before he realized I was behind him. He was turning off a pocket recording device. He wheeled around to give me an angry look.

"You'd use a kid," he said. "That's low."

I looked at him sharply for a minute. Then I said, "You're worried that your little boy, who's Hunter's age, has autism. You're scared this hearing you came to attend will go badly for you and maybe for Agent Weiss. You're scared because you reacted to Claude. You're thinking of asking to transfer into the BVA in Louisiana. You're mad that I know people who can make you back off."

If Lattesta could have pressed himself into the metal of the car, he would've. I'd been a fool because I'd been proud. I should have let him go without a word.

"I wish I could tell you who it was who put me off-limits to the FBI," I said. "It would scare your pants off." In for a penny, in for a pound, right? I turned and went back up the front steps and into the house. A moment later, I heard his car tear down my driveway, probably scattering my beautiful gravel as it went.

Hunter and Claude were laughing in the kitchen, and I found them blowing with straws into the dishwashing water in the sink, which still had some soap bubbles. Hunter was standing on a stool I used to reach the top shelves of the cabinets. It was an unexpectedly happy picture.

"So, Cousin, he's gone?" Claude asked. "Good job, Hunter. I think there's a lake monster under that water!"

Hunter blew even harder, and water drops spattered the curtains. He laughed a little too wildly.

"Okay, kids, enough," I said. This was getting out of hand.

Leave a fairy alone with a child for a few minutes, and this was what happened. I glanced at the clock. Thanks to Hunter's early wake-up call, it was only nine. I didn't expect Remy to come to collect Hunter until late afternoon.

"Let's go to the park, Hunter."

Claude looked disappointed that I'd stopped their fun, but Hunter was game to go somewhere. I grabbed my softball mitt and a ball and retied Hunter's sneakers.

"Am I invited, too?" Claude said, sounding a little miffed.

I was taken by surprise. "Sure, you can come," I said. "That would be great. Maybe you should take your own car, since I don't know what we'll be doing afterward." My self-absorbed cousin genuinely enjoyed being with Hunter. I would never have anticipated this reaction—and truthfully, I don't think he had anticipated it, either. Claude followed me in his Impala as I drove to the park.

I went to Magnolia Creek Park, which stretched on either side of the creek. It was prettier than the little park close to the elementary school. The park wasn't much, of course, since Bon Temps is not exactly a wealthy little town, but it had the standard playground equipment, a quarter-mile walking track, and plenty of open area, picnic tables, and trees. Hunter attacked the jungle gym as if he'd never seen one before, and maybe he hadn't. Red Ditch is smaller and poorer than Bon Temps.

I found that Hunter could climb like a monkey. Claude was ready to steady him at every move. Hunter would've found that annoying if I'd done it. I wasn't sure why that should be, but I knew it to be true.

A car pulled up as I enticed Hunter down from the jungle gym to play ball. Tara got out and came over to see what we were doing.

"Who's your friend, Sookie?" she called.

The tight top she was wearing made Tara look a little bigger than she had when she'd come into the bar to eat lunch. She was wearing some pre-pregnancy shorts scooted down under her belly. I knew extra money wasn't plentiful in the du Rone/Thornton household these days, but I hoped Tara could find money in the budget to get some real maternity clothes before too long. Unfortunately, her clothing store, Tara's Togs, didn't carry maternity stuff.

"This is my cousin Hunter," I said. "Hunter, this is my friend Tara." Claude, who had been swinging on the swing set, chose that moment to leap off and bound over to where we stood. "Tara, this is my cousin Claude."

Now, Tara had known me all her life, and she knew all the members of my family. I gave her high points for absorbing this introduction and giving Hunter a friendly smile, which she then extended to Claude. She must have recognized him—she'd seen him in action. But she never blinked an eye.

"How many months are you?" Claude asked.

"A little more than three months away from delivery," Tara said, and sighed. I guess Tara had gotten used to relative strangers asking her personal questions. She'd told me before that all conversational bars were removed when you were pregnant. "People will ask you anything," she'd said. "And the women'll tell you labor and delivery stories that make your hair curl."

"Do you want to know what you're having?" Claude asked.

That was way out of bounds. "Claude," I said reprovingly. "That's too personal." Fairies just didn't have the same concept of personal information *or* personal space that humans did.

"I apologize," my cousin said, very insincerely. "I thought

you might enjoy knowing before you buy their clothes. You color-code babies, I believe."

"Sure," Tara said abruptly. "What sex is the baby?"

"Both," he said with a smile. "You're having twins, a boy and a girl."

"My doctor's heard only one heartbeat," she said, trying to be gentle about telling him he was wrong.

"Then your doctor is an idiot," Claude said cheerfully. "You have two babies, alive and well."

Tara obviously didn't know what to make of this. "I'll get him to look harder next time I go in," she said. "And I'll tell Sookie to let you know what he says."

Fortunately, Hunter had mostly ignored this conversation. He had just learned how to throw the softball up in the air and catch it, and he was distracted by the effort to put my mitt on his little hand. "Did you play baseball, Aunt Sookie?" he asked.

"Softball," I said. "You bet I did. I played right field. That means I stood way out in the field and waited to see if the girl batting would hit the ball out my way. Then I'd catch it, and I'd throw it in to the pitcher, or whichever player needed it most."

"Your aunt Sookie was the best right fielder in the history of the Lady Falcons," Tara said, squatting down to talk to Hunter eye to eye.

"Well, I had a good time," I said.

"Did you play softball?" Hunter asked Tara.

"No, I came and cheered for Sookie," Tara said, which was the absolute truth, God bless her.

"Here, Hunter," Claude said, and gave the softball an easy toss. "Go get it and throw it back to me."

The unlikely twosome wandered around the park, throwing the ball to each other with very little accuracy. They were having a great time.

"Well, well, well," Tara said. "You have a habit of picking up family in funny places. A cousin? Where'd you get a cousin? He's not a secret by-blow of Jason's, right?"

"He's Hadley's son."

"Oh . . . oh my God." Tara's eyes widened. She looked at Hunter, trying to pick out a likeness to Hadley in his features. "That's not the dad? Impossible."

"No," I said. "That's Claude Crane, and he's my cousin, too."

"He's sure not Hadley's kid," Tara said, laughing. "And Hadley's the only cousin you had that I ever heard of."

"Ah . . . sort of wrong-side-of-the-blanket stuff," I said. It was impossible to explain without casting Gran's integrity into question.

Tara saw how uncomfortable I was with the subject of Claude.

"How are you and the tall blond getting along?"

"We're getting along okay," I said cautiously. "I'm not looking elsewhere."

"I should say not! No woman in her right mind would go out with anyone else if she could have Eric. Beautiful *and* smart." Tara sounded a bit wistful. Well, at least JB was beautiful.

"Eric can be a pain when he wants to be. And talk about baggage!" I tried to picture stepping out on Eric. "If I tried to see someone else, he might . . ."

"Kill that someone else?"

"He sure wouldn't be happy," I said, in a massive understatement.

"So, you want to tell me what's wrong?" Tara put her hand on mine. She's not a toucher, so that meant a lot.

"Truth be told, Tara, I'm not sure." I had an overwhelming feeling that something was askew, something important. But I couldn't put my finger on what that might be.

"Supes?" she said.

I shrugged.

"Well, I got to go into the shop," she said. "McKenna opened for me today, but I can't ask her to do that for me all the time." We said good-bye, happier with each other than we'd been in a long time. I realized that I needed to throw Tara a baby shower, and I couldn't imagine why it hadn't occurred to me before now. I needed to get cracking on the planning. If I made it a surprise shower, and did all the food myself . . . Oh, and I'd have to tell people Tara and JB were expecting twins. I didn't doubt Claude's accuracy for a second.

I thought I would go out into the woods myself, maybe tomorrow. I'd be alone then. I knew that Heidi's nose and eyes—and Basim's, for that matter—were far more acute than mine, but I had an overwhelming impulse to see what I could see. Once again, something stirred in the back of my head, a memory that wasn't a memory. Something to do with the woods . . . with a hurt man in the woods. I shook my head to rid myself of the haziness, and I realized I couldn't hear any voices.

"Claude," I called.

"Here!"

I walked around a clump of bushes and saw the fairy and the little boy enjoying the whirligig. That's what I'd always called it, anyway. It's circular, several kids can stand on it, a few others run around the edges pushing, and then it whirls in a circle until the impetus is gone. Claude was pushing it way too fast, and though Hunter was enjoying it, his grin was looking a little tense, too. I could see the fear in his brain, seeping through the pleasure.

"Whoa, Claude," I said, keeping my voice level. "That's enough speed for a kid." Claude stopped pushing, though he was reluctant. He'd been having a great time himself.

Though Hunter pooh-poohed my warning, I could tell he was relieved. He hugged Claude when Claude told him he had to go to Monroe to open up his club. "What kind of club?" Hunter asked, and I had to give Claude a significant look and keep my head blank.

"See you later, sport," the fairy told the child, and hugged him back.

It was time for an early lunch, so I took Hunter to McDonald's as a big treat. His dad hadn't mentioned any ban on fast food, and I figured one trip was okay.

Hunter loved his Happy Meal, ran the toy car from the container over the tabletop until I was absolutely tired of it, and then wanted to go into the play area. I was sitting on a bench watching him, hoping the joys of the tunnels and the slide would hold him for at least ten more minutes, when another woman came out the door into the fenced area, with a boy about Hunter's age in tow. Though I practically heard the ominous thud of bass drums, I kept a smile pasted on my face and hoped for the best.

After a few seconds of regarding each other warily, the two boys began shouting and running around the small play area together, and I relaxed, but cautiously. I ventured a smile at Mom, but she was brooding off into the distance, and I didn't have to read her mind to see she'd had a bad morning. (I discovered that her dryer had broken down, and she couldn't afford another one for at least two months.)

"Is this your youngest?" I asked, trying to look cheerful and interested.

"Yes, youngest of four," she said, which explained her desperation about the dryer. "All the rest of 'em are at Little League baseball practice. It'll be summer vacation soon, and they'll be home for three months."

Oh. I was out of things to say.

My unwilling companion sank back into her own grim thoughts, and I did my best to stay out. It was a struggle, because she was like a black hole of unhappy thoughts, kind of sucking me in with her.

Hunter came to stand in front of her, regarding her with open-mouthed fascination.

"Hello," the woman said, making a great effort.

"Do you really want to run away?" he asked.

This was definitely an "oh shit" moment. "Hunter, we need to be going," I said quickly. "Come on, now. We're late, late!" And I picked Hunter up and carried him away, though he was squirming and wiggling in protest (and also much heavier than he looked). He actually landed a kick on my thigh, and I almost dropped him.

The mother in the play area was staring after us, her mouth agape, and her little boy had come to stand in front of her, puzzled at his playmate's abrupt departure.

"I was having a good time!" Hunter yelled. "Why do we have to go?"

I looked him straight in the eyes. "Hunter, you be quiet until we're in the car," I said, and I meant every word. Carrying him through the restaurant while he was yelling had focused every eye on us, and I hadn't enjoyed the attention. I'd noticed a couple of people I knew, and there would be questions to answer later. This wasn't Hunter's fault, but it didn't make me feel any kinder.

As I buckled his seat belt, I realized I'd let Hunter get too tired and overexcited, and I made a mental note not to do that again. I could feel his little brain practically jiggling up and down.

Hunter was looking at me as though his heart were broken. "I was having a good time," he said again. "That boy was my friend."

I turned sideways to look him in the face. "Hunter, you said something to his mom that let her know you're different."

He was realistic enough to admit the truth of what I was saying. "She was really mad," he muttered. "Moms leave their kids."

His own mother had left him.

I thought for a second about what I could say. I decided to ignore the darker theme here. Hadley had left Remy and Hunter, and now she was dead and would never return. Those were facts. There was nothing I could do to change them. What Remy wanted me to do was to help Hunter live the rest of his life.

"Hunter, this is hard. I know it. I went through the same thing. You could hear what that mom was thinking, and then you said it out loud."

"But she *was* saying it! In her head!"

"But not out loud."

"That was what she was *saying.*"

"*In her head.*" He was just being stubborn now. "Hunter, you're a very young man. But to make your own life easier, you have to start thinking before you talk."

Hunter's eyes were wide and brimful with tears.

"You have to think, and you have to keep your mouth shut."

Two big tears coursed down his pink cheeks. Oh, geez Louise.

"You can't ask people questions about what you hear from their heads. Remember, we talked about privacy?"

He nodded once uncertainly, and then again with more energy. He remembered.

"People—grown-ups and children—are going to get real upset with you if they know you can read what's in their heads. Because the stuff in someone's head is private. You wouldn't want anyone telling you you're thinking about how bad you need to pee."

Hunter glared at me.

"See? Doesn't feel good, does it?"

"No," he said, grudgingly.

"I want you to grow up as normal as you can," I said. "Growing up with this condition is tough. Do you know any kids with problems everyone can see?"

After a minute, he nodded. "Jenny Vasco," he said. "She has a big mark on her face."

"It's the same thing, except you can hide your difference, and Jenny can't," I said. I was feeling mighty sorry for Jenny Vasco. It seemed wrong to be teaching a little kid that he should be stealthy and secretive, but the world wasn't ready for a mind-reading five-year-old, and probably never would be.

I felt like a mean old witch as I looked at his unhappy and tear-stained face. "We're going to go home and read a story," I said.

"Are you mad at me, Aunt Sookie?" he said, with a hint of a sob.

"No," I said, though I wasn't happy about being kicked. Since he'd know that, I'd better mention it. "I don't appreciate your kicking me, Hunter, but I'm not mad anymore. I'm really mad at the rest of the world, because this is hard on you."

He was silent all the way home. We went inside and sat on the couch after he paid a visit to the bathroom and picked a couple of books from the stash I'd kept. Hunter was asleep before I finished *The Poky Little Puppy*. I gently eased him down on the couch, pulled off his shoes, and got my own book. I read while he napped. I got up from time to time to get some small task done. Hunter slept for almost two hours. I found this an incredibly peaceful time, though if I hadn't had Hunter all day, it might simply have been boring.

After I'd started a load of laundry and tiptoed back into the room, I stood by the sleeping boy and looked down. If I had a child, would my baby have the same problem Hunter had? I hoped not. Of course, if Eric and I continued in our relationship, I would never have a child unless I was artificially inseminated. I tried to picture myself asking Eric how he felt about me being impregnated by an unknown man, and I'm ashamed to say I had to smother a snigger.

Eric was very modern in some respects. He liked the convenience of his cell phone, he loved automatic garage-door openers, and he liked watching the news on television. But artificial insemination . . . I didn't think so. I'd heard his verdict on plastic surgery, and I had a strong feeling he'd consider this in the same category.

"What's funny, Aunt Sookie?" Hunter said.

"Nothing important," I said. "How about some apple slices and some milk?"

"No ice cream?"

"Well, you had a hamburger and French fries and a Coke at lunch. I think we'd better stick to the apple slices."

I put *The Lion King* on while I prepared Hunter's snack, and he sat on the floor in front of the television while he ate. Hunter got tired of the movie (which of course he'd seen before) about halfway through, and after that, I taught him how to play Candy Land. He won the first time.

As we were working our way through a second game, there was a knock. "Daddy!" Hunter shrieked, and pelted for the door. Before I could stop him, he'd pulled it open. I was glad he'd known who the caller was, because it gave me a bad moment. Remy was standing there in a dress shirt, suit pants, and polished lace-ups. He looked like a different man. He was grinning at Hunter as if he hadn't seen his child in days. In a second, the boy was up in his arms.

It was heartwarming. They hugged each other tight. I had a little lump in my throat.

In a second, Hunter was telling Remy about Candy Land, and about McDonald's, and about Claude, and Remy was listening with complete attention. He gave me a quick smile to say he'd greet me in a second, once the torrent of information had slowed down.

"Son, you want to go get all your stuff together? Don't leave anything," Remy cautioned his son. With a quick smile in my direction, Hunter dashed off to the back of the house.

"Did it go okay?" Remy asked, the minute Hunter was out of earshot. Though in a sense Hunter was *never* out of hearing, it would have to do.

"Yes, I think so. He's been so good," I said, resolving to keep the kick to myself. "We had a little problem on the McDonald's playground, but I think it led to a good talk with him."

Remy looked as if a load had just dropped back onto his shoulders. "I'm sorry about that," he said, and I could have—well, kicked myself.

"No, it was only normal stuff, the kind of thing you brought him here so I could help with," I said. "Don't worry about it. My cousin Claude was here, and he played with Hunter at the park, though I was there all the time, of course." I didn't want Remy to think I'd farmed Hunter out to any old person. I tried to think of what else to tell the anxious father. "He ate real good, and he slept just fine. Not long enough," I said, and Remy laughed.

"I know all about that," he told me.

I started to tell Remy that Eric was asleep in the closet and that Hunter had seen him for a few minutes, but I had the confused feeling that Eric would be one man too many. I'd already introduced the idea of Claude, and Remy hadn't been totally delighted to hear about that. A typical dad reaction, I guessed.

"Did the funeral go okay? No last-minute hitches?" You never know what to ask about funerals.

"No one threw themselves into the grave or fainted," Remy said. "That's about all you can hope for. A few skirmishes over a dining room table that all the kids wanted to load into their trucks right then."

I nodded. I'd heard many brooding thoughts through the years about inheritances, and I'd had my own troubles with Jason when Gran died. "People don't always have their nicest face on when it comes to dividing up a household," I said.

I offered Remy a drink, but he smilingly turned me down. He was obviously ready to be alone with his son, and he peppered me with questions about Hunter's manners, which I was able to praise, and his eating habits, which I was able to admire, too. Hunter wasn't a picky kid, and that was a blessing.

Within a few minutes, Hunter had returned to the living room with all his stuff, though I did a quick patrol and found two Duplos that had escaped his notice. Since he'd liked *The Poky Little Puppy* so much, I stuck it in his backpack for him to enjoy at home. After a few more thank-yous, and an unexpected hug from Hunter, they were gone.

I watched Remy's old truck go down the driveway.

The house felt oddly empty.

Of course, Eric was asleep underneath it, but he was dead for a few more hours, and I knew I could rouse him only in the direst of circumstances. Some vampires couldn't wake in the daytime, even if they were set on fire. I pushed that memory away, since it made me shiver. I glanced at the clock. I had part of the sunny afternoon to myself, and it was my day off.

I was in my black-and-white bikini and lying out on the old chaise before you could say, "Sunbathing is bad for you."

Chapter 7

The minute the sun sank, Eric was out of the compartment below the guest-bedroom closet. He picked me up and kissed me thoroughly. I'd already warmed up some TrueBlood for him, and he made a face but gulped it down.

"Who is the child?" he asked.

"Hadley's son," I said. Eric had met Hadley when she'd been going with Sophie-Anne Leclerq, the now finally deceased Queen of Louisiana.

"She was married to a breather?"

"Yes, before she met Sophie-Anne," I said. "A very nice guy named Remy Savoy."

"Is that him I smell? Along with a big scent of fairy?"

Uh-oh. "Yes, Remy came to pick up Hunter this afternoon. I was keeping him because Remy had to go to a family funeral. He didn't think that would be a good place to take a kid." I didn't bring up Hunter's little problem. The fewer who knew about it, the better, and that included Eric.

"And?"

"I meant to tell you this the other night," I said. "My cousin Claude?"

Eric nodded.

"He asked if he could stay here for a while, because he's lonely in his house with both his sisters dead."

"You are letting a man live with you." Eric didn't sound angry—more like he was poised to be angry, if you know what I mean? There was just a little edge in his voice.

"Believe me, he's not interested in me as a woman," I said, though I had a guilty flash of him walking in on me in the bathroom. "He is all about the guys."

"I know you are fully aware of how to take care of a fairy who gives you trouble," Eric said, after an appreciable silence.

I'd killed fairies before. I hadn't particularly wanted to be reminded of that. "Yes," I said. "And if it'll make you feel better, I'll keep a squirt gun loaded with lemon juice on my bedside table." Lemon juice and iron—the fairy weaknesses.

"That would make me feel better," Eric said. "Is it this Claude that Heidi scented on your land? I felt you were very worried, and that's one reason I came over last night."

The blood bond was hard at work. "She says neither of the fairies she tracked was Claude," I said, "and that really worries me. But—"

"It worries me, too." Eric looked down at the empty bottle of TrueBlood, then said, "Sookie, there are things you should know."

"Oh." I'd been about to tell him about the fresh corpse. I was sure he would have led off the discussion with the body if Heidi had mentioned it, and it seemed pretty important to me. I may have sounded a little peeved at being interrupted. Eric gave me a sharp look.

Okay, I was at fault, *excuse me*. I should have been long-ing to be chock-full of information that Eric felt would help me negotiate the minefield of vampire politics. And there were nights I'd have been delighted to learn more about my boyfriend's life. But tonight, after the unusual stresses and strains of Hunter care, what I'd wanted was (again, *excuse me*) to tell him about the body-in-the-woods crisis and then have a good long screw.

Normally, Eric would be down with that program.

But not tonight, apparently.

We sat opposite each other at the kitchen table. I tried not to sigh out loud.

"You remember the summit at Rhodes, and how a sort of strip of states from south to north were invited," Eric began.

I nodded. This didn't sound too promising. My corpse was way more urgent. Not to mention the sex.

"Once we had ventured from one side of the New World to another, and the white breathing population migrated across, too—*we* were the first explorers—a large group of us met to divide things up, for better governing of our own population."

"Were there any Native American vampires here when you came? Hey, were you on the Leif Ericson expedition?"

"No, not my generation. Oddly enough, there were very few Native American vampires. And the ones that were here were different in several ways."

Now, that was pretty interesting, but I could tell Eric wasn't going to stop and fill in the blanks.

"At that first national meeting, about three hundred years ago, there were many disagreements." Eric looked very, very serious.

"No, really?" Vampires arguing? I could yawn.

And he didn't appreciate my sarcasm, either. He raised blond eyebrows, as if to say, "Can I go on and get to the point? Or are you going to give me grief?"

I spread my hands: "Keep on going."

"Instead of dividing the country the way humans would, we included some of the north and some of the south in every division. We thought it would keep the cross-representation going. So the easternmost division, which is mostly the coastal states, is called Moshup Clan, for the Native American mythical figure, and its symbol is a whale."

Okay, maybe I looked a little glazed at that point. "Look it up on the Internet," Eric said impatiently. "Our clan—the states that met in Rhodes compose this one—is Amun, a god from the Egyptian system, and our symbol is a feather, because Amun wore a feathered headdress. Do you remember that we all wore little feather pins there?"

Ah. No. I shook my head.

"Well, it was a busy summit," Eric conceded.

What with the bombs, and the explosions, and all.

"To our west is Zeus, from the Roman system, and a thunderbolt is their symbol, of course."

Sure. I nodded in profound agreement. Eric may have sensed that I was not exactly on board, by then. He gave me a stern look. "Sookie, this is important. As my wife, you must know this."

I wasn't even going to get into that tonight. "Okay, go ahead," I said.

"The fourth clan, the West Coast division, is called Narayana, from early Hinduism, and its symbol is an eye, because Narayana created the sun and moon from his eyes."

I thought of things I'd like to ask, like "Who the hell sat around and picked the stupid names?" But when I ran my questions through my inner censor, each one sounded snarkier than the last. I said, "But there were some vampires at the summit in Rhodes—the Amun Clan summit—that should be in Zeus, right?"

"Yes, good! There are visitors at the summits, if they have some vested interest in a topic under discussion. Or if they are engaged in a lawsuit against someone in that division. Or if they're going to marry someone in the division whose time it is to have a summit." His eyes crinkled at the corners with his smile of approval. *Narayana created the sun from his eyes,* I thought. I smiled back.

"I understand," I said. "So, how come Felipe conquered Louisiana, since we're Amun and he's . . . Ah, is Nevada in Narayana or Zeus?"

"Narayana. He took Louisiana because he wasn't as frightened of Sophie-Anne as everyone else. He planned, and executed quickly and with precision after the governing . . . board . . . of Narayana Clan approved his plan."

"He had to present a plan before he moved on us?"

"That's the way it's done. The kings and queens of Narayana wouldn't want their territory weakened if Felipe failed and Sophie-Anne managed to take Nevada. So he had to outline his plan."

"They didn't think we might want to say something about that plan?"

"Not their concern. If we're weak enough to be taken, then we are fair game. Sophie-Anne was a good leader, and much respected. With her incapacitation, Felipe judged we were weak enough to attack. Stan's lieutenant in Texas has struggled these past few months since Stan was injured in Rhodes, and it's been hard for him to hold on to Texas."

"How would they know how hurt Sophie-Anne was? How hurt Stan is?"

"Spies. We all spy on each other." Eric shrugged. (Big deal. Spies.)

"What if one of the rulers in Narayana had owed some favor to Sophie-Anne and decided to tip her off to the take-over?"

"I'm sure some of them considered it. But with Sophie-Anne so severely wounded, I suppose they decided that the odds lay with Felipe."

This was appalling. "How do you trust anyone?"

"I don't. There are two exceptions. You, and Pam."

"Oh," I said. I tried to imagine feeling like that. "That's awful, Eric."

I thought he'd shrug that off. But instead, he regarded me soberly. "Yes. It's not good."

"Do you know who the spies in Area Five are?"

"Felicia, of course. She is weak, and it's not much of a secret that she must be in the pay of someone; probably Stan in Texas, or Freyda in Oklahoma."

"I don't know Freyda." I'd met Stan. "Is Texas in Zeus or Amun?"

Eric beamed at me. I was his star pupil. "Zeus," he said. "But Stan had to be at the summit because he was proposing to go in with Mississippi on a resort development."

"He sure paid for that," I said. "If they have spies, we have spies, too, right?"

"Of course."

"Who? I'm not missing anyone?"

"You met Rasul in New Orleans, I believe."

I nodded. Rasul had been of Middle Eastern stock, and he'd had quite a sense of humor. "He survived the takeover."

"Yes, because he agreed to become a spy for Victor, and therefore for Felipe. They sent him to Michigan."

"Michigan?"

"There is a very large Arab enclave there, and Rasul fits in well. He tells them he fled the takeover." Eric paused. "You know, his life will be ended if you tell anyone this."

"Oh, duh. I'm not telling anyone any of this. For one thing, the fact that you-all named your little slices of America after gods is just . . ." I shook my head. Really something. I wasn't sure what. Proud? Stupid? Bizarre? "For another thing, I like Rasul." And I thought it was pretty damn smart of him to take the chance to get out from under Victor's thumb, no matter what he'd agreed to do. "Why are you telling me all this, all of a sudden?"

"I think you need to know what's going on around you, my lover." Eric had never looked more serious. "Last night, while I was working, I found myself distracted by the idea that you might suffer for your ignorance. Pam agreed. She's wanted to give you the background of our hierarchy for some weeks. But I thought the knowledge would burden you, and you had enough problems to handle. Pam reminded me that ignorance could get you killed. I value you too much to let yours continue."

My initial thought was that I'd really enjoyed that ignorance, and it would have been okay with me if I'd retained it. Then I had to hop all over myself. Eric was really trying to include me in his life and its ins and outs. And he was trying to help me acclimatize to his world because he considered me a part of it. I tried to feel warm and fuzzy about that.

Finally, I said, "Thanks." I tried to think of intelligent questions to ask. "Um, okay. So the kings and queens of each state in a particular division get together to make decisions and bond—what, every two years?"

Eric was eyeing me cautiously. He could tell not all was well in Sookieville. "Yes," he said. "Unless there's some crisis that calls for an extra meeting. Each state is not a separate kingdom. For instance, there's a ruler of New York City and a ruler of the rest of the state. Florida is also divided."

"Why?" That took me aback. Until I considered. "Oh, lots of tourists. Easy prey. High vampire population."

Eric nodded. "California is in thirds—California Sacramento, California San Jose, and California Los Angeles. On the other hand, North and South Dakota have become one kingdom, since the population is so thin."

I was getting the hang of looking at things through vampire eyes. There'd be more lions where the gazelles crowded around the watering hole. Fewer prey animals, fewer predators. "How does the business of—well, of Amun, say—get conducted between those biennial meetings?" There had to be stuff that came up.

"Message boards, mostly. If we have to have a face-to-face, committees of sheriffs meet, depending on the situation. If I had an argument with the vampire of another sheriff, I'd call that sheriff, and if he wasn't ready to give me satisfaction, his lieutenant would meet with my lieutenant."

"And if that didn't work?"

"We'd kick the dispute up the ladder, to the summit. In between meeting years, there's an informal gathering, with no ceremony or celebration."

I could think of a lot of questions, but they were all of the "what if" variety, and there wasn't any immediate need for me to know the answers.

"Okeydokey," I said. "Well, that was real interesting."

"You don't sound interested. You sound irritated."

"This isn't what I expected when I found out you were sleeping in the house."

"What did you expect?"

"I expected you'd come over here because you couldn't wait an extra minute to have fabulous, mind-blowing sex with me." And to hell with the corpse, for the moment.

"I've told you things for your own good," Eric said soberly. "However, now that that's done, I am as ready as ever to have sex with you, and I can certainly make it mind-blowing."

"Then cut to the chase, honey."

With a movement too fast for me to follow, Eric's shirt was off, and while I was admiring the view, his other clothes followed.

"Do I actually get to chase you?" he asked, his fangs already out.

I made it halfway to the living room before he caught me. But he carried me back to the bedroom.

It was great. Even though I had a niggling anxiety gnawing at me, that gnawing was successfully stifled for a very satisfying forty-five minutes.

Eric liked to lie propped on his elbow, his other hand stroking my stomach. When I protested that since my stomach wasn't completely flat, this made me feel fat, he laughed heartily. "Who wants a bag of bones?" he said, with absolute sincerity. "I don't want to hurt myself on the sharp edges of the woman I'm bedding."

That made me feel better than anything he'd said to me in a long time. "Did women . . . Were women curvier when you were human?" I asked.

"We didn't always have choices about how fat we were," Eric said dryly. "In bad years, we were all skin and bones. In good years, when we could eat, we did."

I felt abashed. "Oh, sorry."

"This is a wonderful century to live in," Eric said. "You can have food anytime you want."

"If you have the money to pay for it."

"Oh, you can steal it," he said. "The point is, the food is here to be had."

"Not in Africa."

"I know people still starve in many parts of the world. But sooner or later, this prosperity will extend everywhere. It just got here first."

I found his optimism amazing. "You really think so?"

"Yes," he said simply. "Braid my hair for me, would you, Sookie?"

I got my hairbrush and an elastic band. Color me silly, but I really enjoyed doing this. Eric sat on the stool in front of my vanity table, and I threw on a robe he'd given me, a beautiful peach-and-white-silk one. I began brushing Eric's long hair. After he said he didn't mind, I got some hair gel and slicked the blond strands back so there wouldn't be any loose hairs ruining the look. I took my time, making the neatest braid I could, and then I tied off the end. Without his hair floating around his face, Eric looked more severe, but just as handsome. I sighed.

"What is this sound coming from you?" he asked, turning from side to side to get several views of himself in the mirror. "Are you not happy with the result?"

"I think you look great," I said. Only the fact that he might accuse me of false modesty kept me from saying, "So what on earth are you doing with me?"

"Now I'll do your hair."

Something in me flinched. The night I'd had sex for the very first time, Bill had brushed my hair until the sensuality of the movement had turned into a very different kind of sensuality. "No, thanks," I said brightly.

I realized that I felt very odd, all of a sudden.

Eric swung around to look up at me. "What's making you so jumpy, Sookie?"

"Hey, what happened to Alaska and Hawaii?" I asked at random. I still had the brush in my hand, and without meaning to, I dropped it. It clattered on the wooden floor.

"What?" Eric looked down at the brush, then up at my face, in some confusion.

"What section are they in? They both in Nakamura?"

"Narayana. No. Alaska is lumped in with the Canadians. They have their own system. Hawaii is autonomous."

"That's just not right." I was genuinely indignant. Then I remembered there was something very important I had to tell Eric. "I guess Heidi reported back to you after she sniffed out my land? She told you about the body?" My hand jerked involuntarily.

Eric was watching my every move, his eyes narrowed. "We already talked about Debbie Pelt. If you really want me to, I'll move her."

I shivered all over. I wanted to tell him that the body was fresh. I'd started out to do that, but somehow I was having trouble formulating my sentence. I felt so peculiar. Eric cocked his head, his eyes locked on my face. "You're behaving very strangely, Sookie."

"Do you think Alcide could tell from the smell that the corpse was Debbie?" I asked. What was wrong with me?

"Not from the scent," he said. "A body is a body. It doesn't retain the distinctive scent that identified it as a particular person, especially after this long. Are you so worried about what Alcide thinks?"

"Not as much as I used to be," I said, babbling on. "Hey, I heard on the radio today that one of the senators from Oklahoma came out as a Were. He said he'd register with some government bureau the day they pried his fangs from his cold, dead corpse."

"I think the backlash from this will benefit vampires," Eric said with some satisfaction. "Of course, we'd always realized the government would want to keep track of us somehow. Now it seems that if the Weres win their fight to be free of supervision, we may be able to do the same."

"You better get dressed," I said. Something bad was going to happen soon, and Eric needed clothes.

He turned and peered at himself in the mirror one last time. "All right," he said, a little surprised. He was still nude and magnificent. But at the moment, I wasn't feeling a bit lusty. I was feeling jangly, and nervous, and worried. I felt like spiders were crawling all over my skin. I didn't know what could be happening to me. I tried to speak but found I couldn't. I made my fingers move in a "hurry up" gesture.

Eric gave me a quick, worried glance and wordlessly began searching for his clothes. He found his pants, and he pulled them on.

I sank down to the floor, my hands on both sides of my head. I thought my skull might detach from my spine. I whimpered. Eric dropped his shirt.

"Can you tell me what's wrong?" he asked, sinking down to the floor beside me.

"Someone's coming," I said. "I feel so *strange*. Someone's coming. Almost here. Someone with your blood." I realized I'd felt a faint, faint trace of this same oddness before, when I'd confronted Bill's maker, Lorena. I hadn't had a blood bond with Bill, or at least not one anything like as binding as the one I had with Eric.

Eric rose to his feet in less than the blink of an eye, and I heard him make a sound deep in his chest. His hands were in white fists. I was huddled against my bed, and he was between me and the open window. In the blink of an eye, I realized there was someone right outside.

"Appius Livius Ocella," Eric said. "It's been a hundred years."

Geez Louise. Eric's maker.

Chapter 8

Between Eric's legs I could see a man, very scarred and very muscular, with dark eyes and hair. I knew he was short because I could only see his head and shoulders. He was wearing jeans and a Black Sabbath T-shirt. I couldn't help it. I giggled.

"Haven't you missed me, Eric?" The Roman's voice had an accent I really couldn't have broken down, it had so many layers.

"Ocella, your presence is always an honor," Eric said. I giggled harder. Eric was lying.

"What is wrong with my wife?" he asked.

"Her senses are confused," the older vampire said. "You have my blood. She's had your blood. And another child of mine is here. The bond between us all is scrambling her thoughts and feelings."

No shit.

"This is my new son, Alexei," Appius Livius Ocella told Eric.

I peered past Eric's legs. The new "son" was a boy of no more than thirteen or fourteen. In fact, I could hardly see his face. I froze, trying not to react.

"Brother," said Eric by way of greeting his new sibling. The words came out level and cold.

I was going to stand up now. I was not going to crouch here any longer. Eric had crowded me into a very small space between the bed and the nightstand, with the bathroom door to my right. He hadn't shifted from his defensive posture.

"Excuse me," I said, with a great effort, and Eric took a step forward to give me room, keeping himself between me and his maker and the boy. I rose to my feet, pushing on the bed to get upright. I still felt fried. I looked Eric's sire right in his dark and liquid eyes. For a fraction of a second, he looked surprised.

"Eric, you need to go to the front door and let them in," I said. "I'll bet they don't really need an invitation."

"Eric, she's rare," said Ocella in his oddly accented English. "Where did you find her?"

"I'm asking you in out of courtesy, because you're Eric's dad," I said. "I could just leave you outside." If I didn't sound as strong as I wanted, at least I didn't sound frightened.

"But my child is in this house, and if he is welcome, so am I. Am I not?" Ocella's thick black brows rose. His nose . . . Well, you could tell why they coined the term "Roman nose." "I waited to come in out of courtesy. We could have appeared in your bedroom."

And the next moment they were inside.

I didn't dignify that with an answer. I spared a glance for

the boy, whose face was absolutely blank. He was no ancient Roman. He hadn't been a vampire a full century, I estimated, and he seemed to come from Germanic stock. His hair was light and short and cut evenly, his eyes were blue, and when he met my own, he inclined his head.

"Your name is Alexei?" I asked.

"Yes," said his maker, while the boy stood mute. "This is Alexei Romanov."

Though the boy didn't react, and neither did Eric, I had a moment of sheer horror. "You *didn't*," I said to Eric's maker, who was about my height. "You *didn't*."

"I tried to save one of his sisters, too, but she was beyond my recall," Ocella said bleakly. His teeth were white and even, though he was missing the one next to his left canine. If you had lost teeth before you became a vampire, they didn't regenerate.

"Sookie, what is it?" Eric was not following, for once.

"The Romanovs," I said, trying to keep my voice hushed as though the boy couldn't hear me from twenty yards away. "The last Russian royal family."

To Eric, the executions of the Romanovs must seem like yesterday, and perhaps not very important in the tapestry of deaths he'd experienced in his thousand years. But he understood that his maker had done something extraordinary. I looked at Ocella without anger, without fear, for just a few seconds, and I saw a man who, finding himself an outcast and lonely, looked for the most outstanding "children" he could find.

"Was Eric the first vampire you made?" I asked Ocella.

He was bemused by what he saw as my brazen attitude. Eric had a stronger reaction. As I felt his fear roll through me,

I understood that Eric had to physically perform whatever Ocella ordered him to do. Before, that had been an abstract concept. Now I realized that if Ocella ordered Eric to kill me, Eric would be compelled to do it.

The Roman decided to answer me. "Yes, he was the first one I brought over successfully. The others I tried to bring over—they died."

"Could we please leave my bedroom and go into the living room?" I said. "This is not the right place to receive visitors." See? I was trying to be polite.

"Yes, I suppose," said the older vampire. "Alexei? Where do you suppose the living room is?"

Alexei half turned and pointed in the right direction.

"Then that's where we'll go, dearest," Ocella said, and Alexei led the way.

I had a moment to look up at Eric, and I knew my face was asking, *"What the hell is going on here?"* But he looked stunned, and helpless. Eric. Helpless. My head was whirling.

When I had a second to think about it, I was pretty nauseated, because Alexei was a child and I was fairly sure that Ocella had a sexual relationship with the boy, as he'd had with Eric. But I wasn't foolish enough to think that I could stop it, or that any protest I made would make the slightest difference. In fact, I was far from sure Alexei himself would thank me for intervening, when I remembered Eric telling me about his desperate attachment to his maker during the first years of his new life as a vampire.

Alexei had been with Ocella for a long time now, at least in human terms. I couldn't remember exactly when the Romanov family had been executed, but I thought it was sometime around 1918, and apparently it had been Ocella

who'd saved the boy from final death. So whatever constituted their relationship, it had been ongoing for more than
eighty years.

All these thoughts flickered through my head, one after
another, as we followed the two visitors. Ocella had said he
could have entered without warning. It would have been nice
if Eric had told me about that. I could see how he might
have hoped that Ocella would never visit, so I was willing to
give Eric a pass . . . but I couldn't help thinking that instead
of his lecture on the ways vampires had sliced up my country according to their own convenience, it would have been
more practical to let me know his maker could appear *in my
bedroom*.

"Please, have a seat," I said, after Ocella and Alexei had
settled on the couch.

"So much sarcasm," said Ocella. "Will you not offer us
hospitality?" His gaze ran up and down me, and though the
color of his eyes was rich and brown, they were utterly cold.

I had a second to realize how glad I was that I'd put a
robe on. I would have rather eaten Alpo than been naked in
front of these two. "I'm not happy with your popping up outside my bedroom window," I said. "You could have come to
the door and knocked, like people with good manners do." I
wasn't telling him anything he didn't already know; vampires
are good at reading people, and the oldest vampires are usually better than humans at telling what humans are feeling.

"Yes, but then I wouldn't have seen such a charming
sight." Ocella let his gaze brush Eric's shirtless body almost
tangibly. Alexei, for the first time, showed an emotion. He
looked scared. Was he afraid Ocella would reject him, throw
him out onto the mercy of the world? Or was he afraid that
Ocella would keep him?

I pitied Alexei from the bottom of my heart, and I feared him just as much.

He was as helpless as Eric.

Ocella had been looking at Alexei with an attention that was almost frightening. "He's already much better," Ocella murmured. "Eric, your presence is doing him so much good."

I'd kind of figured things couldn't get more awkward, but a peremptory knock at the back door followed by a "Sookie, you here?" told me that actually the night could get worse.

My brother, Jason, came in without waiting for me to answer. "Sookie, I saw your light on when I pulled up, so I figured you were awake," he said, and then he stopped abruptly when he realized how much company I had. And what they were.

"Sorry to interrupt, Sook," he said slowly. "Eric, how you doing?"

Eric said, "Jason, this is my . . . This is Appius Livius Ocella, my maker, and his other son Alexei." Eric said it properly, "AP-pi-us Li-WEE-us Oh-KEL-ah."

Jason nodded at both of the newcomers, but he avoided looking directly at the older vampire. Good instinct. "Good evening, O'Kelly. Hey, Alexei. So you're Eric's little brother, huh? Are you a Viking like Eric?"

"No," said the boy faintly. "I am Russian." Alexei's accent was much lighter than the Roman's. He looked at Jason with interest. I hoped he wasn't thinking about biting my brother. The thing about Jason, and what made him so attractive to people (particularly women), was that he practically radiated life. He just seemed to have an extra helping of vigor and vitality, and it was returning with a boom now that the misery of his wife's death was fading. This was his manifestation of the fairy blood in his veins.

"Well, good to meet you-all," Jason said. Then he quit paying attention to the visitors. "Sookie, I came to get that little side table from up in the attic. I came by here once before to pick it up, but you were gone and I didn't have my key with me." Jason kept a key to my house for emergencies, just as I kept a key to his.

I'd forgotten his asking me for the table when we'd had dinner together. At this point, he could have asked me for my bedroom set, and I would have agreed just to get him out of danger. I said, "Sure, I don't need it. Go on up. I don't think it's very far inside the door."

Jason excused himself, and everyone's eyes followed him as he bounded up the stairs. Eric was probably just trying to keep his eyes busy while he thought, but Ocella watched my brother with frank appraisal, and Alexei with a kind of yearning.

"Would you like some TrueBlood?" I asked the vampires, through clenched teeth.

"I suppose, if you won't offer yourself or your brother," the ancient Roman said.

"I won't."

I turned to go to the kitchen.

"I feel your anger," Ocella said.

"I don't care," I said, without turning to face him. I heard Jason coming downstairs, a little more slowly now that he was carrying the table. "Jason, you want to come with me?" I said over my shoulder.

He was more than glad to leave the room. Though he was civil to Eric because he knew I loved him, Jason was not happy in the company of vamps. He put the table down in a corner of the kitchen.

"Sook, what's going on here?"

"Come into my room for a second," I said after I'd gotten the bottles out of my refrigerator. I'd feel a lot better if I had more clothes on. Jason trailed after me. I shut the door once we were inside my bedroom.

"Watch the door. I don't trust that old one," I said, and Jason obligingly turned his back and watched the door while I pulled off the robe, getting into my clothes as fast as I've ever dressed in my life.

"Whoa," Jason said, and I jumped. I turned to see that Alexei had opened the door and would have entered if Jason hadn't been holding it.

"I'm sorry," Alexei said. His voice was a ghost of a voice, a voice that once had been. "I apologize to you, Sookie, and you, Jason."

"Jason, you can let him in. What are you sorry for, Alexei?" I asked. "Come on, let's go to the kitchen and I'll warm up the TrueBlood." We trailed into the kitchen. We were a little farther from the living room, and there was a chance Eric and Ocella wouldn't hear us.

"My master is not always like this. His age, it turns him."

"Turns him into what? A total jerk? A sadist? A child molester?"

A faint smile crossed the boy's face. "At times, all of those," he said succinctly. "But truthfully, I haven't been well myself. That's why we're here."

Jason began to look angry. He likes kids, always has. Even though Alexei could have killed Jason in a second, Jason thought of Alexei as a child. My brother was building up a big mad, actually thinking of charging into the living room to confront Appius Livius Ocella.

"Listen, Alexei, you don't have to stay with that dude if you don't want to," Jason said. "You can stay with me or Sookie, if Eric won't put you up. Nobody's gonna make you stay with someone you don't want to be with." Bless Jason's heart, he sure didn't know what he was talking about.

Alexei smiled, a faint smile that was simply heart-piercing. "Really, he is not so bad. He is a good man, I believe, but from a time you can't imagine. I think you are used to knowing vampires who are trying to . . . mainstream. Master, he is not trying to do this. He is much happier in the shadows. And I must stay with him. Please don't trouble yourselves, but I thank you for your concern. I'm feeling better already now that I'm with my brother. I don't feel as if I'll suddenly do something . . . regrettable."

Jason and I looked at each other. That was enough to make us both worried.

Alexei was looking around the kitchen as if he seldom saw one. I figured that was probably true.

I took the warm bottles out of the microwave and shook them. I put some napkins on the tray with the bottles. Jason got himself a Coke from the refrigerator.

I didn't know what to think about Alexei. He apologized for Ocella like the Roman was his grumpy grandpa, but it was apparent that he was in Ocella's sway. Of course he was; he was Ocella's child in a very real sense.

It was an awfully strange situation, having a figure out of history sitting in your living room. I thought of the horrors he'd experienced, both before and after his death. I thought of his childhood as the tsarevitch, and I knew that despite his hemophilia, that childhood must have contained some glorious moments. I didn't know whether the boy often longed for the love, devotion, and luxury that had surrounded him from birth until the rebellion, or (considering he'd been executed along with his whole immediate family) whether it was possible he saw being a vampire as an improvement over being buried in a pit in the woods in Russia.

Though with the hemophilia, his life expectancy in those days would have been pretty damn short anyway.

Jason added ice to his glass and looked in the cookie jar. I didn't keep cookies anymore, because if I did, I'd eat 'em. He closed the jar sadly. Alexei was watching everything Jason did as if he were observing an animal he'd never seen before.

He noticed me looking at him. "Two men took care of me, two sailors," he said, as though he could read the questions in my mind. "They carried me around when the pain was bad. After the world turned upside down, one of them abused me when he had the chance. But the other died, simply because he was still kind to me. Your brother reminds me a little of that one."

"Sorry about your family," I said awkwardly, since I felt compelled to say something.

He shrugged. "I was glad when they found them and gave the burial," he said. But when I saw his eyes, I knew that his words were a thin layer of ice over a pit of pain.

"Who was that in your coffin?" I asked. Was I being tacky? What on earth else was there to talk about? Jason was looking from Alexei to me, mystified. Jason's idea of history was remembering Jimmy Carter's embarrassing brother.

"When the big grave was found, Master knew they would find my sister and me soon. We overestimated the searchers, perhaps. It took sixteen more years. But in the meantime, we revisited the place where I was buried."

I felt my eyes fill with tears. *The place where I was buried . . .*

He continued, "We had to provide some of my bones for it, because we had learned about DNA by then. Otherwise, of course, we could have found a boy about the right age. . . ."

I really couldn't think of anything remotely normal to say. "So you cut out some of your own bones to put in the grave," I said, my voice clogged and shaky.

"In steps, over time. Everything grew back," he said reassuringly. "We had to burn my bones a little. They had burned Maria and me, and poured acid on us, too."

Finally, I managed, "Why was that necessary? To put your bones there?"

"Master wanted me to be at rest," he said. "He didn't want any sightings. He reasoned that if my bones were found, there would be no more controversy. Of course, by now no one would expect me to be alive anyway, much less looking like I did then. Perhaps we weren't thinking clearly. When you've been out of the world so long . . . And in the first five years after the revolution, I was seen by a couple of people who did recognize me. Master had to take care of them."

That, too, took a minute to sink in. Jason looked nauseated. I wasn't far behind him. But this little chitchat had already taken long enough. I didn't want "Master" to think we were plotting against him.

"Alexei," Appius Livius called in a sharp voice. "Is all well with you?"

"Yes, sir," Alexei said, and hurried back to the Roman.

"Jesus Christ, Shepherd of Judea," I said, and turned to carry the tray of bottles into the living room. Jason was clearly unhappy, but he followed me.

Eric was fixed on Appius Livius Ocella like a 7-Eleven

clerk watches a customer who may have a gun. But he seemed to have relaxed a smidgen, now that he'd had a little time to recover from the shock of his maker's appearance. Through the bond, I felt a wash of overwhelming relief from Eric. After I thought about that, I believed I understood. Eric was relieved beyond measure that the older vampire had brought a bedmate with him. Eric, who had given a pretty good impression of indifference about his many years as Ocella's sexual companion, had had a moment of crazed unwillingness when he actually saw his maker again. Eric was reassembling and rearming himself. He was returning to being Eric, the sheriff, from his abrupt reversion to Eric, the new vampire and love slave.

The way I perceived Eric would never be quite the same again. I knew now what he feared. What I was getting from Eric was that it wasn't so much the physical aspect as the mental; above all else, Eric did not want to be under the control of his maker.

I served each of the vampires a bottle, carefully placing it on a napkin. At least I didn't have to worry about serving an accompanying snack . . . unless Ocella decided all three of them would feed from me. In which case, I had no hope I would survive, and there wouldn't be a damn thing I could do about it. This should have made me the model of discretion. I should have determined to sit there with my ankles crossed and not let butter melt in my mouth.

But it just pissed me off.

Eric's hand twitched, and I knew he was reading my mood. He wanted to tell me to tone it down, to cool off, to come in under the radar. He might not want to be under Ocella's sway again, but he loved the vampire, too. I made myself back down. I hadn't given the Roman a chance. I didn't really know him. I only knew some things I didn't like about him, and there must be some other things I would like or admire. If he'd been Eric's for-real father, I'd have given him lots of chances to prove his worth.

I wondered how clearly Ocella could sense my emotions. He was still tuned in to Eric and always would be, and Eric and I were bonded. But it seemed my feelings didn't carry over; the Roman didn't so much as glance my way. I cast my eyes down. I would have to learn how to be stealthier, and in a hurry. Normally, I was good at hiding what I felt, but the nearness of the ancient vampire and his new protégé, their blood so like Eric's, had thrown me for a loop.

"I'm not sure what to call you," I said, meeting the Roman's eyes. I was trying to mimic my grandmother's best company voice.

"You may call me Appius Livius," he said, "since you are Eric's wife. It took Eric a hundred years to earn the right to call me Appius, rather than Master. Then centuries to be able to call me Ocella."

So only Eric got to call him Ocella. Fine with me. I noticed Alexei was still at the "Master" stage. Alexei was sitting as still as if he'd taken a huge tranquilizer, his synthetic blood sitting on the coffee table in front of him with only a sip missing.

"Thanks," I said, aware that I didn't sound very thankful. I glanced over at my brother. Jason was thinking he had a pretty good idea about what he wanted to call the Roman, but I gave my head a small but definite shake.

"Eric, tell me how you are doing these days," Appius Livius said. He sounded genuinely interested. His hand went over to Alexei, and I saw he was stroking the boy's back, as if

Alexei were a puppy. But I couldn't deny there was affection in the gesture.

"I'm very well. Area Five is prosperous. I was the only Louisiana sheriff to survive the takeover by Felipe de Castro." Eric managed to sound matter-of-fact.

"How did that come about?"

Eric gave the older vampire a rundown on the political situation with Victor Madden. When he thought Appius Livius was up to speed on the Felipe de Castro/Victor Madden situation, Eric asked him, "How did you come to be on hand for the rescue of this young man?" Eric smiled at Alexei.

This would be a story worth listening to, now that I'd heard Alexei's horrifying tale about "salting" his grave. While Alexei Romanov sat by his side in remote silence, Appius told Eric about tracking down the Russian royal family in 1918.

"Though I had expected something of the sort, I had to move much faster than I had anticipated," Appius said. He finished his bottled blood. "The decision to execute them was made so swiftly, conducted at such speed. No one wanted the men to have time to think twice about it. For many of the soldiers, it was a terrible thing they were doing."

"Why did you want to save the Romanovs?" Eric asked, as if Alexei weren't there.

And Appius Livius laughed. He gave great laugh. "I hated the fucking Bolsheviks," he said. "And I had a tie to the boy. Rasputin had been giving him my blood for years. I happened to be in Russia already; you remember the St. Petersburg Massacre?"

Eric nodded. "I do indeed. I had not seen you in many years, and only caught a glimpse of you then." Eric had talked about the St. Petersburg Massacre before. A vampire named Gregory had had madness visited on him by a vengeful maenad, and it had taken twenty vampires to pin him down and then disguise the results.

"After that night, when so many of us worked together to tidy up the scene after Gregory was subdued, I developed a fondness for the Russian vampires—and the Russian people, too." He tacked the Russian people on with a gracious nod toward me and Jason, as representatives of the human race. "The fucking Bolsheviks killed so many of us. I was grieved. The deaths of Fedor and Velislava were particularly hard. They were both great vampires, and hundreds of years old."

"I knew them," Eric said.

"I sent them a message to get out before I started to look for the royal family. I could track Alexei because he'd had my blood. Rasputin knew what we were. Whenever the empress would call him to heal the boy when the hemophilia was very bad, Rasputin would beg some of my blood and the boy would recover. I heard a rumor they were thinking of killing the royal family, and I began following the scent of my blood. When I set out to rescue them, you can imagine how like a crusader I felt!"

They both laughed, and I suddenly understood that the two vampires had actually seen crusaders, the original Christian knight crusaders. When I tried to comprehend how old they were, how much they'd witnessed, how many experiences they'd had that almost no one else walking the earth remembered, it made my head hurt.

"Sook, you got the most interesting company," Jason said.

"Listen, I know you want to go, but if you could stick around for a while, I'd appreciate it," I said. I wasn't happy with having Eric's maker and the poor child Alexei here, and since Alexei was clearly happy with Jason, his presence might help ease this uncomfortable situation.

"I'll just go put the table out in the truck and call Michele," he said. "Alexei, you want to come with me?"

Appius Livius didn't move, but he definitely grew tense. Alexei looked over at the ancient Roman. After a long pause, Appius Livius nodded at the boy. "Alexei, remember your company manners," Appius Livius said softly. Alexei bobbed his head.

Having been given permission, the tsarevitch of Russia went outside with the road-crew worker to stow a table in the back of a pickup.

When I was alone with Eric and his maker, I felt a stab of anxiety. Actually, it was flowing right through the bond I had with Eric. I wasn't the only one around here who was worried. And their conversation appeared to be at a standstill.

"Excuse me, Appius Livius," I said carefully. "Since you were in the right empire at the right time, I wonder if you ever saw Jesus?"

The Roman was staring at the hallway, willing Alexei to reappear. "The carpenter? No, I didn't see him," Appius said, and I could tell he was making an effort to be courteous. "The Jew died right around the time I was changed. As you will appreciate, I had many other things to think of. In fact, I didn't hear the whole myth until some time later when the world began to change as a result of his death."

That would really have been amazing, talking to a creature who'd seen the living God . . . even if he called him a "myth." And I went back to fearing the Roman—not for what he'd done to me, or what he'd done to Eric, or even what he was doing to Alexei, but for what he *might do* to all of us, if he took a mind to. I had always tried to find the good in people, but the best I could say of Appius was that he had good taste in those he picked to become vampires.

While I brooded, Appius was explaining to Eric how conveniently it had worked out in the cellar in Ekaterinburg. Alexei had almost bled out from his wounds, so he'd given the boy a big gulp of his blood—moving at superspeed, and therefore invisible to the execution squad. Then he'd watched from the shadows while the bodies were thrown down a well. The next day, the royal family was dug up again since the murderers feared the uproar that might follow the deaths of the Romanovs.

"I followed them the minute the sun set the next day," Appius said. "They'd stopped to rebury them. Alexei and one of his sisters . . ."

"Maria," Alexei said softly, and I jumped. He had reappeared silently in the living room, standing behind Appius's chair. "It was Maria."

There was a silence. Appius looked hugely relieved. "Yes, of course, dear boy," Appius said, and he did manage to sound as though he cared. "Your sister Maria was completely gone, but there was a tiny spark in you." Alexei put his hand on Appius Livius's shoulder, and Appius Livius reached up to pat him.

"They had shot him many times," he explained to Eric. "Twice in the head. I put my blood directly in the bullet holes." He turned his head to look at the boy behind him. "My blood worked well, since you had lost so much of yours." It was like he was recollecting happy times. Hoo, boy. The Roman turned back to look at Eric and me, and he smiled proudly. But I could see Alexei's face.

Appius Livius genuinely felt that he'd been a savior to Alexei. I wasn't so sure Alexei was totally convinced of that.

"Where's your brother?" Appius Livius suddenly asked,

and I pushed to my feet to go find him. I had put two and two together, and I understood that Eric's maker wanted to be sure Alexei hadn't drained Jason and left him out in the yard.

Jason came into the living room just then, slipping his cell phone into his pocket. He narrowed his eyes. Jason was not a nuance kind of guy, but he could tell when I was unhappy. "Sorry," he said. "Talkin' to Michele."

"Hmmm," I said. I made a mental note that Appius Livius was worried about Alexei being alone with humans, and I knew that should scare me quite a bit. The night was growing older, and I had things to find out. "I hate to change the subject, but there are a few things I need to know."

"What, Sookie?" Eric asked, looking directly at me for the first time since Old Master had popped up. He was pouring caution down the bond between us.

"I just have a couple of questions," I said, smiling as sweetly as I could. "Have you been in this area for any length of time?"

I met the ancient dark eyes again. It was hard to take Appius all in, somehow; I found I couldn't look at him as a cohesive individual. He scared the shit out of me.

"No," he said mildly. "We have not. We've come here from the southwest, from Oklahoma, and we have only just arrived in Louisiana."

"So you wouldn't know anything about the new body buried at the back of my land?"

"No, nothing. Would you like us to go dig it up? Unpleasant, but doable. You are wanting to see who it is?"

That was an unexpected offer. Eric was looking at me very oddly. "I'm sorry, honey," I told him. "I was trying to tell you when our unexpected guests showed up."

"Not Debbie," he said.

"No, Heidi says there's a new burial. But we do need to know who it is, and we need to find out who put it there."

"The Weres," Eric said instantly. "This is the thanks you get for letting them use your land. I'll call Alcide, and we'll have a meeting." Eric looked positively delighted to get the chance to do something bosslike. He whipped out his cell phone and dialed Alcide before I could say anything.

"Eric," he said into the phone by way of identification. "Alcide, we have to talk." I could hear the buzz on the other end of the line.

A moment later Eric said, "That's not good, Alcide, and I am sorry to hear you have troubles. But I have other concerns. What did you do on Sookie's land?"

Oh, crapanola.

"You should come here and see, then. I think some of your people have been bad. Very well, then. I'll see you in ten minutes. I am at her house."

He hung up, looking triumphant. "Alcide was in Bon Temps?" I asked.

"No, but he was on the interstate and nearly at our exit," Eric explained. "He's returning from some meeting in Monroe. The Louisiana packs are trying to present a united front to the government. Since they've never organized before, this is not going to work." Eric snorted, clearly scornful. "The Weres are always—what did you say the other day about FEMA, Sookie? 'A day late and a dollar short,' right? At least he's close, and when he gets here we'll get to the bottom of this."

I sighed, trying to make it discreet and silent. I hadn't realized things would go so far so fast. I asked Eric, Appius Livius, and Alexei if they wanted more TrueBlood, but they turned it down. Jason was looking bored. I glanced at the clock.

"I'm afraid I have only one spot that's suitable for a vampire. Where are you-all planning to sleep, come the dawn? I just want to know in case I need to call around and find a place."

"Sookie," said Eric gently, "I will take Ocella and his son back to my house. They can have the guest coffins there."

Eric ordinarily slept in his bed, because his bedroom was windowless. There were a couple of other coffins in the guest bedroom, sleek fiberglass things that looked sort of like kayaks, which he kept stowed under the beds. The most wrong thing about Alexei and Appius Livius staying with Eric was that if they were there, I was definitely staying here.

"I think your darling would love to come in during the day and sink a stake into our chests," Appius Livius said, as if that were a big joke. "If you think you can do it, young woman, you are welcome to try."

"Oh, not at all," I said, absolutely insincerely. "I wouldn't dream of doing such a thing to Eric's dad." Not a bad idea, though.

Beside me, Eric twitched all over; it was a funny movement, like a dog running in its sleep. "Be polite," he told me, and there was no element of fun in his voice at all. He was giving me an order.

I took a deep breath. It was on the tip of my tongue to rescind Eric's invitation to my house. He'd have to leave, and presumably Appius Livius and Alexei would, too. It was that "presumably" that stopped me. The idea of being alone with Appius Livius even for a second trumped the pleasurable vision of the three vampires walking out backward.

It was probably lucky for all of us that the doorbell rang then. I was out of my seat as if a rocket had fired me. It would be good to have more breathers around.

Alcide was wearing a suit. He was flanked by Annabelle, who was wearing a dark green sheath and heeled pumps, and Jannalynn, Sam's new interest. Jannalynn had a sense of style, though it was a style that left me stunned. She had on a shiny silver dress that barely covered her assets and silver high-heeled sandals that laced up the front. The silver eye shadow over her heavily outlined eyes completed the look. In a scary kind of way, she looked great. Sam certainly dated women who were extraordinary in some way, and he wasn't afraid of strong characters, which was a thought I'd have to save for later. Maybe it was a two-natured thing? Alcide was the same way.

I gave the packleader a hug, and I said hello to Annabelle and to Jannalynn, who gave me a curt nod.

"What is this problem Eric called me about?" Alcide was saying as I stood aside to let them enter. When the Weres realized they were in a room with three vampires, all of them tensed. They'd expected only Eric. When I glanced back at the vampires, I saw they were all standing, too, and even Alexei was on the alert.

Jason said, "Alcide, good to see you. Ladies, looking mighty fine tonight."

I went into high gear. "Hi, you-all!" I said brightly. "It was so nice of you to come at such short notice. Eric, you know Alcide. Alcide, this is Eric's longtime friend Appius Livius Ocella, who's in town visiting with his, ah, protégé, Alexei. Eric, I don't know if you've met Alcide's friend Annabelle, a new pack member, and Jannalynn, who's been in the Long Tooth pack for ages. Jannalynn, we've never had a chance to talk much, but of course Sam talks about you all the time. And I think you all know my brother, Jason."

Whew. I felt like I'd run an introduction marathon. Since vamps don't shake hands, that concluded the opening ceremonies. Then I had to get them all to sit down while I offered them drinks, which no one accepted.

Eric fired the opening volley. "Alcide, one of my trackers went over Sookie's land after Basim al Saud warned her about the strangers he smelled in her woods. Our tracker has found a new body buried there."

Alcide looked at Eric as though he had begun speaking in tongues.

"We didn't kill anyone that night," Alcide said. "Basim said he told Sookie we smelled an old body, and a fairy or two, and a vampire. But he didn't mention a fresh body."

"Yet there's a new burial there now."

"Which we had nothing to do with." Alcide shrugged. "We were there three nights before your tracker smelled the scent of a fresh body."

"It seems quite a huge coincidence, doesn't it? A body on Sookie's land, right after your pack is there?" Eric was looking aggravatingly reasonable.

"Maybe it's more of a coincidence that there was already a body on Sookie's land."

Oh, boy, I *really* didn't want to go there.

Jannalynn was actually snarling at Eric. It was an interesting look, with the eye makeup and all. Annabelle was standing with her arms slightly away from her body, waiting to see which way she needed to jump.

Alexei was staring off into space, which seemed to be his fallback stance, and Appius Livius simply seemed bored.

"I say we should go see who it is," Jason said unexpectedly. I looked at him with approval.

So out we went into the woods to dig up a corpse.

Chapter 9

Alcide changed to some boots he had in the truck, and he shed his tie and coat. Jannalynn wisely took off her spike-heeled sandals and Annabelle her own more modest heels. I gave them both some sneakers of mine, and I offered Jannalynn an old T-shirt to cover her shiny silver dress so it wouldn't snag in the woods. She pulled it over her head. She even said, "Thanks," though she didn't sound actually grateful. I retrieved two shovels from the toolshed. Alcide took one shovel, Eric the other. Jason carried one of those great big flashlights called a lantern that he'd fished out of the toolbox on his truck. The lantern was for my benefit. The vampires could see perfectly well in the dark, and the Weres could see very well, too. Since Jason was a werepanther, he had excellent night vision. I was the blind one in the group.

"Do we know where we're going?" Annabelle said.

"Heidi said it was due east, close to the stream, in a clearing," I said, and we slogged eastward. I kept running into stuff, and after a while Eric handed off his shovel to Jason and crouched so I could cling to his back. I kept my head tucked behind his so branches wouldn't hit me in the face. Our progress was smoother after that.

"I smell it," Jannalynn said suddenly. She was out ahead of us all, as if her job in the pack were to make the way clear for the packleader. She was a different woman out in the woods. Though I couldn't see very well, I could see that. She was quick, sure-footed, and decisive. She darted ahead, and after a moment she called back, "Here it is!"

We got there to find her standing over a patch of dirt in a little clearing. It had been disturbed recently, though an attempt had been made to camouflage that disturbance.

Eric eased me down onto the ground, and Jason shone the lantern at the earth. "It's not . . . ?" I whispered, knowing everyone there could hear me.

"No," Eric said firmly. "Too recent." Not Debbie Pelt. She was elsewhere, in an older grave.

"Only one way to find out who it is," Alcide said. Jason and Alcide began to dig, and since they were both very strong, it went quickly. Alexei came over to stand by me, and it occurred to me that a grave in the woods had to be a bad flashback for him. I put an arm around him as if he were still human, though I noticed that Appius gave me a sardonic look. Alexei's eyes were on the gravediggers, especially Jason. I knew this child could dig the grave with his bare hands as fast as they were digging with shovels, but Alexei looked so frail it was hard to think of him being as strong as other vampires. I wondered how many people had made that mistake in the past few decades, and how many of those had died at Alexei's small hands.

Jason and Alcide could make the dirt fly. While they worked, Annabelle and Jannalynn prowled around the little clearing, probably trying to pick up what scents they could. Despite the rain of two nights ago, there might be something in the areas protected by the trees. Heidi hadn't been looking for a murderer; she'd been trying to make a list of who'd crossed the land. I was thinking that the only creatures who hadn't been tromping through my woods had been regular old humans. If the Weres were lying, a Were could be the killer. Or it could be one of the fae, who were a violent race, as I had observed. Or the killer could be Bill, since Heidi thought the vampire she'd scented was my neighbor.

I hadn't smelled the body while it was under the dirt as the others had, since my sense of smell was only a fraction of theirs. But as the dirt piles grew and the hole got deeper, I could tell it was there. Oh gosh, could I.

I put my hand across my nose, which didn't help at all. I couldn't imagine how the others were enduring it, since it would be so much sharper to their senses. Maybe they were also more practical, or simply more accustomed.

Then both the diggers stopped. "He's wrapped up," Jason said. Alcide bent over and fumbled with something at the bottom of the hole.

"I think I got it pulled apart," Alcide said after a moment.

"Pass me the lantern, Sookie," Jason said, and I tossed it to him. He shone it down. "I don't know this man," he said.

"I do," said Alcide in a strange voice. Annabelle and Jannalynn were at the edge of the grave instantly. I had to brace myself to step forward to look down into the pit.

I recognized him instantly. The three Weres threw back their heads and howled.

"It's the Long Tooth enforcer," I told the vampires. I gagged and had to wait a minute before I could go on. "It's Basim al Saud." The passage of days had made a great difference, but I knew him instantly. Those corkscrew curls I'd envied, the muscled body.

"Shit," screamed Jannalynn, when the howling was done. And that about summed it up.

When the Weres had calmed down, there was a lot to talk about.

"I only met him the once," I said. "Of course, he was fine when he got in the truck with Alcide and Annabelle."

"He told me what he'd smelled on the property, and I told him to tell Sookie," Alcide told Eric. "She had a right to know. We didn't talk about anything in particular on the way back to Shreveport, did we, Annabelle?"

"No," she said, and I could tell she was crying.

"I dropped him off at his apartment. When I called him the next day to go with me to a meeting with our representative, he said he had to pass because he had to work. He was a website designer, and he had a meeting with an important client. I wasn't too happy he couldn't go, but of course, the guy had to make a living." Alcide shrugged.

Annabelle said, "He didn't have to work that day."

There was a moment of silence.

"I was at his apartment when you called," she said, and I could tell the effort she was expending to keep her voice calm and level. "I had been there a few hours."

Wow. Unexpected revelation. Jason had hopped out of the grave, and he and I gave each other big eyes. This was like one of Gran's "stories," the soap operas she'd watched religiously.

Alcide growled. The ritual howling for the dead had brought out the wolf in him.

"I know," Annabelle said. "And we'll talk about it later. I'll take my punishment, which I deserve. But Basim's death is more important than my bad judgment. This is my duty, to tell you what happened. Basim got a phone call before yours, and he didn't want me to hear it. But I heard enough to understand his conversation was with someone who was paying him."

Alcide's growl intensified. Jannalynn was standing close to her pack sister, and the only way I can put it was that she was aimed at Annabelle. She was crouching slightly, her hands curved as if they were about to sprout claws.

Alexei had edged close to Jason, and when the tension kept ratcheting up, Jason's arm slung around the boy's shoulders. Jason was having the same problem separating illusion and reality that I was.

Annabelle flinched at the sound coming from Alcide, but she kept on going. "So Basim made up an excuse to get me out of the apartment, and he took off. I tried to follow him, but I lost him."

"You were suspicious," Jannalynn said. "But you didn't call the packmaster. You didn't call me. You didn't call anyone. We took you in and made you a member of our pack, and you betrayed us." Suddenly, she hit Annabelle in the head with her fist, actually leaping into the air to land the blow. Just like that, Annabelle was on the ground. I gasped, and I wasn't the only one.

But I was the only one who noticed that Jason was straining to hold Alexei back. Something about the violence in the air had sent the boy over the edge. If he'd been a little bigger,

Jason would've been on the ground. I punched Eric in the arm, jerked my head in the direction of the struggle. Eric leaped over to help Jason restrain the boy, who fought and snarled in their arms.

For a moment there was silence in the dark clearing as everyone watched Alexei struggle with his madness. Appius Livius looked profoundly sad. He worked his way into the knot of limbs and wrapped his own arms around his child. "Sshhhhhh," he said. "My son, be still." And gradually Alexei grew quiet.

Alcide's voice was very close to a rumble when he said, "Jannalynn, you are my new second. Annabelle, get up. This is pack business now, and we'll settle it at a pack meeting." He turned his back on us and began moving.

The Weres were simply going to walk out of the woods and drive away. "Excuse me," I said sharply. "There's the little matter of the body being buried on my land. I think there's something pretty damn significant about that."

The Weres stopped walking.

Eric said, "Yes." The one word carried a lot of weight. "Alcide, I believe Sookie and I need to sit in on your pack meeting."

"Only pack members," Jannalynn snapped. "No oneys, no deaders." She was still as small as ever, but with her field promotion to second, she seemed harder and stronger in spirit. She was a ruthless little thing, no doubt about it. I thought Sam was mighty brave, or mighty foolish.

"Alcide?" Eric said quietly.

"Sookie can bring Jason, since he's two-natured," Alcide growled. "She's a oney, but she's a friend of the pack. No vamps."

Eric glanced at my brother. "Jason, will you accompany your sister?"

"Sure," Jason said.

So it was settled. Out of the corner of my eye, I saw Annabelle stagger to her feet and reorient herself. Jannalynn packed a wallop.

"What are you going to do with the body?" I called after Alcide, who was definitely moving out. "Do you want us to cover him back up or what?"

Annabelle took a hesitant step after Jannalynn and Alcide. That was going to be a happy ride back to Shreveport. "Someone will come get him tonight," Jannalynn called over her shoulder. "So there'll be activity in your woods. Don't be alarmed." When Annabelle glanced back, I noticed she was bleeding from one corner of her mouth. I felt the vampires come to attention. In fact, Alexei stepped away from Jason and would have followed her if Appius Livius hadn't kept his grip on the boy.

"Should we cover him back up?" Jason said.

"If they're sending a crew to get him, that seems like wasted effort," I said. "Eric, I'm so glad you sent Heidi. Otherwise . . ." I thought hard. "Listen, if he was buried on my land, it was so he could be found here, right? So there's no telling when someone's going to get a tip to come looking for him."

The only one who seemed to follow my reasoning was Jason, who said, "Okay, we got to get him out of here."

I was flapping my hands in the air, I was so anxious. "We've got to put him somewhere," I said. "We could just set him in the cemetery!"

"Naw, too close," Jason said.

"What about the pond behind your house?" I said.

"Naw, dammit! The fish! I couldn't ever eat those fish again."

"Aaargh," I said. Really!

"Is your time with her usually like this?" Appius Livius asked Eric, who was smart enough not to answer.

"Sookie," he said. "It won't be pleasant, but I think I can fly carrying him if you can suggest a good place to put him."

I felt like my brain was running through a maze and hitting all the dead ends. I actually smacked myself on the side of the head to jog an idea loose. It worked. "Sure, Eric. Put him in the woods right across the road from my driveway. There's a little bit of a driveway left there, but no house. The Weres can use the driveway as a marker when they come to retrieve him. Cause *someone's* coming to find him, and coming soon."

Without further discussion, Eric leaped into the hole and rewrapped Basim in the sheet or whatever the wrapping was. Though the lantern showed me his face was full of disgust, he scooped up the decomposing body and leaped into the air. He was out of view in a second.

"Damn," said Jason, impressed. "Cool."

"Let's fill in this grave," I said. We set to work, with Appius Livius watching. It obviously didn't occur to him that his help would make the job go much faster. Even Alexei shoved in piles of dirt, and he seemed to be having a pretty good time doing it. This was probably as close to a normal activity as the thirteen-year-old had come in some time. Gradually, the hole filled in. It still looked like a grave. The tsarevitch tore at the hard edges with his small hands. I almost protested, but then I saw what he was doing. He reconfigured the grave-shaped dent until it looked like an irregular dent, maybe created by rain or a collapsed mole tunnel. He beamed at us when he'd finished, and Jason clapped him on the back. Jason got a branch and swept it over the area, and then we tossed leaves and branches around. Alexei enjoyed that part, too.

Finally, we gave up. I couldn't think of one more thing to do.

Filthy and frightened, I shouldered one of the shovels and prepared to make my way through the woods. Jason took the other shovel in his right hand, and Alexei took Jason's left hand, as if he were even younger than the child he looked. My brother, though his face was a picture, kept hold of the vampire. Appius Livius at last made himself useful by leading us through the trees and undergrowth with some assurance.

Eric was at the house when we reached it. He'd already thrown his clothes into the garbage and gotten into the shower. Under other circumstances, I would have loved to join him, but it just wasn't possible to feel sexy at the moment. I was grimy and nasty, but I was still the hostess, so I heated up some more TrueBlood for the two visiting vampires and showed them the downstairs bathroom in case they wanted to wash up.

Jason came into the kitchen to tell me that he was going to shove off.

"Let me know when the meeting is," he said in a subdued way. "And I gotta report all this to Calvin, you know."

"I understand," I said, weary to death of politics of all kinds. I wondered if America knew what it was in for when it considered requiring the two-natured to register. America was really better off not having to go through this crap. Human politics were tedious enough.

Jason went out the back door. A second later, I heard his

truck roaring away. Almost as soon as Appius Livius and Alexei had had their drinks, Eric came out of my bedroom in fresh clothes (he kept a change at my house) and smelling very much like my apricot body wash. With his maker around, Eric could hardly have a heart-to-heart with me, assuming he wanted to. He wasn't exactly acting like my honey now that his dad was in the house. There could be several reasons for this. I didn't like any of them.

Soon afterward, the three vampires left for Shreveport. Appius Livius thanked me for my hospitality in such an impassive way that I had no idea whether he was being sarcastic. Eric was as silent as a stone. Alexei, as calm and smiling as if he'd never gone mad, gave me a cold embrace. I had a hard time accepting it with equal calm.

Three seconds after they were out the door, I was on the phone.

"Fangtasia, where all your bloody dreams come true," said a bored female voice.

"Pam. Listen."

"The phone is pressed to my ear. Speak."

"Appius Livius Ocella just dropped in."

"Fuck a zombie!"

I wasn't sure that I'd heard that correctly. "Yes, he's been here. I guess he's your granddad? Anyway, he's got a new protégé with him, and they're heading for Eric's to spend the day."

"What does he want?"

"He hasn't said yet."

"How is Eric?"

"Very tightly wound. Plus, a lot of stuff happened that he'll tell you about."

"Thanks for the warning. I'll go to the house now. You're my favorite breather."

"Oh. Well . . . great."

She hung up. I wondered what preparations she would make. Would the vamps and humans who worked at the Shreveport nightclub go into a cleaning frenzy at Eric's? I'd only seen Pam and Bobby Burnham there, though I assumed some of the crew came in from time to time. Would Pam rush some willing humans over to act as bedtime snacks?

I was too tense to think about going to bed. Whatever Eric's maker was doing here, it wasn't something I was going to like. And I already knew Appius Livius's presence was bad for our relationship. While I was in the shower—and before I picked up the wet towels Eric had left on the floor—I did some serious thinking.

Vampire plotting can be pretty convoluted. But I tried to imagine the significance of the Roman's surprise visit. Surely he hadn't shown up in America, in Louisiana, in Shreveport, just to catch up on the geezer gossip.

Maybe he needed a loan. That wouldn't be too bad. Eric could always make more money. Though I had no idea how Eric stood financially, I had a little nest egg in the bank since Sophie-Anne's estate had paid up the money she'd owed me. And whatever Claudine had had in her checking account would be coming to join it. If Eric needed it, he could have it.

But what if money wasn't the issue? Maybe Appius Livius needed to hole up because he'd gotten in trouble somewhere else. Maybe some Bolshevik vampires were after Alexei! That would be interesting. I could always hope they'd catch up with Appius Livius . . . as long as it wasn't at Eric's house.

Or perhaps Eric's maker had been courted by Felipe de

Castro or Victor Madden because they wanted something from Eric that he hadn't given up yet, and they planned on using Eric's maker to pull his strings.

But here was my most likely scenario: Appius Livius Ocella had dropped by with his "new" boy toy just to mess with Eric's head. That was the guess I was putting my money on. Appius Livius was hard to read. At moments he seemed okay. He seemed to care about Eric, and he seemed to care about Alexei. As for Eric's maker's relationship with Alexei— the boy would have died if Appius Livius hadn't intervened. Given the circumstances—Alexei's witnessing the murders of his entire family and their servants and friends—letting the tsarevitch die might have been a blessing.

I was sure Appius Livius was having sex with Alexei, but it was impossible to tell whether Alexei's passive demeanor came from the fact that he was in an unwanted sexual relationship or from his being permanently traumatized from seeing his family shot multiple times. I shuddered. I dried off and brushed my teeth, hoping I could sleep.

I realized there was another phone call I should make. With great reluctance, I called Bobby Burnham, Eric's daytime guy. Bobby and I had never liked each other. Bobby was weirdly jealous of me, though he didn't have the hots for Eric sexually at all. In Bobby's opinion, I diverted Eric's attention and energy away from its proper focus, which was Bobby and the business affairs he handled for Eric while Eric slept the day away. I was down on Bobby because instead of silently disliking me, he actively tried to make my life more difficult, which was a whole different kettle of fish. But still, we were both in the Eric business.

"Bobby, it's Sookie."

"I got caller ID."

Mr. Sullen. "Bobby, I think you ought to know that Eric's maker is in town. When you go over to get your instructions, be careful." Bobby normally got briefed right before Eric went to ground for the day, unless Eric stayed over at my place.

Bobby took his time with his reply—probably trying to figure out if I was playing some elaborate practical joke on him. "Is he likely to want to bite me?" he asked. "The maker?"

"I don't know what he's going to want, Bobby. I just felt like I ought to give you a heads-up."

"Eric won't let him hurt me," Bobby said confidently.

"Just as general information—if this guy says jump, Eric has to ask how high."

"No way," Bobby said. To Bobby, Eric was the most powerful creature under the moon.

"Way. They gotta mind their maker. This is no lie."

Bobby had to have heard that news item before. I know there's some kind of website or message board for vampires' human assistants. I'm sure they swap all kinds of handy hints about dealing with their employers. Whatever the reason, Bobby didn't argue or accuse me of trying to deceive him, which was a nice change.

"Okay," he said, "I'm ready for 'em. Was . . . What kind of person is Eric's maker?"

"He's not much like a person at all anymore," I said. "And he's got a thirteen-year-old boyfriend who used to be Russian royalty."

After a long silence, Bobby said, "Thanks. It's good to be prepared."

That was the nicest thing he'd ever said to me.

"You're welcome. Good night, Bobby," I said, and we hung up. We'd managed to have an entire civil conversation. Vampires, bringing America together!

I changed into a nightshirt and crawled into bed. I had to try to get some sleep, but it took its own sweet time coming. I kept seeing the light from the lantern dance across the clearing in the woods as the dirt mounded up around the edges of Basim's grave. And I saw the dead Were's face. But eventually, finally, the edges of that face blurred and darkness slid over me.

I slept late and heavily the next day. The minute I woke, I knew someone was in the kitchen cooking. I let my extra sense check it out, and I found that Claude was frying bacon and eggs. There was coffee in the pot, and I didn't need telepathy to know that. I could smell it. The perfume of morning.

After a trip to the bathroom, I stumbled into the hall and made my way into the kitchen. Claude was sitting at the table eating, and I could see there was enough coffee in the pot for me.

"There's food," he said, pointing to the stove.

I got a plate and a mug, and settled in for a good start to my day. I glanced over at the clock. It was Sunday, and Merlotte's wouldn't be open until the afternoon. Sam was trying Sundays again in a limited way, though the whole staff half hoped it wouldn't be profitable. As Claude and I ate in a companionable silence, I realized I felt wonderfully peaceful because Eric was in his day sleep. That meant I didn't have to feel him walking around with me. His problematic sire and his new "brother" were out of it, too. I sighed with relief.

"I saw Dermot last night," Claude said.

Crap! Well, so much for peace. "Where?" I asked.

"He was at the club. Staring at me with longing," Claude said.

"Dermot's gay?"

"No, I don't think so. It wasn't my dick he was thinking of. He wanted to be around another fairy."

"I sure hoped he was gone. Niall told Jason and me that Dermot helped kill my parents. I wish he'd gone into the fae land when it was closing up."

"He would have been killed on sight." Claude took the time to sip some coffee before he added, "No one in the fae world understands Dermot's actions. He should have sided with Niall from the beginning, because he's kin and because he's half-human and Niall wanted to spare humans. But his own self-loathing—or at least that's all I can imagine—led him to take the side of the fairies who really couldn't stand him, and that side lost." Claude looked happy. "So Dermot has cut off his own nose to spite his face. I love that saying. Sometimes humans put things very well."

"Do you think he still means to hurt my brother and me?"

"I don't think he ever intended to hurt you," Claude said, after thinking it over. "I think Dermot is crazy, though he used to be an agreeable guy a few score years ago. I don't know if it's his human side that's gone batshit, or his fae side that's soaked up too many toxins from the human world. I can't even explain his part in killing your parents. The Dermot I used to know would never have done such a thing."

I considered pointing out that truly crazy people can hurt others around them without meaning to, or without even realizing they're doing it. But I didn't. Dermot was my great-uncle, and according to everyone who'd met him, he was nearly a dead ringer for my brother. I admitted to myself I was curious about him. And I wondered about what Niall had said about Dermot having been the one who'd opened the truck doors so my parents could be pulled out and drowned by Neave and Lochlan. Dermot's behavior, the bit that I'd observed, didn't gibe with the horror of that incident. Would Dermot think of me as kin? Were Jason and I fae enough to attract him? I had doubted Bill's assertion that he felt better from my nearness because of my fairy blood.

"Claude, can *you* tell I'm not entirely human? How do I register on the fairy meter?" Fae-dar.

"If you were in a crowd of humans, I could pick you out blindfolded and say you are my kin," Claude said without hesitation. "But if you were in the middle of the fae, I would call you human. It's an elusive scent. Most vamps would think, 'She smells good,' and they'd enjoy being close to you. That would be the extent of it. Once they know you have fairy blood, they can attribute that enjoyment to it."

So Bill really could be comforted by my little streak of fae, at least now that he knew how to identify it. I got up to rinse off my plate and pour another mugful of coffee, and in passing I grabbed Claude's empty plate, too. He didn't thank me.

"I appreciate your cooking," I said. "We haven't talked about how we'll handle grocery expenses or household items."

Claude looked surprised. "I hadn't thought about it," he said.

Well, at least that was honest. "I'll tell you how Amelia and I did it," I said, and in a few sentences I laid out the guidelines. Looking a little stunned, Claude agreed.

I opened the refrigerator. "These two shelves are yours," I said, "and the rest are mine."

"I get it," he said.

Somehow I doubted that. Claude sounded like he was simply trying to give the impression that he understood and agreed. There was a good chance we'd have to have this conversation again. When he'd left to go upstairs, I took care of the dishes—after all, he'd cooked—and after I got dressed, I thought I'd read for a while. But I was too restless to concentrate on my book.

I heard cars coming down the driveway through the woods. I looked out the front window. Two police cars.

I'd been sure this was coming. But my heart sank down to my toes. Sometimes I hated being right. Whoever had killed Basim had planted his body on my land to implicate me in his death. "Claude," I called up the stairs. "Get decent, if you're not. The police are here."

Claude, curious as ever, came down the stairs at a trot. He was wearing jeans and a T-shirt, like me. We went out on the front porch. Bud Dearborn, the sheriff (the regular human sheriff), was in the first car, and Andy Bellefleur and Alcee Beck were in the second. The sheriff and two detectives—I must be a dangerous criminal.

Bud got out of his car slowly, the way he did most things these days. I knew from his thoughts that Bud was increasingly a victim to arthritis, and he had some doubts about his prostate, too. Bud's mashed-in face didn't give any hint about his physical discomfort as he came up to the porch, his heavy belt creaking with the weight of all the things hanging from it.

"Bud, what's up?" I asked. "Not that I'm not glad to see you-all."

"Sookie, we got an anonymous phone call," Bud said. "As you know, law enforcement couldn't solve much without anonymous tips, but I personally don't respect a person who won't tell you who they are."

I nodded.

"Who's your friend?" Andy asked. He looked worn. I'd heard his grandmother, who'd raised him, was on her death-bed. Poor Andy. He'd much rather be there than here. Alcee Beck, the other detective, really didn't like me. He never had, and his dislike had found a good foundation to settle on—his wife had been attacked by a Were who was trying to get to me. Even though I'd taken the guy out, Alcee was down on me. Maybe he was one of the rare people repulsed by my trace of fairy blood, but more likely, he just didn't care for me. There was no point in trying to win him over. I gave him a nod, which he did not return.

"This here is my cousin Claude Crane from Monroe," I said.

"How's he related?" Andy asked. All three of these men knew the skein of blood ties that bound together practically the whole parish.

"It's kind of embarrassing," Claude said. (Nothing would embarrass Claude, but he gave a good imitation.) "I'm from what you call the wrong side of the blanket."

For once, I was grateful to Claude for taking that weight. I cast my eyes down as though I couldn't bear to talk about the shame of it. "Claude and I are trying to get acquainted since we found out we were related," I said.

I could see that fact go into their mental files. "Why y'all here?" I asked. "What did the anonymous caller say?"

"That you had a body buried in your woods." Bud looked away as if he were a little ashamed to say something so outra-geous, but I knew different. After years in law enforcement, Bud knew exactly what human beings could do, even the most normal-looking human beings. Even young blondes with big boobs. Maybe especially them.

"You didn't bring any tracking dogs," Claude observed. I

was kind of hoping that Claude would keep his mouth shut, but I saw I wasn't going to get my wish.

"I think a physical search will do it," Bud said. "The location was real specific." (*And the tracking dogs were expensive to hire,* he thought.)

"Oh my gosh," I said, genuinely startled. "How could this person claim not to be involved if they knew where the body was exactly? I don't get it." I'd hoped Bud would tell me more, but he didn't bite.

Andy shrugged. "We got to go look."

"Look away," I said, with absolute confidence. If they'd brought the dogs, I'd have been sweating bullets that they'd scent Debbie Pelt or the former resting site of Basim. "You'll excuse me if I just stay here in the house while you-all tramp through the woods. I hope you don't pick up too many ticks." Ticks lurked on bushes and weeds, sensing your chemicals and body heat as you passed, then making a leap of faith. I watched Andy tuck his pants into his boots, and Bud and Alcee sprayed themselves.

After the men had disappeared into the woods, Claude said, "You'd better tell me why you're not scared."

"We moved the body last night," I said, and turned to sit down at the desk where I'd installed the computer I'd gotten from Hadley's apartment. Let Claude put that in his pipe and smoke it! After a few seconds, I heard him stomp back up the stairs.

Since I had to wait for the men to come out of the woods, I might as well check my e-mail. A lot of forwarded messages, most of them inspirational or patriotic, from Maxine Fortenberry, Hoyt's mother. I deleted those without reading them. I read an e-mail from Andy Bellefleur's pregnant wife, Halleigh. It was a strange coincidence, hearing from her while her husband was out in back of my house on a wild-goose chase.

Halleigh told me she was feeling great. Just great! But Grandmama Caroline was failing fast, and Halleigh feared Miss Caroline wouldn't live to see her great-grandchild born.

Caroline Bellefleur was very old. Andy and Portia had been brought up in Miss Caroline's house after their parents had died. Miss Caroline had been a widow for longer than she'd been married. I had no memory of Mr. Bellefleur at all, and I was pretty sure Portia and Andy hadn't known him that long. Andy was older than Portia, and Portia was a year older than me, so I estimated that Miss Caroline, who'd once been Renard Parish's finest cook and had made the best chocolate cake in the world, was at least in her nineties.

"Anyway," Halleigh went on, "she wants to find the family Bible more than anything else on this earth. You know she's always got a bee in her bonnet, and now it's finding that Bible, which has been missing for umpty-ump years. I had a wild thought. She thinks way back our family was connected to some branch of the Comptons. Would you ask your neighbor, Mr. Compton, if he would mind very much looking for that old Bible? It seems like a long shot, but she hasn't lost any of her personality though she's physically weak."

That was a nice way of saying that Miss Caroline was bringing up that Bible real often.

I was in a quandary. I knew that Bible was over at the Compton house. And I knew after she studied it, Miss Caroline would find out that she was a direct descendant of Bill Compton. How she'd feel about that was anybody's guess. Did I want to screw with her worldview when the woman was on her deathbed?

On the other hand, did . . . Oh, hell, I was tired of trying to balance everything out, and I had enough on my plate to worry about. In a reckless moment, I forwarded Halleigh's e-mail to Bill. I had come late to e-mail, and I still didn't entirely trust it. But at least I felt I'd put the ball into Bill's court. If he chose to lob it back, well, okay.

After I'd messed around a little on eBay, marveling at the things people were trying to sell, I heard voices in the front yard. I looked out to see Bud, Alcee, and Andy brushing dust and twigs off their clothes. Andy was rubbing at a bite on his neck.

I went outside. "Did you find a body?" I asked them.

"No, we did not," Alcee Beck said. "We did see that people had been back there."

"Well, sure," I said. "But no body?"

"We won't trouble you any further," Bud said shortly.

They left in a cloud of dust. I watched them go, and shivered. I felt like the guillotine had been descending on my neck and had been prevented from cutting off my head only because the rope was too short.

I went back to the computer and sent Alcide an e-mail. It said only, "The police were just here." I figured that would be enough. I knew I wouldn't hear from him until he was ready for me to come to Shreveport.

I was surprised that it took three days to receive a reply from Bill. Those days had been remarkable only for the number of people I hadn't heard from. I hadn't heard from Remy, which wasn't too extraordinary. None of the members of the Long Tooth pack called, so I could only assume they'd retrieved the body of Basim from its new resting place and that they would let me know when the meeting would be held. If someone came into my woods and tried to find out why Basim's body had vanished, I didn't know about it. And I didn't hear from Pam or Bobby Burnham, which was a little worrisome, but still . . . no big.

What did gripe me in a major way was not hearing from Eric. Okay, his (maker, sire, dad) mentor Appius Livius Ocella was in town . . . but geez Louise.

In between sessions of worrying, I looked up Roman names and found that "Appius" was his praenomen, his common name. Livius was his nomen, his family name, handed down from father to son, indicating that he was a member of the Livii family or clan. Ocella was his cognomen, so it was meant to indicate what particular branch of the Livii had borne him; or it could have been given as an honorific for his service in a war. (I had no idea what war that could have been.) As a third possibility, if he'd been adopted into another family, the cognomen would reflect his birth family.

Your name said a lot about you in the Roman world.

I wasted a lot of time finding out all about Appius Livius Ocella's name. I still had no idea what he wanted or what he intended to do to my boyfriend. And those were the things I needed to know the most. I have to say, I was feeling pretty sulky, pugnacious, and sullen (I looked up a few words while I was online). Not a pretty posy of emotions, but I couldn't seem to upgrade to dull unhappiness.

Cousin Claude was making himself scarce, too. I glimpsed him only once in those three days, and that was when I heard him go through the kitchen and out the back door and got up in time to see him getting into his car.

This goes to explain why I was delighted to see Bill at my

back door when the sun had set on the third day after I'd sent him Halleigh's e-mail. He was not looking appreciably better than he had the last time I'd seen him, but he was dressed in a suit and tie and his hair was carefully combed. The Bible was under his arm.

I understood why he was groomed, what he meant to do. "Good," I said.

"Come with me," he said. "It will help if you're there."

"But they'll think . . ." And then I made my mouth shut. It was unworthy to be worrying about the Bellefleurs' assuming Bill and I were a couple again when Caroline Bellefleur was about to meet her maker.

"Would that be so terrible?" he asked with simple dignity.

"No, of course not. I was proud to be your girlfriend," I said, and turned to go back to my room. "Please come in while I change clothes." I'd finished the lunch-and-afternoon shift, and I'd changed to shorts and a T-shirt.

Since I was in a hurry, I changed to an above-the-knee black skirt and a white cap-sleeve fitted blouse I'd gotten on sale at Stage. I slid a red leather belt through the belt loops and got some red sandals from the back of my closet. I fluffed my hair, and I was ready.

I drove us over in my car, which was beginning to need an alignment.

It wasn't a long ride to the Bellefleur mansion; it didn't take long to get anywhere in Bon Temps. We parked in the driveway at the front door, but as we'd driven up I'd glimpsed several cars in the back parking area. I'd seen Andy's car there, and Portia's, too. There was an ancient gray Chevy Chevette parked sort of unobtrusively at the rear, and I wondered if Miss Caroline had a round-the-clock caregiver.

We walked up to the double front doors. Bill didn't think it was appropriate ("seemly" was the word he used) to go to the back, and under the circumstances, I had to agree. Bill walked slowly and with effort. More than once I wanted to offer to carry the heavy Bible but I knew he wouldn't let me, so I saved my breath.

Halleigh answered the door, thank God. She was startled when she saw Bill, but she recovered her poise very quickly and greeted us.

"Halleigh, Mr. Compton has brought the family Bible that Andy's grandmother wants to see," I said, in case Halleigh had gone temporarily blind and hadn't noticed the huge volume. Halleigh was looking a little rough around the edges. Her brown hair was a mess, and her green flowered dress looked almost as tired as her eyes. Presumably, she'd come over to Miss Caroline's after she'd worked all day teaching school. Halleigh was obviously pregnant, something Bill hadn't known, I could tell by the fleeting expression on his face.

"Oh," Halleigh said, her face visibly relaxing with relief. "Mr. Compton, please come in. You have no idea how Miss Caroline's fretted about this." I think Halleigh's reaction was a pretty good indicator of just how much Miss Caroline had fretted.

We stepped into the entrance hall together. The wide flight of stairs was ahead of us and to our left. It curved gracefully up to the second floor. Lots of local brides had had their pictures made on this staircase. I had come down it in heels and a long dress when I'd been a stand-in for a sick bridesmaid at Halleigh and Andy's wedding.

"I think it would be real nice if Bill could give the Bible

to Miss Caroline," I said, before the pause could become awkward. "There's a family connection."

Even Halleigh's excellent manners faltered. "Oh . . . how interesting." Her back stiffened, and I saw Bill appreciating the curve of her pregnancy. A faint smile curved his lips for a second. "I'm sure that would be just fine," Halleigh said, rallying. "Let's just go upstairs."

We went up the stairs after her, and I had to struggle with the impulse to put a hand under Bill's elbow to help him a little. I would have to do something to help Bill. He obviously wasn't getting any better. A little fear crept into my heart.

We walked a little farther along the gallery to the door to the largest bedroom, which was open a discreet few inches. Halleigh stepped in ahead of us.

"Sookie and Mr. Compton have brought the family Bible," she said. "Miss Caroline, can he bring it in?"

"Yes, of course, have him bring it," said a weak voice, and Bill and I walked in.

Miss Caroline was the queen of the room, no doubt about it. Andy and Portia were standing to the right of the bed, and they looked both worried and uneasy as Bill ushered me in. I noticed the absence of Portia's husband, Glen. A middle-aged African-American woman was sitting in a chair to the left of the bed. She was wearing the bright, loose pants and cheerful tunic that nurses favored now. The pattern made her look as though she worked on a pediatric ward. However, in a room decorated in subdued peach and cream, the splash of color was welcome. The nurse was thin and tall, and wore an incredible wig that reminded me of a movie Cleopatra. She nodded to us as we came closer to the bed. Caroline

Bellefleur, who looked like the steel magnolia she was, lay propped up on a dozen pillows in the four-poster bed. There were shadows of exhaustion under her old eyes, and her hands curled in wrinkled claws on the bedspread. But there was still a flicker of interest in her eyes as she looked at us.

"Miss Stackhouse, Mr. Compton, I haven't seen you since the big wedding," she said with an obvious effort. Her voice was thin as paper.

"That was a beautiful occasion, Mrs. Bellefleur," Bill said with an almost equal effort. I only nodded. This was not my conversation to have.

"Please take a seat," the old woman said, and Bill pulled a chair up closer to her bed. I sat a couple of feet back.

"Looks like that Bible is too big for me to handle now," the ancient lady said, with a smile. "It was so nice of you to bring it over. I have sure been wanting to see it. Has it been in your attic? I know we don't have much connection with the Comptons, but I sure wanted to find that old book. Halleigh was nice enough to do some checking for me."

"As a matter of fact, this book was on my coffee table," Bill said gently. "Mrs. Bellefleur—Caroline—my second child was a daughter, Sarah Isabelle."

"Oh my goodness," said Miss Caroline, to indicate she was listening. She didn't seem to know where this was headed, but she was definitely attentive.

"Though I didn't learn this until I read the family page in this Bible after I returned to Bon Temps, my daughter Sarah had four children, though one baby was born dead."

"That happened so often back then," she said.

I glanced over at the Bellefleur grandchildren. Portia and Andy weren't happy that Bill was here, not at all, but they were listening, too. They hadn't spared a glance for me, which was actually just fine. Though they were puzzled by Bill's presence, the focus of their thoughts was the woman who had raised them and the visible fact that she was fading away.

Bill said, "My Sarah's daughter was named Caroline, for her grandmother . . . my wife."

"My name?" Miss Caroline sounded pleased, though her voice was a little weaker.

"Yes, your name. My granddaughter Caroline married a cousin, Matthew Phillips Holliday."

"Why, those are my mother and father." She smiled, which did drastic things to her scores of wrinkles. "So you are . . . Really?" To my amazement, Caroline Bellefleur laughed.

"Your great-grandfather. Yes, I am."

Portia made a sound as though she were choking on a stinkbug. Miss Caroline disregarded her granddaughter entirely, and she didn't look over at Andy—which was lucky, because he was turkey-wattle red.

"Well, if this isn't funny," she said. "I'm as wrinkled as unironed linen, and you're as smooth as a fresh peach." She was genuinely amused. "Great-granddaddy!"

Then a thought seemed to occur to the dying lady. "Was it you arranged for that timely windfall we got?"

"The money couldn't have been put to better use," Bill said gallantly. "The house looks beautiful. Who will live in it after you die?"

Portia gasped, and Andy looked a little taken aback. But I glanced at the nurse. She gave me a brief nod. Miss Caroline's time was very near, and the lady was fully aware of it.

"Well, I think Portia and Glen will stay here," Miss Caroline said slowly. It was evident she was tiring fast. "Halleigh and Andy want to have their baby in their own home, and I don't blame them one bit. You're not saying you're interested in the house?"

"Oh, no, I have my own," Bill reassured her. "And I was glad to give my own family the wherewithal to repair this place. I want my descendants to keep on living here through the years and have many happy times in this place."

"Thank you," Miss Caroline said, and now her voice was barely a whisper.

"Sookie and I must go," Bill said. "You rest easy, now."

"I will," she said, and smiled, though her eyes were closing.

I rose as quietly as I could and slipped out of the room ahead of Bill. I thought Portia and Andy might want to say a few things to Bill. Sure enough, they didn't want to disturb their grandmother, so they followed Bill out onto the gallery.

"Thought you were dating another vampire now?" Andy asked me. He didn't sound as snarky as he usually did.

"I am," I said. "But Bill is still my friend."

Portia had briefly dated Bill, though not because she thought he was cute or anything. I was sure that added to her embarrassment as she stuck out her hand to Bill. Portia needed to brush up on her vampire etiquette. Though Bill looked a little taken aback, he accepted the handshake. "Portia," he said. "Andy. I hope you don't find this too awkward."

I was busting-at-the-seams proud of Bill. It was easy to see where Caroline Bellefleur had gotten her graciousness.

Andy said, "I wouldn't have taken the money if I'd known it came from you." He'd evidently come straight from work, because he was wearing all his gear: a badge and handcuffs clipped to his belt, a holstered gun. He looked pretty formidable, but he was no match for Bill, even as sick as Bill was.

"Andy, I know you're not a fan of the fang. But you're part

of my family, and I know you were raised to respect your elders."

Andy looked completely taken aback.

"That money was to make Caroline happy, and I think it did," Bill continued. "So it served its purpose. I've gotten to see her and to tell her about our relationship, and she has the Bible. I won't burden you with my presence any longer. I would ask that you have the funeral at night so I can attend."

"Who ever heard of a funeral at night?" Andy said.

"Yes, we'll do that." Portia didn't sound warm and welcoming, but she did sound absolutely resolved. "The money made her last few years very happy. She loved restoring the house to its best state, and she loved giving us the wedding here. The Bible is the frosting on the cake. Thank you."

Bill nodded to both of them, and without further ado we left Belle Rive.

Caroline Bellefleur, Bill's great-granddaughter, died in the early hours of the morning.

Bill sat with the family during the funeral, which took place the next night, to the profound amazement of the town.

I sat at the back with Sam.

It wasn't an occasion for tears; without a doubt, Caroline Bellefleur had had a long life—a life not devoid of sorrow, but at least full of moments of compensatory happiness. She had very few remaining contemporaries, and those who were still alive were almost all too tottery to come to her funeral.

The service seemed quite normal until we drove out to the cemetery, which didn't have night lighting—of course—and I saw that temporary lights had been set up around the perimeter of the grave in the Bellefleur plot. That was a strange sight. The minister had a hard time reading the service until a member of the congregation held his own flashlight to the page.

The bright lights in the dark night were an unpleasant reminder of the recovery of Basim al Saud's body. It was hard to think properly about Miss Caroline's life and legacy with all the conjecture rattling around in my head. And why hadn't anything already happened? I felt as though I were living waiting for the other shoe to drop. I wasn't aware my hand had tightened on Sam's arm until he turned to look at me with some alarm. I forced my fingers to relax and bowed my head for the prayer.

The family, I heard, was going to Belle Rive for a buffet meal after the service. I wondered if they'd gotten Bill his favorite blood. Bill looked awful. He was using a cane at the grave site. Something had to be done about finding his sibling, since he wasn't taking action himself. If there was a chance his sibling's blood might cure him, the effort had to be made.

I'd driven to the funeral with Sam, and since my house was so close, I told Sam I'd walk back from the grave site. I'd stuck a little flashlight in my purse, and I reminded Sam I knew the cemetery like the back of my hand. So when all the other attendees took off, including Bill, to go to Belle Rive for the buffet meal, I waited in the shadows until the cemetery employees started filling in the hole, and then I walked through the trees to Bill's house.

I still had a key.

Yes, I knew I was being a terrible busybody. And maybe I was doing the wrong thing. But Bill was wasting away, and I just couldn't sit by and let him do it.

I unlocked the front door and went to Bill's office, which had been the Compton formal dining room. Bill had all

his computer gear set up on a huge table, and he had a rolling chair he'd gotten at Office Depot. A smaller table served
as a mailing station, where Bill prepared copies of his vampire database to send to purchasers. He advertised heavily in vampire magazines—*Fang*, of course, and *Dead Life*,
which appeared in so many languages. Bill's newest marketing effort involved hiring vampires who spoke many different languages to translate all the information so he could
sell foreign-language editions of his worldwide vampire
listing service. As I remembered from a previous visit, there
were a dozen CD copies of his database in cases by his mailing station. I double-checked to make sure I had one that
was in English. Wouldn't do me much good to get one in
Russian.

Of course, Russian reminded me of Alexei, and thinking
of Alexei reminded me all over of how worried/angry/fright-
ened I was about Eric's silence.

I could feel my mouth pinching together in a really
unpleasant expression as I thought about that silence. But I
had to pay attention to my own little problem right now, and
I scooted out of the house, relocked the door, and hoped Bill
wouldn't pick up on my scent in the air.

I went through the cemetery as quickly as if it had been
daytime. When I was in my own kitchen, I looked around for
a good hiding place. I finally fixed on the linen closet in the
hall bathroom as a good spot, and I put the CD under the
stack of clean towels. I didn't think even Claude could use
five towels before I got up the next day.

I checked my answering machine; I checked my cell
phone, which I hadn't taken to the service. No messages. I
undressed slowly, trying to imagine what could have happened to Eric. I'd decided I wouldn't call him, no matter what.

He knew where I was and how to reach me. I hung my black
dress in the closet, put my black heels on the shoe rack, and
then pulled on my Tweety Bird nightshirt, an old favorite.
Then I went to bed, mad as a wet hen.

   And scared.

Chapter 10

Claude hadn't come home the night before. His car wasn't by the back door. I was glad someone had gotten lucky. Then I told myself not to be so pitiful.

"You're doing okay," I said, looking in the mirror so I'd believe it. "Look at you! Great tan, Sook!" I had to be in for the lunch shift, so I got dressed right after I'd eaten breakfast. I retrieved the purloined CD from under the towels. I'd either pay Bill for it or return it, I told myself virtuously. I hadn't really stolen it if I planned to pay for it. Someday. I looked at the clear plastic case in my hands. I wondered how much the FBI would pay for it. Despite all Bill's attempts to make sure only vampires bought the CD, it would be truly amazing if no one else had it.

So I opened it and popped it into my computer. After a preliminary whir, the screen popped up. "The Vampire Directory," it said in Gothic lettering, red on a black screen. Stereotype, anyone?

"Enter your code number," prompted the screen.

Uh-oh.

Then I remembered there'd been a little Post-it on top of the case, and I dug it out of the wastebasket. Yep, this was surely a code. Bill would never have attached the code to the box if he hadn't believed his house was secure, and I felt a pang of guilt. I didn't know what procedure he'd established, but I assumed he put the code in a directory when he mailed out the disc to a happy customer. Or maybe he'd put a "destruct" code on the paper for fools like me, and the whole thing would blow up in my face. I was glad no one else was in the house after I typed in the code and hit Enter, because I dropped to my knees under the desk.

Nothing happened, except some more whirring, and I figured I was safe. I scrambled back into my chair.

The screen was showing me my options. I could search by country of residence, country of origin, name, or last sighting. I clicked on "Residence," and I was prompted: "Which country?" I could pick from a list. After I clicked on "USA," I got another prompt: "What state?" And another list. I clicked on "Louisiana" and then on "Compton." There he was, in a modern picture taken at his house. I recognized the paint color. Bill was smiling stiffly, and he didn't look like a party animal, that's for sure. I wondered how he'd fare with a dating service. I began to read his biography. And sure enough, there at the bottom, I read, "Sired by Lorena Ball of Louisiana, 1870."

But there was no listing for "brothers" or "sisters."

Okay, it wasn't going to be that easy. I clicked on the boldfaced name of Bill's sire, the late, unlamented Lorena. I was curious as to what her entry would say, since Lorena had met the ultimate death, at least until they learned how to resuscitate ashes.

"Lorena Ball," her entry read, with only a drawing. It was a pretty good likeness, I thought, cocking my head as I looked it over. Turned in 1788 in New Orleans . . . lived all across the South but returned to Louisiana after the Civil War . . . had "met the sun," murder by person or persons "unknown." Huh. Bill knew perfectly well who'd killed Lorena, and I could only be glad he hadn't put my name in the directory. I wondered what would have happened to me if he had. See, you think you have enough to worry about, but then you think of a possibility you'd never imagined and you realize you have even *more* problems.

Okay, here we go. . . . "Sired Bill Compton (1870) and Judith Vardamon (1902)."

Judith. So this was Bill's "sister."

After some more clicking and reading, I discovered that Judith Vardamon was still "alive," or at least she had been when Bill had been compiling his database. She lived in Little Rock.

I further discovered I could send her an e-mail. Naturally, she wasn't obliged to answer it.

I stared down at my hands, and I thought hard. I thought about how awful Bill looked. I thought about his pride, and the fact that he hadn't yet contacted this Judith, though he suspected her blood would cure him. Bill wasn't a fool, so there was some good reason he hadn't called this other child of Lorena. I just didn't know that reason. But if Bill had decided she shouldn't be contacted, he knew what he was doing, right? Oh, to hell with it.

I typed in her e-mail address. And moved the cursor down to the topic. Typed "Bill's ill." Thought that looked almost funny. Almost changed it, but didn't. Moved the cursor down to the body of the e-mail, clicked again. Hesitated.

Then I typed, "I'm Bill Compton's neighbor. I don't know how long it's been since you heard from him, but he lives at his old home place in Bon Temps, Louisiana, now. Bill's got silver poisoning. He can't heal without your blood. He doesn't know I'm sending this. We used to date, and we're still friends. I want him to get better." I signed it, because anonymous is not my style.

I clenched my teeth really hard together. I clicked on Send.

As much as I wanted to keep the CD and browse through it, my little code of honor told me I had to return it without enjoying it, because I hadn't paid. So I got Bill's key and put the disc back in its plastic case and started across the cemetery.

I slowed as I drew near to the Bellefleur plot. The flowers were still piled on Miss Caroline's grave. Andy was standing there, staring at a cross made out of red carnations. I thought it was pretty awful, but this was definitely an occasion for the thought to count more than the deed. I didn't think Andy was registering what was right in front of him anyway.

I felt as though "Thief" were burned onto my forehead. I knew Andy wouldn't care if I backed up a truck to Bill's house and loaded up all the furniture and drove off with it. It was my own sense of guilt that was plaguing me.

"Sookie," Andy said. I hadn't realized he'd noticed me.

"Andy," I said cautiously. I wasn't sure where this conversation would go, and I had to leave for work soon. "You still have relatives in town? Or have they left?"

"They're leaving after lunch," he said. "Halleigh had to work on some class preparations this morning, and Glen had to run into his office to catch up on paperwork. This has been hardest on Portia."

"I guess she'll be glad when things get back to normal." That seemed safe enough.

"Yeah. She's got a law practice to run."

"Did the lady who was taking care of Miss Caroline have another job to go to?" Reliable caregivers were as scarce as hens' teeth and far more valuable.

"Doreen? Yeah, she moved right across the garden to Mr. DeWitt's." After an uncomfortable pause, he said, "She kind of got on to me that night, after you-all left. I know I wasn't polite to . . . Bill."

"It's been a hard time for you-all."

"I just . . . It makes me mad that we were getting charity."

"You weren't, Andy. Bill is your family. I know it must feel weird, and I know you don't think much of vampires in general, but he's your great-great-great-grandfather, and he wanted to help out his people. It wouldn't make you feel funny if he'd left you money and he was out here with Miss Caroline under the ground, would it? It's just that Bill's still walking around."

Andy shook his head, as if flies were buzzing around it. His hair was thinning, I noticed. "You know what my grand-mother's last request was?"

I couldn't imagine. "No," I said.

"She left her chocolate cake recipe to the town," he said, and he smiled. "A damn recipe. And you know what, they were as excited at the newspaper when I took that recipe in as if it were Christmas and I'd brought them a map to Jimmy Hoffa's body."

"It's going to be in the paper?" I sounded as thrilled as I felt. I bet there would be at least a hundred chocolate cakes in the oven the day the paper came out.

"See, you're all excited, too," Andy said, sounding five years younger.

"Andy, that's big news," I assured him. "Now, if you'll excuse me, I have to go return something." And I hurried through the rest of the cemetery to Bill's house. I put the CD, complete with its little sticky note, on top of the pile from which I'd taken it, and I skedaddled.

I second-guessed myself, and third-, fourth-, and fifth-guessed, too. At Merlotte's I worked in a kind of haze, concentrating fiercely on getting lunch orders right, being quick, and responding instantly to any request. My other sense told me that despite my efficiency, people weren't glad to see me coming, and really I couldn't blame them.

Tips were low. People were ready to forgive inefficiency, as long as you smiled while you were sloppy. They didn't like the unsmiling, quick-handed me.

I could tell (simply because he thought it so often) that Sam was assuming I'd had a fight with Eric. Holly thought that I was having my period.

And Antoine was an informant.

Our cook had been lost in his own broody mood. I realized how resistant he normally was to my telepathy only when he forgot to be. I was waiting on an order to be up at the hatch, and I was looking at Antoine while he flipped a burger, and I heard directly from him, *Not getting off work to meet that asshole again, he can just stuff it up his butt. I'm not telling him nothing else.* Then Antoine, whom I'd come to respect and admire, flipped the burger onto its waiting bun and turned to the hatch with the plate in his hand. He met my eyes squarely.

Oh shit, he thought.

"Let me talk to you before you do anything," he said, and I knew for sure that he was a traitor.

"No," I said, and turned away, going right to Sam, who was behind the bar washing glasses. "Sam, Antoine is some kind of agent for the government," I said, very quietly.

Sam didn't ask me how I knew, and he didn't question my statement. His mouth pressed into a hard line. "We'll talk to him later," he said. "Thanks, Sook." I regretted now that I hadn't told Sam about the Were buried on my land. I was always sorry when I didn't tell Sam something, it seemed.

I got the plate and took it to the right table without meeting Antoine's eyes.

Some days I hated my ability more than others. Today was one of those days. I had been much happier (though in retrospect, it had been a foolish happiness) when I'd assumed Antoine was a new friend. I wondered if any of the stories he'd told about going through Katrina in the Superdome had been true, or if those had been lies, too. I'd felt such sympathy for him. And I'd never had a hint until now that his persona was false. How could that be?

First, I don't monitor every single thought of every person. I block a lot of it out, in general, and I try especially hard to stay out of the heads of my coworkers. Second, people don't always think about critical stuff in explicit terms. A guy might not think, *I believe I'll get the pistol from under the seat of my truck and shoot Jerry in the head for screwing my wife.* I was much more likely to get an impression of sullen anger, with overtones of violence. Or even a projection of how it might feel to shoot Jerry. But the shooting of Jerry might not have reached the specific planning stage at the moment the shooter was in the bar, when I was privy to his thoughts.

And mostly people *didn't* act on their violent impulses, something I didn't learn until after some very painful incidents as I grew up.

If I spent my life trying to figure out the background of every single thought I heard, I wouldn't have my own life.

At least I had something to think about besides wondering what the hell was happening with Eric and the Long Tooth pack. At the end of my shift, I found myself in Sam's office with Sam and Antoine.

Sam shut the door behind me. He was furious. I didn't blame him. Antoine was mad at himself, mad at me, and defensive with Sam. The atmosphere in the room was choking with anger and frustration and fear.

"Listen, man," Antoine said. He was standing facing Sam. He made Sam look small. "Just listen, okay? After Katrina, I didn't have no place to live and nothing to do. I was trying to find work and keep myself going. I couldn't even get a damn FEMA trailer. Things were going *bad*. So I . . . I borrowed a car, to get to Texas to some relatives. I was gonna dump it where the cops could find it, get it back to the owner. I know it was stupid. I know I shouldn'ta done it. But I was desperate, and I did something dumb."

"Yet you're not in jail," Sam observed. His words were like a whip that barely flicked Antoine, drew a little bit of blood.

Antoine breathed out heavily. "No, I'm not, and I'll tell you why. My uncle is a werewolf, in one of the New Orleans packs. So I knew something about 'em. An FBI agent named Sara Weiss came to talk to me in jail. She was okay. But after she spoke with me once, she brought this guy Lattesta, Tom Lattesta. He said he was based in Rhodes, and I couldn't figure out what he was doing in New Orleans. But he told me that he knew all about my uncle, and he figured that you-all were coming out sooner or later since the vamps did. He knew what you were, that there were other things besides wolves. He knew there'd be a lot of people didn't like hearing that people who were part animal lived in with the rest of us. He described Sookie to me. He said she was something strange, too, and he didn't know what. He sent me here to watch, to see what happened."

Sam and I exchanged glances. I don't know what Sam had anticipated, but this was way more serious than I'd imagined. I figured back. "Tom Lattesta has known all along?" I said. "When did he start thinking there was something wrong with me?" Had it been before he saw the footage from the hotel explosion in Rhodes, which he'd used as the reason for approaching me a few months ago?

"Half the time he's sure you're a fraud. Half the time he thinks you're the real deal."

I turned to my boss. "Sam, he came to my house the other day. Lattesta. He told me that someone close to me, one of the *great* relatives"—I didn't want to get more specific in front of Antoine—"had fixed it so he had to back off."

"That explains why he was so mad," Antoine said, and his face hardened. "That explains a lot."

"What did he tell you to do?" Sam asked.

"Lattesta said the car theft thing was forgotten as long as I kept an eye on Sam and any other people who weren't all the way human who came into the bar. He said he couldn't touch Sookie now, and he was mighty pissed."

Sam looked at me, a question on his face.

"He's sincere," I said.

"Thank you, Sookie," Antoine said. He looked abjectly miserable.

"Okay," Sam said, after looking at Antoine for a few more seconds. "You still have a job."

"No . . . conditions?" Antoine was looking at Sam unbelievingly. "He expects me to keep watching you."

"Not a condition, but a warning. If you tell him one thing more besides the fact that I'm here and running this business, you're outta here, and if I can think of something else to do to you, I will."

Antoine seemed weak with relief. "I'll do my best for you, Sam," he said. "Tell the truth, I'm glad it all came out. It's been sitting heavy on my conscience."

"There'll be a backlash," I said when Sam and I were alone.

"I know. Lattesta will come down on him hard, and Antoine will be tempted to make something up to tell him."

"I think Antoine is a good guy. I hope I'm not wrong." I'd been wrong about people before. In major ways.

"Yeah, I hope he lives up to our expectations." Sam smiled at me suddenly. He has a great smile, and I couldn't help but smile back. "It's good to have faith in people sometimes, give them another chance. And we'll both keep our eyes on him."

I nodded. "Okay. Well, I better get home." I wanted to check my cell phone for messages and my landline, too. And my computer. I was dying for someone to reach out and touch me.

"Is something the matter?" Sam asked. He reached out to give me a tentative pat on the shoulder. "Anything I can do?"

"You're the greatest," I said. "But I'm just trying to get through a bad situation."

"Eric's out of touch?" he said, proving that Sam is one shrewd guesser.

"Yeah," I admitted. "And he's got . . . relatives in town. I don't know what the hell's going on." The word "relatives" jogged my brain. "How are things going in your family, Sam?"

"The divorce is no-fault, and it's going through," he said. "My mom is pretty miserable, but she'll be better as time goes on, I hope. Some of the people in Wright are giving her the cold shoulder. She let Mindy and Craig watch her change."

"What form did she pick?" I'd rather be a shapeshifter than a wereanimal, so I'd have a choice.

"A Scottie, I think. My sister took it real well. Mindy's always been more flexible than Craig."

I thought women were almost always more flexible than men, but I didn't think I needed to say that out loud. Generalizations like that can come back to bite you in the ass. "Deidra's family settled down?"

"It looks like the wedding's back on, as of two nights ago," Sam said. "Her mom and dad finally got that the 'contamination' couldn't spread to Deidra and Craig and their kids, if they have any."

"So you think the wedding will take place?"

"Yeah, I do. You still going to go to Wright with me?"

I started to say, "You still want me to?" but that would have been unduly coy, since he'd just asked me. "When the date is set, you'll have to ask my boss if I can get off work," I told him. "Sam, it may be tacky of me to persist in asking, but why aren't you taking Jannalynn?"

I wasn't imagining the discomfort that emanated from Sam. "She's . . . Well, ah . . . She's . . . I can just tell that she and my mom wouldn't get along. If I do introduce her to my family, I think I better wait until the tension of the wedding isn't part of the picture. My mom's still jangled from the shooting and the divorce, and Jannalynn is . . . not a calm person." In my opinion, if you were dating someone you were clearly embarrassed to introduce to your family, you were probably dating the wrong person. But Sam hadn't asked me for my opinion.

"No, she certainly isn't a calm individual," I said. "And now that she's got those new responsibilities, she's got to be pretty focused on the pack, I guess."

"What? What new responsibilities?"

Uh-oh. "I'm sure she'll tell you all about it," I said. "I guess you haven't seen her in a couple of days, huh?"

"Nope. So we're both down in the dumps," he said.

I was willing to concede I'd been pretty grim, and I smiled at him. "Yeah, that's a big part of it," I said. "With Eric's maker being in town, and him being scarier than Freddy Krueger, I'm pretty much on my own, I guess."

"If we don't hear from our significant others, let's go out tomorrow night. We can hit Crawdad Diner again," Sam said. "Or I can grill us some steaks."

"Sounds good," I told him. And I appreciated his offer. I'd been feeling kind of cast adrift. Jason was apparently busy with Michele (and after all, he'd stayed the other night when I'd half expected him to scoot out of the house), Eric was busy (apparently), Claude was almost never at the house and awake when I was awake, Tara was busy being pregnant, and Amelia had time to send me only the occasional e-mail. Though I didn't mind being by myself from time to time— in fact, I enjoyed it—I'd had a little too much of it lately. And being alone is a lot more fun if it's optional.

Relieved that the conversation with Antoine was over, and wondering what trouble Tom Lattesta might cause in the future, I grabbed my purse from the drawer in Sam's desk and headed for home.

It was a beautiful late afternoon when I pulled up in back of the house. I thought of working out to an exercise DVD before I fixed supper. Claude's car was gone. I hadn't noticed

Jason's truck, so I was surprised to see him sitting on my back steps.

"Hey, Brother!" I called as I got out of the car. "Listen, let me ask you . . ." And then, getting his mental signature, I realized the man sitting on the steps wasn't Jason. I froze. All I could do was stare at my half-fae great-uncle Dermot and wonder if he had come to kill me.

Chapter 11

He could have slain me about sixty times in the seconds I stood there. Despite the fact that he didn't, I still didn't want to take my eyes off him.

"Don't be afraid," Dermot said, rising with a grace that Jason could never have matched. He moved like his joints were machine made and well oiled.

I said through numb lips, "Can't help it."

"I want to explain," he said as he drew nearer.

"Explain?"

"I wanted to get closer to both of you," he said. He was well into my personal space by then. His eyes were blue like Jason's, candid like Jason's, and really, seriously, crazy. *Not* like Jason's. "I was confused."

"About what?" I wanted to keep the conversation going, I surely did, because I didn't know what would happen when it came to a halt.

"About where my loyalties lay," he said, bowing his head as gracefully as a swan.

"Sure. Tell me about that." Oh, if only I had my squirt gun, loaded with lemon juice, in my purse! But I'd promised Eric I'd put it on my nightstand when Claude had come to live with me, so that was where it lay. And the iron trowel was where it was supposed to be, in the toolshed.

"I will," he said, standing close enough that I could smell him. He smelled great. Fairies always do. "I know you met my father, Niall."

I nodded, a very small movement. "Yes," I said, to make sure.

"Did you love him?"

"Yes," I said without hesitation. "I did. I do."

"He's easy to love; he's charming," Dermot said. "My mother, Einin, was beautiful, too. Not a fairy kind of beautiful, like Niall, but she was human-beautiful."

"That's what Niall told me," I said. I was picking my way through a conversational minefield.

"Did he tell you the water fairies murdered my twin?"

"Did Niall tell me your brother was murdered? No, but I heard."

"I saw parts of Fintan's body. Neave and Lochlan had torn him limb from limb."

"They helped drown my parents, too," I said, holding my breath. What would he say?

"I . . ." He struggled to speak, his face desperate. "But I *wasn't there*. I . . . Niall . . ." It was terrible to watch Dermot struggle to speak. I shouldn't have had any mercy for him, since Niall had told me about Dermot's part in my parents' deaths. But I really couldn't endure his pain.

"So how come you ended up siding with Breandan's forces in the war?"

"He told me my father had killed my brother," Dermot said bleakly. "And I believed him. I mistrusted my love for Niall. When I remembered my mother's misery after Niall stopped coming to visit her, I thought Breandan must be right and we weren't meant to mingle with humans. It never seems to turn out well for them. And I hated what I was, half-human. I was never at home anywhere."

"So, are you feeling better now? About being a little bit human?"

"I've come to terms with it. I know my former actions were wrong, and I'm grieved that my father won't let me into Faery." The big blue eyes looked sad. I was too busy trying not to shake to get the full impact.

In a breath, out a breath. Calm, calm. "So now you're thinking Jason and I are okay? You don't want to hurt us anymore?"

He put his arms around me. This was "hug Sookie" season, and no one had told me ahead of time. Fairies were very touchy-feely, and personal space didn't mean anything to them. I would have liked to tell my great-uncle to back off. But I didn't dare. I didn't need to read Dermot's mind to understand that almost anything could set him off, so delicate was his mental balance. I had to stiffen all my resolution to maintain my even breathing so I wouldn't shiver and shake. His nearness and the tension of being in his presence, the huge strength that hummed through his arms, took me back to a dark ruined shack and two psycho fairies who really had deserved their deaths. My shoulders jerked, and I saw a flash of panic in Dermot's eyes. *Calm. Be calm.*

I smiled at him. I have a pretty smile, people tell me, though I know it's a little too bright, a little nuts. However, that suited the conversation perfectly. "The last time you saw Jason . . ." I said, and then couldn't think how to finish.

"I attacked his companion. The beast who'd hurt Jason's wife."

I swallowed hard and smiled some more. "Probably would've been better if you'd explained to Jason why you were going after Mel. And it wasn't Mel who killed her, you know."

"No, it was my own kind that finished her off. But she would have died anyway. He wasn't taking her to get help, you know."

Wasn't much I could say, because his account of what had happened to Crystal was accurate. I noticed I hadn't gotten a coherent response from Dermot on why he'd left Jason in ignorance of Mel's crime. "But you didn't explain to Jason," I said, breathing in and out—in a very soothing way. I hoped. It seemed to me that the longer I touched Dermot, the calmer we both got. And Dermot was markedly more coherent.

"I was very conflicted," he said seriously, unexpectedly borrowing from modern jargon.

Maybe that was as good an answer as I was going to get. I decided to take another tack. "Did you want to see Claude?" I said hopefully. "He's living with me now, just temporarily. He should be back later tonight."

"I'm not the only one, you know," Dermot told me. I looked up and met his mad eyes. I understood that my great-uncle was trying to tell me something. I wished to God I could make him rational. Just for five minutes. I stepped back from him and tried to figure out what he needed.

"You're not the only fairy left out in the human world. I know Claude's here. Someone else is, too?" I would've enjoyed my telepathy for a couple of minutes.

"Yes. *Yes.*" His eyes were pleading with me to understand. I'd risk a direct question. "Who else is on this side of Faery?"

"You don't want to meet him," Dermot assured me. "You have to be careful. He can't decide right now. He's ambivalent."

"Right." Whoever "he" was, he wasn't the only one who had mixed feelings. I wished I knew the right nutcracker that would open up Dermot's head.

"Sometimes he's in your woods." Dermot put his hands on my shoulders and squeezed gently. It was like he was trying to transmit things he couldn't say directly into my flesh.

"I heard about that," I said sourly.

"Don't trust other fairies," Dermot told me. "I shouldn't have."

I felt like a lightbulb had popped on above my head. "Dermot, have you had magic put on you? Like a spell?"

The relief in his eyes was almost palpable. He nodded frantically. "Unless they're at war, fairies don't like to kill other fairies. Except for Neave and Lochlan. They liked to kill everything. But I'm not dead. So there's hope."

Fairies might be reluctant to kill their own kind, but they didn't mind making them insane, apparently. "Is there anything I can do to reverse this spell? Can Claude help?"

"Claude has little magic, I think," Dermot said. "He's been living like a human too long. My dearest niece, I love you. How is your brother?"

We were back in nutty land. God bless poor Dermot. I hugged him, following an impulse. "My brother is happy, Uncle Dermot. He's dating a woman who suits him, and she won't take any shit off him, either. Her name is Michele— like my mom's, but with one *l* instead of two."

Dermot smiled down at me. Hard to say how much of this he was absorbing.

"Dead things love you," Dermot told me, and I made myself keep smiling.

"Eric the vampire? He says he does."

"Other dead things, too. They're pulling on you."

That was a not-so-welcome revelation. Dermot was right. I'd been feeling Eric through our bond, as usual, but there were two other gray presences with me every moment after dark: Alexei and Appius Livius. It was a drain on me, and I hadn't realized it until this moment.

"Tonight," Dermot said, "you'll receive visitors."

So now he was a prophet. "Good ones?"

He shrugged. "That's a matter of taste and expedience."

"Hey, Uncle Dermot? Do you walk around this land very often?"

"Too scared of the other one," he said. "But I try to watch you a little."

I was figuring out if that was a good thing or a bad thing when he vanished. Poof! I saw a kind of blur and then nothing. His hands were on my shoulders, and then they weren't. I assumed the tension of conversing with another person had gotten to Dermot.

Boy. That had been really, really weird.

I glanced around me, thinking I might see some other trace of his passage. He might even decide to return. But nothing happened. There wasn't a sound except the prosaic growl of my stomach, reminding me that I hadn't eaten lunch and that it was now suppertime. I went into the house on shaking legs and collapsed at the table. Conversation with a spy. Interview with an insane fairy. Oh, yes, phone Jason and tell him to be back on fairy watch. That was something I could do sitting down.

After that conversation, I remembered to carry in the newspapers when I got my legs to working again. While I baked a Marie Callender's pot pie, I read the past two days' papers.

Unfortunately, there was a lot of interest on the front page. There had been a gruesome murder in Shreveport, probably gang-related. The victim had been a young black man wearing gang colors, which was like a blinking arrow to the police, but he hadn't been shot. He'd been stabbed multiple times, and then his throat had been slashed. Yuck. Sounded more personal than a gang killing to me. Then the next night the same thing had happened again, this time to a kid of nineteen who wore different gang colors. He'd died the same awful way. I shook my head over the stupidity of young men dying over what I considered nothing, and moved on to a story that I found electrifying and very worrisome.

The tension over the werewolf registration issue was rising. According to the newspapers, the Weres were the big controversy. The stories hardly mentioned the other two-natured, yet I knew at least one werefox, one werebat, two weretigers, a score of werepanthers, and a shapeshifter. Werewolves, the most numerous of the two-natured, were catching the brunt of the backlash. And they were sounding off about it, as they should have.

"Why should I register, as if I were an illegal alien or a dead citizen?" Scott Wacker, an army general, was quoted as saying. "My family has been American for six generations, all of us army people. My daughter's in Iraq. What more do you want?"

The governor of one of the northwestern states said, "We

need to know who's a werewolf and who's not. In the event of an accident, officers need to know, to avoid blood contamination and to aid in identification."

I plunged my spoon into the crust to release some of the heat from the pot pie. I thought that over. *Bullshit,* I concluded.

"That's bushwah," General Wacker responded in the next paragraph. So Wacker and I had something in common. "For one thing, we change back to human form when we're dead. Officers already glove up when they're handling bodies. Identification is not going to be any more of a problem than with the one-natured. Why should it be?"

You go, Wacker.

According to the newspaper, the debate raged from the people in the streets (including some who weren't simply people) to members of Congress, from military personnel to firefighters, from law experts to constitutional scholars.

Instead of thinking globally or nationally, I tried to evaluate the crowd at Merlotte's since the announcement. Had revenue fallen off? Yes, there'd been a slight decrease at first, right after the bar patrons had watched Sam change into a dog and Tray become a wolf, but then people had started drinking as much as they had formerly.

So was this a created crisis, a nothing issue?

Not as much as I would have liked, I decided, having read a few more articles.

Some people really hated the idea that individuals they'd known all their lives had another side, a mysterious life unbeknownst (isn't that a great word? It had been on my Word of the Day calendar the week before) to the general public. That was the impression I'd gotten before, and it seemed that still held true. No one was budging on that position; the Weres got angrier, and the public got more frightened. At least a very vocal part of the public.

There had been demonstrations and riots in Redding, California, and Lansing, Michigan. I wondered if there were going to be riots here or in Shreveport. I found that hard to believe and painful to picture. I looked through the kitchen window at the gathering dusk, as if I expected to see a crowd of villagers with torches marching to Merlotte's.

It was a curiously empty evening. There wasn't much to clean up after I'd eaten, my laundry was up to date, and there was nothing on television I wanted to watch. I checked my e-mail; no message from Judith Vardamon.

There was a message from Alcide. "Sookie, we've set the pack meeting for Monday night at eight at my house. We've been trying to find a shaman for the judging. I'll see you and Jason then." It had been nearly a week since we'd found Basim's body in the woods, and this was the first I'd heard. The pack's "day or two" had stretched into six. And that meant it had been a very long time since I'd heard from Eric.

I called Jason again and left voice mail on his cell phone. I tried not to worry about the pack meeting, but every time I'd been with the whole pack, something violent had happened.

I thought again about the dead man in the grave in the clearing. Who had put him there? Presumably, the killer had wanted Basim's silence, but the body hadn't been planted on my land by mistake.

I read for thirty minutes or so, and then it was full dark and I felt Eric's presence, and then the lesser though undeniable company of the other two vampires. As soon as they woke, I felt tired. This made me so twitchy I broke my own resolution.

I knew that Eric realized I was unhappy and worried. It

was impossible for him not to know that. Maybe he thought by keeping me away he was protecting me. Maybe he didn't know that his maker and Alexei were both in my consciousness. I took a deep breath and called him. The phone rang, and I pressed it to my ear as though I were holding Eric himself. But I thought, and I wouldn't have believed this possible a week ago, *What if he doesn't pick up?*

The phone rang, and I held my breath. After the second ring, Eric answered. "The pack meeting has been set," I blurted.

"Sookie," he said. "Can you come here?"

On my drive to Shreveport, I wondered at least four times if I was doing the right thing. But I concluded that whether I was right or wrong (in running to see Eric when he asked me to) was simply a dead issue. We were both on the ends of the line stretched between us, a line spun from blood. It trumped how we felt about each other at any given moment. I knew he was tired and desperate. He knew I was angry, uneasy, hurt. I wondered, though. If I'd called him and said the same thing, would he have hopped into his car (or into the sky) and arrived on my doorstep?

They were all at Fangtasia, he'd said.

I was shocked to see how few cars were parked in front of the only vampire bar in Shreveport. Fangtasia was a huge tourist draw in a town that was boasting a tourist increase, and I'd expected it to be packed. There were almost as many cars parked in the employee parking at the back as there were at the main door. That had never happened before.

Maxwell Lee, an African-American businessman who also happened to be a vampire, was on duty at the rear entrance, and that was a first, too. The rear door had never been specially guarded, because the vampires were so sure they could take care of themselves. Yet here he was, wearing his usual three-piece suit but doing a task he normally would have considered beneath him. He didn't look resentful; he looked worried.

I said, "Where are they?"

He jerked his head toward the main room of the bar. "I'm glad you're here," he said, and I knew Eric's maker's visit wasn't going well.

So often having out-of-town visitors is awkward, huh? You take them to see the local sights, you try to feed them and keep them entertained, but then you're really wishing they would leave. It wasn't hard to see that Eric was on his last nerve. He was sitting in a booth with Appius Livius Ocella and Alexei. Of course, Alexei looked too young to be in a bar, and that added to the absurdity of the moment.

"Good evening," I said stiffly. "Eric, you wanted to see me?"

Eric scooted over closer to the wall so I'd have plenty of room, and I sat by him. Appius Livius and Alexei both greeted me, Appius with a strained smile and Alexei with more ease. When we were all together, I discovered that being close to them relaxed the tense thread inside me, the thread that bound us all together.

"I've missed you," Eric said so quietly that at first I thought I'd imagined it.

I wouldn't refer to the fact that he'd been completely out of touch for days. He knew that.

It took all my self-control to bite back a few choice words. "As I was trying to tell you over the phone, the pack meeting about Basim has been set for Monday night."

"Where and when?" he said, and there was a note in his

voice that let me know he was not a happy camper. Well, he could pitch his tent right alongside mine.

"At Alcide's house. The one that used to be his dad's. At eight o'clock."

"And Jason's going with you? Without a doubt?"

"I haven't talked to him yet, but I left him a message."

"You've been angry with me."

"I've been worried about you." I couldn't tell him anything about how I'd felt that he didn't already know.

"Yes," Eric said. His voice was empty.

"Eric is an excellent host," the tsarevitch said, as if I expected a report.

I scratched up a smile to offer the boy. "That's good to hear, Alexei. What have you two been doing? I don't think you've ever been to Shreveport before."

"No," Appius Livius said in his curious accent. "We hadn't been here to visit. It's a nice little city. My older son has been doing his best to keep us busy and out of trouble."

Okay, that had been a tad on the sarcastic side. I could tell from Eric's tension that he hadn't entirely succeeded in the "keeping them out of trouble" part of his agenda.

"The World Market is fun. You can get stuff from all over the world there. And Shreveport was the capitol of the Confederacy for a while." Geez Louise, I needed to do better than that. "If you go to the Municipal Auditorium, you can see Elvis's dressing room," I said brightly. I wondered if Bubba ever visited there to see his old stomping grounds.

"I had a very good teenager last night," Alexei said, matching my cheerful tone. As though he'd said he'd run a red light.

I opened my mouth and nothing came out. If I said the

wrong thing, I might be dead right then and there. "Alexei," I said, sounding much calmer than I felt, "you have to watch it. That's against the law here. Your maker and Eric could both suffer for it."

"When I was with my human family, I could do anything I wanted," Alexei said. I really couldn't read his voice at all. "I was so sick, they indulged me."

Eric twitched.

"I can sure understand that," I said. "Any family would be tempted to do that with a sick child. But since you're well now, and you've had lots of years to mature, I know you understand that doing exactly what you want to do is not a good plan." I thought of at least twenty other things I could have said, but I stopped right there. And that was a good thing. Appius Livius looked directly into my eyes and nodded almost imperceptibly.

"I don't look grown up," Alexei said.

Again, too many options on what I could say. The boy— the old, old, boy—definitely expected me to answer. "No, and it's an awful pity what happened to you and your family. But—"

And Alexei reached over, took my hand, and *showed me* what had happened to him and his family. I saw the cellar, the royal family, the doctor, the maid, facing the men who had come to kill them, and I heard the guns fire, and the bullets found their marks; or in the case of the women, they didn't, since the royal women had sewn jewels into their clothes for the escape that never came about. The jewels saved their lives for all of a few seconds, until the soldiers killed each groaning and bleeding and screaming individual. His mother, his father, his sisters, his doctor, his mother's maid, the cook, his father's valet . . . and his dog. And after the shooting, the soldiers went around with bayonets.

I thought I was going to throw up. I swayed where I sat, and Eric's cold arm went around me. Alexei had let go, and I was never gladder of anything in my life. I would not have touched the child again for anything.

"You see," Alexei said triumphantly. "You see! I should be free to go my own way."

"No," I said. And I was proud that my voice was firm. "No matter how we suffer, we have an obligation to others. We have to be unselfish enough to try to live in the right way, so others can get through their own lives without us fouling them up."

Alexei looked rebellious. "That's what Master says, too," he muttered. "More or less."

"Master is right," I said, though the words tasted bad in my mouth.

"Master" waved for the bartender to come over. Felicia slunk up to the table. She was tall and pretty and as gentle as a vampire can be. She had some fresh scars on her neck. "What can I get you-all?" she said. "Sookie, can I bring you a beer or . . . ?"

"Some iced tea would be great, Felicia," I said.

"And some TrueBlood for all of you?" she asked the vampires. "Or, we do have a bottle of Royalty."

Eric's eyes closed, and Felicia realized her blunder. "Okay," she said briskly. "TrueBlood for Eric, tea for Sookie."

"Thank you!" I said, smiling up at the bartender.

Pam strode up to the table. She was trailing the gauzy black costume she wore at Fangtasia, and she was as close to panic as I'd ever seen her. "Excuse me," she said, bowing in the direction of the guests. "Eric, Katherine Boudreaux is visiting Fangtasia tonight. She's with Sallie and a small party."

Eric looked as if he were going to explode. "Tonight," he said, and one word spoke volumes. "With much regret, Ocella, I must ask you and Alexei to go back to my office."

Appius Livius got up without asking for further explanation, and Alexei, to my surprise, followed him without any questions. If Eric had been in the habit of breathing, I would say that he exhaled with relief when his visitors had left his sight. He said a few things in an ancient tongue, but I didn't know which one.

Then a stout, attractive blonde in her forties was standing by the table, another woman right behind her.

"You must be Katherine Boudreaux," I said pleasantly. "I'm Sookie Stackhouse; I'm Eric's girlfriend."

"Hi, honey. I'm Katherine," she said. "This is my partner, Sallie. We're here with some friends who were curious about my job. I try to visit all the vampire workplaces during the year, and we hadn't been to Fangtasia in months. Since I'm based right here in Shreveport, I ought to make it in more often."

"We're so glad you're here," Eric said smoothly. He sounded like his normal self. "Sallie, always good to see you. How's the tax business?"

Sallie, a slim brunette whose hair was just beginning to gray, laughed. "Taxes are booming, as always," she said. "You ought to know, Eric, you pay enough of them."

"It's good to see our vampire citizens getting along with our human citizens," Katherine said heartily, looking around the bar, which was so thinly populated it almost wasn't open. Her blond eyebrows contracted slightly for a moment, but that was the only sign Ms. Boudreaux gave that she noticed Eric's business was down.

Pam said, "Your table is ready!" She swept her hand toward two tables that had been put together for the party, and the state BVA agent said, "Excuse me, Eric. I've gotta go pay attention to my company."

After a shower of pleasantries and pleased-to-meet-yous, we were finally by ourselves, if sitting in a booth in the middle of a bar can be counted as being by ourselves. Pam started over, but Eric checked her with a raised finger. He took my hand with one of his and rested his forehead on his other hand.

"Can you tell me what's up with you?" I said bluntly. "This is awful. It's very hard to have faith in us when I don't know what's happening."

"Ocella has had some business to discuss with me," Eric said. "Some unwelcome business. And as you saw, my half brother is ailing."

"Yes, he shared that with me," I said. It was still hard to believe what I'd seen and suffered with the child, through his memory of the deaths of everyone he'd loved. The tsarevitch of Russia, sole survivor of a mass murder, could use some counseling. Maybe he and Dermot could be in the same therapy group. "You don't go through something like that and come out Mr. Mental Health, but I've never experienced anything like that. I know it must have been hell for him, but I've got to say . . ."

"You don't want to go through it, too," Eric said. "You're not alone in that. It's clearest for us: Ocella, me, you. But he can share that with other people, too. It's not as detailed for them, they tell me. No one wants that memory. We all carry plenty of our own bad memories. I'm afraid that he may not be able to survive as a vampire." He paused, turning the bottle of TrueBlood around and around on the table. "Apparently, it's a nightly grind to get Alexei to do the simplest things. And not to do others. You heard his remark about the teenager. I don't want to go into the details. However . . . have you read the papers lately, the Shreveport papers?"

"You mean *Alexei* might be responsible for those two murders?" I could only sit there staring at Eric. "The stab wounds, the throats? But he's so small and young."

"He's insane," Eric said. "Ocella finally told me that Alexei had had episodes like this before—not as severe. It has led him to consider, very reluctantly, giving Alexei the final death."

"You mean putting him to sleep?" I said, not sure I'd heard him right. "Like a dog?"

Eric looked me straight in the eyes. "Ocella loves the boy, but he cannot be allowed to kill people or other vampires when these fits take him. Such incidents will get into the paper. What if he were caught? What if some Russian recognized him as a result of the notoriety? What would that do to our relationship with the Russian vampires? Most important, Ocella cannot keep track of him every moment. Two times, the boy has gotten out on his own. And two deaths resulted. In my area! He'll subvert all we're trying to do here in the United States. Not that my maker cares about my position in this country," Eric added, a little bitterly.

I gave Eric a sort of heavy pat on the cheek. Not a slap. A heavy pat. "Yeah, let's not forget the *two dead men*," I said. "That Alexei murdered, in a painful and horrible way. I mean, I realize that this is all about him and your maker and your personal cred, but let's spare a tip of the hat to those guys he killed."

Eric shrugged. He was worried and he was at his wit's end, and he didn't care at all about the deaths of two humans. He was probably thankful that Alexei had picked victims who wouldn't attract much sympathy and whose deaths were easily explained. Gang members killed one another all the time, after all. I gave up on making my point. At least partly because I'd had a thought—if Alexei was capable of turning against his own kind, maybe we could steer him onto Victor?

I shuddered. I was creeping myself out. "So your maker brought Alexei to you hoping that you'd have some bright ideas about keeping your half brother alive, teaching him some self-control?"

"Yes. That's one of the reasons he's here."

"Appius Livius having sex with the kid can't be helping Alexei's mental health," I said, since I simply couldn't *not* say it.

"Please understand. In Ocella's time, that was not a consideration," Eric said. "Alexei would be old enough, in those times. And men of a certain station were free to indulge themselves with very little guilt or question. Ocella doesn't think in the modern way about such things. As it happens, Alexei has become so . . . Well, they are not having sex now. Ocella is an honorable man." Eric sounded very intent, very serious, as if he had to persuade me of his maker's integrity. And all this concern was about the man who'd murdered him. But if Eric admired Ocella, respected him, didn't I have to do the same?

And—it popped into my head that Eric wasn't doing anything for his brother that I wouldn't do for mine.

Then I had another unwelcome thought, and my mouth

went dry. "If Appius Livius isn't having sex with Alexei, who *is* he having sex with?" I asked in a small voice.

"I know this is your business, since we're married— something I've insisted on and you've belittled," Eric said, and the bitterness was back in his voice. "I can only tell you that I'm not having sex with my maker. But I would if he told me that was what he wanted. I would have no choice."

I tried to think of a way to round this conversation off, escape with some dignity. "Eric, you're busy with your visitors." Busy in a way I'd never imagined. "I'm going to that meeting at Alcide's Monday night. I'll tell you what happens, when and if you call me. There are a couple of things I need to bring you up to speed on, if you ever have a chance to come to my place to talk." Like Dermot appearing on my doorstep. That was a story Eric would be interested to hear, and God knows I wanted to tell him about it. But now was not the right time.

"If they stay until Tuesday, I'm going to see you no matter what they're doing," Eric told me. He sounded a little more like himself. "We'll make love. I feel like buying you a present."

"That sounds like a great night to me," I said, feeling a surge of hope. "I don't need a present, just you. So I'll see you Tuesday, no matter what. That's what you said, right?"

"That's what I said."

"Okay then, until Tuesday."

"I love you," Eric said in a drained voice. "And you are my wife, in the only way that matters to me."

"Love you, too," I said, passing on the last half of his closing statement because I didn't know what it meant. I got up to go, and Pam appeared by my side to walk me to my car. Out of the corner of my eye, I saw Eric get up and walk over to the Boudreaux table to make sure his important visitors were happy.

Pam said, "He'll ruin Eric if he stays."

"How so?"

"The boy will kill again, and we won't be able to cover it up. He can escape if you so much as blink. He has to be watched constantly. Yet Ocella argues with himself about putting the boy down."

"Pam, let Ocella decide," I warned her. I thought since we were by ourselves I could take the huge liberty of calling Eric's maker by his personal name. "I'm serious. Eric'll have to let him kill you if you take Alexei out."

"You care, don't you?" Pam was unexpectedly touched.

"You're my bud," I said. "Of course I care."

"We are friends," Pam said.

"You know it."

"This isn't going to end well," Pam said, as I got in my car.

I couldn't think of a single thing to say.

She was right.

I ate a Little Debbie cinnamon roll when I got home, just because I thought I deserved one. I was so worried I couldn't even think of going to bed just yet. Alexei had given me his own personal nightmare. I'd never heard of a vampire (or any other being, human or not) being able to transmit a memory like that. It struck me as peculiarly horrible that it should be Alexei who was so "gifted," when he had such a ghastly memory to share. I went though the royal family's excruciating ordeal again. I could understand why the boy was the way he was. But I could also understand why he might have to be— put to sleep. I pushed up from the table, feeling thoroughly exhausted. I was ready for bed. But my plan got altered when the doorbell rang.

You'd think, living out in the country at the end of a long driveway through the woods, that I would have plenty of warning of guests. But that wasn't always the case, especially with supes. I didn't recognize the woman I saw through the peephole, but I knew she was a vampire. That meant she couldn't come in without being invited, so it was safe to find out why she was there. I opened the door, feeling mostly curious.

"Hi, can I help you?" I asked.

She looked me up and down. "Are you Sookie Stackhouse?"

"I am."

"You e-mailed me."

Alexei had blown out my brain cells. I was slow tonight. "Judith Vardamon?"

"The same."

"So Lorena was your sire? Your maker?"

"She was."

"Please come in," I said, and stepped aside. I might have been making a big mistake, but I'd almost given up hope that Judith would respond to my message. Since she'd come all the way here from Little Rock, I thought I owed her that much trust.

Judith raised her eyebrows and stepped over my threshold. "You must love Bill, or else you're a fool," she said.

"Neither, I hope. You want some TrueBlood?"

"Not now, thank you."

"Please, have a seat."

I sat on the edge of the recliner while Judith took the couch. I thought it was incredible that Lorena had "made" both Bill and Judith. I wanted to ask a lot of questions, but I didn't want to offend or irritate this vampire, who'd already done me a huge favor.

"Do you know Bill?" I said, to kick off the talk we had to have.

"Yes, I know him." She seemed cautious, which was odd when I considered how much stronger she was than I.

"You're the younger sister?" She looked to be about thirty, or at least that had been her death age. She had dark brown hair and blue eyes, and she was short and pleasantly round. She was one of the most nonthreatening vampires I'd ever met, at least superficially. And she looked oddly familiar.

"I beg your pardon?"

"Lorena turned you after she turned Bill? Why'd she pick you?"

"You were Bill's lover for some months, I gather? Reading between the lines of your message?" she asked in turn.

"Yes, I was. I'm with someone else now."

"How is it that he never told you how he came to meet Lorena?"

"I don't know. His choice."

"Very strange." She looked openly distrustful.

"You can think it's strange till the cows come home," I said. "I don't know why Bill didn't tell me, but he didn't. If you want to tell me, fine. Tell me. But that's not really important. The important thing is that Bill's not getting well. He got bitten by a fairy with silver-tipped teeth. If he has your blood, he might get over it."

"Did Bill perhaps hint to you that you should ask me?"

"No, ma'am, he didn't. But I hate to see him hurting."

"Has he mentioned my name?"

"Ah. No. I found out by myself so I could get in touch with you. It seems to me that if you're Lorena's get, too, you must have known he was suffering. I find myself wondering why you haven't shown up before."

"I'll tell you why." Judith's voice was ominous.

Oh, great, another tale of pain and suffering. I knew I wasn't going to like this story.

I was right.

Chapter 12

Judith began her story by asking me a question. "Have you ever met Lorena?"

"Yes," I said, and left it at that. Evidently, Judith didn't know exactly how I'd met Lorena, which had been a few seconds before I drove a stake through her heart and ended her long, nasty life.

"Then you know she's ruthless."

I nodded.

"You need to know why I've stayed away from Bill all these years, when I'm very fond of him," Judith said. "Lorena has had a hard life. I wouldn't necessarily believe everything she's told me, but I've heard confirmation of a few parts of it from others." Judith wasn't seeing me anymore; she was looking past me, down the years, I guess.

"How old was she?" I said, just to keep the story rolling.

"By the time Lorena met Bill she had been a vampire for many decades. She had been turned in 1788 by a man named Solomon Brunswick. He met her in a brothel in New Orleans."

"He met her in the obvious way?"

"Not exactly. He was there to take blood from another whore, one who specialized in the odder desires of men. Compared to some of her other customers, a little bite wasn't anything too remarkable."

"Had Solomon been a vampire a long time?" I was curious despite myself. Vampires as living history . . . Well, since they'd come out of the coffin, they'd added a lot to college courses. Bring a vampire to class to tell his or her story, and you got great attendance.

"Solomon had been a vampire for twenty years by then. He became a vampire by accident. He was a sort of tinker. He sold pots and pans, and he mended broken ones. He had other goods that were hard to find in New England then: needles, thread, odds and ends like that. He took his horse and cart from town to town and farm to farm, all by himself. Solomon encountered one of us while he camped in the woods one night. He told me that he survived the first encounter, but the vampire followed him during the night to his next camp and attacked him again. This second attack was a critical one. Solomon was one of the unfortunates who get turned accidentally. Since the vampire who drank from him left him for dead, unaware of the change—or at least, I like to think so—Solomon was untrained and had to learn all by himself."

"Sounds really awful," I said, and I meant that.

She nodded. "It must have been. He worked his way down to New Orleans to avoid people who wondered why he hadn't aged. Where he came upon Lorena. After he'd had his meal, he was leaving out the back when he spotted her in the dark courtyard. She was with a man. The customer tried to leave without paying, and in the blink of an eye Lorena seized him and cut his throat."

That sounded like the Lorena I'd known.

"Solomon was impressed with her savagery and excited by the fresh blood. He grabbed the dying man and drained him, and when he threw the body into the yard of the next house, Lorena was impressed and fascinated. She wanted to be like he was."

"That sounds about right."

Judith smiled faintly. "She was illiterate but tenacious and a tremendous survivor. He was far more intelligent, but he had poor killing skills. By then, he had figured some things out, and so he was able to bring her over. They took blood from each other sometimes, and that gave them the courage to find others like us, to learn what they needed to learn to live well instead of merely surviving. The two of them practiced how to be successful vampires, tested the limits of their new natures, and made an excellent team."

"So Solomon was your grandfather, since he begat Lorena," I said biblically. "What happened after that?"

"Eventually, the bloom went off the rose," Judith said. "Makers and their children stay together longer than a merely sexual couple but not forever. Lorena betrayed Solomon. She was caught with the half-drained body of a dead child, but she was able to play a human woman pretty convincingly. She told the men who grabbed her that Solomon was the one who'd killed the child, that he'd made her carry the body, so the blood was all over her. Solomon barely got out of the town alive—they were in Natchez, Mississippi. He never saw Lorena again. He's never met Bill, either. Lorena found him after the War between the States.

"As Bill later told me, one night Lorena was wandering

through this area. It was much harder then to stay concealed, especially in rural areas. There weren't as many people to hunt you down, true, and there was little or no communication. But strangers were conspicuous and with the thinner population, the choices of prey were less. An individual death was noticed more. A body had to be hidden very carefully, or the death meticulously staged. At least there wasn't much organized law enforcement."

I reminded myself not to look disgusted. This knowledge was nothing new. That was how vampires had lived until a few years ago.

"Lorena saw Bill and his family through the windows of their house." Judith looked away. "She fell in love. For several nights, she listened to the family. During the day she would dig a hole in the woods and bury herself. At night, she'd watch.

"Finally, she decided to act. She realized—even Lorena realized—Bill would never forgive her if she killed his children, so she waited until he came out in the middle of the night to find out why the dog wouldn't stop barking. When Bill came out with his rifle, she crept up behind him and took him."

I thought of Lorena, so close to my own family, right through the woods. . . . She could have come to my great-great-grandparents' place just as easily, and my whole family history would have been different.

"She turned him that night, buried him, and helped him resurrect three nights later."

I couldn't imagine how shattered Bill must have been. Everything gone in the blink of an eye: his whole life taken and altered and given back to him in a terrible form.

"I guess she took him away from here," I said.

"Yes, that was essential. She had arranged a death for him. She'd smeared a clearing with his blood and left his gun there and rags from his clothing. He told me it looked as though a panther had gotten him. So they traveled together, and while he was bound to her, he hated her, too. He was miserable with her, but she remained obsessed with him. After thirty years, she tried to make him happier by killing a woman who looked very much like his wife."

"Oh, gosh," I said, trying not to feel sick. "You, huh?" That was why her face had been vaguely familiar. I'd seen Bill's old family pictures.

Judith nodded. "Evidently, Bill saw me entering a neighbor's house, going to a party with my family. He followed me home and watched me, because the resemblance caught his fancy. When Lorena discovered this new interest, she thought Bill would stay with her if she provided him with a companion."

"I'm sorry," I said. "I'm really, really sorry."

Judith shrugged. "It wasn't Bill's fault, but you'll understand why I had to think about it before I came in answer to your message. Solomon is in Europe now, or I would have asked him to come with me. I dread seeing Lorena again, and I was afraid . . . afraid she would be here, afraid you would have asked her to help Bill, too. Or she might have made up this story to bring me here, for all I knew. Is she . . . Is she around?"

"She's dead. Didn't you know?"

Judith's round blue eyes went wide. She couldn't be any more pale, but her eyes closed for a long moment. "I felt a strong wrench around eighteen months ago. . . . That was Lorena's death?"

I nodded.

"That's why she hasn't summoned me. Oh, this is wonderful, wonderful!"

Judith looked like a different woman.

"I guess I'm a little surprised that Bill didn't get in touch with you to tell you."

"Maybe he thought I would know it. Children and makers are bound. But I wasn't sure. It seemed too good to be true." Judith smiled, and she looked suddenly pretty, even with the fangs. "Where is Bill?"

"He's through the woods." I pointed in the right direction. "In his old home."

"I'll be able to track him once I'm outside," she said happily. "Oh, to be with him without Lorena near!"

Ah. What?

Before, it had been okay for Judith to sit and talk my ear off, but now all of a sudden, she was ready to take off like a scalded cat. I was sitting there with my eyes narrowed, wondering what I'd done.

"I'll heal him, and I'm sure he'll thank you after," she said, and I felt like I'd been dismissed. "Was Bill there when Lorena died?"

"Yeah," I said.

"Did he suffer much punishment for killing her?"

"He didn't kill her," I said. "I did."

She froze, staring at me as if I'd suddenly announced I was King Kong. She said, "I owe you my freedom. Bill must think very highly of you."

"I believe he does," I said. To my embarrassment, she bent to kiss my hand. Her lips were cold.

"Bill and I can be together now," she said. "Finally! I'll see you another night to tell you how grateful I am, but now I have to go to him." And she was out of the house and zipping through the woods to the south before I could say Jack Robinson.

I kind of felt like a very large fist had hit me upside the head.

I would be a total sleaze to feel anything but happy for Bill. Now he could hang around with Judith for centuries, if he wanted to. With the never-aging duplicate of his wife. I made myself smile with gladness.

When looking happy didn't make me happy, I did twenty jumping jacks, then twenty push-ups. *Okay, that's better,* I thought, as I lay on my stomach on the living room floor. Now I was ashamed that my arm muscles were trembling. I remembered the workouts the Lady Falcons softball coach had put us through, and I knew Coach Peterson would kick my butt if she could see me now. On the other hand, I wasn't seventeen anymore.

As I rolled over to lie on my back, I considered that fact soberly. It wasn't the first occasion I'd felt the passage of time, but it was the first occasion that I'd noticed my body had changed into something a little less efficient. I had to contrast that with the lot of the vampires I knew. At least 99 percent of them had become vamps at the peak of their lives. There were a few who had been younger, like Alexei, and a few who had been older, like the Ancient Pythoness, but most of them had ranged in age from sixteen to thirty-five at the time of their first death. They'd never have to apply for Social Security or Medicare. They'd never need to worry about hip replacements or lung cancer or arthritis.

By the time I reached middle age (if I was so lucky, since my life was what you would call "high risk"), I would be slowing down in perceptible ways. After that, the wrinkles would only grow and deepen, my skin would look looser on my bones and sport a spot or two, and my hair would thin out. My chin would sag a little, and my boobs would, too. My joints would ache when I sat too long in one position. I'd have to get reading glasses.

I might develop high blood pressure. I might have a blocked artery. My heart might beat irregularly. When I got the flu, I would be *very* sick. I'd fear Parkinson's, Alzheimer's, a stroke, pneumonia . . . the boogie-bears that hid under the beds of the aging.

What if I told Eric I wanted to be with him forever? Assuming he didn't scream and run as fast as he could in the other direction, assuming he actually changed me, I tried to imagine what being a vampire would be like. I would watch all my friends grow old and die. I would sleep in the hidey-hole in the closet floor myself. If Jason married Michele, she might not like me holding their babies. I would feel the urge to attack people, to bite them; they'd all be walking McBloodburgers to me. I'd think of people as food. I stared up at the ceiling fan and tried to imagine wanting to bite Andy Bellefleur or Holly. Ick.

On the other hand, I'd never be sick again unless someone shot me or bit me with silver, or staked me, or put me out in the sun. I could protect frail humans from danger. I could be with Eric forever . . . except for that bit where vampire couples usually didn't stay together all that long.

Okay, I could still be with Eric for a few years.

How would I make my living? I could only take the later shift at Merlotte's, and that after dark had fallen, if Sam let me keep my job. And Sam, too, would grow old and die. A new owner might not like having a permanent barmaid who could only work one shift. I could go back to college and take night classes and computer classes until I got some kind of degree. In what?

I'd reached the limit of my imagination. I rolled to my knees and rose from the floor, wondering if I was imagining a slight stiffness in my joints.

Sleep was long in coming that night, despite my very long and very scary day. The silence of the house pressed in around me. Claude came home in the wee hours, whistling.

When I got up the next morning, not bright but way too early, I felt sluggish and dispirited. I found two envelopes shoved under my front door on my way to the porch with my coffee. The first note was from Mr. Cataliades, and it had been hand-delivered by his niece Diantha at three a.m., she'd noted on the envelope. I was sorry to miss a chance to talk to Diantha, though I was grateful she hadn't woken me. I opened that envelope first out of sheer curiosity. "Dear Miss Stackhouse," Mr. Cataliades wrote. "Here is a check for the amount in Claudine Crane's account when she passed away. She wanted you to have it."

Short and to the point, which was more than most people I'd talked to recently. I flipped the check over and found that it was for a hundred and fifty thousand dollars.

"Oh my God," I said out loud. "Oh my God." I dropped it because my fingers suddenly lost their power, and the check drifted down to the porch. I scrambled to retrieve it and read it again to make sure I hadn't been mistaken.

"Oh," I said. I was sticking with the classics, because saying anything else seemed to be beyond me. I couldn't even imagine what I would do with so much money. That was beyond me, too. I had to give myself a little space until I could think about this unexpected legacy with any rational plan.

I carried the amazing check into the house and put it in a drawer, terrified something would happen to it before I got it to the bank. Only when I was sure it was safe did I even think of opening my other note, which was from Bill.

I carried it back out to the porch chair and took a gulp of my cooling coffee. I tore open the envelope.

"Dearest Sookie—I didn't want to frighten you by knocking on your door at two in the morning, so I'm leaving this for you to read in the daylight. I wondered why you had been in my house last week. I knew you'd come in, and I knew that sooner or later your motive would become apparent. Your generous heart has given me the cure I needed.

"I never thought I would see Judith after the last time we parted. There were reasons I didn't call her over the years. I understand she told you why Lorena picked her to turn vampire. Lorena didn't ask me before she attacked Judith. Please believe this. I would never condemn someone to our life unless she wanted it and told me so."

Okay, Bill was giving me credit for some complicated thinking. I'd never dreamed of suspecting that Bill had asked Lorena to find him a mate resembling his late wife.

"I would never have been brave enough to contact Judith myself for fear she hated me. I am so glad to see her again. And her blood, freely given, has already worked a great healing in me."

All right! That had been the whole point.

"Judith has agreed to stay for a week so we can 'catch up' with each other. Maybe you will join us some evening? Judith was most impressed with your kindness. Love, Bill."

I forced myself to smile down at the folded piece of paper. I'd just write him right back and tell him how pleased I was that he was better and that he'd renewed his old relationship

with Judith. Of course, I hadn't been happy when he was dating Selah Pumphrey, a human real estate dealer, because we
had only recently broken up, and I knew he didn't really care
about her. Now I was determined to be happy for Bill. I was
not going to be one of those awful people who gets all bent
out of shape when the ex acquires a replacement. That was
hypocritical and selfish to the extreme, and I hoped I was a
better person than that. At least I was determined to provide
a good imitation of such a person.

"Okay," I said to my coffee mug. "That turned out great."

"Would you rather talk to me than to your coffee?" Claude
asked.

I'd heard feet on the creaky stairs through the open window, and I'd registered that another brain was up and working, but I hadn't foreseen that he'd join me on the porch.

"You got in late," I said. "You want me to get you a cup of
coffee? I made plenty."

"No, thank you. I'll have some pineapple juice in a minute. It's a beautiful day." Claude was shirtless. At least he was
wearing drawstring pants with the Dallas Cowboys all over
them. Ha! He wished!

"Yeah," I said, with a marked lack of enthusiasm. Claude
raised one perfectly shaped black eyebrow.

"Who's down in the dumps?" he asked.

"No, I'm very happy."

"Yes, I can see the joy written all over your face. What's
the matter, Cousin?"

"I did get the check from Claudine's estate. God bless her.
That was so generous." I looked up at Claude, putting all my
sincerity into my face. "Claude, I hope you're not mad at me.
That's just . . . so much money. I haven't got a clue what I
want to do with it."

Claude shrugged. "That was what Claudine wished. Now, tell me what's wrong."

"Claude, you'll have to excuse me being surprised that you care. I would've said you didn't give a flying eff how I felt. Now you're being all sweet with Hunter, and you're offering to help me clean out the attic."

"Maybe I'm developing a cousinly concern for you." He raised one eyebrow.

"Maybe pigs will fly."

He laughed. "I'm trying to be more human," he confessed. "Since I'll live out my long existence among humans, apparently, I'm trying to be more . . ."

"Likable?" I supplied.

"Ouch," he said, but he wasn't really hurt. Being hurt would presuppose that he cared about my opinion. And that was something you couldn't be taught, right?

"Where's the boyfriend been?" he asked. "I do so love the smell of vampire around the house."

"Last night was the first time I've seen him in a week. And we didn't have any alone time."

"You two have a fight?" Claude settled one hip on the porch railing, and I could tell he was determined to show me he could be interested in someone else's life.

I felt a certain amount of exasperation. "Claude, I'm drinking my very first cup of coffee, I didn't get a lot of sleep, and I've had a bad few days. Could you just scoot away and take a shower or something?"

He sighed as if I'd broken his heart. "All right, I can take a hint," he said.

"That really wasn't so much a hint as an outright statement."

"Oh, I'll go."

But as he straightened up and took a step toward the door, I realized I did have something else to say. "I take that back. There *is* something we have to talk about," I said. "I haven't had a chance to tell you that Dermot was here."

Claude stood up straight, almost as if he were prepared to bolt. "What did he say? What did he want?"

"I'm not sure what he wanted. I think, like you, he wanted to be close to someone else with a bit of fairy blood. And he wanted to tell me that he was under a spell."

Claude paled. "From whose magic? Has Grandfather come back through the gate?"

"No," I said. "But could a fairy have cast a spell on him before the gate closed? And I think you must know there's another full-blooded fairy on this side of the portal, or gate, whatever you call it." As I understood fairy morals, it was not possible to answer me with a direct lie.

"Dermot is crazy," Claude said. "I have no idea what he'll do next. If he approached you directly, he must be under extreme pressure. You know how ambivalent he is about humans."

"You didn't answer my question."

"No," Claude said. "I didn't. And there's a reason for that." He turned his back to me and looked out over the yard. "I like my head on my shoulders."

"So there *is* someone else around, and you know who it is. Or you know more about putting spells on than you're admitting?"

"I'm not going to talk about it." And Claude went inside. Within minutes, I heard him going out the back of the house, and his car passed by on its way down the drive to Hummingbird Road.

So I had gained a valuable piece of knowledge that was

completely useless. I couldn't summon up the fairy, ask the fairy why he or she was still on this side, what his or her intentions were. But if I had to guess, I would have to say I was pretty sure that Claude wouldn't be this frightened of a sweet fairy who wanted to spread goodness and light. And a really nice fairy wouldn't have put some spell on poor Dermot that made him so discombobulated.

I said a prayer or two, hoping that would restore my normal good mood, but it didn't work today. Possibly I wasn't approaching prayer in the right spirit. Communicating with God isn't the same as taking a happy pill—far from it.

I pulled on a dress and sandals and went to Gran's grave. Having a conversation with her usually reminded me of how levelheaded and wise she'd been. Today all I thought about was her wildly out-of-character indiscretion with a half fairy that had resulted in my dad and his sister, Linda. My grandmother had (maybe) had sex with a half fairy because my grandfather couldn't make babies. So she'd gotten to carry and birth her children, two of them, and she'd raised them with love.

And she'd buried both of them.

As I crouched by the headstone looking down at the grass that was getting thicker on her grave, I wondered if I should draw some meaning from that. You could make a case that Gran had done something she shouldn't have . . . to get something she wasn't supposed to get . . . and after she'd gotten it, she'd lost it in the most painful way imaginable. What could be worse than losing a child? Losing two children.

Or you could decide that everything that had happened was completely at random, that Gran had done the best she could at the moment she'd had to make a decision, and that her decision simply hadn't worked out for reasons equally beyond her control. Constant blame, or constant blamelessness.

There had to be better choices.

I did the best possible thing for me to do. I put in some earrings and went to church. Easter was over, but the flowers on the Methodist altar were still beautiful. The windows were open because the temperature was pleasant. A few clouds were gathering in the west, but nothing to worry about for the next few hours. I listened to every word of the sermon and I sang along with the hymns, though I kept that down to a whisper because I have a terrible voice. It was good for me; it reminded me of Gran and my childhood and faith and clean dresses and Sunday lunch, usually a roast surrounded by potatoes and carrots that Gran put in the oven before we left the house. She would have made a pie or a cake, too.

Church isn't always easy when you can read the minds around you, and I worked very hard on blocking them out and thinking my own thoughts in an attempt to connect to the part of my upbringing, the part of myself, that was good and kind and intent on trying to become better.

When the service was over, I talked to Maxine Fortenberry, who was in seventh heaven over Hoyt and Holly's wedding plans, and I saw Charlsie Tooten toting her grandbaby, and I talked to my insurance agent, Greg Aubert, who had his whole family with him. His daughter turned red when I looked at her, because I knew a few things about her that made her conscience twinge. But I wasn't judging the girl. We all misbehave from time to time. Some of us get caught, and some of us don't.

Sam was in church, too, to my surprise. I'd never seen him there before. As far as I knew, he'd never been to any church in Bon Temps.

"I'm glad to see you," I said, trying not to sound too startled. "You been going somewhere else, or is this a new venture?"

"I just felt it was time," he said. "For one thing, I like church. For another thing, a bad time is coming for us two-natured folks, and I want to make sure everyone in Bon Temps knows I'm an okay guy."

"They'd have to be fools not to know that already," I said quietly. "Good to see you, Sam." I moved off because a couple of people were waiting to talk to my boss, and I understood that he was trying to anchor his position in the community.

I tried not to worry about Eric or anything else the rest of the day. I'd had a text message inviting me to have lunch with Tara and JB, and I was glad to have their company. Tara had gotten Dr. Dinwiddie to check very carefully, and sure enough, he'd found another heartbeat. She and JB were stunned, in a happy way. Tara had fixed creamed chicken to spoon over biscuits, and she'd made a spinach casserole and a fruit salad. I had a great time at their little house, and JB checked my wrists and said they were almost back to normal. Tara was all excited about the baby shower JB's aunt was planning on giving them in Clarice, and she assured me I'd get an invitation. We picked a date for her shower in Bon Temps, and she promised she'd register online.

By the time I got home, I figured I'd better put a load of wash in, and I washed my bath mat, too, and hung it out on the line to dry. While I was outside, I made sure I had my little plastic squirt gun, full of lemon juice, tucked in my pocket. I didn't want to get caught by surprise again. I just couldn't figure out what I'd done to deserve having an apparently (judging by Claude's reaction) hostile fairy tromping around my property.

My cell phone rang as I trailed gloomily back to the house. "Hey, Sis," Jason said. He was cooking on the grill. I could hear the sizzle. "Michele and me are cooking out. You want to come? I got plenty of steak."

"Thanks, but I ate at JB and Tara's. Give me a rain check on that."

"Sure thing. I got your message. Tomorrow at eight, right?"

"Yeah. Let's ride over to Shreveport together."

"Sure. I'll pick you up at seven at your place."

"See you then."

"Gotta go!"

Jason did not like long phone conversations. He'd broken up with girls who wanted to chat while they shaved their legs and painted their nails.

It was not a great commentary on my life that the prospect of meeting with a bunch of unhappy Weres seemed like a good time—or at least an interesting time.

Kennedy was bartending when I got to work the next day. She told me that Sam had a final, take-the-checkbook appointment with his accountant, who'd gotten an extension since Sam had been so late turning all the paperwork over.

Kennedy looked as pretty as she always did. She refused to wear the shorts most of the rest of us wore in warm weather, instead opting for tailored khakis and a fancy belt with her Merlotte's T-shirt. Kennedy's makeup and hair were pageant quality. I glanced automatically at Danny Prideaux's usual barstool. Empty.

"Where's Danny?" I asked when I went to the bar to get a beer for Catfish Hennessy. He was Jason's boss, and I half expected to see Jason come in to join him, but Hoyt and a couple of the other roadwork guys sat at Catfish's table.

"He had to work at his other job today," Kennedy said, trying to sound offhand. "I appreciate Sam making sure I've got protection while I'm working, Sookie, but I really don't think there's going to be any trouble."

The bar door slammed. "I'm here to protest!" yelled a woman who looked like anyone's grandmother. She had a sign, and she hoisted it up. NO COHABITATION WITH ANI-MALS, it read, and you could see that she'd written "cohabitation" while she looked at a dictionary; each letter was written with such care.

"Call the police first," I told Kennedy. "And then Sam. Tell him to get back here no matter *what* he's talking about." Kennedy nodded and turned to the wall phone.

Our protester was wearing a blue and white blouse and red pants she'd probably gotten at Bealls or Stage. She had short permed hair dyed a reasonable brown and wore wire-rimmed glasses and a modest wedding ring on her arthritic fingers. Despite this completely average exterior, I could feel her thoughts burning with the fire of a zealot.

"Ma'am, you need to take yourself outside. This building is privately owned," I said, having no idea if this was a good line to take or not. We'd never had anyone protesting before.

"But it's a public business. Anyone can come inside," she said, as if she were the authority.

Not any more than I was. "No, not if Sam doesn't want them in here, and as his representative, I'm telling you to leave."

"You're not Sam Merlotte, or his wife. You're that girl who dates a vampire," she said venomously.

"I am Sam's right-hand person at this bar," I lied, "and I'm telling you to get out, or I'll put you out."

"You lay one finger on me, and I'll call the law on you," she said, jerking her head.

Rage flared up in me. I really, really don't like threats.

"Kennedy," I said, and in a second she was standing by me. "I'd say between us we're strong enough to pick up this lady and take her out of the bar. What do you say?"

"I'm all for it." Kennedy stared down at the woman as if she were only waiting for the starting gun to go off. "And you're that girl who shot her boyfriend," the woman said, beginning to look properly frightened.

"I am. I was really mad at him, and at the moment I'm pretty pissed off at you," Kennedy said. "You get your butt out of here and take your little sign with you, and you do it right now."

The older woman's courage broke, and she scuttled out, remembering at the last moment to keep her head up and her back straight since she was one of God's soldiers. I got that direct from her head.

Catfish clapped for Kennedy, and a few others joined in, but mostly the bar patrons sat in stunned silence. Then we heard the chanting from the parking lot, and we all surged to the windows.

"Jesus Christ, Shepherd of Judea," I breathed. There were at least thirty protesters in the parking lot. Most of them were middle-aged, but I spotted a few teenagers who should have been in school, and I recognized a couple of guys who I knew to be in their early twenties. I sort of recognized most of the crowd. They attended a "charismatic" church in Clarice, a church that was growing by leaps and bounds (if construction was any indicator). The last time I'd driven by when I was going to have physical therapy with JB, a new activities building had been going up.

I wished they were being active *there*, where they belonged, rather than here. Just as I was about to do something idiotic (like going out in the parking lot), two Bon Temps police cars pulled up, lights flashing. Kevin and Kenya got out. Kevin was skinny and white, and Kenya was round and black. They were both good police officers, and they loved each other dearly . . . but unofficially.

Kevin approached the chanting group with apparent confidence. I couldn't hear what he said, but they all turned to face him and began talking all at once. He held up his hands to pat the air in a "back off and get quiet" gesture, and Kenya circled around to come up behind the group.

"Maybe we should go out there?" Kennedy said.

Kennedy, I noted, was not in the habit of sitting back and letting things take their course. Nothing wrong with being proactive, but this was not the time to escalate the confrontation in the parking lot, and that was what our presence would do. "No, I think we need to stay right here," I said. "There's no point in throwing fuel on the fire." I looked around. None of the patrons were eating or drinking. They were all looking out the windows. I thought of requesting that they sit down at their tables, but there was no point in asking them to do something they clearly weren't going to do, with so much drama going on outside.

Antoine came out of the kitchen and stood by me. He looked at the scene for a long moment. "I didn't have nothing to do with it," he said.

"I never thought you did," I said, surprised. Antoine relaxed, even inside his head. "This is some crazy church action," I said. "They're picketing Merlotte's because Sam is two-natured. But the woman who came in here, she was pretty aware of me and she knew Kennedy's history, too. I hope this is a one-shot. I'd hate to have to deal with protesters all the time."

"Sam'll go broke if this keeps up," Kennedy said in a low voice. "Maybe I should just quit. It's not going to help Sam that I work here."

"Kennedy, don't set yourself up to be a martyr," I said. "They don't like me, either. Everyone who doesn't think I'm crazy thinks there's something supernatural about me. We'd all have to quit, from Sam on down."

She looked at me sharply to make sure I was sincere. She gave me a quick nod. Then she looked out the window again and said, "Uh-oh." Danny Prideaux had pulled up in his 1991 Chrysler LeBaron, a machine he found only slightly less fascinating than he found Kennedy Keyes.

Danny had parked right at the edge of the crowd, and he hopped out and began to hurry toward the bar. I just knew he was coming to check on Kennedy. Either they'd had a police band radio on at the home builders' supply place or Danny had heard the news from a customer. The jungle drums beat fast and furious in Bon Temps. Danny was wearing a gray tank top and jeans and boots, and his broad olive shoulders were gleaming with sweat.

As he strode toward the door, I said, "I think my mouth is watering." Kennedy put her hand over her mouth to stifle a yip of laughter.

"Yeah, he looks pretty good," she said, trying to sound offhand. We both laughed.

But then disaster struck. One of the protesters, angry at being shooed away from Merlotte's, brought his sign down on the hood of the LeBaron. At the sound Danny turned around. He froze for a second, and then he was heading at top speed toward the sinner who'd marred the paint job on his car.

"Oh, no," Kennedy said and hurtled out of the bar as if she'd been fired from a slingshot. "Danny!" she yelled. "Danny! You stop!"

Danny hesitated, turning his head just a fraction to see who was calling him. With a leap that would have done a kangaroo proud, Kennedy was beside him and wrapping her arms around him. He made an impatient movement, as if to shake her off, and then it seemed to dawn on him that Kennedy, whom he'd spent hours admiring, was embracing him. He stood stiffly, his arms at his side, apparently afraid to move.

I couldn't tell what Kennedy was saying to him, but Danny looked down at her face, completely focused on her. One of the demonstrators had forgotten herself enough to get an "Awww" expression on her face, but she snapped out of her lapse into humanity and brandished her sign again.

"Animals go! People stay! We want Congress to show the way!" one of the older demonstrators, a man with a lot of white hair, shouted as I opened the door and stepped out.

"Kevin, get them out of here!" I called. Kevin, whose thin, pale face was creased into unhappy lines, was trying to shepherd the little crowd out of the parking lot.

"Mr. Barlowe," Kevin said to the white-haired man, "what you're doing is illegal, and I could put you in jail. I really don't want to have to do that."

"We're willing to be arrested for our beliefs," the man said. "Isn't that so, you-all?"

Some of the church members didn't look entirely certain of that.

"Maybe you are," Kenya said, "but we got Jane Bodehouse in one of the cells now. She's coming off a bender, and she's throwing up about every five minutes. Believe me, people, you do *not* want to be in there with Jane."

The woman who'd originally come into Merlotte's turned a little green.

"This is private property," Kevin said. "You cannot demonstrate here. If you don't clear this parking lot in three minutes, all of you are under arrest."

It was more like five minutes, but the parking lot was clear of demonstrators when Sam joined us in the parking lot to thank Kevin and Kenya. Since I hadn't seen his truck drive up, his appearance was quite a surprise.

"When did you get back?" I asked.

"Less than ten minutes ago," he said. "I knew if I showed myself, they'd just get pumped up again, so I parked on School Street and walked through the back way."

"Smart," I said. The lunch crowd was leaving Merlotte's, and the incident was already on the track to becoming a local legend. Only one or two of the patrons seemed upset; the rest regarded the demonstration as good entertainment. Catfish Hennessy clapped Sam on the shoulder as he went by, and he wasn't the only one who made an extra effort to show support. I wondered how long the tolerant attitude would last. If the picketers kept it up, a lot of people might decide that coming here simply wasn't worth the trouble.

I didn't need to say any of this out loud. It was written on Sam's face. "Hey," I said, slinging an arm around his shoulders. "They'll go away. You know what you should do? You should call the pastor of that church. They're all from Holy Word Tabernacle in Clarice. You should tell him that you want to come talk to the church. Show them you're a person just like everyone else. I bet that would work."

Then I realized how stiff his shoulders were. Sam was rigid with anger. "I should not have to tell anyone anything," he said. "I'm a citizen of this country. My father was in the army.

I was in the army. I pay my share of taxes. And I'm *not* a person like everyone else. I'm a shifter. And they need to just put that on their plates and eat it." He whirled to go back into his bar.

I flinched, though I knew his anger wasn't directed at me. As I watched Sam stalk away, I reminded myself that none of this was about me. But I couldn't help but feel I had a stake in the outcome of this new development. Not only did I work at Merlotte's, but the woman who'd come in initially had named me as part of the problem.

Furthermore, I still thought approaching the church in person was a good idea. It was reasonable and civil.

Sam wasn't in a reasonable and civil mood, and I could understand that. I just didn't know where he was going to put his anger.

A newspaper reporter came in an hour later and interviewed all of us about "the incident," as he called it. Errol Clayton was a guy in his forties who wrote about half the stories in the little Bon Temps paper. He didn't own it, but he managed it on a shoestring budget. I had no issue with the paper, but of course lots of folks made fun of it. The *Bon Temps Bugle* was frequently called the *Bon Temps Bungle*.

While Errol was waiting for Sam to finish a phone call, I said, "You want a drink, Mr. Clayton?"

"I'd sure appreciate some iced tea, Sookie," he said. "How's that brother of yours?"

"He's doing well."

"Getting over the death of his wife?"

"I think he's come to terms with it," I said, which covered all sorts of ground. "That was a terrible thing."

"Yes, very bad. And it was right here in this parking lot,"

Errol Clayton said, as if I might have forgotten. "And right here, in this parking lot, was where the body of Lafayette Reynold was found."

"That's true, too. But of course, none of that was Sam's fault, or had anything to do with him."

"Never arrested anyone for Crystal's death that I recall."

I reared back to give Errol Clayton a hard stare. "Mr. Clayton, if you've come here to make trouble, you can just leave now. We need things to be better, not worse. Sam is a good man. He goes to the Rotary, he puts an ad in the high school yearbook, he sponsors a baseball team at the Boys and Girls Club every spring, and he helps with the Fourth of July fireworks. Plus, he's a great boss, a veteran, and a tax-paying citizen."

"Merlotte, you got you a fan club," Errol Clayton said to Sam, who'd come to stand right behind me.

"I've got a friend," Sam said quietly. "I'm lucky enough to have a lot of friends and a good business. I sure would hate to see that ruined." I heard an apology in his voice, and I felt his hand pat my shoulder. Feeling much better, I slipped away to do my job, leaving Sam to talk to the newspaperman.

I didn't get a chance to talk to my boss again before I left to go home. I had to stop at the store because I needed a couple of things—Claude had made inroads into my potato chip stash and my cereal, too—and I wasn't just imagining that the store was full of people who were busy talking about what had happened at lunchtime at Merlotte's. There was silence every time I came around a corner, but of course that didn't make any difference to me. I could tell what people were thinking.

Most of them didn't share the beliefs of the demonstrators.

But the mere fact of the incident had set some of the previously indifferent townspeople to thinking about the issue of the two-natured, and about the legislation that proposed to take away some of their rights.

And some of them were all for it.

Chapter 13

Jason was on time, and I climbed up into his truck. I'd changed into blue jeans and a pale blue thin T-shirt I'd bought at Old Navy. It said PEACE in golden Gothic letters. I hoped I didn't look like I was hinting. Jason, in an ever-appropriate New Orleans Saints T-shirt, looked ready for anything.

"Hey, Sook!" He was buzzing with happy anticipation. He'd never been to a Were meeting, of course, and he wasn't aware of how dangerous they could be. Or maybe he was, and that was why he was so excited.

"Jason, I got to tell you a few things about Were gatherings," I said.

"Okay," he said, a bit more soberly.

Aware that I sounded more like his know-it-all older sister instead of his younger sister, I gave him a little lecture. I told Jason that the Weres were touchy, proud, and protocol minded; explained how the Weres could abjure a pack member; emphasized the fact that Basim was a newer pack member who'd been trusted with a position of great responsibility. That he'd betrayed that trust would make the pack even touchier, and they might question Alcide's judgment in picking Basim as enforcer. He might even be challenged. The pack judgment on Annabelle was impossible to predict. "Something pretty awful may happen to her," I warned Jason. "We got to suck it up and accept it."

"You're saying they might physically punish a woman because she cheated on the packleader with another pack officer?" Jason said. "Sookie, you're talking to me like I'm not two-natured, too. You think I don't know all that?"

He was right. That was exactly how I'd been treating him.

I took a deep breath. "I apologize, Jason. I still think about you as my human brother. I don't always remember that you're a lot more. In all honesty, I'm scared. I've seen them kill people before, like I've seen your panthers kill and maim people when they thought that was justice. What scares me is not that you do it, which is bad enough, but that I've come to accept it as just . . . the way you do things if you're two-natured. When those demonstrators were at the bar today, I was so mad at them for hating Weres and shifters without really knowing anything about them. But now I'm wondering how they'd feel if they actually knew more about how packs work; how Gran would feel if she knew I was willing to watch a woman, or anyone, be beaten and maybe killed for an infraction of some rules I don't live by."

Jason was silent for what seemed like a long time. "I think the fact that a few days have passed is a good thing. It's given Alcide time to cool off. I hope the other pack members have had time to think, too," he said finally. And I knew that was all we could say about this, and maybe more than I should have said. We fell silent for a short time.

"Can't you listen in to what they're thinking?" Jason asked.

"Full Weres are pretty hard to read. Some are harder than others. Of course, I'll see what I can get. I can block a lot when I make myself, but if I let my guard down . . ." I shrugged. "This is a case where I want to know everything I can as soon as I can."

"Who do you think killed that dude in the grave?"

"I've given it some thought," I said gently. "I see three main possibilities. But the key to me suspecting all three is that he was buried on my land, and I have to assume that wasn't by chance."

Jason nodded.

"Okay, here goes. Maybe Victor, the new vamp leader of Louisiana, killed Basim. Victor wants to knock Eric out of his position, since Eric's a sheriff. That's a pretty important position."

Jason looked at me like I was an idiot. "I may not know all their fancy titles and all their little secret handshakes," he said, "but I know someone in charge when I see him. If you say this Victor outranks Eric and wants him gone, I believe you."

I had to stop underestimating my brother's shrewdness. "Maybe Victor thought that if I got arrested for murder— since someone tipped off the law that there was a body on my land—Eric would go down with me. Maybe Victor thought that would be enough for their mutual boss to take Eric out of his position."

"Wouldn't it have been better to put the body in Eric's house and call the police?"

"That's a good point. But finding a body in Eric's house

would mean bad press for all vampires. Another idea I had, maybe the killer was Annabelle, who was screwing both Basim and Alcide. Maybe she got jealous, or maybe Basim said he was going to tell. So she killed him, and since they'd just been on my land, she thought of it as a good place to bury a body."

"That's a long way to drive with a body in the trunk," Jason said. He was clearly going to play devil's advocate.

"Sure, it's easy to punch holes in all my ideas," I said, sounding exactly like his little sister. "Once I go to all the work of coming up with them! But you're right. That'd be a risk I wouldn't want to take," I added, on a more mature level.

"Alcide could've done it," Jason said.

"Yeah. He could've. But you were there. Did it seem to you—remotely—like he knew it was going to be Basim?"

"No," he said. "I thought he got a huge shock. But I wasn't looking at Annabelle."

"I wasn't, either. So I don't know how she reacted."

"So you got any other ideas?"

"Yeah," I said. "And this is my least favorite. You know I told you that Heidi the vampire scented fairies in the woods?"

"I did, too," Jason said.

"Maybe I should get you to check out the woods on a regular basis," I said. "Anyway, Claude said it wasn't him, and Heidi confirmed that. But what if Basim saw Claude meeting with another fairy? In the area around the house, where Claude's scent would be natural?"

"When would this have happened?"

"The night the pack was on the property. Claude hadn't moved in then, but he'd come around to see me."

I could see Jason trying to figure out the sequence. "So Basim warned you about the fairies he tracked, but he didn't tell you he'd seen some? I don't think that holds together, Sook."

"You're right," I admitted. "And we still don't know who the other fairy would be. If there are two, and one of them isn't Claude, and the other one is Dermot . . ."

"That leaves one fairy we don't know about."

"Dermot's seriously messed up, Jason."

Jason said, "I'm worried about *all* of 'em."

"Even Claude?"

"Look, how come he showed up now? When you have other fairies in the woods? And does that sound crazy when you say it out loud, or what?"

I laughed. Just a little. "Yeah, it sounds nuts. And I get your point. I don't entirely trust Claude, even if he is a little bit family. I wish I hadn't said yes to him moving in. On the other hand, I don't believe he means to hurt me or you. And he's not *quite* as much of an asshole as I thought he was."

We tried to put together a few more theories about Basim's death, but we could punch too many holes in all of our theories. It passed the time until we arrived.

The house Alcide had moved into when his dad died was a large two-story brick home on large grounds, enhanced with impressive landscaping. The—estate? manor house?—was in a very nice area of Shreveport, of course. In fact, it wasn't too far from Eric's neighborhood. That gnawed at me, thinking of Eric so close to me but in so much trouble.

The confusion of what I was feeling through our blood bond was making me more jittery with every passing night. There were so many people sharing in that bond now, so much feeling going back and forth. It wore me out emotionally. Alexei was the worst. He was a very dead little boy, that was the only way I could put it: a child locked in a permanent grayness, a child who experienced only occasional flashes of pleasure and color in his new "life." After days of experiencing what amounted to an echo of him living in my head, I'd decided the boy was like a tick sucking on the life of Appius Livius, Eric, and now me. He siphoned off a little every day.

Apparently, Appius Livius was so used to Alexei's draining him that he accepted it as part of his existence. Maybe— possibly—the Roman felt responsible for the trouble Alexei caused, since he'd brought him over. If that was Appius Livius's conviction, I thought he was absolutely correct. I was sure that bringing Alexei to Eric, thinking the presence of another "child" would soothe Alexei's psychosis, was a last-ditch effort to cure the boy. And Eric, my lover, was caught in the middle of all this along with all the problems he was staving off involving Victor.

I felt less and less like a good person every day. As we walked from the driveway to Alcide's front door, I admitted to myself that since my visit to Fangtasia, I found myself wishing that all of them would die—Appius Livius, Alexei, Victor.

I had to shove all that into a mental corner, because I had to be on my game to enter a house full of Weres. Jason put his arm around my shoulders and gave me a half hug. "Sometime you'll have to explain to me how come we're doing this," he said. "Because I think I kind of forgot."

I laughed, which was what he'd wanted. I put up a hand to ring the bell, but the door swung open before my finger-tip made contact. Jannalynn was standing there in a sports bra and running shorts. (She always came up with wardrobe choices that startled me.) The running shorts showed concave dips by her hipbones, and I sighed. "Concave" was not a word I'd ever used in relation to my body.

"Getting into the new job?" Jason asked her, stepping

forward. Jannalynn had to either back up or block his way, and she chose to back up.

"I was born for this job," the young Were said.

I had to agree. Jannalynn seemed to love doling out violence. At the same time, I wondered what job she could hold in the real world. She'd been bartending at a Were-owned bar in Shreveport when I'd first seen her, and I knew the owner of that bar had died in the struggle between the packs. "Where are you working now, Jannalynn?" I asked, since there shouldn't be any need to keep that secret that I could see.

"I manage the Hair of the Dog. The ownership passed to Alcide, and he felt I could handle the job. I have some help," she said, which was a confession that surprised me.

Ham, his arm around a pretty brunette in a sundress, was waiting across the foyer by the opened doors to the living room. He patted my shoulder and introduced his companion as Patricia Crimmins. I recognized her as one of the women who'd joined the Long Tooth pack in surrender after the Were war, and I tried to focus on her. But my attention kept straying. Patricia laughed and said, "It's quite a place, isn't it?"

I nodded in silent agreement. I'd never been in the house before, and my eyes were drawn to the French doors on the other side of the big room. There were lights out in the large backyard, which not only was enclosed by a fence that had to be seven feet tall, but was also lined outside with those quick-growing cypresses that shoot up like spears. In the middle of the patio was a fountain, which would make getting a drink easy if you'd turned into a wolf. There was a lot of wrought iron furniture set around on the flagstones, too. Wow. I'd known the Herveauxes were well-to-do, but this was impressive.

The living room itself was very "men's club," all glossy dark leather and paneling, and the fireplace was as big as fireplaces got in this day and age. There were animal heads mounted on the walls, which I thought was kind of amusing. Everyone seemed to have a drink in hand, and I located the bar at the center of the thickest cluster of Weres. I didn't spot Alcide, who because of his height and his presence was usually a standout in any crowd.

I spotted Annabelle. She was in the center of the room on her knees, though she was not constrained in any way. There was an empty space all around her.

"Don't approach," Ham said quietly as I took a step forward. I stopped in my tracks.

"You can talk to her later, probably," Patricia whispered. It was the "probably" that bothered me. But this was pack business, and I was on pack land.

"I'm getting me a beer," Jason said after he'd had a good look at Annabelle's situation. "What do you want, Sook?"

"You need to go upstairs," Jannalynn said very quietly. "Don't drink anything else. Alcide's got a drink for you." She jerked her head toward the stairs to my left. I puckered my brows together, and Jason looked as though he were going to protest, but she jerked her head again.

I found Alcide in a study at the head of the stairs. He was looking out the window. There was a glass of cloudy yellow liquid sitting on the desk blotter.

"What?" I said. I was getting an even worse feeling about this evening than I'd already had.

He turned to face me. His black hair was still in a tumble, and he could have used a shave, but grooming had nothing to do with the charisma that surrounded him like a cocoon. I didn't know if the role had enhanced the man, or if the man had grown into the role, but Alcide had come far from the charming, friendly guy I'd met two winters ago.

"We don't have a shaman anymore," he said with no pre-amble. "We haven't had one for four years. It's hard to find a Were who's willing to take the position, and you have to have the talent for it to even consider it anyway."

"Okay," I said, waiting to see where he was going.

"You're the closest we've got."

If there'd been drums in the background, they would've started an ominous roll. "I'm not a shaman," I said. "In fact, I don't know what a shaman is. And you don't have me."

"That's a term we use for a medicine man or woman," Alcide said. "One with a gift for interpreting and applying magic. It sounded better to us than 'witch.' And this way, we know who we're talking about. If we had a pack shaman, that shaman would drink the stuff in this glass and be able to help us determine the truth of what happened to Basim, and the degree of guilt of everyone involved. Then the pack would decide on proportionate justice."

"What is it?" I asked, pointing at the liquid.

"It's what was left over in the last shaman's stash."

"What is it?"

"It's a drug," he said. "But before you walk out, let me tell you that the last shaman took it several times without any lasting ill effect."

"Lasting."

"Well, he had stomach cramps the next day. But he was able to go back to work the day after that."

"Of course, he was a Were, and he'd be able to eat things I can't eat anyway. What does it do to you? Or rather, what would it do to me?"

"It gives you a different perception of reality. That's what the guy told me. And since I clearly wasn't shaman material, that's *all* he told me."

"Why would I take an unknown drug?" I asked, genuinely curious.

"Because otherwise we'll never get to the bottom of this," Alcide said. "Right now, the only guilty person I can see is Annabelle. She may only be guilty of being unfaithful to me. I hate that, but she doesn't deserve to die for it. But if I can't find out who killed Basim and planted him in your ground, I think the pack will condemn her, since she's the only one who was involved with him. I guess I'd be a good suspect for killing Basim out of jealousy. But I could have done it legally, and I wouldn't have blamed you."

I knew that was true.

"They'll put her to death," he said, harping on the point that would have the most effect on me.

I was almost tough enough to shrug. Almost.

"Can't I try to do this my way?" I said. "Laying my hands on them?"

"You've told me yourself it's hard to get a clear thought from Weres." Alcide said it almost sadly. "Sookie, I'd hoped we'd be a couple one day. Now that I'm packmaster and you're in love with that cold ass Eric, I guess that'll never happen. I thought we might have a chance because you couldn't read my thoughts that clearly. Since I know that, I don't think I can rely on you laying on your hands and getting an accurate reading."

He was right.

"A year ago," I said, "you wouldn't have asked this of me."

"A year ago," he answered, "you wouldn't have hesitated to drink."

I crossed to the desk and tossed it down.

Chapter 14

*I went down the stairs on Alcide's arm. I was already feel-*ing a little swimmy in the head, having taken an illegal drug for the first time in my life.

I was an idiot.

However, I was an increasingly warm and comfortable idiot. A delightful side effect of the shaman's drink was that I couldn't feel Eric and Alexei and Appius Livius with nearly as much immediacy, and the relief was incredible.

A less pleasant side effect was that my legs didn't feel quite real underneath me. Maybe that was why Alcide was keeping such a tight grip on my arm. I remembered what he'd said about his former hope that we'd be a couple one day, and I thought it might be nice to kiss him and remind myself what it felt like. Then I realized I'd better channel those warm and fuzzy feelings into finding out the answers to the puzzles fac-ing Alcide. I directed my feelings, which was an excellent deci-sion. I was so proud of my excellence I could have rolled in it.

The shaman had probably known a few tricks for keeping all this dreaminess focused on the matter at hand. I made a huge effort to sharpen up. In my absence, the group in the living room had swollen in numbers; the whole pack was here. I could feel the totality of it, the completeness.

Eyes turned to look at us as we descended the stairs. Jason looked alarmed, but I gave him a reassuring smile. Something must have been off about it, because his face didn't smooth out.

Alcide's second went to stand by the kneeling Annabelle. Jannalynn threw back her head and gave a series of yips. Now I was standing by my brother, and he was holding on to me. Somehow, Alcide had passed me over to Jason's keeping.

"Geez," Jason muttered. "What's wrong with waving your hand in the air or ringing a triangle?" I could assume yipping was not a summons in the panther pride. That was okay. I smiled at Jason. I felt a lot like Alice in Wonderland after she took a bite of the mushroom.

I was on one side of the empty space around Annabelle, Alcide on the other. He looked around to collect the pack's attention. "We're here tonight with two visitors to decide what to do about Annabelle," he said without a preamble. "We're here to judge whether she had anything to do with the death of Basim, or if that death can be laid at the door of anyone else."

"Why are there visitors?" asked a woman's voice. I tried to find her face, but she was standing so far in the back I couldn't see her. I estimated there were perhaps as many as forty people in the room, ranging in age from sixteen (the change began after puberty) to seventy. Ham and Patricia were to my left, about a quarter of the circle away. Jannalynn had stayed by Annabelle. The few other pack members I knew by name were scattered through the crowd.

"Listen hard," Alcide said, looking directly at me. *Okay, Alcide, message received.* I closed my eyes, and I listened. Well, this was abso-fucking-lutely amazing. I found I knew when his gaze swept the assembled pack members by the ripple of fear that followed. I could *see* the fear. It was dark yellow. "Basim's body was found on Sookie's land," Alcide said. "It was planted there in an attempt to blame her for his death. The police came to search for it right after we removed it."

There was a general surge of surprise . . . from almost everyone.

"You moved the body?" Patricia said. My eyes flew open. Why had Alcide elected to keep that a secret? Because it had been a total shock to Patricia, and to a few others, that Basim's body was *not* still in the clearing. Jason moved up behind me and put his beer down. He knew he needed his hands free. My brother might not be a mental giant, but he had good instincts.

I was amazed at Alcide's cleverness in setting up the scene. I might not get Were thoughts that clearly, but Were emotions . . . That was what he was after. Now that I was concentrating, focusing on the creatures in the room, almost out of my body with the intensity of it, I saw Alcide as a ball of red energy, pulsing and attractive, and all the other Weres were circling around him. I understood for the first time that the packleader was the planet around which all others orbited in the Were universe. The pack members were various shades of red and violet and pink, the colors of their devotion to him. Jannalynn was a blazing streak of intense crimson, her adoration making her almost as bright as Alcide himself. Even Annabelle was a watery cerise, despite her infidelity.

But there were a few spots of green. I held my hand out in front of me as if I were telling the rest of the world to stop while I considered this new interpretation of perception.

"Tonight Sookie is our shaman," Alcide's voice boomed from a distance. I could safely ignore that. I could follow the colors, because they betrayed the person.

Green, look for the green. Though my head remained still and my eyes closed, I turned them somehow to look at the green people. Ham was green. Patricia was green. I looked the other way. There was one more green one, but he fluctuated between pale yellow and faint green. Ha! *Ambivalent,* I told myself wisely. *Not a traitor yet, but doubtful about Alcide's leadership.* The wavering image belonged to a young male, and I dismissed him as insignificant. I looked at Annabelle again. Cerise still, but flickering with amber as her intense fear broke through her loyalty.

I opened my eyes. What was I supposed to say—"They're green, get them!"? I found myself moving, drifting through the pack like a balloon through the trees. Finally, I was right in front of Ham and Patricia. This was where the hands would come in handy. Ha! That was funny! I laughed a little.

"Sookie?" Ham said. Patricia shrank back, letting go of him.

"Don't go anywhere, Patricia," I said, smiling at her. She flinched, ready to run, but a dozen hands grabbed her and held her firmly. I looked up at Ham and put my fingers on his cheeks. If I'd had some finger paint, he'd have looked like a movie Indian on the warpath. "So jealous," I said. "Ham, you told Alcide there were people camping on the stream and that was why the pack needed to run in my woods. You invited those men, didn't you?"

"They—no."

"Oh, I see," I said, touching the tip of his nose. "I see." I could hear his thoughts as clearly as if I were inside his head now. "So they *were* from the government. They were trying to gather information on the Were packs in Louisiana and anything bad the packs might have done. They asked you to bribe an enforcer, a second. To describe all the bad stuff he'd done. So they could push through that bill, the one that'll require you-all to register like aliens. Hamilton Bond—shame on you! You told them to force Basim to tell them stuff, the stuff that had gotten him kicked out of the Houston pack."

"None of this is true, Alcide," Ham said. He was trying to sound all Big Serious Man, but to me he sounded like a squeaky little mouse. "Alcide, I've known you my whole life."

"And you thought that Alcide would make you his second," I said. "Instead, he picked Basim, who already had a track record as an enforcer."

"He got thrown out of Houston," Ham said. "That's how bad he was." The anger broke through, pulsing in gold and black.

"I'd ask him, and I'd know the truth, but I can't now, right? Because you killed him and put him in the cold, cold ground." Actually, it hadn't been all that cold, but I felt I was due a little artistic license. My mind soared and swooped, way above everything. I could see so much! I felt like God. This was fun.

"I didn't kill Basim! Well, maybe I did, but it was because he was screwing our packleader's girlfriend! I couldn't stomach such disloyalty!"

"Beep! Try again!" I fanned my fingers over his cheeks. We needed to know something else, didn't we? Some other question had to be answered.

"He met with a creature in your woods on our moon night," Ham blurted. "He, I don't know what he talked about."

"What kind of creature?"

"I don't know. Some guy. Some . . . I've never seen anything like him. He was really handsome. Like a movie star or something. He had long hair, really pale long hair, and he was there one minute and gone the next. He talked to Basim while Basim was in his wolf form. Basim was by himself. After we ate the deer, I'd fallen asleep on the other side of some laurel bushes. When I woke up, I heard them talking. The other guy was trying to frame you for something because you'd done something to him. I don't know what. Basim was going to kill someone and bury him on your land, and then call the cops. That would take care of you, and then the fair . . ." Ham's voice died away.

"You knew it was a fairy," I said, smiling at Ham. "You knew. So you decided to do the job first."

"It wasn't something Alcide would have wanted Basim to do, right, Alcide?"

Alcide didn't answer, but he was pulsating like a sky-rocket on the periphery of my vision.

"And you told Patricia. And she helped," I said, stroking his face. He wanted to make me stop, but he didn't dare.

"Her sister died in the war! She couldn't accept her new pack. I was the only one who was nice to her, she said."

"Aw, you're so generous to be nice to the pretty Were woman," I said mockingly. "Good Ham! Instead of Basim killing someone and burying them, you killed Basim and buried him. Instead of Basim getting a reward from the fairy, you thought you would get a reward from the fairy. Because fairies are rich, right?" I let my nails dig into his cheek. "Basim wanted the money to get out from under the government guys. You wanted the money just because you wanted the money."

"Basim owed a blood debt in Houston," Ham said. "Basim wouldn't have talked to the anti-Were people for any reason. I can't go to my death with that lie on my soul. Basim wanted to pay off the debt he owed for killing a human who was a friend of the pack. It was an accident, while Basim was in wolf form. The human poked him with a hoe, and Basim killed him."

"I knew about that," Alcide said. He hadn't spoken until now. "I told Basim I would loan him the money."

"I guess he wanted to earn it himself," Ham said miserably. (Misery, I learned, was deep purple.) "He thought he'd meet with the fairy again, find out exactly what the fairy wanted him to do, get a body from a mortuary or a drunk's body from some alley, and plant it on Sookie's land. That would fulfill the letter of what the fairy wanted. No harm would have been done. But instead, I decided . . ." He began sobbing, and his color turned all washed-out gray, the color of faded faith.

"Where were you going to meet him?" I asked. "To get your money? Which you had earned, I'm not saying you didn't." I was proud of how fair I was being. Fairness was blue, of course.

"I was going to meet him at the same spot in your woods," he said. "On the south side by the cemetery. Later tonight."

"Very good," I murmured. "Don't you feel better now?"

"Yes," he said, without a trace of irony in his voice. "I do feel better, and I'm ready to accept the judgment of the pack."

"I'm not," Patricia cried. "I escaped death in the pack war by surrendering. Let me surrender again!" She fell to her knees, like Annabelle. "I beg forgiveness. I'm only guilty of loving the wrong man." Like Annabelle. Patricia bowed her head, and her dark braid fell over one shoulder. She put her clasped hands to her face. Pretty as a picture.

"You didn't love me," Ham said, genuinely shocked. "We *screwed*. You were upset with Alcide because he didn't pick you to bed. I was upset with Alcide because he didn't pick me as his second. That was the sum total of what we had in common!"

"Their colors are certainly getting brighter *now*," I observed. The passion of their mutual accusation was perking up their auras to something combustible. I tried to summarize to myself what I'd learned, but it all came out a jumble. Maybe Jason could help me sort it out later. This shaman stuff was kind of taxing. I felt that soon I would be depleted, as if the end of a race were in sight. "Time to decide," I said, looking at Alcide, whose brilliant red glow was still steady.

"I think Annabelle should be disciplined but not cast out of the pack," Alcide said, and there was a chorus of protest.

"Kill her!" said Jannalynn, her fierce little face determined. She was so ready to do the killing. I wondered if Sam really understood what he'd bitten off in going out with such a ferocious thing. He seemed so far away now.

"This is my reasoning," Alcide said calmly. The room quieted as the pack listened. "According to them," and he pointed at Ham and Patricia, "Annabelle's only guilt is a moral one, in sleeping with two men at the same time while telling one of them she was faithful. We don't know what she told Basim."

Alcide spoke the truth . . . at least, the truth as he saw it. I looked at Annabelle and saw her all: the disciplined woman who was in the Air Force, the practical woman who balanced her pack life with the rest of her life, the woman who lost all her practicality and restraint when it came to sex. Annabelle was a rainbow of colors right now, none of them happy except the vibrating white line of relief that Alcide did not plan to kill her.

"As for Ham and Patricia. Ham is the murderer of a pack member. Instead of an open challenge, he took the path of stealth. That would call for severe punishment, maybe death. We should consider that Basim was a traitor—not only a pack member, but a second, who was willing to deal with someone outside the pack, to plot against the pack interests and against the good name of a friend of the pack," Alcide continued.

"Oh," I murmured to Jason. "That's me."

"And Patricia, who promised to be loyal to this pack, broke her vow," Alcide said. "So she should be cast out forever."

"Packmaster, you're too merciful," Jannalynn said vehemently. "Ham clearly deserves death for his disloyalty. Ham, at least."

There was a long silence, broken by a growing buzz of discussion. I looked around the room, seeing the color of thoughtfulness (brown, of course) turning into all kinds of shades as passions rose. Jason put his arms around me from behind. "You need to back out of this," he whispered, and I could see his words turn pink and curly. He loved me. I put a hand over my mouth so I wouldn't laugh out loud. We stepped backward; one step, two, three, four, five. Then we were standing in the foyer.

"We need to leave," Jason said. "If they're going to kill two good-looking gals like Annabelle and Patricia, I don't want to be around to see it. If we don't see anything, we won't have to testify in court, if it comes to that."

"They won't debate long. I think Annabelle will see tomorrow. Alcide will let Jannalynn persuade him to kill Ham and Patricia," I said. "His colors tell me so."

Jason gaped at me. "I don't know what you took or smoked or inhaled upstairs," he said, "but you need to get out of here now."

"Okay," I said, and suddenly I realized I felt pretty damn bad. I made it outside to Alcide's shrubbery before I threw up. I waited for the second wave to roll over me before I risked getting into Jason's truck.

"What would Gran say about me leaving before I saw the results of what I'd done?" I asked him sadly. "I left after the Were war when Alcide was celebrating his victory. I don't know how you panthers celebrate, but believe me, I didn't want to be around when he fucked one of the Weres. It was bad enough seeing Jannalynn execute the wounded. On the other hand . . ." I lost my train of thought in another wave of sickness, though this one wasn't as violent.

"Gran would say you're not obliged to watch people kill each other, and you didn't cause it, they did," Jason said briskly. I could tell that my brother, though sympathetic, wasn't thrilled about driving me all the way home with my stomach so jittery.

"Listen, can I just drop you by Eric's?" he said. "I know he's gotta have a bathroom or two, and that way my truck can stay clean."

Under any other circumstances I would have refused, since Eric was in such a charged situation. But I felt shaky, and I was still seeing colors. I chewed two antacids from the glove compartment and rinsed my mouth out repeatedly with some Sprite Jason had in the truck. I had to agree that it would be better if I could spend the night in Shreveport.

"I can come back and get you in the morning," Jason offered. "Or maybe his day guy can give you a ride to Bon Temps."

Bobby Burnham would rather transport a flock of turkeys.

While I hesitated, I discovered that now that I wasn't surrounded by Weres, I felt the misery rolling through the blood bond. It was the strongest, most active emotion I'd felt from Eric in days. The misery began to swell as unhappiness and physical pain overwhelmed him.

Jason opened his mouth to ask questions about what I'd taken before the pack meeting. "Get me to Eric's," I said. "Quick, Jason. Something's wrong."

"There, too?" he said plaintively, but we roared out of Alcide's driveway.

I was practically shaking with anxiety when we stopped at the gate so Dan the security guard could give me a look. He hadn't recognized Jason's truck.

"I'm here to see Eric, and this is my brother," I said, trying to act normal.

"Go on through," Dan said, smiling. "It's been a while."

When we pulled into Eric's driveway, I saw that his garage door was open, though the garage light was off. In fact, the house was in total darkness. Maybe everyone was over at Fangtasia. Nope. I knew Eric was there. I simply knew it.

"I don't like this," I said, and sat up a little straighter. I struggled against the effects of the drug. Though I was a little closer to normal since I'd been sick, I still felt as though I were experiencing the world through gauze.

"He don't leave it open?" Jason peered out over his steering wheel.

"No, he *never* leaves it open. And look! The kitchen door is open, too." I got out of the truck, and I heard Jason get out on his side. His truck lights stayed on automatically for a few seconds, so I got to the kitchen door easily enough. I always knocked at Eric's door if he didn't expect me, because I never knew who would be there or what they'd be talking about, but this time I simply pushed the door even wider. I could see a short distance into the kitchen because of the truck lights. The wrongness rolled out in a cloud, that feeling a mixture of the sense I'd been born with and the extra layer of senses the drug had imparted. I was glad Jason was right behind me. I could hear his breathing, way too fast and noisy.

"Eric," I said, very quietly.

No one answered. There was no sound of any kind.

I stepped into the kitchen just as Jason's truck lights went off. There were streetlights out on the street, and they supplied a dim glow. "Eric?" I called. "Where are you?" Tension made my voice crack. Something was awfully wrong.

"In here," he said from farther in the house, and my heart clenched.

"Thank you, God," I said, and my hand went out to the wall switch. I flicked it down, flooding the room with light. I looked around. The kitchen was pristine, as always.

So the awful things hadn't happened here.

I crept from the kitchen into Eric's big living room. I knew immediately that someone had died here. There were bloodstains everywhere. Some of them were still wet. Some of them dripped. I heard Jason's breath catch in his throat.

Eric was sitting on the couch, his head in his hands. There was no one else alive in the room.

Though the smell of blood was almost choking me, I was by him in a second. "Honey?" I said. "Look at me."

When he raised his head, I could see a terrible gash across his forehead. He'd bled copiously from the head wound. There was dried blood all over his face. When he straightened, I could see the blood on his white shirt. The head wound was healing, but the other one . . . "What's under the shirt?" I said.

"My ribs are broken and they've come through," he said. "They'll heal, but it'll take time. You'll have to push them back into place."

"Tell me what's happened," I said, trying very hard to sound calm. Of course, he knew I wasn't.

"Dead guy over here," Jason called. "Human."

"Who is it, Eric?" I eased his bare feet up onto the sofa so he could lie down.

"It's Bobby," he said. "I tried to get him out of here in time, but he was so sure there was something he could do to help me." Eric sounded incredibly tired.

"Who killed him?" I hadn't even scanned for other beings in this house, and I almost gasped at my own carelessness.

"Alexei snapped," Eric said. "Tonight he left his room when Ocella came in here to talk to me. I knew Bobby was still in the house, but I simply didn't think about his being in danger. Felicia was here, too, and Pam."

"Why was Felicia here?" I asked, because Eric didn't ask his staff to his house, as a rule. Felicia, the Fangtasia bartender, had been lowest on the vampire totem pole.

"She was dating Bobby. He had some papers I needed to sign, and she'd just come over with him."

"So Felicia . . . ?"

"Part of a vampire left over here," Jason called. "Looks like the rest has flaked away."

"She's gone to her final death," Eric told me.

"Oh, I'm so sorry!" I put my arms around him, and after a second, his shoulders relaxed. I had never seen Eric so defeated. Even the awful night we'd been surrounded by the vampires of Las Vegas and forced to surrender to Victor, the night he'd thought we might all die, he'd had that spark of determination and vigor. But at the moment he was literally overwhelmed with depression and anger and helplessness. Thanks to his damn *maker*, whose ego had required he bring back a traumatized boy from the dead.

"Where's Alexei now?" I asked, making my voice as brisk as I could manage. "Where's Appius? Is he still alive?" To hell with the two-name requirement. I thought it would be great if Alexei had been helpful enough to kill the old vampire, save me the trouble.

"I don't know." Eric sounded completely defeated.

"Why not?" I was genuinely shocked. "He's your maker, buddy! You'd know if he died. If I've been feeling you three for a week, I know you've been feeling him even stronger." Judith had said she'd felt a tug the day of Lorena's death, though she hadn't understood what it meant. Eric had been alive for so long, maybe it would actually cause him physical harm if Appius died. In a snap, I completely reversed my thinking. Appius should live until Eric recovered from his wounds. "You need to get out of here and go find him!"

"He asked me not to follow when he went after Alexei. He doesn't want us all to die."

"So you're just going to sit home because he said so? When you don't know where they are or what they're doing, or who they're doing it to?" I didn't know what I wanted Eric to actually do. The drug was still coasting through my system, though it was slightly weaker—I was only seeing colors where they shouldn't be every now and then. But I had very little control over my thoughts and my speech. I was simply trying to get Eric to act like Eric. And I wanted him to stop bleeding. And I wanted Jason to come push Eric's bones back in because I could see them sticking out.

"Ocella asked this of me," Eric said, and he glared at me.

"So, he *asked*? That doesn't sound like a direct order to me. It sounds like a request. Correct me if I'm wrong," I said, as snarkily as I could.

"No," Eric said through clenched teeth. I could feel his anger rising. "It was *not* a direct order."

"Jason!" I yelled. My brother appeared, looking very grim. "Please push Eric's ribs back in," I said, which is another sentence I never thought I'd hear myself saying. Without a word, but with a hard-set mouth, Jason put his hands on each side of the gaping wound. He looked at Eric's nose, and said, "Ready?" Without waiting for an answer, he pushed in.

Eric made an awful noise, but I noticed the bleeding stopped and the healing began. Jason looked down at his reddened hands and went to find a bathroom.

"Well, then?" I said, handing Eric an open bottle of True-Blood that had been left on the coffee table. He made a face, but gulped it down. "What are you gonna do?"

"Later on we'll have words about this," he said. He gave me a look.

"Fine with me!" I glared right back and went off on an irrational tangent. "And while you're listing the things you should be doing, where's the cleaning crew?"

"Bobby . . ." he began, and then stopped short.

Bobby would have called the cleaning crew for Eric.

"Okay, how's about I do that part," I said, and wondered where to find a phone book.

"He kept a list of important numbers in the right-hand desk drawer in my office," Eric said, very quietly.

I found the name of the vampire cleaning service based midway between Shreveport and Baton Rouge, Fangster Cleanup. Since it was vampire run, they'd be open. A male answered the phone immediately, and I described the problem. "We'll be there in three hours, if the homeowner can guarantee us a safe sleeping place in case the job runs over," he said.

"No problem." There was no telling where the other two resident vampires were or if they'd survive to return before the dawn. If they did, they could all sleep in Eric's big bed or in the other light-tight bedroom, if the coffins were required. I thought there were a couple of the fiberglass pods stashed in the laundry room, too.

Now the carpets and the furniture would be cleaned. We just had to make sure no one else died tonight. After I hung up I felt super efficient but strangely empty, which I attributed to having lost everything that had been in my stomach. Since I was so light, I floated when I walked. Okay, maybe I still had more drug in me than I'd thought.

Then it suddenly hit me—Eric had said that Pam was in the house, too. Where was she? "Jason," I yelled, "please, please—find Pam."

I returned to the foul-smelling living room, marched over to the windows, and opened them. I swung around to face my boyfriend, who before this night had been many things: Arrogant, quick thinking, strong willed, secretive, and tricky were only the short list. But he'd never been indecisive, and he'd never been hopeless.

"What's the plan?" I asked him.

He was looking a little better now that Jason had done his thing. I couldn't see any bones anymore. "There isn't one," Eric said, but at least he looked guilty about it.

"What's the *plan*?" I asked again.

"I told you. I haven't made a plan. I don't know what to do. Ocella may be dead by now, if Alexei was clever enough to waylay him." Eric's bloody tears ran down his cheeks.

"Bzzzzzt!" I made the noise of a buzzer going off. "You'd know if Appius Livius was dead. He's your maker. *What's the plan?*"

Eric shot to his feet, with only a slight wince. Good. I'd goaded him upright. "I haven't got one!" he roared. "No matter what I do, someone will die!"

"With *no* plan, someone's going to die. And you know it. Someone's probably dying right this second! Alexei is crazy! Let's *have a plan*." I threw my hands up in the air.

"Why do you smell strange?" He'd finally taken in the PEACE T-shirt. "You smell of Were and of drugs. And you've been sick."

"I've already been through hell tonight," I said, maybe overstating a little bit. "And now I get to go through it twice, because *someone's* got to get your Viking butt on the road."

"What am I supposed to do?" he said, in a strangely reasonable voice.

"So you're okay with Alexei killing Appius? I mean, I sure am, but I would've thought you would've objected. Guess I was wrong."

Jason staggered in. "I found Pam," he said. He sat down very suddenly on an armchair. "She needed blood."

"But she's moving?"

"Only barely. She's cut, her ribs are kicked in, and her left arm and her right leg are broken."

"Oh God," I said, and dashed back to find her. I definitely hadn't been thinking straight because of the drugs, or she would've been my first priority once I found Eric alive. She'd begun crawling to the living room from the bathroom, where Alexei had evidently trapped her. The knife slashes were the most obvious injury, but Jason had been right about the broken bones. And this was after she'd had Jason's blood.

"Don't say anything," she grunted. "He caught me unawares. I am . . . so . . . stupid. How is Eric?"

"He's going to be okay. Can I help you up?"

"No," she said bitterly. "I prefer to drag myself along the hardwood floor."

"Bitch," I said, squatting to help her up. It was hard work, but since Jason had donated so much blood to Pam, I hated to ask him for help. We staggered into the living room.

"Who would have thought Alexei could do so much damage? He's so puny, and you're a great fighter."

"Flattery," she said, her voice ragged, "is not effective at this point. It was my fault. The little shit was following Bobby around, and I saw he'd gotten a knife from the kitchen. I tried to corner him while Bobby got out of the house. To give Ocella a chance to cool the boy down. But he went for me. He's fast as a snake."

I was beginning to doubt I could get Pam to the couch.

Eric rose unsteadily and put his arm around her. Between us, we maneuvered her over to the couch he'd vacated.

"Do you need my blood?" he asked her. "I thank you for doing your best to stop him."

"He's my kin, too," Pam said, settling back on a pillow with relief. "Through you, I'm related to that little murderer." Eric made a gesture with his wrist. "No, you need all your blood if you're going after him. I'm healing."

"Since you got a few pints of mine," Jason said weakly, with a ghost of his usual swagger.

"It was good. Thank you, panther," she said, and I thought my brother smirked a little; but just then, his cell phone rang. I knew the ring tone; it was from a song he loved, Queen's "We Are the Champions." Jason extricated the phone from his pocket and opened it. "Hey," he said, and then he listened.

"You okay?" he asked.

He listened some more.

"Okay. Thanks, honey. You stay inside, lock the doors, and don't answer them until you hear my voice. Wait, wait! Until you hear my cell phone! Okay?"

Jason flipped the phone shut. "That was Michele," he said. "Alexei was just at my house looking for me. She went to the door, but when she saw he was a deader, she didn't ask him in. He told her he wants to warm himself in my life, whatever that means. He'd tracked me there from your house by my smell." Jason looked self-conscious, as if he were afraid he'd forgotten to put on deodorant.

"Did the older one come after him?" I asked. I leaned against a handy wall. I was beginning to feel really ragged.

"Yeah, within a minute."

"What did Michele tell them?"

"She told 'em to go back to your house. She figured if they were vamps, they were some problem of yours." That was Michele, all right.

My cell was out in Jason's truck. I used his to call my house. Claude answered. "What are you doing there?" I said.

"We're closed on Monday," he said. "Why'd you call if you didn't want me to answer?"

"Claude, there is a very bad vamp headed to the house. And he can come in, he's been there before," I said. "You gotta get out. *Get in your car and get out.*"

Alexei's psychotic break plus Claude's fairy allure to vampires: This was a deadly combination. The night, apparently, was still not over. I wondered if it ever would be. For an awful moment, I looked into an endless nightmare of wandering from crisis to crisis, always one step behind.

"Give me your keys, Jason," I said. "You're in no shape to drive after your blood donation, and Eric's still healing. I don't want to drive his car." My brother fished his keys from his pocket and tossed them to me, and I was grateful for someone who didn't argue.

"I'm coming," Eric said, and pushed to his feet once more. Pam had shut her eyes, but they flew open as she realized we were leaving.

"All right," I said, since I would take any help I could get. Even a weak Eric was stronger than almost anything. I told Jason about the cleanup crew that was coming, and then we were out the door and into the truck with Pam still protesting that if we loaded her in she would heal along the way.

I drove, and I drove fast. There was no point in asking if Eric could fly so he could get there faster, because I knew he couldn't. Eric and I didn't talk along the way. We had either too much to say, or not enough. When we were about four minutes away from the house, Eric doubled over with pain. It wasn't his. I got a backwash of it from him. Something big had happened. We were rocketing down the driveway to my house less than forty-five minutes after we'd left Shreveport, which was pretty damn good.

The security light in my front yard illuminated a strange

scene. A pale-haired fairy I'd never seen before was standing back-to-back with Claude. The one I didn't know had a long, thin sword. Claude had two of my longest kitchen knives, one in each hand. Alexei, who appeared to be unarmed, was circling them like a small white killing machine. He was naked and covered in splotches, which were all shades of red. Ocella was lying sprawled on the gravel. His head was covered in dark blood. That seemed to be the theme of the night.

We skidded to a stop and scrambled out of Jason's truck. Alexei smiled, so he knew we were there, but he didn't stop his circling. "You didn't bring Jason," he called. "I wanted to see him."

"He had to give Pam a lot of blood to keep her from dying," I said. "He was too weak."

"He should have let her pass away," Alexei called, and darted under the sword to give the unknown fairy a hard fist to the stomach. Though Alexei had a knife, he seemed to be feeling playful. The fairy swung the sword faster than I could follow with my eyes, and it nicked Alexei, adding another rivulet to the blood already coursing down his chest.

"Can you please stop?" I asked. I staggered, because I seemed to have run out of steam. Eric put his arm around me.

"No," Alexei said in his high boy's voice. "Eric's love for you is pouring through our bond, Sookie, but I can't stop. This is the best I've felt in decades." He did feel wonderful; I could feel that coming through the bond. Though the drugs had temporarily deadened it, now I was feeling nuances, and there was such a contradictory bundle of them that it was like standing in a wind that kept changing directions.

Eric was trying to ease us over to where his maker lay. "Ocella," he said, "do you live?"

Ocella opened one black eye behind a mask of blood. He said, "For the first time in centuries, I think I wish I didn't."

I think I wish you didn't, too, I thought, and I felt him glance at me.

"She'll kill me with no compunction, that one," the Roman said, almost sounding amused. In the same voice he said, "Alexei has severed my spinal column, and until it heals, I will not be able to move."

"Alexei, please don't kill the fairies," I said. "That's my cousin Claude, and I don't have much family left."

"Who's the other one?" the boy asked, making an incredible leap to pull at Claude's hair and vault the other fairy, whose sword was not quick enough this time.

"I have no idea," I said. I started to add that he was no friend of mine and was probably an enemy, since I figured he was the one who'd been colluding with Basim, but I didn't want to see anyone else die . . . except possibly Appius Livius.

"I am Colman," the fairy bellowed. "I am of the sky fae, and my child is dead because of you, woman!"

Oh.

This was the father of Claudine's baby.

When Eric's arms left me, I had to struggle to stay on my feet. Alexei did one of his darting runs into the circle of blades, punching Colman's leg so hard that the fairy almost went down. I wondered if Colman's leg had broken. But while Alexei was close, Claude managed to stab backward and wound Alexei in the spot right below his shoulder. It would have killed the boy if he'd been human. As it was, Alexei nearly slipped on the gravel but managed to scrabble to his feet and keep on going. Vampire or not, the boy was tiring. I didn't dare look away to see what Eric was doing, where he was.

I had an idea. Under its impetus, I ran into the house, though I couldn't run in a straight line and I had to stop and breathe on my way up the porch steps.

In a drawer in my night table was the silver chain I'd gotten so long ago when the drainers had kidnapped Bill for his blood. I grabbed the chain, staggered back out of the house with it concealed in my hand behind my back, and edged near to the three combatants—but closest of all to the dancing, whirling Alexei. Even in that short time I'd been gone, he seemed to have gotten a little slower—but Colman was down on one knee.

I hated my plan, but this had to stop.

The next time the boy came by I was ready, with plenty of slack in the chain I was gripping with both hands. I swung my arms up, then down, the slack of the chain landing around Alexei's neck. I crossed my hands and pulled. Then Alexei was on the ground and screaming, and a shaved moment after that, Eric was there with a tree branch he'd broken off. He raised both arms and brought them down. The second after that, Alexei, tsarevitch of Russia, had gone to his final death.

I panted, because I was too exhausted to cry, and I sank to the ground. The two fairies gradually dropped their battle stances. Claude helped Colman stand, and they put their hands on each others' shoulders.

Eric stood between the fairies and me, keeping a watchful eye on them. Colman was my enemy, no doubt about that, and Eric was being cautious. I took advantage of the fact that he wasn't looking at me to pull the stake from Alexei and crawl over to the helpless Appius. He watched me coming with a smile.

"I want to kill you right now," I said, very quietly. "I want you dead so bad."

"Since you've stopped to speak to me, I know you're not going to do it." He said that with the utmost confidence. "You won't keep Eric, either."

I wanted to prove him wrong on both counts. But there'd been so much death and blood already that night. I hesitated. Then I raised the broken bit of branch. For the first time, Appius looked a little worried—or maybe he was simply resigned.

"Don't," Eric said.

I might still have done it if there hadn't been pleading in his voice.

"You know what you could do that would actually be some help, Appius Livius?" I said. There was a shout from Eric. Appius Livius's eyes flickered past me, and I *felt* him tell me to move. I thrust myself off to the side with every ounce of strength left in my body. The sword intended for me went right into Appius Livius, and it was a fairy blade. The Roman went into convulsions instantly, as the area around the wound blackened with shocking rapidity. Colman, who had been looking down at his accidental murder victim with shocked eyes, stiffened, and his shoulders went back. He began to topple, and I saw that there was a dagger between them. Eric shoved the quivering Colman away.

"Ocella!" Eric screamed, terror in his voice. Suddenly, Appius Livius went still.

"Well, all right," I said wearily, and turned my heavy head to see who had thrown the knife. Claude was looking down at the two blades still in his hands as if he expected to see one of them vanish.

Color us puzzled.

Eric seized the wounded Colman and latched on to his neck. Fairies are incredibly attractive to vampires—their blood, that is—and Eric had a great reason to kill this fairy. He wasn't holding back at all, and it was pretty gross. The gulping, the blood running down Colman's neck, his glazed eyes . . . Both of them had glazed eyes, I realized. Eric's were full of bloodlust, and Colman's were becoming full of death. Colman had been too weakened by his many wounds to fight Eric off. Eric was looking rosier by the second.

Claude limped over to sit on the grass beside me. He put my knives carefully on the ground by me, as if I'd been badgering him for their return. "I was trying to persuade him to go home," my cousin said. "I saw him only once or twice. He had an elaborate scheme to put you in a human jail. He planned to kill you until he saw you with the child Hunter in the park. He thought of taking the child, but even in a rage he couldn't do it."

"You moved in to protect me," I said. That was amazing, from someone as selfish as Claude.

"My sister loved you," Claude said. "Colman was fond of Claudine, and very proud she chose him to father her child."

"I guess he was one of Niall's followers." He'd said he was one of the sky fairies.

"Yes, 'Colman' means 'dove.'"

It didn't make any difference now. I was sorry for him. "He had to know nothing I said would have stopped Claudine from doing what she thought was right," I said.

"He knew," Claude admitted. "That was why he couldn't

bring himself to kill you, even before he saw the child. That's why he talked to the werewolf, concocted such an indirect scheme." He sighed. "If Colman had really been convinced you caused Claudine's death, nothing would have stopped him."

"I would have stopped him," said a new voice, and Jason stepped out of the woods. No, it was Dermot.

"Okay, *you* threw the knife," I said. "Thanks, Dermot. Are you okay?"

"I hope. . . ." Dermot looked at us pleadingly.

"Colman had a spell on him," Claude observed. "At least, I think so."

"He said you didn't have a lot of magic," I said to Claude. "He told me about the spell, as close as he could say it. I thought it must be the other fairy, Colman, who put it on him. But since Colman is dead, I would have thought that would break the spell."

Claude frowned. "Dermot, so it wasn't Colman who laid the spell?"

Dermot sank to the ground in front of us. "So much longer," he said elliptically. I puzzled over that for a moment.

"He was spelled much longer ago," I said, finally feeling a little throb of excitement. "Are you saying that you were spelled months ago?"

Dermot seized my hand in his left and took Claude's hand in his right.

Claude said, "I think he means that he's been spelled for much longer. For years." Tears rolled down Dermot's cheeks.

"I bet you money that Niall did it," I said. "He probably had it all worked out in his head. Dermot deserved it for, I don't know, having qualms about his fairy legacy or something."

"My grandfather is very loving but not very . . . tolerant," Claude said.

"You know how they undo spells in fairy tales?" I said.

"Yes, I have heard that humans tell fairy tales," Claude said. "So, tell me how they say to break spells."

"In the fairy tales, a kiss does it."

"Easily done," Claude said, and as if we had practiced synchronized kissing, we leaned forward and kissed Dermot.

And it worked. He shuddered all over, then looked at us both, intelligence flooding his eyes. He began to weep in earnest, and after a moment Claude got to his knees and helped Dermot up. "I'll see you in a while," he said. Then he guided Dermot into the house.

Eric and I were alone. Eric had sunk onto his haunches a little distance from the three bodies in my front yard.

"This is positively Shakespearean," I said, looking around at the remains and the blood soaking into the ground. Alexei's corpse was already flaking away, but much more slowly than that of his ancient maker. Now that Alexei had met his final death, the pathetic bones in his grave in Russia would vanish, too. Eric had cast the body of the fairy onto the gravel, where it began to turn to dust, in the way fairies did. It was quite different from vampire disintegration, but just as handy. I realized I wouldn't have three corpses to hide. I was so tired from the sum total of a truly horrific day that I found it the happy moment of the past few hours. Eric looked and smelled like something out of a horror movie. Our eyes met. He looked away first.

"Ocella taught me everything about being a vampire," Eric said very quietly. "He taught me how to feed, how to hide, when it was safe to mingle with humans. He taught me how to make love with men, and later he freed me to make love with women. He protected me and loved me. He caused me pain for decades. He gave me life. My maker is dead." He spoke as if he could scarcely believe it, didn't know how to feel. His eyes lingered on the crumbling mass of flakes that had been Appius Livius Ocella.

"Yes," I said, trying not to sound happy. "He is. And I didn't do it."

"But you would have," Eric said.

"I was thinking about it," I said. There was no point in denying it.

"What were you going to ask him?"

"Before Colman stabbed him?" Though "stabbed" was hardly the right word. "Transfixed" was more accurate. Yes, "transfixed." My brain was moving like a turtle.

"Well," I said. "I was going to tell him I'd be glad to let him live if he'd kill Victor Madden for you."

I'd startled Eric, as much as anyone as wiped out as he was could be startled. "That would have been good," he said slowly. "That was a good idea, Sookie."

"Yeah, well. Not gonna happen."

"You were right," Eric said, still in that very slow voice. "This is just like the end of one of Shakespeare's plays."

"We're the people left standing. Yay for us."

"I'm free," Eric said. He closed his eyes. Thanks to the last traces of the drug, I could practically watch the fairy blood zinging through his system. I could see his energy level picking up. Everything physically wrong with him had healed, and now with the rush of Colman's blood he was forgetting his grief for his maker and his brother, and feeling only the relief of being free of them. "I feel so good." He actually drew a breath of the night air, still tainted with the odors of blood and death. He seemed to savor the smell. "You are my dearest," he said, his eyes manic blue.

"I'm glad to hear that," I said, utterly unable to smile.

"I have to return to Shreveport to see about Pam, to arrange for the things I must do now that Ocella is dead," Eric said. "But as soon as I can, we'll be together again, and we'll make up for our lost time."

"Sounds good to me," I said. We were alone in our bond once more, though it wasn't as strong as it had been because we hadn't renewed it. But I wasn't about to suggest that to Eric, not tonight. He looked up, inhaled again, and launched himself into the night sky.

When all the bodies had completely disintegrated, I got to my feet and went into the house, the very flesh on my bones feeling as if it could fall off from weariness. I told myself that I should feel a certain measure of triumph. I wasn't dead; my enemies were. But in the void left by the drug, I felt only a certain grim satisfaction. I could hear my great-uncle and my cousin talking in the hall bathroom, and the water running, before I shut my own bathroom door. After I'd showered and was ready for bed, I opened the door to my room to find them waiting for me.

"We want to climb in with you," Dermot said. "We'll all sleep better."

That seemed incredibly weird and creepy to me—or maybe I only thought it should have. I was simply too tired to argue. I climbed in the bed. Claude got in on one side of me, Dermot on the other. Just when I was thinking I would never be able to sleep, that this situation was too odd and too wrong, I felt a kind of blissful relaxation roll through my body, a kind of unfamiliar comfort. I was with family. I was with blood.

And I slept.

Turn the page for a special preview
of Charlaine Harris's next
Sookie Stackhouse novel

DEAD RECKONING

Available in May 2011 from Ace Books!

The attic had been kept locked until the day after my grandmother died. I'd found her key and opened it that awful day to look for her wedding dress, having the crazy idea she should be buried in it. I'd taken one step inside and then turned and walked out, leaving the door unsecured behind me.

Now, two years later, I pushed that door open again. The hinges creaked as ominously as if it were midnight on Halloween instead of a sunny Wednesday morning at the end of May. The broad floorboards protested under my feet as I stepped over the threshold. There were dark shapes all around me, and a very faint musty odor—the smell of old things long forgotten.

When the second story had been added to the original Stackhouse home decades before, the new floor had been divided into bedrooms, but perhaps a third of it had been relegated to storage space after the largest generation of Stackhouses had thinned out. Since Jason and I had come to live with my grandparents after our parents had died, the attic door had been kept locked. Gran hadn't wanted to clean up after us if we decided the attic was a great place to play.

Now I owned the house, and the key was on a ribbon around my neck. There were only three Stackhouse descendants—Jason, me, and my deceased cousin Hadley's son, a little boy named Hunter.

I waved my hand around in the shadowy gloom to find the hanging chain, grasped it, and pulled. An overhead bulb illuminated decades of family castoffs.

Cousin Claude and Great-Uncle Dermot stepped in behind me. Dermot exhaled so loudly it was almost a snort. Claude looked grim. I was sure he was regretting his offer to help me clean out the attic. But I wasn't going to let my cousin off the hook, not when there was another able-bodied male available to help. For now, Dermot went where Claude went, so I had two for the price of one. I couldn't predict how long the situation would hold. I'd suddenly realized that morning that soon it would be too hot to spend time in the upstairs room. The window unit my friend Amelia had installed in one of the bedrooms kept the living spaces tolerable, but of course we'd never wasted money putting one in the attic.

"How shall we go about this?" Dermot asked. He was blond and Claude was dark; they looked like gorgeous bookends. I'd asked Claude once how old he was, to find he had only the vaguest idea. The fae don't keep track of time the same way we do, but Claude was at least a century older than me. He was a kid compared to Dermot; my great-uncle thought he was seven hundred years my senior. Not a wrinkle, not a gray hair, not a droop anywhere, on either of them.

Since they were much more fairy than me—I was only

one-eighth—we all seemed to be about the same age, our late twenties. But that would change in a few years. I would look older than my ancient kin. Though Dermot looked very like my brother, Jason, I'd realized the day before that Jason had crow's-feet at the corners of his eyes. Dermot might not ever show even that token of aging.

Pulling myself back into the here and now, I said, "I suggest we carry things down to the living room. It's so much brighter down there; it'll be easier to see what's worth keeping and what isn't. After we get everything out of the attic, I can clean it up after you two leave for work." Claude owned a strip club in Monroe and drove over every day, and Dermot went where Claude went. As always . . .

"We've got three hours," Claude said.

"Let's get to work," I said, my lips curving upward in a bright and cheerful smile. That's my fallback expression.

About an hour later, I was having second thoughts, but it was too late to back out of the task. (Getting to watch Claude and Dermot shirtless made the work a lot more interesting.) My family has lived in this house since there have been Stackhouses in Renard Parish. And that's been well over a hundred and fifty years. We've saved things.

The living room began to fill up in a hurry. There were boxes of books, trunks full of clothes, furniture, vases. The Stackhouse family had never been rich, and apparently we'd always thought we could find a use for anything, no matter how battered or broken, if we kept it long enough. Even the two fairies wanted to take a break after maneuvering an incredibly heavy wooden desk down the narrow staircase. We all sat on the front porch. The guys sat on the railing, and I slumped down on the swing.

"We could just pile it all in the yard and burn it," Claude

suggested. He wasn't joking. Claude's sense of humor was quirky at best, minuscule the rest of the time.

"No!" I tried not to sound as irritated as I felt. "I know this stuff is not valuable, but if other Stackhouses thought it ought to be stored up there, I at least owe them the courtesy of having a look at all of it."

"Dearest great-niece," Dermot said, "I'm afraid Claude has a point. Saying this debris is 'not valuable' is being kind." Once you heard Dermot talk, you knew his resemblance to Jason was strictly superficial.

I glowered at the fairies. "Of course to you two most of this would be trash, but to humans it might have some value," I said. "I may call the theater group in Shreveport to see if they want any of the clothes or furniture."

Claude shrugged. "That'll get rid of some of it," he said. "But most of the fabric isn't even good for rags." We'd put some boxes out on the porch when the living room began to be impassable, and he poked one with his toe. The label said the contents were curtains, but I could only guess what they'd originally looked like.

"You're right," I admitted. I pushed with my feet, not too energetically, and swung for a minute. Dermot went in the house and returned with a glass of peach tea with lots of ice in it. He handed it to me silently. I thanked him and stared dismally at all the old things someone had once treasured. "Okay, we'll start a burn pile," I said, bowing to common sense. "Round back, where I usually burn the leaves?"

Dermot and Claude glared at me.

"Okay, right here on the gravel is fine," I said. The last time my driveway had been graveled, the parking area in front of the house, outlined with landscape timbers, had gotten a fresh load, too. "It's not like I get a lot of visitors."

By the time Dermot and Claude knocked off to shower and change for work, the parking area contained a substantial mound of useless items waiting for the torch. Stackhouse wives had stored extra sheets and coverlets, and most of them were in the same ragged condition as the curtains. To my deeper regret, many of the books were mildewed and mouse-chewed. I sighed and added them to the pile, though the very idea of burning books made me queasy. But broken furniture, rotted umbrellas, spotted place mats, an ancient leather suitcase with big holes in it . . . no one would ever need these items again.

The pictures we'd uncovered—framed, in albums, or loose—we placed in a box in the living room. Documents were sorted into another box. I'd found some old dolls, too. I knew from television that people collected dolls, and perhaps these were worth something. There were some old guns, too, and a sword. Where was *Antiques Roadshow* when you needed it?

Later that evening at Merlotte's, I told my boss Sam about my day. Sam, a compact man who was actually immensely strong, was dusting the bottles behind the bar. We weren't very busy that night. In fact, business hadn't been good for the past few weeks. I didn't know if the slump was due to the chicken processing plant closing or the fact that some people objected to Sam being a shapeshifter. (The two-natured had tried to emulate the successful transition of the vampires, but it hadn't gone so well.) And there was a new bar, Vic's Redneck Roadhouse, about ten miles west off the Interstate. I'd heard the Redneck Roadhouse held all kinds of wet T-shirt contests, beer pong tournaments, and a promotion called "Bring in a Bubba Night"—crap like that.

Popular crap. Crap that raked in the customers.

Whatever the reasons, Sam and I had time to talk about attics and antiques.

"There's a store called Splendide in Shreveport," Sam said. "Both the owners are appraisers. You could give them a call."

"How'd you know that?" Okay, maybe that wasn't so tactful.

"Well, I do know a few things besides tending bar," Sam said, giving me a sideways look.

I had to refill a pitcher of beer for one of my tables. When I returned I said, "Of course you know all kinds of stuff. I just didn't know you were into antiques."

"I'm not. But Jannalynn is. Splendide's her favorite place to shop."

I blinked, trying not to look as disconcerted as I felt. Jannalynn Hopper, who'd been dating Sam for a few weeks now, was so ferocious she'd been named the Long Tooth pack enforcer—though she was only twenty-one and about as big as a seventh-grader. It was hard to imagine Jannalynn restoring a vintage picture frame or planning to fit a plantation sideboard into her place in Shreveport. (Come to think of it, I had no idea where she lived. Did Jannalynn actually have a house?)

"I sure wouldn't have guessed that," I said, making myself smile at Sam. It was my personal opinion that Jannalynn was not good enough for Sam.

Of course, I kept that to myself. Glass houses, stones; right? I was dating a vampire whose kill list would top Jannalynn's for sure, since Eric was over a thousand years old. In one of those awful moments you have at random, I realized that everyone I'd ever dated—though granted, that was a short list—was a killer.

And so was I.

I had to shake this off in a hurry, or I'd be in a melancholy funk all evening.

"You have a name and phone number for this shop?" I hoped the antiques dealers would agree to come to Bon Temps. I'd have to rent a U-Haul to get all the attic contents to Shreveport.

"Yeah, I got it in my office," Sam said. "I was talking to Brenda, the female half of the partnership, about getting Jannalynn something special for her birthday. It's coming right up. Brenda—Brenda Hesterman—called this morning to tell me she had a few things for me to look at."

"Maybe we could go see her tomorrow?" I suggested. "I have things piled all over the living room and some out on the front porch, and the good weather won't last forever."

"Would Jason want any of it?" Sam asked diffidently. "I'm just saying, family stuff."

"He got a piecrust table around a month ago," I said. "But I guess I should ask him." I thought about it. The house and its contents were mine, since Gran had left it to me. Hmmmm. Well, first things first. "Let's ask Ms. Hesterman if she'll come give a look. If there's pieces that are worth anything, I can think about it."

"Okay," Sam said. "Sounds good. Pick you up tomorrow at ten?"

That was a little early for me to be up and dressed since I was working the late shift, but I agreed.

Sam sounded pleased. "You can tell me what you think about whatever Brenda shows me. It'll be good to have a woman's opinion." He ran a hand over his hair, which (as usual) was a mess. A few weeks ago he'd cut it real short, and now it was in an awkward stage of growing back. Sam's hair is a pretty color, sort of strawberry blond; but since it's naturally curly, now that it was growing out it couldn't seem to pick a direction. I suppressed an urge to whip out a brush and make sense out of it. That was not something an employee should do to her boss's head.

Kennedy Keyes and Danny Prideaux, who worked for Sam part time as substitute bartender and bouncer, respectively, came in to climb on two of the empty barstools. Kennedy is beautiful. She was first runner-up to Miss Louisiana a few years ago, and she still looks like a beauty pageant queen. Her chestnut hair's all glossy and thick, and the ends wouldn't dare to split. Her makeup is meticulous. She has manicures and pedicures on a regular basis. She wouldn't buy a garment at Wal-Mart if her life depended on it.

A few years ago her future, which should have included a country club marriage in the next parish and a big inheritance from her daddy, had been derailed from its path when she'd served time for manslaughter.

Along with pretty nearly everyone I knew, I figured her boyfriend had had it coming, after I saw the pictures of her face swelling black and blue in her mug shots. But she'd confessed to shooting him when she called 911, and his family had a little clout, so there was no way Kennedy could walk. She'd gotten a light sentence and time off for good behavior, since she'd taught deportment and grooming to the other inmates. Eventually, Kennedy had done her time. When she'd gotten out, she'd rented a little apartment in Bon Temps, where she had an aunt, Marcia Albanese. Sam had offered her a job pretty much right after he met her, and she'd accepted on the spot.

"Hey, man," Danny said to Sam. "Fix us two mojitos?"

Sam got the mint out of the refrigerator and set to work. I handed him the sliced limes when he was almost through with the drinks.

"What are you all up to tonight?" I asked. "You look mighty pretty, Kennedy."

"I finally lost ten pounds!" she said, and when Sam deposited her glass in front of her, she lifted it to toast with Danny. "To my former figure! May I be on the road to getting it back!"

Danny shook his head. He said, "Hey! You don't need to do anything to look beautiful." I had to turn away so I wouldn't say, *Awwww.* Danny was one tough guy who couldn't have grown up in a more different environment than Kennedy—the only experience they'd had in common was jail—but boy, he was carrying a big torch for her. I could feel the heat from where I stood. You didn't have to be telepathic to see Danny's devotion.

We hadn't drawn the curtains on the front window yet, and when I realized it was dark outside, I started forward. Though I was looking out from the bright bar to the dark parking lot, there were lights out there, and something was moving . . . moving fast. Toward the bar. I had a slice of a second to think *Odd*, and then caught the flicker of flame.

"Down!" I yelled, but the word hadn't even gotten all the way out of my mouth when the window shattered and the bottle with its fiery head landed on a table where no one was sitting, breaking the napkin holder and scattering the salt and pepper shakers. Burning napkins flared out from the point of impact to drift down to the floor and the chairs and the people. The table itself was a mass of fire almost instantly.

Danny moved faster than I'd ever seen a human move. He swept Kennedy off her stool, flipped up the pass-through, and shoved her down behind the bar. There was a brief log-jam as Sam, moving even faster, grabbed the fire extinguisher from the wall and tried to leap through the pass-through to start spraying.

I felt heat on my thighs and looked down to see that my apron had been ignited by one of the napkins. I'm ashamed to say that I screamed. Sam swiveled around to spray me and then turned back to the flames. The customers were yelling, dodging flames, running into the passage that led past the bathrooms and Sam's office through to the back parking lot. One of our perpetual customers, Jane Bodehouse, was bleeding heavily, her hand clapped to her lacerated scalp. She'd been sitting by the window, not her usual place at the bar, so I figured she'd been cut by flying glass. Jane staggered and would have fallen if I hadn't grabbed her arm.

"Go that way," I yelled in her ear, and shoved her in the right direction. Sam was spraying the biggest flame, aiming at the base of it in the approved manner, but the napkins that had floated away were causing lots of little fires. I grabbed the pitcher of water and the pitcher of tea off the bar and began methodically tracking the flames on the floor. The pitchers were full, and I managed to be pretty effective.

One of the window curtains was on fire, and I took three steps, aimed carefully, and tossed the remaining tea. The flame didn't quite die out. I grabbed a glass of water from a table and got much closer to the fire than I wanted to. Flinching the whole time, I poured the liquid down the steaming curtain. I felt an odd flicker of warmth behind me and smelled something disgusting. A powerful gust of chemicals made a strange sensation against my back. I turned to try to figure out what had happened and saw Sam whirling away with the extinguisher.

I found myself looking through the serving hatch into the kitchen. Antoine, the cook, was shutting down all the appliances. Smart. I could hear the fire engine in the distance, but I was too busy looking for yellow flickers to feel much relief. My eyes, streaming with tears from the smoke and the chemicals, were darting around like pinballs as I tried to spot flames, and I was coughing like crazy. Sam had run to retrieve the second extinguisher from his office, and he returned holding it ready. We rocked from side to side on our feet, ready to leap into action to extinguish the next flicker.

Neither of us spotted anything else.

Sam aimed one more blast at the bottle that had caused the fire, and then he put down the extinguisher. He leaned over to plant his hands on his thighs and inhaled raggedly. He began coughing. After a second, he bent down to the bottle.

"Don't touch it," I said urgently, and his hand stopped halfway down.

"Of course not," he said, chiding himself, and he straightened up. "Did you see who threw it?"

"No," I said. We were the only people left in the bar. I could hear the fire engine getting closer and closer, so I knew we had only a minute more to talk to each other alone. "Coulda been the same people who've been demonstrating out in the parking lot. I don't know that the church members are into firebombs, though." Not everyone in the area was pleased to know there were such creatures as werewolves and shapeshifters following the Great Reveal, and the Holy Word Tabernacle in Clarice had been sending its members to demonstrate at Merlotte's from time to time.

"Sookie," Sam said, "Sorry about your hair."

"What about it?" I said, lifting my hand to my head. The

shock was setting in now. I had a hard time making my hand mind my directions.

"The end of your ponytail got singed," Sam said. And he sat down very suddenly. That seemed like a good idea.

"So that's what smells so bad," I said, and collapsed on the floor beside him. We had our backs against the base of the bar, since the stools had gotten scattered in the melee of the rush out the back door. My *hair* was burned off. I felt tears run down my cheeks. I knew it was stupid, but I couldn't help it.

Sam took my hand and gripped it, and we were still sitting like that when the firefighters rushed in. Even though Merlotte's is outside the city limits, we got the official town firefighters, not the volunteers.

"I don't think you need the hose," Sam called. "I think it's out." He was anxious to prevent any more damage to the bar.

Truman La Salle, the fire chief, said, "You two need first aid?" But his eyes were busy, and his words were almost absentminded.

"I'm okay," I said, after a glance at Sam. "But Jane's out back with a cut on her head, from the glass. Sam?"

"Maybe my right hand got a little burned," he said, and his mouth compressed as if he was just now feeling the pain. He released my hand to rub his left over his right, and he definitely winced this time.

"You need to take care of that," I advised him. "Burns hurt like the devil."

"Yeah, I'm figuring that out," he said, his eyes squeezing shut.

Bud Dearborn came in as soon as Truman yelled, "Okay!" The sheriff must have been in bed, because he had a thrown-together look and was minus his hat, a reliable part of his wardrobe. Sheriff Dearborn was probably in his late fifties by now, and he showed every minute of it. He'd always looked like a Pekinese. Now he looked like a gray one. He spent a few minutes going around the bar, watching where his feet went, almost sniffing the disarray in the bar. Finally he was satisfied and came up to stand in front of me.

"What you been up to now?" he asked.

"Someone threw a firebomb in the window," I said. "None of my doing." I was too shocked to sound angry.

"Sam, they aiming for you?" the sheriff asked. He wandered off without waiting for an answer.

Sam got up slowly and turned to reach his left hand to me. I gripped it and he pulled. Since Sam's much stronger than he looks, I was on my feet in a jiffy.

Time stood still for a few minutes. I had to think that I was maybe a bit in shock.

As Sheriff Dearborn completed his slow and careful circuit of the bar, he arrived back at Sam and me.

By then we had another sheriff to deal with.

Eric Northman, my boyfriend and the vampire sheriff of Area Five, which included Bon Temps, came through the door so quickly that when Bud and Truman realized he was there, they jumped, and I thought Bud was going to draw his weapon. Eric gripped my shoulders and bent to peer into my face. "Are you hurt?" he demanded.

It was like his concern gave me permission to drop my bravery. I felt a tear run down my cheek. Just one. "My apron caught fire, but I think my legs are okay," I said, making a huge effort to sound calm. "I only lost a little hair. So I didn't come out of it too bad. Bud, Truman, I can't remember if you've met my boyfriend, Eric Northman from Shreveport." There were several iffy facts in that sentence.

"How'd you know there was trouble here, Mr. Northman?" Truman asked.

"Sookie called me on her cell phone," Eric said. That was a lie, but I didn't exactly want to explain our blood bond to our fire chief and our sheriff, and Eric would never volunteer any information to humans.

One of the most wonderful, and the most appalling, things about Eric loving me is that he didn't give a shit about anyone else. He ignored the damaged bar, Sam's burns, and the police and firefighters (who were keeping track of him from the corners of their eyes) still inspecting the building.

Eric circled me to evaluate the hair situation. After a long moment, he said, "I'm going to look at your legs. Then we'll find a doctor and a beautician." His voice was absolutely cold and steady, but I knew he was volcanically angry. It rolled through the bond between us, just as my fear and shock had alerted him to my danger.

"Honey, we have other things to think about," I said, forcing myself to smile, forcing myself to sound calm. One corner of my brain pictured a pink ambulance screeching to a halt outside to disgorge emergency beauticians with cases of scissors, combs, and hair spray. "Dealing with a little hair damage can wait until tomorrow. It's a lot more important to find out who did this and why."

Eric glared at Sam as if the attack were Sam's responsibility. "Yes, his bar is far more important than your safety and well-being," he said. Sam looked astonished at this rebuke, and the beginnings of anger flickered across his face.

"If Sam hadn't been so quick with the fire extinguisher, we'd all have been in bad shape," I said, keeping up with the calm and the smiling. "In fact, both the bar and the people in it would have been in a lot more trouble." I was running out of faux serenity, and of course Eric realized it.

"I'm taking you home," he said.

"Not until I talk to her." Bud showed considerable courage in asserting himself. Eric was scary enough when he was in a *good* mood, much less when his fangs ran out as they did now. Strong emotion does that to a vamp.

"Honey," I said, holding on to my own temper with an effort. I put my arm around Eric's waist, and tried again. "Honey, Bud and Truman are in charge here, and they have their rules to follow. I'm okay." Though I was trembling, which of course he could feel.

"You were frightened," Eric said. I felt his own rage that something had happened to me that he had not been able to prevent. I suppressed a sigh at having to babysit Eric's emotions when I wanted to be free to have my own nervous breakdown. Vampires are nothing if not possessive when they've claimed someone as theirs, but they're also usually anxious to blend into the human population, not cause any unnecessary waves. This was an overreaction.

Eric was mad, sure, but normally he was also quite pragmatic. He knew I wasn't seriously hurt. I looked up at him, puzzled. My big Viking hadn't been himself in a week or two. Something other than the death of his maker was bothering him, but I hadn't built up enough courage to ask him what was wrong. I'd cut myself some slack. I'd simply wanted to enjoy the peace we'd shared for a few weeks.

Maybe that had been a mistake. Something big was pressing on him, and all this anger was a by-product.

"How'd you get here so quick?" Bud asked Eric.

"I flew," Eric said casually, and Bud and Truman gave each

other a wide-eyed look. Eric had had the ability for (give or take) a thousand years, so he disregarded their amazement. He was focused on me, his fangs still out.

They couldn't know that Eric had felt the swell of my terror the minute I'd seen the running figure. I hadn't had to call him when the incident was over. "The sooner we get all this settled," I said, baring my teeth right back at him in a terrible smile, "the sooner we can leave." I was trying, not so subtly, to send Eric a message. He finally calmed down enough to get my subtext.

"Of course, my darling," he said. "You're absolutely right." But his hand took mine and squeezed too hard, and his eyes were so brilliant they looked like little blue lanterns.

Bud and Truman looked mighty relieved. The tension ratcheted down a few notches. Vampires equal drama.

While Sam was getting his hands treated and Truman was taking pictures of what remained of the bottle, Bud asked me what I'd seen.

"I caught a glimpse of someone out in the parking lot running toward the building, and then the bottle came through the window," I said. "I don't know who threw it. After the window broke and the fire spread from all the lit napkins, I didn't notice anything but the people trying to leave and Sam trying to put it out."

Bud asked me the same thing several times in several different ways, but I couldn't help him any more than I already had.

"Why do you think someone would do this to Merlotte's, to Sam?" Bud asked.

"I don't understand it," I said. "You know, we had those demonstrators from the church in the parking lot a few weeks ago. They've only come back once since then. I can't imagine any of them making a—was that a Molotov cocktail?"

"How you know about those, Sookie?"

"Well, one, I read books. Two, Terry doesn't talk about the war much, but every so now and then he does talk about weapons." Terry Bellefleur, Detective Andy Bellefleur's cousin, was a decorated and damaged Vietnam veteran. He cleaned the bar when everyone was gone and came in occasionally to substitute for Sam. Sometimes he just hung at the bar watching people come in and out. Terry did not have much of a social life.

As soon as Bud declared himself satisfied, Eric and I went to my car. He took the keys from my shaking hand. I got in the passenger side. He was right. I shouldn't drive until I'd recovered from the shock.

Eric had been busy on his cell phone while I was talking to Bud, and I wasn't totally surprised to see a car parked in front of my house. It was Pam's, and she had a passenger.

Eric pulled around back where I always park, and I scrambled out of the car to hurry through the house to unlock the front door. Eric followed me at a leisurely pace. We hadn't exchanged a word on the short drive. He was preoccupied and still dealing with his temper. I was shocked by the whole incident. Now I felt a little more like myself as I went out on the porch to call, "Come in!"

Pam and her passenger got out. He was a young human, maybe twenty-one, and thin to the point of emaciation. His hair was dyed blue and cut in an extremely geometric way, rather as if he'd put a box on his head, knocked it sideways, then trimmed around the edges. What didn't fit inside the lines had been shaved.

It was eye-catching, I'll say that.

Pam smiled at the expression on my face, which I hastily transformed into something more welcoming. Pam has been a vampire since Victoria was on the English throne, and she's been Eric's right hand since he called her in from her wanderings in northern America. He's her maker.

"Hello," I said to the young man as he entered the front door. He was extremely nervous. His eyes darted to me, away from me, took in Eric, and then kind of strafed the room to absorb it. A flicker of contempt crossed his clean-shaven face as he took in the cluttered living room, which was never more than homey even when it was clean.

Pam thumped him on the back of his head. "Speak when you're spoken to, Immanuel!" she growled. She was standing slightly behind him, so he couldn't see her when she winked at me.

"Hello, ma'am," he said to me, taking a step forward. His nose twitched. Pam said, "You smell, Sookie."

"It was the fire," I explained.

"You can tell me about it in a moment," she said, her pale eyebrows shooting up. "Sookie, this man is Immanuel Earnest," she said. "He cuts hair at Death by Fashion in Shreveport. He's brother to my lover, Miriam."

That was a lot of information in three sentences. I scrambled to absorb it.

Eric was eyeing Immanuel's coiffure with fascinated disgust. "*This* is the one you brought to correct Sookie's hair?" he said to Pam. His lips were pressed together in a very tight line. I could feel his skepticism pulsing along the line that bound us.

"Miriam says he is the best," Pam said, shrugging. "I haven't had a haircut in a hundred fifty years. How would I know?"

"Look at him!"

I began to be a little worried. Even for the circumstances,

Eric was in a foul mood. "I like his tattoos," I said. "The colors are real pretty."

Aside from his extreme haircut, Immanuel was covered with very sophisticated tattoos. No "MOM" or "BETTY SUE" or naked ladies; elaborate and colorful designs extended from wrists to shoulders. He'd look dressed even when he was naked. The hairdresser had a flat leather case tucked under one of his skinny arms.

"So, you're going to cut off the bad parts?" I said brightly.

"Of your hair," he said carefully. (I wasn't sure I'd needed that particular reassurance.) He glanced at me, then back down at the floor. "Do you have a high stool?"

"Yes, in the kitchen," I said. When I'd rebuilt my burned-out kitchen, custom had made me buy a high stool like the one my Gran had perched on while she talked on the old telephone. The new phone was cordless, and I didn't need to stay in the kitchen when I used it, but the counter simply hadn't looked right without a stool beside it.

My three guests trailed behind me, and I dragged the stool into the middle of the floor. There was just enough room for everyone when Pam and Eric sat on the other side of the table. Eric was glowering at Immanuel in an ominous way, and Pam was simply waiting to be entertained by our emotional upheavals.

I clambered up on the stool and made myself sit with a straight back. My legs were smarting, my eyes were prickly, and my throat was scratchy. But I forced myself to smile at the hairstylist. Immanuel was real nervous. You don't want that in a person with sharp scissors.

Immanuel took the elastic band off my ponytail. There was a long silence while he regarded the damage. He wasn't thinking good thoughts. My vanity got hold of me. "Is it very bad?" I asked, trying to keep my voice from quavering. Reaction was definitely getting the upper hand, now that I was safe at home.

"I'm going to have to take off about three inches," he said quietly, as if he were telling me a relative was terminally ill.

To my shame, I reacted much the same way as if that had been the news. I could feel tears well up in my eyes, and my lips were quivering. *Ridiculous!* I told myself. My eyes slewed left when Immanuel set his leather case on the kitchen table. He unzipped it and took out a comb. There were also several pairs of scissors in special loops and an electric trimmer with its cord neatly coiled. Have hair care, will travel.

Pam was texting with incredible speed. She was smiling as though her message were pretty damn funny. Eric stared at me, thinking many dark thoughts. I couldn't read 'em, but I could sure tell he was unhappy in a major way.

I sighed and returned my gaze to straight ahead. I loved Eric, but at the moment I wanted him to take his broodiness and shove it. I felt Immanuel's touch on my hair as he began combing it out. It felt strange when it reached the end of its length, and a little tug and a funny sound let me know that some of my burned hair had fallen to the floor as the comb reached it.

"It's damaged beyond repair," Immanuel murmured. "I'll cut. Then you wash. Then I cut again."

"You must quit this job," Eric said abruptly, and Immanuel's comb stopped moving until he realized Eric was talking to me.

I wanted to throw something heavy at my honeybun. And I wanted it to smack him right in his stubborn, handsome head. "We'll talk later," I said, not looking at him.

"What will happen next? You're too vulnerable!"

"We'll talk *later*."

Out of the corner of my eye, I saw Pam look away so Eric wouldn't see her smirk.

"Doesn't she need something around her?" Eric snarled at Immanuel. "Covering her clothes?"

"Eric," I said, "since I'm all smelly and smoky and covered with fire extinguisher stuff, I don't think keeping my clothes free of burned hair is a big deal."

Eric didn't snort, but he came close. However, he did seem to pick up on my feeling that he was being a total pain, and he shut up and got a hold on himself.

The relief was tremendous.

Immanuel, whose hands were surprisingly steady for someone cooped up in a kitchen with two vampires (one remarkably irritable) and a charred barmaid, combed until my hair was smooth as it could be. Then he picked up his scissors. I could feel the hairdresser focusing completely on his task. Immanuel was a champion at concentration, I discovered, since his mind lay open to me.

It really didn't take long. The burned bits drifted to the floor like sad snowflakes.

"You need to go shower now, and come back with clean wet hair," Immanuel said. "After that, I'll even it up. Where's your broom, your dustpan?"

I told him where to find them, and then I went into my bedroom, passing through it to my own bathroom. I wondered if Eric would join me, since I knew from past experience that he liked my shower. The way I felt, it would be far better if he stayed in the kitchen.

I pulled off my smelly clothes and ran the water as hot as I could stand it. It was a relief to step into the tub and let the heat and wetness flow over me. When the warm water hit my legs it stung. For a few moments I wasn't appreciative or happy about anything. I just remembered how scared I'd been. But after I'd dealt with that, I had something on my mind.

The figure I'd spotted running toward the bar, bottle in hand—I couldn't be completely sure, but I suspected it had not been human.

EDITED BY
#1 *NEW YORK TIMES* BESTSELLING AUTHOR

CHARLAINE HARRIS
&
TONI L. P. KELNER

HOME IMPROVEMENT: UNDEAD EDITION

There's nothing quite like a home renovation for finding
skeletons in the closet—or witches in the attic. And if the
home in question belongs to a vampire, a wizard, a
ghost or even a demon, the possibility of DIY
going bad is very, very high...

**ALL-NEW ORIGINAL TALES
OF HAUNTED HOME REPAIR BY**

CHARLAINE HARRIS
PATRICIA BRIGGS
VICTOR GISCHLER
JAMES GRADY
HEATHER GRAHAM
SIMON R. GREEN
STACIA KANE
TONI L. P. KELNER
E. E. KNIGHT
ROCHELLE KRICH
MELISSA MARR
SEANAN McGUIRE
SUZANNE McLEOD
S. J. ROZAN

Coming August 2011 from Ace Books

Includes a never-before-published
SOOKIE STACKHOUSE story!

penguin.com

M808T1110

Now on **HBO**®,
True Blood®, the original series
based on the Sookie Stackhouse novels
from

Charlaine Harris

DEAD UNTIL DARK

Sookie Stackhouse is a small-time cocktail waitress in small-town Louisiana. She's quiet, keeps
to herself, and doesn't get out much. Not because
she's not pretty. She is. It's just that, well, Sookie
has this sort of "disability." She can read minds.
And that doesn't make her too dateable. Then
along comes Bill. He's tall, dark, handsome—and
Sookie can't hear a word he's thinking, making
him her perfect match.

But Bill has a disability of his own: He's a vampire
with a bad reputation. He hangs with a seriously
creepy crowd, all suspected of—big surprise—
murder. And when one of Sookie's coworkers is
killed, she fears she's next.

M336T0111

THE COMPLETE THIRD SEASON

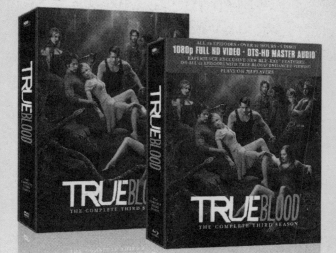

COMING IN JUNE
TO DVD, BLU-RAY™
AND DIGITAL DOWNLOAD

"ONE OF THE FINEST
ITALIAN COOKBOOKS EVER
TO APPEAR IN ENGLISH."
Craig Claiborne

"MARCELLA HAZAN
IS SYNONYMOUS
WITH ITALIAN CUISINE."
James Beard

"THE BEST NORTHERN ITALIAN
COOKBOOK TO BE PUBLISHED YET
. . . likely to do for Italian
cuisine what Julia Child
did for French."
Ms.

"Her recipes are wrought with a
craftsperson's pride. They contain a
teacher's attention to detail without
becoming ponderous. They are in short
a pleasure to work with."
The Washington Post

THE CLASSIC ITALIAN COOKBOOK
The Art of Italian Cooking
and the Italian Art of Eating

Also by Marcella Hazan
Published by Ballantine Books:

MORE CLASSIC ITALIAN COOKING

Marcella Hazan

The Classic Italian Cookbook

The Art of Italian Cooking
and the Italian Art of Eating

BALLANTINE BOOKS • NEW YORK

THE CLASSIC ITALIAN COOKBOOK
The Art of Italian Cooking and
the Italian Art of Eating

Copyright © 1973 by Marcella Hazan

Illustrations Copyright © 1984 by Susan Gaber

All rights reserved under International and Pan-American Copyright Conventions. Published in the United States by Ballantine Books, a division of Random House, Inc., New York, and simultaneously in Canada by Random House of Canada Limited, Toronto.

The excerpt on *Bollito misto*, pages 311–312, is from *The Passionate Epicure* by Marcel Rouff, copyright © 1962 by E. P. Dutton & Co., Inc., publishers, and is used with their permission.

Library of Congress Catalog Card Number: 75-39785

ISBN 0-345-31402-6

This edition published by arrangement with Alfred A. Knopf, Inc.

Originally published by Harper's Magazine Press.

Manufactured in the United States of America

First Ballantine Books Edition: February 1984
Fourteenth Printing: April 1992

Pattern Design by Asher Kingsley

To Victor, my husband, *con tutto il mio amore e profonda tenerezza*. Without his confidence I would not have started this work, without his support I would soon have abandoned it, without his hand next to mine I could not have given it its final form and expression. His name really belongs on the title page.

Contents

Illustrations

Acknowledgments

It is impossible for cooks ever to give a full account of their debts. Our skills, our tastes, our discoveries, all rest upon the compressed layers of experience of family, friends, chance acquaintances, other cooks, and the long ranks of the generations that have preceded us.

I regret that time and an ungrateful memory have blurred the identity of some of my benefactors. Among them are a deft and patient woman in the vegetable market at the foot of the Quirinale hill, turning from her work to give me the best artichoke-trimming demonstration I have ever seen, and a perfect recipe for making artichokes *alla romana*. The fishermen of my home town, making their dinner on the cobblestone dock after unloading and selling their catch, broiling their fish to absolute perfection. The maids of my youth, working in my father's and my uncle's houses, from whose superb, natural skills I was learning how to cook, unawares, as I discovered many years later.

Fortunately, not all my creditors need to remain anonymous. First, and most important among them, are my family. My father's mother, Nonna Polini, whose handmade pasta remains the paragon to which I must compare every other. My father, Fin, who was skilled and true in everything he put his hand to. My mother, Maria Leonelli, who is still the best cook in the family, my aunt Licia Conconi, who taught me how to make *polenta*, and my cousin Armando Sabbadini. I am grateful too to my mother-in-law, Julia Hazan, through whom I discovered a remarkable new world of cooking.

I should also like to express my debt to Ada Boni, whose *Talismano della Felicità* was indeed a happy talisman in the early period of my marriage, when I first faced alone the mysteries of the kitchen and the expectations of a food-loving husband.

I am further indebted for recipes and assistance to Ginesio Albonetti of La Griglia D'Oro, Cesenatico; "Zia" Ines Anzuoni; Maria Bartoli; Evio Battellani, creator of the Scrigno di Venere and master of Al Cantunzein, Bologna's temple of pasta; Vittorio Boldrini, of Cesenatico's Pesce Spada; Stella Donati, of Star food products; Claudia Fioravanti; Marchese Giuseppe Gavotti, chancellor of the Accademia Italiana della Cucina, sage and witty gentleman of Italian gastronomy; Lorenza Magnani; Roberto Moglia; Pietro Molesini, owner-chef of Al Caminetto, Padriciano (Trieste); Pietro Piromallo of Bologna; Cavaliere Renato Ramponi, chef de cuisine of Florence's Grand Hotel; Silvano Renna of L'Osteriaccia at Cusercoli; Vittorio Rocchi of the non-pareil Rocca di Bazzano restaurant; Bruna Saglio; Valeria and Maria Luisa Simili of Bologna's great bakery; and Bruno Tasselli, of Bologna's Pappagallo.

To Lucia Parini, for her irreplaceable and skillful assistance, I owe special thanks.

I am also particularly grateful to Grace Chu, from whom I learned about teaching cooking; to my students, whose experiences have contributed so much to this book; and to Craig Claiborne, whose warm interest has been chiefly responsible for my cooking having come to public notice.

As for the making of the book, my gratitude forever goes to my editor and publisher, Peter Mollman, for his generous and never-flagging support, to Jane Mollman for her saintly patience and her sensitive, informed reading of the manuscript, and to George Koizumi, for the liveliest and clearest illustrations with which a cookbook author has ever had her recipes illuminated.

Preface

Nothing significant exists under Italy's sun that is not touched by art. Its food is twice blessed because it is the product of two arts, the art of cooking and the art of eating. While each nourishes the other, they are in no way identical accomplishments. The art of cooking produces the dishes, but it is the art of eating that transforms them into a meal.

Through the art of eating, an Italian meal becomes a precisely orchestrated event, where the products of the season, the traditions of place, the intuitions of the cook, and the knowledgeable joy of the participants are combined into one of the most satisfying experiences of which our senses are capable.

I hope that these pages will reward those looking for new dishes with which to please themselves and their friends. But I have tried to put something more here. In my classes I attempt to demonstrate not only how to make dishes but how to make meals. I hope that this book can be used to that same end, and that it will help its readers discover some of the happiness and beauty of the total Italian food experience.

M. H.

New York City
December, 1972

INTRODUCTION

ITALIAN COOKING:
WHERE DOES IT COME FROM?

The first useful thing to know about Italian cooking is that, as such, it actually doesn't exist. "Italian cooking" is an expression of convenience rarely used by Italians. The cooking of Italy is really the cooking of its regions, regions that until 1861 were separate, independent, and usually hostile states. They submitted to different rulers, they were protected by sovereign armies and navies, and they developed their own cultural traditions and, of course, their own special and distinct approaches to food.

The unique features of each region and of the individual towns and cities within it can still be easily observed when one travels through Italy today. These are living differences that appear in the physical cast of the people, in their temperament, in their spoken language, and, most clearly, in their cooking.

The cooking of Venice, for example, is so distant from that of Naples, although they are both Italian cities specializing in seafood, that not a single authentic dish from the one is to be found on the other's table. There are unbridgeable differences between Bologna and Florence, each the capital of its own region, yet only sixty miles apart. There are also subtle but substantial distinctions to be made between the cooking of Bologna and of other cities in its

1

region, such as Cesena, fifty-two miles away, Parma, fifty-six miles, or Modena, just twenty-three miles to the north.

It isn't only from the inconstant contours of political geography that cooking in Italy has taken its many forms. Even more significant has been the forceful shaping it has received from the two dominant elements of the Italian landscape—the mountains and the sea.

Italy is a peninsula shaped like a full-length boot that has stepped into the Mediterranean and Adriatic seas up to its thigh. There it is fastened to the rest of Europe by an uninterrupted chain of the tallest mountains on the continent, the Alps. At the base of the Alps spreads Italy's only extensive plain, which reaches from Venice on the Adriatic coast westward through Lombardy and into Piedmont. This is the dairy zone of Italy, and the best-irrigated land. The cooking fat is butter, almost exclusively, and rice or corn mush (polenta) are the staples. Up to a few years ago, when thousands of workers from the south came north to find jobs in Turin and Milan, macaroni was virtually unknown here.

The northern plain gives out just before touching the Mediterranean shore, where it reaches the foothills of the other great mountain chain of Italy, the Apennines. This chain extends from north to south for the whole length of the country like the massive, protruding spine of some immense beast. It is composed of gentle, softly rounded hills sloping toward the seas on the eastern and western flanks and, in the central crest, of tall, forbidding stone peaks. Huddled within the links of this chain are countless valleys, isolated from each other until modern times like so many Shangri-las, giving birth to men, cultures, and cooking styles profoundly different in character.

To a certain extent, the Apennine range helps determine that variety of climates which has also favored diversity in cooking. Turin, the capital of Piedmont, standing in the open plain at the foot of the Alps, has winters more severe than Copenhagen. The Ligurian coast, just a few miles to the west, nestles against the Apennines, which intercept the cold Alpine winds and allow the soft Mediterranean breezes to create that mild, pleasant climate which has made the Riviera famous. Here flowers abound, the olive begins to flourish, and the fragrance of fresh herbs invades nearly every dish.

On the eastern side of the same Apennines that hug the

Riviera coast lies the richest gastronomic region in Italy, Emilia-Romagna. Its capital, Bologna, is probably the only city in all Italy whose name is instantly associated in the Italian mind not with monuments, not with artists, not with heroes, but with food.

Emilia-Romagna is almost evenly divided between mountainous land and flat, with the Apennines at its back and at its feet the last remaining corner of the northern plain rolling out to the Adriatic. This Emilian plain is extraordinarily fertile land enriched by the alluvial deposits of the countless Apennine torrents that have run through it toward the sea. It leads all Italy in the production of wheat, which perhaps explains why here it is almost heresy to sit down to a meal that doesn't include a dish of homemade pasta. The vegetables of Emilia-Romagna may well be the tastiest in the world, surpassing even the quality of French produce. The fruit from its perfumed orchards is so remarkable in flavor that local consumers must compete with foreign markets for it. Italy's best hams and sausages are made here and also some of its richest dairy products, among which is the greatest Italian cheese, Parmesan.

In Emilia-Romagna the sea has been as bountiful as the land. The Adriatic, perhaps because it contains less salt than the Mediterranean, perhaps because it is constantly purified by fresh waters from Alpine streams, produces fish famous in all Italy for its fine delicate flesh. When a restaurant in any part of Italy offers fish from the Adriatic it makes sure its patrons know it. Since the quality of the fish is so fine it requires little enhancement in the kitchen, and Adriatic fish cookery has become the essence of masterful simplicity. Nowhere else except perhaps in Japan is fish fried or broiled so simply and well.

In crossing Emilia-Romagna's southern border into Tuscany every aspect of cooking seems to have turned over and, like an embossed coin, landed on its reverse side. Tuscany's whole approach to the preparation of food is in such sharp contrast to that of Bologna that their differences seem to sum up two main and contrary manifestations of Italian character.

Out of the abundance of the Bolognese kitchen comes cooking that is exuberant, prodigal with precious ingredients, and wholly baroque in its restless exploration of every agreeable combination of texture and flavor. The Florentine, careful and calculating, is a man who knows the measure of all things, and his cooking is an austerely composed play upon essential and unadorned themes.

Bologna will sauté veal in butter, stuff it with the finest mountain ham, coat it with aged Parmesan, simmer it in sauce, and smother it with the costliest truffles. Florence takes a T-bone steak of noble size and grills it quickly over a blazing fire, adding nothing but the aroma of freshly ground pepper and olive oil. Both are triumphs.

From Tuscany down, the Apennines and their foothills in their southward march spread nearly from coast to coast so that the rest of Italy is almost entirely mountainous. As a result, two major changes take place in cooking. First, as it is cheaper and simpler on a hillside to cultivate a grove of olive trees than to raise a herd of dairy cows, olive oil supplants butter as the dominant cooking fat. Second, as we get farther away from the rich wheat fields of Emilia-Romagna, soft, homemade egg and flour pasta gives way to the more economical, mass-produced, eggless hard macaroni, the staple of the south.

From Naples south the climate becomes considerably warmer. A harsher sun bakes the land, inflames the temper of the inhabitants, and ignites their sauces. At the toe-tip of the peninsula and in the heart of Sicily there is little rainfall, and most of that only in the winter months. The lands are parched by harsh, burning winds and the temperatures are sometimes higher than in southern Florida and Texas. The food is as extreme as the climate. The colors of the vegetables are intense and violent, the pastas are so pungent that they often need no topping of cheese, and the sweets are of the most overpowering richness.

There is no need here and certainly there is no room to examine in greater detail all the richly varied forms that history and geography have pressed upon the cooking of Italy. What is important is to be aware that these differences exist and that behind the screen of the too-familiar term "Italian cooking" lies concealed, waiting to be discovered, a multitude of riches.

THE ITALIAN ART OF EATING

Not everyone in Italy may know how to cook, but nearly everyone knows how to eat. Eating in Italy is one more manifestation of the Italian's age-old gift of making art out of life.

The Italian art of eating is sustained by a life measured in nature's rhythms, a life that falls in with the slow wheelings of the seasons, a life in which, until very recently, produce and fish reached the table not many hours after having been taken from the soil or the sea.

It is an art that has also been abetted by the custom of shutting down the whole country at midday for two hours or more. Fathers come home from work and children from school, and there is sufficient time for the whole family to celebrate, not just the most important meal, but more likely also the most important event of the day.

There probably has been no influence, not even religion, so effective in creating a rich family life, in maintaining a civilized link between the generations, as this daily sharing of a common joy. Eating in Italy is essentially a family art, practiced for and by the family. The finest accomplishments of the home cook are not reserved like the good silver and china for special occasions or for impressing guests, but are offered daily for the pleasure and happiness of the family group.

The best cooking in Italy is not, as in France, to be found in restaurants, but in the home. One of the reasons that Italian restaurants here are generally so poor is that they do not have Italian home cooking with which to compete. The finest restaurants in Italy are not those glittering establishments known to every traveler, but the very small, family-run *trattorie* of ten or twelve tables that offer home cooking only slightly revised by commercial adaptations. Here the menus are unnecessary, sometimes nonexistent, and almost always illegible. Patrons know exactly what they want, and in ordering a meal they are evoking patterns established countless times at home.

Italian food may be a midnight spaghetti snack after the theater, a pizza and a glass of wine, a cool salad on a sultry summer noon. But an Italian *meal* is something else entirely;

5

it is a many-layered experience far richer and more complete than this.

Out of the potentially infinite combinations of first and second courses, of side dishes, of sauces and seasonings, an Italian meal, whether it is set out at home for the entire family or consumed in solitary communion in a restaurant, emerges as a complex composition free of discordant notes. Its elements may vary according to the season and the unique desires of the moment, but their relationships are governed by a harmonious and nearly invariable arrangement.

There is no main course to an Italian meal. With some very rare exceptions, such as *ossobuco* with *risotto*, the concept of a single dominant course is entirely foreign to the Italian way of eating. There are, at a minimum, two principal courses, which are never, never brought to the table at the same time.

The first course may be pasta either in broth or with sauce, or it can be a risotto or a soup. *Minestra*, which is the Italian for "soup," is also used to mean the first course whether it is a soup or not. This is because, to the Italian mind, the first course, even when it is sauced pasta or *risotto*, is still a soup in the sense that it is served in a deep dish and that it always precedes and never accompanies the meat, fowl, or fish course.

After there has been sufficient time to relish and consume the first course, to salute its passing with some wine, and to regroup the taste buds for the next encounter, the second course comes to the table. The choice of the second course is usually a development of the theme established by the first. The reverse may also be true, when the first course is chosen in anticipation of what the second will be. If the second course is going to be beef braised in wine, you will not preface it with spaghetti in clam sauce or with a dish of *lasagne* heavily laced with meat. You might prefer a *risotto* with asparagus, with zucchini, or with plain Parmesan cheese. Or a dish of green *gnocchi*. Or a light potato soup. If you are going to start with *tagliatelle alla bolognese* (homemade noodles with meat sauce), you might want to give your palate some relief by following with a simple roast of veal or chicken. On the other hand, you would not choose a second course so bland, such as steamed fish, that it could not stand up to the impact of the first.

The second course is often attended by one or two vegetable side dishes, which sometimes may develop into a full course of their own. The special pleasures of the Italian table are never keener or more apparent than in this moment when the vegetables appear. In Italian menus the word for a vegetable side dish is *contorno*, which can be translated literally as "contour." This reveals exactly what role vegetables play, because it is the choice of vegetables that defines the meal, that gives it shape, that encircles it with the flavors, textures, and colors of the season.

The sober winter taste, the austere whites and gray-greens of artichokes, cardoons, celery, cauliflower; the sweetness and the tender hues of spring in the first asparagus, the earliest peas, baby carrots, young fava beans; the voluptuous gifts of summer: the luscious eggplant, the glossy green pepper, the sun-reddened tomato, the succulent zucchini; the tart and scented taste of autumn in leeks, finocchio, fresh spinach, red cabbage; these do more than quiet our hunger. Through their presence the act of eating becomes a way of sharing our life with nature. And this is precisely what is at the heart of the Italian art of eating.

An Italian meal is a story told from nature, taking its rhythms, its humors, its bounty and turning them into episodes for the senses. As nature is not a one-act play, so an Italian meal cannot rest on a single dish. It is instead a lively sequence of events, alternating the crisp with the soft and yielding, the pungent with the bland, the variable with the staple, the elaborate with the simple.

It takes a theme such as "fish," states it very gently in a simple antipasto of tender, boiled young squid delicately seasoned with olive oil, parsley, and lemon, contrasts it with a rich and creamy shrimp risotto, and restates it with a superbly broiled bass that sums up every pure and natural quality with which fish has been endowed. All this subsides in a tart salad of seasonal greens and closes on the sweet, liquid note of fresh sliced fruit in wine.

This book has been organized in the same sequence as an Italian meal: first courses first, second courses second, side dishes. Antipasti lead the procession, salads and dessert close it. Recipes for one course carry suggestions on how to choose a course to follow or precede it. The most suitable vegetable accompaniment is suggested with the second course. Through this constant reminder of those patterns which form the Italian way of eating I hope the reader will discover that there is something more significant to an Italian meal than a single overpowering dish oozing sauce and melted cheese.

In the relationships of its varied parts an Italian meal develops something very close to the essence of civilized life itself. No dish overwhelms another, either in quantity or flavor, each leaves room for new appeals to the eye and palate, each fresh sensation of taste, color, and texture interlaces a lingering recollection of the last.

Of course, no one expects that the Italian way of eating can be wholly absorbed into everyday American life. Even in Italy it is succumbing to the onrushing uniformity of an industrial society. In Blake's phrase, man's brain is making the world unlivable for man's spirit. Yet, it is possible even from the tumultuous center of the busiest city life to summon up the life-enhancing magic of the Italian art of eating. What it requires is generosity. You must give liberally of time, of patience, of the best raw materials. What it returns is worth all you have to give.

INGREDIENTS

The character of a cuisine is determined more by basic approach than by ingredients. Ingredients come and go, depending on popular taste and the changing patterns of commerce. It is a picture that emerges more clearly as one steps away from it. It is hard to imagine Italian cooking, and that of Naples in particular, without tomatoes. And Venetians would go into shock if they were deprived of *polenta*. But tomatoes and corn are both fairly recent newcomers to the two venerable cuisines. In the recipes of this book I have introduced shallots, which, although they are an ancient Mediterranean commodity, are not generally available in Italy. Yet they adapt themselves with perfect grace to Italian cooking, and in many instances are preferable to onions.

This is not said to encourage indifference to a precise choice of ingredients but rather to discourage an exaggerated dependence on them. A heavy hand with the garlic or the tomato sauce does not make Italian cooking. There is no question that there are certain components without which it would be impossible to reproduce the taste of Italian cooking as we know it today. Fortunately, these are all available here in some form. In the following list, some of the most important ones are briefly considered.

BAY LEAVES

Alloro

Bay leaves go very nicely with roasts of meat and chicken. Adding them to the fire when broiling fish over charcoal is also a nice touch. Buy them whole from Greek or Italian grocers and store them in a tightly closed glass jar in a cool cupboard.

BROTH

Brodo

Broth is almost as necessary to Italian cooking as stock is to French cooking, although Italian broth is much thinner and less concentrated in flavor than stock. All you need for broth is a few vegetables, some beef, veal, and chicken bones, and, ideally, some good scraps of meat and chicken. If you are doing *ossobuco* (Braised Veal Shanks, Milan Style, page 246) have the butcher saw the bony ends off the shanks, and save them for a broth. Do the same when boning a breast of chicken. If you are not ready to cook these scraps immediately, store them in the freezer and make your broth when you have a nice assortment of bones and meat trimmings. A broth keeps indefinitely in the refrigerator if you boil it for 15 minutes every 3 or 4 days. Or you may freeze it for longer periods. You should always have some on hand.

HOMEMADE MEAT BROTH

Makes about 1½ quarts of broth

1 teaspoon salt
1 carrot, peeled
1 small yellow onion, peeled
1 stalk celery
¼ sweet green pepper

1 canned Italian tomato
1 small potato, peeled
6 to 8 cups assorted bones and meat scraps

Put all the ingredients in a stockpot and cover with cold water by 2 inches. Set the cover askew and bring to a boil. When boiling, regulate the heat so that the liquid cooks at the barest simmer. From time to time, but especially during the first few minutes, skim off the scum that rises to the surface. Cook for 2 to 3 hours, without ever letting the liquid come to a steady boil. Strain the broth into a glass or porcelain container and allow to cool uncovered. When cool, store, uncovered, in the refrigerator. When the fat on the surface has hardened, remove it.

If you have not used it up after 4 days, bring the broth to a boil for 10 minutes, allow it to cool, and refrigerate again. If in the meantime you have accumulated other good scraps of meat and bones, add them to the broth, add more vegetables (all but the tomato), add enough water to cover by about 2 inches, and repeat the whole cooking process. In this manner you will never be without good homemade broth.

NOTE
Do not use lamb or pork bones unless you need a particularly strong-tasting broth.

LUGANEGA SAUSAGE

One of the most serious shortcomings of Italian food stores is their lack of good fresh sausages. I have tried every variety of so-called Italian sausages without ever finding any that were acceptable. The only exception is a sausage available in long, continuous coils, not separated into links, called *luganega*. Even this is a qualified exception, because pork butchers here do not make *luganega* as they do in Italy, with pork shoulder and Parmesan cheese. However, it is milder and more honest in taste than all other local Italian sausages, and you can expect very satisfactory results from it.

MORTADELLA

Mortadella is Bologna's most famous pork product, and many Italians consider it the finest sausage in Italy. A well-made *mortadella* is very smooth in texture and possesses a subtle and delicate savoriness. It consists of various cuts of pork finely ground, boiled, and larded. It is delicious in a sandwich, excellent in a plate of mixed cold cuts, and necessary to the cooking of many Bolognese dishes. *Mortadella* is the largest of sausages, in Bologna often reaching a girth of 18 inches or more. Here it is less than half that size. Unfortunately, local mortadella is, at best, an only partially satisfactory imitation of the original product. We must be content that it is available at all, and make use of it. When buying it, do not let your grocer slice it too thin. It should be cut at least ⅛ inch thick.

DRIED WILD MUSHROOMS

Funghi secchi

In the fall and spring one of the most thrilling sights in Italian markets is that of mountains of orange, cream-colored, and nut-brown wild mushrooms fresh from the woods. Ah, the haunting aroma of giant mushroom caps, sautéed with oil, garlic, and parsley! Alas, we are well protected from such temptations here. But while we cannot buy fresh wild mushrooms, their woodsy fragrance has been captured in the dried variety. Drying deprives the mushroom of its succulence but compensates for this by concentrating its flavor. Dried mushrooms can no longer be used as a vegetable, but they are a marvelous seasoning for sauces, *risotto*, meat, and chicken. They are available in Italian groceries, and sometimes at the supermarket. When buying them, look for large, creamy-brown sections. Avoid the dark brown, crumbly kind. Choice mushrooms are expensive, but a little goes a long way. If stored in a tightly closed metal box, they will keep indefinitely.

The water in which dried mushrooms are reconstituted is full of flavor and should never be discarded. Wherever dried mushrooms are called for, the recipe will indicate how the water is to be used.

OLIVE OIL

Olio d'oliva

In the center and south of Italy, in the islands, and along both coasts, olive oil is the fundamental cooking fat. Unlike peanut oil or other vegetable oils, olive oil has a decided taste, which should not be used indiscriminately. The recipes in this book reflect the current trend of Italian cooking by using olive oil only where its presence is essential. In those circumstances where its flavor would be obtrusive and unnecessary to the harmony of a dish it has been supplanted by vegetable oil. However, where raw oil is required, as in salads, the use of anything but olive oil is inconceivable.

Most olive oil packed for export has been so highly refined that it has only the faintest suggestion of olives. This is true of nearly all the widely distributed brands. A recipe calling for olive oil will not be entirely successful with such thin, impalpable oil. Good olive oil should have both the color and taste of the green olive, and that is what you should look for. You are most likely to find it in the green, fruity oils from Sicily, such as Madre Sicilia or Due Sicilie.

After you open the can, decant the oil into a large glass bottle or ceramic jug and leave it uncorked. It will keep indefinitely.

PANCETTA

Pancetta is exactly the same cut of pork as bacon, except that it is not smoked. Instead, it is cured in salt and spices. It comes tightly rolled up in a salami shape, and it is sliced to order. The convenient way to buy it is to get ¼ to ½ pound in thin slices and an equal amount in a single slice. For some recipes you will use the slices just as they are, while for others you will cut the larger piece into cubes or strips. *Pancetta* keeps up to three weeks in the refrigerator, if carefully sealed in plastic wrap.

When it is of good quality, *pancetta* can be eaten as it is, like prosciutto or any other cold cut. In Italian cooking it is used as a flavoring agent in sauces, pasta fillings, vegetables, and roasts. When used next to veal it bastes it as it cooks, and keeps it from drying.

There are no exact substitutes for *pancetta*, but if it is not obtainable you can replace it with prosciutto or unsmoked ham. As far as I know, *pancetta* is available only in Italian food stores.

PARMESAN CHEESE

Parmigiano-reggiano

This precious cheese, which is an inseparable part of much Italian cooking, is produced by just five small provinces in the old Duchy of Parma, now absorbed into Emilia. It is made only during the mild months of the year, from spring through fall, when the cows can amble out and feed upon the richest pasture in Italy. It is aged at least two years, but good food shops in Italy carry Parmesan that is three or four years old, and even older.

Parmesan is straw yellow in color and has a mellow, rounded, slightly salty taste. It is the finest cheese for cooking because it melts without running and without disintegrating into a rubbery tangle. It has no peer, of course, for grating over pasta, and when it is freshly cut it deserves to be eaten as it is, accompanied by the best red wine you can afford.

When buying Parmesan cheese, ask to look at it and taste it before it is cut for you. If it is whitish and dry, and leaves a bitter aftertaste, do not buy it or, if you must, buy as little as you can get away with. If it is pale yellow, slightly moist on the tongue, and pleasantly salty, invest in a good-sized piece. A three-pound piece of properly wrapped Parmesan will keep for a few weeks in the refrigerator.

How to Store Parmesan

To maintain the freshness of Parmesan cheese you must prevent its moisture from escaping. As soon as you get it home, wrap the cheese in a double or triple thickness of aluminum foil. Make sure the foil is not torn at any point and that it is tightly sealed. Keep it on the bottom shelf of the refrigerator.

Parmesan is usually sold with some of its crust. When cutting off a piece, always cut it with part of the crust attached, because the cheese left next to the crust tends to dry faster. Do not discard the crust. Wrap it and store it like the cheese and save it to use in soups. Do not grate much more cheese than you need. Grated cheese does not keep.

After you have had the cheese a while, you may notice that it has become drier and whiter. If this happens, moisten a piece of cheesecloth and twist it until it is no more than damp. Wrap it around the cheese, then wrap and seal with aluminum foil. Refrigerate overnight. The following day remove the cheesecloth and rewrap with just aluminum foil.

The recipes in this book call for freshly grated Parmesan cheese. Do not under any circumstances use ready-grated cheese sold in jars. Even if this commercially grated cheese were of good quality, which it is not, it would have lost all its flavor long before getting to the market. It is of no interest whatever to Italian cooking.

PARSLEY

Prezzemolo

All Italian vegetable stores, and now many supermarkets, carry Italian parsley. It has a larger, less curly leaf than regular parsley, and a better developed, yet less pungent fragrance. The stem is milder than the leaf, and can sometimes be substituted for the leaves for a more toned-down flavor. For Italian cooking you really should use Italian parsley, but if it is not available don't let it worry you. The other variety is quite satisfactory.

PEPPER

Pepe

Ready-ground pepper is one of those modern conveniences that keep giving progress a bad name. Why it exists I do not know. It is certainly no more work to twist a pepper mill than to brandish a shaker, but there is an enormous difference in the result. The aroma of pepper is short-lived. All that you get with ready-ground pepper is some of its pungency.

Black pepper is the whole fruit of the pepper plant. White pepper is simply black pepper stripped of its shell. White pepper is stronger, but black pepper is used more frequently in Italian cooking because it is more aromatic. Unless you are addicted to pepper, do not buy a large amount at one time. Its flavor is perishable.

RICE

Riso

Italian rice is thicker and shorter than American rice. It takes a little longer to cook, but it has more "tooth" and body. It is ideal for *risotto* because the grains adhere creamily to each other without surrendering their individual firmness. It is excellent also for all Italian soups.

"Arborio" is the generic name of the most commonly imported variety of Italian rice. It is available here under more than one brand name, and can be obtained not only from Italian groceries but also from the food shops of many department stores.

RICOTTA

Ricotta is a soft, bland, white milk product made from whey, that watery part of the milk which separates from the curd when this is made into cheese. Large use of it is made in Emilia, where it is put into delicate fillings for pasta. Also famous are the ricotta cheesecakes of the south. Fresh, true ricotta can be obtained at a few Italian food stores. It is extremely perishable, and even under refrigeration it should be used within 24 to 48 hours. A passable substitute is the more long-lived whole-milk ricotta readily available at most supermarkets.

Perhaps because they are so similar in appearance, some authors suggest that ricotta and cottage cheese are interchangeable. This is a most grievous error. Cottage cheese is completely un-Italian in taste, and should not be contemplated as a replacement for ricotta.

ROMANO CHEESE

Pecorino romano

Romano is Italy's oldest cheese, whose beginnings probably coincide with those of Rome. It is a hard grating cheese made from sheep's milk, hence also called *pecorino*. It is very much sharper than Parmesan and, when grated, breaks down into smaller, more powdery granules. It is not to be considered a zestier alternative to Parmesan. The aggressiveness of Romano enhances such spicy dishes as Bucatini with Pancetta, Tomatoes, and Hot Pepper (page 100), but it would be out of character and strike a jarring note in Tuscan soups, delicate Bolognese pastas, or the *risotti* of the north.

Romano does not make an agreeable table cheese.

ROSEMARY

Rosmarino

This herb is so frequently used to flavor roasted meat or chicken that in Italy the fragrance of rosemary in the house almost invariably means that there is a roast in progress in the kitchen. It is an easy herb to grow in a window box. In the spring, many plant stores will sell you a well-started pot of rosemary that will continue to grow and furnish you with fresh branches for years. Lacking this, you can use dried whole leaves, but avoid the powder.

SAGE

Salvia

The gray-green furry leaves of the sage plant are an excellent flavoring for meat and chicken and have a particular affinity for veal cooked with white wine. If you can grow your own sage or buy it fresh, it is preferable to the dried variety. But dried whole sage leaves can be quite satisfactory. Buy them in branches from Italian or Greek grocers. They will keep almost indefinitely when stored in a tightly closed glass jar or a plastic bag in a cool cupboard. Do not buy powdered sage—it is perfectly useless.

SEMOLINA

Semolino

Farina or semolina, known in Italian as *semolino*, is the coarse-grained particles of durum wheat, the same wheat from which spaghetti and other macaroni is made. Imported Italian *semolino* can be ordered from Italian groceries, and if you are fond of semolina *gnocchi* you'd be well advised to buy a substantial quantity that you can keep on hand. Italian *semolino* has more body and color than the American variety and it gives markedly superior results. Do not confuse *semolino* with quick-cooking breakfast farina.

SWEET MARJORAM AND ORÉGANO

Maggiorana e origano

Marjoram and orégano are closely related plants. Marjoram is considerably milder than orégano, and is used on occasion in northern and central cooking, in soups and braised meats. Orégano is virtually never used outside of southern cooking, where it appears frequently in tomato sauces, and sometimes with fish or salads.

WATER

Acqua

Water is the phantom ingredient in much Italian cooking. One of my students once protested, "When you add water, you add nothing!" But that is precisely why we use it. Italian cooking is the art of giving expression to the undisguised flavors of its ingredients. In many circumstances, an overindulgence in stock, wine, or other flavored liquids would tinge the complexion of a dish with an artificial glow. That is why some recipes will direct that if the quantity of broth used is not sufficient, you should continue cooking with water, as needed. We sometimes use water for deglazing, because it lasts just long enough to help scrape loose the cooking residues stuck to the pan, and then evaporates without a trace. Whenever broth or wine has a part in developing the flavor of a dish, it is in the recipe. Otherwise use water.

SOME NOTES ON KITCHEN EQUIPMENT

La Batteria di cucina

This is not a full-scale discussion of kitchen equipment, a subject that has been handled very competently in many other cook books. It is principally a list of those tools that are particularly necessary to Italian cooking and are sometimes missing from otherwise well-furnished kitchens.

POTS AND PANS

I tegami

The traditional pan of Italian peasant kitchens is made of earthenware. It is unsurpassed for cooking beans and all vegetables, to which aluminum sometimes imparts a harsh, metallic taste. Earthenware is excellent also for stews, fricassees, and slow-simmered sauces. The drawback to earthenware, aside from its fragility, is that it is porous and absorbs some of the cooking fat. If used frequently, it need not cause any concern. If used at long intervals, however, the fat may turn rancid and give off a disagreeable odor.

The best all-purpose cooking ware is heavy, enameled cast iron. It transmits and retains heat magnificently, it is suited to all foods, it is both oven-safe and flameproof, and you can usually serve directly from it at the table. It is also very easy to clean. Have several sizes and shapes available. Little ones are perfect for making a small amount of sauce. Oval casseroles with lids are all but indispensable for long, narrow roasts. Low, open baking pans are what you need for gratinéing vegetables. Two rectangular pans, 2½ to 3 inches high, in different lengths and widths, can be used for *lasagne*.

Absolutely necessary for Italian cooking is a series of heavy frying pans or skillets. You should have at least three—small, medium, and large. They should have very solid, thick bottoms, to help prevent scorching. There are some aluminum alloys that give you thickness without excessive weight. It is also useful to have at least one heavy cast-iron skillet, excellent for all high-temperature frying and for pan-broiling steaks.

For cooking pasta, you need a pot that will comfortably contain at least four quarts of water plus the pasta.

An asparagus cooker makes it considerably simpler to cook asparagus perfectly, and it is useful for other purposes, such as making broth. If you do not have one, you can use a fish poacher, which is indispensable for poaching fish whole. Do not use the poacher for high-temperature cooking, because it is usually made of thin-gauge metal.

CUTTING TOOLS

Per tagliare

In addition to the usual assortment of knives (which should include, incidentally, two or three well-honed paring knives), you need one with a large, flat, well-balanced blade for cutting pasta. A Chinese cleaver is perfect.

A sharp, efficient peeler, because, for Italian dishes, vegetables and fruit frequently require peeling.

A straight pastry wheel for cutting *tortelloni* and other pasta, and a fluted wheel for *pappardelle* noodles.

A half-moon for effortless chopping of vegetables.

ODDS AND ENDS

Aggegi vari

A meat pounder for flattening *scaloppine* and cutlets.
One or more large hardwood chopping boards.
Several wooden spoons with handles of varying lengths.

A large ladle for soups, and a small one for degreasing sauces.

A long-handled fork for turning frying food without getting too close to the pan.

A slotted spatula and a slotted spoon for retrieving food from cooking fat.

A deep slotted spoon for retrieving *gnocchi* and other pasta. The Chinese stores have lovely ones made of bamboo and wire.

A large pasta colander with handles which you can stand in the basin when draining pasta.

A three-footed ring which will fit into any pan and convert it into the bottom half of a double boiler.

A food mill with three different disks. (A blender is not a satisfactory substitute because it flattens out textures to a greater degree than is desirable for Italian dishes.)

Whisks in different sizes.

A rotary grater for Parmesan cheese.

A four-sided grater for vegetables, mozzarella, nutmeg, and so on.

An Italian rolling pin for pasta (see page 107).

A pepper mill.

Italian coffeepots in two-, four-, and six-cup sizes.

SAUCES

Le Salse

This is the briefest chapter in the book because, outside of pasta dishes, sauces are used infrequently in Italian cooking. Most fish, meat, and fowl courses stand or fall on their own merits, with no more sauce to enhance their appeal than can be gleaned from loosening the residues or thickening the cooking juices they leave in the pan. Unlike classic French cuisine, Italian cooking has no basic central sauces, branching off and spreading their network throughout the repertory.

The most important Italian sauces are those used for pasta. In Italian, however, they are not even called *salsa* (the Italian for sauce). The correct term is *sugo*, for which there is no accurate English equivalent. There is an infinite number of them, but for an Italian cook, they do not have an independent existence of their own; they are a natural outgrowth of the dish in which they appear. For this reason, and to help steer the reader away from unsuccessful pairings, pasta and its sauces are taken up together in the chapter on first courses. Here you will find just four recipes: mayonnaise, béchamel, piquant green sauce, and red sauce.

There is no need to discuss the uses of mayonnaise, which

go well beyond the boundaries of any cuisine. In Italy it is used with many cold dishes, especially cold poached fish. It is indispensable in the preparation of the tuna sauce that is part of one of the most splendid of all cold meat dishes, *vitello tonnato*, Sliced Cold Veal with Tuna Sauce (page 265).

Béchamel, despite its name, is a thoroughly Italian sauce. It is a key element in many pasta and vegetable dishes. The technique for béchamel given here produces a particularly fine, silken white sauce that you might want to use even for non-Italian recipes.

The piquant sauce and the red sauce are traditionally served with Mixed Boiled Meats (page 311), but they are very nice, too, with simple pan-broiled steaks or breaded veal cutlets. The piquant sauce is also an excellent sauce for fish, such as a fine cold, poached striped bass.

MAYONNAISE

Maionese

I can't imagine anyone with a serious interest in food using anything but homemade mayonnaise. Once you've had a little practice, it becomes one of the easiest and quickest sauces you can make. You can even prepare it two or three days ahead of time, storing it in the refrigerator in a small bowl tightly sealed with plastic wrap. Let it return to room temperature before using it. Mayonnaise can make or break any recipe of which it is a part. The commercial variety is so sugary and watery that it is beneath discussion.

You can make mayonnaise with olive oil or vegetable oil. It is lighter and more delicate with vegetable oil, but with fish olive oil is best. Use a pale yellow-green olive oil, such as the oil from Lucca or the Riviera. The deeper-green variety from the south of Italy or from Spain gives mayonnaise a somewhat bitter taste.

A most important point to remember when making mayonnaise is to have all the ingredients at room temperature. The bowl in which the eggs will be beaten and the blades of the electric beater should also be warmed up by dipping them in hot water and drying them quickly.

Makes over 1 cup.

2 egg yolks	2 tablespoons lemon
Salt	juice, approximately
1 to 1⅓ cups olive oil or	
vegetable oil (see	
note below)	

1. In a round-bottomed bowl, and using an electric beater set at medium speed, beat the egg yolks together with ¼ teaspoon salt until the yolks are very pale yellow and the consistency of thick cream. (Until you acquire more confidence in making mayonnaise, you might want to use the low setting on the beater.)

2. Add oil, drop by drop, while beating constantly. Stop pouring oil every few seconds, while you continue beating, until you see that all the oil you've added has been absorbed by the egg yolks and there is none floating free. Continue dribbling in oil and beating until the sauce has become quite thick. Add a teaspoon or less of lemon juice and continue beating. This will thin out the sauce a little. Add more oil, at a slightly faster pace than before, stopping from time to time while you continue beating to allow the egg yolks to absorb the oil completely. When the sauce becomes too thick add more lemon juice, until you've added the full 2 tablespoons. When you have finished adding all the oil, the mayonnaise is done.

3. Taste for salt, which it will surely need, and lemon. If the sauce is to be used for fish you will want it a bit on the tart side. Mix in any addition of salt or lemon with the beater.

REMEMBER:
- all ingredients must be at room temperature.
- the egg yolks must be beaten until they are pale yellow and creamy before adding oil.
- the oil must be added drop by drop until the sauce thickens.

And finally, *note*: Don't exceed ⅔ cup of oil per egg yolk. If you have no experience with making mayonnaise do not use more than ½ *cup of oil per egg yolk* the first few times.

BÉCHAMEL SAUCE

Salsa balsamella

Long before the French christened it "béchamel," a sauce
of flour and milk cooked in butter, called *balsamella*, was
a part of the cooking of Romagna. It is essential to many of
its pastas and vegetables, and such an unquestionably native
dish as *lasagne* could not exist without it.

Balsamella is possibly the simplest and most quickly made
of sauces. The only problem it poses is the formation of
lumps. If you add the milk as directed, a little bit at a time,
off the heat, beating the sauce constantly with a wooden
spoon, you should have absolutely no difficulty in producing
a perfectly smooth *balsamella* every time.

Makes 1⅔ cups medium-thick sauce

2 cups milk	3 tablespoons all-purpose
4 tablespoons butter	flour
	¼ teaspoon salt

1. In a small pan, heat the milk until it comes to the
very edge of a boil.
2. While you are heating the milk, melt the butter over
low heat in a heavy enameled iron saucepan of 4 to 6 cups'
capacity.
3. When the butter is melted, add all the flour, stirring
constantly with a wooden spoon. Let the flour and butter
bubble for 2 minutes, without ceasing to stir. Do not let
the flour become colored.
4. Turn off the heat and add the hot milk 2 tablespoons
at a time, stirring it constantly into the flour-and-butter
mixture. As soon as the first 2 tablespoons have been incorporated into the mixture, add another 2 tablespoons,
always stirring with your trusty spoon. When you have added
½ cup of milk to the mixture, you can start adding ¼
cup at a time, until you have added it all. (Never add more
than ¼ cup at one time.)
5. When all the milk has been incorporated, turn on the
heat to low, add the salt, and stir-cook until the sauce is as
dense as thick cream. If you need it thicker, cook and stir

a little while longer. If you need it thinner, cook a little less.

NOTE

When the sauce cools, it sets, and you will not be able to spread it. Therefore, inasmuch as it takes so little time to prepare, it is best to make it just before you are ready to use it. If you must make it in advance, reheat it slowly, stirring constantly until it is the right consistency again. Béchamel sauce can also be refrigerated.

PIQUANT GREEN SAUCE

Salsa verde

This is a tart green sauce that is always served with boiled meats (page 311) and often with boiled or steamed fish. If you are making it for meat, use vinegar; if for fish, lemon juice. You may vary the proportions according to taste, increasing the vinegar or lemon if you like it tarter, and adding salt when necessary.

For 4 servings

2½ tablespoons finely chopped parsley
2 tablespoons finely chopped capers
6 flat anchovy fillets, mashed in a mortar or bowl, OR 1 tablespoon anchovy paste
½ teaspoon very finely chopped garlic
½ teaspoon strong mustard, Dijon or German

½ teaspoon red wine vinegar (approximately), if the sauce will be used on meat OR 1 tablespoon strained lemon juice (approximately), if the sauce is for fish
½ cup olive oil
Salt, if necessary

1. Put the parsley, capers, mashed anchovy fillets, garlic, and mustard in a bowl and stir, mixing thoroughly. Add the vinegar or lemon juice and stir again. Add the olive oil, beating it vigorously into the other ingredients.

2. Taste for salt and for piquancy. (Add vinegar or lemon juice if you want it tarter, but add very small amounts at a time.)

NOTE
This sauce can be refrigerated for up to a week. Stir it well again before serving. It can also be used as dressing for Hard-Boiled Eggs with Piquant Sauce (page 42), but in that case you must hold back some of the oil.

RED SAUCE

Salsa rossa

This is an alternative to green sauce as an accompaniment to boiled meats. It is mellower, and it is served warm. Also excellent with Breaded Veal Cutlets, Milan Style (page 260) and with broiled steaks, it can be prepared ahead of time and refrigerated up to two weeks, but it must always be warmed up before serving.

For 4 servings

5 medium yellow onions, peeled and sliced thin
¼ cup vegetable oil
2 green peppers

2 cups canned Italian tomatoes, with their juice
A pinch of chopped hot red pepper
½ teaspoon salt

1. Cook the sliced onions in a saucepan with the oil over moderate heat until wilted and soft but not brown.
2. Remove the inner core and seeds from the green peppers. Peel the peppers with a potato peeler, and cut into ½-inch slices. Add to the wilted onions in the saucepan and continue cooking over moderate heat.
3. When the onions and peppers have been reduced by half in bulk, add the tomatoes, the hot pepper, and the salt. Continue cooking over low to moderate heat for 25 to 30 minutes, or until the tomatoes and oil separate. Taste for salt. Warm and stir just before serving.

ANTIPASTI

Antipasti are the rogues of the Italian table. Nothing in all gastronomy plays so boldly upon the eye to excite the palate and set gastric juices in motion. The most appropriate place for antipasti is in a restaurant, where they are usually strategically displayed so that they can cast their spell on every arriving patron.

They are far less frequently a part of the home meal. When served at home, antipasti usually consist of one or more of the wonderful Italian pork products: prosciutto, *mortadella*, *coppa*, mountain salami, dried sausages. Prosciutto is sometimes served with fruit. There can be no finer antipasto than sweet prosciutto with ripe figs or cantaloupe.

What is an antipasto on one occasion is not necessarily that on another. You will see more antipasti in the index than you will find in this chapter. This is because of the flexibility of many Italian dishes. For example, such an elegant antipasto as Cold Sliced Veal with Tuna Sauce (page 265) can be an excellent second course, and it is among the second courses that you will find it.

All together, there are not as many antipasti here as in other books, perhaps, or as are offered by some restaurants.

There are, however, a few more than are customarily prepared in an Italian home. Too much emphasis on antipasti puts a slightly commercial stress on an Italian meal. Use antipasti liberally for parties and buffets. But in the intimacy of a family meal use them wisely—which is to say, sparingly.

BAKED OYSTERS WITH OIL AND PARSLEY

Ostriche alla moda di Taranto

For 6 persons

Rock salt or well-washed
    pebbles
36 oysters, thoroughly
    washed and
    scrubbed, shucked,
    and each placed on
    a half shell

1½ tablespoons fine, dry
    unflavored bread
    crumbs
Freshly ground pepper,
    a twist of the mill
    for each oyster
¼ cup olive oil
Lemon juice

1. Preheat the oven to 500°.

2. Choose enough bake-and-serve pans to accommodate the oysters in one layer. Spread the rock salt or pebbles— the pebbles sold by Japanese stores can be very decorative—on the bottom of the pans. (The salt or pebbles serve both to keep the oysters from tipping and to retain heat.)

3. Arrange the oysters side by side in one layer in the pans. Top each oyster with a sprinkling of bread crumbs, a grinding of pepper, and a few drops of olive oil.

4. Place the oysters in the uppermost level of the preheated oven for 3 minutes. Before serving, moisten each oyster with a few drops of lemon juice.

BAKED OYSTERS WITH PARMESAN CHEESE

Ostriche alla parmigiana

For 6 persons

Rock salt or well-washed
    pebbles
36 oysters, thoroughly
    washed and
    scrubbed, shucked,
    and each placed on
    a half shell
6 tablespoons freshly
    grated Parmesan
    cheese

1 tablespoon fine, dry
    unflavored bread
    crumbs
Freshly ground pepper,
    a twist of the mill
    for each oyster
2½ tablespoons butter

1. Preheat the oven to 500°.
2. Spread the rock salt or pebbles on the bottom of enough bake-and-serve pans to accommodate the oysters in one layer. (See explanation in Step 2 of preceding recipe.)
3. Arrange the oysters side by side in the pans. Top each oyster with ½ teaspoon of grated cheese, a tiny pinch of bread crumbs, a grinding of pepper, and a dot of butter.
4. Place in the uppermost level of the preheated oven for 5 minutes. Serve piping hot.

COLD SALMON FOAM

Spuma fredda di salmone

For 6 persons

15 ounces canned salmon
¼ cup olive oil
2 tablespoons lemon
    juice
A pinch of salt

Freshly ground pepper,
    about 6 twists of the
    mill
1½ cups very cold
    whipping cream

1. Drain the salmon and look it over carefully for bones and bits of skin. Using a fork, crumble it in a mixing bowl. Add the oil, lemon juice, a little pinch of salt, and the pepper

and beat them into the salmon until you've obtained a smooth, evenly blended mixture.

2. In a cold mixing bowl, whip the cream with a whisk or electric beater until it is stiff. Delicately fold the cream into the salmon mixture until it is completely incorporated. Refrigerate for at least 2 hours, but preferably not more than 24.

NOTE

One attractive way of presenting this is to spoon each individual serving onto a lettuce leaf, making a small, rounded mound. Garnish it then by placing a black olive (not the sharp Greek variety) on the mound's peak, and standing a tomato slice and a lemon slice at divergent angles on either side of it. You can use this as a spread for canapés with cocktails or serve it as antipasto.

BROILED MUSSELS AND CLAMS ON THE HALF SHELL

Cozze e vongole passate ai ferri

For 4 to 6 persons

2 dozen littleneck clams, the tiniest you can find, cleaned as directed on page 50
2 dozen mussels, cleaned as directed on page 53
3 tablespoons finely chopped parsley
½ teaspoon finely chopped garlic
⅓ cup olive oil
½ cup fine, dry unflavored bread crumbs
1 canned Italian tomato, drained and cut into 2 dozen small strips
Lemon wedges

1. Put the clams and mussels in separate covered pots over high heat until they open their shells. Bear in mind that mussels open up much faster than clams, and take care to remove both mussels and clams from the heat as soon as they are open, or they will become tough. Detach the clams and mussels from their shells, setting aside half the clam shells and half the mussel shells. Rinse off the clams one by one in their own juice to remove all traces of sand.

2. Preheat the broiler.

3. Put the parsley, garlic, olive oil, and bread crumbs in a mixing bowl and add the clams and mussels. Mix well until both clams and mussels are thoroughly coated and let stand at least 20 minutes. (If you feel you will have trouble later distinguishing the clams from the mussels, divide the marinating ingredients into two parts and use two separate bowls.)

4. Wash the clam and mussel shells. In each half shell place one of its respective mollusks. Distribute the leftover marinade in the mixing bowl among all the clams and mussels and top each clam with a sliver of tomato. Place on the broiling pan and run under the hot broiler for just a few minutes, until a light crust forms. Serve hot, with wedges of lemon on the side.

ANCHOVIES

Acciughe

The heady fragrance of anchovies carries into the cooking of every Italian region, from Piedmont to Sicily. Southerners may use them with more abandon than central or northern Italians, but there is no good kitchen in Italy that gets along entirely without anchovies. The best anchovies you can use are those you fillet at home. Canned fillets or paste are a blessed convenience when you have nothing else available, but they cannot come close to the fuller, mellower flavor of homemade fillets. Fillets are made from whole, salt-cured anchovies, and, if you have access to a Greek grocer, that is the ideal place to buy them, although you can find them also at some Italian and other ethnic groceries. They are sold loose, by weight, out of a large can. If the can has been started recently, you are in luck, because the anchovies in the upper half of the can are always the best. The others tend to be saltier and drier. You should fillet the anchovies and steep them in oil as soon as possible, and no later than 24 hours after buying them, otherwise they will dry.

ANCHOVIES IN OIL

Whole salt-cured anchovies
(½ pound whole anchovies will yield about 4 servings of fillets)
Olive oil

1. Although all anchovies are not equally salty, it is best to begin by rinsing them quickly in cold running water to remove excess salt. Wipe dry with paper towels.

2. Spread some waxed paper or a flattened brown paper bag on the work counter. Lay the anchovies on the paper, and, grasping each by the tail, gently scrape off its skin with a knife. Remove the dorsal fin and the bones attached to it.

3. Using the knife, separate the anchovy into two halves and remove the spine. Place the fillets in a shallow rectangular dish. As soon as you have a full layer of fillets, cover with olive oil. You can build up several layers in the same dish, but make sure that they are all completely covered by oil. If you are not going to use them immediately, refrigerate them. They will keep for 10 days to 2 weeks.

NOTE
When the oil congeals in the refrigerator it turns into a yellowish-green solid. This doesn't mean it has gone bad. When it reaches room temperature again, it will return to a liquid.

MENU SUGGESTIONS

Aside from their many uses in cooking, anchovy fillets make a marvelous antipasto, the irresistible aroma of which will move the most indolent appetite. You may use them on canapés, of course, just as you would use canned fillets. But these homemade fillets are perfect just by themselves. Serve them with sweet butter, and slices of good crusty French or Italian bread. Follow with a substantial dish that won't be thrown off balance by the rather overwhelming flavor of the anchovies. Two suggestions: Bucatini with Pancetta, Tomatoes, and Hot Pepper (page 100), or Thin Spaghetti with Eggplant (page 94).

PEPPERS AND ANCHOVIES

Peperoni e acciughe

Here broiled sweet peppers and anchovies are steeped together in oil until they soften and there is an exchange of flavors. The peppers acquire pungency, while letting the anchovies share in their sweetness. The result is most appetizing, especially as a prelude to a robust meal.

Approximately 8 servings

8 medium sweet peppers, green, yellow, or red	Freshly ground pepper
	Orégano
	3 tablespoons capers
16 large or 20 medium flat anchovy fillets, preferably the home-prepared variety (preceding page)	4 cloves garlic, lightly crushed with a heavy knife handle and peeled
	Olive oil
Salt	

1. Place the peppers under a hot broiler. When the skin swells and is partially charred on one side, turn another side toward the flame. When all the skin is blistered and slightly charred, remove the peppers, and peel them while still hot.

2. Cut the peeled peppers lengthwise into strips 1½ to 2 inches wide, removing all the seeds and the pulpy inner core. Pat the strips dry with a cloth or paper towels.

3. Choose a serving dish that will hold the peppers in 4 layers. Arrange a layer of peppers on the bottom. Place 4 to 5 anchovies over the peppers. Add a tiny pinch of salt, a liberal grinding of pepper, a small pinch of orégano, a few capers, and one crushed garlic clove. Repeat until you have used up all the peppers and anchovies. Add enough olive oil to cover the top layer.

4. Put the dish in the refrigerator for 4 hours or more, then bring to room temperature before serving. If you are preparing these peppers several days ahead of time, remove the garlic after 24 hours.

TOMATOES STUFFED
WITH TUNA AND CAPERS

Pomodori ripieni di tonno

For 6 persons

6 large, ripe, round,
 meaty tomatoes
Salt
2 seven-ounce cans
 Italian tuna, packed
 in olive oil
Mayonnaise (page 23)
 made using 1 large
 egg yolk, ½ cup
 olive oil, and 2
 tablespoons lemon
 juice

2 teaspoons strong
 mustard, Dijon or
 German
1½ tablespoons capers,
 the tinier the better
Garnishes as suggested
 below

1. Slice off the tops of the tomatoes. Remove all the
seeds and some of the dividing walls, leaving just three or
four large sections. Salt lightly and put the tomatoes open
end down on a platter, allowing their liquid to drain away.

2. In a bowl, mash the tuna to a pulp with a fork. Add
the mayonnaise, holding back 1 or 2 tablespoons, add the
mustard and the capers. Mix with a fork to a uniform consistency. Taste and correct for salt.

3. Shake off the excess liquid from the tomatoes, but
don't squeeze them. Stuff to the very top with the tuna
mixture. Seal the tops with the remaining mayonnaise, and
garnish with an olive slice, a strip of green or red pepper,
a ring of capers, or parsley leaves. Serve at room temperature or slightly chilled.

TOMATOES STUFFED WITH SHRIMP

Pomodori coi gamberetti

For 6 persons

6 large, ripe, round, meaty tomatoes	1½ tablespoons capers, the tinier the better
¾ pound small shrimps	1 teaspoon strong mustard, Dijon or German
1 tablespoon red wine vinegar	Parsley
Salt	
Mayonnaise (page 23) made with 1 large egg yolk, ½ cup olive oil, and 2½ to 3 tablespoons lemon juice	

1. Prepare the tomatoes as indicated on the preceding page.

2. Rinse the shrimps in cold water. Bring 2 quarts of water with the 1 tablespoon of vinegar and 1 tablespoon of salt to a boil. Drop in the shrimps and cook for just 2 minutes after the water returns to a boil. Drain, peel, and devein the shrimps and set aside to cool.

3. Pick out six of the best-looking, best-shaped shrimps and set aside. Chop the rest of the shrimps roughly. Put them in a bowl and mix the chopped shrimps with the mayonnaise, capers, and mustard.

4. Shake off the excess liquid from the tomatoes, but don't squeeze them. Stuff to the top with the shrimp-and-mayonnaise mixture. Garnish each tomato with a shrimp and one or two parsley leaves. Serve at cool room temperature or slightly chilled.

SHRIMPS WITH OIL AND LEMON

Gamberetti all'olio e limone

In Italy, very tiny fresh-caught shrimps are used to prepare this simple but sublime antipasto. The shrimps are boiled very briefly with vegetables, then steeped in olive oil and lemon juice. There is nothing more to it than that, but I've known people whose memories turn to *gamberetti all'olio e limone* with keener joy than they feel toward anything else they had in Italy. Although our ocean shrimps do not have the same sweetness as the tiny shrimps of the Adriatic, they can be very good all the same. For this recipe you should try to use the smallest fresh shrimps you can find.

For 6 persons

1 stalk celery
1 carrot, peeled
2 tablespoons red wine vinegar
Salt
1½ pounds small fresh shrimps, washed in cold water but left unpeeled

½ cup olive oil
¼ cup lemon juice
Freshly ground pepper to taste (optional)

1. Put the celery, carrot, vinegar, and 1 tablespoon of salt in a saucepan with 2 to 3 quarts of water and bring to a rapid boil.

2. Add the unpeeled shrimps. If very small, not over ½ inch in diameter, they will be cooked shortly after the water returns to a boil; medium shrimp cook in about 2 to 3 minutes.

3. When cooked, drain the shrimps, peel, and devein. Put them in a shallow bowl and add the oil, lemon juice, 1 teaspoon salt (or more to taste), and optional pepper while the shrimps are still warm. Mix well and let them steep in the seasonings at room temperature for 1 to 1½ hours before serving. Serve with crusty French or Italian bread or with thinly sliced, good-quality white bread, lightly toasted.

NOTE
This dish is far better if never chilled, but if necessary it can be prepared a day ahead of time and kept in the refrigerator under plastic wrap. Always return it to room temperature before serving, however.

TASTY CARROT STICKS

Bastoncini di carota marinati

For 4 persons

¼ pound carrots
1 small clove garlic,
    lightly crushed with
    a heavy knife handle
    and peeled

Salt and freshly ground
    pepper to taste
¼ teaspoon orégano
1 tablespoon red wine
    vinegar
Olive oil, enough to
    cover

1. Peel the carrots, cut them in 2-inch lengths, and cook them in boiling salted water for about 10 or 12 minutes. (Cooking time varies according to the thickness and freshness of the carrots. In order to cook the carrots uniformly put the thickest parts into the water first, then the thinner, tapered ends. You want the carrots tender but quite firm for this recipe because the marinade will continue to soften them.)

2. Drain the cooked carrots, and cut lengthwise into small sticks about ¼ inch thick. Place in a small, deep serving dish.

3. Bury the garlic in the carrots. Add salt and pepper to taste, the orégano and vinegar and enough olive oil to just cover the carrots.

4. Refrigerate and allow to marinate at least overnight, removing the garlic after 24 hours. Serve at room temperature.

MENU SUGGESTIONS

This is a tangy and rustic appetizer. It can be part of an antipasto composed of such other dishes as Anchovies in Oil (page 33), Peppers and Anchovies (page 34), and Tuna and Bean Salad (page 402).

HOT ANCHOVY-FLAVORED
DIP FOR VEGETABLES

Bagna caôda

One of the most frequent observations on Italian food is that it is based mainly on peasant cooking. Like many of the commonly held beliefs about Italian cooking, this is not entirely true, but it is a fact that some of the glories of the Italian table were first created in peasant kitchens. Typical of these is *bagna caôda*, a hot dip for raw vegetables. It is a perfect illustration of the gastronomic genius of the Italian peasant. The materials are only those most easily available to him: oil, butter, garlic, a few anchovies in brine, and his own vegetables. The preparation is quick and direct: the garlic is sautéed for the briefest of moments, the anchovies are cooked just long enough to dissolve them, and the vegetables to be dipped into the sauce are raw. The result is a heartening, restorative dish of immensely satisfying flavor.

Eating *bagna caôda* is a two-handed affair. One hand takes a vegetable, the other bread, dipping them alternately in the sauce. The only interruption in this resolute rhythm is for long, slaking swallows of young, lively wine.

In peasant kitchens, *bagna caôda* is prepared in an earthenware pot, kept warm over drowsily glowing coals while everyone gathers around and dips. When the vegetables are finished, the fire is stirred up and eggs are broken into the pot and scrambled with the rest of the sauce. Today in the smart *trattorie* of Piedmont, *bagna caôda* is served in individual earthenware chafing dishes with built-in candle warmers. At home I prefer to make and serve *bagna caôda* in a single pot. It is both better for the sauce and more fun. But however you do it, it is important that the dip be kept warm the entire time that one is eating. The heat should be kept at a minimum, at no more than candle-warmer intensity, because the dip must not continue to cook after it is prepared. An earthenware pot is all but indispensable for *bagna caôda*. If you don't already have one, this is the best of reasons for getting one.

For 6 to 8 persons

¾ cup olive oil	8 to 10 flat anchovy
3 tablespoons butter	fillets, chopped
2 teaspoons finely	1 teaspoon salt
chopped garlic	

Heat the oil and butter until the butter is thoroughly liquefied and barely begins to foam. (Don't wait for the foam to subside or the butter will be too hot.) Add the garlic and sauté very briefly. It must not take on any color. Add the anchovies and cook over very low heat, stirring frequently, until the anchovies dissolve into a paste. Add the salt, stir, and bring to the table along with raw vegetables, as prepared below.

THE VEGETABLES

cardoons   The traditional vegetable for *bagna caôda* is a very tender, sweet, dwarf cardoon found in many sections of Piedmont. The large cardoon available here in Italian vegetable markets is tougher and often bitter. You might try using just the heart, however, which can be quite nice at times. Wash it thoroughly and cut into four sections, like a celery heart. Rub the cut parts with a little lemon juice or the cardoon will discolor.

artichokes   You don't need to trim artichokes for *bagna caôda* as you do for recipes where they are cooked. Rinse the artichoke in cold water and serve it whole. One pulls off a leaf at a time, dips it, and bites off just the tender part.

broccoli   Cut off the florets and put aside for use in any recipe for cooked broccoli. Serve just the stalks, after peeling the tough outer skin.

spinach   Use only young, crisp spinach. Wash very thoroughly and at length in several changes of cold water until the water shows no trace of soil. Serve with the stems on because they provide a hold for dipping.

zucchini   Only very fresh, small, young, glossy-skinned zucchini are suitable. Wash thoroughly in cold water, lightly

scraping the skin to remove any embedded soil. Cut lengthwise into sections 1 inch thick.

sweet peppers Wash in cold water and cut into quarter
sections. Remove the seeds and the pulpy inner core.

celery Discard any bruised or tough outer stalks. Wash
very carefully in cold water.

carrots Scrape or peel clean and cut lengthwise into sections ½ inch thick.

radishes Cut off the root tips, wash in cold water, and
serve with stems and leaves, attractive and helpful for dipping, left on.

asparagus This is a vegetable you will never see served
with *bagna caôda* in Piedmont. The very thought scandal-
izes my Piedmontese friends. *Bagna caôda* is a winter dish,
asparagus is a spring vegetable, and never the twain, et
cetera. It is a pity for them, because I have never tasted
any better vegetable with this dip. Use the freshest asparagus you can find, with the crispest stalks and tightest buds.
Trim it and peel it as directed on page 341. Wash it with
cold water and add a generous quantity of it to the vegetable
bowl because it will be very popular.
    This is not necessarily a definitive list of vegetables suit-
able for *bagna caôda*. You should feel free to make your
own discoveries. Remember, though, this is a dip for vegetables freshly picked at the peak of their development. Use
only the youngest, sweetest vegetables available, and serve
as wide a variety of them as possible. And before serving
pat all the vegetables dry with a towel.

MENU SUGGESTIONS

Depending on the variety and quantity of vegetables you
use, *bagna caôda* can be practically a meal on its own, and
would need nothing more to complete it than an Open-
Faced Italian Omelet with Cheese (page 316) or with Tomatoes, Onions, and Basil (page 320). If you would like to
work it into a fuller meal, however, follow it with Beef

Braised in Red Wine Sauce (page 231), Casserole-Roasted Lamb with Juniper Berries (page 269), Baby Lamb Chops Fried in Parmesan Cheese Batter (page 272), Charcoal-Broiled Chicken Marinated in Pepper, Oil, and Lemon (page 297), or Broiled Pork Liver Wrapped in Caul Fat (page 292). A perfect alternative to all these is a magnificent American roast beef.

HARD-BOILED EGGS WITH PIQUANT SAUCE

Uova sode in salsa verde

For 6 persons

6 eggs (U.S. Large)
2 tablespoons olive oil
½ tablespoon chopped capers
1 tablespoon chopped parsley
1 teaspoon anchovy paste
¼ teaspoon finely chopped garlic
¼ teaspoon strong mustard, Dijon or German
A small pinch of salt
12 small strips of pimento

1. Put the eggs in cold water and bring to a boil. Boil slowly for 10 minutes, then set aside to cool. When cool, remove the shells, and cut the eggs in half lengthwise. Carefully remove the yolks without damaging the whites. Set aside the whites.

2. Combine the egg yolks and the remaining ingredients, except for the pimento and the reserved egg whites, in a bowl. Using a fork, mash to a creamy, uniform consistency. Divide into 12 equal parts and spoon into the cavities of the reserved egg whites. Garnish each with a strip of pimento.

NOTE
These can be prepared ahead of time and refrigerated, but serve at room temperature.

STUFFED MUSHROOMS WITH BÉCHAMEL SAUCE

Funghi ripieni

For 6 persons

12 large mushrooms
2½ tablespoons butter
1 tablespoon finely
   chopped shallots or
   yellow onion
3 tablespoons chopped
   prosciutto or cooked
   ham
Salt
Freshly ground pepper,
   about 4 twists of the
   mill

A thick Béchamel Sauce
   made with: 1½
   tablespoons flour,
   1½ tablespoons
   butter, ¼ teaspoon
   salt, and 1 cup milk
   (page 25)
3 tablespoons freshly
   grated Parmesan
   cheese
Fine, dry unflavored
   bread crumbs

1. Slice off the ends of the mushroom stems. Wipe the mushrooms clean with a damp cloth. If there are still traces of soil, wash each mushroom carefully under cold running water, working quickly. Dry well with a towel. Detach the stems and chop them fine.

2. Preheat the oven to 500°.

3. In a skillet, sauté the chopped shallots or onion in 2½ tablespoons butter over medium-high heat until pale gold in color. Add the chopped prosciutto and sauté for about a minute. Add the finely chopped mushroom stems, salt, and pepper and cook, stirring, for 2 to 3 minutes. Tilt the skillet and draw off all the fat with a spoon.

4. In a bowl, mix the contents of the skillet with the warm béchamel. Add the grated Parmesan and mix again.

5. Place the mushroom caps, bottoms up, in a butter-smeared baking dish. Sprinkle lightly with salt, fill with the béchamel stuffing, sprinkle with bread crumbs, and dot each cap with butter. Place in the upper third of the preheated oven and bake for 15 minutes, or until a slight crust has formed. Allow to settle for about 10 minutes before serving.

MUSHROOM AND CHEESE SALAD

Insalata di funghi e formaggio

In October and November, when the wild mushrooms are gathered in the woods at the foothills of the Alps, the choicest, firmest mushrooms go into delicious and wildly expensive salads with white truffles and cheese. We don't have white truffles here, and wild mushrooms are virtually never seen in the markets, but we have a limitless supply of excellent cultivated mushrooms and Swiss cheese. This is not a replica of the Italian original, but it can stand on its own merits as a very appealing antipasto.

For 4 persons

½ pound very crisp, white fresh mushrooms
Juice of ½ lemon
⅔ cup Swiss cheese cut into strips 1 inch long, ¼ inch wide, and ⅛ inch thick

3 tablespoons olive oil
Salt to taste
Freshly ground pepper, a liberal quantity, to taste

1. Detach the mushroom stems from the caps. Save the stems for another recipe. Wipe the caps clean with a damp cloth, then cut into slices ⅛ inch thick. Put the slices in a salad bowl and moisten them with some lemon juice to keep them from discoloring. (You can prepare these as much as 30 to 45 minutes ahead of time.)
2. When ready to serve, add the strips of Swiss cheese to the bowl and toss with the olive oil, salt, and pepper.

BRESAOLA

Bresaola is a specialty of the Valtellina, a fertile valley at the northernmost edge of Lombardy. It is a whole beef filet, cured in salt and air-dried, a little tarter yet more delicate than prosciutto. Sliced thin it is one of the finest and most elegant of antipasti. It can precede any meal, whether hearty or light.

Although Valtellina *bresaola* is not available here, many specialty food shops carry a nearly identical product, Switzerland's Grison. Grison is compressed into a rectangular loaf, while *bresaola* maintains the original round, tapered shape of the filet. This makes Grison somewhat drier than *bresaola*, but otherwise it is a completely acceptable substitute.

It should be served as quickly as possible after it is sliced, at most within 24 hours, or else it will become dry and turn sharp.

Serve it with olive oil, enough to moisten each slice, a few drops of lemon juice, and freshly ground pepper.

FRIED MORTADELLA, PANCETTA, AND CHEESE TIDBITS

Bocconcini fritti

This is a savory hot antipasto that can also be served before meals with an apéritif, or as part of a buffet. In Bologna and its province it is often a prelude to the *grande fritto misto*, the great platter of mixed fried meats and vegetables, found on page 322.

For 6 persons

¼ pound Swiss cheese, in one piece	2 eggs, lightly beaten, in a bowl
¼ pound *mortadella*, in one piece	1 cup fine, dry unflavored bread crumbs, spread on a dish or on waxed paper
¼ pound *pancetta*, thinly sliced	
1 cup all-purpose flour spread on a dish or on waxed paper	Vegetable oil, enough to come at least 1 inch up the side of the skillet

1. Cut one-third of the cheese into 1-inch cubes and the rest into ½-inch cubes. Set aside.

2. Cut two-thirds of the *mortadella* into cubes whose sides are as wide as the slice is thick. Cut the rest of the slice into thin strips 2 inches long and about ½ inch wide.

3. Cut the *pancetta* into strips as close as possible in size to the *mortadella* strips.

4. Wrap part of the smaller cheese cubes with strips of *pancetta*, and the others with strips of *mortadella*. Fasten with toothpicks. You now have four kinds of tidbits ready to coat and fry: cheese wrapped in *pancetta*, cheese wrapped in *mortadella*, cheese cubes, and *mortadella* cubes.

5. Roll the tidbits in flour, dip them in egg, then roll them in bread crumbs. (You can prepare them up to this point 3 or 4 hours ahead of time, if you like.)

6. Choose not too large a skillet, so as not to waste oil, then pour in enough oil to come at least 1 inch up the sides of the pan. Heat the oil over high heat.

7. When the oil is very hot, slip in as many of the tidbits as will fit loosely in the pan. Fry until golden brown on both sides, then transfer to paper towels to drain. Continue until you've fried all the tidbits. (Caution: handle them with tongs, not with a fork. The prongs of a fork might puncture the crust on the cheese and it will run out.)

ROMAN GARLIC BREAD

Bruschetta

Although here it is known as garlic bread, the most important ingredient in *bruschetta* is not garlic but olive oil. The origin of *bruschetta* in Italy is probably nearly as old as that of olive oil itself. Each winter in ancient Rome one's first taste of the freshly pressed, dense, green olive oil was most likely an oil-soaked piece of bread that may or may not have been rubbed with garlic. In modern times *bruschetta* became a staple of the poor man's *trattoria*, where it went a long way in making up for the frugality of the fare. When eating in *trattorie* became the fashionable thing to do, *bruschetta* found its way into polite society. The name *bruschetta* comes from *bruscare*, which means "to roast over coals," the original and still the best way of toasting the bread.

For 6 persons

12 slices Italian whole-
    wheat bread (*pane
    integrale*), 1½ inches
    thick, 3 to 4 inches
    wide
4 to 5 cloves garlic,
    lightly crushed with
    a heavy knife handle
    and peeled

½ cup olive oil, as green
    and dense as you
    can find, preferably
    Sicilian olive oil
Salt and freshly ground
    pepper to taste

1. Preheat the broiler.
2. Toast the bread on both sides to a golden brown under
the hot broiler.
3. Rub one side of the toast while still hot with garlic.
Discard the garlic as it dries up and take a fresh clove. Put
the toast on a platter, garlic-rubbed side facing up, and pour
a thin stream of olive oil over it. Not a few drops, but enough
to soak each slice very lightly. Add a sprinkling of salt and
a healthy twist or two of freshly ground pepper per slice.
The toast is best served while still warm.

FIRST COURSES

I Primi

The first course in an Italian meal is almost always a pasta, a *risotto*, or a soup. Occasionally, but not frequently, a vegetable, an antipasto, or a fish course may become the first course, but no pasta or soup is ever turned into a side dish or second course. Sometimes one finds *risotto* incorporated into the second course, as when Risotto, Milan Style (page 173) is combined with *ossobuco* (Braised Veal Shanks, Milan Style, page 246). But these instances are very rare.

First courses are, justifiably, the best-known feature of Italian cooking. Into them, Italians have poured most of their culinary genius and inventiveness. Although the temptation is strong to give as many as possible of these incredibly varied and attractive dishes, it will not be done here. Rather than take a breathless junket through the whole landscape of Italian first courses, I thought it would be more profitable for those with a more than casual interest in good cooking to tarry over a few selected areas and explore them in depth.

Italy's most original and important contribution to cooking is the vast repertory of homemade pasta. However, every treatment I have seen of it has been cursory, inadequate, or, even worse, misleading. Here, with the first fully detailed exposition of the subject in English, I have tried to give even the most inexperienced cook easy access to the techniques and the inexhaustible satisfactions of homemade pasta. The step-by-step analysis of both hand-made and machine-made egg pasta should guide any willing beginner safely past the early difficulties toward a well-grounded proficiency in making pasta at home. Once you have mastered the fundamentally simple mechanics of rolling out a thin sheet of egg-pasta dough, you can move on to execute any one of dozens of delicious variations on the pasta theme.

Risotto, another uniquely Italian preparation that approaches pasta in variety and importance, is also examined in detail. The basic *risotto* technique is clearly set down, and you are shown how it can be developed into nine different *risotti*. With taste and ingenuity you can expand this, as Italian families do, into your own personal *risotto* repertory.

You will also find recipes for three varieties of *gnocchi*—potato, semolina, and spinach and ricotta—along with seven different ways of serving them.

In this chapter, too, are some of the heroic country soups of Tuscany, as well as several other traditional soups, including an unusual clam soup and a little-known sauerkraut soup from Trieste.

Macaroni pasta deserves and has been given whole volumes. I have given here fresh versions of some of the best-known sauces as well as several less familiar ones. There are six different tomato sauces and, altogether, twenty-seven different sauces for both homemade and macaroni pasta.

I wish there had been room for more. Perhaps you will be encouraged by what you find here to discover other dishes at their source. But even if you never go beyond the material in this chapter, you will still possess a larger variety of first courses than do most regional Italian cooks.

CLAM SOUP

Zuppa di vongole

Clams, unlike oysters and most mussels, often contain some sand. There are methods for eliminating the sand, such as allowing the clams to stand for long periods in cold water so that they can open up and disgorge it or trapping the sand by straining the cooked clam juices. In terms of flavor, however, when clams are to be served in their shells, as in this soup, neither method is as satisfactory as letting the clams release their juices directly into the sauce. There may be a little sand, but this quickly settles to the bottom of the pot, and with a little care in lifting out the clams and spooning the sauce into the soup plates it will all be left behind.

For 4 persons

3 dozen littleneck clams
    in their shells, the
    tiniest you can find
1½ tablespoons finely
    chopped shallots or
    yellow onion
½ cup olive oil
2 teaspoons finely
    chopped garlic

2 tablespoons finely
    chopped parsley
¼ teaspoon cornstarch
    dissolved in ⅔ cup
    dry white wine
Toasted Italian whole-
    wheat bread (*pane
    integrale*), 1 slice
    per serving

1. Set the clams in a large basin or sink filled with cold water. Let stand for 5 minutes, then drain and refill the basin with clean water. Scrub the clams vigorously with a coarse, stiff brush or by rubbing them one against the other. When they are all scrubbed, drain and fill basin again with clean water. Repeat these steps for 20 or 30 minutes, until you see that the water in the basin remains clear. Transfer the cleaned clams to a bowl.

2. Choose a heavy casserole large enough to contain the clams later. (Remember that they more than double in volume when open.) Over medium heat sauté the shallots in

the olive oil until translucent. Add the garlic. When it has colored lightly add the parsley and stir two or three times. Add the cornstarch and wine, turn the heat to high, and cook briskly for 2 minutes.

3. Drop in the clams. Stir, basting them lightly, and cover tightly. Continue cooking over high heat and stir the clams from time to time so that they all cook evenly. When their shells open, they will release their juices, and they will be done.

4. Place a slice of bread in each individual soup plate. Ladle the clams and sauce over the bread, taking care not to scoop up the liquid from the bottom of the pot because it probably contains sand.

NOTE

In Italy we bring the pot to the table and serve the clams a few at a time so that they don't get cold.

MENU SUGGESTIONS

This is an all-purpose first course that can be followed by any fish course, giving the preference, however, to robust rather than delicate flavors. It goes well with Poached Halibut with Parsley Sauce (page 203), Fish Broiled the Adriatic Way (page 214), Stuffed Squid Braised in White Wine (page 221), or Stewed Squid (page 219).

VELVETY CLAM SOUP WITH MUSHROOMS

Zuppa di vongole vellutata

This clam soup from the northern Adriatic coast is a considerable departure from traditional Italian methods of doing shellfish. The clam broth is enriched with eggs, milk, and butter, and completely eschews garlic. You can think of it as a sort of chowder with a special Italian taste.

For 4 persons

3 dozen littleneck clams,
     the tiniest you can
     find
2 tablespoons olive oil
1 tablespoon finely
     chopped shallots or
     yellow onion
3 tablespoons butter
½ pound mushrooms,
     thinly sliced
⅛ teaspoon salt

3 to 4 twists of the
     pepper mill
3 egg yolks
⅓ cup milk
1 cup chicken broth,
     homemade or
     canned
1 tablespoon cornstarch
     dissolved in 1 cup
     warm water

1. Follow the directions for washing and scrubbing clams
(page 50).
2. Heat the clams with the olive oil in a covered saucepan
over medium-high heat until they open their shells. Give
them a vigorous shake or turn them so that they will all
heat evenly (some clams are more obstinate than others
about opening). When most of them have opened up, it
would be best to remove the open clams while waiting for
the stubborn ones; otherwise they will become tough as
they linger in the pan. Remove the clams from their shells
and rinse off any sand on the meat by dipping them briefly
one at a time in their own juice. Unless the clams are exceptionally small, cut them up into two or more pieces and
set aside. Strain the clam juices through a sieve lined with
paper towels and set aside.
3. In a skillet, sauté the shallots in 1½ tablespoons of
the butter over medium-high heat. When the shallots have
turned pale gold, add the sliced mushrooms, salt, pepper,
and sauté briskly for about 3 minutes. Remove from the
heat and set aside.
4. In a small bowl mash the remaining 1½ tablespoons
of butter until soft and creamy. Set aside.
5. Put the egg yolks in a serving bowl or soup tureen
and beat them lightly with a fork or whisk, gradually adding
the milk. Swirl in the softened butter.
6. In a medium-sized stockpot or casserole bring the
chicken broth to a boil. Mix in the dissolved cornstarch, a

little bit at a time. Add the strained clam juices, the contents of the skillet, and the clams. Pour the hot soup, in tiny quantities at first, into the bowl or tureen containing the egg-yolk mixture. Beat rapidly with the whisk as you pour, gradually increasing the quantities of soup until it has all been added to the bowl. Serve immediately with *crostini* made from two to three slices of bread (Fried Bread Squares for Soup, page 84).

MENU SUGGESTIONS

Follow this soup with a fish course having a crisp, straightforward taste, such as Shrimp Brochettes, Adriatic Style (page 215), Fish Broiled the Adriatic Way (page 214), or Fried Squid (page 223).

MUSSEL SOUP

Zuppa di cozze

The two most important things to know about the proper preparation of mussels are, first, that you must take your time to clean them, and, second, that it takes virtually no time at all to cook them.

To get mussels clean you must scrub them thoroughly under cold running water with a coarse, stiff brush or rub them one against another until you have removed all traces of dirt and slime. It takes rather a long time because there is a surprising amount of obstinate slime on each mussel, but once you are past this tedious part the rest of the work goes quickly and the result is completely rewarding. Discard all the mussels that are not tightly closed and any that feel much lighter or heavier than the rest. With a sharp paring knife, cut off the tough, ropelike tufts that protrude from the shells. The mussels are now clean and ready.

There are cooks who let the mussels stand for a long time in a bucket of water. Inasmuch as fine, fresh mussels very rarely contain sand, this step is wholly unnecessary. Not only that, but in allowing the mussels to unclench their shells in water you lose much of their precious, tasty juice.

For 4 persons

1½ teaspoons chopped garlic	2 pounds fresh mussels, cleaned and scrubbed as directed above
⅓ cup olive oil	
1 tablespoon coarsely chopped parsley	
1 cup canned Italian tomatoes, drained and cut up	4 slices Italian whole-wheat bread (*pane integrale*), toasted and (optional) rubbed with garlic
⅛ teaspoon chopped hot red pepper	

1. Choose a casserole large enough to contain the mussels later. Sauté the garlic in the oil over moderate heat until it has colored lightly. Add the parsley, stir once or twice, then add the cut-up tomatoes and the chopped hot pepper. Cook, uncovered, at a gentle simmer for about 25 minutes, or until the tomatoes and oil separate.

2. Add the mussels, cover the casserole, raise the heat to high, and cook until the mussels open their shells, about 3 to 5 minutes. To get all the mussels to cook evenly, grasp the casserole with both hands, holding the cover down tight, and jerk it two or three times.

3. Put the 4 slices of toasted bread in 4 soup dishes and ladle the mussels, with all their sauce, over the bread. Serve piping hot.

MENU SUGGESTIONS

There is as much joy for the eye as for the palate here in the delicate, amber mussel within its glossy jet-black shell balanced against the exuberance of the tomato sauce. As a first course, this can precede any fish course that is not sauced with tomato. Broiled or fried fish would be my first choice, but an excellent second course could also be Pan-Roasted Mackerel with Rosemary and Garlic (page 205). If you want to precede it with an antipasto, try Peppers and Anchovies (page 34).

CREAMY POTATO SOUP WITH CARROTS AND CELERY

Minestrina tricolore

This lovely soup is a study in delicate contrasts. The name, *minestrina tricolore*, or "tricolor" soup, comes from the creamed potato, the orange flecks of carrot, and the parsley, which recall the colors of the Italian flag. Its character comes from the interruption of its smooth, velvety consistency by the crisp specks of sautéed carrot and celery. It is quite artless and good.

For 4 to 6 persons

1½ pounds potatoes, peeled and roughly diced

3 tablespoons finely chopped yellow onion

2 tablespoons butter

3 tablespoons vegetable oil

3 tablespoons finely chopped carrot

3 tablespoons finely chopped celery

5 tablespoons freshly grated Parmesan cheese

1 cup milk

2 cups Homemade Meat Broth (page 10) OR ½ cup canned beef broth mixed with 1½ cups water

Salt to taste

2 tablespoons chopped parsley

1. Put the potatoes and just enough cold water to cover in a stockpot. Cover, bring to a boil, and cook at a moderate boil until the potatoes are tender. Purée the potatoes, with their liquid, through a food mill back into the pot. Set aside.

2. In a skillet sauté the chopped onion, with all the butter and oil, over medium heat until pale gold in color. Add the chopped carrot and celery and cook for about 2 minutes, but not long enough to let the vegetables become soft, since you want them to be crunchy in the soup.

3. Add the entire contents of the skillet to the puréed potatoes in the pot. Turn on the heat to medium and add the grated Parmesan cheese, the milk, and the broth. Stir and cook at a steady simmer for a few minutes, until the

cooking fat floating on the surface is dispersed throughout the soup and the consistency of the soup is that of liquid cream. Add salt to taste. (Bear in mind that this soup will thicken as it cools in the plate. If the soup is too dense, simply add equal parts of broth and milk, as required.) When done, mix in the parsley off the heat. Serve in warm soup plates, with *crostini* (Fried Bread Squares for Soup, page 84) and additional freshly grated Parmesan cheese on the side.

MENU SUGGESTIONS

This is a very pleasant soup that gets along well with virtually any meat or fowl second course. Avoid dishes with cream or milk, and very sharp tomato sauces, however. A nice combination would be with Breaded Veal Cutlets, Milan Style (page 260), Chicken Fricassee with Dried Wild Mushrooms (page 300), or any of the simple roasts.

POTATO AND ONION SOUP

Zuppa di patate e cipolle

For 6 persons

1½ pounds yellow onions, peeled and very thinly sliced	3½ cups Homemade Meat Broth (page 10) (approximately)
3 tablespoons butter	OR 3 cups water (approximately) plus ½ cup canned beef bouillon
3 tablespoons vegetable oil	
Salt	
2 pounds boiling potatoes, peeled and diced into ¼-inch cubes	3 tablespoons freshly grated Parmesan cheese

1. In an uncovered skillet, cook the onion, with all the butter and oil and a dash of salt, over moderate heat. Cook gently and slowly, allowing the onion gradually to wilt. Cook until it turns light brown. Turn off the heat and set aside. Do not remove the onion from the skillet.

2. Boil the diced potato in 3 cups of the homemade broth or 3 cups of water. Add a little salt. Do not boil too rapidly.

3. When the potato is tender add all the onion from the skillet, together with its cooking fat. Loosen any of the cooking residue from the bottom of the skillet with some of the hot liquid in which the potatoes have cooked and add it to the soup.

4. Add the remaining ½ cup homemade broth or ½ cup canned bouillon and bring to a gentle boil. With a wooden spoon mash part of the potatoes against the side of the pot and mix into the boiling liquid. Continue cooking for 8 to 10 minutes. Check the soup for density. If at this point it is too thick (it's supposed to be a soup, not a purée), add homemade broth or water as required.

5. Turn off the heat. Add the grated Parmesan cheese, stirring it into the soup. Taste and correct for salt. Serve with a small bowl of freshly grated Parmesan cheese on the side.

MENU SUGGESTIONS

This soup goes well with meat courses that have a hearty country character. Try it with Meat Loaf Braised in White Wine with Dried Wild Mushrooms (page 238), either of the veal stews on pages 262–264, Roast Pork with Bay Leaves (page 275), or Fried Calf's Brains (page 289).

RICE AND PEAS

Risi e bisi

No one else in Italy cooks rice in so many different ways as the Venetians. They have at least several dozen basic dishes, not counting individual variations, where rice is combined with every likely vegetable, meat, fowl, or fish. Of all of them, the one Venetians have always loved the best has been *risi e bisi*. In the days of the Republic of Venice, *risi e bisi* was the first dish served at the dinner given by the doges each April 25 in honor of Saint Mark. Those, of course, were the earliest, youngest peas of the season, which are the best to use for *risi e bisi*. But one can also make it with later, larger peas, the ones Venetians call *senatori*. You may use frozen peas, if you must, and this recipe shows you how, but until you've made it with choice fresh peas your *risi e bisi* will be a tolerable but slightly blurred copy of the original.

Risi e bisi is not *risotto* with peas. It is a soup, although a very thick one. Some cooks make it thick enough to eat with a fork, but it is at its best when it is fairly runny, with just enough liquid to require a spoon.

For 4 persons

2 tablespoons chopped yellow onion	3½ cups Homemade Meat Broth (page 10) for fresh peas, 3 cups for frozen (see note below)
¼ cup butter	
2 pounds fresh peas (unshelled weight) OR 1 ten-ounce package frozen peas, thawed	1 cup raw rice, preferably Italian Arborio rice
Salt	2 tablespoons chopped parsley
	½ cup freshly grated Parmesan cheese

NOTE

This is one of those dishes that really demand the flavor and delicacy of homemade broth. If you absolutely must use store-bought broth, use canned chicken broth in the following proportions: *for fresh peas*, 1 cup broth mixed with 2½ cups water; *for frozen peas*, 1 cup broth mixed with 2 cups water.

1. Put the onion in a stockpot with the butter and sauté over medium heat until pale gold.

2. *If you are using fresh peas*, add the peas and 1 teaspoon salt, and sauté for 2 minutes, stirring frequently. Add 3 cups of broth, cover, and cook at a very moderate boil for 10 minutes. Add the rice, parsley, and the remaining ½ cup broth, stir, cover, and cook at a slow boil for 15 minutes, or until the rice is tender but *al dente*, firm to the bite. Stir from time to time while cooking, and taste and correct for salt.

If you are using thawed frozen peas, add the peas and

1 teaspoon salt and sauté for 2 minutes, stirring frequently. Add the broth and bring to a boil. Add the rice and parsley, stir, cover, and cook at a slow boil for 15 minutes, or until the rice is tender but *al dente*, firm to the bite. Stir from time to time while cooking and taste and correct for salt.

3. Just before serving, add the grated cheese, mixing it into the soup.

MENU SUGGESTIONS

The ideal coupling for *risi e bisi* is that other well-known Venetian specialty, Sautéed Calf's Liver with Onions, Venetian Style (page 286). It can also precede Fish Broiled the Adriatic Way (page 214), Shrimp Brochettes, Adriatic Style (page 215), or Sautéed Chicken Breast Fillets with Lemon and Parsley (page 303). Otherwise, it will go well with any meat or fowl dish, saving those, of course, that incorporate peas.

RICE AND CELERY SOUP

Minestra di sedano e riso

For 4 persons

2 cups diced celery stalks (see Step 1 below)
⅓ cup olive oil
1 teaspoon salt
2 tablespoons finely chopped yellow onion
2 tablespoons butter
1 cup raw rice, preferably Italian Arborio rice

2 cups Homemade Meat Broth (page 10) OR 1 cup canned beef broth mixed with 1 cup water
3 tablespoons freshly grated Parmesan cheese
2 tablespoons chopped parsley

1. Wash the celery stalks well, strip them of most of their strings with a vegetable peeler, and dice. Put the diced celery, olive oil, and salt in a saucepan and add enough water to cover. Bring to a steady simmer, cover, and cook until the celery is tender but not soft. Turn off the heat but do not drain.

2. Put the chopped onion in another saucepan or stockpot with the butter and sauté over medium heat until pale gold but not browned.

3. Add half the celery to the saucepan with the onion, using a slotted spoon. Sauté the celery for 2 or 3 minutes, then add the rice and stir it until it is well coated. Add all the broth.

4. Purée the rest of the celery, with all its cooking liquid, through a food mill directly into the saucepan containing the rice. Bring to a steady simmer, cover, and cook until the rice is tender but firm to the bite, about 15 to 20 minutes.

5. Swirl in the grated cheese, turn off the heat, add the chopped parsley, and mix. Serve promptly, before the rice becomes too soft.

MENU SUGGESTIONS

This tasty but not overwhelming soup would be a good choice if you are going to follow with Meat Balls (page 236), Black-Eyed Peas and Sausages with Tomato Sauce (page 279), Honeycomb Tripe with Parmesan Cheese (page 282), or Oxtail Braised with Wine and Vegetables (page 280), which has a delicious touch of celery of its own.

ESCAROLE AND RICE SOUP

Zuppa di scarola e riso

Scarola is a broad-leafed salad green from the chicory family. It is marvelous in soup as well as in salads. There are probably as many ways to cook it as there are leaves in a head of escarole, but many make it either too bland and retiring or else too aggressively flavored. This version, where the escarole is first briefly sautéed in butter with lightly browned onions, stays at a happy distance from the two extremes.

For 4 persons

1 head of escarole (¾ to
    1 pound)
2 tablespoons finely
    chopped yellow
    onion
¼ cup butter
Salt
3½ cups Homemade
    Meat Broth, (page
    10) OR 1 cup canned
    chicken broth mixed

with 2½ cups water,
    OR 2 chicken
    bouillon cubes
    dissolved in 3½ cups
    water
½ cup raw rice,
    preferably Italian
    Arborio rice
3 tablespoons freshly
    grated Parmesan
    cheese

1. Detach all the escarole leaves from the head and discard any that are bruised, wilted, or discolored. Wash all the rest in various changes of cold water until thoroughly clean. Cut into ribbons ½ inch wide and set aside.

2. In a stockpot sauté the chopped onion in the butter over medium heat until nicely browned. Add the escarole and a light sprinkling of salt. Briefly sauté the escarole, stirring it once or twice, then add ½ cup of the broth, cover the pot, and cook over very low heat until the escarole is tender—from 25 minutes to more than three-quarters of an hour, depending on the freshness and tenderness of the escarole.

3. When the escarole is tender, add the rest of the broth, raise the heat slightly, and cover. When the broth comes to a boil, add the rice and cover. Cook for 15 to 20 minutes, stirring from time to time, until the rice is *al dente*, firm to the bite. Off the heat, mix in the Parmesan cheese. Taste and correct for salt, spoon into soup plates, and serve.

NOTE
Don't cook the soup ahead of time with the rice in it. The rice will become mushy. If you must do it ahead of time, stop at the end of step 2. About 25 minutes before serving, add the 3 cups of broth to the escarole, bring to a boil, and finish cooking as in step 3.

MENU SUGGESTIONS

Follow the suggestions for Rice and Celery Soup (page 59). This can also precede Casserole-Roasted Lamb with Juniper Berries (page 269).

SPINACH SOUP

Minestrina di spinaci

For 5 or 6 persons

2 ten-ounce packages
   frozen leaf spinach,
   thawed, OR 2 pounds
   fresh spinach
4 tablespoons butter
2 cups Homemade Meat
   Broth (page 10) OR 1
   cup canned chicken
   broth mixed with 1
   cup water

2 cups milk
¼ teaspoon nutmeg
5 tablespoons freshly
   grated Parmesan
   cheese
Salt, if necessary

1. Cook, squeeze dry, and chop the spinach as directed on page 145.

2. Put the chopped, cooked spinach and the butter in a stockpot. Sauté the spinach over medium heat for 2 to 3 minutes.

3. Add the broth, milk, and nutmeg. Bring to a simmer, stirring frequently.

4. Add the Parmesan cheese and cook for 1 more minute, stirring two to three times. Taste for salt. Serve immediately, with *crostini*, Fried Bread Squares for Soup (page 84) on the side.

MENU SUGGESTIONS

This soup can precede any meat or fowl. It goes particularly well with any of the roasts of lamb on pages 268–271, Baby Lamb Chops Fried in Parmesan Cheese Batter (page 272), Fried Calf's Brains (page 289), or Fried Breaded Calf's Liver (page 288).

VEGETABLE SOUP

Minestrone di Romagna

A vegetable soup will tell you where you are in Italy almost as precisely as a map. There are the soups of the south, leaning heavily on tomato, garlic, and oil, sometimes containing pasta; there are those of the center, heavily fortified with beans; the soups of the north, with rice; those of the Riviera, with fresh herbs; and there are nearly as many variations in between as there are local cooks. In Romagna, very little is put into *minestrone* beyond a variety of seasonal vegetables, whose separate characteristics give way and intermingle through very slow cooking in broth. The result is a soup of mellow, dense flavor that recalls no vegetable in particular but all of them at once.

It is not necessary to prepare all the vegetables ahead of time although you may do so if it suits you. The vegetables don't go into the pot all at once, but in the sequence indicated, and while one vegetable is slowly cooking in oil and butter you can peel and cut another. I find this method more efficient and less tedious than preparing all the vegetables at one time, and somehow it produces a better-tasting soup. In any event, cook each vegetable 2 or 3 minutes, at least, before adding the next.

For 6 to 8 persons

½ cup olive oil
3 tablespoons butter
1 cup thinly sliced yellow
    onion
1 cup diced carrots
1 cup diced celery
2 cups peeled, diced
    potatoes
1½ cups fresh white
    beans, if available,
    OR 1½ cups canned
    cannellini beans or
    Great Northern
    beans OR ¾ cup
    dried white beans,
    cooked as directed
    on page 74
2 cups diced zucchini
    (about 2 medium
    zucchini) (see note
    below)

1 cup diced green beans
3 cups shredded
    cabbage, preferably
    Savoy cabbage
6 cups Homemade Meat
    Broth (page 10) OR 2
    cups canned beef
    broth mixed with 4
    cups water
The crust from a 1- or 2-
    pound piece of
    Parmesan cheese,
    carefully scraped
    clean (optional)
⅔ cup canned Italian
    tomatoes, with their
    juice
⅓ cup freshly grated
    Parmesan cheese

1. Choose a stockpot large enough for all the ingredients. Put in the oil, butter, and sliced onion and cook over medium-low heat until the onion wilts and is pale gold in color but not browned. Add the diced carrots and cook for 2 to 3 minutes, stirring once or twice. Repeat this procedure with the celery, potatoes, white beans (if you are using the fresh beans), zucchini, and green beans, cooking each one a few minutes and stirring. Then add the shredded cabbage and cook for about 6 minutes, giving the pot an occasional stir.

2. Add the broth, the cheese crust, the tomatoes and their juice, and a little bit of salt. (Go easy on the salt, especially if you are using canned broth. You can correct the seasoning later.) Cover and cook at a very slow boil for at least 3 hours. If necessary, you can stop the cooking at any time and resume it later on. (*Minestrone* must never be thin and watery, so cook until it is soupy thick. If you should find that the soup is becoming *too* thick, you can add another cup of homemade broth or water. Do not add more canned broth.)

3. Fifteen minutes before the soup is done, add the canned or cooked dry beans (if you are not using fresh ones). Just before turning off the heat, remove the cheese crust, swirl in the grated cheese, then taste and correct for salt.

NOTE

Before dicing the zucchini, scrub it thoroughly in cold water to remove all soil—and if still in doubt, peel it.

Minestrone, unlike most cooked vegetable dishes, is even better when warmed up the next day. It keeps up to a week in the refrigerator.

MENU SUGGESTIONS

Minestrone goes very well with roasts of all kinds, particularly lamb. You can safely follow it with any meat course that doesn't include any vegetables.

COLD VEGETABLE SOUP WITH RICE, MILAN STYLE

Minestrone freddo alla milanese

One of the few consolations of a hot Milan summer is this basil-scented cold *minestrone*. The *trattorie* make it fresh every morning, fill the soup plates, and set them out along with the rest of the day's specialties displayed near the entrance: fresh-picked vegetables, a poached fish, mountain prosciutto, sweet melons. By noontime the *minestrone* is precisely the right temperature and consistency, and shortly thereafter it is all snapped up.

This is the most beautiful way in which one can revive leftover *minestrone*, and, of course, not only can it be made ahead of time, it *must* be made ahead of time.

For 4 persons

2 cups leftover Vegetable
    Soup (page 63)
2 cups water
½ cup raw rice,
    preferably Italian
    Arborio rice
1 teaspoon salt

Freshly ground pepper,
    about 8 twists of the
    mill
¼ cup freshly grated
    Parmesan cheese
8 good-sized fresh basil
    leaves, cut into 4 or
    5 strips each

1. In a stockpot, bring the soup and 2 cups of water to a boil. Add the rice, stirring it with a wooden spoon. When the soup returns to a boil, add the salt and pepper, cover the pot, and turn the heat down to medium low. Stir from time to time. Test the rice after 10 to 12 minutes. It should be very firm, because it will continue to soften as it cools in the plate. Taste and correct for salt.

2. When the rice is done, ladle the soup into four individual soup plates, add the grated cheese and the basil, mix well, and allow to cool. Serve at room temperature.

NOTE
Never refrigerate the soup; always serve it the same day it is made.

MENU SUGGESTIONS

Bear in mind that this is a warm-weather dish. The second course could be a cold boiled fish with mayonnaise, Cold Sliced Veal with Tuna Sauce (page 265), Sautéed Veal Scaloppine with Lemon Sauce (page 252).

MINESTRONE, COLD OR HOT, WITH PESTO

COLD MINESTRONE (COLD VEGETABLE SOUP WITH RICE, MILAN STYLE, PRECEDING PAGE):

When the rice is done, at the end of Step 1, swirl in 1 tablespoon of *pesto* (page 132). Ladle into individual soup plates, omitting the basil in Step 2.

HOT MINESTRONE (VEGETABLE SOUP, PAGE 66):

Add 1½ to 2 tablespoons of *pesto* (page 139) at the end of Step 3. If you are making the soup ahead of time, add the *pesto* when reheating, just before serving.

PASSATELLI

Passatelli consists of eggs, Parmesan cheese, and bread crumbs formed into short, thick, cylindrical strands by pressing the mixture through a special tool. The strands are then boiled very briefly in homemade meat broth. The original tool can be replaced by a food mill, but the homemade broth is absolutely essential and cannot be replaced by canned bouillon.

This soup is native only to the Romagna section of Emilia, a narrow strip of territory east of Bologna, bordering on the Adriatic Sea. The *romagnoli* want their food to be satisfying but simple and delicate in taste. This soup is all these things and, moreover, extremely quick to prepare.

For 6 persons

7 cups broth from Mixed
    Boiled Meats
    (page 311) or
    Homemade Meat
    Broth
    (page 10)
¾ cup freshly grated
    Parmesan cheese

⅓ cup fine, dry
    unflavored bread
    crumbs
¼ teaspoon nutmeg
    (see note below)
2 eggs

1. Bring the broth to a steady, moderate boil in an uncovered pot. While the broth is coming to a boil, combine the grated Parmesan, the bread crumbs, and the nutmeg on a pastry board or large cutting block. Make a mound with a well in the center. Break the eggs open into the well and knead all the ingredients together. It should have the tender granular consistency of cooked cornmeal mush (*polenta*). (If, as sometimes happens, the eggs are a bit on the large side, you may have to add a little more Parmesan and bread crumbs.)

2. Put the disk with the largest holes into your food mill. When the broth boils, press the Parmesan-bread-crumb-and-egg mixture through the mill directly into the boiling broth. Cook at a slow boil for a minute or two at the most. Turn off the heat and allow to rest for 4 to 5 minutes, then ladle into warm soup plates and serve with a bowl of freshly grated Parmesan on the side.

NOTE

The nutmeg can be increased slightly, according to taste, but the flavor of nutmeg should never be more than hinted at.

MENU SUGGESTIONS

The natural second course for *passatelli* is Mixed Boiled Meats (page 311), which should have produced the broth for the soup. If you are making *passatelli* with other broth, you can follow it with any simple roasted meat or fowl.

SPLIT GREEN PEA AND POTATO SOUP

Zuppa di piselli secchi e patate

This is a good, simple soup. It requires so little looking after that I usually make it on the side while I am cooking other things. When it is done, I put it away in the refrigerator, where it keeps perfectly for several days, and then I have a marvelous soup on hand, all ready to heat up at a moment's notice. There is something comforting about having a robust soup like this one to fall back on, especially on a blustery winter evening. The only thing to look out for when reheating is that the soup should not become too thick. If it does, just add some more broth or water.

For 6 persons

½ one-pound package of split green peas, washed and drained	2 tablespoons chopped yellow onion
2 medium potatoes, peeled and roughly cut up	3 tablespoons olive oil
	3 tablespoons butter
5 cups Homemade Meat Broth (page 10) OR 1 cup canned beef broth mixed with 4 cups water OR 1 bouillon cube dissolved in 5 cups water	3 tablespoons freshly grated Parmesan cheese
	Salt

1. Cook the split peas and potatoes at a moderate boil in 3 cups of the broth until both are quite tender. Then purée the peas and potatoes, with their cooking liquid, through a food mill and into a stockpot.

2. Put the onion in a small skillet along with the oil and butter and sauté over medium-high heat until a rich golden color.

3. Add all the contents of the skillet to the stockpot; then add the remaining 2 cups of broth and bring to a moderate boil. Cook, stirring occasionally, until the oil and butter are dissolved in the broth. Just before turning off the heat, mix in the grated cheese, then taste and correct for salt. Serve with additional grated cheese and *crostini* (Fried Bread Squares for Soup, page 84) on the side.

NOTE

If you are doing the soup in advance, add the cheese only when you reheat it. Allow the soup to cool thoroughly before refrigerating.

MENU SUGGESTIONS

Any roasted meat or fowl would make an excellent second course. Other possibilities are Left-Over Boiled Beef with Sautéed Onions (page 233), Meat Balls (page 236), Little Veal "Bundles" with Anchovies and Cheese (page 256), Veal Stew with Sage and White Wine (page 262), Boiled Cotechino Sausage, if you are not serving it with lentils (page 277), Stewed Rabbit with White Wine (page 309), or Fried Breaded Calf's Liver (page 288).

LENTIL SOUP

Zuppa di lenticchie

For 4 persons

2 tablespoons finely chopped yellow onion

3 tablespoons olive oil

3 tablespoons butter

2 tablespoons finely chopped celery

2 tablespoons finely chopped carrot

⅓ cup shredded *pancetta*, prosciutto, OR unsmoked ham

1 cup canned Italian tomatoes, cut up, with their juice

½ one-pound package of dried lentils, washed and drained

4 cups Homemade Meat Broth (page 10) OR 1 cup canned beef broth mixed with 3 cups water

Salt, if necessary

Freshly ground pepper, 4 to 6 twists of the mill

3 tablespoons freshly grated Parmesan cheese

1. Put the onion in a stockpot with the oil and 2 tablespoons of the butter and sauté over medium-high heat until a light golden brown.

2. Add the celery and carrot and continue sautéing for 2 to 3 minutes, stirring from time to time.

3. Add the shredded *pancetta*, and sauté for 1 more minute.

4. Add the cut-up tomatoes and their juice, and adjust the heat so that they cook at a gentle simmer for 25 minutes, uncovered. Stir from time to time with a wooden spoon.

5. Add the lentils, stirring and turning them two or three times, then add the broth, salt (easy on the salt if you are using canned broth), and pepper. Cover and cook, at a steady simmer, until the lentils are tender. (Cooking time is about 45 minutes, but it varies greatly from lentils to lentils, so that the only reliable method is to taste them. Note, too, that some lentils absorb a surprising amount of

liquid. If this happens add more homemade broth or water
to keep the soup from getting too thick.)

6. When the lentils are cooked, correct for salt; then,
off the heat, swirl in the remaining tablespoon of butter and
the grated cheese. Serve with additional freshly grated cheese
on the side.

MENU SUGGESTIONS

This sturdy soup can precede any meat dish that does
not have a strong tomato presence. Good choices would be
Beef Braised in Red Wine Sauce (page 231), Left-Over Boiled
Beef with Sautéed Onions (page 233), Veal Stew with Sage
and White Wine (page 262), Roast Spring Lamb with White
Wine (page 268), Pork Loin Braised in Milk (page 274),
Roast Pork with Bay Leaves (page 275), any of the roasted,
broiled, or fricasseed chickens (except the one with tomatoes), and Sautéed Calf's Liver with Onions, Venetian Style
(page 286).

RICE AND LENTIL SOUP

Zuppa di lenticchie e riso

Lentil soup can be made in large batches and frozen.
When reheating it, you can vary the basic formula through
the simple and pleasant addition of rice.

For 6 persons

Lentil Soup (page 73)
1½ cups Homemade
    Meat Broth
    (page 10) OR ½ cup
    canned beef broth
    mixed with 1 cup
    water

½ cup raw rice,
    preferably Italian
    Arborio rice
Salt, if necessary

Bring the soup to a boil, then add the broth. When the
soup comes to a boil again, add the rice and stir with a
wooden spoon. Cook at a moderate boil until the rice is
tender but firm to the bite, about 15 minutes. (If the rice

you are using absorbs too much liquid, add more homemade broth or water.) Taste and correct for salt. Serve with freshly grated Parmesan cheese on the side.

MENU SUGGESTIONS

Follow the ones for Lentil Soup (preceding page).

BEANS AND SAUERKRAUT SOUP

La Jota

Trieste has long been the most passionately Italian of cities, but this stout bean soup of hers with potatoes, sauerkraut, and bacon speaks with an unmistakable accent from her Austro-Hungarian past.

An important step in the preparation of the soup is the slow stewing of the sauerkraut to blunt its sharpness. Although *Jota* requires much slow cooking, it can be done at your convenience because the soup should be served at least a day later to give its flavors time for full development. If you must, you can even interrupt its preparation at the end of any step, allow the soup to cool, refrigerate it, and the following day resume cooking where you left off.

When completed, *Jota* is enriched with a final flavoring called *pestà*. Although the components differ—this *pestà* contains salt pork so finely chopped that it is nearly reduced to a paste, hence the name—this procedure strongly recalls the addition of flavored oil in Tuscan bean soups.

For 8 persons

2 pounds fresh cranberry beans (unshelled weight) (see note, page 77)

¼ pound bacon, in 1-inch strips

1 pound sauerkraut, drained

½ teaspoon cumin

¾ pound pork's head OR pork rind

1 cup peeled, coarsely diced potato (1 medium potato)

1 teaspoon salt

3 tablespoons cornmeal

THE PESTÀ:

¼ cup finely chopped
  salt pork
1 tablespoon chopped
  yellow onion

1 teaspoon chopped
  garlic
2 teaspoons salt
3 teaspoons all-purpose
  flour

1. Shell the beans, rinse them in cold water, and put them in a pot with 3 cups of water. Bring to a boil, then cover and adjust the heat so that they cook at a very slow boil. Cook until tender, about 45 minutes, depending on the beans. When done, set them aside in their own liquid.

2. While the beans are cooking, sauté the bacon in a medium saucepan over moderate heat for 2 to 3 minutes. Add the drained sauerkraut and the ½ teaspoon cumin, mix with the bacon, and cook in the bacon fat for about 2 minutes. Then add 1 cup water, cover the pan, and cook at very low heat for 1 hour. At the end of an hour the sauerkraut should be very much reduced in volume and there should be no liquid in the pan. If there is still some left, uncover the pan and allow the liquid to evaporate over medium heat.

3. While the beans are cooking and the sauerkraut is stewing, put the pork's head or pork rind in a stockpot with 1 quart of water and bring to a boil. After it has boiled for 5 minutes, drain, discarding the cooking liquid, and cut the head or rind into ¾- to 1-inch-wide strips. (Do not be alarmed if it is very tough. It will soften away to a creamy consistency in later cooking.)

4. Return the cut-up pork to the stockpot. Add the diced potato, 3 cups of water, and 1 teaspoon salt. Cover and cook at a slow but steady boil for 1 hour.

5. Add the beans with their cooking liquid, cover, and cook at a very slow, quiet boil for 30 minutes.

6. Add the sauerkraut. Cover, and cook, always at a very slow boil, for 1 hour.

7. Add the cornmeal in a thin stream, stirring it thoroughly into the soup, add 2 cups of water, cover, and cook at the same slow boil for 1 hour. Stir from time to time.

8. When the soup is nearing completion, prepare the *pestà*. Put the chopped salt pork and the onion in a small saucepan and sauté over medium heat until the onion is

pale gold. Add the garlic and sauté it until it is nicely colored. Then add 2 teaspoons salt and the flour, 1 tablespoon at a time, stirring it thoroughly and cooking it until it, too, is a rich, blond color.

9. Add the *pestà* to the soup, stirring thoroughly, and simmer for 20 minutes more before serving.

MENU SUGGESTIONS

This is a "heavyweight" among soups and should be balanced in the second course by broiled or roasted meat or fowl. A substantial but suitable meat course with a congenial Triestine flavor is Braised Veal Shanks, Trieste Style (page 249).

COOKING DRIED BEANS

When fresh beans are not available, most Italian cooks use dried beans rather than canned, precooked beans. Dried beans are not only much more economical than canned beans, but, when properly cooked, they have better texture than the generally mushy canned variety. You can buy packed dried beans in all supermarkets, but in many cities there are Greek and other stores that sell them loose, by weight. These are a still better buy than the prepacked beans, and usually offer a far broader selection.

Dried beans should always be soaked before cooking, otherwise their skins will burst before the beans become tender. There are many techniques for cooking dried beans. The following has given consistently successful results, especially with Great Northern beans or kidney beans, which are the closest to the white beans that usually go into Italian soups.

1. Put the desired quantity of beans in a bowl and cover them by 2 inches with cold water. Let them soak overnight in a warm place, such as over the pilot flame of a gas stove. (In this instance, be careful not to use a plastic bowl!)

2. The following day, preheat the oven to 325°.

3. Rinse and drain the beans, put them in a flameproof casserole, and cover with cold water by 2 inches.

4. Bring the beans to a moderate boil on top of the stove, then cover the pot and place in the middle level of the

preheated oven. Cook until tender, about 40 to 60 minutes, depending on the beans. Keep them in their liquid until you are ready to use them.

BEAN SOUP WITH PARSLEY AND GARLIC

Zuppa di cannellini con aglio e prezzemolo

This is indeed a bean lover's bean soup. It is virtually all beans, with very little liquid, and just a whiff of garlic. It is thick enough to be served as a side dish next to a good roast. If you like it thinner all you have to do is add a little more broth or water.

For 4 to 6 persons

1 teaspoon chopped garlic
½ cup olive oil
2 tablespoons chopped parsley
2 cups dried white kidney beans or other white beans, cooked as directed on page 74 and drained, OR 2 twenty-ounce cans white kidney beans or other white beans, drained

Salt
Freshly ground pepper, about 8 twists of the mill
1 cup Homemade Meat Broth (page 10), OR canned chicken broth, OR water
Toasted Italian bread

1. Put the garlic in a stockpot with the olive oil and sauté over medium heat until just lightly colored.
2. Add the parsley, stir two or three times, then add the drained, cooked beans, ½ teaspoon salt, and pepper. Cover and simmer gently for about 6 minutes.
3. Put about ½ cup of beans from the pot into a food mill and purée them back into the pot, together with the broth or water. Simmer for another 6 minutes, then taste and correct for salt. Serve over slices of toasted Italian bread.

This needs to be balanced by a fairly substantial, forth-right second course. Serve it before any roasted meat or fowl, or before Honeycomb Tripe with Parmesan Cheese (page 282) or Sautéed Calf's Liver with Onions, Venetian Style (page 286).

BEANS AND PASTA SOUP

Pasta e fagioli

For 6 persons

2 tablespoons chopped
    yellow onion
¼ cup olive oil (slightly
    less if there is much
    fat on the pork you
    are using)
3 tablespoons chopped
    carrot
3 tablespoons chopped
    celery
3 or 4 pork ribs OR a
    ham bone with some
    meat on them OR 2
    small pork chops
⅔ cup canned Italian
    tomatoes, cut up,
    with their juice
2 pounds fresh cranberry
    beans (unshelled
    weight) (see note
    below)

3 cups Homemade Meat
    Broth (page 10)
    (approximately) OR 1
    cup canned beef
    broth mixed with 2
    cups water
    (approximately)
Salt
Freshly ground pepper,
    about 6 twists of the
    mill
Maltagliati (page 116),
    made with 1 egg and
    ¾ cup all-purpose
    flour (basic pasta
    recipe, page 108),
    OR 6 ounces small,
    tubular macaroni
2 tablespoons freshly
    grated Parmesan
    cheese

1. Put the onion in a stockpot with the oil and sauté over medium heat until pale gold.

2. Add the carrot, celery, and pork and sauté for about 10 minutes, stirring the vegetables and turning the pork from time to time.

3. Add the chopped tomatoes and their juice, turn the heat down to medium low, and cook for 10 minutes.

4. If you are using fresh cranberry beans, shell the beans, rinse them in cold water, and add to the pot. Stir two or three times, then add the broth. Cover the pot, adjust the heat so that the liquid is bubbling at a very moderate boil, but at a bit more than a simmer, and cook for 45 minutes to 1 hour, or until the beans are tender. (If you are using precooked beans, cook the tomatoes for 20 minutes instead of 10, as in Step 3, then add the drained beans. Let the beans cook in the tomatoes for 5 minutes, stirring thoroughly, then add the broth and bring to a moderate boil.)

5. Scoop up about ½ cup of beans and mash them through a food mill back into the pot.

6. Add salt and pepper. (If you are using canned broth, taste carefully for salt, because some canned bouillon can be very salty.)

7. Check the soup for density; add more homemade broth or water if needed, and bring the liquid to a steady boil. Add the pasta. If you are using fresh egg pasta, stop the cooking 1 minute after you've dropped it in. If you are using dried pasta or macaroni, taste for doneness and stop the cooking when the pasta is very firm to the bite. (The soup should rest for about 10 minutes before serving, so if you do not stop the cooking when the pasta is very firm it will be quite mushy by the time it gets to the table.) Just before serving, swirl in the grated cheese.

NOTE

Cranberry beans are pink-and-white marbled beans, and they add a wonderful flavor to this soup. If they are not available use 1 cup dried Great Northern beans, cooked as directed on page 74, or 1 twenty-ounce can white kidney beans or other white beans, drained.

The soup can be prepared entirely ahead of time up to, but not including, Step 7. Add the pasta only when you are going to serve the soup.

MENU SUGGESTIONS

This fine, comforting soup can precede any substantial dish of meat or fowl. Particularly nice would be Pan-Broiled

Steak with Marsala and Hot Pepper Sauce (page 229), Braised
Veal Shanks, Trieste Style (page 249), Roast Spring Lamb
with White Wine (page 268), Roast Pork with Bay Leaves
(page 275), Chicken Fricassee with Dried Wild Mushrooms
(page 300), Stewed Rabbit with White Wine (page 309), or
Sautéed Calf's Liver with Onions, Venetian Style (page 286).

RED CABBAGE SOUP

Zuppa di cavolo nero

This is as much a pork-and-beans dish as it is a cabbage
soup, and, along with *cassoulet*, it has an honored place in
that robust family of Mediterranean dishes using beans and
pork or beans and lamb. It is a Tuscan specialty, as are so
many bean dishes in Italy, and every Tuscan cook has a
personal version of it. A constant element of this and many
other Tuscan soups is the garlic- and rosemary-flavored hot
oil that is added to the soup just before serving.

You should not hesitate to take some freedom with the
basic recipe, varying its proportions of sausage, beans, and
cabbage according to taste. In the recipe as given here,
soup, meat course, and vegetable are combined in one hearty
dish that is a meal in itself. It can be made even heartier
by increasing the quantity of sausage. On the other hand,
you can eliminate the sausage altogether, substituting for
it any piece of pork on a bone, and increase the quantity of
broth to make a true soup that will fit as a first course into
a substantial country menu.

This dish develops even better flavor when warmed up
one or two days later, which means that you can prepare it
entirely in advance at the most convenient time on your
schedule.

For 6 persons

¼ pound fresh pork rind
½ teaspoon chopped garlic
2 tablespoons chopped yellow onion
2 tablespoons thinly shredded *pancetta*
¼ cup olive oil
1 pound red cabbage, coarsely shredded
⅓ cup chopped celery
3 tablespoons canned Italian tomato, drained and coarsely chopped
A tiny pinch of thyme
3 cups Homemade Meat Broth (page 10) (approximately) OR 1 cup canned beef broth mixed with 2 cups water (approximately)
Salt
Freshly ground pepper, 6 to 8 twists of the mill
½ pound *luganega* sausage OR other mild sausage
1 cup dried Great Northern beans or other white beans, cooked as directed on page 74 and drained, OR 1 twenty-ounce can white kidney beans, *cannellini*, OR other white beans, drained

FOR THE FLAVORED OIL:

2 large or 3 medium cloves garlic, lightly crushed with a heavy knife handle and peeled
¼ cup olive oil
½ teaspoon chopped rosemary leaves

1. Put the pork rind in a small saucepan, cover by about 1 inch with cold water, and bring to a boil. After it has boiled for 1 minute, drain and allow to cool. Cut into strips about ½ inch wide and 2 to 3 inches long and set aside.

2. Put the garlic, onion, and *pancetta* in a stockpot with the oil and sauté over medium heat until the onion and garlic are very lightly colored.

3. Add the shredded cabbage, the chopped celery, the pork rind, the tomato, and a tiny pinch of thyme. Cook over medium-low heat until the cabbage has completely wilted. Stir thoroughly from time to time.

4. When the cabbage has become soft, add the broth, 2 teaspoons salt, and pepper, cover the pot, and cook at

very low heat for 2 to 2½ hours. This cooking may be done at various stages, spread over two or three days. In fact the soup acquires even better flavor when reheated in this manner.

5. Off the heat, uncover the pot, tilt it slightly, and draw off as much as possible of the fat that rises to the surface.

6. Brown the sausage in a small pan for 6 to 8 minutes over medium-low heat. They need no other fat than that which they throw off, which you will discard after they are browned on all sides.

7. Return the pot to the burner and bring to a simmer. Add the browned sausages, drained of their fat. Purée half the cooked beans into the pot, and stir well. Cover and simmer for 15 minutes.

8. Add the remaining whole beans and correct for desired thickness by adding more homemade broth or water. Taste and correct for salt. Cover and simmer for 10 more minutes. (The soup may be prepared entirely ahead of time up to and including this point. Always return it to a simmer before proceeding with the next step.)

9. Put the crushed garlic cloves and the oil in a small pan and sauté over lively heat until the garlic is nicely browned. Add the chopped rosemary, turn off the heat, and stir two or three times. Pour the oil through a sieve into the soup pot, cover, and simmer for 15 minutes more. Serve with good, crusty Italian or French bread.

MENU SUGGESTIONS

If you are using this as a meal-in-itself dish, you might still precede it with either of the baked oyster dishes on pages 29–30, Broiled Mussels and Clams on the Half Shell (page 31), Peppers and Anchovies (page 34), Mushroom and Cheese Salad (page 44), or a platter of assorted cold cuts. If you decide to omit the sausages and use this as soup, it can precede any roast of meat or fowl, and would also go well with Meat Loaf Braised in White Wine with Dried Wild Mushrooms (page 238), Fried Breaded Calf's Liver (page 288), or Broiled Pork Liver Wrapped in Caul Fat (page 292). This would make a good, stout weekend dinner in the country, with the possibility of a long walk later to work it off.

CHICK-PEA SOUP

Zuppa di ceci

This savory soup can be made entirely ahead of time, refrigerated for as long as ten days, and it will lose none of its taste or aroma when warmed up. Many like to purée the whole soup through a food mill, in which case it may become necessary to add a little more broth until the soup has the consistency of cream. It is served then with *crostini* (Fried Bread Squares for Soup, page 84). If you try this soup and like it, make more than you need the next time. You will then be able to use it again as the base for Chick-pea and Pasta Soup (page 83) or Chick-peas and Rice Soup (page 82).

For 4 to 6 persons

¾ cup dried chick-peas
 OR 2 sixteen-ounce
 cans chick-peas
4 whole cloves garlic,
 peeled
⅓ cup olive oil
1½ teaspoons finely
 crushed rosemary
 leaves, almost
 powder fine
⅔ cup canned Italian
 tomatoes, roughly
 chopped, with their
 juice

1 cup Homemade Meat
 Broth (page 10) OR 1
 bouillon cube
 dissolved in 1 cup
 water
Salt, if necessary
Freshly ground pepper,
 about 4 twists of the
 mill

1. If you are using dried chick-peas you must first soak them overnight. Put them in a large enough bowl, add water to cover by 2 inches, and let them soak all night in a warm corner of the kitchen. (Over the gas pilot would be an excellent place, but do not use a plastic bowl.)

2. The following morning preheat the oven to 325°. Discard the water in which the chick-peas have soaked, put them in a medium-sized stockpot, add enough water to come up 1 inch above the chick-peas (do *not* add salt), and bring them to a boil on top of the stove. Cover tightly and

cook in the middle level of the oven for 1½ hours, or until the chick-peas are tender. (At this stage they are almost exactly equivalent to the canned variety, except that they are not salted and have slightly better texture. Canned chick-peas are very convenient, but they are also considerably more expensive. Which ones to use will have to be your decision. It doesn't matter to the soup.) I always peel chick-peas before using them in soup, but it is a chore, and if you'd rather put up with the peels than with the chore you can omit it.

3. Sauté the garlic cloves in the olive oil in a heavy casserole over medium-high heat. When the garlic is well browned remove it. Add the crushed rosemary leaves to the oil, stir, then add the chopped tomatoes with their juice. Cook over medium heat for about 20 to 25 minutes, or until the tomatoes separate from the oil.

4. Add the drained chick-peas and cook for 5 minutes, turning them in the sauce. Add the broth or the dissolved bouillon cube, bring to a boil, cover, and keep at a steady, moderate boil for 15 minutes. Taste and correct for salt, add freshly ground pepper, and allow to boil about 1 minute more, uncovered. Serve hot.

NOTE:
If you are making the soup ahead of time, add the salt and pepper when you warm it up.

CHICK-PEAS AND RICE SOUP

Zuppa di ceci e riso

For 8 persons

Chick-Pea Soup (page 81)
3 cups Homemade Meat
    Broth (page 10)
    (approximately) OR 2
    bouillon cubes
    dissolved in 3 cups
    water
    (approximately)

1 cup raw rice
Salt, if necessary

1. Purée the basic chick-pea soup through a food mill into a stockpot. Add the broth and bring to a boil. Add the rice, stir, cover the pot, and cook at a steady but moderate boil. Stir from time to time, and after 10 or 12 minutes check to see if more broth is required. (Some types of rice absorb more liquid than others, and the soup must be fairly liquid or it isn't a soup.)

2. The soup is done when the rice is tender but firm, from 15 to more than 20 minutes, according to the type of rice you are using. Taste and correct for salt. Allow to rest for a minute or two, then spoon into soup plates and serve.

NOTE

This soup, or any other that contains rice, cannot be prepared ahead of time because the rice will become mushy.

CHICK-PEAS AND PASTA SOUP

Zuppa di ceci e maltagliati

For 8 persons

Chick-pea Soup (page 81)
2 cups Homemade Meat
    Broth (page 10)
    (approximately) OR 2
    bouillon cubes
    dissolved in 2 cups
    water
    (approximately)

Maltagliati (page 116),
    made with 1 egg and
    ¾ cup of flour (basic
    pasta recipe, page
    108), OR ½ pound
    small macaroni
Salt, if necessary
2 to 3 tablespoons freshly
    grated Parmesan
    cheese

1. Purée about one-third of the basic soup through a food mill into a stockpot. Add the rest of the soup and all the broth and bring to a boil. Add the pasta, stir, cover the pot, and cook at a steady but moderate boil. If you are using freshly made pasta, watch it carefully because it cooks very rapidly, in a minute or less. Whatever pasta you may be using, stop the cooking when it is very firm to the bite, because the pasta continues to soften even after the heat is turned off. With store-bought macaroni you may have to

add some liquid while cooking, if the soup becomes too thick.

2. Taste and correct for salt. Allow the soup to bubble for a few brief moments after you add the salt, then turn off the heat and mix in the grated cheese. (Remember that Parmesan cheese is salty, so regulate the amount you add by the saltiness of the soup.) Allow to rest for a minute or two, spoon into soup plates, and serve.

NOTE

This soup cannot be prepared ahead of time because the pasta would become too soft.

MENU SUGGESTIONS

These chick-pea soups, like all the bean soups, call for a substantial meat course to follow. Any of the lamb roasts on pages 268–272, or the Roast Pork with Bay Leaves (page 275), would be perfect. Broiled steak would be excellent too.

FRIED BREAD SQUARES FOR SOUP

Crostini di pane per minestra

For 4 persons

4 slices firm-bodied, good-quality white bread	Vegetable oil, enough to come ½ inch up the side of the pan

1. Cut away the crusts from the bread and cut the slices into ½-inch squares.

2. Choose a medium-sized skillet. (Inasmuch as you need oil to a depth of ½ inch, it is wasteful to choose too broad a skillet. If the bread doesn't fit in all at one time, it doesn't matter. Bread browns very rapidly and it can be done a few pieces at a time.) Heat the oil in the skillet over moderately high heat. It should become hot enough so that the bread sizzles when it goes in. Test it first with one square. When the oil is hot, put in as much bread as will fit loosely in a single layer. Turn the heat down, because bread will burn quickly if the oil gets too hot, move the squares around in

the pan, and as soon as they turn a light-gold color transfer them with a slotted spoon or spatula to paper towels to drain. Finish doing all the squares, adjusting the heat as necessary so that the bread will brown lightly without burning.

NOTE
Crostini can be prepared several hours ahead of time. After more than a day, however, they take on a stale, rancid taste.

HOW TO COOK PASTA

There is probably no single cooking process in any of the world's cuisines simpler than the boiling of pasta. This very simplicity appears to have had an unsettling effect on some writers, to judge from the curiously elaborate and often misleading procedures described in many Italian cook books. One book tells you to drop pasta into boiling water a little bit at a time. Another counsels you to lift it painstakingly strand by strand when draining it. A third suggests you can keep pasta warm in a 200° oven until you are ready to sauce it. Ah, pasta, what sins have been committed in thy name! Here is the way it is really done.

Water   It is important to cook pasta in abundant water, but it is not necessary to drown it. Italians calculate 1 liter of water per 100 grams of pasta. This works out to slightly more than 4 quarts for 1 pound of pasta. Stick to just 4 quarts of water for every pound of pasta. It will be quite sufficient.

Salt   When the water comes to a boil, add 1½ heaping tablespoons of salt for every 4 quarts of water. If the sauce you are going to be using is very bland, you may put in an additional ½ tablespoon of salt.

When and how to put in the pasta   Put in the pasta when the salted water has come to a rapid boil. Add all the pasta at once. When you put it in a little at a time, it cannot cook evenly. If you are cooking long pasta, such as spaghetti or *perciatelli*, after dropping it in the pot you must bend it in the middle with a wooden spoon to force the strands entirely under water. Never, never break spaghetti in two. Stir the pasta with a wooden spoon to keep it from sticking together. Cover the pot after you put in the pasta to accelerate the water's return to a boil. Watch it, lest it boil over. When it returns to a boil, uncover, and cook at a lively but not too fierce a boil, until it is *al dente*.

Al dente   *Al dente* means "firm to the bite," and that is how Italians eat pasta. Unfortunately, they are the only ones who do. Of course, it is not easy to switch to firm pasta when one is used to having it soft and mushy, and it is very tempting to ingratiate oneself with one's readers by not pressing the issue. The whole point of pasta, however, is its texture and consistency, and overcooking destroys these. Soft pasta is no more fit to eat than a limp and soggy slice of bread.

In the course of civilization's long and erratic march, no other discovery has done more than, or possibly as much as, pasta has to promote man's happiness. It is therefore well worth learning how to turn it out at its best.

No foolproof cooking times can be given, but you can begin by ignoring those on the box. They are invariably excessive. There are so many variables, such as the type and make of pasta, the hardness and quantity of water, the heat source, even the altitude (it is impossible to make good pasta at over 4,500 feet above sea level), that the only dependable procedure is to taste the pasta frequently while it boils. As soon as pasta begins to lose its stiffness and becomes just tender enough so that you can bite through without snapping it, it is done. You should try at first to stop the cooking when you think the pasta is still a little underdone. Do not be afraid to stop too early. It is probably already overcooked, and, in any case, it will continue to soften until it is served. Once you have learned to cook and eat pasta *al dente*, you'll accept it no other way.

Draining, saucing, and serving pasta   The instant pasta is done you must stop its cooking and drain it. Adding a glass of cold water to the pot as you turn off the heat is helpful, but it is not necessary if you are very quick about emptying the pot into the pasta colander. Give the colander a few vigorous sideways and up-and-down jerks to drain the pasta of all its water. Transfer the pasta without delay to a warm serving bowl. If grated cheese is called for, add it at this point and mix it into the pasta. The pasta's heat will melt it partially so that it will blend creamily with the sauce. Add the sauce and toss the pasta rapidly with two forks or a fork and spoon, coating it thoroughly with sauce. Add a thick pat of butter, unless you are using a sauce dominated by olive oil, toss briefly, and bring to the table immediately, serving it in warm soup plates. *Note*: There are two important points to remember in this whole operation:

1. The instant pasta is done, drain it, sauce it, and serve it with the briefest interval possible, because pasta continues to soften at every stage from the colander to the table.

2. Sauce the pasta thoroughly, but avoid prolonged tossings and exaggerated liftings of strands into the air, because there is one thing worse than soft pasta and that is cold pasta.

Reheating   As a rule, pasta cannot be reheated, but some kinds of leftover pasta, such as *rigatoni* or *ziti*, can be turned into a very successful dish when baked (page 105).

Choosing pasta shapes   Although all macaroni pasta is made from the same, identical dough, the end result is determined by shape and size. Spaghetti is probably the most successful vehicle for the greatest variety of sauces. Thin spaghetti (spaghettini) is best for seafood sauces and for any sauce whose principal fat is olive oil. Regular spaghetti is ideal for butter-based white sauces or tomato sauces. The one sauce that somehow doesn't work very well with spaghetti is meat sauce. With meat sauce you ought to choose a substantial, stubby cut of pasta, such as *rigatoni*. Try it also with shells (*conchiglie*); their openings will trap little bits of meat. *Fusilli* and *rotelle* are splendid with dense, spicy cream and meat sauces, such as the sausage sauce on page 104, which cling deliciously to all their twists and curls. There are hundreds of pasta shapes, of which a dozen or more are easily available. You ought to experiment with all the ones you find, and develop your own favorite liaisons of pasta and sauce.

I strongly recommend that you try imported Italian pasta. It is vastly superior to domestic pasta because it really cooks to and holds that absolutely perfect degree of toothy tenderness which deserves to be called *al dente*. It also swells considerably in the cooking, which means that pound for pound it will go farther than American-made pasta. Such excellent brands as De Cecco and Carmine Russo are easily available at all well-stocked Italian groceries, in a broad variety of shapes and cuts.

FIVE TOMATO SAUCES FOR SPAGHETTI AND OTHER PASTA

Sughi di pomodoro

We have all heard about the decline of the fresh tomato. To judge by the plastic-wrapped examples in the supermarkets not even the worst reports are exaggerated. The poor tomato is picked half ripe, gassed, shuttled great distances, and artificially quickened back to life. One who has never tasted a tomato honestly ripened on the vine by the heat of the summer sun cannot possibly believe that this is one of agricultural man's greatest triumphs, one of the most glorious products he has ever grown.

The situation is difficult, but not entirely hopeless. It is still possible to make a good sauce from fresh tomatoes, and it is something that everyone should experience before real tomatoes disappear altogether. You will have to limit yourself, in making these sauces, to those few weeks of the year when the tomatoes on the market are likely to be locally grown. The best tomatoes for this purpose, and those on which the recipes here are based, are the long, narrow plum tomatoes. They should feel reasonably firm, but yielding, not wooden to the touch. And they should be an even, intense red. If you use other varieties of tomatoes, you may have to increase the quantities, depending on how watery they are.

When choice, ripe, fresh tomatoes are not available, a good tomato sauce can be made with canned imported Italian plum tomatoes. I find the tomatoes of San Marzano superior to all others, especially the ones packed by Luigi Vitelli, which are sweet and full-flavored. At the foot of each of the following five recipes there are instructions on how to substitute canned tomatoes for fresh.

TOMATO SAUCE I

Of the three basic tomato sauces given here, this is the most concentrated and the most strongly flavored. It goes well with all macaroni pasta.

For 6 servings

2 pounds fresh, ripe
    plum tomatoes
½ cup olive oil
⅓ cup finely chopped
    yellow onion

⅓ cup finely chopped
    carrot
⅓ cup finely chopped
    celery
2 teaspoons salt
¼ teaspoon granulated
    sugar

1. Wash the tomatoes in cold water. Cut them in half, lengthwise. Cook in a covered saucepan or stockpot at a steady simmer for 10 minutes. Uncover and simmer gently for 1½ hours more.

2. Purée the tomatoes through a food mill into a bowl. Discard the seeds and skin.

3. Rinse and dry the saucepan. Put in the olive oil, then add the chopped onion, and lightly sauté over medium heat until just translucent, not browned. Add the carrot and celery and sauté for another minute. Add the puréed tomato, the salt, and the sugar, and cook at a gentle simmer, uncovered, for 20 minutes. Stir from time to time while cooking.

If using canned tomatoes: use 2 cups tomatoes with their juice, omit Steps 1 and 2, and simmer 45 minutes instead of 20.

TOMATO SAUCE II

Although this sauce is made with the same ingredients as Tomato Sauce I, it has a fresher, more delicate flavor. There are two reasons for this. First, the tomato is cooked much less, just enough to concentrate it, but not so long that its garden-sweet taste is altered. Second, the vegetables are cooked right along with the tomato instead of undergoing a preliminary sautéing in oil. It is an excellent all-purpose sauce for every kind of pasta, from spaghettini to such thicker, stubby cuts as *penne* or *ziti*.

For 6 servings

2 pounds fresh, ripe
    plum tomatoes
⅔ cup chopped carrot
⅔ cup chopped celery

⅔ cup chopped onion
Salt
¼ teaspoon granulated
    sugar
½ cup olive oil

1. Wash the tomatoes in cold water. Cut them in half, lengthwise. Cook in a covered stockpot or saucepan over medium heat for 10 minutes.
2. Add the carrot, celery, onion, 2 teaspoons salt, and sugar and cook at a steady simmer, uncovered, for 30 minutes.
3. Purée everything through a food mill, return to the pan, add the olive oil, and cook at a steady simmer, uncovered, for 15 minutes more. Taste and correct for salt.

If using canned tomatoes: Use 2 cups tomatoes and their juice. Start the recipe at Step 2, cooking the tomatoes with the vegetables as directed.

TOMATO SAUCE III

This is the simplest and freshest of all tomato sauces. It has no vegetables, except an onion. The onion is not sautéed, it is not chopped, it is only cut in two and cooked together with the tomato. Except for salt and a tiny amount of sugar, the sauce has no seasonings. It has no olive oil, only butter. What does it have? Pure, sweet tomato taste, at its most appealing. It is an unsurpassed sauce for potato *gnocchi*, and it is excellent with spaghetti, *penne*, and *ziti*.

For 6 servings

2 pounds fresh, ripe
   plum tomatoes
¼ pound butter

1 medium yellow onion,
   peeled and halved
Salt
¼ teaspoon granulated
   sugar

1. Wash the tomatoes in cold water. Cut them in half, lengthwise. Cook in a covered stockpot or saucepan until they have simmered for 10 minutes.
2. Purée the tomatoes through a food mill back into the pot. Add the butter, onion, 1½ teaspoons salt, and sugar and cook at a slow but steady simmer, uncovered, for 45 minutes. Taste and correct for salt. Discard the onion.

If using canned tomatoes: Use 2 cups tomatoes and their juice, and start the recipe at Step 2.

TOMATO SAUCE WITH MARJORAM AND CHEESE

The fragrance of marjoram and the slight piquancy of Romano cheese make this a particularly appetizing sauce for summer. It is excellent with *perciatelli* and spaghetti.

For 6 servings

Tomato Sauce II (page
   90)
2 teaspoons marjoram
2 tablespoons freshly
   grated Parmesan
   cheese

2 tablespoons freshly
   grated Romano
   pecorino cheese
1 tablespoon olive oil

1. Bring the tomato sauce to a simmer. Add the marjoram, stir, and simmer for 8 to 10 minutes.
2. When the pasta is ready to be seasoned, mix both grated cheeses and the olive oil into the sauce, off the heat. Stir thoroughly but rapidly and pour over the pasta. Serve the pasta with additional grated Parmesan cheese on the side.

TOMATO SAUCE WITH ROSEMARY
AND PANCETTA

This savory sauce is particularly good with stubby cuts of macaroni, such as *maccheroncini*, *ziti*, or *penne*. It is also excellent with *spaghettini*.

For 6 to 8 servings

All the ingredients of
   Tomato Sauce II
   (page 90)
2 teaspoons finely
   chopped dried
   rosemary leaves

½ cup thin strips of
   rolled *pancetta*, ⅛
   inch wide by 2
   inches long

1. Make Tomato Sauce II, up to and including puréeing the cooked tomatoes and vegetables. Then proceed as follows.

2. Heat up the olive oil in a small skillet over medium-high heat. When hot, add the chopped rosemary and the *pancetta* strips. Sauté for 1 minute, stirring constantly. Transfer all the contents of the skillet to a saucepan, together with the puréed tomatoes, and cook at a steady simmer, uncovered, for 15 minutes. Taste and correct for salt.

THIN SPAGHETTI WITH FRESH BASIL
AND TOMATO SAUCE

Spaghettini alla carrettiera

Carretti were hand- or mule-driven carts in which wine and produce were brought into Rome from the surrounding hills. The *carrettieri*, the cart drivers, were notoriously underpaid and had to improvise inexpensive but satisfying meals that could be quickly prepared in the intervals between treks to and from the city.

There are many versions of *spaghettini alla carrettiera*. This is evidently a spring and summer version, because it calls for a large quantity of fresh basil. It has a very fresh, unlabored taste. Don't be put off by the amount of garlic required. It simmers in the sauce without browning so that its flavor comes through very gently. In Rome, one would use very ripe, small sauce tomatoes called *casalini*, which thicken quickly in cooking. For our purposes, a good-quality canned Italian plum tomato is best.

For 4 persons

1 large bunch fresh basil, preferably with the smallest possible leaves

2 cups canned Italian plum tomatoes, seeded, drained, and coarsely chopped

5 large cloves garlic, peeled and chopped fine

⅓ cup olive oil, more if desired

Salt

Freshly ground pepper, about 6 twists of the mill

1 pound *spaghettini*

1. Pull off all the basil leaves from the stalks, rinse them briefly in cold water, and roughly chop them. The yield should be about 1½ to 2 cups.

2. Put the chopped basil, tomatoes, garlic, the ⅓ cup olive oil, 1 teaspoon salt, and pepper in an uncovered saucepan and cook over medium-high heat for 15 minutes. Taste and correct for salt.

3. Drop the *spaghettini* in 4 quarts of boiling salted water. Since thin spaghetti cook very rapidly, begin testing them early for doneness. They should be truly *al dente*, very firm to the bite.

4. Drain the *spaghettini* in a large colander, giving the colander two or three vigorous upward jerks to make all the water run off, and transfer quickly to a large hot bowl. Add the sauce, mixing it thoroughly into the *spaghettini*. You may, if you wish, add a few drops of raw olive oil. Serve immediately.

NOTE
No grated cheese is called for.

If you want to precede this with an antipasto, try either some cold Sautéed Mushrooms with Garlic and Parsley (page 365), or Peppers and Anchovies (page 34). As a second course, serve Pan Roast of Veal (Page 241), Roast Pork with Bay Leaves (page 275), or Chicken Fricassee with Dried Wild Mushrooms (page 300). Avoid any second course with tomatoes.

THIN SPAGHETTI WITH EGGPLANT

Spaghettini con le melanzane

For 4 persons

1 medium eggplant (about 1 pound)	1¾ cups canned Italian tomatoes
1½ teaspoons finely chopped garlic	⅛ teaspoon finely chopped hot red pepper or less, to taste
3 tablespoons olive oil	
2 tablespoons finely chopped parsley	Salt
	1 pound *spaghettini*

1. Trim, slice, salt, and fry the eggplant according to the instructions for Fried Eggplant (page 358). Set aside to drain on paper towels.
2. In a medium-sized saucepan sauté the garlic in olive oil over moderate heat just until the garlic begins to color lightly. Stirring rapidly, add the parsley, tomatoes, chopped hot pepper, and ¼ teaspoon salt. Cook, uncovered, for about 25 minutes, or until the tomatoes have separated from the oil and turned to sauce.
3. Cut the fried eggplant slices into slivers about ½ inch wide. When the sauce is ready, add the eggplant slivers and cook for 2 or 3 minutes more. Taste for salt. (You can prepare the sauce three or four days in advance if you like.)
4. Drop the *spaghettini* into 4 quarts of boiling salted water. Since thin spaghetti cook very rapidly and continue to soften even after draining, you must be ready to stop the cooking when the *spaghettini* are still quite firm.
5. Put a small quantity of the sauce in a warm serving

bowl. Add the drained *spaghettini*, mix, add the rest of the sauce quickly, mix again, and serve immediately.

NOTE
This dish does not call for a topping of grated cheese.

MENU SUGGESTIONS

This can precede the peppery Pan-Broiled Steak With Marsala and Hot Pepper Sauce (page 228), Braised Veal Shanks, Trieste Style (page 249), any roast of lamb (pages 268–272), Roast Chicken with Rosemary (page 296), or Broiled Pork Liver Wrapped in Caul Fat (page 292). If you want an appetizer, try Mushroom and Cheese Salad (page 44).

THIN SPAGHETTI WITH RED CLAM SAUCE

Spaghettini alle vongole

For 4 persons

1 dozen littleneck clams, the tiniest you can find
1½ teaspoons finely chopped garlic
3 tablespoons olive oil
1 teaspoon chopped anchovy fillets or anchovy paste
1½ tablespoons finely chopped parsley

2 cups canned Italian tomatoes, coarsely chopped, with their juice
Salt
Freshly ground pepper, about 6 twists of the mill
1 pound *spaghettini*

1. Wash and scrub the clams thoroughly as directed on page 50. Heat them over high heat in a covered pan until they open their shells. Detach the clams from the shells and rinse off any sand on the meat by dipping them briefly one at a time in their own juice. Unless the clams are exceptionally small, cut them up into two or more pieces and set aside. Strain the clam juices through a sieve lined with paper towels and set aside.

2. In a saucepan, sauté the garlic in the olive oil over medium heat. When the garlic has colored lightly, add the chopped anchovies or paste and stir. Add the chopped parsley, stir, then add the chopped tomatoes with their juice

and the strained clam juices. Cook, uncovered, at a gentle simmer for about 25 minutes, or until the tomatoes and oil separate. Taste and correct for salt, then add the pepper. Off the heat, mix in the chopped clams. (If you are preparing the sauce ahead of time, hold back the clams until after you've warmed up the sauce; otherwise they will become tough and rubbery. Film them with a little olive oil to keep them moist.)

3. Drop the *spaghettini* into 4 quarts of boiling salted water and cook until *al dente*, firm to the bite. (*Spaghettini* cook very rapidly and should be eaten even slightly more *al dente* than other pasta.) Drain the pasta immediately when cooked. Transfer to a warm bowl and mix in the sauce, thoroughly seasoning all the strands. Serve right away.

NOTE
No grated cheese is called for in this recipe.

MENU SUGGESTIONS

For an antipasto: Shrimps with Oil and Lemon (page 36), or Broiled Mussels and Clams on the Half Shell (page 31). As a second course, Fish Broiled the Adriatic Way (page 214) would be perfect, and so would Fried Squid (page 223) or, if you've skipped the shrimp antipasto, Shrimp Brochettes, Adriatic Style (page 215), or Poached Halibut with Parsley Sauce (page 203).

THIN SPAGHETTI WITH ANCHOVY AND TOMATO SAUCE

Spaghettini al sugo di pomodoro e acciughe

For 4 persons

1 teaspoon chopped
    garlic
⅓ cup olive oil
4 flat anchovy fillets,
    coarsely chopped
2 tablespoons chopped
    parsley

1½ cups canned Italian
    tomatoes, chopped,
    with their juice
Salt
Freshly ground pepper,
    6 to 8 twists of the
    mill
1 pound *spaghettini*

1. Put the garlic in a small saucepan with the oil and sauté over medium heat until it has colored lightly.

2. Add the chopped anchovies and parsley and sauté for another 30 seconds, stirring constantly.

3. Add the tomatoes, ½ teaspoon salt, and pepper. Stir, and adjust the heat so that the sauce cooks at a gentle but steady simmer for 25 minutes. Stir frequently. Taste and correct for salt.

4. Bring 4 quarts of water to a boil, add 1½ tablespoons salt, drop in the *spaghettini*, and cook until *al dente*, firm to the bite. Drain, transfer promptly to a warm bowl, mix thoroughly with the sauce, and serve at once.

NOTE

Although the sauce takes only slighty more time to do than does cooking the pasta, it may be prepared in advance, and reheated before using.

MENU SUGGESTIONS

Follow those given for Thin Spaghetti with Red Clam Sauce (page 95).

SPAGHETTI WITH TUNA SAUCE

Spaghetti al tonno

For 4 or 5 persons

½ teaspoon finely
    chopped garlic
5 tablespoons olive oil
3 tablespoons finely
    chopped parsley
1½ cups canned Italian
    tomatoes, coarsely
    chopped, with their
    juice

10 ounces Italian tuna OR
    domestic tuna
    packed in oil,
    drained
Salt
Freshly ground pepper,
    about 6 twists of the
    mill
3 tablespoons butter
1 pound spaghetti

1. In a skillet, sauté the garlic, with all the olive oil, over medium heat until it has colored lightly. Add the chopped parsley, stir, and cook for another half minute. Add the chopped tomatoes and their juice, stir well, lower

the heat, and cook at a steady, gentle simmer, uncovered, for about 25 minutes, or until the tomatoes separate from the oil.

2. While the tomato sauce is simmering, drain the tuna and break it up into small pieces with a fork. When the tomato sauce is done, add the tuna to it, mixing it well into the sauce. Add just a light sprinkling of salt, bearing in mind that the tuna is already salty, add pepper, and cook at a gentle simmer, uncovered, for 5 minutes. Taste and correct for salt, turn off the heat, and swirl in the butter.

3. Drop the spaghetti into 4 quarts of boiling salted water and cook until *al dente*, very firm to the bite. Drain and transfer immediately to a warm serving bowl. Mix in all the sauce and serve immediately.

NOTE
The sauce may be prepared entirely ahead of time and refrigerated for one or two days. Add the butter, however, only after it has been reheated. No grated cheese is called for with this sauce.

MENU SUGGESTIONS

Antipasto: Broiled Mussels and Clams on the Half Shell (page 31). Second course: Pan-Roasted Mackerel with Rosemary and Garlic (page 205), Shrimp Brochettes, Adriatic Style (page 215), or Fish Broiled the Adriatic Way (page 214). Avoid tomato or cream sauces.

SPAGHETTI WITH GARLIC AND OIL

Spaghetti "ajo e ojo"

This is one of the easiest, quickest, and tastiest pasta dishes you can prepare. Its humble origins are in the shanty towns of Rome, but it is now a universal favorite, especially among Rome's chic insomniacs, who depend upon a wee hours' *spaghettata* to see them through the night until their early-morning bedtime.

In most versions, crushed garlic cloves are sautéed in olive oil until they are nearly black. They are then discarded and the spaghetti is seasoned with the flavored oil. In this recipe the garlic is chopped, sautéed lightly, and left in the oil to be added to the spaghetti. The result is a fuller yet milder taste of garlic, with no trace of bitterness.

For 4 persons

½ cup plus 1 tablespoon
   olive oil
2 teaspoons very finely
   chopped garlic
Salt

1 pound spaghetti OR
   spaghettini
Freshly ground pepper,
   6 to 8 twists of the
   mill
2 tablespoons chopped
   parsley

1. The sauce can be prepared in the time it takes to bring the water for the spaghetti to a boil. When you've turned on the heat under the water, put the ½ cup oil, the garlic, and 2 teaspoons of salt in a very small saucepan. Sauté the garlic over very low heat, stirring frequently, until it slowly becomes a rich, golden color.
2. Drop the spaghetti into the boiling salted water and cook until tender but *al dente*, very firm to the bite. Drain immediately, transfer to a warm bowl, and add the oil and garlic sauce. Toss rapidly, coating all the strands, adding pepper and parsley. Mix the remaining tablespoon of olive oil into the spaghetti and serve.

MENU SUGGESTIONS

Aside from its *dolce vita* standing as a late-night snack, Spaghetti with Garlic and Oil is an easy introduction to any plain but hearty second course, whether it is fish, meat, or fowl. Avoid following it with dishes that have a bold garlic taste, which would be monotonous, or a delicate sauce, which would be lost on the palate after the brashness of the spaghetti. Specially recommended would be Thin Pan-Broiled Steaks with Tomatoes and Olives (page 230), Beef Patties with Anchovies and Mozzarella (page 234), Meat Balls (page 236), or Veal Scaloppine with Tomatoes (page 253).

BUCATINI WITH PANCETTA, TOMATOES, AND HOT PEPPER

Bucatini all'Amatriciana

For 4 persons

1 medium yellow onion,
    chopped fine
2 tablespoons butter
3 tablespoons vegetable
    oil
1 slice rolled *pancetta*, ¼
    inch thick, cut into
    strips ½ inch wide
    and 1 inch long
1½ cups canned Italian
    tomatoes
½ to 1 small dried hot
    red pepper,
    chopped fine

Salt
1 pound *bucatini* OR
    perciatelli (thick,
    hollow spaghetti)
3 tablespoons freshly
    grated Parmesan
    cheese
1 tablespoon freshly
    grated Romano
    pecorino cheese,
    more if desired

1. Sauté the onion in a saucepan with all the butter and oil until it is pale gold. Add the strips of *pancetta* and sauté for about a minute. Add the tomatoes, chopped hot pepper, and 1½ teaspoons salt. Cook over medium heat, uncovered. The sauce is done when the tomatoes and the cooking fats separate, about 25 minutes. Turn off the heat and taste for salt.

2. Drop the *bucatini* into 4 quarts boiling salted water. Stop the cooking when very firm, very *al dente*, and drain immediately. (Although large in diameter, the *bucatini* are hollow and have very thin sides, and they quickly turn from firm to soft. They will continue to soften as they are being seasoned and while they rest in the serving bowl.)

3. Transfer the cooked *bucatini* to a warm serving bowl, add the sauce, and mix. Add the Parmesan and the Romano and mix very thoroughly. Taste for salt and spiciness. If you like it somewhat sharper you can add a little more Romano, but not so much as to overwhelm the other flavors.

Antipasto: ideally, good Italian salami, if you can find it. Or the Braised Artichokes with Mortadella Stuffing (page 331). A perfect second course would be Casserole-Roasted Lamb with Juniper Berries (page 269). Other suggestions: Roast Chicken with Rosemary (page 296), Meat Loaf Braised in White Wine with Dried Wild Mushrooms (page 238), or Sautéed Calf's Liver with Onions, Venetian Style (page 286).

FUSILLI WITH CREAMY ZUCCHINI AND BASIL SAUCE

Fusilli alla pappone

For 4 persons

1 pound zucchini
Vegetable oil, enough to come ½ inch up the side of a medium skillet
1 pound *fusilli* (spiral spaghetti)
3 tablespoons butter
3 tablespoons olive oil
1 teaspoon all-purpose flour dissolved in ⅓ cup milk
Salt

⅔ cup roughly chopped fresh basil
1 egg yolk, beaten lightly with a fork
½ cup freshly grated Parmesan cheese
¼ cup freshly grated Romano *pecorino* cheese (see note below)

1. Wash the zucchini as directed on page 377 and cut into sticks about 3 inches long and ⅛ inch thick.

2. Heat the vegetable oil in a skillet over medium-high heat. Fry the zucchini sticks, a few at a time, so that they are not crowded. Fry them until they are a light-brown color, not too dark, turning them occasionally. As each batch is done, transfer to paper towels to drain.

3. Drop the *fusilli* into 4 quarts of boiling salted water, stirring with a wooden spoon. It will cook while you prepare the sauce.

4. In another skillet, melt half the butter and add all the

olive oil. When the butter begins to foam, turn the heat down to medium low, and stir in the flour-and-milk mixture, a little bit at a time. Cook, stirring constantly, for 30 seconds. Add the fried zucchini sticks, turning them two or three times, then add ¼ teaspoon salt and the chopped basil. Cook long enough to turn everything once or twice. Off the heat, swirl in the remaining butter. Rapidly mix in the egg yolk, then all the grated cheese. Taste and correct for salt.

5. Cook the *fusilli* until *al dente*, firm to the bite. Drain, transfer to a warm serving bowl, toss with all the sauce, and serve immediately.

NOTE

You may increase the quantity of Romano and decrease the Parmesan if you prefer a more piquant cheese flavor.

MENU SUGGESTIONS

Antipasti: none is required. This is a rather rich sauce, and the palate should be kept limber enough to deal with it. Second courses: Pan-Broiled Steak with Marsala and Hot Pepper Sauce (page 228), Veal Stew with Sage and White Wine (page 262), Baby Lamb Chops Fried in Parmesan Cheese Batter (page 272), or Pan-Roasted Chicken with Garlic, Rosemary, and White Wine (page 294).

PENNE WITH A SAUCE OF TOMATOES AND DRIED WILD MUSHROOMS

Penne al sugo di pomodoro e funghi secchi

For 4 persons

1 ounce dried wild
  mushrooms
2 tablespoons finely
  chopped shallots or
  yellow onion
1 tablespoon vegetable
  oil
4 tablespoons butter
2 tablespoons ¼-inch-
  wide strips of
  pancetta, prosciutto,
  or unsmoked ham

1½ cups canned Italian
  tomatoes, cut up,
  with their juice
Salt
Freshly ground pepper,
  about 4 twists of the
  mill
1 pound *penne* OR other
  short tubular pasta,
  such as *mezzani* OR
  ziti

1. Put the mushrooms to soak in 1 cup lukewarm water for about 30 minutes. When they have finished soaking, lift out the mushrooms but do not discard the water. Rinse the mushrooms in several changes of cold water and set aside. Strain the water from the soak through a sieve lined with paper towels and set aside.

2. Put the shallots in a small saucepan with the oil and butter and sauté over medium heat until pale gold.

3. Add the *pancetta*, and continue sautéing for another minute or two, stirring several times.

4. Add the cut-up tomatoes and their juice, the mushrooms, the strained liquid from the mushroom soak, ¼ teaspoon salt, and pepper, and cook, uncovered, at a gentle simmer for 45 minutes. Stir with a wooden spoon from time to time.

5. Drop the pasta into boiling salted water and cook until tender but *al dente*, firm to the bite. Drain, giving the colander a few vigorous up-and-down shakes to let all the water run off. Transfer to a warm serving bowl, pour all the sauce over the pasta, and mix thoroughly but rapidly. Serve immediately, with a bowl of freshly grated Parmesan cheese on the side.

You can follow this with any second course of meat or fowl that does not contain tomatoes or mushrooms. Particularly good choices would be broiled steak, Pan Roast of Veal (page 241), Roast Spring Lamb with White Wine (page 268), Charcoal-Broiled Chicken Marinated in Pepper, Oil, and Lemon (page 297), or the Broiled Pork Liver Wrapped in Caul Fat (page 292).

CONCHIGLIE WITH SAUSAGE AND CREAM SAUCE

Conchiglie con il sugo per la gramigna

Gramigna is both a kind of crab grass and a thin, short tubular macaroni with which one usually serves this sauce. *Gramigna*, to my knowledge, is not available here, but this creamy, tasty sauce is every bit as delectable with *conchiglie*, *fusilli*, or *rotelle*: any pasta whose twists or cavities can trap little morsels of sausage and cream. Use a mild, sweet sausage. Avoid any sausage containing hot peppers, fennel seeds, or other pungent spices. *Luganega* is best, but you may substitute other sweet sausages if you can't find *luganega*. Breakfast sausage or German bratwurst are acceptable alternatives.

For 4 persons

6 to 8 ounces *luganega* sausage
1½ tablespoons chopped shallots OR yellow onion
2 tablespoons butter
2 tablespoons vegetable oil

Freshly ground pepper, about 4 twists of the mill
⅔ cup heavy cream
Salt
1 pound *conchiglie, fusilli,* OR *rotelle*

1. Skin the sausage and crumble it as fine as possible.
2. Put the shallots in a small saucepan with the butter and oil and sauté until pale gold.

3. Add the crumbled sausage meat and sauté it for 10 minutes, stirring frequently.

4. Add the pepper and the cream, turn up the heat to medium high, and cook until the cream has thickened. Stir frequently while cooking. Taste and correct for salt.

5. Drop the *conchiglie* into 4 quarts of boiling salted water and stir with a wooden spoon. When *al dente*, firm to the bite, drain, giving the colander a few vigorous up-and-down jerks to shake all the water out of the *conchiglie*'s cavities. Transfer to a warm serving bowl, toss with all the sauce, and serve immediately, with a little freshly grated Parmesan cheese on the side.

MENU SUGGESTIONS

No antipasti are recommended. Suitable second courses could be the Beef Braised in Red Wine Sauce (page 231), the Roast Spring Lamb with White Wine (page 268), the Breaded Veal Cutlets, Milan Style (page 260), or the Charcoal-Broiled Chicken Marinated in Pepper, Oil, and Lemon (page 297).

BAKED RIGATONI WITH MEAT SAUCE

Rigatoni al forno col ragù

For 6 persons

1 pound *rigatoni* OR similar-cut pasta, such as *mezzani*, *ziti*, OR *penne*	A medium-thick Béchamel Sauce (page 25)
Salt	6 tablespoons freshly grated Parmesan cheese
2 cups Meat Sauce, Bolognese Style (page 120)	2 tablespoons butter

1. Preheat the oven to 400°.

2. Drop the pasta into 4 quarts of boiling salted water and cook until just *al dente*, firm to the bite. (It should be a shade firmer than you would ordinarily cook it because it will soften more as it bakes in the oven.) Drain and transfer to a large mixing bowl.

3. Add the meat sauce, the béchamel sauce, and 4 ta-

blespoons of the grated cheese to the pasta. Mix thoroughly. Transfer to a butter-smeared bake-and-serve dish. Level the top with a spatula, sprinkle it with the remaining 2 tablespoons grated cheese, and dot with butter. Place in the uppermost level of the oven and bake for 10 minutes. Allow to settle a few minutes before serving.

MENU SUGGESTIONS

Follow this with Rolled Stuffed Breast of Veal (page 254), Sautéed Veal Chops with Sage and White Wine (page 272), Pork Loin Braised in Milk (page 284), Stewed Rabbit with White Wine (page 320), or Pan-Roasted Squab (page 319).

HOMEMADE EGG PASTA

La Sfoglia
(Pasta all'uovo fatta in casa)

Macaroni pasta is factory made with flour and water. In homemade pasta, eggs take the place of water and hands replace machines. Although egg pasta is now produced in almost every Italian province, it is the specialty of Emilia-Romagna, and even today the pasta produced there is incontestably the finest in Italy. Until comparatively recent times, spaghetti and other macaroni were nearly unknown to the Emilian table. The only pasta consumed was homemade pasta, and it was made fresh every day in virtually every home. My grandmother, who died at ninety-three, made pasta for us daily until the last few years of her life. At the end, when, instead of homemade pasta, an occasional dish of macaroni would appear on our table, she would be saddened and perplexed by our declining taste.

There is no denying that, for a beginner, making pasta at home takes time, patience, and a considerable amount of physical effort. The rewards are such, however, that you should be persuaded to make the attempt. When you have mastered basic pasta dough you will have immediate access to some of the most miraculous creations in all gastronomy: *fettuccine, tagliatelle, tortellini, cappelletti, cappellacci, tortelloni, cannelloni, lasagne, garganelli,* and all their glorious variations. As you become skillful, you will discover, too, that the fresh egg pasta you are making at home is not only vastly better than what you can buy in any store, but that it is also superior to what you are likely to eat in any restaurant this side of the Alps.

WHAT YOU NEED TO MAKE PASTA

- A steady surface on which to work, 24 inches deep, 36 inches wide, preferably unvarnished wood, but it can well be formica. Marble is not too satisfactory.
- A rolling pin, 1½ inches in diameter, 32 inches long. This is the ideal size for pasta. You will probably not find it in any store, but you can easily have one cut for you from hardwood at a good lumber supply house. Make sure the ends are sanded and smooth.
  Before using a new rolling pin, wash it with soap and water and rinse. Dry thoroughly with a soft towel and let dry further in the warmth of the kitchen. Then dampen a cloth in olive oil or lightly grease your hands and rub oil over the entire surface of the pin. Do not overgrease. When the oil has been absorbed, lightly rub some flour over the pin. This procedure should be repeated every dozen or so times that the rolling pin is used.
- A broad-bladed, well-balanced knife. A Chinese cleaver is excellent.
- A place protected from draughts and not overheated. Pasta dough must not dry out too quickly while you are working on it.

THE INGREDIENTS

Although no one making pasta in Italy ever really measures out flour, the traditionally accepted formula corresponds to 1 level cup of flour for every egg. I have experimented with this, as well as with other proportions, and I have found that, with American flour, the best results are obtained using ¾ cup of flour for every U.S. Large egg. This must not be considered an inflexible rule, however, because eggs vary in size, and in flour-absorption qualities. Start with ¾ cup of flour per egg. If you find that the egg will take a little more flour, add it. It is easier for beginners to work with less than with more flour, because the dough stays softer and easier to handle. If you keep it too soft, however, it may also become a problem, because very soft dough is likely to stick and tear. Until you develop a feel for the right consistency, you are safest with these recommended proportions:

*3 or 4 persons**	*5 or 6 persons**	*7 or 8 persons**
2 eggs	3 eggs	4 eggs
1½ cups all-purpose flour	2¼ cups all-purpose flour	3 cups all-purpose flour

For stuffed pasta, such as *tortellini*, add 1 teaspoon of milk for each egg used. This is to make the pasta easier to seal. In Emilia-Romagna we never add oil, water, or salt to pasta dough.

HANDMADE EGG PASTA (BASIC RECIPE)**

There are four steps in making a sheet of egg-pasta dough from eggs and flour. In the first step the eggs are combined with as much flour as they will take without becoming stiff and dry. In the second, the eggs and flour are kneaded to a smooth, elastic consistency. In the third, the dough is opened out with the rolling pin to a circular sheet about ⅛ inch thick. In the last step the sheet is wrapped around the pin and stretched again and again until it is almost paper thin and transparent. All together, it should take a reasonably skillful person less than 25 minutes. Here is a detailed description of each step:

1. Pour out the flour on the working surface, shape it into a mound, and make a well in the center of the mound. Put the whole eggs in the well. If you are making stuffed pasta, and the recipe calls for milk, add the milk. Beat the eggs lightly

---

*These servings for flat pasta only. Stuffed pasta goes further. See individual recipes for yield.
**See also page 117 for homemade pasta made on the pasta machine.

with your fingers or with a fork, for a minute or two. Start mixing flour into the eggs with a circular motion, drawing the flour from the inside wall of the well. Use one hand for mixing, the other for supporting the outside wall of the well, lest it collapse and let the eggs run through. When the eggs cease to be runny, tumble the rest of the flour over them, and, working with palms and fingertips, push and squeeze the eggs and flour until they are a well-combined but somewhat crumbly paste. If the eggs were very large, or had exceptional flour-absorption qualities, the mass may be on the moist and sticky side. Add as much flour as the mass will absorb without becoming stiff and dry, but do not exceed 1 cup of flour per egg.

2. Set the egg and flour mass to one side and scrape off every last crumb of caked flour from the working surface and from your hands. Wash and dry your hands. Knead the mass, pressing against it with the heel of your palm, folding it over and turning it again and again. After 8 to 10 minutes it should be a smooth, compact, and elastic ball of dough. Pat it into a flattish bunlike shape. (If you are making a lot of pasta and using more than 2 eggs, divide the mass in two and keep one half covered between 2 soup plates while you roll out and thin the other half. When you've become more experienced, you can try doing the entire mass at one time.)

3. Dust the work surface lightly with flour. Open out the ball of dough with the rolling pin, starting to roll at about one-third of the way in on the ball, rolling forward, away from you. Rotate the dough one quarter turn after every roll so that it opens out into an even, circular shape. As it begins to flatten out, gradually lessen the degree of rotation after each roll, but don't lose control of the shape. It must stay as round as possible. Don't press the dough *against* the work surface. Roll it *out and away*, without putting weight on it. Stop when you have rolled out a sheet ⅛ inch thick.

4. This last step is the hardest one for beginners to learn. But it doesn't require particular skills; it is all a question of getting the right motion. Once you have it you have mastered pasta, and you will never again give it a second thought. The objective is to give the pasta sheet its final thinning out by stretching it with a sideways pressure of your hands as you

PASTA

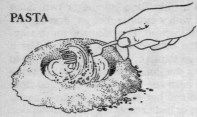

Beat the eggs, and mix them with
the flour drawn from the inside wall
of the well.

Knead the dough, pressing it
with the heel of your palm...

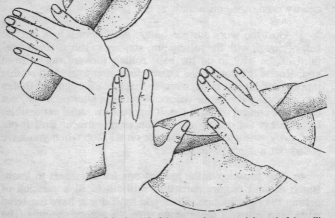

Make the dough into a ball, and
open out the ball with the rolling
pin. Always roll away from you,
turning the dough as it begins to
flatten out.

Curl the far end of the pasta sheet around the end of the rolling
pin and roll it toward you.

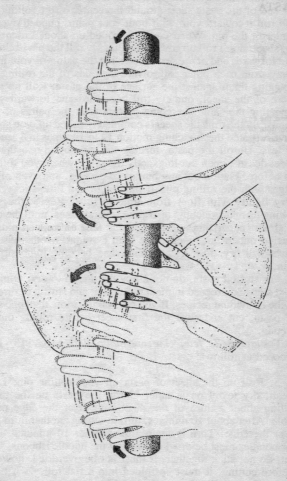

Giving the pasta sheet a final thinning out: move hands back and forth, quickly and lightly, over the length of the rolling pin. At the same time roll the pin backward and forward to thin the sheet evenly.

wrap it around the rolling pin. Here is how you do it. Curl the far end of the pasta sheet around the center of the rolling pin, and roll it toward you, with both your palms cupped over the center of the pin. When you have rolled up about a quarter of the sheet, don't roll up any more. Quickly roll the pin backward and forward, and *at the same time* slide the palms of your hands away from each other and toward the ends of the rolling pin, dragging them against the surface of the pasta. Roll up some more of the sheet, quickly roll backward and forward while repeating the same stretching motion with the palms of your hands. By the time the sheet is completely rolled up, you should have repeated the stretching motion 12 to 14 times in 8 seconds or less. Unroll the pasta, turning the pin slightly so that the sheet doesn't open out to exactly the place where you rolled it up before. Flatten out any bumps or creases, and even off the edges with the rolling pin. If the dough is a little sticky, dust very lightly with flour from time to time. Repeat the same rolling up and stretching operation several times, until the pasta is almost paper thin and transparent. The entire step must be carried out in not much more than 8 minutes, otherwise the pasta will dry, lose its elasticity, and become impossible to thin.

For stuffed pasta, do not allow the dough to dry. Omit the next step and proceed immediately to cut and stuff it as directed in the individual recipes. If you are making more than one sheet of pasta, cut and stuff the first sheet before rolling out the second.

For *tagliatelle*, *fettuccine*, and *maltagliati* (pages 113 – 117), proceed as follows:

5. Roll up the sheet of pasta on your rolling pin. Lay a clean, dry towel on a table. Unroll the pasta on the towel, letting about a third of the sheet hang over the edge of the table. After about 10 minutes, turn it, letting another third hang over the edge. Turn it again after another 10 minutes. Pasta for noodles must be dried out so that the noodle ribbons, when cut, do not stick together. It must not be overdried, however. Before cutting, it must be folded into a flat roll, so it has to stay soft and pliable enough to fold without cracking. When the surface of the pasta begins to take on a leathery look it is ready for folding and cutting. This drying process usually takes about 30 minutes but in a very hot room it can take as little as 15 or 20 minutes.

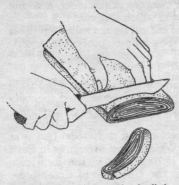

For tagliatelle, fettuccine, and maltagliati: Hold the roll loosely with one hand, and with the other hold the knife so that the flat part of the blade leans against your knuckles.

Open out the noodles, and let dry for 5 minutes before cooking.

6. Roll up the pasta on the rolling pin and unroll it on the work surface. Fold it over and over into a flat roll about 3 inches wide. Place one hand on the roll, with fingertips partly drawn back under your knuckles. Hold the knife with your other hand, crosswise to the roll, leaning the flat part of the blade against your knuckles. Cut the pasta to the width desired, pulling back your knuckles after each cut and following them with the flat side of the blade. Keep your knuckles high and don't lift the knife above them. (This method gives you perfect control of the knife and is almost completely accident-proof.) When you have cut the entire roll, open out the noodles on a clean, dry towel and allow them to firm up for 5 minutes. They are then ready to cook. Gather them up with the towel and let them slide into the boiling water.

FLAT PASTA
TAGLIATELLE, AND OTHER NOODLES

There are two broad catergories of egg pasta. There is stuffed pasta, such as *tortellini*, *tortelloni*, *cannelloni*, and *lasagne*, and there is non-stuffed pasta, which includes all varieties of noodles. We refer to this last category as flat pasta, and here are the most important shapes in which it is cut.

All of the following shapes are cut from a rolled-up sheet of homemade pasta dough. (See Step 6, preceding page.)

TAGLIATELLE

Tagliatelle are the long, narrow noodles, and it is probably the best-known cut of all. This is the uncontested specialty of Bologna. Of all their many contributions to civilized life, there is probably none for which the Bolognese have any higher regard or greater affection than *tagliatelle*. Just as at the International Bureau of Weights and Measures in Paris the standard of the meter is deposited in the form of a platinum bar, in Bologna, at the Chamber of Commerce, there is a sealed glass case wherein the ideal width and thickness of *tagliatelle* are embodied in a solid gold noodle. According to the Accademia Italiana della Cucina (Italian Academy of Cooking), the correct dimensions of raw *tagliatelle* are: thickness, 1 millimeter (slightly more than 1/32 inch), and width, 6 millimeters (slightly less than 1/4 inch). This sort of precision deserves our wonder and admiration, but, inasmuch as we are not making yardsticks, we are only making noodles, we can permit ourselves some elasticity.

The most desirable width, in terms of wrapping-around-the-sauce ability and of plumpness in the plate, hovers around 1/4 inch. No need to worry, however, if you exceed it slightly. The thickness is simply that of the thinnest pasta dough you are able to produce. If you are using the pasta machine, this entire discussion is academic because the cutting blades and the rollers predetermine width and thickness.

Tagliatelle is best served Bolognese fashion, with Meat Sauce, Bolognese Style (page 120).

FETTUCCINE

This is the term Romans use for noodles, and it is commonly assumed that they are precisely the same as *tagliatelle*, except for the name. The fact is, however, that *fettuccine*, as Romans are accustomed to eat them, are somewhat narrower and thicker than *tagliatelle*. I find this slightly stouter

SOME BASIC PASTA SHAPES

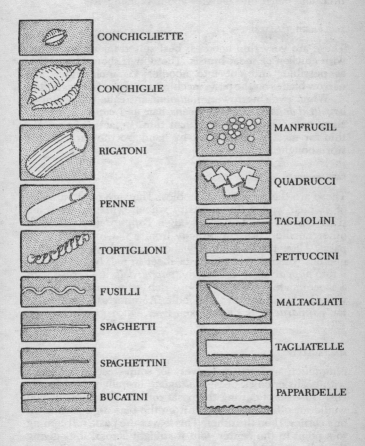

CONCHIGLIETTE

CONCHIGLIE

RIGATONI

PENNE

TORTIGLIONI

FUSILLI

SPAGHETTI

SPAGHETTINI

BUCATINI

MANFRUGIL

QUADRUCCI

TAGLIOLINI

FETTUCCINI

MALTAGLIATI

TAGLIATELLE

PAPPARDELLE

noodle ideally suited to carry sauces in which heavy cream is an essential ingredient.

For *fettuccine*, keep your pasta dough not quite paper thin, and cut it into noodles about ⅛ inch wide.

TAGLIOLINI, TAGLIARINI

These are very thin noodles, best suited for use in soups, with chicken or meat broths. The dough should be as thin as possible, and cut into noodles ¹⁄₁₆ inch wide. The narrow blades on the pasta machine are perfect for *tagliolini*.

When even narrower, *tagliolini* are called *capellini* or *capelli d'angelo*. *Capello* means hair and *capelli d'angelo*, angel hair. They are indeed hair thin. In fact, they are too thin for most people to cut by hand, so they are usually store bought.

PAPPARDELLE

These are the broadest of noodles. They are cut to a width of ⅝ inch with a fluted pastry wheel, which gives them their characteristic crimped edge. *Pappardelle*, unlike all other noodles, are cut directly from a flat, open sheet of pasta. Allow the dough to dry about half as long as for other noodles, then divide the pasta sheet in half before cutting it into *pappardelle*. In Tuscany, *pappardelle* are served with a sauce made from hare, whose rich, gamy taste goes well with the broadness of the noodle. Another excellent sauce for *pappardelle* is the chicken-liver sauce given on page 130.

MALTAGLIATI

Maltagliati are used exclusively for soups, especially soups with beans or chick-peas. *Maltagliati* literally means "badly cut." Instead of cutting the pasta roll straight across as you would for other noodles, cut it on the bias, first cutting off one corner, then the other. This leaves the pasta roll coming to a point in the center. Cut it straight across, thus giving the roll a straight edge again, then cut off the corners once more as before. At its broadest point, *maltagliati* should be about ½ inch wide or less, but precision, as the name indicates, is not terribly important.

There is no bean soup calling for pasta that is not immensely improved when you use homemade *maltagliati* instead of commercial macaroni. Like all noodles, maltagliati easily keeps for a month without refrigeration, so that you can always have a supply on hand.

QUADRUCCI

The name means "little squares," and that is exactly what they are. They are made by first cutting the pasta into *tagliatelle* noodles, then cutting the still-folded ribbons crosswise into squares. It makes a fine, delicate pasta for use with a good, clear meat or chicken broth.

HOMEMADE PASTA USING THE PASTA MACHINE

The pasta machine kneads and thins out pasta and cuts it, if you wish, into two different noodle widths. It is truly effortless, but, unfortunately, machine pasta is not really as fine as the handmade kind. Something happens to its composition as it goes through the steel rollers that gives the dough an ever so slightly slippery texture. Moreover, the machine gives you only one degree of thinness, whereas for *fettuccine*, for example, you might want the pasta a little thicker, or for stuffed pasta a little thinner. These considerations aside, however, machine pasta can be quite good; it is certainly superior to the commercial variety and it is far better than having no homemade pasta at all.

1. Combine the eggs and flour exactly as in Step 1 of the handmade pasta recipe (page 108).

2. The smooth steel rollers at one end of the machine knead, roll out, and thin the dough. The first setting, at which the rollers are widest apart, is for kneading. Pull off a piece of the egg and flour mass about the size of a lemon, keeping the rest of the mass covered between two soup plates. Feed the mass through the rollers 8 to 10 times, until it is smooth and elastic. Each time after you knead it, fold it over and turn it before feeding it through the rollers again, so that it will be kneaded evenly.

3. Shift the rollers to the next setting and pass the kneaded

dough through. Do not fold the dough. Lower the setting again, and feed through once more. Go down all the settings, feeding the dough once through each setting until it is thoroughly thinned out. If the dough is sticky, dust it lightly with flour.

4. If you are making stuffed pasta, proceed immediately to cut the dough and stuff it as directed in the recipes. For noodles, allow the pasta to dry on a clean towel for at least 15 minutes. Before cutting, trim the dough to a workable length, no more than 24 inches.

5. For *tagliatelle* (page 113), feed the dough through the broad cutting blades. The narrow blades are suitable only for making the *tagliolini*, very thin noodles, best served in broth. For *fettuccine* or *maltagliati*, fold the dough into a flat roll and cut it by hand as directed in Step 6 of the handmade pasta recipe (page 113).

KEEPING HOMEMADE PASTA

Uncooked flat noodle pasta, such as *tagliatelle*, *fettuccine*, *tagliolini*, *maltagliati*, and so on, keeps a very long time, even a long as a month or more, without refrigeration. Allow the opened-out noodles to dry thoroughly. When dry transfer to a platter or large soup bowl. (Handle carefully, because pasta is very brittle at this stage and breaks easily.) Put away, uncovered, in a dry, cool cupboard. Use exactly as you would fresh pasta, except that it will take somewhat longer to cook.

Although stuffed pasta can also be made ahead of time, it does not keep as long as noodle pasta. How long it keeps depends on the stuffing. Follow the suggestions at the end of each recipe.

COOKING HOMEMADE PASTA

Follow the same procedure as for macaroni pasta. If the pasta is to be seasoned with a very delicate sauce, add a bit more salt to the water in which it boils.

People who are doing it for the first time are always astonished to see how quickly fresh egg pasta cooks. As a general rule, fresh flat pasta is done within 5 to 10 *seconds* after the water in which it has been dropped returns to a boil. Stuffed pasta takes a while longer, and all dried pasta takes much longer, several minutes at least. Taste it frequently as it boils to avoid overcooking.

Always stir pasta with a wooden spoon immediately after dropping it in the pot, or it may stick together.

SPINACH PASTA

Pasta verde

Spinach is added to pasta dough to color it and to make it slightly softer and creamier. It doesn't significantly alter its flavor. You can use green pasta exactly as you would yellow pasta. It is found most frequently in the form of *lasagne* (page 136) or *tagliatelle* (page 113), but *cappelletti* (page 147), *tortelloni* (page 154), and *garganelli* (page 160) can also be very successful when made with spinach pasta. Green pasta is particularly attractive when served with Tomato and Cream Sauce (page 153), or any sauce in which the white of cream and béchamel or the red of tomato predominates.

Spinach pasta is made with precisely the same technique used for yellow pasta.

½ ten-ounce package frozen leaf spinach, thawed, OR ½ pound fresh spinach	2 eggs
¼ teaspoon salt	1½ cups all-purpose flour, approximately

1. If you are using frozen spinach, cook it with ¼ teaspoon salt in a covered pan over medium heat for 5 minutes. Drain and let cool.

If you are using fresh spinach, try to choose young, tender spinach. Remove all the stems, and discard any leaves that are not perfectly green and crisp. Wash it in a basin of cold water, changing the water several times until it shows no traces of soil. Cook it with ¼ teaspoon of salt in a covered pan over medium heat with just the water that clings to the leaves. Cook until tender, 15 minutes or more, then drain and allow to cool.

Squeeze the cooked spinach with your hands as dry as you can, then chop it very fine.

2. Pour the flour on the work surface, shape it into a mound, and make a well in the center. Put the whole eggs and the chopped spinach in the well, and lightly beat the eggs and the spinach together, using your fingers or a fork. Add flour gradually to the egg and spinach mixture, drawing it in from the inside wall of the well. Since it is impossible to estimate in advance exactly how much flour the egg and spinach will absorb, simply work it into the egg and spinach mixture gradually until the mixture has incorporated as much flour as possible without becoming stiff and dry. When the mass is ready for kneading, proceed exactly as though it were yellow pasta. Refer to Step 2 of the basic recipe (page 109), or knead it and thin it out in the pasta machine (page 117).

NOTE

If you are making stuffed pasta, do *not* add milk to spinach pasta. It is soft enough to seal well without it. Cooking times for spinach pasta are slightly shorter than for yellow pasta.

MEAT SAUCE, BOLOGNESE STYLE

Ragù

Ragù is not to be confused with *ragoût*. A *ragoût* is a French meat stew, while *ragù* is Bologna's meat sauce for seasoning its homemade pasta. The only thing they share is a common and justified origin in the verb *ragoûter*, which means "to excite the appetite."

A properly made *ragù* clinging to the folds of homemade noodles is one of the most satisfying experiences accessible to the sense of taste. It is no doubt one of the great attractions of the enchanting city of Bologna, and the Bolognese claim one cannot make a true *ragù* anywhere else. This may be so, but with a little care, we can come very close to it. There are three essential points you must remember to make a successful *ragù*:

• The meat must be sautéed just barely long enough to lose its raw color. It must not brown or it will lose delicacy.

- It must be cooked in milk *before* the tomatoes are added. This keeps the meat creamier and sweeter tasting.
- It must cook at the merest simmer for a long, long time. The minimum is 3½ hours; 5 is better.

The union of *tagliatelle* and *ragù* (following page) is a marriage made in heaven, but *ragù* is also very good with *tortellini*, it is indispensable in *lasagne*, and it is excellent with such macaroni as *rigatoni*, *ziti*, *conchiglie*, and *rotelle*. Whenever a menu lists pasta *alla bolognese*, that means it is served with *ragù*.

For 6 servings, or 2¼ to 2½ cups

2 tablespoons chopped yellow onion
3 tablespoons olive oil
3 tablespoons butter
2 tablespoons chopped celery
2 tablespoons chopped carrot
¾ pound ground lean beef, preferably chuck or the meat from the neck

Salt
1 cup dry white wine
½ cup milk
⅛ teaspoon nutmeg
2 cups canned Italian tomatoes, roughly chopped, with their juice

1. An earthenware pot should be your first choice for making *ragù*. If you don't have one available, use a heavy, enameled cast-iron casserole, the deepest one you have (to keep the *ragù* from reducing too quickly). Put in the chopped onion, with all the oil and butter, and sauté briefly over medium heat until just translucent. Add the celery and carrot and cook gently for 2 minutes.

2. Add the ground beef, crumbling it in the pot with a fork. Add 1 teaspoon salt, stir, and cook only until the meat has lost its raw, red color. Add the wine, turn the heat up to medium high, and cook, stirring occasionally, until all the wine has evaporated.

3. Turn the heat down to medium, add the milk and the nutmeg, and cook until the milk has evaporated. Stir frequently.

4. When the milk has evaporated, add the tomatoes and stir thoroughly. When the tomatoes have started to bubble, turn the heat down until the sauce cooks at the laziest simmer, just

an occasional bubble. Cook, uncovered, for a minimum of 3½ to 4 hours, stirring occasionally. Taste and correct for salt. (If you cannot watch the sauce for such a long stretch, you can turn off the heat and resume cooking it later on. But do finish cooking it in one day.)

NOTE

Ragù can be kept in the refrigerator for up to 5 days, or frozen. Reheat until it simmers for about 15 minutes before using.

TAGLIATELLE WITH BOLOGNESE MEAT SAUCE

Tagliatelle alla bolognese

For 6 persons

2 to 2½ cups Meat Sauce, Bolognese Style (previous page)	1½ tablespoons salt
	1 tablespoon butter
Tagliatelle (page 113), made with 3 eggs and 2¼ cups all-purpose flour (basic pasta recipe, page 108)	½ cup freshly grated Parmesan cheese

1. Heat 4 to 5 quarts of water and, while it is coming to a boil, bring the sauce to a very gentle simmer, stirring it well.

2. When the water boils, add the salt, then all the noodles, and stir with a wooden spoon. If the pasta is fresh, it will be done within 5 to 10 *seconds* after the water returns to a boil. Drain immediately and shake the colander well.

3. Spoon a little bit of hot sauce onto the bottom of a warm serving platter, add the noodles, pour the rest of the sauce over them, and toss the noodles with the sauce, the butter, and the grated cheese. Serve without delay, with additional freshly grated cheese on the side.

MENU SUGGESTIONS

For an authentic Bolognese meal, follow with Sautéed Turkey Breast Fillets with Ham, Cheese, and White Truffles (page 305). Other second courses could be Pan Roast of Veal (page

241), Roast Spring Lamb with White Wine (page 268), Pan-Roasted Chicken with Garlic, Rosemary, and White Wine (page 294), or Stewed Rabbit with White Wine (page 309).

FETTUCCINE TOSSED IN CREAM AND BUTTER

Fettuccine all'Alfredo

There actually was an Alfredo, in whose Roman restaurant this lovely dish became famous. Alfredo had a gold fork and spoon with which he gave a final toss to each serving of *fettuccine* before it was sent to the table. Despite its southern origin, this dish has now become a fixture of those Italian restaurants abroad specializing in northern cuisine. Although it is astonishingly simple, it isn't often that one finds it done well. Its essential requirements are homemade—better yet handmade—pasta cooked very firm, and good-quality fresh heavy cream.

For 5 or 6 persons

1 cup heavy cream
3 tablespoons butter
Salt
Fettuccine (page 114), made with 3 eggs and 2¼ cups all-purpose flour (basic pasta recipe, page 108)

⅔ cup freshly grated Parmesan cheese
Freshly ground pepper, 4 to 6 twists of the mill
A very tiny grating of nutmeg

1. Choose an enameled cast-iron pan, or other flameproof cook-and-serve ware, that can later accommodate all the cooked *fettuccine* comfortably. Put in ⅔ cup of the cream and all the butter and simmer over medium heat for less than a minute, until the butter and cream have thickened. Turn off the heat.

2. Bring 4 quarts of water to a boil. Add 2 tablespoons of salt, then drop in the *fettuccine* and cover the pot until the water returns to a boil. If the *fettuccine* are fresh, they will be done a few seconds after the water returns to a boil. If dry, they will take a little longer. (Cook the *fettuccine* even firmer than usual,

because they will be cooked some more in the pan.) Drain immediately and thoroughly when done, and transfer to the pan containing the butter and cream.

3. Turn on the heat under the pan to low, and toss the *fettuccine*, coating them with sauce. Add the rest of the cream, all the grated cheese, ½ teaspoon salt, the pepper, and nutmeg. Toss briefly until the cream has thickened and the *fettuccine* are well coated. Taste and correct for salt. Serve immediately from the pan, with a bowl of additional grated cheese on the side.

MENU SUGGESTIONS

For an elegant dinner you can precede this with an antipasto of Baked Stuffed Zucchini Boats (page 380) or Mushroom and Cheese Salad (page 44). The second course may be Beef Braised in Red Wine Sauce (page 231), Sautéed Veal Chops with Sage and White Wine (page 261), Sautéed Veal Scaloppine with Marsala (page 251), Sweetbreads Braised with Tomatoes and Peas (page 284), Sautéed Chicken Livers with Sage (page 293), or any roast in this book, *except* for pork braised in milk.

YELLOW AND GREEN NOODLES WITH CREAM, HAM, AND MUSHROOM SAUCE

Paglia e fieno alla ghiotta

Paglia e fieno, "straw and hay," is the bucolic, but self-effacing name of one of the most exquisite of pasta dishes. It is a combination of narrow yellow and spinach noodles, served with a cream sauce. Sautéed tiny fresh peas are usually a part of the sauce, but a less common version, using mushrooms, is given here. I think it would be a pity to limit one's enjoyment of this elegant dish to those rare occasions when very young, freshly picked peas appear on the market, and in this sauce, I much prefer the lovely, rounded taste of good mushrooms to the indifferent presence of frozen, canned, or mealy middle-aged peas. You may substitute prosciutto for the ham, but it will give you a somewhat sharper flavor and coarser texture.

For 6 to 8 persons

¾ pound crisp, white mushrooms	¾ cup heavy cream
2 tablespoons finely chopped shallots or yellow onion	*Fettuccine* (page 114), made with 2 eggs and 1½ cups all-purpose flour (basic pasta recipe, page 108)
6 tablespoons butter	
Salt	
Freshly ground pepper, about 6 twists of the mill	Spinach Pasta (page 119), cut into *fettuccine*
6 ounces unsmoked ham, shredded	½ cup freshly grated Parmesan cheese

1. Slice off the ends of the mushroom stems. Wipe the mushrooms clean with a damp cloth. If there are still traces of soil, wash very rapidly in cold running water and dry thoroughly with a towel. Dice into ¼-inch cubes and set aside.

2. Choose a skillet that can later accommodate the mushrooms loosely. Put in the chopped shallots and half the butter and sauté over medium heat until the shallots have turned pale gold in color. Turn the heat up to high and add the diced mushrooms. When the mushrooms have absorbed all the butter, briefly turn the heat down to low, add 1 teaspoon salt and the pepper, and shake the pan, moving and tossing the mushrooms. As soon as the mushroom juices come to the surface, which happens quickly, turn the heat up to high and cook the mushrooms for about 3 minutes, stirring frequently. Turn the heat down to medium, add the ham, and cook it for less than a minute, stirring as it cooks. Add half the heavy cream, and cook just long enough for the cream to thicken slightly. Taste and correct for salt. Turn off the heat and set aside.

3. Choose an enameled iron pan or other flameproof serving dish that can later accommodate all the noodles without piling them too high. Put in the rest of the butter and the cream and turn on the heat to low. When the butter is melted and incorporated into the cream, turn off the heat and proceed to boil the pasta.

4. Spinach pasta cooks faster than yellow pasta, so the two pastas must be boiled in separate pots. Bring 4 quarts of water in each pot to a boil and add 1 tablespoon of salt to each. First drop the yellow noodles in one pot, and stir them with a wooden

spoon. Immediately after, drop the spinach noodles in the other pot and stir them with the spoon. Taste the spinach noodles for doneness 5 seconds or so after the water returns to a boil. They should be quite, quite firm because they will continue to soften up while cooking with the sauce. Drain well and transfer to the waiting pan. Immediately after, drain the yellow noodles and transfer them to the same pan. (Be very sure not to overcook the noodles. It is safer to err on the side of underdone than overdone.)

5. Turn on the heat to low and start tossing the noodles, coating them with butter and cream. Add half the mushroom sauce, mixing it well with the noodle strands. Add the grated cheese and mix it into the noodles. (This entire step should not take more than a minute.) Turn off the heat. Make a slight depression in the center of the mound of noodles and pour in the rest of the mushroom sauce. Serve immediately, with a bowl of additional grated cheese on the side.

MENU SUGGESTIONS

Follow the suggestions given for Fettuccine Tossed in Cream and Butter (page 123).

FETTUCCINE WITH GORGONZOLA SAUCE

Fettuccine al gorgonzola

This sauce is both creamy and piquant, two qualities that are seldom combined in Italian cooking. Its mild piquancy comes from gorgonzola, Italy's incomparable blue cheese. The sauce works best when the gorgonzola is creamy and mellow. Look for cheese that is warm white in color, soft, and, preferably, recently cut. Avoid dry, crumbly, or yellowish cheese. You can try substituting domestic gorgonzola or other blue cheeses, if you are so inclined, but you will never achieve the perfectly balanced texture and flavor of this sauce with any cheese but choice Italian gorgonzola.

Besides *fettuccine*, *garganelli* (Homemade Macaroni, page 160) and Potato Gnocchi (page 185) are absolutely lovely with gorgonzola sauce.

For 6 persons

4 ounces gorgonzola
⅓ cup milk
3 tablespoons butter
Salt
Fettuccine (page 114)
      made with 3 eggs
      and 2½ cups all-
      purpose flour (basic
      pasta recipe, page
      108)

¼ cup heavy cream
⅓ cup freshly grated
      Parmesan cheese

1. Choose a shallow enameled iron pan, or other flame-proof serving dish, that can later accommodate all the pasta. Put in the gorgonzola, milk, butter, and 2 teaspoons salt and turn on the heat to low. Mash the gorgonzola with a wooden spoon, and stir to incorporate it into the milk and butter. Cook for about 1 minute, until the sauce has a dense, creamy consistency. Turn off the heat and set aside until you are almost ready to add the pasta.

2. Bring 4 quarts of water to a boil. Add 2 tablespoons of salt, then drop in the *fettuccine* and cover the pot until the water returns to a boil. If the *fettuccine* are fresh, they will be done a few seconds after the water returns to a boil. If dry, they will take a little longer.

3. Just seconds before the pasta is done, turn on the heat under the sauce to low, and stir in the heavy cream. Add the drained, cooked pasta (if you are doing *gnocchi*, add each batch as it is done) and toss it with the sauce. Add all the grated cheese and mix it into the pasta. Serve immediately, directly from the pan, with a bowl of additional grated cheese on the side.

MENU SUGGESTIONS

It would be a pity to cancel out this marvelous sauce by following it with another highly flavored dish. A good choice for the second course would be the Pan Roast of Veal (page 241), Breaded Veal Cutlets, Milan Style (page 260), the Baby Lamb Chops Fried in Parmesan Cheese Batter (page 272), or the Sautéed Chicken Breast Fillets with Lemon and Parsley (page 303).

FETTUCCINE WITH WHITE CLAM SAUCE

Fettuccine al sugo di vongole bianco

This is a tomato-less sauce that includes two ingredients rarely used in Italian clam sauces: butter and cheese. But this departure from tradition is justified and successful because it adds smoothness and delicacy to the sauce. On the Adriatic, where I first came across it, this sauce is served with the clams still in their shells. The size of full-grown Adriatic clams, however, is little more than a thumbnail. If you tried it with husky American ocean clams, you might have difficulty in accommodating the pasta in the same dish.

For 4 persons

2 dozen littleneck clams, the tiniest you can find
1 tablespoon chopped shallots OR yellow onion
½ cup olive oil
1 teaspoon chopped garlic
2 tablespoons chopped parsley
¼ teaspoon chopped dried hot red pepper

1 tablespoon butter
2 tablespoons freshly grated Parmesan cheese
Salt
¼ cup white wine
Fettuccine (page 114), made with 2 eggs and 1½ cups all-purpose flour (basic pasta recipe, page 108)

1. Wash and scrub the clams as directed on page 53, then put in a covered saucepan over high heat. As the clams open up, shuck them and put them in a small bowl. When all the clams have been shucked, pour the juices from the pan over them and set aside.
2. Put the shallots in a small saucepan with the oil and sauté over medium-high heat until translucent.
3. Add the garlic and sauté until lightly colored.
4. Add the parsley and hot pepper, stir three or four times, then add the wine. Allow the wine to boil until it

has evaporated by half, then turn off the heat. (The sauce may be prepared several hours ahead of time up to this point.)

5. Rinse the clams one by one in their own juice and chop into small pieces.

6. Filter the clam juices through a sieve lined with paper towels. You should have about ⅔ cup of liquid. If there is more, discard it. Add the liquid to the sauce and boil until it is reduced by half.

7. Add the clams, turn them quickly in the hot sauce, and turn off the heat. Add the butter and cheese, mixing thoroughly. Taste and correct for salt. (No salt at all may be required, especially in the summer, when clams seem to be saltier.)

8. Add 1½ teaspoons salt to 4 quarts rapidly boiling water, then drop in the pasta and drain as soon as it is tender but *al dente*, firm to the bite. (If you are using freshly made pasta, remember that it is done a few seconds after the water returns to a boil.)

9. The moment the pasta is drained, transfer it to a warm serving bowl, add the sauce (previously reheated if no longer hot), toss thoroughly but rapidly, and serve immediately. Additional grated cheese may be served on the side if desired.

NOTE

The sauce is also excellent with spaghetti or with *garganelli* (Homemade Macaroni, page 160).

MENU SUGGESTIONS

This can be preceded by Shrimps with Oil and Lemon (page 36), the Herb-Flavored Seafood Salad (page 405), or Cold Sautéed Trout in Orange Marinade (page 210). The second course could be Fish Broiled the Adriatic Way (page 214) or the Baked Striped Bass and Shellfish Sealed in Foil (page 201).

PAPPARDELLE WITH CHICKEN-LIVER SAUCE

Pappardelle con il ragù di fegatini

Pappardelle are the broadest of the long noodles. In Tuscany and elsewhere they are often served with a sauce made from stewed hare. Another good condiment for *pappardelle* is this magnificent sauce of chicken livers. The same sauce is also quite good with regular noodles (*tagliatelle*, page 113). In the Molded Risotto with Parmesan Cheese and Chicken-Liver Sauce (page 172), it makes a very elegant and delicious first course.

For 4 persons

½ pound chicken livers
2 tablespoons chopped
    shallots OR yellow
    onion
3 tablespoons olive oil
2 tablespoons butter
¼ teaspoon finely
    chopped garlic
3 tablespoons diced
    pancetta, prosciutto,
    OR unsmoked ham
1½ teaspoons chopped
    sage
¼ pound ground lean
    beef

Salt
Freshly ground pepper,
    6 to 8 twists of the
    mill
1 teaspoon tomato paste
    dissolved in ¼ cup
    dry white vermouth
Pappardelle (page 116),
    made with 2 eggs
    and 1½ cups all-
    purpose flour (basic
    pasta recipe, page
    108)

1. Clean the chicken livers of any greenish spots and particles of fat, then wash them, cut them each up into 3 or 4 pieces, and dry them thoroughly on paper towels. Set aside.

2. Put the shallots in a small saucepan with the oil and butter, and sauté lightly over medium heat until translucent.

3. Add the garlic, but do not allow it to become colored. Stir two or three times, then add the diced *pancetta* and the chopped sage leaves. Sauté for about half a minute and stir.

4. Add the ground meat, crumbling it with a fork, and cook until it has completely lost its raw red color.

5. Add 1 teaspoon salt and the pepper and turn the heat up to medium high. Add the chicken livers and stir and cook until they have lost their raw color.

6. Add the tomato paste and vermouth mixture, stir well, and cook for about 8 to 10 minutes. Taste and correct for salt.

7. When the sauce is nearly done, drop the pasta into 4 quarts of boiling water that contains 1 tablespoon salt. Drain as soon as it is tender but *al dente*, firm to the bite. (If you are using fresh, moist pasta, remember that it is done just a few seconds after the water returns to a boil.)

8. The moment the pasta is drained, transfer it to a warm platter, add the sauce, toss thoroughly but rapidly, and serve immediately, with grated Parmesan cheese on the side, if desired.

NOTE
You should time the preparation of this sauce so that it is ready to use the moment the pasta is cooked. If it has been prepared a bit ahead of time and has cooled, it should be reheated very gently. On no account should it be prepared long in advance or refrigerated, because the chicken livers would stiffen, lose delicacy, and acquire sharpness.

MENU SUGGESTIONS

The second course should be a fine meat dish, not strongly seasoned. It can be broiled steak, Beef Braised with Red Wine Sauce (page 231), Pan Roast of Veal (page 241), Breaded Veal Cutlets, Milan Style (page 260), Roast Spring Lamb with White Wine (page 268), or Baby Lamp Chops Fried in Parmesan Cheese Batter (page 272).

GENOESE BASIL SAUCE
FOR PASTA AND SOUP

Pesto

If the definition of poetry allowed that it could be composed with the products of the field as well as with words, *pesto* would be in every anthology. Like much good poetry, *pesto* is made of simple stuff. It is simply fresh basil, garlic, cheese, and olive oil hand ground into sauce. There is nothing more to it than that, but every spoonful is loaded with the magic fragrances of the Riviera.

The Genoese, who invented it, insist that authentic *pesto* cannot be made without their own small-leaved basil and a marble mortar. This is true and it isn't. It is true that Genoese basil is particularly fragrant, partly because of the soil but, even more important, because of the very salty Mediterranean breezes that bathe it as it grows. It is also true that grinding the basil into the marble of the mortar somehow releases more of its flavor than other methods. But, with all this, *pesto* is such an inspired invention that it survives almost anything, including our minty, large-leafed basil and the electric blender.

Two recipes are given here, one for the blender and one for the mortar. The ingredients are identical, the difference is one of procedure. You should try, at least once, to make pesto in a mortar, because of the greater character of its texture and its indubitably richer flavor. But blender *pesto* is still so good that we should enjoy it with a clear conscience whenever we don't have the time or the patience for the mortar. Also, since fresh basil has a brief season, and *pesto* keeps quite well in the freezer, the blender is absolutely invaluable for making a large supply to keep on hand.

In Genoa, they use equal quantities of Parmesan cheese and of a special, mildly tangy Sardinian cheese made of sheep's milk. The Romano *pecorino* cheese available here is considerably sharper than Sardo *pecorino*. You must therefore increase the proportion of Parmesan to *pecorino*, or you will throw the fine equilibrium of flavors in *pesto* out of balance. The proportion I suggest is 4 parts Parmesan to 1 part Romano. As you become familiar with *pesto* you can adjust this to taste. A well-rounded *pesto* is *never* made with all Parmesan or all *pecorino*.

The old, traditional recipes do not mention pine nuts or butter. But modern *pesto* invariably includes them, and so does this recipe.

Potato Gnocchi (page 185) are delicious with *pesto*, and so is spaghetti. The Genoese use it with *fettuccine*, which they call *trenette* (page 135), and it can be a spectacular addition to cold or hot *minestrone* (page 66).

BLENDER PESTO

Enough for about 6 servings of pasta

2 cups fresh basil leaves
    (see note below)
½ cup olive oil
2 tablespoons pine nuts
2 cloves garlic, lightly
    crushed with a
    heavy knife handle
    and peeled

1 teaspoon salt
½ cup freshly grated
    Parmesan cheese
2 tablespoons freshly
    grated Romano
    pecorino cheese
3 tablespoons butter,
    softened to room
    temperature

1. Put the basil, olive oil, pine nuts, garlic cloves, and salt in the blender and mix at high speed. Stop from time to time and scrape the ingredients down toward the bottom of the blender cup with a rubber spatula.

2. When the ingredients are evenly blended, pour into a bowl and beat in the two grated cheeses by hand. (This is not much work, and it results in more interesting texture and better flavor than you get when you mix in the cheese in the blender.) When the cheese has been evenly incorporated into the other ingredients, beat in the softened butter.

3. Before spooning the *pesto* over pasta, add to it a tablespoon or so of the hot water in which the pasta has boiled.

NOTE
The quantity of basil in most recipes is given in terms of whole leaves. American basil, however, varies greatly in leaf sizes. There are small, medium, and very large leaves, and they all pack differently in the measuring cup. For the sake of accurate measurement, I suggest that you tear all but the tiniest leaves into two or more small pieces. Be gentle, so as not to crush the basil. This would discolor it and waste the first, fresh droplets of juice.

MORTAR PESTO

Same yield as blender pesto

2 cups fresh basil leaves
    (see note above)
2 tablespoons pine nuts
2 cloves garlic, lightly
    crushed with a
    heavy knife handle
    and peeled
A pinch of coarse salt

½ cup freshly grated
    Parmesan cheese
2 tablespoons freshly
    grated Romano
    pecorino cheese
½ cup olive oil
3 tablespoons butter,
    softened to room
    temperature

1. Choose a large marble mortar with a hardwood pestle. Put the basil, pine nuts, garlic, and coarse salt in the mortar. Without pounding, but using a rotary movement and grinding the ingredients against the sides of the mortar, crush all the ingredients with the pestle.

2. When the ingredients in the mortar have been ground into a paste, add both grated cheeses, continuing to grind with the pestle until the mixture is evenly blended.

3. Put aside the pestle. Add the olive oil, a few drops at a time at first, beating it into the mixture with a wooden spoon. Then, when all the oil has been added, beat in the butter with the spoon.

4. As with blender *pesto*, add 1 or 2 tablespoons of hot water from the pasta pot before using.

MAKING PESTO FOR THE FREEZER

1. Mix all the ingredients in the blender as directed in Step 1 of blender *pesto*. Do *not* add the cheese or butter. Spoon the contents of the blender cup into a jar. If you are doubling or tripling the recipe, divide it into as many jars. Seal tightly and freeze.

2. Before using, thaw overnight in the refrigerator. When completely thawed, beat in the grated cheeses and the butter as in Step 2 of blender *pesto*. Adding the cheese at this time, rather than before freezing, is no more work and it gives the sauce a much fresher flavor.

In Genoa, *pesto* is traditionally served with *fettuccine*, which the Genoese call *trenette*. *Trenette* are cooked and served together with boiled, sliced potatoes. Here is how to make them:

TRENETTE WITH POTATOES AND PESTO

Trenette col pesto

For 6 persons

1½ tablespoons salt
3 medium potatoes,
   peeled and thinly
   sliced
Fettuccine (page 114),
   made with 2 eggs
   and 1½ cups
   all-purpose flour
   (basic pasta recipe,
   page 108)

Genoese Basil Sauce for
   Pasta and Soup
   (previous page)

1. In 4 to 5 quarts water, to which 1½ tablespoons salt have been added, boil the sliced potatoes until nearly tender.

2. Add the *fettuccine*. If the pasta is fresh, it will be done 5 to 10 seconds after the water returns to a boil. Drain

both *fettuccine* and potatoes, transfer to a warm platter, and toss the *fettuccine* with the *pesto*. Serve immediately.

MENU SUGGESTIONS FOR TRENETTE, GNOCCHI,
AND SPAGHETTI WITH PESTO

Pesto is compatible with fish, and any pasta seasoned with *pesto* can be followed by Fish Broiled the Adriatic Way (page 214), or Shrimp Brochettes, Adriatic Style (page 215). Other suitable second courses are Little Veal "Bundles" with Anchovies and Cheese (page 256), the Rolled Breast of Chicken Fillets Stuffed with Pork (page 304), the Baby Lamb Chops Fried in Parmesan Cheese Batter (page 272), Fried Calf's Brains (page 289), and Fried Breaded Calf's Liver (page 288).

BAKED GREEN LASAGNE WITH MEAT SAUCE

Lasagne verdi al forno

Although this classic *lasagne* as we make it in Romagna is richly laced with meat sauce and béchamel, it is almost austere compared to the southern variety that is popular here. In the expatriate southern style, *lasagne* spills over with sausages, meat balls, ricotta, mozzarella, hard-boiled eggs, and anything else personal inclination may suggest. *Lasagne* in Romagna is not intended as a catchall. While acting as a vehicle for a moderate amount of meat sauce, the pasta maintains its own clearly established character. The béchamel that is added should be no more than is necessary to bind the layers and maintain moistness during baking.

It is extremely important to avoid overcooking *lasagne*. Mushy *lasagne* is an abomination. And do not use boxed macaroni *lasagne* for this recipe. *Lasagne* is never, but simply never, made with anything but homemade pasta dough.

For 6 persons

2¼ cups Meat Sauce
   Bolognese Style
   (page 120)
Béchamel Sauce (page
   25), made with 3
   cups milk, 6
   tablespoons butter,
   4½ tablespoons all-
   purpose flour, and
   ¼ teaspoon salt. It
   should be fairly
   thin, with the
   consistency of sour
   cream.

A sheet of Spinach Pasta
   (page 119)
1 tablespoon salt
⅔ cup freshly grated
   Parmesan cheese
2 tablespoons butter

1. Prepare the meat sauce and béchamel and set aside.

2. If you are making the pasta by hand, roll out a sheet that is not quite paper thin. Cut the dough into rectangular strips about 4½ inches wide and 11 inches long. Do not allow it to dry any longer than it takes to bring 4 quarts of water to a boil. While the water is coming to a boil, lay some clean, dry towels flat on the work counter and set a bowl of cold water near you at the range. When the water boils, add the salt, then drop in 4 of the pasta strips. Stir with a wooden spoon. Cook for just 10 seconds after the water returns to a boil, then retrieve the pasta with a large slotted spoon, dip it in the bowl, and rinse it with cold water. Wring each strip very gently by hand and lay it flat on the towel. Cook all the pasta in the same manner, including the trimmings. When it is all laid out on the towel, pat it dry on top with another towel.

3. Preheat the oven to 450°.

4. Choose a 14-inch bake-and-serve *lasagne* pan. Smear the bottom with a little bit of meat sauce, skimming it from the top, where there is more fat. Place a single layer of pasta in the pan, overlapping the strips, if necessary, no more than ¼ inch. (Do not prop up the edges of the pasta along the sides of the pan. It will become dry and tough there.) Spread enough sauce on the pasta to dot it with meat, then spread béchamel over the meat sauce. Before sprinkling cheese, taste the béchamel and meat sauce

coating. If it is on the salty side, sprinkle the grated cheese sparsely. If it is rather bland, sprinkle the cheese freely. Add another layer of pasta and coat it as before. (Do not make more than 6 thin layers of pasta at the maximum, since *lasagne* shouldn't be too thick, and do not build up the layers any higher than ½ inch from the top of the pan.) Use the trimmings to plug up any gaps in the layers. Coat the top layer with béchamel, sprinkle with cheese, and dot lightly with butter.

5. Bake on the uppermost rack of the oven for 10 to 15 minutes, until a light, golden crust forms on top. Do not bake for more than 15 minutes. If after 10 minutes' baking you see that no crust is beginning to form, raise the oven temperature for the next 5 minutes.

6. Allow *lasagne* to settle 5 to 8 minutes before serving. Serve directly from the pan.

MENU SUGGESTIONS

A very nice preliminary to green *lasagne* is sweet prosciutto, served with a slice of ripe cantaloupe. A suitable second course would be Rolled Stuffed Breast of Veal (page 244), Roast Spring Lamb with White Wine (page 268), Sautéed Lamb Kidneys with White Wine (page 290), Roast Chicken with Rosemary (page 296), or Stewed Rabbit with White Wine (page 309).

YELLOW PASTA SHELLS STUFFED WITH SPINACH FETTUCCINE

Lo scrigno di Venere

This breathtakingly beautiful dish is a bonus for those of you who have learned to make pasta by hand. The large sheet of yellow pasta required cannot be turned out by machine. The sheet is used to form individual shells of yellow pasta to be filled with spinach *fettuccine* seasoned with a sauce of ham, béchamel, and dried wild mushrooms, then sealed and baked. It calls for quite a bit of work, but the weight of your efforts will drop from your shoulders at the joyous surprise your family and friends will show as they unwrap their individual pasta shells.

It is very important to understand the rhythm of the recipe. Read it carefully and do not start on it until you feel you know exactly how the work is to be organized, so that everything will fall into the right place at the right time.

For 6 persons

3 ounces dried wild
    mushrooms
1 cup Béchamel Sauce
    (page 25) (see Step
    2, below)
Spinach pasta (page 119),
    cut by hand into
    fettuccine (page 114)
2 tablespoons chopped
    shallots or yellow
    onion
4½ tablespoons butter
Salt

⅔ cup unsmoked ham,
    cut into ¼-inch
    strips
1 cup heavy cream
A sheet of homemade
    pasta dough (page
    108), made with 3
    eggs and 2¼ cups
    flour
⅓ cup freshly grated
    Parmesan cheese
6 gratin pans, about 4½
    inches in diameter

1. Put the dried mushrooms in a small bowl with 1½ cups lukewarm water. They must soak at least 30 minutes.

2. Make the thin béchamel sauce (keeping it thin by cooking it little; it should have the consistency of thin sour cream). Set aside off the heat, over a pan filled with hot water.

3. Prepare the spinach pasta, rolling it out either by hand or by machine, but cutting it into *fettuccine* by hand.

4. Remove the mushrooms from their soak, but do not discard the water. Strain the water through a sieve lined with paper towels and set aside. Rinse the mushrooms in cold running water, chop each into two or three pieces, and set aside.

5. Put shallots in a saucepan with 3 tablespoons of the butter and sauté over medium heat until pale gold.

6. Add the mushrooms, their water, and 1½ teaspoons salt. Cook at a simmer until their liquid has evaporated.

7. Add the ham, stir three or four times, and add the heavy cream. Cook briefly until the cream thickens slightly; then turn off the heat and set aside.

8. Prepare the sheet of yellow pasta, rolling it out as thin as possible by hand. Let the dough dry for 10 minutes.

9. Choose a pot cover 8 inches in diameter. Lay the sheet of pasta flat and cut it into 6 disks with the pot cover. (The leftover pasta can be cut up, dried, and used in a soup.)

10. Bring 4 quarts of water to a boil, add 1 tablespoon salt, and drop in the pasta disks, cooking them two at a time. While the water is coming to a boil, lay some clean, dry towels flat on your work counter and set a bowl of cold water near the stove. Cook the pasta for 20 to 30 seconds after the water returns to a boil, then retrieve it with a slotted spoon, dip it in the bowl, rinsing with cold water, wring it out gently by hand, and open it up flat on a towel.

11. Bring another 4 to 5 quarts of water to a boil, add 1 tablespoon salt, and drop in the spinach *fettuccine*.

12. While the water is coming to a boil, warm up the ham and mushroom sauce. When it has simmered for a minute or so, turn the heat down to very low, and add all the grated cheese, mixing it thoroughly into the sauce. Turn off the heat.

13. Keep an eye on the spinach *fettuccine*. It will be done a few seconds after the water returns to a boil. When done, drain and season immediately with the ham and mushroom sauce. Set aside 6 single strands of *fettuccine*, and divide the rest of the *fettuccine* into 6 portions.

14. Preheat the oven to 450°.

15. Take the gratin pans and smear the remaining butter on the bottom of each; then, working on a large, flat platter, coat a pasta disk on both sides with some of the béchamel sauce. Place the disk in one of the pans, centering it, and letting its edges hang over the sides. Put one of the portions of *fettuccine* in the center of the disk. Make sure it has its share of sauce. Keep the *fettuccine* fairly loose—do not press them down. Pick up the disk at the edges and close it by folding the edges toward the center. Fasten the folds at the top with a toothpick, then wrap one of the single strands of *fettuccine* around the toothpick as decoratively as you can. Repeat the operation until you have filled and

sealed all 6 pasta disks. (You can prepare the shells up to this point in the morning for the evening, if you like.)

16. Put the pans with the shells in the uppermost level of the preheated oven. Bake for 5 to 8 minutes, or until a light brown crust forms on the edges of the folds.

17. Transfer each shell from its pan to a soup plate, lifting it carefully with two metal spatulas. Remove the toothpick without disturbing the decorative *fettuccina*. Serve at once.

MENU SUGGESTIONS

This magnificent presentation should be followed by a simple but elegant second course. My first choice would be Pan-Roasted Squab (page 308). Other possibilities are Sautéed Breaded Veal Chops (page 258), Sautéed Veal Chops with Sage and White Wine (page 261), Sautéed Chicken Breast Fillets with Lemon and Parsley (page 303), or a fine whole roasted chicken. If you want to precede the shells with an antipasto, serve Baked Oysters with Oil and Parsley (page 29), Cold Salmon Foam (page 30), or Bresaola (page 44).

MEAT-STUFFED PASTA ROLLS

Cannelloni

This is among the few homemade egg pasta dishes that are not native to Emilia-Romagna. It may have originated in Piedmont. *Cannelloni* is one of the most elegant of pastas, but although a number of ingredients and several different steps are involved, it is not a difficult dish to produce. In fact, it is probably the easiest of all stuffed pastas to make.

The pasta for *cannelloni* is given the briefest of boils before being stuffed. It is then seasoned with a simplified meat sauce and topped with a thin béchamel sauce. The second and final cooking takes place in the oven.

For 6 persons

Béchamel Sauce (page 25), made with 2 cups milk, ¼ cup butter, 3 tablespoons all-purpose flour, and ¼ teaspoon salt

THE STUFFING:

1½ tablespoons finely chopped yellow onion
2 tablespoons olive oil
6 ounces lean ground beef
Salt
½ cup chopped *mortadella* OR unsmoked ham

1 egg yolk
½ teaspoon nutmeg
1½ cups freshly grated Parmesan cheese
1¼ cups fresh ricotta

THE MEAT SAUCE:

1 tablespoon finely chopped yellow onion
2 tablespoons olive oil

6 ounces lean ground beef
1 teaspoon salt
½ cup canned Italian tomatoes, chopped, with their juice

A sheet of homemade pasta dough (page 108), using 2 eggs and 1½ cups all-purpose flour

1 tablespoon salt
⅓ cup freshly grated Parmesan cheese
¼ cup butter

1. Make the béchamel sauce. It should be rather thin, with a consistency similar to that of sour cream. Set aside.

2. To make the stuffing, put the chopped onion in a saucepan or a skillet with the olive oil and cook over medium heat until translucent but not colored. Add the ground beef, turn the heat down to medium low, and cook it without letting it brown. Crumble the meat with a fork as it cooks.

When it loses its raw red color, cook it for 1 minute more without browning. Transfer the meat with a perforated ladle or colander to a mixing bowl, carrying with it as little of the cooking fat as possible. Add 1½ teaspoons salt, chopped *mortadella*, egg yolk, nutmeg, grated cheese, ricotta, and ¼ cup of the béchamel sauce. Mix thoroughly. Taste and correct for salt and set aside.

3. To make the meat sauce, put the chopped onion in a saucepan with the olive oil and sauté over medium heat until very pale gold in color. Add the meat, turn the heat down to medium low, and cook without browning, exactly as you did for the stuffing. Add the salt and the chopped tomatoes and their juice and cook at the barest simmer for 45 minutes. Set aside.

4. Prepare the pasta dough, and, if you are making it by hand, make it as thin as possible. (The pasta machine has only one setting for thinness.) Cut the pasta into rectangles 3 inches by 4 inches. Do not allow it to dry any longer than it takes to bring 4 quarts of water to a boil. While the water is coming to a boil, lay one or more clean, dry towels open flat on the work counter, and set a bowl of cold water not far from the stove. When the water comes to a boil, add the salt, then drop in 5 of the pasta strips. Stir with a wooden spoon. When the water returns to a boil, wait 20 seconds, then retrieve the pasta with a large slotted spoon, dip it and rinse it in the cold water, then spread it on the dry towel. Cook all the pasta strips, no more than 5 at a time, in the same manner. When all the pasta is laid out on the towel, pat it dry with another towel.

5. Preheat the oven to 400°.

6. Take a bake-and-serve pan 9 inches by 14 inches and butter the bottom. To stuff the pasta, I find a wood cutting block very comfortable to work on, but a large platter or any clean, flat surface will do. Lay a pasta strip flat and spread a tablespoon of stuffing on it, covering the whole strip except for a ½-inch border all around. Roll the strip up on its narrow side, keeping it somewhat loose. Lay it in the baking pan with its folded-over edge facing down. Proceed until you've used up either all the pasta or all the stuffing. (Somehow it's hard to make them come out exactly even.) Squeeze the *cannelloni* in tightly, if you have to, but don't overlap them.

7. Spread the meat sauce over the *cannelloni*, coating them evenly with sauce. Spread the béchamel sauce over this. Sprinkle with the grated cheese and dot with the butter. Bake on the next-to-highest rack in the oven for 15 minutes, or until a very light, golden crust forms. (Do not in any case exceed 20 minutes, or it will be overcooked.) Allow to settle for about 10 to 15 minutes, then serve. Although the *cannelloni* are already richly seasoned, you might have some extra grated cheese available at the table.

MENU SUGGESTIONS

Bresaola (page 44) would be a fine antipasto with which to precede *cannelloni*. As a second course you could follow with Beef Braised in Red Wine Sauce (page 241), Rolled Stuffed Breast of Veal (page 244), Hothouse Lamb, Roman Style (page 271), Or Pan-Roasted Squab (page 308).

SLICED PASTA ROLL WITH SPINACH FILLING

Il rotolo di pasta

In this dish an entire sheet of pasta dough is rolled up with spinach stuffing, wrapped in cheesecloth, and boiled. When cool it is sliced like a roast, seasoned with a béchamel and tomato sauce, and baked very briefly in a very hot oven. It is a delicious change of pace from all the familiar pasta dishes, and it lends itself to a very attractive presentation.

For 6 persons

½ recipe Tomato Sauce III (page 90)
2 ten-ounce packages frozen leaf spinach, thawed, OR 2 pounds fresh spinach
Salt
2 tablespoons finely chopped yellow onion
6 tablespoons butter

3½ to 4 tablespoons chopped prosciutto, unsmoked ham, OR *mortadella*
1 heaping cup fresh whole-milk ricotta
1 cup freshly grated Parmesan cheese
¼ teaspoon nutmeg
1 egg yolk

A sheet of homemade pasta dough (page 108), made with 2 eggs and 1½ cups all-purpose flour

Medium-thick Béchamel Sauce (page 25), made with 1 cup milk, 2 tablespoons butter, 1½ tablespoons all-purpose flour, and ⅛ teaspoon salt
⅓ cup freshly grated Parmesan cheese

1. Prepare the tomato sauce and set aside.

2. If you are using frozen spinach, cook the thawed spinach in a covered pan with ½ teaspoon of salt for 5 minutes.

If you are using fresh spinach, discard any wilted or discolored leaves and all the stems. Wash in a basin in several changes of cold water until the water shows no trace of soil. Cook with just the water that clings to the leaves in a covered pan with ½ teaspoon of salt for 15 minutes, or until tender.

Drain the spinach, squeeze lightly to remove most of its moisture, and chop roughly. Set aside.

3. In a skillet, sauté the onion, with ¼ cup butter, over medium heat. When the onion turns pale gold in color, add the chopped prosciutto and sauté for about 30 seconds more. Then add the chopped, cooked spinach and sauté it for 2 to 3 minutes. You will find that all the butter has been absorbed.

4. Transfer the contents of the skillet to a mixing bowl, and add the ricotta, 1 cup grated Parmesan cheese, nutmeg, and, last of all, the egg yolk. Mix all the ingredients with a fork until they are well combined. Taste and correct for salt.

5. Make the pasta as directed in the basic recipe, then roll out as thin a sheet of pasta as you can and lay it flat in front of you. Spread the filling over the pasta, starting about 3 inches in from the edge near you. The filling should cover all but a ¼-inch border all around the sheet, and the 3-inch border near you. Fold this 3-inch border over the filling, and continue to fold until you've rolled up all the pasta. Wrap the pasta roll tightly in a cheesecloth, tying the two ends securely with string. (If you are using the pasta machine, follow exactly the same stuffing procedure, except

that you will have to make several short rolls instead of one long one. Each roll must be wrapped in cheesecloth separately.)

6. If you've made a single long roll you will need a fish poacher or other long, deep pan that can accommodate the pasta and 3 to 4 quarts of water. If you have several short rolls, a large stockpot or kettle will do. Bring the water to a boil, add 1 tablespoon of salt, then put in the pasta roll or rolls and cook at a gentle but steady boil for 20 minutes. Lift out the pasta. If it is a single long roll use the fish retriever in the poacher or two slotted spoons or spatulas, to make sure it doesn't split in the middle. Unwrap the pasta while it is hot and set aside to cool.

7. Preheat the oven to 400°.

8. While the pasta cools, prepare the béchamel, and when ready mix it with the already prepared tomato sauce. When the pasta is cool, cut it like a roast into slices about ¾ inch thick.

9. Choose a bake-and-serve dish that can accommodate the pasta slices in a single layer. Lightly smear the bottom of the dish with 2 to 3 tablespoons of sauce. Arrange the slices in the dish slightly overlapping, like shingles. Pour the rest of the sauce over the pasta, then sprinkle ⅓ cup grated Parmesan cheese over the sauce and dot lightly with the remaining 2 tablespoons butter. Bake on the uppermost rack of the oven for 15 minutes. Allow to settle 6 to 8 minutes, then serve from the baking dish.

NOTE

After this dish has been entirely assembled it can wait several hours (but not overnight) at room temperature before going into the oven.

MENU SUGGESTIONS

An excellent choice for a second course would be any of the three lamb roasts on pages 268–272. Also suitable would be Pan-Roasted Chicken with Garlic, Rosemary, and White Wine (page 294), Roast Chicken with Rosemary (page 296), or Stewed Rabbit with White Wine (page 309). Avoid any dish that has a decided tomato presence.

CAPPELLETTI FILLED WITH MEAT AND CHEESE

Cappelletti

In the Romagna section of Emilia-Romagna, *cappelletti* served in capon broth is the traditional dish for Christmas and New Year's Day. We usually prepare all the *cappelletti* for both occasions at one time, on Christmas Eve. Since this means a production of several hundred *cappelletti*, everyone in the family, children included, moves into the kitchen to stuff and wrap dumplings. Children, in fact, are ideal for the job because their narrow, tapered fingers permit them to wrap the tightest, smallest dumplings. When you set out to make *cappelletti*, try to make a family event out of it. The work goes quickly, it is fun, and it engenders respect for quality and beauty in food.

If you travel out of Romagna a dozen miles or less into the province of Bologna, the word *cappelletti* has little meaning. But the Bolognese have a virtually identical product called *tortellini*. The stuffings will vary, but then no two families make stuffing exactly the same way. The basic difference is one of shape. While the pasta for *tortellini* is cut into disks, that for *cappelletti* is cut into squares. This gives *cappelletti* its characteristic resemblance to little peaked hats, which is precisely what its name means.

Makes about 200 cappelletti *(see note below)*

2 tablespoons butter
¼ pound lean pork loin, diced into ½-inch cubes
Salt and freshly ground pepper
5½ ounces chicken breast, boned, trimmed of all fat, and diced into ½-inch cubes
3 tablespoons *mortadella*, finely chopped

1¼ cups fresh ricotta
1 egg yolk
1 cup freshly grated Parmesan cheese
½ teaspoon nutmeg
Homemade pasta dough (page 108) made with 4 eggs, 3 cups all-purpose flour, and 1 tablespoon milk

1. Melt the butter in a skillet over medium heat. Just as the foam begins to subside, add the pork, seasoning it with ½ teaspoon salt and 3 or 4 twists of the pepper mill. Cook gently for about 10 minutes, browning it on all sides. Remove from the skillet with a slotted spoon and set aside to cool. Add the chicken to the skillet, seasoning it with ½ teaspoon salt and another 3 or 4 twists of the pepper mill. Brown it on all sides, remembering that chicken breast cooks very rapidly, in about 2 to 3 minutes, depending on the thickness. Remove from the skillet with a slotted spoon and set aside to cool, together with the pork.

2. When the pork and chicken are cool, chop them by hand as fine as possible. (Do not "blender" them or machine-grind them. The filling should not be so homogenized that the character and texture of the meat do not come through.) Put the chopped meat into a bowl and combine it with the *mortadella*, fresh ricotta, egg yolk, grated cheese, and nutmeg. Mix thoroughly until all the ingredients are evenly amalgamated. Taste and correct for salt.

3. Prepare the dough as directed in the basic recipe. If you are rolling and stretching it by hand, divide the kneaded mass in two, rolling out one half while keeping the other half covered between two soup plates. (Pasta for dumplings needs no drying; on the contrary, it should be quite soft.) As soon as you've rolled out the first half of the mass into as thin a sheet of dough as possible, cut and stuff the dough as directed below. Then roll out the other half of the mass. (If you are using the pasta machine, cut and stuff each strip of dough as soon as it is thinned out.)

4. Fold the sheet of pasta dough loosely two or three times, leaving a few inches of it not rolled up. Keeping the rest of the dough under a towel, cut a continuous strip 1½ inches wide from the unfolded part. Trim the strip so that it is perfectly straight. (You can let the trimmings dry and use them on another occasion in soup.) If you are making machine pasta, cut the dough into similar 1½-inch strips. You can adjust the width of the strip about ¼ inch either way so you won't have too much to trim away.

CAPPELLETTI

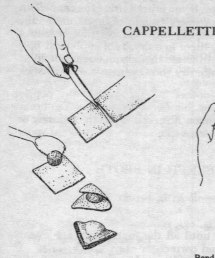

Bend a cappelletti around the finger
and press one corner around the other.

Cappelletti: On 1½-inch squares
of dough, put about ¼ teaspoon
of filling. Fold each square diagonally, with the edges not quite
meeting. Press down firmly to seal
the edges.

5. Cut the strip into 1½-inch squares. Put about ¼
teaspoon of the filling in the center of each square. Fold
the square in half, diagonally across, forming a triangle. The
upper edges should not quite meet the lower, but should
stop about ⅛ inch short. Press down firmly to seal the
sides. Pick up the triangle at one end of its long base, holding
it between your thumb and index finger with the tip of the
triangle pointing upward. Grasp the other end of the base
with the other hand and wrap the base around the index
finger of the first hand until the two ends meet. Press them
firmly together. As you are folding the dumpling around
your finger, make sure the peaked part doesn't hang down.
Force it to fold toward you so that, as you close the dumpling, its peak points in the same direction as your fingertip.

6. As you make the dumplings, set them out in neat rows on a dry clean towel. If you are not using the *cappelletti* immediately, turn them every couple of hours until they are uniformly dry. When dry they will keep for at least a week. In Italy we keep them in a dry, cool cupboard, but, if you prefer, you can refrigerate them in an open container. Make sure they are quite dry, however, or they will stick to each other.

NOTE

Calculate 16 to 18 a person if served in broth, 2 dozen or more apiece if served with sauce.

CAPPELLETTI IN BROTH

Cappelletti in brodo

For 6 persons

2½ quarts Homemade Meat Broth (page 10) (see note below)	100 *cappelletti* (page 147), approximately

Bring the broth to a boil. Drop in the *cappelletti* and stir gently from time to time with a wooden spoon. Fresh *cappelletti* cook very much faster than the dry ones; so, if fresh, taste for doneness 5 minutes after the broth returns to a boil. If dry, it may take more than three times as long. (For cooking dry *cappelletti*, it is advisable to increase the amount of broth by ½ cup, because some is lost through evaporation.) When the *cappelletti* are done—they should be firm but thoroughly cooked—ladle them into individual soup plates along with the broth. Serve immediately, with a bowl of grated Parmesan cheese on the side.

NOTE

2½ quarts of the broth is the amount you need for cooking the pasta. If any is left over, it can be refrigerated or frozen and used again.

MENU SUGGESTIONS

You can precede *cappelletti* in broth with good-quality mixed cold cuts such as prosciutto, *mortadella*, and Tuscan-type salami. Or you can make your own Fried Mortadella, Pancetta, and Cheese Tidbits (page 45). An obviously suitable second course is Mixed Boiled Meats (page 311), but they also go well with Beef Braised in Red Wine Sauce (page 231), Sautéed Turkey Breast Fillets with Ham, Cheese, and White Truffles (page 305), Pork Loin Braised in Milk (page 274), or Chicken Fricassee with Dried Wild Mushrooms (page 300).

CAPPELLETTI WITH BUTTER AND HEAVY CREAM

Cappelletti con la panna

For 6 persons

1 tablespoon olive oil	3 tablespoons butter
2 tablespoons salt	½ cup freshly grated
150 *cappelletti* (page 147)	Parmesan cheese
⅔ cup heavy cream	

1. Bring 4 quarts of water, containing 1 tablespoon of olive oil, to a boil. Add 2 tablespoons of salt, then drop in the *cappelletti*.

2. While the *cappelletti* are cooking, choose an enameled cast-iron or other flameproof cook-and-serve pan that will later accommodate all the *cappelletti* without stacking them too high. Put in half the cream and all the butter and simmer over moderate heat for less than a minute, until the cream and butter have thickened. Turn off the heat.

3. Fresh *cappelletti* are done within 5 minutes after the water returns to a boil, while dry *cappelletti* may take 15 to 20 minutes. When done—they should be firm, but cooked throughout—transfer them with a large slotted spoon or colander to the pan containing the cream and butter and turn the heat on to low. Turn the *cappelletti* to coat them all with the cream and butter sauce. Add the rest of the cream and all the grated cheese, and continue turning the *cappelletti* until they are evenly coated and all the cream has thickened. Serve immediately from the same pan, with a bowl of additional grated cheese on the side.

MENU SUGGESTIONS

See the ones for Fettuccine Tossed in Cream and Butter (page 123).

TORTELLINI

Some people prefer the rounder, more compact shape of *tortellini*. If you would like to make *tortellini alla panna* or *tortellini in brodo*, follow every direction in the above recipes except for cutting the pasta. Instead of cutting the pasta into squares, cut it into 2-inch disks, using juice glass, cookie cutter, or any circular instrument with that diameter. The disks are stuffed, folded, wrapped, and sealed exactly as the squares are.

TORTELLINI FILLED WITH PARSLEY AND RICOTTA

Tortellini di prezzemolo

For 4 to 6 persons

⅓ cup finely chopped parsley, preferably Italian parsley
1¼ cups fresh ricotta
1 cup freshly grated Parmesan cheese
Salt
1 egg yolk

¼ teaspoon nutmeg
A sheet of homemade pasta dough (page 113), made with 3 eggs, 2¼ cups all-purpose flour, and 1 tablespoon milk

1. Combine all the filling ingredients—parsley, ricotta, grated Parmesan cheese, ½ teaspoon salt, egg yolk, and nutmeg—in a mixing bowl and mix well with a fork. Taste and correct for salt, then set aside.

2. Prepare the pasta as directed in the basic recipe and roll out the thinnest sheet of pasta dough you can (if you are doing it by hand). Thereafter, follow all the cutting, stuffing, and wrapping directions for *cappelletti* (pages 147–151). There is only one difference, and that is that the pasta is cut into disks instead of squares. This recipe calls for

TORTELLINI

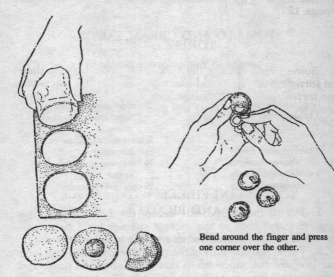

Bend around the finger and press one corner over the other.

Tortellini begin as circles. When stuffed and folded over, the edges do not come exactly together.

tortellini slightly larger than the meat-filled variety, which means the disks should be between 2¼ and 2½ inches in diameter. (If you have no cutter quite that size, you should be able to find a glass that will do.)

NOTE

Parsley-and-ricotta filling will not keep, so you should plan to cook the *tortellini* the same day you make them. The best way to serve these delicate dumplings is with cream and butter. Follow exactly the same method given for Cappelletti with Butter and Heavy Cream (page 151). Or for a soft touch of color and a bit more flavor, try the lovely, pale Tomato and Cream Sauce given below.

Follow those given for Fettuccine Tossed in Cream and Butter (page 123).

TOMATO AND CREAM SAUCE

Sugo di pomodoro e panna

For 6 servings

¼ pound butter
3 tablespoons finely chopped yellow onion
3 tablespoons finely chopped carrot
3 tablespoons finely chopped celery

2½ cups canned Italian tomatoes, with their juice
2 teaspoons salt, more if necessary
¼ teaspoon granulated sugar
½ cup heavy cream

1. Put all the ingredients except the heavy cream in a saucepan and cook at the merest simmer for 1 hour, uncovered. Stir from time to time with a wooden spoon.
2. Purée the contents of the pan through a food mill (you can prepare the sauce up to this point ahead of time, and refrigerate it for a few days or freeze it) into a saucepan and bring to a simmer, stirring with a wooden spoon. Add the heavy cream and stir-cook for 1 minute more. Taste and correct for salt. Use immediately.

In addition to Tortellini Filled with Parsley and Ricotta, this sauce is excellent with *cappelletti* (page 147), Tortelloni Filled with Swiss Chard (page 154), and Spinach and Ricotta Gnocchi (page 189). It is not disagreeable with macaroni pasta, but it is perhaps too delicate. Second courses following pasta seasoned with this sauce could be Pan Roast of Veal (page 241), Sautéed Veal Chops with Sage and White Wine (page 261), Breaded Veal Cutlets, Milan Style (page 260), Roast Spring Lamb with White Wine (page 268), and any of the chicken dishes that do not contain tomato.

TORTELLONI FILLED WITH SWISS CHARD

Tortelloni di biete

For 5 or 6 persons

2 large bunches Swiss
 chard (see note
 below)
Salt
2½ tablespoons finely
 chopped yellow
 onion
3½ tablespoons
 prosciutto, rolled
 pancetta, OR
 unsmoked ham
¼ cup butter
1 cup fresh ricotta

1 egg yolk
⅔ cup freshly grated
 Parmesan cheese
¼ to ½ teaspoon nutmeg
A sheet of homemade
 pasta dough (page
 108) made with 2
 eggs, 1½ cups all-
 purpose flour, and 2
 teaspoons milk

1. Pull the Swiss chard leaves from the stalks, discarding
any bruised or discolored leaves. If the chard is mature and
the stalks are large and white, save them to make Swiss
Chard Stalks with Parmesan Cheese (page 357). Wash the
leaves in a basin in several changes of cold water until the
water shows no soil deposit. Lift up the leaves and transfer
them to a saucepan or stockpot without shaking them. (The
water that clings to the leaves is all the water they need for
cooking.) Add ¼ teaspoon salt, cover the pot, and cook
over medium heat until tender, approximately 15 minutes,
depending on the freshness of the chard. Drain, squeeze
out all the moisture you can, and chop the chard very fine.
Set aside.

2. In a small skillet, sauté the chopped onion and prosciutto, in the butter, over medium heat. After less than a
minute, add the chopped, cooked Swiss chard leaves and a
small pinch of salt, and cook for 2 to 3 minutes more, until
all the butter has been absorbed.

3. Transfer the contents of the skillet to a mixing bowl.
Add the ricotta, egg yolk, grated Parmesan cheese, and

nutmeg, and mix thoroughly with a fork until all the ingredients have been well combined. Taste and correct for salt and nutmeg.

4. If you are hand-making the pasta, roll out the thinnest sheet of dough you can. Do not allow it to dry. Fold the sheet loosely two or three times, leaving about 5 inches of it extended away from you and keeping the near, folded part covered with a towel. Trim the farthest edge of the sheet so that it is perfectly straight. Dot the pasta with shallow teaspoonfuls of filling, spacing them 1½ inches apart, and setting them in a straight row 2¼ inches from the trimmed edge of the sheet. Pick up the edge and fold it toward you over the stuffing, which should then remain enclosed in the middle of a long tube. Detach this folded-over part from the pasta sheet, using a pastry cutter. Then divide it into squares, cutting straight across between each bulge of filling. Each square will have 3 cut edges. Press them firmly together, moistening them if necessary, to make sure they are tightly sealed. (If you are making machine pasta, stuff and cut each strip of dough as it is thinned out by the machine before kneading and thinning out more pasta.) Repeat the operation until you've run out of pasta or stuffing. (It is virtually impossible to make them come out exactly the same, but leftover pasta can be cut into *maltagliati* (page 116) and used in soup. Leftover stuffing makes a tasty sandwich spread.) For cooking instructions, see following recipe.

The flavor of all cooked leaf vegetables is noticeably impaired by any attempt at conservation; therefore you must use this pasta the same day you make it.

NOTE

Although Swiss chard has a sweeter, more delicate taste than spinach, it is not always as readily available. In case you can't find chard, spinach makes a very satisfactory substitute. Use either 2 ten-ounce packages of frozen leaf spinach or 2 pounds fresh spinach.

For frozen spinach, first thaw the spinach, then cook it slowly in a covered pan for 5 minutes with ¼ teaspoon salt.

For fresh spinach, remove the stems and discard any wilted leaves. Wash in a basin in several changes of cold water until the water shows no trace of soil. Cook in a covered saucepan with ¼ teaspoon salt and whatever water clings to the leaves for 15 to 20 minutes or until tender.

Drain the cooked spinach, squeeze most of the moisture out of it, chop it very fine, and use it exactly as directed for Swiss chard.

TORTELLONI WITH BUTTER AND CHEESE

Tortelloni al burro e formaggio

This is the simplest way pasta is served in Italy, and it is marvelously well suited to the delicate taste of *tortelloni*. It is also an excellent way to serve spaghetti.

For 5 or 6 persons

1 tablespoon olive oil	¼ pound butter
2 tablespoons salt	1 cup freshly grated
Tortelloni Filled with	Parmesan cheese
Swiss Chard (page	
154)	

1. Bring 4 quarts water containing 1 tablespoon oil to a boil. Add 2 tablespoons salt, then the *tortelloni*. Cover until the water returns to a boil.

2. While the *tortelloni* are cooking, cut 1 stick (¼ pound) butter into thin strips and put in a very warm serving bowl.

3. As soon as the *tortelloni* are cooked *al dente*, firm to the bite, about 5 minutes after the water returns to a boil, transfer them with a large slotted spoon or colander to the bowl containing the butter. Add the grated cheese and toss, coating all the *tortelloni* with butter and cheese. Serve immediately, with a bowl of additional grated cheese on the side.

MENU SUGGESTIONS

There is really no meat course that is incompatible with a butter-and-cheese-seasoned pasta. The chard filling is quite delicate, however, and deserves a not-too-pungent successor. I would avoid anything with sharp tomato and orégano flavoring.

TORTELLONI WITH BUTTER AND HEAVY CREAM

Use the same method given for Cappelletti with Butter and Heavy Cream (page 151).

TORTELLONI WITH TOMATO AND CREAM SAUCE

Cook the *tortelloni* as directed above for the butter-and-cheese sauce, but season with Tomato and Cream Sauce (page 153).

CAPPELLACCI FILLED WITH SWEET POTATOES AND PARSLEY

Cappellacci del Nuovo Mondo

One of the pleasantest memories of my university days in Ferrara is of the leisurely hours spent at the dinner table with friends, where food and talk gave us release from the pressures of exams and the anxieties of impending adulthood. Often these meals started with a dish of *cappellacci di zucca*, pasta dumplings filled with pumpkin. This is a specialty of Ferrara that is not made elsewhere in Italy, or even in Emilia-Romagna, except in the homes or *trattorie* of expatriate Ferrarese.

The pumpkin used in Ferrara looks very much like American pumpkin. It is yellow, flat, and broad, with a diameter of about 16 inches. It has a unique, beautifully rounded taste that is difficult to describe. It is sweet, but savory, not cloying. I have tried to make *cappellacci* here using pumpkin, Hubbard squash, acorn squash, and any other variety of squash I could find, but I have always found the taste flat and disappointing. Some time ago, at a Thanksgiving dinner, with my thoughts far from home, a biteful of sweet potatoes suddenly brought back to me Ferrara and its *cappellacci*. The following day my long-suffering family was trying out a new dish under the sun, Italian egg pasta with American sweet potato filling. It went over well then, and has since become our favorite dish to spring on unsuspecting newly arrived Italian guests.

It is not, of course, Ferrara's *cappellacci*, but it makes good use of the same idea, that of combining pasta with a sweet vegetable filling. It may also encourage you to give expression to your own inventiveness and special tastes through the traditional techniques of homemade pasta.

For 5 or 6 persons

1¾ pounds sweet
   potatoes (not yams)
1¼ cups freshly grated
   Parmesan cheese
3 tablespoons finely
   chopped parsley
2 tablespoons chopped
   mortadella,
   prosciutto, or
   unsmoked ham

1 egg yolk
½ teaspoon nutmeg
½ teaspoon salt
A sheet of homemade
   pasta dough (page
   108), made with 2
   eggs, 1½ cups all-
   purpose flour, and 2
   teaspoons milk

1. Preheat the oven to 450°.
2. Put the potatoes to bake in the middle level of the oven. After 20 minutes turn the thermostat down to 400° Cook for another 35 to 40 minutes, or until the potatoes are very tender when pierced with a fork.
3. Turn off the oven. Remove the potatoes and split them in half, lengthwise. Return the potatoes to the oven, cut side facing up, and leave the oven door slightly ajar. Remove the potatoes after 10 minutes.
4. Peel the potatoes and purée them through a food mill into a bowl. Add all the other ingredients, except of course the pasta, and mix thoroughly with a fork until the mixture is smooth and evenly blended. Taste and correct for salt.
5. Prepare the pasta as directed in the basic recipe and proceed to cut it and stuff it exactly as directed in Step 4 of Tortelloni Filled with Swiss Chard on page 154.

CAPPELLACCI WITH BUTTER AND CHEESE

Follow the directions for Tortelloni with Butter and Cheese (page 157).

CAPPELLACCI WITH MEAT SAUCE

Cappellacci are also very good with Meat Sauce, Bolognese Style (page 120). Calculate about 2 cups sauce for this quantity of pasta.

MENU SUGGESTIONS

Antipasti: Bresaola (page 44), Fried Mortadella, Pancetta, and Cheese Tidbits (page 45), or mixed Italian cold cuts. If you want to turn this into an Italian Thanksgiving dinner, roast turkey makes an excellent second course. Otherwise, all the other roasts of veal, lamb, pork, or chicken given here are good choices. Also suitable is Broiled Pork Liver Wrapped in Caul Fat (page 292), or Lamb Kidneys with White Wine (page 290)

HOMEMADE MACARONI

Garganelli

Garganelli is macaroni made by hand from egg pasta. Looking somewhat like a grooved version of *penne* or *ziti*, it is native to that section of Emilia called Romagna, and it demonstrates that for the *romagnoli*, even when it comes to macaroni, there is no pasta like homemade egg pasta. I can't justify *garganelli* to anyone who measures the advantages of a dish by the speed with which it can be prepared. But I do recommend it to those who do not regret the time spent in producing pasta whose superb texture and lovely hand-turned shape cannot be duplicated by anything bought in a box.

If you have a long, rainy afternoon on your hands, or if you have friends helping you, make a large amount of dough.

GARGANELLI

Garganelli are made by rolling pasta squares over a comb.

Garganelli will keep for weeks after it dries, and you can make enough to have a supply on hand.

For 6 to 8 persons

Homemade pasta dough (page 108), using 4 eggs and 3 cups all-purpose flour	1 tablespoon salt

1. Roll out the thinnest sheet of pasta that you can, if you are making it by hand. Fold the sheet into a loose roll and cover it, leaving just a few inches exposed. Cut this exposed part into 1½-inch squares. (If you are machine-making the pasta, cut each thinned-out strip of dough into squares and roll into *garganelli*, as directed below, before kneading and rolling out more dough.)

2. Have ready a dowel or smooth, round pencil, ¼ inch in diameter and 6 to 7 inches long. Take a large, absolutely clean comb, with teeth at least 1½ inches long (the closest equivalent to the original wooden tool, which is, in fact, called *pettine*, or "comb") and lay it flat on the table, with the teeth pointing away from you. Lay a pasta square diagonally on the comb, so that one corner points in the same direction as the

teeth, another toward you. Place the dowel on the square and parallel to the comb. Curl the corner of the square facing you around the dowel and, with a gentle downard pressure, push the dowel away from you and off the comb. Curled around the dowel you will have a single macaroni with a lightly ridged surface. Tip the dowel on its end and the macaroni will slide off. Proceed until all the dough has been cut and rolled into macaroni.

3. *Garganelli* are boiled like all other pasta, then served with your choice of sauce (see note below). Boil up to 6 servings of *garganelli* in 4 quarts of water with 1 tablespoon of salt. Add more water for more servings, as needed. *Garganelli*, like all other egg pasta, will cook much faster when fresh and soft than when dry, so, if fresh, start tasting them for doneness 20 to 30 seconds after the water returns to a boil. (Do not overcook. It would be a pity to have gone to all the trouble of making *garganelli* and then ruin them by overcooking.)

NOTE

The ideal sauces for *garganelli* are without a doubt Meat Sauce, Bolognese Style (page 120), and Gorgonzola Sauce (page 126). Another excellent sauce is the white clam sauce on page 128. I also find *garganelli* particularly good with Broccoli and Anchovy Sauce for Orecchiette and Other Pasta (page 164). This sauce is unknown in Romagna, just as *garganelli* is unknown in Apulia, where the sauce comes from. But the two hit it off beautifully together.

MENU SUGGESTIONS

If you are using meat sauce, Braised Veal Shanks, Trieste Style (page 249), Little Veal "Bundles" with Anchovies and Cheese (page 256), any of the three lamb roasts on pages 268–72, or Chicken Fricassee with Dried Wild Mushrooms (page 300) are good choices for the second course. If you are using the Broccoli and Anchovy Sauce, see the suggestions under that recipe (page 164). If white clam sauce, see the suggestions under the recipe for Fettuccine with White Clam Sauce (page 128).

HOMEMADE PASTA FROM APULIA

Orecchiette

The territory of Apulia extends over the entire heel and half the instep of the Italian boot. It is a region of glorious coastlines, of bleached, agonizingly beautiful towns, and a tough, ancient race of shepherds and fishermen. They say of Bari, their principal port, that if Paris had had the sea it would have been a little Bari. There is a similar lack of understatement in Apulian food. The favorite Apulian vegetables are cabbage, cauliflower, peppers, and broccoli. Hot pepper is used freely, anchovies appear in nearly every variety of dish short of dessert, everything is cooked in dense, fruity Apulian olive oil, and a hard, piquant ricotta is grated for seasoning pasta.

Apulia, like Emilia-Romagna, has a strong tradition of homemade pasta. It is made without eggs, just hard durum wheat flour and water, which makes a firmer, chewier, less delicate dough than the Emilian *sfoglia*. It is better suited, however, to its native, highly flavored sauces. Like all pasta, it comes in many shapes. The best known outside Apulia is '*recchie*, in Italian *orecchiette*, or "little ears." These are small disks of pasta given their earlike shape by a rotary pressure of the thumb. The broccoli and anchovy sauce that follows this recipe is an ideal sauce for *orecchiette*.

For 6 persons

1 cup semolina, preferably the imported Italian kind called *semolino*	½ teaspoon salt
	Up to 1 cup of lukewarm water, as required
2 cups all-purpose flour	

1. Combine the semolina, flour, and salt and pour them on your work surface, making a mound with a well in the center. Add a few tablespoons of water at a time, incorporating it with the flour until the flour has absorbed as much water as possible without becoming stiff and dry. (The consistency should not be sticky, but it should be somewhat

softer than that of egg pasta.) Knead the mass until it is smooth and elastic.

2. Keeping the rest of the dough covered with a cloth or a soup bowl, pull off a ball about the size of a lemon from the kneaded dough. Roll the ball into a sausagelike cylinder about ¾ inch thick. Slice it into disks ¹⁄₁₆ inch thick. Place a disk in the cupped palm of one hand and, with a rotary pressure of the thumb of the other hand, make a depression in the center slightly broadening the disks to a width of about 1 to 1¼ inches. The shape should be that of a very shallow mushroom cap, with edges slightly thicker than the center. Repeat the procedure until you've used up all the dough.

NOTE

Orecchiette can be used fresh or allowed to dry and kept a month or more in a dry cupboard. This pasta takes considerably longer than egg pasta to cook, but it is cooked in exactly the same manner, in abundant salted boiling water.

BROCCOLI AND ANCHOVY SAUCE FOR ORECCHIETTE AND OTHER PASTA

Sugo di broccoli e acciughe

For 4 servings

2 cups fresh broccoli florets
Salt
6 tablespoons olive oil OR ¼ cup olive oil plus 2 tablespoons butter (see note below)
6 large or 8 medium flat anchovy fillets, chopped

Freshly ground pepper, 8 to 10 twists of the mill
1 tablespoon butter
6 tablespoons freshly grated Parmesan cheese
6 tablespoons freshly grated Romano *pecorino* cheese

1. Wash the broccoli florets in cold water. Bring 2 quarts of water to a boil, add ¼ teaspoon salt and florets. Cover and cook at a moderate boil until tender, about 7 to 8 minutes. Drain and set aside.

2. Put ¼ cup oil (if you are adding butter later) or all the oil (if you are using no butter) in a skillet with the

chopped anchovies. Cook over medium heat, mashing the anchovies with a wooden spoon until they dissolve into a paste. Add the broccoli florets, the pepper, and, if you are using it, the 2 tablespoons butter. Turn the broccoli in the anchovy sauce as you sauté it lightly for 4 to 5 minutes. Taste and correct for salt. (If the anchovies were very salty, none may be needed.)

3. Add the sauce to the cooked pasta, plus 1 tablespoon of butter and the two grated cheeses. Mix the grated cheese thoroughly into the hot pasta. Serve immediately. No additional cheese is required at the table.

NOTE

The *pugliesi*, who invented this sauce, use only olive oil. I find that a little bit of butter makes the sauce creamier and smoother.

MENU SUGGESTIONS

A fish antipasto has a natural affinity with this sauce. Try Broiled Mussels and Clams on the Half Shell (page 31), or Shrimps with Oil and Lemon (page 36). For a second course, any of the three lamb roasts on pages 268–72 or Roast Pork with Bay Leaves (page 275) would be suitable.

ITALIAN PANCAKES

Crespelle

Italians make very thin pancakes that they use as they would use *cannelloni*, stuffing them with a variety of fillings and transforming them into yet another series of pasta dishes.

Two traditional fillings are given here, one with spinach and prosciutto, and another with meat sauce. Once you have tried them and acquired experience and self-confidence, you should experiment with your own formulas, using other vegetables, such as thinly sliced artichoke hearts, or other meat ingredients, such as chicken livers. Remember that the fillings must always be completely cooked before the *crespelle* are stuffed, and that you need a certain amount of béchamel sauce for creamy liaison.

Makes 16 to 18 crespelle

THE BATTER:

1 cup milk	2 eggs
Generous ¾ cup all-purpose flour	⅛ teaspoon salt

FOR COOKING THE CRESPELLE:

1 to 2 tablespoons butter

1. Put the milk in a bowl and add the flour gradually, sifting it through a sieve. Beat with a fork or whisk until all the flour and milk are evenly blended. Add the two eggs and salt, beating them until they are thoroughly incorporated into the mixture.

2. Put ½ teaspoon butter in a heavy 8-inch skillet, melting it over medium-low heat. Rotate the pan so that the bottom is evenly coated with butter.

3. When the butter is fully melted but not brown, pour 2 tablespoons of batter over the center of the pan. Quickly lift the pan away from the burner and tip it in several directions with a seesaw motion so that the batter covers the whole bottom.

4. Return the skillet to the fire. Cook until the pancake has set and turned a pale-brown color on one side. Turn it with a spatula and brown it very lightly on the other side; then transfer it to a platter.

5. Coat the bottom of the skillet with a tiny amount of butter, half what you used at first, and proceed as above until all the pancake batter is used up.

NOTE

In order to pour the batter all at once into the pan without scooping it up tablespoon by tablespoon, mark off 2 tablespoons with tape on a small measuring cup or juice glass and fill it in advance, refilling it while you do the pancakes.

Crespelle may be made hours, or even days, in advance, if refrigerated and interleaved with plastic wrap or waxed paper. They may even be frozen.

ITALIAN PANCAKES FILLED WITH SPINACH

Crespelle alla fiorentina

For 4 persons

1 pound fresh spinach OR
   1 ten-ounce package
   frozen leaf spinach,
   thawed
3 tablespoons finely
   chopped yellow
   onion
4 tablespoons butter
½ cup chopped
   prosciutto,
   mortadella, or
   unsmoked ham

1¼ cups freshly grated
   Parmesan cheese
¼ teaspoon nutmeg
1 cup plus 5 tablespoons
   Béchamel Sauce
   (page 25)
Salt
Crespelle (Italian
   Pancakes, previous
   page)

1. Cook, drain, squeeze most of the moisture out of the spinach and chop as directed in Sliced Pasta Roll with Spinach Filling (page 144).
2. Put the chopped onion in a small skillet with 2 tablespoons of the butter and sauté over medium heat until pale gold.
3. Add the chopped prosciutto, stir, and sauté lightly for less than a minute.
4. Add the chopped spinach and cook for 2 to 3 minutes, stirring constantly, until it has completely absorbed all the butter.
5. Transfer the contents of the skillet to a mixing bowl, and combine with 1 cup of the grated cheese, the nutmeg, the 5 tablespoons béchamel, and ¼ teaspoon salt. Mix thoroughly, then taste and correct for salt.
6. Preheat the oven to 450°.
7. Lightly smear the bottom of a flameproof bake-and-serve dish with butter. Lay one of the *crespelle* on a flat, clean work surface and spread a skimpy tablespoon of filling over it, leaving a ½-inch border uncovered. Roll up the *crespella*, keeping it loose and rather flat. Place it in the bottom of the dish, with its folded-over end facing down. Proceed until you have filled and rolled up all the *crespelle*,

arranging them in a single layer in the baking dish and keeping them not too tightly packed.

8. Spread the remaining 1 cup of béchamel sauce over the *crespelle*. Make sure the ends of the *crespelle* rolls are well covered, and that there is some béchamel in between them. Sprinkle with ¼ cup grated cheese and dot lightly with butter.

9. Place in the uppermost level of the preheated oven for 5 minutes, then run under the broiler for less than a minute, until a light crust has formed. Allow to settle for a minute or so, then serve from the same dish.

MENU SUGGESTIONS

This can precede any meat or fowl, except those very boldly seasoned.

ITALIAN PANCAKES FILLED WITH MEAT SAUCE

Crespelle con il ragù

For 4 persons

1½ cups Meat Sauce, Bolognese Style (page 120)	*Crespelle* (Italian Pancakes, page 165)
½ cup plus 2 tablespoons Béchamel Sauce (page 25)	⅓ cup freshly grated Parmesan cheese
¼ teaspoon nutmeg	2 tablespoons butter

1. Draw off all the fat that floats to the surface of the meat sauce, then combine 1 cup of the meat sauce with 2 tablespoons of the béchamel and the nutmeg in a bowl.

2. Preheat the oven to 450°.

3. Stuff the *crespelle* and arrange them in a lightly buttered flameproof bake-and-serve dish, following the directions in Step 7 of the preceding recipe.

4. Mix the remaining ½ cup meat sauce with the ½ cup béchamel and spread it over the *crespelle*. Sprinkle with the grated cheese, dot lightly with butter, and place

in the uppermost level of the preheated oven for 5 minutes, then run under the broiler for less than a minute, until a light crust has formed. Allow to settle for a minute or so, then serve from the same dish.

MENU SUGGESTIONS

Follow the suggestions given for Meat-Stuffed Pasta Rolls (page 141).

RISOTTO

Risotto is a uniquely Italian technique for cooking rice. There are so many things you can do with *risotto* that it is almost a cuisine all by itself. Unfortunately, it is the most misunderstood of all the well-known Italian dishes. The French seem to believe it is the same thing as rice pilaf. Others think it is just rice boiled in broth with seasonings. If you have never had it except in restaurants, you have very likely never had a true *risotto*. Restaurant *risotto*, even in Italy, is usually precooked rice pilaf that is given a *risotto* treatment before serving. It can even be reasonably good sometimes, but genuine *risotto* is quite another thing.

Risotto can be made with almost any ingredient added to the rice: shellfish, game, chicken livers, sausages, vegetables, herbs, cheese. The variations are inexhaustible, yet they are all produced through this one basic technique.

THE BASIC RISOTTO TECHNIQUE

In making *risotto*, the objective is to cause rice to absorb, a little at a time, enough hot broth until it swells and forms a creamy union of tender, yet firm grains. The following outline can be used as a guide for all *risotto* recipes.

1. Sauté chopped onion in butter and oil until the onion is very lightly colored.

2. Add rice, and sauté it for 1 to 2 minutes. Stir to coat it well with cooking fat.

3. Add ½ cup of simmering broth and stir while cooking, until the rice absorbs the liquid and wipes the sides of the pot as you stir. When the rice dries out, add another ½ cup of simmering broth and continue to stir-cook. You must be steadfast and tireless in your stirring, always loosening the rice from the entire bottom surface of the pot; otherwise it will stick. Add liquid as the rice dries out, but don't "drown" the rice. Remember, *risotto* is not boiled rice.

4. Correct heat is very important in making *risotto*. It should be very lively, but if the liquid evaporates too rapidly the rice cannot cook evenly. It will be soft outside and chalky inside. If the heat is too slow, the rice becomes gluey, which is even worse. Regulate the heat so that, if you are using Italian rice, it will cook in about 30 minutes' time. The *risotto* is done when the rice is tender but *al dente*, firm to the bite. You must be able to judge when the rice is close to doneness, so that as it finishes cooking you won't swamp it with excess liquid. Until you acquire experience with *risotto*, it is safer, after 20 minutes' cooking, to reduce the dose of broth to ¼ cup at a time, at frequent intervals. When cooked, the rice should be creamily bound together, neither dry nor runny.

PREPARING IT AHEAD OF TIME

Once *risotto* is made it must be served. It cannot be warmed up. If absolutely necessary, however, you can partially cook it several hours ahead of time. This is an unorthodox method, but it works.

1. Cook the rice to the halfway point, when the outside is almost tender but the inside is quite hard. Allow it to dry out before removing it from the heat, being careful that it doesn't stick. Spread it very thinly on a large cold platter.

2. A quarter of an hour or so before serving, melt 1 tablespoon of butter in a casserole. Add the rice and stir, coating it well with butter. Add ½ cup of simmering broth and resume cooking it in the normal manner until done.

HOW MUCH BROTH TO USE

The quantity of liquid given in the following recipes for *risotto* should be considered an approximate amount. You may end up using less or slightly more than indicated, but this is not significant. There are too many variables involved to be able to establish a "correct" amount of liquid. What is important is never to cook *risotto* with too much liquid *at one time*, and to bring it to its final tender but firm-to-the-bite stage so that it is creamy but not saturated.

RISOTTO WITH PARMESAN CHEESE

Risotto alla parmigiana

This is the purest and perhaps the finest of all *risotti*. The only major ingredient added to the rice and broth is Parmesan cheese. In Italian cooking, you should never use anything except good-quality, freshly grated Parmesan cheese, but for this particular *risotto* you should make a special effort to obtain authentic, aged, Italian *parmigiano-reggiano* from the best supplier you know.

During the truffle season in Italy, the *risotto* is crowned at the table with thinly sliced fresh white truffles. Fresh truffles are sometimes available here for a few days in late November or early December. If you should have a chance at a nice large truffle, do get it for this *risotto*. It is going to set you back a considerable amount, but you are not likely to regret it.

4 servings

5 cups Homemade Meat
    Broth (page 10) OR 1
    cup canned chicken
    broth mixed with 4
    cups water
2 tablespoons finely
    chopped shallots OR
    yellow onion

3 tablespoons butter
2 tablespoons vegetable
    oil
1½ cups raw Italian
    Arborio rice
½ heaping cup freshly
    grated Parmesan
    cheese
Salt, if necessary

1. Bring the broth to a slow, steady simmer.

2. Put the shallots in a heavy-bottomed casserole with 2 tablespoons of the butter and all the oil and sauté over medium-high heat until translucent but not browned.

3. Add the rice and stir until it is well coated. Sauté lightly, then add ½ cup of the simmering broth. Proceed according to the basic directions for making *risotto* (page 180), adding ½ cup of simmering broth as the rice dries out, and stirring it very frequently to prevent it from sticking. (If you run out of broth, continue with water.)

4. When you estimate that the rice is about 5 minutes away from being done, add all the grated cheese and the remaining tablespoon of butter. Mix well. Taste and correct for salt. Remember, when the cooking nears the end, not to add too much broth at one time. The *risotto* should be creamy but not runny. Serve immediately, with additional grated cheese, if desired, on the side.

MENU SUGGESTIONS

There is virtually no second course of meat, fowl, or variety meats that cannot follow this *risotto*. It can complement a delicate dish such as Sautéed Veal Scaloppine with Marsala (page 251), or hold its own before something as earthy as Oxtail Braised with Wine and Vegetables (page 280). It goes especially well before Sweetbreads Braised with Tomatoes and Peas (page 284), or Sautéed Chicken Livers with Sage (page 293). Do avoid any dishes with cheese. It would create monotony.

MOLDED RISOTTO WITH PARMESAN CHEESE AND CHICKEN-LIVER SAUCE

Anello di risotto alla parmigiana con il ragù di fegatini

In this elegant combination of a creamy white *risotto* with a dark and lovely sauce you have what Italians would call *un boccone da cardinale*, "a morsel fit for a cardinal." In Italy the church has always been known for its patronage of the arts.

For 4 or 5 persons

Risotto with Parmesan Cheese (page 171), made with 2 tablespoons butter and 1 tablespoon oil and omitting the butter at the end	**Chicken-liver sauce (page 130), made with only 2 tablespoons olive oil and 1 tablespoon butter**

Lightly butter a 6-cup ring mold. When the *risotto* is done, spoon it all into the ring mold and tamp it down. Invert the mold over a serving platter and lift it away, leaving a ring of *risotto* on the platter. Pour all the sauce in the center of the ring, and serve immediately.

MENU SUGGESTIONS

Follow the ones given for Pappardelle with Chicken-Liver Sauce (page 130).

RISOTTO, MILAN STYLE

Risotto alla milanese

For 6 persons

1 quart Homemade Meat Broth (page 10) OR 1 cup canned chicken broth mixed with 3 cups of water	2 cups raw Italian Arborio rice
2 tablespoons diced beef marrow, *pancetta*, OR prosciutto	⅓ teaspoon powdered saffron OR ½ teaspoon chopped whole saffron, dissolved in 1½ cups hot broth or water
2 tablespoons finely chopped shallots OR yellow onion	Salt, if necessary
5 tablespoons butter	Freshly ground pepper, about 4 twists of the mill or more to taste
2 tablespoons vegetable oil	¼ cup freshly grated Parmesan cheese

1. Bring the broth to a slow, steady simmer.

2. In a heavy-bottomed casserole, over medium-high heat, sauté the beef marrow and shallots in 3 tablespoons of the butter and all the oil. As soon as the shallots become translucent, add the rice and stir until it is well coated. Sauté lightly for a few moments and then add ½ cup of the simmering broth, about a ladleful. Proceed according to the basic directions for making *risotto* (page 169), adding a ladleful of hot broth as the rice dries out, and stirring it very frequently to prevent it from sticking. After 15 minutes add half the dissolved saffron. When the rice has dried out, add the rest of the saffron. (The later you add the saffron, the stronger the taste and aroma of saffron will be at the end. Herbs that call too much attention to themselves are a rude intrusion upon the general harmony of a dish, but if you like a stronger saffron presence wait another 5 to 8 minutes before adding the diluted saffron. But be careful it doesn't upstage your *risotto*.) When the saffron liquid has been absorbed, finish cooking the *risotto* with hot broth. (If you run out of broth, add water.)

3. When the rice is done, tender but *al dente*, firm to the bite, taste for salt. (If the broth was salty, you might not need any. Consider, too, the saltiness of the cheese you will be adding.) Add a few twists of pepper to taste, and turn off the heat. Add 2 tablespoons of butter and all the cheese and mix thoroughly. Spoon into a hot platter and serve with a bowl of freshly grated cheese on the side.

MENU SUGGESTIONS

Risotto Milan Style is traditionally served with Braised Veal Shanks, Milan Style (page 246), one of the rare instances when a first course is served together with the meat course in an Italian menu. It is a well-justified exception, because the two dishes are an ideal complement to each other. This *risotto* can also be served as a regular first course when the second course is a roasted or braised meat or fowl.

RISOTTO WITH DRIED WILD MUSHROOMS

Risotto coi funghi secchi

For 6 persons

1 ounce imported dried wild mushrooms	3 tablespoons vegetable oil
1 quart Homemade Meat Broth (page 10) OR 1 cup canned chicken broth mixed with 3 cups of water	2 cups raw Italian Arborio rice
	¼ cup freshly grated Parmesan cheese
2 tablespoons finely chopped shallots OR yellow onion	Salt, if necessary
	Freshly grated pepper, about 4 twists of the mill
4 tablespoons butter	

1. Soak the mushrooms in 2 cups of lukewarm water for at least 30 minutes before cooking. After the liquid turns very dark strain it through a sieve lined with paper towels and set aside. Continue soaking and rinsing the mushrooms in frequent changes of water until the mushrooms are soft and thoroughly free of soil.

2. Bring the broth or the canned broth and water to a slow, steady simmer.

3. In a heavy-bottomed casserole, over medium-high heat, sauté the chopped shallots or onion in half the butter and all the oil until translucent but not brown. Add the rice and stir until it is well coated. Sauté lightly for a few moments and then add a ladleful, ½ cup, of the simmering broth. Proceed according to the basic directions for making *risotto* (page 169), adding 1 ladleful of hot liquid as the rice dries out, and stirring it very frequently to prevent it from sticking. When the rice has cooked for 10 to 12 minutes add the mushrooms and ½ cup of the strained mushroom liquid. As it becomes absorbed, add more of the mushroom liquid, ½ cup at a time. After you've used up the mushroom liquid finish cooking the rice with hot broth. (If you run out of broth, add water.)

4. When the rice is done, turn off the heat and mix in the grated Parmesan and the rest of the butter. Taste and

correct for salt. (If the broth was very salty, you may not need any salt at all.) Add a few twists of pepper and mix. Spoon the rice into a hot serving platter and serve immediately with a bowl of freshly grated cheese on the side.

It is perhaps easier to say what second courses to avoid than to indicate which ones to choose. Stay away from any dish with mushrooms, of course, and also from other sharply competitive flavors, such as the Thin Pan-Broiled Steaks with Tomatoes and Olives (page 230) and Veal Scaloppine with Tomatoes (page 253) or Casserole-Roasted Lamb with Juniper Berries (page 269). Otherwise, all roasts, stews, and fricassees of meat and fowl are good choices. Particularly good are all the sautéed veal dishes.

RISOTTO WITH MEAT SAUCE

Risotto col ragù

For 4 persons

5 cups Homemade Meat Broth (page 10) OR 1 cup canned chicken broth mixed with 4 cups water	1½ cups raw Italian Arborio rice
	Salt, if necessary
	3 tablespoons freshly grated Parmesan cheese
1 cup Meat Sauce, Bolognese Style (page 120)	1 tablespoon butter

1. Bring the broth to a slow, steady simmer.
2. Heat the meat sauce in a heavy, open casserole over medium heat. When it is hot and simmering, add the rice and stir until it is thoroughly mixed into the meat sauce. Cook for a few moments longer, then add a ladleful, ½ cup, of simmering broth. Proceed according to the basic directions for making *risotto* (page 169), adding a ladleful

of simmering broth as the rice dries out, and stirring it very frequently to prevent it from sticking. (If you run out of broth, continue with water.) When the rice is done, tender yet *al dente*, firm to the bite, taste for salt. If you find it is on the salty side, reduce or omit the grated cheese. Turn off the heat and swirl in 1 tablespoon of butter. Transfer to a hot platter and serve.

MENU SUGGESTIONS

The meat sauce makes this a very substantial *risotto*. Choose a lighter second course, such as Sautéed Veal Scaloppine with Lemon Sauce (page 252) or with Marsala (page 251). The Charcoal-Broiled Chicken Marinated in Pepper, Oil, and Lemon (page 297) would also be a good choice.

RISOTTO WITH LUGANEGA SAUSAGE

Risotto con la luganega

For 6 persons

5 cups Homemade Meat Broth (page 10) OR 1 cup canned chicken broth mixed with 4 cups water	2 cups raw Italian Arborio rice
2 tablespoons finely chopped shallots OR yellow onion	¾ pound *luganega* sausage
	¼ cup dry white wine
	Salt, if necessary
	Freshly ground pepper, about 5 or 6 twists of the mill
3 tablespoons butter	
2 tablespoons vegetable oil	3 tablespoons freshly grated Parmesan cheese

1. Bring the broth to a slow, steady simmer.
2. In a heavy-bottomed casserole, over medium-high heat, sauté the chopped shallots with 2 tablespoons of butter and all the oil. When translucent, add the rice and stir until

it is well coated. Sauté lightly for a few moments, then add a ladleful, ½ cup, of the simmering broth. Proceed according to the basic instructions for making *risotto* (page 169), adding a ladleful of hot broth as the rice dries out, and stirring it very frequently to prevent it from sticking.

3. While the rice is cooking, cut the *luganega* into 2-inch lengths and cook it in a skillet over medium-high heat with the wine. After the wine has evaporated, continue browning the sausage in its own fat for 12 to 15 minutes. Remove and set aside, but do not discard the juices in the skillet.

4. When the rice is done, tender, but *al dente*, firm to the bite, taste for salt. (You might not need any if the broth was salty. Consider too the saltiness of the cheese you will be adding.) Add a few twists of pepper to taste and turn off the heat. Add the tablespoon of butter and all the cheese and mix thoroughly. Spoon into a hot platter.

5. Tip the skillet in which the sausage was cooked and draw off all but 2 tablespoons of the fat. Add 2 tablespoons of water, turn the heat to high, and while the water boils away scrape up and loosen any residue stuck to the pan. Return the sausages to the pan for a few moments, turning them as they warm up. Make a slight depression in the center of the mound of *risotto* on the platter, and on it place the sausages and their sauce. Serve immediately.

NOTE

Additional grated cheese is not usually called for with this *risotto*, but it is best to have some in a bowl at the table to suit individual taste.

MENU SUGGESTIONS

This *risotto* can precede any roasted or braised meat except pork. It is also good before chicken, if simply roasted or broiled, such as in the Charcoal-Broiled Chicken Marinated in Pepper, Oil, and Lemon (page 297).

RISOTTO WITH ASPARAGUS

Risotto con gli asparagi

For 6 persons

1 pound fresh asparagus
Homemade Meat Broth
    (page 10) OR 1 cup
    canned chicken
    broth mixed with
    water, sufficient to
    come to 5 cups
    liquid when added
    to the water in
    which the asparagus
    has cooked (see Step
    3)
2 tablespoons finely
    chopped shallots or
    yellow onion

5 tablespoons butter
3 tablespoons vegetable
    oil
2 cups raw Italian
    Arborio rice
Salt, if necessary
Freshly ground pepper,
    about 4 twists of the
    mill
¼ cup freshly grated
    Parmesan cheese
1 tablespoon finely
    chopped parsley

1. Trim, wash, and boil the asparagus, following the instructions for cooking asparagus on page 341. Drain, reserving the cooking liquid, and set aside to cool.
2. When the asparagus is cool, cut into ½-inch pieces, utilizing as much of the stalk as possible. If the very bottom of the stalk is tough and stringy, keep just the tender inner core, scraping it up with a knife.
3. Add the broth to the water in which the asparagus cooked and bring to a slow, steady simmer.
4. In a heavy-bottomed casserole, over medium-high heat, sauté the shallots in 3 tablespoons of the butter and all the oil until translucent. Add the cut-up asparagus and sauté lightly for 2 minutes, stirring frequently. Add the rice and stir until it is thoroughly coated. Sauté lightly for a few moments, then add a ladleful, ½ cup, of the simmering broth. Proceed according to the basic directions for making *risotto* (page 169), adding a ladleful of hot broth as the rice dries out, and stirring it very frequently to prevent it from sticking. (If you should run out of broth, continue with water.)
5. When the rice reaches the proper consistency, tender

but *al dente*, firm to the bite, taste it to see if it requires salt. Add a few twists of freshly ground pepper to taste. Turn off the heat and mix in the remaining 2 tablespoons of butter and all the grated cheese. Add the chopped parsley and mix. Spoon the rice onto a hot serving platter and serve. At the table it can be topped with a little more freshly grated Parmesan cheese.

MENU SUGGESTIONS

Follow the suggestions for Risotto with Zucchini, below. Of course you won't accompany the second course with any side dish of asparagus.

RISOTTO WITH ZUCCHINI

Risotto con le zucchine

For 4 persons

4 medium zucchini or 6 small ones (see note below)	3 tablespoons butter
	1½ cups raw Italian Arborio rice
3 tablespoons coarsely chopped yellow onion	Freshly ground pepper, about 4 twists of the mill
5 tablespoons vegetable oil	1 tablespoon finely chopped parsley
½ teaspoon finely chopped garlic	3 tablespoons freshly grated Parmesan cheese
Salt	
5 cups Homemade Meat Broth (page 10) OR 1 cup canned chicken broth mixed with 4 cups water	

1. Carefully wash or scrape the zucchini clean and slice into disks ½ inch thick. Set aside.

2. In a medium-sized skillet (9-inch) sauté the onion with 3 tablespoons of the oil over medium-high heat. When the onion becomes translucent, add the chopped garlic, and as soon as it colors lightly, add the sliced zucchini and turn the heat down to medium low. Add a tiny pinch of salt after

10 or 12 minutes. The zucchini are done when they turn a rich golden color, usually about 30 minutes. (You can prepare them ahead of time, several hours or a few days, if you refrigerate them tightly covered with plastic wrap.)

3. Bring the broth or canned broth and water to a slow, steady simmer. Transfer the zucchini to a heavy-bottomed casserole, leaving behind in the pan as much of the cooking fat as possible. Add 2 tablespoons butter and the remaining 2 tablespoons oil to the casserole and turn the heat to high. When the fat and zucchini begin to bubble, add the rice and stir until it is well coated. Sauté lightly for about 1 minute, then add a ladleful, ½ cup, of the simmering broth. Proceed according to the basic directions for making *risotto* (page 169), adding 1 ladleful of hot liquid as the rice dries out, and stirring it very frequently to keep it from sticking. (If you run out of broth, add water.)

4. When the rice is done, tender but *al dente*, firm to the bite, taste for salt. (If the broth was very salty, you might not need any. Bear in mind, too, that the Parmesan cheese you will add is salty.) Turn off the heat, add a few twists of pepper, the tablespoon of butter, the chopped parsley, and the grated Parmesan and mix thoroughly. Spoon onto a hot platter and serve immediately, with a bowl of freshly grated cheese on the side.

NOTE

If you've made the Zucchini Stuffed with Meat and Cheese on page 382, use the chopped cores of 8 to 10 zucchini.

MENU SUGGESTIONS

Any meat or chicken roast will make a fine second course, as would Sautéed Lamb Kidneys with White Wine (page 290), Fried Breaded Calf's Liver (page 288), and Sautéed Chicken Livers with Sage (page 293). Avoid stews or fricassees containing vegetables, and don't accompany the second course with any side dish of zucchini.

RISOTTO WITH CLAMS

Risotto con le vongole

For 6 persons

3 dozen littleneck clams,
   the tiniest you can
   find
1 tablespoon finely
   chopped yellow
   onion
5 tablespoons olive oil
2 teaspoons finely
   chopped garlic

2 tablespoons chopped
   parsley
2 cups raw Italian
   Arborio rice
⅓ cup dry white wine
Salt and freshly ground
   pepper to taste

1. Wash and scrub the clams thoroughly, according to the directions on page 50. Heat them over high heat in a covered pan until they open their shells, giving them a vigorous shake or turning them so that they will heat up more evenly. (Some clams are more stubborn about opening up than others.) When most of them have opened up, it is best to remove them while waiting for the tardy ones; otherwise they will become tough as they linger in the pan. Remove the clams from their shells and rinse off any sand on the meat by dipping them briefly one at a time in their own juice. Unless the clams are exceptionally small, cut them up in two or more pieces and set aside. Strain the clam juices through a sieve lined with paper towels and set aside.

2. Bring 5 cups of water to a slow, steady simmer.

3. In a heavy-bottomed casserole, sauté the chopped onion in the olive oil over medium-high heat. When translucent, add the garlic and sauté until it colors lightly. Add the parsley, stir, then add the rice and stir until it is well coated with the oil. Sauté lightly for a few moments and then add the wine. When the wine has evaporated and the rice dries out, add the strained clam juices. As the rice dries out, add a ladleful, ½ cup, of the simmering water. Proceed according to the basic directions for making *risotto* (page 169), adding a ladleful of simmering water as the rice

dries out, and stirring it very frequently to prevent it from sticking. After 15 or 20 minutes add salt and pepper to taste.

4. When the rice is done, tender but *al dente*, firm to the bite, taste and correct for salt and pepper. Add the clams, mixing them into the hot rice; then turn off the heat and spoon the rice onto a hot platter. Serve immediately.

NOTE

This *risotto*, as is true of all pastas and soups with a seafood base, does not call for grated cheese.

MENU SUGGESTIONS

For a complete fish dinner, you can start with Baked Oysters with Oil and Parsley (page 29), or Cold Salmon Foam (page 30), as an antipasto. Follow the *risotto* with Fish Broiled the Adriatic Way (page 214). Other second courses could be Stuffed Squid Braised in White Wine (page 221), or the Fillet of Sole with Piquant Tomato Sauce (page 208).

RICE WITH FRESH BASIL AND MOZZARELLA CHEESE

Riso filante con la mozzarella

This is nothing more than boiled rice and fresh basil enmeshed in the fine tangles of melted mozzarella. It is another example of how, in Italian cooking, simple handling of the simplest ingredients results in a dish interesting in texture, lovely to look at, and, best of all, delicious.

For 4 persons

1 tablespoon salt	1¼ cups mozzarella
1½ cups raw rice,	cheese, shredded on
preferably Italian	the largest holes of
Arborio rice	the grater
6 tablespoons butter, cut	⅔ cup freshly grated
up	Parmesan cheese
2 tablespoons shredded	
fresh basil OR 1	
tablespoon chopped	
parsley	

1. Bring 3 quarts of water to a boil, add the salt, then the rice, and mix with a wooden spoon. Cover the pot and cook at a moderate but steady boil until rice is tender but *al dente*, firm to the bite. (Depending on the rice, it should take about 15 to 20 minutes.) While cooking, stir from time to time with a wooden spoon.

2. Drain and transfer the rice to a warm serving bowl. Mix in the cut-up butter; then add the basil (or parsley) and mix.

3. Add the shredded mozzarella and mix quickly and thoroughly. (The heat of the rice unravels the mozzarella, forming a soft, fluffy skein of cheese and rice flecked with basil green.)

4. Add the grated Parmesan cheese, stir two or three times, and serve immediately.

MENU SUGGESTIONS

This would be very nice before a second course of Thin Pan-Broiled Steaks with Tomatoes and Olives (page 230), Veal Scaloppine with Tomatoes (page 253), Veal Rolls in Tomato Sauce (page 255), Veal Stew with Tomatoes and Peas (page 264), or Chicken Fricassee with Green Peppers and Tomatoes (page 299). Actually it can precede any kind of meat or fowl—roasted, braised, fried, or sautéed—as long as it isn't made with cheese or milk.

POTATO GNOCCHI

Gnocchi di patate

Most recipes for potato *gnocchi* call for one or more egg yolks. I find that the eggless version produces finer *gnocchi*. Eggs may make them easier to handle, but they also make them tough and rubbery. Eggless *gnocchi* are light, fluffy and less filling. *Gnocchi* can be seasoned with almost any sauce. Three particularly happy combinations are *gnocchi* with Tomato Sauce III (page 90), with Pesto (page 132), or with Gorgonzola Sauce (page 126).

For 4 to 6 persons

1½ pounds boiling potatoes (not Idaho potatoes or new potatoes)
1 cup all-purpose flour

Tomato Sauce III (page 90), OR Pesto (page 132), OR Gorgonzola Sauce (page 126)
⅔ cup freshly grated Parmesan cheese, more if necessary

1. Boil the potatoes, unpeeled, in abundant water. (Do not test them too often while cooking by puncturing them with a fork or they will become waterlogged.) When cooked, drain them, and peel as soon as you can handle them. Purée them through a food mill or potato ricer while still warm.

2. Add most of the flour to the mashed potatoes and knead into a smooth mixture. (Some potatoes take more flour than others, so it is best not to add all the flour at once.) Stop adding flour when the mixture is soft, smooth, and still slightly sticky. Shape it into sausage-like rolls about as thick as your thumb, then cut the rolls into ¾-inch lengths.

3. This step is more complicated to explain than it is to execute. At first, just go through the motions until you feel you've understood the mechanics of the step. Then start on the *gnocchi*—but without losing heart if the first few don't turn out quite right. You will soon acquire the knack and

do a whole mess of *gnocchi* in two or three minutes. (And, in working with *gnocchi*, it will make your life much easier if you remember to dust repeatedly with flour the *gnocchi*, your hands, and any surface you are working on.)

Take a fork with long, rounded, slim prongs. Working over a counter, hold the fork sideways—that is, with the prongs pointing from left to right (or right to left) and with the concave side facing you. With the other hand, place a dumpling on the inside curve of the fork just below the points of the prongs and press it against the prongs with the tip of the index finger pointing directly at and perpendicular to the fork. While pressing the dumpling with your finger, flip it away from the prong tips, and toward the handle of the fork. Don't drag it, flip it. As it rolls to the base of the prongs, let it drop to the counter. The dumpling will then be somewhat crescent-shaped, with ridges on one side formed by the prongs, and a deep depression on the other formed by your finger. (This is not just a capricious decorative exercise. It serves to thin out the middle section of the dumpling so that it will cook more evenly, and to create little grooved traps in its surface for the sauce to sink into and make the *gnocchi* tastier.)

4. Drop the *gnocchi*, about 2 dozen at a time, into 5 quarts or more of boiling salted water. In a very short time they will float to the surface. Let them cook just 8 or 10 seconds more, then lift them out with a slotted spoon and transfer to a heated platter. Season with a little of the sauce you are using. (If you are using the tomato sauce, add a light sprinkling of grated cheese.) Drop more *gnocchi* in the boiling water and repeat the whole process until they are cooked. When all the *gnocchi* are done, pour the rest of the sauce over them and mix in all the grated cheese. Serve hot.

MENU SUGGESTIONS

If sauced with *pesto*, see the suggestions for Trenette with Potatoes and Pesto (page 135). If sauced with tomato sauce: Beef Braised in Red Wine Sauce (page 231), Braised Veal Shanks, Trieste Style (page 249), Rolled Stuffed Breast of Veal (page 244), Casserole-Roasted Lamb with Juniper Berries (page 269), Sautéed Calf's Liver with Onions, Venetian Style (page 286), or Rolled Breast of Chicken Fillets Stuffed with Pork (page 304) are some suitable second courses. If sauced with gorgonzola, see the suggestions for Fettuccine with Gorgonzola Sauce (page 126).

BAKED SEMOLINA GNOCCHI

Gnocchi alla romana

Although many Romans will maintain that semolina *gnocchi* are not *alla romana*, this dish can be traced back directly to Imperial Rome. Apicius gives a recipe for *gnocchi* made of semolina milk exactly like these, then fried and served with honey. All that has changed substantially since then is the cooking method and the seasoning.

For 4 to 6 persons

1 quart milk
1 heaping cup semolina,
    preferably imported
    Italian *semolino*. If
    possible, avoid using
    quick-cooking
    breakfast farina.

1 cup freshly grated
    Parmesan cheese
2 teaspoons salt
2 egg yolks
7 tablespoons butter

1. Heat the milk in a heavy saucepan over moderate heat until it is just short of boiling. Lower the heat and add the semolina, pouring it in a thin, slow stream and beating it steadily into the milk with a whisk. Continue beating until it forms a thick mass on the whisk as it turns (about 10 minutes). Remove from the heat.

2. Add ⅔ cup of the grated cheese, salt, the 2 egg yolks, and 2 tablespoons of butter to the semolina. Mix rapidly, to avoid coagulating the egg, until all the ingredients are well blended.

3. Moisten a formica or marble surface with cold water and spoon out the semolina mixture, using a metal spatula

or a broad-bladed knife to spread it to a thickness of approximately ⅜ inch. (Dip the spatula or knife into the cold water from time to time.) Let the semolina cool completely, about 30 to 40 minutes.

4. Preheat the oven to 450°.

5. With a 1½-inch biscuit cutter, or with a small glass of approximately the same diameter, cut the semolina mixture into disks, moistening the cutting tool from time to time in cold water to make the cuts easier and neater.

6. Smear the bottom of a rectangular or oval bake-and-serve dish with butter. Lift off the small four-sided sections of semolina in between the disks and lay them on the bottom of the baking dish. Dot with butter and sprinkle with grated Parmesan. Over this arrange all the disks in a single layer, overlapping them like roof tiles. Dot with butter and sprinkle with the remaining grated cheese. Place on the uppermost rack of the oven and bake for 15 minutes or until a light golden crust has formed. If after 15 minutes the crust hasn't formed, turn the oven thermostat up to 500° and bake for 5 more minutes. Allow to settle a few minutes before serving.

NOTE

The entire dish can be prepared up to two days ahead of time before baking if it is refrigerated and covered with plastic wrap.

MENU SUGGESTIONS

This is a dish of uncomplicated taste and texture that can precede any meat dish or fowl. It is a particularly fitting first course when the second course is Hothouse Lamb, Roman Style (page 271). Sweetbreads Braised with Tomatoes and Peas (page 284) or Rolled Breast of Chicken Fillets Stuffed with Pork (page 304) are also excellent choices. For an antipasto you might have the Artichokes, Roman Style (page 326), or the Mushroom and Cheese Salad (page 44).

SPINACH AND RICOTTA GNOCCHI

Gnocchi verdi

For 4 persons

1 tablespoon finely
    chopped yellow
    onion
2 tablespoons butter
2 tablespoons very finely
    chopped *mortadella*,
    pancetta, OR
    unsmoked ham
1 ten-ounce package
    frozen leaf spinach,
    thawed, OR 1 pound
    fresh spinach,
    prepared as directed
    on page 145

Salt
¾ cup fresh ricotta
⅔ cup all-purpose flour
2 egg yolks
1 cup freshly grated
    Parmesan cheese
¼ teaspoon nutmeg

1. Put the onion in a skillet with the butter and sauté over medium heat until pale gold.

2. Add the chopped *mortadella* and continue sautéing just long enough to stir 3 to 4 times, combining the *mortadella* well with the onion and butter.

3. Add the spinach and ¼ teaspoon salt and sauté for 5 to 6 minutes, stirring frequently. (The spinach will absorb all the butter, but it is not necessary to add any more.)

4. Transfer the entire contents of the skillet to a mixing bowl. Add the ricotta and flour, mixing thoroughly with a wooden spoon. Add the egg yolks, grated cheese, and nutmeg, and incorporate them thoroughly into the mixture with the spoon. Taste and correct for salt.

5. Make small pellets out of the mixture, shaping them quickly in the palm of your hand. Ideally they should be about ½ inch in diameter, but if this size is too small for you to handle, or the job too tedious, you can make them as large as ¾ inch. (The smaller the better, however, because they cook more quickly and stay softer.) When the mixture begins to stick to your hands, dust your hands lightly with flour.

6. Cook the *gnocchi* as indicated in the three recipes that follow.

GREEN GNOCCHI GRATINÉED WITH BUTTER AND CHEESE

Gnocchi verdi al burro e formaggio

For 4 persons

1½ tablespoons salt
Spinach and Ricotta
    Gnocchi (preceding
    recipe)

4½ tablespoons butter
½ cup freshly grated
    Parmesan cheese

1. Preheat the oven to 375°.
2. Bring 4 quarts of water to a boil. Add the salt, then drop in the *gnocchi*, a few at one time. Two to three minutes after the water returns to a boil, retrieve the *gnocchi* with a slotted spoon and place in a butter-smeared bake-and-serve dish. Add more *gnocchi* to the boiling water, repeating the above procedure, until all the *gnocchi* are cooked and in the baking dish.
3. Melt the butter in a small pan and pour it over the *gnocchi*.
4. Sprinkle all the grated cheese over the *gnocchi*. Place the dish on the uppermost rack of the oven for about 5 minutes, until the cheese has melted. Allow to settle for a few minutes before serving, then serve directly from the baking dish, with additional grated cheese on the side.

MENU SUGGESTIONS

Follow with any roast: beef, veal, lamb, pork, or fowl. Other excellent choices for the second course would be Beef Braised in Red Wine Sauce (page 231), Veal Rolls in Tomato Sauce (page 255), Chicken Fricassee with Green Peppers and Tomatoes (page 299), Sautéed Calf's Liver with Onions, Venetian Style (page 286), or Fried Breaded Calf's Liver (page 288).

GREEN GNOCCHI IN BROTH

Gnocchi verdi in brodo

If you have very good homemade broth on hand, made from beef, veal, and/or chicken, you can make a delicious and elegant soup with green *gnocchi*. Served as soup, *gnocchi* go quite a bit further, so calculate about 6 ample servings, using the same quantity of *gnocchi* produced with the basic recipe.

For 6 persons

2 quarts homemade
    broth
Spinach and Ricotta
    Gnocchi (page 189)

Bring the broth to a boil. Drop in all the *gnocchi* and cook for 3 to 4 minutes after the broth has returned to a boil. Ladle into soup plates and serve with a bowl of freshly grated Parmesan cheese on the side.

MENU SUGGESTIONS

If the broth comes from meat boiled for the occasion, a platter of Mixed Boiled Meats (page 311) would be the ideal second course. Otherwise, follow the suggestions given for Green Gnocchi Gratinéed with Butter and Cheese (page 190). Especially indicated would be a substantial dish, such as Beef Braised in Red Wine Sauce (page 231).

GREEN GNOCCHI WITH TOMATO AND CREAM SAUCE

Gnocchi verdi con sugo di pomodoro e panna

For 4 persons

Tomato and Cream
    Sauce (page 153)
2 tablespoons salt

Spinach and Ricotta
    Gnocchi (page 189)

1. Keep the sauce warm as you prepare the rest of the dish.

2. Bring 4 quarts of water to a boil. Add the salt, then the *gnocchi*, a few at a time. Three to four minutes after the water returns to a boil, retrieve the *gnocchi* with a slotted spoon, and place on a hot serving platter. Season with a little bit of sauce. Add more *gnocchi* to the boiling water, repeating the above procedure, until all the *gnocchi* are cooked and sauced. Pour any remaining sauce over the *gnocchi*, and serve immediately, with a bowl of freshly grated Parmesan cheese on the side.

MENU SUGGESTIONS

The perfect second course would be a roast of veal, either the Pan Roast of Veal (page 241) or the Rolled Stuffed Breast of Veal (page 244). Also suitable is the Pan-Roasted Chicken with Garlic, Rosemary, and White Wine (page 294) or Roast Chicken with Rosemary (page 296). Avoid any second course that is pungent or includes tomatoes.

POLENTA

For the past three centuries *polenta* has been the staff of life in much of Lombardy and all of Venetia, particularly in Friuli, that northern region of Venetia which arches toward Yugoslavia.

To call *polenta* a cornmeal mush is a most indelicate use of language. In country kitchens, *polenta* was more than food, it was a rite. It was made daily in an unlined copper kettle, the *paiolo*, which was always kept hanging at the ready on a hook in the center of the fireplace. The hearth was usually large enough to accommodate a bench on which the family sat, warming itself at the fire, making talk, watching the glittering cornmeal stream into the boiling kettle, encouraging the tireless stirring of the cook. When the *polenta* was done, there was a moment of joy as it was poured out in a steaming, golden circle on the beechwood top of the *madia*, a cupboard where bread and flour was stored.

Italy's great nineteenth-century novelist, Alessandro Manzoni, described it as looking like a harvest moon coming out of the mist. The image is almost Japanese.

The uses of *polenta* are infinite, and although it is always listed among the first courses, it cannot be neatly labeled a First Course, Second Course, or Side Dish. It can be any of the three. When piping hot it can be eaten alone, with butter and cheese. Or it can accompany any stewed, braised, or roasted meat or fowl. With game birds it is divine. When it has cooled and hardened, it can be fried, broiled, or sliced and baked with a variety of fillings.

There are two basic types of *polenta* flour. One is fine-grained, the other coarse. The coarse-grained is the one used in these recipes because of its more interesting, robust texture. Some traditional Italian recipes tell you to stir *polenta* for an hour or even more. But with a modern stove this is completely unnecessary. In the method given below, 20 minutes' stirring after all the cornmeal has been added will produce absolutely perfect *polenta*.

BASIC METHOD FOR MAKING POLENTA

1 tablespoon salt   2 cups coarse-grained
                                     cornmeal

1. Bring 6½ cups of water to a boil in a large, heavy kettle.

2. Add the salt, turn the heat down to medium low so that the water is just simmering, and add the cornmeal in a very thin stream, stirring with a stout, long wooden spoon. The stream of cornmeal must be so thin that you can see the individual grains. A good way to do it is to let a fistful of cornmeal run through nearly closed fingers. Never stop stirring, and keep the water at a slow, steady simmer.

3. Continue stirring for 20 minutes after all the cornmeal has been added. The *polenta* is done when it tears away from the sides of the pot as you stir.

4. When done, pour the *polenta* onto a large wooden block or a platter. Allow it to cool first if you are going to slice it in preparation for subsequent cooking. Otherwise, serve it piping hot.

NOTE

It may happen that some of the *polenta* sticks to the bottom of the pot. Cover the bottom with water and let it soak for 25 minutes. The *polenta* will then wash away easily.

POLENTA WITH SAUSAGES

Polenta con la luganega

For 4 to 6 persons

2 tablespoons chopped yellow onion	1 pound *luganega* sausage or other sweet sausage, cut into 3-inch lengths
3 tablespoons olive oil	
3 tablespoons chopped carrot	
3 tablespoons chopped celery	1 cup canned Italian tomatoes, cut up, with their juice
¼ pound sliced *pancetta*, cut into strips ½ inch wide	Polenta (previous page)

1. Put the onion in a saucepan with the oil and sauté over medium heat until pale gold.

2. Add the carrot, celery, and *pancetta*. Sauté for 3 to 4 minutes, stirring frequently.

3. Add the sausages and cook for 10 minutes, always at medium heat, turning them from time to time.

4. Add the tomatoes and their juice and cook at a gentle simmer for 25 minutes, stirring from time to time. Cover the pan and transfer to a 200° oven to stay warm while you prepare the *polenta*.

5. When the *polenta* is done, pour it onto a large platter. Make a depression in the center and pour in the sausages and all their sauce. Serve immediately.

MENU SUGGESTIONS

This is a second course, but *polenta* takes the place of pasta or rice, so you can omit the first course. It is quite appropriate to precede this with a plate of mixed Italian cold cuts, such as prosciutto, good salami, and *mortadella*. Another excellent antipasto would be Peppers and Anchovies (page 34).

POLENTA WITH BUTTER AND CHEESE

Polenta al burro e formaggio

For 4 to 6 persons

Polenta (page 193),
  cooked with an
  additional ½ cup of
  water to keep it a
  little thinner

¼ pound butter
6 tablespoons freshly
  grated Parmesan
  cheese

Pour the *polenta* onto a warm platter and mix with the butter and cheese. Serve promptly.

MENU SUGGESTIONS

In this case *polenta* is served as a first course, and may be followed by any meat or fowl. Particularly suitable are the roasts of lamb, pork, or chicken.

FRIED POLENTA

Polenta fritta

For 4 to 6 persons or more, depending on how it is used

Polenta (page 193)
Vegetable oil, enough to come ¾ inch up the side of a skillet

1. Prepare the *polenta* as directed in the basic recipe and allow it to cool completely and become firm. Divide it into four parts, then cut these into slices ½ inch thick. (The traditional way to cut *polenta* is with a tautly held thread.)
2. Heat the oil in a skillet over high heat. When the oil is very hot, slide in as many slices of *polenta* as will fit comfortably. Fry until a transparent, not colored, crust forms on one side, then turn them and do the other side. Transfer to paper towels to drain.

Fried *polenta* is ideal as a component of the Mixed Fried Meats, Vegetables, Cheese, Cream, and Fruit (page 322). It can also accompany Sautéed Calf's Liver with Onions, Venetian Style (page 286), or any roasted meat or fowl. In this case, a soup rather than pasta or rice would be preferable as a first course.

POLENTA WITH GORGONZOLA

Polenta col gorgonzola

Polenta prepared in this manner is excellent as an antipasto or as a nourishing snack.

Polenta (page 193),
    allowed to cool and
    sliced as in Fried
    Polenta, above

Gorgonzola or any ripe,
    tangy cheese

1. Preheat the broiler to its maximum setting.
2. Toast the *polenta* slices under the broiler until they are a light, spotty brown on both sides. Spread the cheese on one side of the hot, toasted slices and serve immediately.

BAKED POLENTA WITH MEAT SAUCE

Polenta pasticciata

For 6 persons

Béchamel Sauce (page
    25) (see Step 2,
    below)
Polenta (page 193),
    allowed to cool

2 cups Meat Sauce,
    Bolognese Style
    (page 120)
⅔ cup freshly grated
    Parmesan cheese
1 tablespoon butter

1. Preheat the oven to 450°.
2. Make the béchamel, keeping it on the thin side by

cooking it less. It should have the consistency of sour cream. Set aside.

3. Slice the cold *polenta* horizontally into 3 layers, each about ½ inch high. Watch both sides of the *polenta* mass as you cut to make sure you are slicing evenly.

4. Lightly butter an 11-inch *lasagne* pan. Cover with a layer of *polenta*, patching where necessary to cover uniformly.

5. Spread béchamel sauce over the *polenta*, then spread the meat sauce and sprinkle with Parmesan cheese. Cover this with another layer of *polenta* and repeat the operation, leaving just enough béchamel, meat sauce, and Parmesan cheese for a light topping over the next and final layer of *polenta*. Dot the top lightly with butter.

6. Bake in the uppermost level of the preheated oven for 10 to 15 minutes, until a light crust has formed on top. Remove from the oven and allow to settle for about 5 minutes before serving.

NOTE

You may prepare this entirely ahead of time up to the point the dish is ready for the oven. It may be refrigerated overnight, but it should be returned to room temperature before baking.

MENU SUGGESTIONS

Follow the ones given for Baked Green Lasagne with Meat Sauce (page 136), which this dish strongly resembles.

SECOND COURSES

I Secondi

While Italian first courses owe their luxuriance to the fertile imagination of the home cook, the austerity of the second courses is the legacy of the hunter and the fisherman. Strike everything broiled or roasted from a list of Italian second courses and you would be left with a very brief list indeed. This should be no cause for regret, however. If the second courses were as exuberant as the pastas, an Italian meal would exhaust both our enjoyment and our digestion.

Next to broiling and roasting, sautéing and frying are the most important cooking methods, and they are all amply represented in this chapter.

The section on fish is relatively brief, which may startle anyone familiar with the excellence and (before polluted waters) the abundance of Italian fish. But while green beans, chicken, and even veal may give roughly the same results here that they do in Italy, there is very little in American waters that resembles Italian fish. Not one of our species of shellfish coincides with an Italian one. No matter what you might read in restaurant menus, there are no *scampi* here. Also missing are other delectable crustaceans such as *mazzancolle*, *langostini*, and *cannocchie*. Very tiny shrimps do exist but are rarely seen fresh in the markets. We do not have the tiny, peppery clams of the Adriatic, or the sweet succulent ones of the Tyrrhenian. We do not have sea dates or sea truffles, or miniature squid and cuttlefish, or the small red mullet. And we have nothing that can approach the Adriatic sole, the world's finest flat fish.

Some of the varieties of ocean fish, however, do lend themselves to an Italian taste in cooking. The finest local fish in my opinion is the striped bass. There is a beautiful recipe for baked striped bass stuffed with shellfish and sealed in foil that would not turn out any better with any Italian fish. Fresh young halibut and red snapper are other excellent fish for which specific recipes are given. There is a general recipe for broiling fish that will give an Italian flavor to the fish already mentioned, as well as to such other varieties as sea bass, porgy, and pompano. For the adventurous, and for those who already know it and like it, there is a brief section on squid. Local squid is not very different from large Italian squid, and the recipes included here should give very happy results. Fish soup is, by definition, a collection of what fish is available. There is a recipe for it in this chapter that should be successful wherever you might be, as long as it is close to a source of good salt-water fish.

The quality of Italian meat is often, but unjustly, maligned. It is true that beef in the south and certain parts of the north can be perfectly terrible, but in those regions cattle is used first for labor, then for food. For meat the people raise lambs, and the delectable *abbacchi* of Rome or kids of Apulia can make one forget filet mignon. Lamb can be butchered at various ages, and the flavor and cooking methods vary accordingly. There are three substantially different lamb roasts in this chapter. One is for hothouse or baby lamb, which is nearly as young as Roman *abbacchio*, another is for slightly older spring lamb, and the third is for the more mature, generally available standard lamb.

There is superb beef in Italy, and it is found in Tuscany. Beef from Val di Chiana cattle can hold its own with Burgundy's Charolais, Japan's Wadakin, or our own Black Angus. The most famous cut of beef in Italy is Florence's T-bone steak, known as *fiorentina*, whose simple but special cooking method is given here. Piedmont also produces good beef, and the Beef Braised in Red Wine Sauce in this chapter is a Piedmontese specialty.

Piedmont, along with Lombardy, produces marvelous, milky veal. Italy's veal dishes are probably its best-known contribution to meat courses, and in this chapter there are, in fact, more recipes for veal than for any other meat. Veal when cut into *scaloppine* has its own special tempo of cooking. It is done very briefly, and at quick, high heat. Today there is far better veal being marketed in this country than ever before. With care in the buying and cooking, it is now possible to produce veal dishes of a very high order.

Italian chicken dishes have always had a universal appeal. They are uncomplicated, easygoing, and invariably charming. Here there are two simple roasts, a tasty, peppery broiled chicken, and two typically Italian fricassees with vegetables. Chicken and turkey breast fillets are very much an Italian specialty. You will find a clear and detailed explanation of a technique for making fillets that can be adapted for any recipe calling for chicken or turkey breasts. This is followed by three examples of how the technique is used in Italian cooking, including Bologna's famous turkey breast fillets with ham, cheese, and truffles.

Close to the end of the chapter, there is a section on variety meats. Those who already include them in their cooking will find some newly edited classic dishes, and some less familiar ones. Those who do not may look the other way, but they should be encouraged to give one of them a try, at least once.

Italians make an excellent open-faced omelet which is called a *frittata*, but they have kept the secret of it at home. Restaurant *frittata* is more often than not stiff and leathery, which has led travelers to conclude that Italians cannot cook eggs. In the last section of this chapter you will find a full explanation of the method—practically the opposite of that of a French omelet—and six excellent examples of *frittate*. If you follow the instructions carefully, you will find that a *frittata* can be every bit as delectable as an omelet, but with more of a country flavor. With a *frittata* it is easier to serve a number of people than with omelets, which are difficult to make with a large quantity of eggs. If you already know how to make omelets, learn how to make *frittate*, and your repertory will have been doubled.

BAKED STRIPED BASS AND SHELLFISH SEALED IN FOIL

Branzino al cartoccio con frutti di mare

This fish is stuffed with mussels, shrimp, and oysters, sealed in heavy foil, and oven braised. Its flesh remains extraordinarily juicy and becomes delicately flavored with a fresh sea fragrance. The ideal way to prepare it is to completely remove the bones while leaving the fish intact. At the table you'll then be able to cut it into neat, boneless slices, which makes it so much more attractive to serve and agreeable to eat. Here is how you do it:

There is a slit in the fish's belly made by the dealer when he cleans out its intestinal cavity. With a sharp knife extend this slit for the whole length of the fish from head to tail. This will expose the entire backbone, from the upper half of which extend the rib bones imbedded in the belly. Using your fingers and a small knife pry these rib bones loose and detach them. With the same technique, loosen the backbone, separating it from the flesh around it. Now carefully bend the head, snapping off the backbone at that end, then do the same with the tail. At this point you will be able to lift away the entire backbone. If you don't feel up to doing this yourself, you should be able to persuade your fish dealer to do it for you. But make sure he slits open the fish on only one side, the belly side.

If you wish, you can substitute red snapper for the striped bass.

For 6 persons

12 mussels, cleaned as
   directed on page 53
6 medium or 12 tiny
   shrimps
6 oysters, unshelled
2 tablespoons chopped
   parsley
2 cloves garlic, lightly
   crushed with a
   heavy knife handle
   and peeled
½ cup olive oil
⅓ cup fine, dry
   unflavored bread
   crumbs

2 tablespoons thinly
   sliced yellow onion
Juice of 1 medium lemon
2½ teaspoons salt
Freshly ground pepper,
   5 or 6 twists of the
   pepper mill
1 striped bass OR red
   snapper (3 to 3½
   pounds), boned as
   directed above

1. Put the mussels in a covered pan over high heat until their shells open, just a few minutes. Detach the mussels from their shells and put them in a mixing bowl large enough to hold all the ingredients except the fish. Strain the juices from the mussels left in the pan into the mixing bowl, using a sieve lined with a thickness of paper towel.

2. Peel and devein the shrimp. Wash them thoroughly in cold water and pat dry. If they are extra large, slice them in half lengthwise. Drop them into the mixing bowl.

3. Shuck the oysters and add them and their juices to the mixing bowl. Add all the other ingredients, except for the fish, to the bowl. Mix thoroughly, but not roughly, so as not to bruise the shellfish.

4. Preheat the oven to 475°.

5. Wash the fish in cold running water inside and out. Pat thoroughly dry with paper towels.

6. Spread a double thickness of heavy-duty aluminum foil on the bottom of a long, shallow baking dish, remembering that the piece of foil must be large enough to close over the fish at all points. Spread some of the liquid from the mixture in the bowl on the bottom of the foil. Place the fish in the center and stuff it with all the ingredients from the bowl, reserving some of the liquid, with which you will now coat the outside of the fish. Fold the foil over the fish and seal it tightly with a double lengthwise fold, making

sure the corners are tightly tucked in. Place in the upper third of the oven and bake for about 40 minutes. When cooked the fish will be very tender and soaked in cooking juices.

7. Allow the fish to rest 10 minutes in the sealed foil, then place the whole package on a serving platter. (Unveiling the fish at the table can be very dramatic, but it can also be quite messy. Don't do it unless you have a little serving table on the side. Also, don't lift the fish out of the foil, because it has no bones and will break up.) Cut the foil open and trim it with scissors down to the edge of the platter. Bring the fish to the table whole and slice it as you would a roast.

MENU SUGGESTIONS

You can build a very fine fish dinner around this dish. For antipasti you can start with the Cold Salmon Foam (page 30), the Herb-Flavored Seafood Salad (page 405), or the Tomatoes Stuffed with Tuna and Capers (page 35). Choose a first course with *pesto*, either Trenette with Potatoes and Pesto (page 135) or Potato Gnocchi (page 185). No vegetable side dish is required. Follow the fish with a green salad, or a Green Bean Salad (page 397).

POACHED HALIBUT WITH PARSLEY SAUCE

Pesce da taglio con salsa di prezzemolo

For 4 persons

THE FISH:

½ medium yellow onion, sliced thin
1 stalk celery
2 or 3 sprigs parsley
1 bay leaf

⅛ teaspoon fennel seeds
1 cup dry white wine
½ teaspoon salt
2 pounds halibut, cut in one slice, bone removed

THE SAUCE:

1 tablespoon finely
   chopped yellow
   onion
2½ tablespoons butter
2 tablespoons olive oil
2 tablespoons finely
   chopped parsley
½ teaspoon finely
   chopped garlic
1 tablespoon chopped
   capers

2 teaspoons anchovy
   paste
2 teaspoons all-purpose
   flour dissolved in ½
   cup broth or, with 1
   bouillon cube, in ½
   cup hot water
2 tablespoons red wine
   vinegar
Salt to taste
Freshly ground pepper,
   about 4 twists of the
   mill

THE GARNISH:

2 hard-boiled eggs, sliced
1 lemon, sliced into ¼-
   inch disks
Parsley leaves

Gherkins, sliced
   lengthwise but left
   whole at one end so
   they can be fanned
   out

1. Put the sliced onion, the celery stalk, parsley sprigs,
bay leaf, fennel seeds, white wine, salt, and 1 quart water
in a deep saucepan. Bring to a boil and let bubble at a
moderate pace for about 15 minutes. There must be enough
liquid to cover the fish; if you feel it is insufficient, add more
water. Meanwhile, wash the fish in cold water and pat dry.
When the poaching liquid has bubbled for 15 minutes, add
the fish, cover the pan, and cook at a slow simmer for 10
to 12 minutes. Turn off the heat, but don't remove the fish
from the pan. Let it sit in the poaching liquid while you
prepare the sauce.

2. In a small saucepan sauté the chopped onion, with
1½ tablespoons of the butter and all the oil, over medium
heat until translucent but not browned. Add the chopped
parsley, garlic, capers, and anchovy paste. Stir well and
sauté lightly for a few moments. Add the flour-broth mixture
a tablespoon at a time, stirring thoroughly, then add the
vinegar. Stir and keep at a moderate boil for 2 minutes.
Taste and correct for salt, then add the pepper. Off the
heat, swirl in the remaining tablespoon of butter.

3. Remove the fish from the pan, lifting it carefully so that it doesn't break up (try using two metal spatulas), and place it on a warm serving platter. Pour the sauce over it and garnish with hard-boiled egg slices, lemon slices topped with parsley leaves, and fanned-out sliced gherkins. Serve immediately.

MENU SUGGESTIONS

For antipasto, Cold Salmon Foam (page 30) or the Baked Oysters with Parmesan Cheese (page 30). First course, a Risotto with Clams (page 182), or the Fettuccine with White Clam Sauce (page 128). No vegetable side dish, just a green salad after the fish.

PAN-ROASTED MACKEREL WITH ROSEMARY AND GARLIC

Sgomberi in tegame con rosmarino e aglio

In the small fishing towns along the Adriatic coast this is a very popular way of cooking mackerel; the slow cooking in oil keeps its firm flesh tender and juicy and the subdued taste of rosemary and garlic make mackerel's robust flavor gentler and very appealing.

For 4 persons

⅓ cup olive oil
4 cloves garlic, peeled
4 mackerel (about ¾ pound each), cleaned but with heads and tails on

1 three-inch sprig fresh rosemary or 1 teaspoon dried rosemary, crumbled
Salt and freshly ground pepper to taste
Juice of ½ lemon
Lemon wedges

1. Wash the mackerel under cold running water and pat dry.
2. Heat the oil in a casserole and lightly sauté the garlic.

3. Add the mackerel and rosemary and lower the heat to medium. Brown the fish well on each side but take care that it doesn't stick to the pan. (Should it stick, be careful as you turn it so it doesn't break up.) Season each side with salt and pepper.

4. When the fish is nicely browned add the lemon juice, cover with a tight-fitting lid, turn the heat down to low, and cook slowly for approximately 15 minutes, or until tender. Serve piping hot, with wedges of lemon on the side.

MENU SUGGESTIONS

As a first course, Clam Soup (page 50), Thin Spaghetti with Red Clam Sauce (page 95), Thin Spaghetti with Anchovy and Tomato Sauce (page 96), or Risotto with Clams (page 182). No vegetables. Follow the fish with Mixed Salad (page 393), or Zucchini Salad (page 399).

RED SNAPPER WITH SAUTÉED MUSHROOMS

Pagello con i funghi trifolati

In this recipe the fish is slowly simmered in wine and broth with a flavor base of sautéed vegetables, anchovy, parsley, and bay leaves. It is then combined with mushrooms sautéed in the classic Italian manner with oil, garlic, and parsley. Although the flavorings in this dish are numerous, they are used in minuscule quantities, and are calculated to set off rather than cloak the delicacy and sweetness of the fish.

For 4 persons

THE SAUTÉED MUSHROOMS:

3 tablespoons olive oil
½ teaspoon chopped
    garlic
½ pound crisp, fresh
    mushrooms

3 teaspoons chopped
    parsley
¼ teaspoon salt

THE FISH:

3 tablespoons olive oil
1 tablespoon butter
2 tablespoons finely
    chopped yellow
    onion
2 tablespoons finely
    chopped carrot
1 large clove garlic,
    lightly crushed with
    a heavy knife handle
    and peeled
1 teaspoon chopped flat
    anchovy fillet
2 teaspoons chopped
    parsley
½ bay leaf, crumbled
⅓ cup dry white wine

1 red snapper (2 to 2½
    pounds), cleaned,
    scaled, and washed,
    but with head and
    tail left on
1 teaspoon salt
Freshly ground pepper,
    4 to 6 twists of the
    mill
½ cup Homemade Meat
    Broth (page 10) OR
    ¼ cup canned beef
    broth mixed with ¼
    cup water OR ½
    bouillon cube
    dissolved in ½ cup
    warm water

1. Using the ingredients listed above, prepare and cook the mushrooms as directed on page 365. Set aside after cooking.

2. In a skillet just large enough for the fish, put the olive oil, butter, onion, and carrot. Cook over medium-low heat until the onion is translucent but not browned.

3. Add the garlic and chopped anchovy. Cook, stirring, for a minute or two, until the anchovy has dissolved and the garlic has released some of its fragrance; then add the parsley and cook long enough to stir everything once or twice.

4. Add the bay leaf and the wine. Cook, stirring frequently, until the wine has evaporated by half.

5. Add the red snapper, half the salt and pepper, and all the broth, and put a cover on the skillet, setting it slightly askew. Cook, keeping the heat always at medium low, and after about 10 minutes, slightly longer if the fish is larger, turn the fish over carefully (possibly using two metal spatulas) so that it stays intact, and add the rest of the salt and pepper. After it has cooked another 10 minutes on the second side, add the mushroom mixture, drained of its oil. Cover the pan and let the mushrooms and fish cook together for no more than a minute. Serve piping hot.

Antipasto to precede this dish could be Baked Oysters with Oil and Parsley (page 29), Cold Salmon Foam (page 30), or Shrimps with Oil and Lemon (page 36). Avoid the ones that are very salty or highly flavored. As a first course after the antipasto, an excellent choice would be Fettucine with White Clam Sauce (page 128), spaghetti with the same sauce or with Red Clam Sauce (page 95), or Risotto with Clams (page 182). No vegetable accompaniment is required. Follow the fish with Mixed Salad (page 393).

FILLET OF SOLE WITH PIQUANT TOMATO SAUCE

Filetti di sogliola con pomodoro e capperi

I am not very fond of American sole, and the reason is that it isn't really sole, it is flounder. Flounder has none of the firm, compact texture of true sole, and only a trace of its delicate taste. Crisply fried Adriatic sole is simply one of the best things it is possible to eat, but I wouldn't try it with flounder. The best one can do with flounder is to take the edge off its awkwardness through the graces of a seductive sauce. The following version relies on the unabashed charms of a tangy tomato sauce, and, if you are partial to sole, you'll find it works quite well.

For 6 persons

⅔ cup thinly sliced yellow onion
5 tablespoons olive oil
1½ teaspoons finely chopped garlic
1 teaspoon orégano
2 tablespoons very tiny capers, or larger capers roughly chopped

1 cup canned Italian tomatoes, cut up, with their juice
Salt to taste
Freshly ground pepper, about 6 twists of the mill
2 pounds fresh sole fillets, preferably grey sole

1. Put the sliced onion in a skillet with the olive oil and cook over medium heat until soft and pale gold in color. Add the garlic, and when it has colored lightly add the orégano and capers, stirring once or twice. Add the cut-up tomatoes and their juice, salt, and pepper. Stir well and cook at a steady simmer for 15 to 20 minutes, or until the tomatoes and the oil separate.

2. Preheat the oven to 450°.

3. Rinse the fish fillets in cold water and blot dry. The fillets are going to be arranged in a single layer in a baking dish, folded over end to end and slightly overlapping. Choose a bake-and-serve dish just large enough for the job, and smear the bottom with about a tablespoon of the tomato sauce. Dip each fillet on both sides in the sauce in the skillet, then fold it and arrange it in the baking dish as directed above. Pour the remaining sauce over the fillets, and place the dish in the uppermost level of the oven: Cook for no more than 5 to 8 minutes, depending upon the thickness of the fillets. (Don't overcook, or the fish will become dry.)

4. When you remove the dish from the oven you may find that the fish has thrown off liquid, thinning out the sauce. If this happens, tilt the dish and spoon all the sauce and liquid into a small pan. Boil it rapidly until it is sufficiently concentrated, then pour it back over the fish. Serve immediately.

MENU SUGGESTIONS

The first course could be Risotto with Clams (page 182), Fettuccine with White Clam Sauce (page 128), or Spaghetti with Garlic and Oil (page 98). If you want an antipasto, serve Shrimps with Oil and Lemon (page 36). Follow the fish with Mixed Salad (page 393) or Green Bean Salad (page 397).

COLD SAUTEED TROUT IN ORANGE MARINADE

Trota marinata all'arancio

Long ago Italian lakes and rivers were busy with trout and other delicious small fish. A day's catch used to result in a large mess of fried fish for dinner, and marinating it was a genial way to cope with the leftovers. Fish treated this way is so remarkably good that soon people started to fry it especially for the purpose of marinating it.

There are many widely different marinades. The one most frequently published is the one in which garlic, vinegar, and herbs are the principal ingredients. It is very popular, but I find it rather aggressive. The marinade given here is elegantly flavored with orange, lemon, and vermouth. It settles fragrantly but gently into the delicate flesh of trout, perch, or other fresh-water fish.

For 6 persons

3 trout, perch, or other freshwater fish (about ¾ pound each), cleaned and scaled, but with heads and tails left on
½ cup olive oil
½ cup or less all-purpose flour, spread on a dish or on waxed paper
2 tablespoons finely chopped yellow onion
1 cup dry white Italian vermouth

2 tablespoons chopped orange peel
½ cup freshly squeezed orange juice
Juice of 1 lemon
1 tablespoon salt
Freshly ground black pepper, about 6 twists of the mill
1½ tablespoons chopped parsley
Unpeeled orange slices (optional)

1. Wash the trout in cold water and pat dry thoroughly with paper towels.

2. Heat the oil in a skillet over medium heat. When the oil is hot, dip both sides of the trout lightly in flour and slip into the skillet. (If all the trout won't fit into the skillet at one time, dip in flour just the ones you are ready to fry.)

3. Brown the fish well on one side, then on the other, calculating about 5 minutes for the first side and 4 minutes for the other. Transfer the fish to a deep dish large enough to contain them in a single layer. Reserve the oil in the skillet.

4. With a very sharp knife, make two or three small diagonal cuts in the skin on both sides of each fish. Be careful not to tear the skin apart, and do not cut into the flesh.

5. Put the chopped onion in the skillet in which you fried the fish and sauté it in the same oil, over medium heat, until pale gold. Add the vermouth and the orange peel and let the vermouth boil for 15 or 20 seconds. Stir, then add the orange juice, lemon juice, salt, and pepper. Let everything bubble for about 30 seconds, stirring two or three times. Add the chopped parsley, stir again once or twice, then pour the entire contents of the skillet over the trout.

6. Plan to serve the trout no earlier than the following day. Let the fish soak in the marinade for at least 6 hours at room temperature, then refrigerate. (They will keep in the refrigerator for 3 to 4 days; after that they lose their fresh taste.) Take them out sufficiently ahead of time to serve them at room temperature. If you like, you may garnish them with unpeeled orange slices.

MENU SUGGESTIONS

This is a fine antipasto for an elegant fish dinner. It can be followed by Fettuccine with White Clam Sauce (page 128) or Trenette with Potatoes and Pesto (page 135), and then by Fish Broiled the Adriatic Way (page 214), or Baked Striped Bass and Shellfish Sealed in Foil (page 201).

You can also promote the trout to a second course, preceded by Cold Salmon Foam (page 30), and/or Potato Gnocchi (page 185) with Genoese Basil Sauce for Pasta and Soup (page 132), or Velvety Clam Soup with Mushrooms (page 51). Follow with Green Bean Salad (page 397) or Mixed Salad (page 393).

TUNA SALAMI

Salame di tonno

In this recipe tuna is combined with mashed potatoes and eggs to form a salami-like roll, which is then slowly simmered with vegetables, herbs, and white wine. It is served cold, sliced, with a caper and anchovy mayonnaise. The tuna completely loses its tinned, salty taste and acquires an elegance of texture and flavor that is pointed up but not overwhelmed by the seasonings.

For 6 persons

1 medium potato
2 seven-ounce cans
    imported Italian
    tuna packed in olive
    oil, drained
¼ cup freshly grated
    Parmesan cheese

1 whole egg plus 1 white
Freshly ground pepper,
    about 6 twists of the
    mill
Cheesecloth

THE FLAVORED BROTH:

½ medium yellow onion,
    sliced thin
1 stalk celery
1 carrot

6 parsley sprigs, stems
    only
Salt
1 cup dry white wine

A MAYONNAISE (PAGE 23) MADE WITH:

1 egg yolk
2 tablespoons lemon
    juice

⅔ cup olive oil
½ teaspoon salt

WHEN THE MAYONNAISE IS MADE, INCORPORATE THE FOLLOWING:

2 tablespoons chopped
    capers
¼ teaspoon anchovy
    paste

Sliced black olives

1. Boil the potato, unpeeled, until it is tender. Drain, peel, and mash through a potato ricer or food mill.

2. Mash the tuna in a bowl. Add the grated cheese, the whole egg plus the egg white, the pepper, and the mashed potato.

3. Moisten a piece of cheesecloth, wring it until it is just damp, and lay it out flat on the work counter. Place the tuna mixture at one end of the cloth, shaping it into a salami-like roll about 2½ inches in diameter. Wrap it in the cheesecloth, covering it with at least two layers. Tie the ends securely with string.

4. Put the sliced onion, celery stalk, carrot, parsley stems, ½ teaspoon salt, and the wine in a saucepan or oval casserole, together with the tuna roll. Add enough water to cover by about 1 inch. Cover the pot and bring to a boil. When it reaches a boil, adjust the heat so that it cooks at the gentlest of simmers. Cook for 45 minutes.

5. When cooked, remove the tuna roll and, as soon as you can handle it, unwrap it gently. Set aside to cool completely.

6. While the tuna is cooling, make a mayonnaise with the egg yolk, lemon juice, olive oil, and ½ teaspoon salt, according to the directions on page 23. Incorporate the chopped capers and anchovy paste.

7. Cut the cold tuna roll into slices ⅜ inch thick. Arrange the slices on a platter, overlapping them very slightly. Cover the slices with the caper- and anchovy-flavored mayonnaise and garnish with black olive slices running the length of the platter, over the center of each slice of tuna.

MENU SUGGESTIONS

This is a very attractive dish for a buffet. It can also be combined with a salad to make a very light meal for a hot summer day, and it can be presented as a lovely antipasto before Fish Broiled the Adriatic Way (see next page).

FISH BROILED THE ADRIATIC WAY

Pesce ai ferri alla moda dell'Adriatico

Broiling fish over a charcoal or wood fire is the favorite way of doing fish along the Adriatic. Before broiling, the fish is steeped in a marinade of olive oil, lemon juice, salt, and bread crumbs for an hour or more. This not only enhances the flavor of the fish, but keeps it from drying out while cooking.

For 4 persons

2½ to 3 pounds fish, either whole, with head and tail left on, OR thick slices of larger fish
2 teaspoons salt
¼ cup olive oil
2 tablespoons lemon juice
6 tablespoons fine, dry unflavored bread crumbs

½ teaspoon rosemary (optional; for use only on such dark-fleshed fish as mackerel or bluefish)
1 or 2 bay leaves (optional)
Lemon wedges

1. If you are using a whole fish, scale and clean it, wash it in cold water, and dry it thoroughly on paper towels.

2. Salt the fish on both sides, put it on a platter, and add the olive oil and lemon juice. Turn the fish two or three times to coat it well. Add the bread crumbs, turning the fish again until it is well coated. If you are preparing a dark-fleshed fish, add the rosemary. Marinate for 1 to 2 hours at room temperature, turning and basting the fish from time to time. Save the marinade.

3. If you are doing the fish in the broiler, preheat it to the maximum at least 15 minutes before cooking. If you are doing the fish over charcoal, the fire must also be ready 15 minutes ahead of time. Throw a bay leaf or two in the fire just before setting the fish on the charcoal grill.

4. Put the fish on the grill at a distance of 4 to 5 inches

from the source of heat. Broil on both sides, until done. (Cooking times vary greatly, depending on the thickness of the fish and the intensity of the heat. You must learn to judge it time by time. A 3-pound striped bass, for example, should be done in about 20 minutes. Do not overcook or it will become dry, nor undercook, because partly done fish is most disagreeable. The flesh should come away easily from the bone and show no traces of translucent, raw pink color.) Baste the fish occasionally while it broils with the leftover marinade. Serve piping hot, with lemon wedges.

MENU SUGGESTIONS

You can precede broiled fish with any pasta or rice with a seafood sauce. Other suggestions for a first course: Mussel Soup (page 53), Clam Soup (page 50), or Velvety Clam Soup with Mushrooms (page 51), Cold Vegetable Soup with Rice, Milan Style (page 65), Thin Spaghetti with Anchovy and Tomato Sauce (page 96), Spaghetti with Genoese Basil Sauce for Pasta and Soup (page 132), or Trenette with Potatoes and Pesto (page 135), Spaghetti with Garlic and Oil (page 98), or Spaghetti with Tomato Sauce III (page 90). You can accompany it, if you like, with Diced Pan-Roasted Potatoes (page 372), but with no other vegetables. Follow with any raw salad or with the Zucchini Salad (page 399). If you'd like an antipasto, choose among Shrimps with Oil and Lemon (page 36), Herb-Flavored Seafood Salad (page 405), or Baked Oysters with Oil and Parsley (page 29).

SHRIMP BROCHETTES, ADRIATIC STYLE

Spiedini di gamberi dell'Adriatico

I have tasted many versions of this very simple dish in seafood and Italian restaurants here, but I have never come across any that recall the delicate balance of flavors and the juicy texture of the shrimps that fishermen cook all along the Adriatic. You must start, of course, with very good-quality shrimps from a reputable fish market, fresh if possible. Do not try to make do with the bags of frozen shrimps from the supermarket freezer. Aside from the shrimps, however, the success of this dish depends upon how you apply the coating of oil and bread crumbs. There must be just enough oil to coat the shrimps, but not so much as to drench them. There must be enough bread crumbs to retain the oil and to form a light protective covering over the delicate flesh, but not so much as to bury the shrimps under a thick, gross crust. Follow the proportions indicated below, but bear in mind that the quantities are approximate. If you use larger shrimps you will need less oil and crumbs because there is less total surface per pound to be coated. Also, some bread crumbs go further than others, depending upon how absorbent they are. An essential ingredient is your good judgment.

For 6 persons

1½ pounds small shrimps
3½ tablespoons olive oil
3½ tablespoons vegetable oil
⅔ cup fine, dry unflavored bread crumbs
½ teaspoon very finely chopped garlic

2 teaspoons finely chopped parsley
¾ teaspoon salt
Freshly ground pepper, 5 or 6 twists of the mill
Lemon wedges

1. Preheat the broiler to its maximum setting. (The broiler must be heated at least 15 minutes before the shrimps are to be cooked.)

2. Shell and devein the shrimps. Wash in cold water and pat thoroughly dry with paper towels.

3. Put the shrimps in a comfortably large mixing bowl. Add as much of the two oils (mixed in equal parts) and of the bread crumbs as you need to obtain an even, light, creamy coating on all the shrimps. (Do not add it all at once because it may not be necessary, but if you are working with very tiny shrimps, you may need even more. In that case, always use 1 part olive oil to 1 part vegetable oil.) When the shrimps are well coated, add the chopped garlic, parsley, salt, and pepper and mix well. Allow the shrimps to steep in the marinade for at least 20 minutes at room temperature.

4. Have ready some flat, double-edged skewers. Skewer

the shrimps lengthwise, 5 or more shrimps per brochette, depending upon the size. As you skewer each shrimp, curl and bend one end inward so that the skewer goes through the shrimp at three points. This is to make sure that the shrimps won't slip as you turn the skewer.

5. These shrimps require brisk, rapid cooking. Wait until the broiler has been on for 15 minutes. Cook the shrimps no more than 3 minutes on one side and 2 minutes on the other, and even less if the shrimps are very small. Each side is done as soon as a crisp, golden crust forms.

6. Serve piping hot, on the skewers, with lemon wedges on the side.

MENU SUGGESTIONS

Very tiny shrimps broiled in this manner are a frequent part of Italian "shore dinners," served together with a mixture of broiled and fried fish. American shrimps are frequently sufficiently large to suffice as a course of their own. The dish can be preceded by a Risotto with Clams (page 182), Clam Soup (page 50), Mussel Soup (page 53), or Trenette with Potatoes and Pesto (page 135). Generally no vegetable is served with it, but the Sautéed Mushrooms with Garlic and Parsley (page 365) can be a very agreeable accompaniment. Follow the shrimp with Mixed Salad (page 393).

SQUID

Calamari

It is odd how New Englanders, who consume clams by the ton, dread the thought of eating another excellent mollusk, the squid. Actually, the flesh of the squid, when properly cooked, is far more delicate and tender than most clams. It is no accident that fish-loving countries from Italy to Japan regard the squid and its numerous relatives as one of the sea's most delectable offerings. If you are open minded about experimenting with food, you will be well rewarded by the taste of squid.

The squid most commonly available here corresponds to the large Italian squid, *Calamari* and *calamaroni*. Its sac, exclusive of tentacles, measures from 3½ inches to 6 or 7 inches in length. It is available either fresh or frozen, and both are good. In Italy, freshly caught large squid is kept in the refrigerator one or two days before cooking, to relax its rigid flesh. In this country it is probably already that old before it reaches the market. Use squid only when it is a pure, milky white in color. The tastiest, sweetest squid, whether fresh or frozen, comes to the markets in early spring.

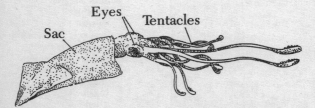

HOW TO CLEAN SQUID

Your dealer will clean squid if you ask him, but he rarely does a thorough job. It is much better to do the whole thing at home rather than to pick up where he has left off.

Hold the sac in one hand, and, with the other, firmly but gently pull off the tentacles. If you are not too abrupt, all the contents of the sac should come away attached to the tentacles. Cut the tentacles above the eyes, reserve the tentacles, and discard everything else from the eyes down.

Remove the quill-like bone from the sac, and thoroughly wash out the inside of the sac, removing anything it may still contain. Peel off the sac's outer skin, which comes off quite easily if the job is done under cold running water. Also under running water, peel off as much of the skin on the tentacles as will come off.

Rinse both sac and tentacles in several changes of cold water, until the water runs clear. Dry thoroughly. The squid is now ready for cooking.

STEWED SQUID WITH TOMATOES AND PEAS

Calamari e piselli alla livornese

For 4 to 6 persons

- 1½ tablespoons finely chopped yellow onion
- 3 tablespoons olive oil
- 1½ teaspoons finely chopped garlic
- 1 tablespoon finely chopped parsley
- ¾ cup canned Italian tomatoes, coarsely chopped, with their juice
- 2 pounds smallest possible squid, cleaned and prepared for cooking as directed above
- Salt and freshly ground pepper to taste
- 2 pounds fresh peas (unshelled weight) or 1 ten-ounce package frozen peas, thawed

1. Put the onion in a flameproof casserole with the olive oil and sauté over medium heat until it begins to turn pale gold. Add the garlic and sauté until it colors lightly but does not brown. Add the parsley, stir once or twice, then add the tomatoes. Cook at a gentle simmer for 10 minutes.

2. Slice the squid sacs into rings about ¾ inch to 1 inch wide. Divide the tentacle cluster into two parts. Add all the squid to the casserole; then add the salt and pepper, stir, cover, and cook at a gentle simmer for 30 minutes.

3. If you are using fresh peas, add them to the casserole at this time. Cover and continue cooking until the squid is tender, about another 20 minutes. (Cooking times, however, vary considerably, depending on the size and toughness of the squid, so test from time to time with a fork. When the squid is easily pierced, it is done.) If you are using thawed frozen peas, add them to the casserole when the squid is practically done, because they need only a few minutes' cooking. Taste and correct for salt and pepper before serving.

NOTE

This stewed squid can be prepared entirely ahead of time and refrigerated up to 2 days. Warm up slowly just before serving.

MENU SUGGESTIONS

Serve Broiled Mussels and Clams on the Half Shell (page 31), Peppers and Anchovies (page 34), or even some Shrimp Brochettes, Adriatic Style (page 215) as an antipasto. Skip the first course, because you will be sopping up lots of bread with the tasty sauce. No vegetables, of course. Follow with Shredded Carrot Salad (page 392).

STUFFED SQUID BRAISED IN WHITE WINE

Calamari ripieni stufati al vino bianco

For 6 persons

6 large squid (the sac should measure 4½ to 5 inches, not including the tentacles)

THE STUFFING:

1 tablespoon olive oil, approximately
2 tablespoons finely chopped parsley
½ teaspoon finely chopped garlic, or more to taste
1 whole egg, lightly beaten

2½ tablespoons freshly grated Parmesan cheese
¼ cup fine, dry, unflavored bread crumbs
½ teaspoon salt
Freshly ground pepper, about 6 twists of the pepper mill

THE BRAISING LIQUID:

Olive oil, enough to come ¼ inch up the side of the skillet
4 whole cloves garlic, peeled

½ cup canned Italian tomatoes, coarsely chopped, with their juice
½ teaspoon finely chopped garlic
¼ cup dry white wine

1. Clean and prepare the squid as directed on page 220.
2. Chop the squid tentacles very fine. In a bowl, mix them with all the stuffing ingredients until you have a smooth, even mixture. There should be just enough olive oil in the mixture to make it slightly glossy. If it doesn't have this light surface gloss, add more olive oil.

3. Divide the stuffing into 6 equal parts and spoon it into the squid sacs. (Do not overstuff, because the squid shrinks as it cooks and too much stuffing may cause it to burst.) Sew up each opening tightly with darning needle and thread—and be sure to put the needle safely away as soon as you are finished using it or it may disappear into the sauce.

4. Choose a skillet large enough to hold the squid in a single layer and coat the bottom with just enough olive oil to come ¼ inch up the side of the pan. Heat the oil over medium-high heat and sauté the garlic cloves until golden brown. Discard the garlic and put in the stuffed squid. Brown the squid well on all sides, then add the chopped tomatoes with their juice, the chopped garlic, and the wine. Cover tightly and cook over low heat for 30 to 40 minutes. The squid is done when it feels tender at the pricking of a fork.

5. Remove the squid to a cutting board and allow to settle for a few minutes. Slice away just enough from the sewn-up end to remove the thread and cut the rest into slices ½ inch thick. Arrange the slices on a warm serving platter so that each squid sac is recomposed. Warm up the sauce in the skillet, pour over the sliced squid, and serve immediately.

NOTE

This dish can be prepared 4 or 5 days ahead of time and refrigerated. Warm it up as follows: Preheat the oven to 300°. Transfer the squid and the sauce to a bake-and-serve dish, add 2 to 3 tablespoons of water, and place in the middle level of the oven. Turn and baste the slices as they warm up, being careful that they don't break up. Serve when warm.

MENU SUGGESTIONS

If you wish to serve a vegetable side dish with the squid, the most suitable would be steamed potatoes. It is quite sufficient, however, to serve Zucchini Salad (page 399) or mixed greens afterwards. It can be preceded by Fettuccine with White Clam Sauce (page 128), or Risotto with Clams (page 182). I have found that Bresaola (page 44), with its tart, clean taste, makes an ideal prelude to this rather robust dish.

FRIED SQUID

Calamari fritti

One of the most prized delicacies along the Adriatic is very tiny squid, often no more than 1½ inches long, fried whole in hot oil. They are incredibly tender and sweet, and, should you find yourself on the Adriatic coast, do not miss your chance to eat them. Although not quite so tender and delicate, our larger local squid can be very good indeed when fried, but it must first be cut up into rings.

For 4 persons

3 pounds squid	**Salt**
Vegetable oil, enough to	**Lemon wedges**
come 1 inch up the	
side of the pan	
1 cup all-purpose flour,	
spread on waxed	
paper or on a platter	

1. Clean the squid as directed on page 230, drying it thoroughly on paper towels. Cut the squid sacs into rings about ⅜ inch wide and separate the tenacle cluster into two parts. Make sure it is all very thoroughly dried.

2. Heat the oil over high heat.

3. When the oil is very hot, dip the squid in the flour, shake off the excess, and slip into the pan. Do not put in any more at one time than will fit loosely in the skillet. Cover the skillet with a spatter screen, since squid has a tendency to burst while frying.

4. As soon as the squid is fried to a tawny gold on one side, turn it. When both sides are done, transfer to paper towels to drain. Sprinkle with salt and serve with lemon wedges on the side.

Fried squid can be preceded by Broiled Mussels and Clams on the Half Shell (page 31), Herb-Flavored Seafood Salad (page 405), Clam Soup (page 50), or Thin Spaghetti or Fettuccine with White Clam Sauce (page 128), with Red Clam Sauce (page 95), or with Tuna Sauce (page 97). Follow with Mixed Salad (page 393) or Zucchini Salad (page 399).

MY FATHER'S FISH SOUP

Il brodetto di papi

Fish soup is one of the most ancient dishes of the Mediterranean. In Italy, every coast town has its own traditional version. On the Tuscan coast it is called *cacciucco*, on the Adriatic side it is called *brodetto* ("little broth"), and elsewhere simply *zuppa di pesce*. To describe every variety of *cacciucco* or *brodetto* would take a larger volume than this one because it changes not just from town to town but from family to family. One of the best soups I've ever tasted is my father's, for which he acquired a considerable reputation in his lifetime. It has the merit of achieving an over-all hearty flavor without the individual delicacy and character of each fish being overwhelmed. My father would use a large variety of small fish, nine or more different kinds, but in this country we have to make do with a smaller variety of larger fish. Ocean fish is quite different from that of the Adriatic, but this is no cause for despair. The very idea behind fish soup is that it can turn virtually any combination of fish into a succulent and satisfying dish. This particular soup does it as well as any I've ever tried.

You need at least 3 to 4 heads for this recipe, so buy as many small whole fish as you can find; otherwise, your fish dealer can probably supply you with a few heads. The greater the variety, the tastier and more interesting the soup becomes. If you use dark-fleshed, fatty fish such as mackerel, bluefish, or eel, it adds to the flavor of the soup, but use it in small quantities. I have been very successful with porgy, sea bass, red snapper, salmon, halibut, scrod, and striped bass. If you can find it, by all means include sculpin. American sole or flounder adds very little to the soup, and it always has a most disagreeably submissive consistency.

For 6 to 8 persons

3 to 4 pounds assorted fresh fish, cleaned and scaled

½ pound or more shrimps in their shells

1 pound squid, cleaned and prepared for cooking as directed on page 220

½ dozen littleneck clams

½ dozen mussels

3 tablespoons finely chopped yellow onion

6 tablespoons olive oil

1½ teaspoons chopped garlic

3 tablespoons chopped parsley

½ cup dry white wine

1 cup canned Italian tomatoes, cut up, with their juice

Salt

Freshly ground pepper, about 10 twists of the mill

1. Wash all the fish under cold running water. Cut off the heads and set aside. Cut the larger fish into slices 3 to 3½ inches wide and set aside. (Fish no longer than 6½ inches can be kept whole.) Wash the shrimps very thoroughly in cold water, but do not remove the shells. Set aside.

2. Divide the squid's tentacle cluster into 2 or 3 parts. Slice the sacs into rings 1 inch wide. Set aside.

3. Wash and scrub the clams and mussels very thoroughly, according to the directions on pages 50 and 53. Heat the clams and mussels in separate, covered pans over medium-high heat until they open. Remove the clams from their shells, filter their juices through a sieve lined with paper towels, and set aside. Remove the mussels from their shells. Tipping the pan, gently draw off with a spoon all but the bottom, murky part of the mussel juices and set aside.

4. Choose a skillet large enough to contain all the fish later in one layer. Lightly sauté the onion in the olive oil over medium heat until translucent, then add the chopped garlic and continue sautéing until it colors lightly. Add the chopped parsley and stir two or three times, then add the wine and raise the heat to high. When the wine has boiled briskly for about

30 seconds, add the chopped tomatoes with their juice. Stir, turn the heat down to a gentle simmer, and cook for about 25 minutes, or until the tomatoes and oil separate.

5. Add the fish heads, ½ tablespoon salt and the ground pepper, then cover the pan and cook for 10 to 12 minutes over medium heat, turning the heads over after 5 or 6 minutes. Remove the heads from the pan and pass them through a food mill. Add the puréed heads to the pan, together with the sliced squid and their tentacles. Cover and cook at a slow, steady simmer for 30 or 40 minutes, or until the squid are tender and easily pierced by a fork. Add the fish, holding back the smallest and tenderest pieces for 1 or 2 minutes, then add another ½ tablespoon salt and all the juices from the clams and mussels. Cover and cook over medium heat for 10 minutes, turning and basting the fish once or twice. After 5 minutes' cooking add the whole, unshelled shrimps. Add the clams and mussels at the very last, giving them just enough time to warm up. Taste and correct for salt. Serve hot, with plenty of good country-style Italian bread for dunking into the broth.

NOTE

The ideal pot for *brodetto* is dark red earthenware. It cooks the soup to perfection and is charming to serve from at the table. If your pan is not suitable for serving, transfer the fish with some delicacy (otherwise it will break up into unattractive bits) to a hot, deep serving platter. Spoon all the sauce and shellfish over it.

MENU SUGGESTIONS

This is both soup and second course, a meal in itself. If you want to make more of an event out of it, precede it with Shrimp Brochettes, Adriatic Style (page 215), or Shrimps with Oil and Lemon (page 36), or Mushroom and Cheese Salad (page 44). Follow the soup with Green Bean Salad (page 397), or Zucchini Salad (page 399).

STEAK BROILED THE FLORENTINE WAY

La fiorentina

Beans and beef are Tuscany's most celebrated contributions to the Italian table. Even before the discovery of America, Florence was famous for its T-bone steak, known in Italy simply as a *fiorentina*. Although the particular flavor and texture of a *fiorentina* cannot be duplicated with any other meat but that of Tuscan-raised Val di Chiana beef, a fine American beefsteak, prepared the Florentine way, can be spectacularly good.

Nothing could be more straightforward than the preparation of a *fiorentina*, but it is often misunderstood outside of Tuscany, even by Italians. The error that is made most frequently is to marinate the steak in oil before broiling, which will make even the finest meat taste of tallow. Here is how the Florentines do it.

For 2 persons

½ teaspoon peppercorns, crushed in a mortar or inside a cloth with a heavy blunt object	1 T-bone steak, 1½ inches thick Salt Olive oil

1. Rub the peppercorns into both sides of the meat.
2. Broil the steak, over a very hot hardwood or charcoal fire, to the desired doneness. (A *fiorentina* should be very rare.) Salt the steak on the broiled side as you turn it.
3. When the steak is done, but while it is still on the grill, moisten it very lightly on both sides with a few drops of olive oil. Serve immediately.

MENU SUGGESTIONS

A *fiorentina* fits perfectly into any American steak dinner. In an Italian menu it might be preceded by any of the bean or chick-pea soups, by Pappardelle with Chicken-Liver Sauce (page 130), Risotto with Parmesan Cheese (page 171), or, skipping the first course, by Artichokes Roman Style (page 326), or Fava Beans, Roman Style (page 346). The vegetable accompaniment (if you started with soup or pasta), can be Sautéed Peas with Prosciutto, Florentine Style (page 368), Sautéed Spinach (page 373), or Sliced Zucchini with Garlic and Tomatoes (page 379). In Florence, in the spring, the salad would be Green Bean Salad (page 397).

PAN-BROILED STEAK WITH MARSALA AND HOT PEPPER SAUCE

Bistecca alla diavola

While Italians may have anticipated by a few centuries Americans' predilection for steaks broiled over coals, they have not overlooked the virtues of pan-broiling. It often gives brilliant results, as in this fiery steak whose own cooking juices are turned into a peppery sauce with a little help from such Italian ingredients as Marsala, garlic, fennel seeds, tomato paste, and, of course, *peperoncino rosso*, hot red pepper.

For 4 persons

4 shell steaks or any other good steak cut (about 3 pounds), ¾ inch thick	1 teaspoon fennel seeds
	1 tablespoon tomato paste diluted in 1 tablespoon water
¼ cup olive oil	
Salt and freshly ground pepper to taste	¼ teaspoon chopped hot red pepper (see note below)
½ cup dry Marsala	
½ cup dry red wine	2 tablespoons chopped parsley
1½ teaspoons finely chopped garlic	

1. Choose a skillet large enough to accommodate the steaks in a single layer. Put in the olive oil, and tilt the pan in several directions so that the bottom is well coated. Heat the oil over high heat until a haze forms over it, then put in the meat. Cook the steaks 3 minutes on one side, and 2 to 3 minutes on the other, for rare meat. Regulate the heat to make sure the oil

doesn't burn. When done, transfer the steaks to a warm platter, and season with salt and pepper.

2. Tip the pan, and, with a spoon, remove all but 1½ to 2 tablespoons of fat. Turn on the heat again to high and add the Marsala and the red wine. Boil the wine for about 30 seconds, while scraping the pan with a wooden spoon to loosen any cooking residues.

3. Add the garlic, cook just long enough to stir 2 or 3 times, then add the fennel seeds and stir again for a few seconds.

4. Add the diluted tomato paste and the chopped red pepper. Turn the heat down to medium and stir-cook for about 1 minute, until the sauce is thick and syrupy.

5. Return the steaks to the pan, just long enough to turn them in the hot sauce. Transfer steaks and sauce to a hot platter, sprinkle the parsley over the meat, and serve immediately.

NOTE

Don't use the crushed red pepper in jars, unless you absolutely can't find the tiny, dried, whole red peppers. These are available at most Italian, Greek, or Latin American groceries.

MENU SUGGESTIONS

As a first course choose either vegetable *risotto* (pages 179–84), or Molded Risotto with Parmesan Cheese and Chicken Liver Sauce (page 172), or Fusilli with Creamy Zucchini and Basil Sauce (page 101), or any of the stuffed pastas on pages 147–54 as long as they are not sauced with tomato or meat sauce. Or you can have a vegetable first course, such as Artichokes, Roman Style (page 326), or Baked Stuffed Zucchini Boats (page 380). If you are not having pasta, Potato Croquettes with Crisp-Fried Noodles (page 371) are a good accompaniment. Other vegetable suggestions: Zucchini Fried in Flour-and-Water Batter (page 377), Sautéed Green Beans with Butter and Cheese (page 348), and Gratinéed Jerusalem Artichokes (page 340).

THIN PAN-BROILED STEAKS WITH
TOMATOES AND OLIVES

Fettine di manzo alla sorrentina

This tasty southern dish utilizes thin slices of beef and can be quite successful with inexpensive cuts of meat. It takes 25 minutes or less if you start from scratch and no more than 5 minutes if the sauce has been prepared ahead of time.

For 4 persons

½ medium yellow onion, sliced thin
Olive oil, sufficient to come ¼ inch up the side of the pan
2 medium cloves garlic, peeled and diced
⅔ cup canned Italian tomatoes, roughly chopped, with their juice
1 dozen black Greek olives, pitted and quartered

¼ teaspoon orégano
Salt to taste
Freshly ground pepper, 6 to 8 twists of the mill
1 pound beef steaks, preferably chuck or chicken steaks, sliced ¼ inch thick, pounded, and edges notched to keep from curling

1. In a good-sized skillet (the broader the skillet, the faster the sauce will thicken), slowly sauté the sliced onion in the olive oil, letting it wilt gradually. As it takes on a pale gold color, add the diced garlic. Continue sautéing until the garlic has colored lightly, then add the tomatoes, olives, orégano, salt, and pepper. Stir and cook at a lively simmer until the tomatoes and oil separate, about 15 minutes or more. (The sauce may be prepared ahead of time up to this point.) Turn the heat down, keeping the sauce at the barest simmer.

2. Heat up a heavy iron skillet until it is smoking hot. Quickly grease the bottom with an oil-soaked cloth or paper towel. Put in the beef slices and cook just long enough to

brown the meat well on both sides. As you turn the meat, season it with salt and pepper. (Do not overcook or the thinly sliced steaks will become tough.) Transfer the browned meat first to the simmering sauce, turning it quickly and basting it with sauce, then to a hot platter, pouring the sauce over the meat. Serve immediately.

MENU SUGGESTIONS

An excellent first course would be Spaghetti with Garlic and Oil (page 98), or Baked Semolina Gnocchi (page 187). Avoid any pasta with either tomato or cream sauce. Escarole and Rice Soup (page 60), and the Rice and Lentil Soup (page 71) are also good choices for the first course. For the vegetable, Braised Artichokes and Peas (page 335) or Braised Artichokes and Leeks (page 336) would temper nicely the piquancy of the tomatoes and olives.

BEEF BRAISED IN RED WINE SAUCE

Stracotto al Barolo

For 6 persons

Vegetable oil
1 beef roast (4 pounds), preferably chuck
1 tablespoon butter
3 tablespoons coarsely chopped yellow onion
2 tablespoons coarsely chopped carrot
2 tablespoons coarsely chopped celery
1½ cups dry red wine (see note below)

1 cup Homemade Meat Broth (page 10) OR canned beef bouillon, more if necessary
1½ tablespoons canned Italian tomatoes, chopped
A pinch of thyme
⅛ teaspoon marjoram
Salt and freshly ground pepper to taste

1. Preheat the oven to 350°.

2. Pour enough oil into a heavy, medium-sized skillet to just cover the bottom. Turn on the heat to moderately high, and when the oil is quite hot slip in the meat. Brown well on all sides. Transfer the meat to a platter and set aside.

3. Choose a casserole, with a tight-fitting lid, just large enough to contain the meat. Put in 2 tablespoons of vegetable oil, the butter, and the chopped vegetables, and over moderate heat sauté the vegetables lightly, stirring from time to time. The vegetables should wilt and color lightly, but should not brown. Turn off the heat and put in the well-browned meat.

4. Tip the skillet, and with a spoon draw off and discard as much of the fat as possible. Add the wine, turn the heat to high, and boil for less than a minute, scraping up and loosening the browning residue stuck to the pan. Add this to the meat in the casserole.

5. Add the broth or canned bouillon to the casserole. It should come two-thirds up the side of the meat; add more if it doesn't. Add the tomatoes, thyme, marjoram, salt, and pepper. Turn the heat to high and bring to a boil, then cover the pot and place it in the middle level of the preheated oven. Braise for about 3 hours, every 20 minutes or so turning the meat and basting it with its liquid, and making sure it is cooking at a steady, slow simmer. (If it is not, regulate the heat accordingly.) At times, either because the cover doesn't fit tightly or because of the texture of the meat, you'll find all the liquid has evaporated or been absorbed. If this happens before the meat is cooked, add 3 or 4 tablespoons of warm water. The meat is cooked when it feels very tender at the pricking of a knife or fork.

6. Remove the meat to a cutting board. If the cooking liquid is too thin and has not reduced to less than ⅔ cup, place the casserole on the stove and boil the liquid over high heat until it has thickened, loosening any residue that may be stuck to the pot. Taste the sauce, adding salt and pepper if necessary. Slice the meat and place on a warm platter, with the slices slightly overlapping. Pour all the sauce over the meat and serve promptly.

NOTE
The ideal wine to use is Barbera or Barolo, which have the right amount of acidity combined with full-bodied flavor. If neither is available a good, stout California Pinot Noir will give excellent results.

MENU SUGGESTIONS

Any first course that is not too pungent in flavor, and does not have fish, can precede this substantial beef dish. All three varieties of *gnocchi* (pages 185, 187, and 189) are suitable, as are some of the more delicate pastas, such as Tortelloni Filled with Swiss Chard (page 154) and Fettuccine Tossed in Cream and Butter (page 123). Risotto with Parmesan Cheese (page 171), or either of the vegetable *risotti* (pages 179–181) are excellent. Or try the nice little Creamy Potato Soup with Carrots and Celery (page 55) or Lentil Soup (page 70). For vegetables, any of the butter and cheese ones will do, such as the Swiss Chard Stalks with Parmesan Cheese (page 357), or the fried vegetables, such as Crisp-Fried Whole Artichokes (page 332) or Fried Asparagus (page 345)

LEFTOVER BOILED BEEF WITH SAUTÉED ONIONS

Il bollito rifatto con le cipolle

The art of serving leftovers is not a highly developed one in Italy, perhaps because portions tend to be small and appetites large. An exception is this savory way to refurbish leftover boiled beef. It comes from Florence, where, from the time Florentines have been Florentines, nothing has ever been thrown away.

For 4 persons

3 cups thinly sliced yellow onions	1 bouillon cube dissolved in ½ cup Homemade Meat Broth (page 10) or in ½ cup water
¼ cup olive oil	
1 pound boiled beef (approximately), cut into slices ⅜ inch thick	
Salt	1 or 2 tablespoons leftover juices from any beef or veal roast (optional)
Freshly ground pepper, 4 to 6 twists of the mill	

1. Put the sliced onions in a skillet with the olive oil and cook slowly over medium-low heat until a light brown color.

2. Add the sliced beef, 2 teaspoons salt, the pepper, broth, and the optional roasting juices. Cover the pan and cook at a gentle simmer for 10 minutes. Uncover, raise the heat to medium, and cook until the broth has completely evaporated. Taste and correct for salt. Serve piping hot.

NOTE

This method is also successful with leftover broiled steak.

MENU SUGGESTIONS

Precede this with hearty Chick-Pea Soup (page 81), or any of the good country soups such as Bean Soup with Parsley and Garlic (page 75), or Bean and Pasta Soup (page 76). Follow with a salad.

BEEF PATTIES WITH ANCHOVIES AND MOZZARELLA

Polpette alla pizzaiola

Although it is very far from being a national dish, Italians do eat "hamburger." This is particularly true of some areas of the south where the beef is rather tough and it is chopped to make it tender. The following version of "hamburger," in its frank, zesty taste, in the simplicity of its approach, and in its decorative appearance, is undeniably Italian.

For 6 persons

1 3-by-3 inch piece white bread, crust removed

3 tablespoons milk

1½ pounds lean beef, preferably chuck, ground

1 egg

Salt

¾ cup fine, dry unflavored bread crumbs, spread on a dinner plate or on waxed paper

¼ cup vegetable oil

6 canned Italian tomatoes, opened flat, without seeds and juice

1 teaspoon orégano

6 slices mozzarella, 4 inches square, ¼ inch thick

12 flat anchovy fillets

1. Preheat the oven to 400°.
2. In a saucer or small bowl, soak the bread in the milk and mash it to a cream with a fork. Put the meat in a bowl, add the bread and milk mush, the egg, and 1 teaspoon salt, and knead with your hands until all the ingredients are well mixed.
3. Divide the meat mixture into 6 patties 1½ inches high and turn them over in the bread crumbs.
4. Over medium heat, heat the oil in a skillet until the meat sizzles when it is slipped in. Add the meat patties and cook 4 minutes on each side, handling them delicately when you turn them over so they don't break up. When done, transfer to a butter-smeared baking dish.
5. Cover each patty with a flattened tomato, reserving a small strip of each tomato, no larger than ½ inch, to be used for garnish. Season lightly with salt and a pinch of orégano. Over each tomato place a slice of mozzarella, and over the mozzarella place two anchovy fillets in the form of a cross. Where the anchovies meet place the reserved strip of tomato. Put the dish in the uppermost level of the oven and bake for 15 minutes, or until the mozzarella melts.

NOTE

These patties can be prepared several hours ahead of time before they are put in the oven.

MENU SUGGESTIONS

The Split Green Pea and Potato Soup (page 68), Lentil Soup (page 70), Risotto with Parmesan Cheese (page 171), and Spaghetti with Fresh Basil and Tomato Sauce (page 92) are all good choices for the first course. An excellent vegetable accompaniment would be any of the ones sautéed with garlic, such as Sautéed Spinach (page 373), Sautéed Broccoli With Garlic (page 350), Sautéed Mushrooms With Garlic and Parsley (page 365), Sautéed Diced Eggplant (page 360), or Sautéed Jerusalem Artichokes (page 339).

MEATBALLS

Polpettine

For 4 persons

⅓ cup milk	3 tablespoons freshly grated Parmesan cheese
1 slice firm, fine-quality white bread, crust removed	Vegetable Oil
1 pound lean beef, preferably from the neck, ground	Salt
	Freshly ground pepper, 3 to 4 twists of the mill
1 tablespoon finely chopped yellow onion	Fine, dry unflavored bread crumbs
1 tablespoon chopped parsley	1 cup canned Italian tomatoes, cut up, with their juice
1 egg	
A tiny pinch of nutmeg or marjoram	

1. Put the milk and the bread in a saucepan and bring to a boil. Mash the bread with a fork and blend it uniformly into the milk. Set aside and let cool before proceeding with the next step.

2. In a mixing bowl put the chopped meat, onion, par-

sley, egg, nutmeg or marjoram, grated Parmesan, 1 table-spoon of oil, the bread and milk mush, 1 teaspoon of salt, and the pepper. Mix everything thoroughly but gently by hand.

3. Gently, without squeezing, shape the mixture into small round balls about 1 inch in diameter. Roll the meatballs lightly in the bread crumbs.

4. Choose a skillet, large enough to hold all the meatballs in a single layer, with a cover. Pour in oil until it is ¼ inch deep. Turn on the heat to medium high, and when the oil is quite hot slip in the meatballs. (Sliding them in with a broad spatula is a good way of doing it. Dropping them in will splatter hot oil over you and your kitchen floor.) Brown the meatballs on all sides, turning them carefully so that they don't break up or stick to the pan.

5. When well browned turn off the heat, tip the pan slightly, and remove as much of the fat that floats to the surface as you can with a spoon. Turn on the heat to medium, add the chopped tomatoes with their juice and ¼ teaspoon of salt, and turn the meatballs over once or twice with care, so that they don't break up. Cover the skillet and cook until the tomato has thickened into sauce, about 25 minutes. While cooking, turn the meatballs over from time to time, and taste for salt.

NOTE
The meatballs can be prepared entirely ahead of time and refrigerated for several days.

MENU SUGGESTIONS

A Creamy Potato Soup with Carrots and Celery (page 55), Potato and Onion Soup (page 56), Rice and Celery Soup (page 59), or Escarole and Rice Soup (page 60) would be a good first course here. For vegetables serve Sautéed Peas with Prosciutto, Florentine Style (page 368), or any of the fried vegetables (pages 334, 345, 364, and 377).

MEAT LOAF BRAISED IN WHITE WINE WITH DRIED WILD MUSHROOMS

Polpettone alla toscana

This juicy and beautifully flavored meat loaf is from Tuscany, whose Chianina beef is the best in Italy. It should be made with a fine, lean cut of beef, all of whose fat has been removed before chopping. The loaf should be firmly packed, not loose and crumbly, so that when it is cooked it can be cut into thin, elegant, compact slices.

For 4 to 5 persons

1 ounce imported dried wild mushrooms
1 pound lean beef, ground
A 2-by-2-inch square piece good-quality white bread, crust removed
1 tablespoon milk
1 tablespoon finely chopped yellow onion
2 teaspoons salt
Freshly ground pepper, about 6 twists of the mill
2 tablespoons chopped prosciutto, or *pancetta*, or *mortadella*, or if you really can't obtain any of these, unsmoked ham

⅓ cup freshly grated Parmesan cheese
¼ teaspoon finely chopped garlic
1 egg yolk
¾ cup fine, dry unflavored bread crumbs, spread on a platter or waxed paper
1 tablespoon butter
2 tablespoons vegetable oil
⅓ cup dry white wine
2 tablespoons tomato paste

1. Put the dried mushrooms in a small bowl or large tumbler with 1 cup of lukewarm water. Let them soak at least 20 minutes.

2. Put the chopped meat in a bowl, loosening it up with a fork.

3. Put the bread and milk in a small pan. Over medium heat, mash it with a fork until it is creamy. Add it to the meat in the bowl, along with the chopped onion, salt, pepper, chopped prosciutto, grated cheese, and chopped garlic. Mix gently but thoroughly by hand until all the ingredients have been incorporated into the meat. Add the egg yolk, mixing it into the other ingredients. Shape the meat into a single, firmly packed ball. Place the ball of meat on any flat surface, a cutting block or large platter, and roll it into a compact salami-like loaf about 2½ inches thick. Tap it with the palm of your hand to drive out any air bubbles. Roll the loaf in the bread crumbs until it is evenly coated.

4. Drain the mushrooms, reserving the water in which they have soaked. (Remember that they should have soaked at least 20 minutes.) Strain the dark liquid through a fine sieve lined with paper towels and set aside. Rinse the mushrooms in several changes of clean, cold water. Chop them roughly and set aside.

5. Choose a heavy-bottomed, preferably oval casserole, just large enough for the meat. Over medium heat, heat all the butter and oil. When the butter foam subsides, add the meat loaf and brown it well on all sides, handling the meat carefully at all times lest the loaf break up.

6. When the meat has been evenly browned, add the wine and raise the heat to medium high. Boil the wine briskly until it is reduced by half. Turn the loaf carefully once or twice.

7. Turn the heat down to medium low and add the chopped mushrooms. Warm up the strained mushroom liquid in a small pan and stir the tomato paste into it. When the tomato paste is thoroughly diluted, add to the meat. Cover and cook at a steady simmer, turning and basting the meat once or twice. After 30 minutes, set the cover slightly askew and cook for another 30 minutes, turning the meat at least once.

8. Transfer the meat loaf to a cutting board and allow to settle for a few minutes before cutting into slices about ⅜ inch thick. Meanwhile, if the sauce in the pot is a little too thin, boil it rapidly, uncovered, over high heat until it is

sufficiently concentrated. Spoon a little bit of sauce over the bottom of a warm serving platter, arrange the meat loaf slices in the platter, partly overlapping, then pour the rest of the sauce over the meat.

MENU SUGGESTIONS

This deserves a robust Tuscan soup as a first course. Choose any of the chick-pea soups (pages 81–83), the Bean Soup with Parsley and Garlic (page 75), the Beans and Pasta Soup (page 76) or Red Cabbage Soup (page 78). Also suitable are Baked Semolina Gnocchi (page 187) or Risotto with Parmesan Cheese (page 171). For a vegetable, accompany with Fried Finocchio (page 364), Zucchini Fried in Flour-and-Water Batter (page 377), or Crisp-Fried Whole Artichokes (page 332).

VEAL

Vitello

Italy's finest veal comes from entirely milk-fed calves less than three months old. The meat is faintly rosy, nearly white, extraordinarily fine-grained, and almost perfectly lean.

Up to a few years ago, comparable veal was not marketed in this country. Only large, partially grazed or grain-fed animals whose flesh was deep pink and sometimes even lightly marbled with fat, were butchered. This is still a commonly distributed type of veal, but some markets and most of the better butchers now sell meat that approaches, even if it does not quite reach, the quality of northern Italian veal. If you buy it carefully, looking for meat that is very pale pink in color, you can attempt with confidence any of the delicious preparations to which veal lends itself.

PAN ROAST OF VEAL

Arrosto di vitello

If there is any dish in Italy that comes close to being a part of every family's repertory, it is probably this exquisitely simple pan-roasted veal. There is an infinite number of ways of roasting veal more elaborately, but there is none that produces more savory or succulent, tender meat. The success of this method lies in slow, watchful cooking, carefully regulating the amount of liquid so that there is just enough to keep the veal from drying out but not so much as to saturate it and dilute its flavor.

The best-looking roast comes from the top round, which some butchers will prepare for you. Rolled, boned shoulder of veal also makes an excellent and considerably less expensive roast.

For 6 persons

2 pounds roast of veal, boned

3 medium cloves garlic, lightly crushed with the handle of a knife and peeled

1 teaspoon rosemary leaves

Freshly ground pepper, about 8 to 10 twists of the mill OR ¼ teaspoon crushed peppercorns

2 tablespoons vegetable oil

2 tablespoons butter

1 teaspoon salt

⅔ cup dry white wine

1. If the roast is to be rolled, spread on it the garlic, rosemary, and pepper while it is flat, then roll and tie it securely. If it is a solid piece, pierce it at several points with a sharp, narrow-bladed knife and insert the rosemary and garlic. (You will season it with pepper later.) Tie it securely.

2. Choose a heavy-bottomed saucepan or casserole, preferably oval, just large enough for the meat. Heat the oil and butter over medium-high heat, and when the butter foam begins to subside add the meat and brown it well on all sides for about 15 minutes. Sprinkle the meat with salt and, if it was omitted before, pepper.

3. Cook just long enough to turn the roast once and then add the wine. As soon as the wine comes to a boil, lower the heat so that it is barely simmering, set the cover askew, and cook until the meat is tender when pierced by a fork, about 1½ to 2 hours. Turn the roast from time to time, and if the cooking liquid dries up add 1 or 2 tablespoons of warm water.

4. When the roast is done, transfer it to a cutting board. If there is no liquid left in the pan, put in ½ cup of water. Evaporate the water rapidly over high heat while loosening the cooking residues stuck to the pan. All together you should have about a spoonful of sauce per serving, so, if there is too much liquid left, concentrate it quickly over high heat. Cut the roast into slices no more than ¼ inch thick. Arrange them on a warm platter, spoon the sauce over them, and serve immediately.

MENU SUGGESTIONS

This roast really presents no problems over the choice of a first course. I would exclude none, except those with fish or with a very spicy sauce. Particularly nice with roast veal is the Tagliatelle with Bolognese Meat Sauce (page 122). Other pasta suggestions: Thin Spaghetti with Fresh Basil and Tomato (page 92) or Cappellacci Filled with Sweet Potatoes and Parsley (page 158). Most vegetables are also a suitable accompaniment. Sweet and Sour Onions (page 367) would be ideal. Other suggestions: Sautéed Peas with Prosciutto, Florentine Style (page 368), either of the sautéed mushrooms (pages 365–367), Sautéed Spinach (page 373), or any of the vegetables with butter and cheese, such as the carrots on page 351.

ROLLED STUFFED BREAST OF VEAL

Petto di vitello arrotolato

Roast boned breast of veal is an ideal way to enjoy the tenderness and delicate taste of veal without paying its usually steep price. It is an attractive-looking dish, and not at all complicated to prepare. If you are irredeemably opposed to dressing your own cuts of meat, you can have the butcher bone the breast for you. But be sure to take the bones home with you, as they make an excellent veal stock or addition to meat broth. Boning it yourself, however, is quite simple, it keeps the cost down, and it can even be enjoyable.

Lay the piece of breast on the work counter, ribs down, and, slipping the blade of a sharp knife between the meat and the bones, work carefully, detaching all the meat in a single, flat, uninterrupted piece. Remove all gristly bits and loose patches of skin, leaving just the single layer of skin that adheres to and covers the meat.

For 4 to 6 persons

1 piece breast of veal (4½ to 5 pounds with bones, about 1¾ pounds boned), bones removed as directed above
Salt
Freshly ground pepper, about 4 to 6 twists of the mill
¼ pound rolled *pancetta* (see note below)

2 whole cloves garlic, peeled
½ teaspoon dried rosemary leaves
2½ tablespoons butter
1 tablespoon vegetable oil
1 cup dry white wine, approximately

1. Remove the bones from the veal as directed above, then lay the boned meat flat. Sprinkle lightly with salt, add pepper, cover with a layer of sliced *pancetta*, place on it the two garlic cloves spaced apart, and sprinkle the rosemary leaves over all. Roll the meat up tightly, jelly-roll fashion, and fasten securely with string.

2. Heat the butter and oil over medium heat in a heavy-bottomed casserole just large enough to contain the veal. When the butter foam subsides, add the meat and brown well on all sides. Season lightly with salt, add enough wine to come one-third of the way up the side of the meat, and turn the heat up to high. Let the wine boil briskly for about 10 seconds, turning the meat in it, then turn the heat down to medium low and set the cover on, slightly askew. Cook until tender when pierced by a fork, about 1¾ to 2 hours. Turn and baste the meat from time to time. If it is sticking, add a couple of tablespoons of warm water.

3. Transfer the veal to a carving board. Allow it to settle for a minute or two and then cut into slices ⅜ inch thick. (As you slice, look for the garlic cloves and remove them.) Arrange the slices on a warm platter.

4. Tilt the casserole and remove all but 2 or 3 tablespoons of fat. Add 2 tablespoons of water, turn the heat on to high, and while the water evaporates scrape up and loosen any cooking residue stuck to the pan. Pour over the sliced veal and serve immediately.

NOTE

If *pancetta* is not available, prosciutto or cooked ham are acceptable, although not equally satisfactory, substitutes.

MENU SUGGESTIONS

The same general observations hold true for this roast that were made for the pan roast on page 243. In addition, one should bear in mind that this one has *pancetta* (or prosciutto), so it would be better to avoid any first course or vegetable accompaniment that is thickly laced with either *pancetta* or prosciutto. Particularly ideal first courses here would be Rice and Peas (page 57), Baked Rigatoni with Meat Sauce (page 105), Risotto with Parmesan Cheese (page 171), or either vegetable *risotto* (pages 179–180).

BRAISED VEAL SHANKS, MILAN STYLE

Ossobuco alla milanese (oss bus)

Ossobuco, oss bus in Milanese dialect, literally means "bone with a hole," or hollow bone. It is made with the shanks of milk-fed veal, very slowly braised in broth with vegetables and herbs, and it turns, when done, into one of the most tender morsels of meat one can eat. A properly cooked *ossobuco* needs no knife; it can be broken up with a fork. The hind shanks are better than the front ones for *ossobuco* because they are meatier and more tender. When the butcher prepares your shanks, have him saw off the two ends, which contain mostly bone and little meat (you can use them in a broth). Have him cut the shanks into pieces no more than 2 inches long, the size at which *ossobuco* cooks best, making sure he doesn't remove the skin enveloping the shanks. It helps to hold the *ossobuco* together and it has a delectable, creamy consistency when cooked.

For 6 persons

1 cup finely chopped yellow onion
⅔ cup finely chopped carrot
⅔ cup finely chopped celery
¼ cup butter
1 teaspoon finely chopped garlic
2 strips lemon peel
½ cup vegetable oil
2 shanks of veal, sawed into 8 pieces about 2 inches long, each securely tied around the middle
¾ cup all-purpose flour, spread on a plate or on waxed paper

1 cup dry white wine
1½ cups Homemade Meat Broth (page 10) OR canned beef broth, approximately
1½ cups canned Italian tomatoes coarsely chopped, with their juice
¼ teaspoon dried thyme
4 leaves fresh basil (optional)
2 bay leaves
2 or 3 sprigs parsley
Freshly ground pepper, about 6 twists of the mill
Salt, if necessary

1. Preheat the oven to 350°.

2. Choose a heavy casserole with a tight-fitting lid that is just large enough to contain the veal pieces later in a single layer. (If you do not have a casserole large enough for all the veal, use two small ones, dividing the chopped vegetables and butter in two equal parts, but adding 1 extra tablespoon of butter per casserole.) Put in the onion, carrot, celery, and butter and cook over medium heat for 8 to 10 minutes, until the vegetables soften and wilt. Add the chopped garlic and lemon peel at the end. Remove from the heat.

3. Heat the oil in a skillet over medium-high heat. Turn the trussed pieces of veal in the flour, shaking off any excess. When the oil is quite hot (test it with the corner of one of the pieces of veal: a moderate sizzle means the heat is just right), brown the veal on all sides. (Brown the veal as soon as it has been dipped in flour, otherwise the flour may dampen and the meat won't brown properly.) Stand the pieces of veal side by side on top of the vegetables in the casserole.

4. Tip the skillet and draw off nearly all the fat with a spoon. Add the wine and boil briskly for about 3 minutes, scraping up and loosening any browning residue stuck to the pan. Pour over the pieces of veal in the casserole.

5. In the same skillet, bring the broth to a simmer and pour into the casserole. Add the chopped tomatoes with their juice, the thyme, basil, bay leaves, parsley, pepper, and salt. (Hold off on salt until after cooking if you are using canned beef broth. It is sometimes very salty.) The broth should come up to the top of the veal pieces. If it does not, add more.

6. Bring the contents of the casserole to a simmer on top of the stove. Cover tightly and place in the lower third of the preheated oven. Cook for about 2 hours, carefully turning and basting the veal pieces every 20 minutes. When done, they should be very tender when pricked with a fork, and their sauce should be dense and creamy. (If, while the veal is still cooking, there is not enough liquid in the casserole, you may add up to ⅓ cup of warm water. If the reverse is true, and the sauce is too thin when the veal is done, remove the meat to a warm platter, place the uncovered casserole on top of the stove, and over high heat

briskly boil the sauce until it thickens.) Pour the sauce over the veal and serve piping hot.

NOTE

When transferring the veal pieces to the serving platter, carefully remove the trussing strings without breaking up the shanks.

GREMOLADA

The traditional recipe for *ossobuco* calls for a garnish of herbs, grated lemon peel, and garlic called *gremolada*, which is added to the veal shanks as they finish cooking. Tradition deserves respect, but art demands sincerity, and cooking is, above all else, an art. In the light of modern taste, I find that the *gremolada* overloads with unnecessary pungency a beautifully balanced and richly flavored dish. I never serve *ossobuco* with *gremolada*. If you feel, however, that you absolutely must try it for yourself, here are the recommended ingredients:

1 teaspoon grated lemon peel

¼ teaspoon very finely chopped garlic

1 tablespoon finely chopped parsley

Some old recipes also include sage and rosemary, but that, I think, is going too far. *Gremolada* is sprinkled over the veal shanks just as they finish cooking.

MENU SUGGESTIONS

The natural accompaniment for *ossobuco* is Risotto, Milan Style (page 173), as was noted under that recipe. It is not served separately, but together with *ossobuco*. If you would just as soon not have *risotto*, you can precede *ossobuco* with Potato Gnocchi (page 185) with Gorgonzola Sauce (page 126), or with Artichokes, Roman Style (page 326). *Ossobuco* can be served without any vegetables on the side, but if you are willing to make the effort, Sautéed Peas with Prosciutto, Florentine Style (page 368) make a very happy accompaniment. Follow *ossobuco* with a fine salad. An excellent one would be Jerusalem Artichoke and Spinach Salad (page 391).

BRAISED VEAL SHANKS, TRIESTE STYLE

Lo "schinco"

This is the same cut that in Milan is sawed into 2-inch pieces and called *ossobuco*. In Trieste the shanks are cooked whole and flavored with anchovies, which give the dish a decidedly different texture and character from *ossobuco*, although still every bit as tender. It is served whole, in all its magnificence, and carved at the table.

As in *ossobuco*, the hind shanks are to be preferred because they are more tender. Have the butcher saw off the two joints at the end where there is no meat.

For 6 persons

½ cup chopped yellow onion
3 tablespoons olive oil
3 tablespoons butter
2 veal shanks
2 cloves garlic, crushed lightly with a knife handle and peeled
1 teaspoon salt

Freshly ground pepper, about 6 twists of the mill
⅓ cup dry white wine
4 large or 6 medium flat anchovy fillets
1½ cups Homemade Meat Broth (page 10) OR ½ cup canned beef broth mixed with 1 cup water

1. Preheat the oven to 350°.
2. Choose a heavy casserole, preferably oval, just large enough for the shanks. Put in the onion with the oil and butter, and sauté over medium heat until pale gold.
3. Add the shanks, garlic, salt, pepper, and wine. Simmer the wine for about 1 minute, turning the shanks once or twice. Add the anchovies and the broth, cover, and bring to a boil. Transfer the casserole to the preheated oven and cook for 2 hours, or until the meat is extremely tender. (It should come easily off the bone.) Turn and baste the shanks every 20 minutes. (While the meat is cooking, if you find that the cooking liquids have dried up, you may add ⅓ cup warm water. If, on the contrary, the meat is done but

the cooking juices are too thin, return to the stove, uncover, turn on the heat to high and boil until the juices are concentrated.)

NOTE

This dish can be prepared entirely ahead of time, refrigerated, and reheated like *ossobuco*.

MENU SUGGESTIONS

Another specialty of Trieste is Beans and Sauerkraut Soup (page 72), which makes an ideal choice for a first course here. Also excellent would be Potato Gnocchi (page 185) with Gorgonzola Sauce (page 126) or Risotto with Parmesan Cheese (page 171). Any of the fried vegetables, such as Zucchini Fried in Flour and Water Batter (page 377) or Fried Whole Artichokes (page 322), is a suitable accompaniment, and so is Sweet and Sour Onions (page 367).

SCALOPPINE

The perfect *scaloppina* is cut across the grain from the top round. It is cut a shade more than ¼ inch thick and flattened to a shade less than ¼ inch. It is a solid slice of meat without any muscle separations. The problem lies in finding a butcher to cut it. I have discussed this with many American butchers, and I know exactly the answer yours will give you. With varying degrees of politeness it will be, "That is not the way we do it." One solution is to allow the butcher to cut a thin slice across the entire leg, which you can then divide into its separate muscles. This, however, will give you *scaloppine* of uneven texture and, while acceptable, will not be wholly satisfactory. A better alternative is to look for the kind of butcher who is willing to cooperate with you, and give you what you want—at a price. It may be expensive, but it will save you much heartache.

Once you have found this paragon, make sure not only

that he cuts the *scaloppine* from a single muscle but also that he cuts them across the grain. If *scaloppine* are cut any other way, the muscle fibers will contract in the cooking, producing a wavy, shrunken, tough slice of meat.

SAUTÉED VEAL SCALOPPINE WITH MARSALA

Scaloppine di vitello al Marsala

For 4 persons

3 tablespoons vegetable oil
1 pound veal *scaloppine*, very thinly sliced and pounded flat
¾ cup all-purpose flour, spread on a dinner plate or waxed paper

½ teaspoon salt
Freshly ground pepper, 5 to 6 twists of the mill
½ cup dry Marsala
3 tablespoons butter

1. Heat the oil over medium-high heat in a heavy skillet.

2. Dip the veal *scaloppine* in flour, coating them on both sides and shaking off any excess. When the oil is quite hot slip the *scaloppine* into the pan and quickly brown them on both sides, which should take less than a minute for each side if the oil is hot enough. (If you can't get all of them into your skillet at one time, do them a few at a time but dip them in flour only as you are ready to brown them, otherwise the flour will get soggy and the *scaloppine* won't brown properly.) Transfer the browned meat to a warm platter and season with salt and pepper.

3. Tip the skillet and draw off most of the fat with a spoon. Turn the heat on to high, add the Marsala, and boil briskly for less than a minute, scraping up and loosening any cooking residue stuck to the pan. Add the butter and any juices that may have been thrown off by the *scaloppine* in the platter. When the sauce thickens, turn the heat down to low and add the *scaloppine*, turning them and basting them with sauce once or twice. Transfer meat and sauce to a warm platter and serve immediately.

An elegant first course would be Italian Pancakes Filled with Spinach (page 167), Meat-Stuffed Pasta Rolls (page 141), or Yellow and Green Noodles with Cream, Ham, and Mushroom Sauce (page 124). Risotto with Parmesan Cheese (page 171) or either vegetable *risotto* (pages 171–181) would also be a good choice. The vegetable: Sautéed Green Beans with Butter and Cheese (page 348) or Sautéed Finocchio with Butter and Cheese (page 362).

SAUTÉED VEAL SCALOPPINE WITH LEMON SAUCE

Scaloppine di vitello al limone

For 4 persons

2 tablespoons vegetable oil
¼ cup butter
1 pound veal *scaloppine*, thinly sliced and pounded flat
¾ cup all-purpose flour, spread on a dish or on waxed paper

Salt and freshly ground pepper to taste
2 tablespoons lemon juice
2 tablespoons finely chopped parsley
½ lemon, thinly sliced

1. Heat the oil and 2 tablespoons of the butter in a skillet, over medium-high heat. (It should be quite hot. Thinly sliced veal must cook quickly or it will become leathery.)

2. Dip both sides of the *scaloppine* in flour and shake off the excess. Slip the *scaloppine*, no more than will fit comfortably in the skillet at one time, into the pan. If the oil is hot enough the meat should sizzle.

3. Cook the *scaloppine* until they are lightly browned on one side, then turn and brown the other side. (If they are very thin they should be completely cooked in about 1 minute.) When done, transfer to a warm platter and season with salt and pepper.

4. Off the heat, add the lemon juice to the skillet, scraping loose the cooking residue. Swirl in the remaining 2

tablespoons of butter. Add the parsley, stirring it into the sauce.

5. Add the *scaloppine*, turning them in the sauce. Turn on the heat to medium very briefly, just long enough to warm up the sauce and *scaloppine* together—but do not overdo it, because the *scaloppine* are already cooked.

6. Transfer the *scaloppine* to a warm platter, pour the sauce over them, garnish with the lemon slices, and serve immediately.

MENU SUGGESTIONS

These exquisite *scaloppine* should be preceded by a first course that has both delicacy and character. It could be spaghetti with Tomato Sauce III (page 90), Fettuccine Tossed in Cream and Butter (page 123), Tortelloni Filled with Swiss Chard (page 154), with either Butter and Cheese (page 157) or Tomato and Cream Sauce (page 153), Risotto with Asparagus (page 179), Rice and Peas (page 57), or Spinach and Ricotta Gnocchi (page 189), with either of the two sauces recommended. Some of the vegetables that can accompany the *scaloppine* are Fried Artichoke Wedges (page 334), Gratinéed Jerusalem Artichokes (page 340), Sautéed Green Beans with Butter and Cheese (page 348), Cauliflower Gratinéed with Butter and Cheese (page 353), and Zucchini Fried in Flour and Water Batter (page 377).

VEAL SCALOPPINE WITH TOMATOES

Scaloppine di vitello alla pizzaiola

For 4 persons

2½ tablespoons vegetable oil

3 cloves garlic, peeled

1 pound veal *scaloppine*, very thinly sliced and pounded flat

¾ cup all-purpose flour, spread on a dinner plate or waxed paper

Salt

Freshly ground pepper, 4 to 5 twists of the mill

⅓ cup white wine

3 teaspoons tomato paste diluted in ½ cup warm water

1 tablespoon butter

½ teaspoon orégano

2 tablespoons capers

1. In a heavy-bottomed skillet heat the oil over high heat and sauté the garlic cloves. When they are browned, remove them.

2. Dip both sides of the veal *scaloppine* in the flour, shake off the excess, and sauté very rapidly on both sides in the hot oil. (Do not overcook. It is sufficient to brown them lightly, which should take a minute or less each side. And never dip the *scaloppine* in flour until you are just ready to cook them. If you do it ahead of time the flour becomes damp and they won't brown properly.) Transfer the *scaloppine* to a warm platter and season with salt and pepper.

3. Tip the skillet and draw off most of the fat with a spoon. Turn on the heat to moderately high, add the wine, and scrape up and loosen the cooking residue in the pan. Then add the diluted tomato paste, stir, add the butter, stir, and continue cooking for a few minutes, until the liquids thicken into sauce. Add the orégano and the capers, stirring them into the sauce. Cook for another minute, then add the sautéed *scaloppine*, turning them quickly once or twice in the sauce. Transfer to a warm platter, pouring the sauce over the veal, and serve immediately.

MENU SUGGESTIONS

This is a zesty but amiable second course that can follow practically any soup or *risotto* and any pasta that does not carry a cream-based sauce or a tomato sauce. It is ideally accompanied by green vegetables sautéed in oil such as the Sautéed Spinach on page 373 or the Finocchio Braised in Olive Oil on page 363.

VEAL ROLLS IN TOMATO SAUCE

Rollatini di vitello al pomodoro

For 4 persons

1 pound veal *scaloppine*, very thinly sliced and pounded flat	2 tablespoons vegetable oil
¼ pound rolled *pancetta*, sliced very thin	Salt to taste
5 tablespoons freshly grated Parmesan cheese	Freshly ground pepper, about 4 twists of the mill
¼ cup butter	½ cup dry white wine
	1 tablespoon tomato paste with just enough warm water to dilute it

1. If the *scaloppine* are unusually large, cut them down to about 5 inches in length and 3½ to 4 inches in width. (If some pieces are irregular it doesn't really matter; it is better to use them than to waste them.) Over each *scaloppina* lay enough *pancetta* to cover. Sprinkle with grated cheese and roll up into a tight, compact roll. Fasten each roll with one or two toothpicks. Insert the toothpicks not across the roll, but into it along the length, so that the roll can turn in the pan.

2. In a heavy skillet, heat up 3 tablespoons of butter and all the oil over medium-high heat. When the butter foam subsides, add the veal rolls and brown quickly on all sides. Transfer the veal to a warm platter, remove the toothpicks, and season with salt and pepper.

3. Add the wine to the skillet, turn the heat to high, and boil briskly for about 2 minutes, scraping up and loosening any browning residue stuck to the pan. Add the diluted tomato paste, stir, turn the heat down to medium, and cook for several minutes, until the tomato separates from the cooking fat. Return the veal rolls to the skillet and warm them up for a minute, turning them in the sauce. Off heat, swirl in the remaining tablespoon of butter. Transfer to a very warm serving platter and serve without delay.

NOTE

This dish can be prepared entirely ahead of time and refrigerated for a few days in its sauce. When making ahead of time, do not remove the toothpicks at the end of Step 2. You will need them to hold the veal rolls together while they warm up.

To reheat, remove the meat from the sauce and allow time to return to room temperature, meanwhile preheating the oven to 325°. Add 1 tablespoon of water to the sauce and bring it to a simmer on the stove. Return the meat to the pan, cover, and warm up in the oven. Turn the rolls once or twice while reheating.

Rollatini take some time to heat up inside. They must be hot through and through before serving. Remove from the oven when they feel quite hot at the touch of a finger.

MENU SUGGESTIONS

First course: Tortelloni with Butter and Cheese (page 157), Italian Pancakes Filled with Spinach (page 167), Trenette with Potatoes and Pesto (page 135), or Rice and Peas (page 57). Choose white vegetables such as Gratinéed Jerusalem Artichokes (page 340), Fried Finocchio (page 364), or Braised and Gratinéed Celery with Parmesan Cheese (page 354).

LITTLE VEAL "BUNDLES" WITH ANCHOVIES AND CHEESE

Fagottini di vitello leccabaffi

These veal "bundles" are made of very thin *scaloppine* coated with a sauce of anchovies and tomato and a layer of cheese. The cheese should be bland to balance the pungency of the anchovies. The *scaloppine* are then rolled and tightly trussed up and cooked very rapidly over high heat, first with butter, then with a little Marsala.

For 6 persons

5 tablespoons butter
8 large or 10 medium flat anchovy fillets
¼ cup chopped parsley
6 tablespoons canned Italian tomatoes, drained and seeds removed
Freshly ground pepper, about 12 twists of the mill
1½ pounds veal *scaloppine*, very thinly sliced and pounded flat
½ teaspoon salt

8 ounces mozzarella, preferably smoked mozzarella, or Bel Paese cheese, cut into slices ⅛ inch thick or grated on the largest holes of the grater
½ cup all-purpose flour, spread on a dish or on waxed paper
1 cup dry Marsala

1. Put 2 tablespoons of the butter and all the anchovies in a very small saucepan, and, over very low heat, mash the anchovies to a pulp with a fork.

2. Add the chopped parsley, the tomatoes, and the pepper, turn the heat up to medium, and cook, stirring frequently, until the tomato thickens into sauce.

3. Lay the veal *scaloppine* flat, sprinkle them with salt, spread the sauce over them, and cover, except for a ¼-inch edge all around, with a layer of cheese. Roll up the *scaloppine*, push the ends in, and truss tightly, running the string both around the rolls and over the ends.

4. In a skillet that can later accommodate all the bundles without crowding, melt the remaining 3 tablespoons of butter over medium-high heat. When the butter foam begins to subside, roll the *scaloppine* lightly in the flour, shaking off the excess, and slide them into the skillet. Brown on all sides for about 2 minutes. (If a little cheese oozes out of the rolls, it is quite all right. It enriches the sauce, and the floating white shreds of cheese are very attractive.) When the meat is well browned, add the Marsala and turn the heat up to high. While the wine boils, turn the veal rolls, and scrape up any browning residue in the pan. Cook for 2 to 3 minutes, stirring constantly, until the wine and other cooking juices have turned into a creamy sauce. Transfer the meat and sauce to a warm platter and serve immediately.

This can be part of a meal that starts with a fish antipasto, such as Broiled Mussels and Clams on the Half Shell (page 31), Shrimps with Oil and Lemon (page 36), or Baked Oysters with Oil and Parsley (page 29). The first course can be Spaghetti with Garlic and Oil (page 98) or Trenette with Potatoes and Pesto (page 135). For vegetable: Fried Finocchio (page 364), Sautéed Jerusalem Artichokes (page 339), or Sautéed Diced Eggplant (page 360).

SAUTÉED BREADED VEAL CHOPS

Costolette alla milanese

A breaded veal chop *alla milanese* is, at its best, the most perfect thing that one can do with veal. When skillfully done, the tender, juicy eye of the chop is enveloped by a delectable crust, very thin and very crisp. It is cooked entirely in butter, and the trick one must learn is to keep the butter hot enough long enough to cook the meat all the way through, but not so hot that it will burn.

The greatest problem we have in doing this dish is that of getting the right kind of chop. The only correct cut is the rib chop. In Italy, where veal comes from a very small animal, each rib yields a single chop, which is flattened to make it broad and thin. Only the eye is left on the bone, and a sufficient length of the rib is left on to give the appearance of a handle. American veal is much larger and the meat on a single rib is too thick for one chop. This means that out of one rib you must have the butcher prepare two chops, one with the handle, one without. The tail of the chop should be trimmed away, leaving a clean, round eye. Since you must pay for the trimmings, take them home and use them for broth. The chops should be pounded flat, but, before pounding the one with the bone, the butcher must knock off the corner where the rib meets the backbone.

It will be a rather expensive cut of meat, and it won't be quite a Milanese-looking chop, but you will have a beautiful piece of veal. If you give its preparation the necessary care, the result should amply reward your efforts and expense.

For 6 persons

3 veal rib chops, divided
    into 6 chops and
    pounded flat
2 eggs, lightly beaten
    with 1 teaspoon salt,
    in a soup plate

1½ cups fine, dry
    unflavored bread
    crumbs, spread on a
    dish or on waxed
    paper
6 tablespoons butter

1. Dip each chop in the beaten eggs, coating both sides, and letting excess egg flow back into the plate as you pull the chop away. Dredge the chops in the bread crumbs, pressing the crumbs with your hands into the surface of both sides of the chops.

2. Choose a skillet that can later contain the chops in a single layer. Put in the butter and melt it over medium-low heat. When the butter foam subsides, slip the chops into the skillet. Cook for 3 minutes on one side, until a dark golden crust has formed, then turn and cook for another 3 minutes on the other side, watching the butter to make sure it does not burn and adjusting the heat if necessary. When done, transfer the chops to a warm platter and serve immediately.

MENU SUGGESTIONS

Breaded veal chops will fit with complete assurance into any menu, whether plain and sturdy or delicately balanced. They make an especially nice second course when preceded by one of the fine homemade pastas, such as Tortellini Filled with Parsley and Ricotta (page 152) with Tomato and Cream Sauce (page 153), or by Risotto with Zucchini (page 180) or Risotto with Asparagus (page 179). Potato Gnocchi (page 185) or Spinach and Ricotta Gnocchi (page 189) are also excellent choices for the first course. But you can just as easily serve a substantial soup, such as Beans and Pasta Soup (page 76), or macaroni pasta, such as Fusilli with Creamy Zucchini and Basil Sauce (page 101).

There is simply no vegetable that will not go with these chops. The tastiest accompaniment is Fried Eggplant (page 358) combined with Oven-Browned Tomatoes (page 374). Other good pairings are Sautéed Mushrooms with Garlic and Parsley (page 365), Sweet and Sour Onions (page 367),

Sautéed Peas with Prosciutto, Florentine Style (page 368), and Sautéed Green Beans with Butter and Cheese (page 348).

BREADED VEAL CUTLETS, MILAN STYLE

Cotolette alla milanese

In Italian cooking, *cotolette*, or cutlets, are not so much the cut of meat as the method by which it is cooked. A *cotoletta* is often a slice of veal, cut like a *scaloppina*, but it can also be a slice of turkey or chicken breast, or beef, or even eggplant. It is dipped in beaten egg, dredged in bread crumbs, and fried in very hot oil.

For 6 persons

1½ pounds veal *scaloppine*, sliced ¼ inch thick and pounded flat

2 whole eggs, lightly beaten, in a soup plate

2 cups fine, dry unflavored bread crumbs, spread on a

dinner plate or on waxed paper

Vegetable oil and butter, just enough to come ⅜ inch up the side of the skillet (see note below)

¾ teaspoon salt

Lemon wedges

1. Dip each veal slice very lightly on both sides in the eggs and then into the bread crumbs. As you turn the cutlet over in the bread crumbs, tap it into the bread crumbs with the palm of your hand to get a better adherence of the crumbs to the meat. Shake off all excess loose crumbs and pile the breaded slices on a dish until you are ready to cook them. (You may prepare them up to this point a few hours ahead of time.)

2. Heat the oil and butter in a heavy skillet over medium-high heat. (To make sure the fat is hot enough, test it with the end of a cutlet. If it sizzles, it's ready.) Cook as many cutlets at one time as will fit in a single layer in the skillet. When they brown on one side, quickly turn them

over. Remove them just as soon as they are brown and crisp
on both sides, which will be very quickly. (Do not cook any
longer than it takes to brown them or the meat will become
dry.) Place the browned cutlets on paper towels, which will
absorb any excess fat, and sprinkle with salt. Serve piping
hot with lemon wedges, or with Red Sauce (page 27).

NOTE

The quantity of cooking fat obviously depends upon the size
of the pan, but the proportions are always 2 parts of vegetable oil to 1 part of butter.

MENU SUGGESTIONS

Follow the ones given for Sautéed Breaded Veal Chops
(previous page), but avoid tomatoes in the first course or
vegetable if you are using the Red Sauce.

SAUTÉED VEAL CHOPS WITH SAGE
AND WHITE WINE

Nodini di vitello alla salvia

For 4 persons

3 tablespoons vegetable oil	12 dried sage leaves
4 veal loin chops, cut ¾ inch thick	½ teaspoon salt
¾ cup all-purpose flour, spread on a dinner plate or on waxed paper	Freshly gound pepper, about 4 twists of the mill
	⅓ cup dry white wine
	2 tablespoons butter

1. Heat the oil in a heavy-bottomed skillet over medium-
high heat.
2. Turn the chops over in the flour, coating both sides,
and shake off any excess. (Do not coat meat with flour until
you are ready to sauté it. The flour becomes damp and the
meat does not brown properly.)
3. Slip the chops and the sage into the hot oil. Cook for

about 8 to 10 minutes all together, turning the chops two or three times so that they cook evenly on both sides. (Veal shouldn't cook too long or it will become dry. The meat is done when it is rosy pink on the inside when cut.) When cooked, remove to a warm platter and add salt and pepper.

4. Tilt the skillet and draw away most of the fat with a spoon. Add the wine and turn the heat to high. Boil rapidly until the liquid has almost completely evaporated and become a little syrupy. While boiling, loosen any cooking residue in the pan and add what juice the chops may have thrown off in the platter. When the wine has almost completely evaporated and thickened, turn the heat to very low and mix in the butter. Return the chops to the skillet for a few moments, turning them over in the sauce. Transfer them to a warm serving platter, pour the remainder of the sauce over them, and serve immediately.

MENU SUGGESTIONS

First course: Baked Rigatoni with Meat Sauce (page 105), Meat-Stuffed Pasta Rolls (page 141), Baked Green Lasagne with Meat Sauce (page 136), Homemade Macaroni (page 160) with Meat Sauce, Bolognese Style (page 120), Spinach and Ricotta Gnocchi (page 189) or Italian Pancakes Filled with Spinach (page 167). A lovely vegetable accompaniment would be Braised Artichokes and Peas (page 335), Asparagus with Parmesan Cheese (page 343), or the Baked Stuffed Zucchini Boats (page 380).

VEAL STEW WITH SAGE AND WHITE WINE

Spezzatino di vitello alla salvia

The preferred cuts for Italian veal stew are the shoulder and the shanks. Avoid the round, which makes a dry and uninteresting stew.

For 4 persons

2 tablespoons finely
   chopped shallots or
   yellow onion
2 tablespoons vegetable
   oil
2 tablespoons butter
1½ pounds shank or
   shoulder of veal,
   boned and rather
   lean, cut into 1-inch
   cubes

¾ cup all-purpose flour,
   spread on a dinner
   plate or on waxed
   paper
18 medium dried sage
   leaves
⅔ cup dry white wine
½ teaspoon salt
Freshly ground pepper,
   about 4 twists of the
   mill

1. In a deep skillet, sauté the shallots in the oil and butter over medium-high heat until translucent but not browned.

2. Dip the pieces of veal in the flour, coating them on all sides and shaking off excess flour. Add to the skillet, together with the sage leaves, and brown well on all sides. (If all the meat won't fit into the skillet at one time you can brown a few pieces at a time, but dip them in the flour only when you are ready to put them in the skillet or the flour coating will get soggy and the meat won't brown properly.) Transfer the meat to a warm platter when browned.

3. When all the meat has been browned, turn up the heat to high, add the wine to the skillet, and boil briskly for about 30 seconds, scraping up and loosening any cooking residue in the pan. Turn the heat down to medium and add the browned meat, salt, and pepper. Cover and cook gently for about 1 hour, turning and basting the meat from time to time, adding a little warm water if necessary. The meat is done when it is tender at the pricking of a fork. Serve immediately.

NOTE

This stew can be prepared entirely ahead of time and refrigerated for several days in a Pyrex or enamelware container with a cover. It can then be warmed up, covered, in the same container, in a 325° preheated oven. Add 2 tablespoons of water when warming it up.

Follow the first-course suggestion for Sautéed Veal Chops with Sage and White Wine (page 261). Also indicated would be Risotto with Asparagus (page 179), or Risotto with Zucchini (page 185). An ideal vegetable is Sautéed Mushrooms with Heavy Cream (page 366), which, after cooking, can be mixed with the veal stew. The combination also makes a fine hot buffet dish.

VEAL STEW WITH TOMATOES AND PEAS

Spezzatino di vitello coi piselli

For 4 persons

2 tablespoons chopped shallots or yellow onion	Freshly ground pepper, about 6 twists of the mill
3 tablespoons vegetable oil	1 cup canned Italian tomatoes, coarsely chopped, with their juice
2 tablespoons butter	
1½ pounds boneless veal for stewing (see preceding recipe), cut into 1½-inch cubes	2 pounds fresh peas (unshelled weight) or 1 ten-ounce package frozen small peas, thawed
2 teaspoons salt	

1. Put the chopped shallots in a heavy casserole with the oil and butter and sauté over medium heat until pale gold.

2. Put in the pieces of veal, browning them well on all sides. (There are two points to bear in mind when browning the meat: it should be thoroughly dry, and it should not be crowded in the pot. If it does not all fit in at once, do a few pieces at a time. Remove the first batch as it is done and then add the others.)

3. Return all the meat to the pot, add 2 teaspoons salt, the pepper, and the chopped tomatoes with their juice. When the tomatoes begin to boil, cover the pot and adjust

the heat so that the tomatoes are barely simmering. Cook until the veal is very tender when pricked with a fork, as little as 1 hour from the time you've covered the pot if it is very young, fine veal. (More often, however, it will be closer to 1½ hours. Actually, a little extra slow cooking doesn't do it any harm.)

4. The peas must be added to the stew before it is completely cooked. If you are using fresh peas, calculate 15 or more minutes' cooking time for the peas, depending on their size and freshness. Add them when the meat has begun to turn tender but is still rather firm. If you are using thawed frozen peas, add them when the veal is tender nearly through and through. Frozen peas take only about 5 minutes or less to cook. Taste and correct for salt.

NOTE
The stew can be prepared completely ahead of time and refrigerated for several days. Reheat over medium heat when ready to serve.

MENU SUGGESTIONS

A perfect choice for the first course is Risotto with Parmesan Cheese (page 171). Also to be recommended is Rice with Fresh Basil and Mozzarella Cheese (page 183). If the occasion seems to call for a soup, try either Potato and Onion Soup (page 56) or Passatelli (page 67). No vegetable is required.

COLD SLICED VEAL WITH TUNA SAUCE

Vitello tonnato

This is one of the loveliest and most versatile of all cold dishes. It is an ideal second course for a summer menu, a beautiful antipasto for an elegant dinner, a very successful party dish for small or large buffets. It requires quite some time and patience in the preparation, but, since it must be prepared at least 24 hours in advance, you can set your own pace and make it at your convenience.

Vitello tonnato is common to both Lombardy and Piedmont, and there are many ways of making it. Most recipes call for braising the veal either partly or wholly in white wine. You may try it if you like. I find it gives the dish a tarter flavor than it really needs.

In this recipe, do not under any circumstances use prepared, commercial mayonnaise.

Veal tends to be dry. To keep it tender and juicy, cook it in just enough water to cover (the method indicated below—put the meat in, add water to just cover, and then remove the meat—is the simplest way to gauge the exact amount); add veal to its cooking liquid only when the liquid is boiling; *never* add salt to the liquid; allow the meat to cool in its own broth.

For 6 to 8 persons

2 to 2½ pounds lean, boneless veal roast, preferably top round, firmly tied
1 medium carrot
1 stalk celery, without leaves
1 medium yellow onion
4 sprigs parsley
1 bay leaf

THE TUNA SAUCE:

Mayonnaise (page 23), made with 2 egg yolks, 1¼ cups olive oil, 2 to 3 tablespoons lemon juice, ¼ teaspoon salt
1 seven-ounce can Italian tuna in olive oil
5 flat anchovy fillets
1¼ cups olive oil
3 tablespoons lemon juice
3 tablespoons tiny capers
Salt, if necessary

1. In a pot just large enough to contain the veal, put in the veal, the carrot, celery, onion, parsley, bay leaf, and just enough water to cover. Now *remove the veal and set aside*. Bring the water to a boil, add the meat, and when the water comes to a boil again, cover the pot, reduce the heat, and keep at a gentle simmer for 2 hours. (If you are using a larger piece of veal, cook proportionately longer.)

Remove the pot from the heat and allow the meat to cool in its broth.

2. Prepare the mayonnaise according to the recipe on page 23, remembering that all ingredients for the mayonnaise must be at room temperature.

3. In a blender mix the tuna, anchovies, olive oil, lemon juice, and the capers at high speed for a few seconds until they attain a creamy consistency. Remove the mixture from the blender jar and fold it carefully but thoroughly into the mayonnaise. Taste to see if any salt is required. (None may be necessary, depending upon how salty the anchovies and capers are.)

4. When the meat is quite cold, transfer it to a cutting board, remove the strings, and cut into thin and uniform slices.

5. Smear the bottom of a serving platter with some of the tuna sauce. Arrange the veal slices over this in a single layer, edge to edge. Cover the layer well with sauce. Lay more veal over this and cover again with sauce; set aside enough sauce to cover well the topmost layer. (The more layers you make the better. It prevents the veal from drying.)

6. Refrigerate for 24 hours, covered with plastic wrap. (It keeps beautifully for up to 2 weeks.) Before serving you may garnish it with lemon slices, olive slices, whole capers, and parsley leaves.

MENU SUGGESTIONS

If you are using this as a second course, precede it with Cold Vegetable Soup with Rice, Milan Style (page 65), Rice and Peas (page 57), or Trenette with Potatoes and Pesto (page 135). No vegetable, but follow it with a simple salad, such as Green Bean Salad (page 397).

As an introduction to a memorable meal, follow it with Molded Risotto with Parmesan Cheese and Chicken-Liver Sauce (page 172), and follow the *risotto* with Pan-Roasted Squab (page 308).

ROAST SPRING LAMB WITH WHITE WINE

Arrosto di agnello pasquale col vino bianco

In most of Italy, lamb is a seasonal dish. It is usually consumed at Eastertime, when it is around four months old. The following traditional Easter recipe from Emilia-Romagna is not quite as highly flavored as Hothouse Lamb, Roman Style (page 271), but it brings out all the tenderness and delicacy of spring lamb.

For 4 persons

1¾ to 2 pounds spring lamb, preferably shoulder, including some chops	½ teaspoon rosemary leaves
3 tablespoons vegetable oil	½ teaspoon salt
2 tablespoons butter	Freshly ground pepper, about 6 twists of the mill
3 whole cloves garlic, peeled	⅔ cup dry white wine

1. If the lamb is too large to fit into your largest saucepan in one piece, cut it in two or three parts. Wash in cold running water, and pat thoroughly dry with paper towels.

2. Heat the oil and the butter in the saucepan over medium-high heat. When the butter foam begins to subside, add the lamb, the garlic, and the rosemary. Brown the lamb well on all sides. (Make sure the garlic doesn't become too brown. If you see that it is darkening too fast, set it on top of the lamb.)

3. When the lamb is nicely browned, especially on the skin side, add salt, pepper, and all the white wine. Turn the heat up to high for a minute or less, enough to turn the lamb over twice. Cover the pan, turn the heat down to low, and cook the lamb at a very gentle simmer for 1½ or 2 hours, turning the lamb from time to time. (If you find that there is not enough cooking liquid in the pan and the meat is sticking to the bottom, add 2 or 3 tablespoons of warm water.)

4. The lamb is done when it feels very tender when

pierced by a fork and the meat begins to come away from the bone. Transfer the lamb to a warm serving platter. Tip the pan, drawing off with a spoon all but 1 or 2 tablespoons of fat. Add 2 tablespoons of water, raise the heat to high, and while the water evaporates scrape up and loosen all the cooking residue in the pan. Pour this over the lamb and serve immediately.

MENU SUGGESTIONS

As a first course, if you'd like to omit the pasta, you can serve Artichokes, Roman Style (page 326), Braised Artichokes with Mortadella Stuffing (page 331), or Fava Beans, Roman Style (page 346). If you are having pasta, these can be either antipasti or vegetable side dishes. For pasta, choose something robust, such as Bucatini with Pancetta, Tomatoes, and Hot Pepper (page 100), Homemade Pasta from Apulia (page 163) with Broccoli and Anchovy Sauce (page 164), Thin Spaghetti with Eggplant (page 94), Fusilli with Creamy Zucchini and Basil Sauce (page 101), or Baked Green Lasagne with Meat Sauce (page 136). Aside from the vegetables mentioned above, other suitable vegetables are Fried Finocchio (page 364) or Zucchini Fried in Flour-and-Water Batter (page 377).

CASSEROLE-ROASTED LAMB WITH JUNIPER BERRIES

Arrosto di agnello al ginepro

In this recipe the meat is simmered right from the start with the vegetables, wine, and flavorings. There is no browning and no liquid or cooking fat to add, because the meat supplies its own fat and juices as it cooks. There is practically nothing to do but watch the pot occasionally. Juniper berries, which are easily found at most spice counters, are absolutely essential to the full-bodied flavor of this dish. Most of the lamb commonly available throughout the year is mature lamb, and this method is particularly successful with it, because it transforms it into meat as tender as that of baby lamb or kid. Allow at least 3½ hours' cooking time.

For 4 persons

2½ pounds leg of lamb,
    preferably butt end,
    bone in
1 tablespoon chopped
    carrot
2 tablespoons chopped
    yellow onion
1 tablespoon chopped
    celery
1 cup dry white wine
2 cloves garlic, lightly
    crushed with a knife
    handle and peeled

½ teaspoon rosemary
    leaves
1½ teaspoons juniper
    berries
2 teaspoons salt
Freshly ground pepper,
    4 to 6 twists of the
    mill

1. Put all the ingredients into a heavy casserole. Cover and cook on top of the stove at low heat for 2 hours, turning the meat every 45 minutes.

2. At this point the lamb should have thrown off a considerable amount of liquid. Set the cover askew, and cook for another 1½ hours at slightly higher heat. The meat should now be very tender at the pricking of a fork. If there is still too much liquid, uncover completely, raise the heat to high, and boil it until it is a little more concentrated. At the end the meat must be a rich brown in color.

3. Off the heat, tilt the casserole and draw off as much of the fat as you can with a spoon. (You can use it as cooking fat for Diced Pan-Roasted Potatoes, page 387.) If you are not serving the roast immediately, do not degrease until after you have reheated it.

MENU SUGGESTIONS

This is the most highly flavored of the three lamb roasts and requires a first course that is interesting but not too aggressive. I suggest Vegetable Soup (page 63), the Molded Risotto with Parmesan Cheese and Chicken-Liver Sauce (page 172), Cappellacci Filled with Sweet Potatoes and Parsley (page 158), or Bean Soup with Parsley and Garlic (page 75). As a vegetable: Fried Cauliflower (page 354), Fried Asparagus (page 345), Sautéed Spinach (page 373), or Sautéed Broccoli with Garlic (page 350).

HOTHOUSE LAMB, ROMAN STYLE

Abbacchio alla cacciatora

Abbacchio is a very young, milk-fed lamb, taken when it is just one month old. Its flesh is nearly as pale as veal, and it is so delicate and tender that in texture it is almost closer to chicken than to lamb. In this recipe it is slowly pan roasted, and flavored with sage, rosemary, a faint amount of garlic, and anchovies. It is one of Rome's most celebrated specialties.

Such young lamb is never available in American markets, but some butchers here carry what they call hothouse lamb. It is two to three months old, somewhat older than *abbacchio*, but still entirely milk fed. If you find it, by all means try it. Cook it as directed here and you will come remarkably close to the taste of the best Roman *abbacchio*. If hothouse lamb is not available, don't give up. Any young lamb lends itself successfully to this recipe. What you should avoid is the coarser, stronger-tasting meat of mature lamb.

For 6 persons

2 tablespoons cooking fat, preferably lard
3 pounds shoulder and/or leg of very young lamb, boned and cut into 2-inch cubes
½ teaspoon salt
Freshly ground pepper, 6 to 8 twists of the mill
½ teaspoon chopped dried sage leaves
½ teaspoon finely chopped garlic
1 teaspoon chopped dried rosemary leaves
2 teaspoons all-purpose flour
½ cup vinegar
⅓ cup water
4 large anchovy fillets, chopped

1. In a saucepan, melt the lard over medium-high heat. Put in the lamb pieces and brown well on all sides.

2. Add the salt, pepper, sage, garlic, and rosemary and continue to cook briskly for another minute or so, long enough to turn all the pieces once.

3. Dust the lamb with flour, sifting it through a sieve. Continue cooking at lively heat, turning each piece once. The meat will have turned a rather dark color.

4. Add the vinegar and boil it briskly, turning up the heat, for 30 seconds. Add the water, cover the pan, lower the heat, and cook at a very gentle simmer for about 1 hour. (The exact cooking time depends entirely on the age of the lamb. When done it should be very tender at the pricking of a fork.) Turn the meat from time to time as it cooks. If there is not sufficient cooking liquid, add 2 to 3 tablespoons of water.

5. When the lamb is done, take 2 or 3 tablespoons of sauce from the pan and put it in a small bowl, together with the chopped anchovies. Mash the anchovies with a spoon or a pestle, then spoon over the lamb in the pan. Turn and baste the lamb with its sauce over very low heat for about 30 seconds. Transfer to a warm platter and serve immediately.

MENU SUGGESTIONS

First course: Baked Semolina Gnocchi (page 187), Sliced Pasta Roll with Spinach Filling (page 144), Spaghetti with Garlic and Oil (page 98), or Pappardelle with Chicken-Liver Sauce (page 130). Vegetable Crisp-Fried Whole Artichokes (page 332), Fava Beans, Roman Style (page 346), or Diced Pan-Roasted Potatoes (page 372).

BABY LAMB CHOPS FRIED IN PARMESAN CHEESE BATTER

Costolettine di agnello fritte

You will never know how succulent lamb chops can be until you've fried them in this egg-and-cheese batter. The crust, which is crisp and delicious, seals in all the sweetness and tenderness of young lamb. The younger the lamb you use, the sweeter and more delicate will be its flavor and texture in frying. But this recipe can be executed also with standard lamb. The chops must be no more than one rib thick. Have the butcher knock off the corner bone and remove the backbone, leaving just the rib. Ideally, he should flatten the eye of the chop for you, but as I've never found an American butcher willing to do this to lamb, avoid wrangling and do it yourself at home with a meat pounder or cleaver.

For 6 persons

12 single rib chops, partly boned and flattened as directed above

½ cup freshly grated Parmesan cheese, spread on a dish or on waxed paper

2 eggs, lightly beaten in a deep dish

1 cup fine, dry unflavored bread crumbs, spread on a dish or on waxed paper

Vegetable oil, enough to come ¼ inch up the side of the skillet

Salt

Freshly ground pepper, about 6 twists of the mill

1. Turn both sides of the chops in the Parmesan cheese, then give the chops a tap to shake off the excess. Dip them immediately into the beaten eggs, letting any excess egg flow back into the dish. Then turn the chops in the bread crumbs, coating both sides and tapping them again to shake off all excess. (You can prepare the chops up to this point as much as an hour ahead of time, or, if you refrigerate them, even 3 or 4 hours. If refrigerated, allow to return to room temperature before frying.)

2. Heat the oil in the skillet over medium heat until it is very hot. Fry as many chops at one time as will fit loosely in the skillet. As soon as they have formed a nice crust on one side, season with salt and pepper and turn them. Add salt and pepper to the other side. Transfer to a warm platter as soon as the second side has formed a crust and do the next batch. (If it is truly young lamb and cut very thin, it should take, altogether, 4 to 5 minutes to cook. If the lamb is a little older or the chops are a bit thick, it may take a few moments longer.) Serve piping hot.

Homemade pastas are ideal with these crisp, tender chops, but any soup, *risotto*, or macaroni will make a suitable first course, as long as it has no fish in it. Almost all vegetables are a suitable accompaniment, but particularly nice are Sautéed Peas with Prosciutto, Florentine Style (page 368), Fava Beans, Roman Style (page 346), the Celery and Potatoes Braised in Olive Oil (page 356), and Fried Zucchini with Vinegar (page 378).

PORK LOIN BRAISED IN MILK

Arrosto di maiale al latte

Whenever I teach this dish I am greeted by more or less polite skepticism, which usually turns to enthusiasm at the first taste. Pork cooked by this method turns out to be exceptionally tender and juicy. It is quite delicate in flavor because it loses all its fat and the milk, as such, disappears, to be replaced by clusters of delicious, nut-brown sauce.

For 6 persons

2 tablespoons butter	1 teaspoon salt
2 tablespoons vegetable oil	Freshly ground pepper, 3 or 4 twists of the mill
2 pounds pork loin in one piece, with some fat on it, securely tied	2½ cups milk

1. Heat the butter and oil over medium-high heat in a casserole large enough to just contain the pork. When the butter foam subsides add the meat, fat side facing down. Brown thoroughly on all sides, lowering the heat if the butter starts to turn dark brown.

2. Add the salt, pepper, and milk. (Add the milk slowly, otherwise it may boil over.) Shortly after the milk comes to a boil, turn the heat down to medium, cover, but not tightly, with the lid partly askew, and cook slowly for about 1½ to 2 hours, until the meat is easily pierced by a fork. Turn

and baste the meat from time to time, and, if necessary, add a little milk. By the time the meat is cooked the milk should have coagulated into small nut-brown clusters. If it is still pale in color, uncover the pot, raise the heat to high, and cook briskly until it darkens.

3. Remove the meat to a cutting board and allow to cool off slightly for a few minutes. Remove the trussing string, carve into slices ⅜ inch thick, and arrange them on a warm platter. Draw off most of the fat from the pot with a spoon and discard, being careful not to discard any of the coagulated milk clusters. Taste and correct for salt. (There may be as much as 1 to 1½ cups of fat to be removed.) Add 2 or 3 tablespoons of warm water, turn the heat to high, and boil away the water while scraping and loosening all the cooking residue in the pot. Spoon the sauce over the sliced pork and serve immediately.

MENU SUGGESTIONS

This is a Bolognese dish, and is often preceded by Tagliatelle with Bolognese Meat Sauce (page 122) or Baked Green Lasagne with Meat Sauce (page 136). If this appears to be too substantial, try the Baked Semolina Gnocchi (page 187), or an assortment of Italian cold cuts. As a vegetable Fried Artichoke Wedges (page 334) or Crisp-Fried Whole Artichokes (page 332) are excellent accompaniments.

ROAST PORK WITH BAY LEAVES

Arrosto di maiale all'alloro

For 6 persons

2 pounds boneless pork loin	1 teaspoon whole peppercorns
3 tablespoons butter	3 bay leaves, medium size
2 tablespoons vegetable oil	½ cup red wine vinegar
Salt	

1. Choose a good heavy pot, preferably enameled cast iron, just large enough to contain the meat, and provided with a close-fitting lid. Heat the butter and oil together at

medium-high heat. When the butter foam begins to subside, put in the meat and brown it well on all sides.

2. When the meat is well browned, salt it on all sides, then add the peppercorns, bay leaves, and vinegar. Turn up the heat for as long as it takes to scrape up all the cooking residue from the bottom. (Do not allow the vinegar to evaporate more than slightly.) Turn the heat down to low, cover the pot, and cook slowly for at least 2 hours, until a fork easily pierces the meat. (Check from time to time to make sure that the liquid in the pot has not completely dried up. If it has you can add, as required, 2 or 3 tablespoons of water.)

3. Place the meat on a cutting board and cut into slices ¼ to ⅜ inch thick. Arrange the slices, slightly overlapping, on a warm serving platter.

4. Tip the pot, removing most, but not all, the fat with a spoon. Remove the bay leaves and pour the sauce from the pot over the meat. (If there should be any cooking residue in the bottom of the pot, put in 2 tablespoons of water and scrape it loose over high heat. Add to the sauce.)

MENU SUGGESTIONS

This goes well with Escarole and Rice Soup (page 60), Vegetable Soup (page 63), Beans and Pasta Soup (page 76), or any of the chick-pea soups on pages 81–83. If you want a macaroni pasta, try Thin Spaghetti with Fresh Basil and Tomato Sauce (page 92), Penne with a Sauce of Tomatoes and Dried Wild Mushrooms (page 103) or Bucatini with Pancetta, Tomatoes, and Hot Pepper (page 100). Accompany with Sautéed Jerusalem Artichokes (page 339), Braised Artichokes and Leeks (page 336), or any of the finocchio dishes on pages 362–64

BOILED COTECHINO SAUSAGE WITH LENTILS

Cotechino con le lenticchie

Cotechino has always been a specialty of that section of Emilia called Romagna, but now it is also made in other Emilian provinces, Modena especially. It is a large, fresh pork sausage about 3 inches in diameter and 8 to 9 inches long. The name *cotechino* comes from *cotica*, the Italian word for pork rind, which is an essential ingredient in this sausage. It also contains meat from the shoulder, cheek, and neck, and it is seasoned with salt, pepper, nutmeg, and cloves. There are slight variations, of course, according to the maker. In the finest *cotechino* only the pork rind is ground; the meat is mashed in a special mortar. A skillfully made *cotechino* when properly cooked is exquisitely tender, with an almost creamy texture, and it is more delicate in taste than you might expect from any pork sausage. Unfortunately, many Italian pork butchers in this country make *cotechino* according to their own lights, and the result is a sausage drier and sharper than it should be. From time to time one does find a reasonably good *cotechino*, and it is well worth searching for. *Cotechino* with lentils makes a wonderful country dish for family and friends, and it is specially heartening on a cold winter day.

For 6 persons

1 *cotechino* sausage	1 cup lentils, rinsed in
1 tablespoon chopped	cold water and
yellow onion	drained
2 tablespoons vegetable	Salt
oil	Freshly ground pepper,
1 tablespoon chopped	4 twists of the mill
celery	

1. Let the *cotechino* soak overnight, or at least 4 hours, in abundant cold water.

2. Put the *cotechino* in a stockpot large enough to contain it comfortably. Add at least 3 quarts of cold water, cover,

and bring to a boil. Cook at a very slow boil for 2½ hours. (Do not prod it with a fork. You must not puncture the skin while it cooks.) When the *cotechino* is done, turn off the heat and allow it to rest in its cooking liquid for 30 minutes before serving. Do not remove it from its liquid until you are ready to slice it.

3. Start doing the lentils about 1½ hours after the *cotechino* has been cooking. Bring 1 quart of water to a simmer. Meanwhile, in a heavy-bottomed casserole, sauté the chopped onion, in the oil, over medium-high heat until pale gold in color. Add the chopped celery and sauté it for about 1 minute.

4. Add the lentils and stir until they are well coated with oil. Add enough simmering water to cover the lentils, turn the heat down to medium low so that the lentils cook at the gentlest simmer, cover the pot, and cook for 30 to 40 minutes, or until the lentils are tender. Add water from time to time so that the lentils are always just covered. (It will improve the taste of the lentils if, in addition to water, you use a ladleful or two of the liquid in which the *cotechino* is cooking.)

5. When the lentils are nearly done, do not add any more water. They must absorb all their cooking liquid before serving. Do not be concerned if some of the lentils burst their skins and become a bit mashed-looking. If there is still some liquid in the pot when they reach tenderness, uncover, turn up the heat, and quickly evaporate it while stirring the lentils. Add salt and pepper to taste.

6. Transfer the *cotechino* to a cutting board and cut into slices ½ inch thick. Spoon the lentils onto a heated platter and arrange the *cotechino* slices on top.

NOTE

If the lentils should cook much faster than anticipated and the *cotechino* is not yet ready, set them aside and warm them up before serving, over medium heat, uncovered, adding a small amount of *cotechino* broth.

MENU SUGGESTIONS

All this needs is a good soup to go before it: Passatelli (page 67), Rice and Celery Soup (page 59), or Escarole and Rice Soup (page 60).

BLACK-EYED PEAS AND SAUSAGES
WITH TOMATO SAUCE

Fagioli dall'occhio con salsicce

For 4 persons

2 tablespoons chopped yellow onion	1 pound *luganega* sausage or other sweet sausage, such as bratwurst or breakfast sausage
¼ cup olive oil	
¼ teaspoon chopped garlic	
⅓ cup chopped carrot	
⅓ cup chopped celery	1 cup dried black-eyed peas, soaked in lukewarm water for at least 1 hour before cooking
1 cup canned Italian tomatoes, coarsely chopped, with their juice	
	Salt and freshly ground pepper, if necessary

1. Use an earthenware casserole if you have one. Otherwise, choose a heavy saucepan, preferably of enameled cast iron. Put in the chopped onion, along with the olive oil, and sauté over medium heat until pale gold. Add the garlic and sauté until it has colored lightly. Add the carrot and celery and cook for about 5 minutes, stirring occasionally. Add the chopped tomatoes with their juice, turn the heat down to medium low, and cook at a gentle, slow simmer for 20 minutes.

2. Preheat the oven to 350°.

3. Puncture the sausage skins in several places with a fork. If you are using *luganega*, cut it into 2½-inch lengths. Add the sausage to the pot and cook at a slow simmer for 15 minutes.

4. Add the peas and enough water to cover them well. Cover and bring to a steady simmer. Transfer to the middle level of the preheated oven and cook for 1½ hours, or until the peas are tender, remembering that cooking times vary according to the peas and some peas do cook faster than others. Look into the pot from time to time to make sure that there is enough cooking liquid. If there is not, you can add ½ cup warm water at a time, as needed. (If,

on the contrary, the beans are cooked and the cooking liquid is too watery, return the pot to the stove, uncover, turn on the heat to high, and boil until the liquid is concentrated.)

5. Tip the pot and draw off most of the fat with a spoon. Taste the peas and correct for salt and pepper. (Seasoning varies greatly, according to the sausages.)

NOTE

If you are not serving it immediately, you can prepare the entire dish ahead of time. It keeps in the refrigerator for several days. Reheat either on the stove at low heat or in a 250° oven.

MENU SUGGESTIONS

Precede with a hot vegetable soup, as suggested for Boiled *Cotechino* Sausage with Lentils (page 277).

OXTAIL BRAISED WITH WINE AND VEGETABLES

Coda alla vaccinara

If you go to Rome and want to eat as the Romans do, you might include in your plans a meal at one of the *trattorie* near the slaughterhouse where they specialize in this dish. *Coda alla vaccinara* is as genuinely Roman as its name. *Vaccinaro*, although now it means "tanner," was the old local name for "butcher." And truly it is a hearty butcher's dish. Oxtail is not for picky filet mignon eaters, but it will satisfy those who appreciate the flavor and body that meat always has when it comes from next to the joints and bones.

For 4 to 5 persons

½ pound pork rind
⅓ cup olive oil
1 tablespoon cooking fat, preferably lard
¼ cup chopped parsley
½ teaspoon chopped garlic
⅔ cup chopped yellow onion
⅔ cup chopped carrot
2½ pounds oxtail, cut at the joints and, if frozen, thawed overnight in the refrigerator

1½ cups dry white wine
½ cup canned Italian tomatoes, seeded, drained, and coarsely chopped
1½ teaspoons salt
Freshly ground pepper, 8 to 10 twists of the mill
1½ cups very coarsely chopped celery

1. Rinse the pork rind in cold water. Bring water to a boil in a pan. Drop in the pork rind. When the water returns to a boil, drain and let the rind cool. When cool, cut it into 1-inch-long strips and set aside.

2. Preheat the oven to 350°.

3. Choose a heavy casserole, large enough to contain all the ingredients in the recipe. Put in the olive oil, lard, parsley, garlic, onion, and carrot. Sauté lightly over medium heat for 10 minutes, stirring frequently.

4. Raise the heat to medium high, then add the oxtail pieces and the pork rind. Brown the meat well on all sides for about 8 minutes.

5. Add the wine, but pour it gradually, or it may boil over. Boil the wine for 2 to 3 minutes, turning the meat once or twice.

6. Add the chopped tomatoes, 1 cup water, salt, and pepper. When the contents of the casserole have come to a steady simmer, cover the pot and place it in the middle level of the preheated oven. Cook for 1½ hours, turning the meat every 30 minutes.

7. Add the cut-up celery to the casserole, mixing it well in the meat and juices. Cook for 45 minutes more in the oven, turning the contents of the pot at least twice. At this point, the meat should be very tender and come easily off the bone. (Some cooks cook the meat much longer and boil

the celery before adding it to the meat. I find that 2¼ to 2½ hours are quite sufficient to make oxtail tender enough to cut with a fork. And boiling the celery results in a partial loss of the flavor that is characteristic of the dish.)

8. Before serving, tip the casserole and draw off as much fat as possible with a spoon.

NOTE

This dish can be prepared entirely ahead of time and warmed up on top of the stove at medium heat just before serving. It will keep in the refrigerator for several days.

MENU SUGGESTIONS

A good country soup is the best first course here: Lentil Soup (page 70), Bean Soup with Parsley and Garlic (page 75), or Beans and Pasta Soup (page 76). If you would rather have a pasta, choose either Spaghetti with Garlic and Oil (page 98) or Bucatini with Pancetta, Tomatoes, and Hot Pepper (page 100). No vegetables need accompany this dish, but follow it with a nice cleansing Mixed Salad (page 393) or Finocchio Salad (page 392).

HONEYCOMB TRIPE WITH PARMESAN CHEESE

Trippa alla parmigiana

To a great many Americans tripe is a mysterious and not particularly appealing dish. Actually, it is just a muscle, the stomach muscle, and a delicious one at that. Little of the meat we routinely eat is so savory, so succulently tender, or has such an appetizing fragrance as a well-prepared dish of tripe. To those who can approach a new experience without tension or preconceptions, I firmly recommend it. Fortunately, the greatest drawback to making tripe at home—its long and tedious scrubbing, soaking, and preliminary blanching—has been completely overcome by the appearance of ready-to-cook honeycomb tripe at many frozen-meat counters. This is an excellent product with which you can confidently prepare any of the great regional Italian tripe dishes.

For 6 persons

2 pounds frozen
   honeycomb tripe,
   thawed
1 small carrot
1 small onion
1 stalk celery
½ cup olive oil
3 tablespoons butter
½ cup chopped yellow
   onion
½ cup chopped celery
½ cup chopped carrot
2 cloves garlic, lightly
   crushed with a knife
   handle and peeled
1 tablespoon chopped
   parsley
¼ teaspoon chopped
   rosemary
⅔ cup dry white wine
1 cup canned Italian
   tomatoes, with their
   juice
Freshly ground pepper,
   about 8 to 10 twists
   of the mill
2 teaspoons salt
1 cup Homemade Meath
   Broth (page 10) OR
   ⅓ cup canned beef
   broth mixed with ⅔
   cup water
¾ cup freshly grated
   Parmesan cheese

1. Rinse the tripe thoroughly under cold running water and set aside.

2. Bring 3 quarts of water to a boil with the whole carrot, onion, and celery. Add the tripe, cover, and cook at a moderate boil for 15 minutes. Drain and place the tripe in a bowl with enough cold water to cover. Soak until the tripe is thoroughly cool, then cut it into strips ½ inch wide by 3 to 4 inches long. Set aside.

3. Preheat the oven to 325°.

4. In a heavy casserole put the olive oil, 1 tablespoon of the butter, and the chopped onion, celery, and carrot, and cook slowly over medium-low heat for about 5 minutes, or until the vegetables have slightly wilted. Add the crushed garlic, parsley, and rosemary and cook just long enough to stir everything well two or three times.

5. Add the tripe, stirring it into the vegetables and seasonings, and cook it for 5 minutes. Add the white wine and raise the heat to medium high, boiling the wine for 30 seconds.

6. Add the tomatoes and their juice, the pepper, salt, and broth and bring to a light boil. Cover the pot and bake in the middle level of the preheated oven for 2 to 2½ hours. (Look in on the tripe from time to time to make sure there is sufficient liquid in the pot. If the liquid is drying

too fast, add 2 to 3 tablespoons of water.) Taste the tripe for doneness after 2 hours. It should be very tender but pleasantly chewy and easily cut with a fork.

7. When done, remove from the oven and swirl in the remaining 2 tablespoons of butter and the grated cheese. Serve piping hot.

NOTE

A more fiery version of the same dish can be achieved by adding ¼ teaspoon of chopped hot red pepper, or slightly more, to taste, before the tripe goes into the oven.

Tripe is just as delicious when reheated. It keeps perfectly in the refrigerator for 4 to 5 days.

MENU SUGGESTIONS

The earthy flavor of tripe goes best with a hearty soup such as Beans and Pasta Soup (page 76), any of the chickpea soups on pages 81–83, or Vegetable Soup (page 63). If you want pasta, choose Spaghetti with Garlic and Oil (page 98). No vegetables are needed. Follow with Mixed Salad (page 393), Finocchio Salad (page 392), or Boiled Cauliflower Salad (page 398).

SWEETBREADS BRAISED WITH TOMATOES AND PEAS

Animelle con pomodori e piselli

In the Italian preparation of sweetbreads you must have a firm, light, patient hand to peel off the thin membrane in which they are wrapped. We don't soak them in water for several hours to whiten them because the Italian approach rarely alters or tones down the natural characteristics of an ingredient. In the version below the sweetbreads are very briefly blanched, sautéed in butter and oil, then cooked slowly with tomatoes and peas. They are quite tender when cooked and very delicate in flavor, somewhat tastier and firmer than brains. They are perfectly complemented by the sweet taste of very young peas.

For 4 to 6 persons

1½ pounds sweetbreads
½ carrot, peeled
1 stalk celery
1 tablespoon vinegar
Salt
2½ tablespoons chopped
    shallots or yellow
    onion
4 tablespoons butter
1 tablespoon vegetable
    oil

⅔ cup canned Italian
    tomatoes, coarsely
    chopped, with their
    juice
2 pounds fresh, young
    peas (unshelled
    weight) or 1 ten-
    ounce package
    frozen small, early
    peas, thawed
Freshly ground pepper,
    2 to 3 twists of the
    mill

1. Working under cold running water, peel off as much of the membrane surrounding the sweetbreads as you can. If you are patient and careful you should be able to pull virtually all of it off. When finished rinse the sweetbreads under cold running water.

2. In a saucepan put enough cold water to cover the sweetbreads later and add the carrot, celery, vinegar, and a pinch of salt. Bring the water to a boil, add the sweetbreads, and cook at a very gentle simmer for 6 minutes. Drain the sweetbreads and, while still warm, pull off any remaining bits of membrane. (The sweetbreads may be prepared a day ahead of time up to this point and refrigerated under plastic wrap.) When cold, cut the sweetbreads into smaller-than-bite-sized chunks, about 1 inch thick.

3. In a deep skillet or casserole, sauté the shallots, in the butter and oil, over medium heat until pale gold but not browned. Add the sweetbreads and sauté until lightly browned on all sides. Add the chopped tomatoes with their juice and continue cooking over moderate heat, keeping the tomatoes at a gentle simmer.

4. After 20 minutes add the shelled fresh peas, ½ teaspoon salt, and pepper, mixing well with the sweetbreads and tomato. (If you are using frozen peas wait another 15 minutes before adding the thawed peas.) Cover and cook at a gentle simmer for 20 more minutes. Taste and correct for salt and pepper, and serve while hot. (If the sauce is too thin, transfer the sweetbreads with a slotted spoon to a warm

platter and rapidly reduce the sauce over high heat, then pour the sauce and peas over the sweetbreads and serve immediately.)

MENU SUGGESTIONS

Sweetbreads may also be served in individual pastry shells or over slices of toasted fine white bread. They can follow a first course of soup, pasta, or *risotto* that does not have a strong tomato presence. Risotto with Parmesan Cheese (page 171) would be an excellent choice. Avoid any spicy or very hearty first course that would be out of balance with the delicate taste of the sweetbreads.

SAUTÉED CALF'S LIVER WITH ONIONS, VENETIAN STYLE

Fegato alla veneziana

What you need for *fegato alla veneziana* is, above everything else, a butcher able and willing to slice calf's liver to an even thinness of ¼ inch. The thinner liver is, the faster it cooks, and the faster it cooks, the sweeter it tastes. This is the whole point of *fegato alla veneziana*. Another essential requirement is that the liver come from a very young, milk-fed animal, less than three months old. Liver from young calves is of a pale, clear, rosy color. As the animal gets older, the liver becomes darker, tougher, and sharper in taste. Of course, you can use the technique of *fegato alla veneziana* with what calf's liver you have available. But if you ever find access to younger liver and a cooperative butcher, don't pass up the opportunity to discover what a joy this dish can be at its best.

For 4 persons

1½ pounds calf's liver, very thinly sliced
3 tablespoons vegetable oil
3 cups thinly sliced yellow onion

Salt
Freshly ground pepper, about 6 twists of the mill

1. Remove the thin skin tissue around the liver slices and any large gristly tubes. (Traditionally, liver for *fegato alla veneziana* is cut at this point into bite-sized pieces about 1½ inches wide. You may do this if you like. I find the larger slices easier to turn while cooking, and I skip this step, unless I am having Venetians to dinner.)

2. Choose a skillet that can later accommodate all the liver in a single layer without crowding. Put in all the oil and sliced onion and cook over medium-low heat for about 15 to 20 minutes. The onion should be limp and nicely browned. (You can prepare everything several hours ahead of time, up to and including this point.)

3. Remove the onion from the skillet with a slotted spoon or spatula, and set aside. Don't be concerned if two or three slivers of onion are left in the skillet. What is important is that you should still have oil in the skillet.

4. Turn the heat to high, and when the oil is very hot put in the liver. (The oil should be very hot in order to cook the liver rapidly.) As soon as the liver loses its raw, reddish color, turn it, add a large pinch of salt and some pepper, and return the onions to the skillet. Give everything one more turn, transfer to a warm platter, and serve immediately.

NOTE

It takes almost longer to read this than to cook the liver. If it is the proper thinness, the liver is done in less than a minute.

MENU SUGGESTIONS

For a first course, it would be hard to improve on Rice and Peas (page 57). Rice and Lentil Soup (page 71), Risotto with Zucchini (page 180), and Risotto with Asparagus (page 179) are also good choices. If you want a vegetable, Fried Tomatoes (page 375) go well with liver.

FRIED BREADED CALF'S LIVER

Fegato di vitello fritto

For 4 persons

Vegetable oil, enough to
    thickly coat the
    bottom of the skillet
2 tablespoons butter
1½ pounds thinly sliced
    calf's liver

¾ cup fine, dry
    unflavored bread
    crumbs, spread on a
    dish or on waxed
    paper
Salt and freshly ground
    pepper to taste
Lemon wedges

1. Heat the oil and the butter in a skillet over high heat.

2. Press the slices of liver into the bread crumbs with the palm of your hand, turning to coat both sides. Shake off excess crumbs. As soon as the butter foam subsides, slip the breaded liver into the skillet.

3. When the liver is lightly and crisply browned on one side, turn it and do the other side. (If it is as thin as recommended, it should take about 30 seconds for each side. If it is thicker, it will take just a little longer.) When done, the liver should be pink and very tender inside.

4. As each slice is done, place on paper towels to drain and season with salt and pepper. Serve piping hot, with lemon wedges.

MENU SUGGESTIONS

First Course: any *risotto* with vegetables (pages 179–181) or Risotto with Parmesan Cheese (page 171). Other possibilities are Italian Pancakes Filled with Meat Sauce (page 168), Conchiglie with Sausage and Cream Sauce (page 104), Beans and Sauerkraut Soup (page 72), or Spinach Soup (page 62). For a vegetable choose Sautéed Diced Eggplant (page 360) or Oven-Browned Tomatoes (page 374).

FRIED CALF'S BRAINS

Cervella fritta

This is the favorite way of doing brains in Italy. The brains are first cooked with vegetables, then sliced and fried. Frying points up their lovely texture. As one bites, the thin, golden armor of their crust gives way to yield the delectable core in all its tenderness.

For 4 persons

1 calf's brain (about 1 pound)
½ carrot, peeled
½ yellow onion, peeled
½ stalk celery
1 tablespoon vinegar
1 teaspoon salt
1 egg, lightly beaten with 1 teaspoon salt, in a bowl

1 cup fine, dry unflavored bread crumbs, spread on a dish or on waxed paper
Vegetable oil, enough to come ½ inch up the side of the pan
Lemon wedges

1. Wash the brain thoroughly in cold water, then let soak in cold water for 10 minutes. Drain, and carefully remove as much as possible of the surrounding membrane and the protruding blood vessels.

2. Put the carrot, onion, celery, vinegar, and 1 teaspoon of salt in a saucepan with 6 cups of water and bring to a boil.

3. Drop in the brain, and when the water has returned to a boil cover the pan and adjust the heat so that the liquid bubbles very slowly but steadily. Cook for 20 minutes.

4. Drain, and let the brain cool completely. When cool, refrigerate for about 10 minutes, or until they are very firm. (You may even prepare them ahead of time, in the morning, and refrigerate until shortly before you are ready to fry. If refrigerating brains for several hours, cover them with plastic wrap.)

5. Cut the brain into broad, larger-than-bite-size pieces, about ½ inch thick.

6. First dip the slices in egg, letting the excess flow back into the bowl, then turn them in bread crumbs.

7. Heat the oil in a skillet over high heat. When the oil is very hot, slip the coated slices into the pan. (Do not put in any more at one time than will fit loosely.) Fry until golden brown on one side, then do the other side. When a nice crust has formed on both sides, transfer to paper towels to drain. When all the slices are done, serve immediately, with lemon wedges on the side.

MENU SUGGESTIONS

Fried brains can be one of the components of Mixed Fried Meats, Vegetable, Cheese, Cream, and Fruit (page 322). If it is going to be a second course on its own, it can be preceded by a soup, such as Escarole and Rice Soup (page 60) or Spinach Soup (page 62), or by Fettuccine Tossed in Cream and Butter (page 123), Meat-Stuffed Pasta Rolls (page 141), Rice and Peas (page 57), or any *risotto*, except those with chicken livers or with clams. It can then be accompanied by any one of the fried vegetables, and Sautéed Green Beans with Butter and Cheese (page 348), Sautéed Mushrooms with Garlic and Parsley (page 365), or Sautéed Broccoli with Garlic (page 350).

SAUTEED LAMB KIDNEYS WITH WHITE WINE

Rognoncini trifolati al vino bianco

When I started teaching I was not aware of the American aversion to organs. I found it out when my students nearly walked out on me the first time I taught this dish. They stayed on, however, and, after discovering how tasty and fine kidneys can be, many of them welcomed this addition to their repertoire. For anyone still unfamiliar with organs this delicate way of preparing kidneys could be a good way to embark on a most delicious experience.

For 4 to 6 persons

20 lamb kidneys	Salt to taste
3 tablespoons vinegar	Freshly ground pepper,
¼ cup vegetable oil	6 to 8 twists of the
2 tablespoons finely	mill
chopped shallots or	½ teaspoon cornstarch
yellow onion	⅔ cup dry white wine
½ teaspoon finely	
chopped garlic	
2 tablespoons finely	
chopped parsley	

1. Split the kidneys in half and wash briefly under cold running water. To a china or earthenware bowl of water large enough to contain them add the vinegar, then the kidneys. Let the kidneys soak for at least 30 minutes, then drain and pat dry with paper towels. Cut them into very thin slices and try to remove as many of the small white vessels as possible.

2. Heat the oil in a heavy-bottomed skillet and sauté the shallots until pale gold. Add the chopped garlic, stir two or three times, add the parsley, and immediately after add the sliced kidneys.

3. Raise the heat to high, add salt and pepper, and stir so that the kidneys are well coated with the sautéed shallots and with the garlic and parsley. As soon as the kidneys have lost their raw red color, transfer them to a warm platter. (It is very important not to overcook kidneys. Tiny lamb kidneys, in particular, cook very rapidly.)

4. Mix the cornstarch into the wine and add to the skillet. Bring to a rapid boil over high heat, taking care to scrape up all the cooking residue stuck to the bottom of the pan. Add any juice the kidneys may have left in their platter. When the sauce starts to thicken, add the kidneys and stir quickly, cooking them just a moment more. Serve with their sauce while still hot.

MENU SUGGESTIONS

Any first course that has character but is not overbearingly sharp goes well with kidneys. Any of the following makes a good choice: Potato Gnocchi (page 185) with either Tomato Sauce III (page 90) or Gorgonzola Sauce (page 126),

Cappelletti with Butter and Heavy Cream (page 151), Italian Pancakes Filled with Spinach (page 167), Rice and Peas (page 57). Vegetable: Braised Artichokes and Leeks (page 336) or Braised Artichokes and Peas (page 335).

BROILED PORK LIVER WRAPPED IN CAUL FAT

Fegatelli di maiale con la rete

This is a classic Tuscan dish, and it is delicious. Like all Tuscan grills it is extremely simple. The one important point to remember is not to overcook the liver. Perfectly broiled liver is pink, juicy, and sweet tasting. Caul fat, or pork net, is a fatty membrane enveloping the intestines. It acts as a self-baster for the liver. It is so inexpensive that it is well worth buying a large piece and utilizing the best parts of it for the wrappers.

For 6 persons

A large piece of caul fat (about 1 pound)
1½ pounds pork liver

Salt and freshly ground pepper to taste
Bay leaves

1. Preheat the broiler to its maximum.
2. Soak the caul fat in lukewarm water for 2 or 3 minutes, until it loosens up. Change the water a few times to rinse and clean the membrane. Lay the membrane on a dry cloth and carefully open it up. Cut the best parts of it into rectangles 5 by 7 inches. (Do not bother patching small pieces together.)
3. Remove any skin or tough, exposed vessels from the liver. Wash the liver in cold water and pat thoroughly dry. Cut it into sections about 3 inches long, 2 inches wide, and ⅝ inch thick.
4. Season the sections of liver with a good pinch of salt and at least a grinding of pepper each. Place a bay leaf on each section and wrap each section with one of the caul-fat

wrappers, tucking the ends under as you wrap. Fasten each piece of liver with a toothpick.

5. Place in the hot broiler, which should have been on for at least 15 minutes, so that it is searing hot when you put in the liver. Turn the liver after 2½ to 3 minutes. Do not cook more than 4 or 5 minutes all together. Serve piping hot.

MENU SUGGESTIONS

This dish is absolutely sensational cooked outdoors over charcoal. It can be part of a mixed grill with steaks and chops. Indoors, precede it with Bean Soup with Parsley and Garlic (page 75), Potato and Onion Soup (page 56), or Split Green Peas and Potato Soup (page 68). Accompany the liver with Cauliflower Gratinéed with Butter and Cheese (page 353), Swiss Chard Stalks with Parmesan Cheese (page 357), or Braised Artichokes and Leeks (page 336).

SAUTÉED CHICKEN LIVERS WITH SAGE

Fegatini di pollo alla salvia

For 6 persons

1½ pounds chicken livers	⅓ cup dry white wine
2 tablespoons finely chopped shallots OR yellow onion	Salt to taste
	Freshly ground pepper, about 4 twists of the mill
¼ cup butter	
1 dozen dried sage leaves	

1. Examine the livers carefully for green spots and cut them out. Remove any bits of fat and wash the livers thoroughly in cold water. Dry well on paper towels.

2. In a skillet, sauté the shallots in the butter over medium heat. When they turn pale gold, raise the heat and add the sage leaves and chicken livers. Cook over high heat for just a few minutes, stirring frequently, until the livers

lose their raw, red color. Transfer the livers to a warm platter.

3. Add the wine to the skillet and boil briskly until it has almost completely evaporated. Scrape up and loosen any cooking residue in the pan. Add any liquid the livers may have thrown off in the platter, and allow it to evaporate.

4. Return the chicken livers to the pan, turn them rapidly for a few moments over high heat, add salt and pepper, and transfer to a warm serving platter. Serve immediately.

MENU SUGGESTIONS

These chicken livers go so well with Italian Mashed Potatoes with Parmesan Cheese (page 369) that you can dispense with a pasta first course without any regrets. You can precede them with Stuffed Mushrooms with Béchamel Sauce (page 43), Artichokes, Roman Style (page 326), or Baked Stuffed Zucchini Boats (page 380). If you want to vary this arrangement, choose Rice and Celery Soup (page 59) or Spinach Soup (page 62) as a first course and accompany the livers with Carrots with Parmesan Cheese (page 351).

PAN-ROASTED CHICKEN WITH GARLIC, ROSEMARY, AND WHITE WINE

Pollo arrosto in tegame

Reliable ovens are only a recent addition to the Italian kitchen, and consequently, traditional roasts are done either on the spit or in a pan on top of the stove. In this recipe the chicken is entirely pan roasted, with just enough liquid to keep it from drying out. As in almost all Italian roasts, it is flavored with garlic and a hint of rosemary. It is one of the simplest and tastiest ways of doing chicken, and, if you use a young frying chicken, you should have the roasted chicken on the table in less than 45 minutes from the time you start preparing it.

For 4 persons

2 tablespoons butter
2 tablespoons vegetable
   oil
2 to 3 cloves garlic,
   peeled
1 frying chicken (2½
   pounds), washed in
   cold water,
   quartered, and
   thoroughly dried in
   a towel

A small branch of fresh
   rosemary, cut in
   two, OR ½ teaspoon
   dried rosemary
   leaves
Salt
Freshly ground pepper,
   about 6 twists of the
   mill
½ cup dry white wine

1. Heat the butter and oil in a deep skillet or sauté pan over medium-high heat. When the butter foam begins to subside, add the garlic and the chicken quarters, skin side down. When the chicken is well browned on one side, turn the pieces over and add the rosemary. If the garlic starts to blacken, remove it. If, however, it stays a deep golden brown, leave it in until the chicken is cooked. Control the heat so that the cooking fat stays hot but doesn't burn.

2. When you have browned the chicken well on all sides, add a large pinch of salt, the pepper, and the wine. Allow the wine to bubble rapidly for 2 to 3 minutes, then lower the heat until it is just simmering, and cover the pan. Cook slowly until the chicken is tender at the pricking of a fork. (A young fryer should take about 30 to 35 minutes.) Turn the chicken two or three times while cooking. (If you see that the cooking liquid has dried up, you can add 1 to 2 tablespoons of water as needed.)

3. Transfer the chicken to a warm serving platter, removing the garlic from the pan if you haven't done it earlier. Tilt the pan, drawing off all but 2 tablespoons of fat with a spoon. Return the pan to high heat, adding 2 to 3 tablespoons of water, and scraping up the cooking juices in the pan. Pour these over the chicken and serve.

MENU SUGGESTIONS

You can precede this with soup, such as Rice and Celery Soup (page 59), Escarole and Rice Soup (page 60), or Spinach Soup (page 62). If you'd like a pasta, any of these would be a good choice: Penne with a Sauce of Tomatoes and Dried Wild Mushrooms (page 103), Baked Rigatoni with Meat Sauce (page 105), Tagliatelle with Bolognese Meat Sauce (page 122), Meat-Stuffed Pasta Rolls (page 141), Risotto with Parmesan Cheese (page 171), Riscotto with Meat Sauce (page 176), Rice and Peas (page 57). If the first course was soup, you can accompany the chicken with Diced Pan-Roasted Potatoes (page 372) or Italian Mashed Potatoes with Parmesan Cheese (page 369). If you had pasta, a good vegetable accompaniment would be Sautéed Green Beans with Butter and Cheese (page 348), Sautéed Peas with Prosciutto, Florentine Style (page 368), or Carrots with Parmesan Cheese (page 351).

ROAST CHICKEN WITH ROSEMARY

Pollo arrosto al forno con rosmarino

For 4 persons

3 cloves garlic, peeled	Salt
1 heaping teaspoon dried rosemary leaves	Freshly ground pepper, about 8 twists of the mill
1 frying chicken (about 2½ pounds), washed and thoroughly dried in a towel	¼ cup vegetable oil

1. Preheat the oven to 375°.

2. Put all the garlic and half the rosemary into the bird's cavity. Add a large pinch of salt and a few grindings of pepper.

3. Rub about half the oil over the outside of the chicken, and sprinkle with salt, some more pepper, and the rest of the rosemary.

4. Put the chicken and the rest of the oil in a roasting pan and place it in the middle level of the preheated oven. Turn the chicken and baste it with the fat and cooking juices in the pan every 15 minutes. Cook for about 1 hour, or until the skin is well browned and crisp.

5. Transfer the chicken to a warm platter. Tip the pan

and draw off all but 1 tablespoon of fat with a spoon. Place the pan over the stove burner, turn on the heat to high, add 1 to 2 tablespoons of water, and while it boils away scrape up all the cooking residue. Pour over the chicken and serve immediately.

MENU SUGGESTIONS

Follow the ones given for Pan-Roasted Chicken with Garlic, Rosemary, and White Wine (page 294).

CHARCOAL-BROILED CHICKEN MARINATED IN PEPPER, OIL, AND LEMON

Pollo alla diavola

This peppery chicken should be very satisfying to an outdoor appetite. It is a famous Roman specialty that has now become popular in most of Italy. The chicken is opened flat, rubbed liberally with crushed peppercorns, and marinated in oil and lemon juice. Many cooks omit the lemon juice until the chicken is cooked, but I find that it enhances the texture and fragrance of the chicken when it goes in the marinade. If you are picnicking, you can prepare the chicken at home, put it in a plastic bag, stow it in a portable refrigerator or insulated food bag, and when your charcoal fire in the wilderness is ready the chicken is ready. Don't skimp on the pepper, or it won't be *alla diavola*, "hot as the devil."

Although charcoal is the ideal fire for chicken *alla diavola*, it is delicious even on an indoor broiler. Preheat the broiler to its maximum setting at least 15 minutes ahead of time.

For 4 persons

1 broiling chicken (about 2 pounds)
⅓ cup lemon juice
1 tablespoon crushed peppercorns

3 tablespoons olive oil
2 teaspoons salt

1. Lay the chicken on the flat surface with the breast facing down and split it open along the entire backbone. Crack the breastbone from the inside. Spread the chicken as flat as you can with your hands. Turn it over so the breast faces you. Cut the wings and legs where they join the body, but without detaching them—just enough to spread them flat. Turn the chicken over again, with the inside of the carcass facing you, and pound it as flat as possible, using a cleaver or large meat flattener. It should have something of a butterfly shape.

2. Put the chicken in a deep dish. Pour the lemon juice over the chicken, then add the peppercorns and the olive oil. Cover the dish and let it marinate for at least 2 hours. Uncover and baste from time to time.

3. When the fire is ready, sprinkle the chicken with salt and place on the grill (which should be about 5 inches above the charcoal), skin side toward the fire. Broil until the skin has turned light brown, then turn it over on the other side, basting with marinade liquid from time to time. Turn it over after about 10 minutes and cook briefly once again on each side, until the thigh is tender at the pricking of a fork. (All together it should take about 35 minutes.) If the marinating liquid should run out before the chicken is done, baste with a teaspoonful of olive oil from time to time. Season with a pinch of crushed pepper before serving.

MENU SUGGESTIONS

If cooked outdoors, some or all of the Charcoal-Broiled Vegetables (page 384), would be lovely with this chicken. Indoors, a first course can be any soup, *risotto*, or pasta that does not have fish or cream in it. You can't go wrong with any vegetable, but a good combination is the Green Beans with Peppers and Tomatoes (page 349) or Fried Eggplant (page 358), together with Oven-Browned Tomatoes (page 374).

CHICKEN FRICASSEE WITH GREEN PEPPERS AND TOMATOES

Pollo alla cacciatora

For 4 or 5 persons

Frying chicken (2½ to 3 pounds), cut into 4 to 6 pieces

3 tablespoons vegetable oil

1 cup all-purpose flour, spread on a dinner plate or on waxed paper

Salt

Freshly ground pepper, 4 to 6 twists of the mill

⅔ cup dry white wine

⅓ cup thinly sliced yellow onion

1 green pepper, with seeds removed, cut into thin strips

1 medium carrot, sliced very thin

½ stalk celery, cut into thin strips

1 clove garlic, peeled and chopped very fine

⅔ cup canned Italian tomatoes, coarsely chopped, with their juice

1. Wash the chicken pieces in cold running water and pat dry very thoroughly with paper towels.

2. Choose a skillet large enough to contain all the chicken pieces comfortably, without crowding. Heat the oil in the skillet over moderately high heat. Turn the chicken pieces in the flour, coating both sides and shaking off the excess, and put in the skillet, skin side down. When one side has turned golden brown, turn the pieces over and brown the other side. When nicely browned on all sides, transfer them to a warm platter and add salt and pepper.

3. Tip the skillet and draw off most of the fat with a spoon. Turn the heat to high, add the wine, and boil rapidly until it is reduced by half. Scrape up and loosen any cooking residue in the pan. Lower the heat to medium, add the sliced onion, and cook for about 5 minutes, stirring two or three times. Add the browned chicken pieces, all but the breasts. (Breasts cook faster, so they can be added later.)

Add the sliced pepper, carrot, celery, garlic, and the chopped tomatoes and their juice. Adjust to a low simmer and cover. After 9 to 10 minutes add the breasts and continue cooking until tender, about 30 minutes. Turn and baste the chicken a few times while cooking.

4. Transfer the chicken to a warm serving platter. If the sauce in the pan is too thin, raise the heat to high and boil it briskly until it thickens, stirring as it boils. Pour the sauce over the chicken and serve immediately.

NOTE

If prepared ahead of time, let the chicken cool in its sauce. When reheating, simmer very slowly, covered, for a few minutes, just until the chicken is hot.

MENU SUGGESTIONS

A good choice for a first course would be a simple Risotto with Parmesan Cheese (page 171). Other possibilities are Beans and Pasta Soup (page 76), Potato Gnocchi with Pesto (page 185), Rice with Fresh Basil and Mozzarella Cheese (page 183), or Tagliatelle with Bolognese Meat Sauce (page 122). No vegetable is called for, but instead of the usual raw salad you might serve Mixed Cooked Vegetable Salad (page 400).

CHICKEN FRICASSEE WITH DRIED WILD MUSHROOMS

Pollo coi funghi secchi

The key ingredient in this succulent dish is dried wild mushrooms. Nothing can be substituted for them that will yield the same full-flavored taste and rich woodsy aroma. The mushrooms with the most delicate flavor and finest texture are the creamy brown variety in large pieces. The very dark, crumbly chips are much cheaper but not quite so agreeable.

For 4 persons

1 ounce imported dried wild mushrooms	Salt and freshly ground pepper to taste
1 frying chicken (about 2½ pounds)	½ cup dry white wine
3 tablespoons vegetable oil	3 tablespoons canned Italian tomatoes, coarsely chopped
3 tablespoons butter	

1. Place the mushrooms in ⅔ cup lukewarm water. Let soak at least 15 to 20 minutes.

2. Wash the chicken under cold running water. Cut into quarters and pat thoroughly dry.

3. Remove the mushrooms, reserving the water in which they have soaked. Filter the water by straining it through a paper towel placed in a fine sieve, and set aside. Rinse the mushrooms in cold running water three or four times, then chop them roughly and set aside.

4. In a heavy-bottomed skillet heat all the oil and 2 tablespoons of the butter. When the butter foam subsides, add the chicken quarters and brown them well on all sides over medium heat. Add salt and pepper, turning the chicken once or twice. Add the wine.

5. When the wine has evaporated add the chopped mushrooms, the water they have soaked in, and the chopped peeled tomatoes. Cover the skillet and cook at gentle heat for about 30 minutes, or until the chicken is tender. Turn the chicken pieces over from time to time.

6. Transfer the chicken to a warm platter. Tip the pan and draw off most of the fat with a spoon. If the sauce in the pan is too thin, boil it over high heat until it is concentrated. Off the heat, swirl in the remaining tablespoon of butter and pour the sauce over the chicken.

MENU SUGGESTIONS

A perfect first course would be Italian Pancakes Filled with Spinach (page 167). Other good choices: Baked Green Lasagne with Meat Sauce (page 136), Fettuccine with Gorgonzola Sauce (page 126), Conchiglie with Sausage and Cream Sauce (page 104), Creamy Potato Soup with Carrots and Celery (page 55), Cappellacci filled with Sweet Potatoes and Parsley (page 158), or Risotto with Luganega Sausage (page 177). For a vegetable: Fried Finocchio (page 364), Crisp-Fried Whole Artichokes (page 332), or one of the vegetables with butter and cheese, such as Carrots with Parmesan Cheese (page 351).

FILLETS OF BREAST OF CHICKEN

Petti di pollo

This is the Italian method of filleting chicken breasts. It produces very thin slices of chicken that cook very rapidly and remain extraordinarily juicy and tender. Once you've acquired the knack of separating the two muscles that make up each side of the breast the whole procedure becomes very simple. The result in terms of texture and flavor is so fine that you will probably adopt this method of filleting for any recipe calling for suprêmes of chicken.

1. Slip your fingers underneath the skin and pull it entirely away from the breast. It comes off quite easily. Be sure you also remove the thin membrane that adheres to the breast underneath the skin.

2. Run a finger along the broad upper part of the breast from the center bone toward the side and feel for an opening. You will find a spot where the finger enters easily without resistance. This is where the two muscles meet, and the probing, lifting action of your fingers has separated them. Detach them from the bone with a small sharp knife. You will obtain from each side of the breast two separate pieces, one small and tapered, the other flatter, larger, and somewhat triangular in shape.

3. The smaller piece has a white tendon that must be pulled out. With one hand grasp the tendon where it protrudes, with the other take a knife and push with the blade against the flesh where it meets the tendon. Pull the tendon out. It should come easily. Nothing else needs to be done to this piece.

4. Lay the larger piece on a cutting board with the side that was next to the bone facing down. Hold it flat with the palm of one hand. With the other hand take a sharp knife

and slice the breast with the blade moving parallel to the
cutting board, thus dividing the piece into two even slices
of half the original thickness. Watch both sides of the piece
while slicing to make sure you are slicing it evenly.

You now have from each half breast three tender fillets
ready for cooking.

SAUTÉED CHICKEN BREAST FILLETS
WITH LEMON AND PARSLEY

Petti di pollo alla senese

For 4 to 5 persons

1 tablespoon vegetable oil	Freshly ground pepper, about 4 twists of the mill
5 tablespoons butter	Juice of 1 lemon
3 whole chicken breasts, filleted as directed above	3 tablespoons chopped parsley
Salt to taste	1 lemon, thinly sliced

1. Heat the oil and 3 tablespoons of the butter in a skillet
over medium-high heat. When the butter foam begins to
subside, sauté the chicken fillets on both sides very briefly.
(They will be cooked in 2 minutes at most.)

2. Remove the fillets to a warm platter and add salt and
pepper.

3. Add the lemon juice to the skillet and turn on the
heat to medium. Loosen all the cooking residue from the
bottom of the pan, adding 1 or 2 tablespoons of water if
necessary. Add the parsley and the remaining 2 tablespoons
butter to the cooking juices. Stir three or four times. Lower
the heat to a minimum and add the cooked chicken fillets,
turning them over quickly in the sauce once or twice.

4. Transfer the fillets to a warm serving platter and pour
the cooking juices from the skillet over them. Serve garnished with lemon slices.

MENU SUGGESTIONS

First course: Tortellini Filled with Parsley and Ricotta
(page 152) with Tomato and Cream Sauce (page 153), Risotto

with Dried Wild Mushrooms (page 175), or Spinach and Ricotta Gnocchi (page 189). Vegetable: Sautéed Peas with Prosciutto, Florentine Style (page 368), Fava Beans, Roman Style (page 346), or Sautéed Mushrooms with Garlic and Parsley (page 365).

ROLLED BREAST OF CHICKEN FILLETS STUFFED WITH PORK

Rollatini di petto di pollo e maiale

For 4 to 6 persons

2 cloves garlic, lightly crushed with a heavy knife handle and peeled
3 tablespoons vegetable oil
½ pound any lean cut pork, ground
Salt
Freshly ground pepper, about 6 twists of the mill

1 teaspoon dried rosemary leaves
2 large whole breasts of chicken, filleted as directed on page 302
2 tablespoons butter
½ cup dry white wine

1. In a skillet, sauté the crushed garlic cloves in the oil over medium heat. When the garlic has colored lightly, add the ground pork, a large pinch of salt, the pepper, and rosemary. Stir, and sauté the meat for 10 minutes, crumbling it with a fork as it cooks. Then, with a perforated ladle or slotted spoon, transfer the meat to a dish and allow to cool. Discard all but 2½ to 3 tablespoons of fat from the skillet.

2. Lay the chicken breast fillets flat and sprinkle very lightly with salt and pepper. Spread the sautéed ground pork on the fillets, and roll each fillet up tightly. Tie up each roll securely with string as though you were preparing miniature roasts. (You can prepare the dish up to this point several hours ahead of time.)

3. Add the butter to the skillet in which you cooked the pork and turn the heat up to medium high. When the butter foam begins to subside, put in the stuffed chicken rolls. Brown well on all sides, but do not overcook. Remember,

it takes about 2 minutes to cook filleted chicken breasts. When the rolls are well browned, transfer them to a warm platter and remove the strings. Add the wine to the skillet, turn the heat to high, and loosen any cooking residue in the pan. When the wine has evaporated, pour the sauce over the chicken rolls, and serve hot.

MENU SUGGESTIONS

A first course that goes well here is Risotto with Dried Mushrooms (page 175). Other possibilities are Baked Semolina Gnocchi (page 187), Baked Rigatoni with Meat Sauce (page 105), or Penne with a Sauce of Tomatoes and Dried Wild Mushrooms (page 103). A good choice for vegetables would be Cauliflower Gratinéed with Butter and Cheese (page 353), Fried Cauliflower (page 354), Fried Finocchio (page 364), or Gratinéed Jerusalem Artichokes (page 340).

SAUTÉED TURKEY BREAST FILLETS WITH HAM, CHEESE, AND WHITE TRUFFLES

Cotoletta di tacchino alla bolognese

This is Bologna's most celebrated meat course, in which the delicate, almost neutral taste of veal or breast of turkey is used as a foil for perhaps the three finest products in the Italian larder: aged Parmesan cheese, sweet Parma ham, and the fresh white truffles of Alba. No one who has tasted this dish in Bologna in late fall, when the white truffles are in season, could possibly forget it. Of the three ingredients, only Parmesan cheese is available here, so it is obvious that our *cotoletta alla bolognese* will be only a distant cousin of the original. However, even with local materials, this is still a most attractive dish and well worth doing.

The old recipes call for thinly sliced veal or turkey breast to be lightly sautéed, then bound to slices of ham, truffles, and cheese, and simmered in beef stock or tomato sauce in a covered pan. Today the last step is omitted and the cutlet is run briefly into the oven just long enough to melt the cheese. This is an improvement over the old method, which tended to produce a flabbier texture and a less fresh-tasting liaison of the ingredients.

Fresh white truffles are virtually unobtainable here, except in New York for a short-lived moment in late November or early December, and at prohibitive prices. Canned white truffles, although expensive, are easily available throughout the year at all gourmet shops or by mail from Italian groceries and some department stores. Some cans contain marvelous truffles, while others, unfortunately, are nearly tasteless. The can should release a powerful fragrance when you open it, and the truffle should be a creamy beige color It is a rather blind item, but you must take your chances because the presence of truffles, however weakened by canning, is absolutely essential to *cotoletta alla bolognese*. Without it the dish is gross and banal, and you'd be better advised to invest time and effort in something more promising.

For 4 to 5 persons

1¼ pounds turkey breast, thawed if frozen
1 tablespoon vegetable oil
¼ cup butter
¾ cup all-purpose flour, spread on a dish or on waxed paper
Freshly ground pepper, about 4 twists of the mill
1 one-ounce can white Alba truffles, or more, if you are not daunted by the price

⅓ cup dry Marsala or dry white wine
2 tablespoons freshly grated Parmesan cheese
¼ pound thinly sliced prosciutto
6 ounces Parmesan cheese (approximately), cut into slivers or shavings using a vegetable peeler
1 tablespoon butter

1. Fillet the turkey breast, using the same method suggested for chicken breasts (page 302). Cut the fillets into slices ¼ inch thick.

2. Melt the butter and oil in a skillet over medium-high heat.

3. When the butter foam begins to subside, turn the turkey slices in the flour, coating both sides and shaking off any excess, and slip the turkey into the skillet. If the slices are no more than ¼ inch thick, they should cook very

quickly, about 1 to 1½ minutes per side. Sauté as many slices at one time as will fit comfortably into the skillet, coating them with flour just before putting them in. As they are done, transfer to a warm platter and add the pepper.

4. Preheat the oven to 400°.

5. Open the can of truffles and pour the liquid it contains into the skillet. Turn on the heat to medium and stir for a minute or so, scraping up and loosening the cooking residue in the pan.

6. Add the Marsala or wine and partly exaporate it for a minute or two over medium heat. Stir it as it thickens.

7. Choose a baking dish that can accommodate all the turkey slices in a single layer. Smear the bottom with about 1 tablespoon of sauce from the skillet, then put in the turkey slices, laying them close together but not overlapping.

8. Distribute the grated cheese over the turkey, sprinkling a little over each slice, then cover each slice with prosciutto. Slice the truffles very thin, using a vegetable peeler, and distribute over the prosciutto. Cover each turkey slice with the slivered Parmesan cheese. (Some recipes suggest Fontina or Bel Paese cheese, but only Parmesan is part of an authentic *cotoletta alla bolognese*.) Pour the rest of the sauce from the skillet over the cheese and put a tiny dot of butter on each slice.

9. Place the dish in the uppermost level of the preheated oven for 6 to 8 minutes, or until the cheese melts. Serve piping hot from the same dish.

NOTE

The prosciutto and cheese should be sufficiently salty to make any addition of salt unnecessary. If, as sometimes happens, either the prosciutto or the Parmesan or both lack salt, salt can be added at the table.

MENU SUGGESTIONS

Tagliatelle with Bolognese Meat Sauce (page 122) is a natural combination with this dish, but other excellent choices would be Cappelletti with Butter and Heavy Cream (page 151), or Spinach and Ricotta Gnocchi (page 189). One or two fried vegetables would complete it to perfection: Fried Artichoke Wedges (page 334), and Fried Tomatoes (page 375).

PAN-ROASTED SQUAB

Piccioncini in tegame

For 4 to 6 persons (see note below)

4 fresh squab (about 1
  pound each),
  cleaned and plucked
2 dozen medium-dried
  sage leaves
4 strips of *pancetta*, 1½
  inches long, ½ inch
  wide, and ¼ inch
  thick

Salt and freshly ground
  pepper
3 tablespoons butter
2 tablespoons vegetable
  oil
⅔ cup dry white wine

1. Remove all the organs from the birds' interiors. Reserve the livers but discard the hearts and gizzards (or hold them for a *risotto*). Wash the squab in cold running water and pat dry thoroughly inside and out. Stuff the cavity of each bird with 2 sage leaves, 1 strip of *pancetta*, and 1 liver, and season with 2 pinches of salt and a twist of pepper.

2. In a skillet large enough to hold all the squab, heat up the butter and oil over medium-high heat. When the butter foam subsides, add the remaining sage leaves and then the squab. Brown the squab evenly on all sides and season with salt and pepper. Add the wine. Turn the heat up to high, allowing the wine to boil briskly for 30 to 40 seconds. While the wine is bubbling turn and baste the squab, then lower the heat to medium low and cover the skillet. Turn the birds every 15 minutes. They should be tender and done in 1 hour.

3. Transfer the squab to a warm platter. If you are serving ½ bird per person, halve them with poultry scissors. Tip the pan and draw off some of the cooking fat with a spoon. Add 2 tablespoons of warm water, turn the heat to high, and while the water evaporates scrape up and loosen any cooking residue in the pan. Pour over the squab and serve.

NOTE

A generous portion would be 1 whole squab per person. If you are having a substantial first course, however, ½ squab per person is quite adequate. The remaining squabs can be divided up for second helpings among the hungrier guests.

MENU SUGGESTIONS

The happiest accompaniment for squab and for any game is Polenta (page 193). When serving *polenta* you do not serve pasta as a first course. You can start the meal with very good-quality prosciutto, sliced thick, or with Artichokes, Roman Style (page 326), or Crisp-Fried Whole Artichokes (page 332). If you are not serving *polenta*, an excellent first course would be *risotto*, either Risotto with Dried Wild Mushrooms (page 175) or Molded Risotto with Parmesan Cheese and Chicken-Liver Sauce (page 172), Cappelletti in Broth (page 150), or Tortelloni with Butter and Cheese (page 157). A good vegetable side dish would be Sautéed Peas with Prosciutto, Florentine Style (page 368), Sweet and Sour Onions (page 367), Sautéed Finocchio with Butter and Cheese (page 362), or Sautéed Jerusalem Artichokes (page 339).

STEWED RABBIT WITH WHITE WINE

Coniglio in padella

Now that factory chicken has completely replaced free-roaming yard-raised chicken, one of the best tasting "fowls" you can eat is rabbit. Rabbit meat is lean and not as flabby as most chicken, and its taste is somewhere in between very good breast of chicken and veal. Frozen young rabbit of excellent quality is now widely available cut up in ready-to-cook pieces. It is so good that there is really little need to bother dismembering whole fresh rabbit. I recommend it without reservation.

In France and Germany rabbit is sometimes subjected to a lengthy preliminary marinade which gives it somewhat the taste of game and partly breaks down its texture. The method given here is very straightforward. Without sautéing, rabbit is stewed in practically nothing but its own juices. It is then simmered in white wine with a little rosemary and a touch of tomato. It is a familiar northern Italian approach, and it succeeds marvelously well in drawing out the delicate flavor of rabbit and in maintaining its fine texture intact.

For 6 persons

3 to 3½ pounds frozen cut-up rabbit, thawed overnight in the refrigerator (see note below)	1½ teaspoons rosemary
	2 teaspoons salt
	Freshly ground pepper, 6 to 8 twists of the mill
½ cup olive oil	1 bouillon cube
¼ cup finely diced celery	2 tablespoons tomato paste
1 clove garlic, peeled	
⅔ cup dry white wine	¼ teaspoon sugar

1. Rinse the rabbit pieces in cold running water and pat thoroughly dry with paper towels.

2. Choose a deep covered skillet large enough to contain all the rabbit pieces in a single layer. Put in the oil, celery, garlic, and the rabbit, cover, and cook over low heat for 2 hours. Turn the meat once or twice, but do not leave uncovered.

3. After 2 hours, you will find that the rabbit has thrown off a great deal of liquid. Uncover the pan, turn up the heat to medium, and cook until all the liquid has evaporated. Turn the meat from time to time. When the liquid has evaporated, add the wine, rosemary, salt, and pepper. Simmer, uncovered, until the wine has evaporated. Dissolve the bouillon cube, tomato paste, and sugar in ⅔ cup warm water, pour it over the rabbit, and cook gently for another 12 to 15 minutes, turning and basting the rabbit two or three times. Serve immediately or reheat gently before serving.

NOTE

Do not use wild rabbit in this recipe, only rabbit raised for food.

If using fresh rabbit, soak in abundant cold water for 12 hours or more, then rinse in several changes of cold water and thoroughly pat dry. It may be refrigerated while soaking.

The rabbit may be prepared entirely ahead of time. When reheating, add 2 to 3 tablespoons of water and warm up slowly in a covered pan over low heat, turning the meat from time to time.

Although this goes well with most soups—and *risotti*, except those with fish—your best choice for first courses is among the homemade pastas: Tagliatelle with Bolognese Meat Sauce (page 122), Baked Green Lasagne with Meat Sauce (page 136), or Cappelletti in Broth (page 150). A fine soup would be Passatelli (page 67). For vegetables, the most congenial are Fried Finocchio (page 364), Zucchini Fried in Flour-and-Water Batter (page 377), or Fried Artichoke Wedges (page 334).

MIXED BOILED MEATS

Bollito misto

When friends and acquaintances about to go to Italy ask what dishes they should eat, among my recommendations, especially if they are going to be in Emilia, Lombardy, or Piedmont, is *bollito misto*, mixed boiled meats. "*Boiled meat?*" they say, their incredulity soon overtaken by disdain. I am afraid it is a piece of advice that has done little to advance my reputation for culinary sagacity.

This makes me think of an episode in *The Passionate Epicure*, Marcel Rouff's legend of that prodigious gastronome, Dodin-Bouffant. Dodin had been the guest of the Prince of Eurasia, who, in the anxiety to parade the richness of his table before this most discerning of gourmets, overwhelmed him with a vulgar and grandiloquent display of pretentious courses. Dodin countered by inviting the Prince and some friends to dine with him at home. When his guests were seated, trembling in anticipation of the feast that awaited them, Dodin announced his menu. Not only was it astonishingly brief, but its principal course was to be a "boiled beef garnished with its own vegetables." This is what follows:

The Prince, reflecting that this meagre program would hardly have provided the first course of his ordinary meals, wondered inwardly whether he should countenance having been brought from so far in order to eat boiled beef which, at home, he left to the servants' hall. . . .

It arrived at last, that fearsome boiled beef, scorned, reviled, insulting to the Prince and to all gastronomy, Dodin-Bouffant's boiled beef, prodigiously imposing, borne . . . upon an immensely long dish . . . held so high aloft at arms' length, that at first the anxious guests could see nothing whatsoever. But when, cautiously and with purposeful slowness, it was placed upon the table there were several minutes of genuine astonishment. Each guest's return to self-possession was marked by personal rhythms and reactions. Rabaz and Magot mentally scourged themselves for having doubted the Master; Trifouille was seized with panic before the display of such genius; Beaubois trembled with emotion. As for the Prince of Eurasia, he wavered between the noble desire to create Dodin-Bouffant a Duke immediately, as Napoleon had wished to do for Corneille, a wild urge to offer the gastronome half his fortune and half his realm to take over the reins of his gustatory administration, the irritation of being taught a lesson which was now crystal clear, and his haste to cut into the marvel which laid before him its intoxicating promises.

The beef itself, lightly rubbed with saltpetre and then gone over with salt, was carved into slices of a flesh so fine that its mouth-melting texture could actually be seen. The aroma it gave forth was not only that of beef-juice smoking like incense, but the energetic smell of tarragon with which it was impregnated and the few, very few, cubes of transparent, immaculate bacon in the larding. The rather thick slices, their velvety quality guessed at by every lip, rested languidly upon a pillow made of a wide slice of sausage, coarsely chopped, in which the finest veal escorted pork, chopped herbs, thyme, chervil. . . . This delicate triumph of pork-butchery was itself supported by ample cuts from the breast and wing fillets of farm chickens, boiled in their own juice with a shin of veal, rubbed with mint and wild thyme. And, to prop up this triple and magnificent accumulation, behind the white flesh of the fowls (fed exclusively upon bread and milk), was the stout, robust support of a generous layer of fresh goose liver simply cooked in Chambertin. . . . Each guest was to extract, in one stroke, between spoon and fork, the quadruple enchantment which was his share. . . . Congenial wholehearted enjoyment could now give itself free rein. . . . They might abandon themselves, in all contentment, to the pleasures of taste, and to that sweet, confident friendship which beckons to well-born men after meals worthy of the name.

An Italian platter of mixed boiled meats, although not as profusely aromatic as Dodin's boiled beef, has many points in common with it. Like Dodin's dish it includes veal, chicken, and a pork sausage, Modena's *zampone*. But what a sausage it is! No pork product in the world can approach its miraculously creamy texture or the poise of its perfectly balanced delicacy and savoriness. Dodin would have been enraptured. There is no *foie gras*, of course, but there is calf's head, which yields a very fine, tender, gelatinous supplement to the corpulence of the other meats.

Restaurants that feature *bollito misto* present it in a special cart, somewhat resembling an English roast beef cart, which carries the different meats in separate compartments filled with steaming broth. The meat is carved at tableside, as roast beef is in England, and served with a piquant green sauce or a red tomato and pepper sauce or both. In Italy, a proper *bollito misto* is virtually synonymous with a restaurant of the first rank.

The recipe given below is for a complete *bollito misto*. It is a fine recipe if you are serving at least eighteen people. If you are not, you will want to scale it down. You can reduce it by more than half simply by omitting the tongue and the *cotechino*. If any of the beef, chicken, or veal is left over, it can be cut up and used in a salad. The beef can also be used in the recipe on page 234.

For 18 persons or more

2 medium carrots, peeled
2 stalks celery
1 medium yellow onion, peeled
1 medium potato, peeled
½ green pepper, cored and seeded
1 beef tongue (about 3 to 3½ pounds)
2 pounds beef brisket, rump roast, or bottom round
2 tablespoons salt

3 tablespoons canned Italian tomatoes
2 pounds veal brisket, rump roast, or bottom round
½ calf's head
1 chicken (2½ pounds)
1 *cotechino* sausage, boiled separately, as directed on page 277, and kept warm in its own broth

1. Choose a stockpot or kettle large enough to hold all the above ingredients, except for the *cotechino*. (It is very important in a *bollito misto* to have all the meats cook together because each lends part of its flavor to the others.

However, if you just cannot manage in one pot, divide the vegetables in two parts, and cook the beef and tongue in one kettle, and all the other meats in another.) Since in an Italian *bollito* the meat is put into liquid that is already boiling, begin by putting all the vegetables, except the tomatoes, into the kettle and enough water to cover the meat later. Bring to a boil.

2. Add the tongue and beef brisket, cover, and return to a boil. Adjust the heat so that the liquid is just barely simmering. Skim off the scum that comes to surface for the first few minutes. Add the salt and the tomatoes.

3. After 1 hour of very slow simmering, remove the tongue for peeling. It is easier to peel the tongue if you can handle it while it is still very hot; otherwise wait a few moments for it to cool off slightly. Slit the skin all around the top of the tongue and peel it away with your fingers. (There is a second skin beneath this that does not peel off. It will be cut off later in one's own dish after the tongue has been sliced.) Trim away all the fat and gristle from the butt of the tongue, and return it to the pot.

4. Add the veal, then, when the veal has simmered for 1 hour, add the calf's head.

5. After another 45 minutes' simmering, add the chicken. When the chicken has simmered for 45 minutes to 1 hour, the *bollito* is done. Leave it in its broth, and it will stay warm enough to serve for 1 hour after you turn off the heat. If you are serving it much later, reheat by bringing the broth to a slow simmer for about 10 minutes. Turn the pieces of meat once or twice, changing their position in the kettle.

6. A steaming platter with an arrangement of all the boiled meats in slices is a beautiful and enticing thing to see. The juicy texture of boiled meat, however, is very short-lived outside of its broth. There are two solutions. One, slice only part of the meat and serve it, keeping the rest in the kettle until you are ready for another round. Or, even more successful, if less elegant, bring the kettle to the table (or transfer all the meat and enough broth to cover to a large tureen), pull out one piece at a time, carving as much of it as desired, and then return it to the protection of its broth. The *cotechino*, as mentioned earlier, should be kept in its own broth until it is time to slice and serve it. Serve *bollito misto* with one of two sauces on the side: Piquant

Green Sauce (page 26) or Red Sauce (page 27), or both, if you like.

NOTE
Calf's head is usually sold whole, but if you are on good terms with your butcher he should be willing to let you have a half. In case you've never used it before, calf's head is sold completely boned and ready for cooking. If the brains are included they should be removed. Use them for Fried Calf's Brains (page 289).

The following are approximate cooking times for the meats in this recipe, calculated from the moment the liquid they are in comes to a simmer:

beef—3½ hours   calf's head—1½ hours
tongue—3½ hours   chicken—45 minutes
veal—1¾ hours

MENU SUGGESTIONS

Any light soup with a vegetable can precede *bollito misto*. An ideal combination is Passatelli (page 67), cooked in part of the *bollito's* broth, or Cappelletti in Broth (page 150).

OPEN-FACED ITALIAN OMELETS

Frittate

In some texts, the Italian *frittata* has become partly confused with French omelets. Actually, the technique for *frittata* differs in three very important ways from that for making omelets.

• Whereas an omelet is cooked very briefly over high heat, a *frittata* is cooked slowly over very low heat.
• An omelet is creamy and moist, just short of runny. A *frittata* is firm and set, although by no means stiff and dry.

• An omelet is rolled or folded over into an oval, tapered shape. A *frittata* is flat and perfectly round.

Because a *frittata* is cooked over low heat, there is less danger of sticking. You do not need to set aside a special pan for *frittate*, but it is essential to use a very good, heavy-bottomed skillet that transmits and retains heat evenly.

A *frittata* must be cooked on both sides. To do this, some people flip it in mid-air like a flapjack. Others turn it over on a dish and then slide it back into the pan. I have found that the least perilous and most effective way is to run it under the broiler for about 20 seconds to cook the top side once the underside is done.

You can incorporate into *frittate* an endless number of fillings, such as cheese, vegetables, herbs, and ham. The following *frittata al formaggio* illustrates the basic *frittata* technique, which remains exactly the same no matter what filling you use.

OPEN-FACED ITALIAN OMELET WITH CHEESE

Frittata al formaggio

For 4 persons

6 eggs (U.S. Extra Large)	1 cup freshly grated Parmesan cheese or Swiss cheese
¼ teaspoon salt	
Freshly ground pepper, about 4 twists of the mill	3 tablespoons butter

1. Beat the eggs in a bowl until the yolks and whites are blended. Add the salt, pepper, and grated cheese, beating them into the eggs.

2. Melt the butter in a 12-inch skillet over medium heat. When the butter begins to foam, well before it becomes colored, add the eggs and turn the heat down as low as possible. When the eggs have set and thickened and only the top surface is runny, about 15 minutes of very slow cooking, run the skillet under the broiler for 30 seconds to 1 minute, or until the top face of the *frittata* has set. (When

done the *frittata* should be set, but soft. It should not be browned either on the bottom or top side.)

3. Loosen the *frittata* with a spatula and slide it onto a warm platter. Cut it into four pielike wedges and serve.

MENU SUGGESTIONS

In Italy, a *frittata* usually appears at the evening meal, which is the light meal of the day. It takes the place of meat or fowl and is preceded by a light soup, or a dish of prosciutto or assorted cold cuts. Here the situation is reversed, and *frittata* obviously makes a fine dish around which you can plan a light lunch. For a hearty country dinner, however, Open-Faced Italian Omelet with Cheese (previous page) can be a satisfying second course when preceded by Hot, Anchovy-Flavored Dip for Vegetables (page 39).

OPEN-FACED ITALIAN OMELET WITH ARTICHOKES

Frittata di carciofi

For 4 persons

1 large or 2 medium artichokes	Freshly ground pepper, 6 twists of the mill
1 teaspoon finely chopped garlic	5 eggs (U.S. Extra Large)
2 tablespoons olive oil	3 tablespoons freshly grated Parmesan cheese
2 tablespoons finely chopped parsley	
Salt	3 tablespoons butter

1. Trim the artichokes as directed on page 335. Then cut them lengthwise into the thinnest possible slices.

2. In a skillet, sauté the garlic, with all the oil, over medium heat until it has colored lightly. Add the sliced artichokes, the parsley, a small pinch of salt, and half the pepper, and sauté for about 1 minute, or long enough to turn the artichokes two or three times. Add ⅓ cup water, cover the pan, and cook until the artichokes are very tender. If they are young and fresh, it may take just 15 minutes or

less. (In this case there might be some water left in the pan. Uncover the pan and evaporate the water over high heat while stirring the artichokes.) If the artichokes are tough, it may take twice as long to cook them. (In which case, if all the water evaporates before they are done, add 2 or 3 tablespoons of water.) When done, drain them completely of oil and set aside to cool.

3. Beat the eggs in a bowl until the yolks and whites are blended. Add the artichokes, another small pinch of salt, the rest of the pepper, and all the grated cheese, and mix thoroughly.

4. In a 12-inch skillet, melt the butter over medium heat. When it begins to foam, and well before it becomes colored, add the egg-and-artichoke mixture, turn the heat down as low as possible, and proceed exactly as directed in Steps 2 and 3 of Open-Faced Italian Omelet with Cheese (page 316).

OPEN-FACED ITALIAN OMELET WITH ASPARAGUS

Frittata di asparagi

For 4 persons

1 pound asparagus
5 eggs (U.S. Extra
    Large)
¼ teaspoon salt
Freshly ground pepper,
    4 to 6 twists of the
    mill

⅔ cup freshly grated
    Parmesan cheese
3 tablespoons butter

1. Trim, peel, and boil the asparagus as directed on page 341; then drain and allow to cool.

2. Cut the cooled asparagus into ½-inch lengths, utilizing as much of the stalk as possible.

3. Beat the eggs in a bowl until the yolks and whites are blended. Add the cut asparagus and the salt, pepper, and grated cheese and mix everything thoroughly.

4. In a 10- or 12-inch skillet, melt the butter over medium heat. When it begins to foam, and well before it becomes colored, add the egg-and-asparagus mixture, turn the heat down as low as possible, and proceed exactly as directed in Steps 2 and 3 of Open-Faced Italian Omelet with Cheese (page 316).

OPEN-FACED ITALIAN OMELET
WITH GREEN BEANS

Frittata con fagiolini verdi

For 4 persons

5 eggs (U.S. Extra Large)	1½ cups coarsely chopped boiled green beans (see page 347)
½ teaspoon salt	
Freshly ground pepper, 6 to 8 twists of the mill	1 cup freshly grated Parmesan cheese
	3 tablespoons butter

1. Beat the eggs in a bowl until the yolks and whites are blended.

2. Add the salt, pepper, green beans, and grated cheese and mix thoroughly.

3. Melt the butter in a 12-inch skillet over medium heat. When it begins to foam, and well before it becomes colored, add the egg-and-green-bean mixture, making sure the green beans are evenly distributed, not bunched up all at one end. Turn the heat down as low as possible and proceed exactly as directed in Steps 2 and 3 of Open-Faced Italian Omelet with Cheese (page 316).

OPEN-FACED ITALIAN OMELET WITH
TOMATO, ONIONS, AND BASIL

Frittata al pomodoro e basilico

For 4 persons

3 cups thinly sliced yellow onion	2 tablespoons freshly grated Parmesan cheese
⅓ cup olive oil	
1 cup canned Italian tomatoes, drained and roughly chopped	Freshly ground pepper, 6 twists of the mill
	½ cup roughly chopped fresh basil
2 teaspoons salt	3 tablespoons butter
5 eggs (U.S. Extra Large)	

1. Cook the sliced onion, with all the oil, in a medium skillet over low heat until it is completely wilted and has turned a rich golden-brown color.

2. Add the tomatoes and ½ teaspoon of the salt. Raise the heat to medium and cook for 8 minutes, stirring frequently. Turn off the heat and tilt the pan, gathering the tomatoes and onion at the up-ended side of the pan to drain them of oil. When the oil has drained off, transfer the vegetables to a bowl and allow to cool.

3. Beat the eggs in a bowl until the yolks and whites are blended. Using a slotted spoon, add the tomatoes and onion, and then add the remaining 1½ teaspoons of salt, the grated cheese, pepper, and chopped basil, and beat everything into the eggs.

4. Melt the butter in a 12-inch skillet over medium heat. When the butter begins to foam, and well before it becomes colored, add the eggs, turn the heat down to minimum, and proceed exactly as directed in Steps 2 and 3 of Open-Faced Italian Omelet with Cheese (page 316).

OPEN-FACED ITALIAN OMELET WITH ZUCCHINI

Frittata di zucchine

For 4 persons

1 cup thinly sliced yellow onion	Freshly ground pepper, 7 or 8 twists of the mill
¼ cup vegetable oil	
3 medium zucchini (or zucchini cores; see note below)	6 fresh basil leaves, roughly chopped, OR, if basil is not in season, 1 tablespoon finely chopped parsley
½ teaspoon salt	
4 eggs (U.S. Extra Large)	
⅔ cup freshly grated Parmesan cheese	3 tablespoons butter

1. Cook the sliced onion, with all the oil, in a medium skillet over low heat until it is completely wilted and has turned a rich golden-brown color.

2. While the onion is cooking, cut off the ends of the zucchini and wash thoroughly in cold water. If not absolutely fresh, with a very smooth glossy skin, peel the skin to remove all traces of imbedded soil. Slice into disks ¼ inch thick. If you are using zucchini cores, chop them roughly.

3. When the onion is cooked, add the zucchini and the salt. Cook over medium heat until lightly browned—or, if you are using the cores, until they have turned into a light-brown, creamy paste. When done, turn off the heat and tilt the pan lightly, pushing the zucchini and onion toward the upended side of the pan. When the oil has drained off, remove the vegetables to a bowl to cool.

4. Beat the eggs in a bowl until the yolks and whites are blended. Add the grated cheese and, with a slotted spoon, the zucchini and onion. Beat everything into the eggs, adding the pepper and basil or parsley at the end.

5. Melt the butter in a 10-inch skillet over medium heat. When the butter begins to foam, and well before it becomes colored, add the egg-and-zucchini mixture, turn the heat down as low as possible, and proceed exactly as described

in Steps 2 and 3 of Italian Open-Faced Omelet with Cheese (page 316).

NOTE
If you have made Zucchini Stuffed with Meat and Cheese (page 382), you can use the leftover cores of 6 or 7 zucchini for this recipe.

MIXED FRIED MEATS, VEGETABLES, CHEESE, CREAM, AND FRUIT

Il Grande Fritto Misto

Brillat-Savarin has given the very best description of frying, defining its action as that of a surprise. Perfectly fried food is "surprised" in hot fat, which quickly imprisons its natural flavor and texture intact within a crisp, light crust. Successful frying requires a generous quantity of very hot fat. Never add fat after you've started frying. Butter, even when clarified, does not tolerate very high temperatures, and it is not, as a rule, suitable for quick frying. The most convenient medium to use is vegetable oil.

Italians are the masters of the frying pan, and fried cheese, meat, vegetables, fruit, taken singly, are frequent components of an Italian meal. Moreover, in some sections of Italy, and in Emilia-Romagna in particular, an entire meal, from first course to fruit, can be based exclusively on fried dishes. This tour de force is known as *il grande fritto misto*. It is a menu that requires from its creator not just skill, but great self-abnegation. Fried foods must be consumed hot, and while the cook fries the guests eat. In Naples it is called *frienno magnanno*, "frying and eating," which is also used idiomatically as an equivalent of "said and done."

For obvious reasons, a *grande fritto misto*, like a *bollito misto*, is consumed more frequently these days in a restaurant than at home. But if you have help in the kitchen and feel like trying it, here is a list of recipes scattered throughout this book that you can pull together into a truly memorable meal.

The first course
Fried Mortadella, Pancetta, and Cheese Tidbits (page 45)

The second course
An assortment of as many as possible of the following, in
reduced quantities:
Breaded Veal Cutlets, Milan Style (page 260), served cut
    into small squares
Baby Lamb Chops Fried in Parmesan Cheese Batter (page
    272)
Fried Breaded Calf's Liver (page 288), served cut into small
    squares
Fried Calf's Brains (page 289)
Fried Artichoke Wedges (page 334)
Fried Asparagus (page 345)
Fried Tomatoes (page 375)
Fried Finocchio (page 364)
Zucchini Fried in Flour-and-Water Batter (page 377) and/
    or Fried Zucchini Blossoms (page 383)
Fried Cauliflower (page 354)
Fried Sweet Cream (page 426), an absolutely indispensable
    part of any *fritto misto*
Fried Polenta (page 195)

Desserts and fruit
Apple Fritters (page 418)

VEGETABLES

Le Verdure

I cannot imagine Italy without its vegetable stalls, filling ancient squares and animating dusty side streets with mounds of fabulous forms in purple, green, red, gold, and orange. In a land heavy with man's monuments, these are the soil's own masterworks.

Perhaps one day the vitality of these still-flourishing markets will be replaced by the pallor of deep-freeze counters, those cemeteries of food, where produce is sealed up in waxed boxes marked, like some tombstones, with photographs of the departed. But I hope it never happens. I would sooner be deprived of all the marvels of Micheangelo.

The quality of Italy's produce is matchless. Only that of France comes close. It is not surprising that, in Italian cooking, the richness and variety of vegetable dishes approaches that of the first courses. Sometimes a vegetable will even take the place of a first course, or of the second. Frequently a boiled vegetable, such as green beans or asparagus, is used as salad. Most often the vegetable is a side dish. Except when fish is served, it is always an essential part of every meal.

In Italian cooking, vegetables can be boiled, braised,

fried, sautéed, gratinéed, baked, and even broiled. Every one of these procedures is illustrated in this chapter, including a recipe for charcoal-broiled vegetables.

In a typically Italian approach, the vegetable is first boiled, then given a finish in the skillet or in the oven with butter and Parmesan cheese. Sometimes, instead of the butter-and-cheese treatment, a boiled vegetable such as spinach or broccoli is sautéed with garlic and olive oil. Frying is another favorite treatment for vegetables, and several examples are given, with different batters.

Trifolare is an expression you will find in all Italian cook books, and vegetables *trifolati* appear on nearly every restaurant menu. When vegetables are *trifolati*, they are thinly sliced and sautéed with garlic, oil, and parsley, a method very successful with mushrooms. You will find the recipe for it here, as well as a similar one for Jerusalem artichokes.

The Jerusalem artichoke is a native American tuber that is now happily settled in certain sections of northern Italy, where it is highly prized. In the following chapter you will be shown how it can be used in a salad.

There are three recipes for finocchio, a vegetable universally popular in Italy. Very good finocchio is available here, it is not terribly difficult to prepare, and it can be an enjoyable addition to your vegetable repertory.

The longest single section of this chapter deals with artichokes. Italians take great pleasure in this extraordinary relative of the thistle, and have found many fascinating ways to cook it. Among the recipes for artichokes given here you will find one of the oldest and still one of the best, *carciofi alla giudia* (crisp-fried whole artichokes), which dates back to Jewish cooking in the ghetto of ancient Rome.

Preparing and cooking vegetables takes time, patience, and care. Do not waste your efforts on second-rate materials. Buy carefully, avoiding any vegetable that is wilted, badly bruised, ill assorted, tired-looking, soggy, flabby, or overgrown. Shopping for good fresh vegetables in this country may be frustrating at times, but that does not mean that we must deliver ourselves up in thralldom to the frozen-food shelves. On any one marketing day there are always available two or more fresh vegetables of respectable quality. Limit yourself as much as possible to vegetables that are in season. They are more likely to be locally grown and fresher,

or, at any rate, richer in flavor. Try not to decide in advance
what you are going to cook but, rather, buy the best-quality
vegetables you can find and then choose a recipe to suit.

ARTICHOKES, ROMAN STYLE

Carciofi alla romana

In Italy one finds two basic types of artichokes. One is
purplish in color, with long, narrow, tapered leaves spiked
at the tips. It is well worth looking out for if you are traveling
in the northern and central part of Italy in the winter and
spring because it is truly extraordinary in flavor and texture.
However, it is not available here, so we will not discuss it
further. The other type of artichoke is very common in the
south, where it is called *mammola*. It has a stout, globelike
shape, it is green, and it is very similar to the artichokes
found in this country. One of the most attractive and appetizing ways of preparing these artichokes is *alla romana*,
Roman style, and it is particularly well suited to American
artichokes.

For 4 persons

4 large artichokes	½ teaspoon crumbled
½ lemon	mint leaves
3 tablespoons finely	½ teaspoon salt
chopped parsley	½ cup olive oil
1½ teaspoons finely	
chopped garlic	

1. Artichokes *alla romana* are served with the stems
attached, so be careful not to snap them off while trimming
the artichokes. Begin preparing an artichoke by bending
back and snapping off the outer leaves. Do not pull the
leaves off all the way to the base, because the whitish bottom
of the leaf is tender, and edible. As you get deeper into the
artichoke, the leaves will snap off farther and farther from
the base. Keep pulling off leaves until you expose a central
cone of leaves that are green only at the tips and whose
paler, whitish base is at least 1½ inches high.

Slice at least an inch off the top of the entire central cone, eliminating all the green part. Don't be afraid to trim too much—you are eliminating only the tough, inedible portions. Rub with the lemon half, squeezing juice over the cut portions of the artichoke so that they won't discolor.

You can now look into the center of the artichoke, where you will find at the bottom some very small, pale leaves with prickly tips curving inward. Cut off all the little leaves and scrape away the fuzzy "choke" beneath them, being careful not to cut away any of the heart or the other tender parts. (A rounded point on the knife can be helpful.) Return to the outside of the artichoke and pare away the green parts of the leaves at the base, leaving only the white.

All there is left to trim now is the outer part of the stem. Turning the artichoke upside down, you will note from the bottom of the stem that the stem has a whitish core surrounded by a layer of green. Trim away all the green up to the base of the artichoke, keeping only the white part. Be careful not to detach the stem, and always rub the cut portions with lemon juice so that they will not discolor.

2. In a bowl, mix the chopped parsley, the chopped garlic, the mint leaves, and the salt. Set aside one-third of the mixture and press the rest into the cavity of each artichoke, rubbing it well into the sides of the cavity.

3. Choose a heavy-bottomed casserole just large enough to contain the artichokes, which are to go in standing, and provided with a tight-fitting lid. Place the artichokes, tops facing down and stems pointing upward, in the casserole. Rub the rest of the parsley, garlic, and mint mixture on the outside of the artichokes. Add all the oil and enough water to cover one-third of the artichoke leaves, *not* the stems. Soak two thicknesses of paper towels in water. (Since the moist towels help to keep steam that cooks the stems inside the pot, they must be wide enough to cover the casserole.) Place the towels over the casserole and put the lid over the paper towels. Bend the corners of the towels back over the lid. Cook over medium heat for about 35 to 40 minutes, or until tender and easily pierced by a fork.

Cooking times vary according to the freshness and tenderness of the artichokes. (If the artichokes are tough and take long to cook, you may have to add 2 or 3 tablespoons of water from time to time. If they cook rapidly and there

ROMAN STYLE ARTICHOKE

PREPARING AN ARTICHOKE

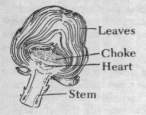

— Leaves

— Choke
— Heart

— Stem

1. Cross section of an artichoke

2. As you get deeper into the artichoke, the leaves will snap off farther from the base. Keep snapping off leaves until you expose a central cone of leaves. The paler, whitish base of the leaves should be at least 1½ inches high.

3. Slice about an inch off the top of the central cone, enough to eliminate all the green part.

4. In the center of the artichoke, you will see at the bottom some very small, pale leaves with purple, prickly tips curving inward. Cut off all these little leaves and scrape away the fuzzy "choke" beneath. Be careful not to cut away any of the heart.

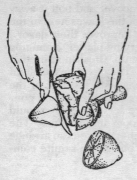

5. Pare away the green outer parts of the leaves at the base of the artichoke, leaving the white and continuing to rub the cut portion with the lemon half.

6. Taking care not to break the stem, trim away its outer green layer, leaving only the whitish cone.

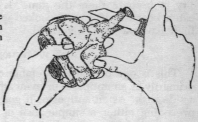

7. The finished product

is too much water left in the pot, uncover and boil it away rapidly. Do not worry if the edges of the leaves next to the bottom of the pot start to brown; it improves their flavor.)

4. Transfer the artichokes to a serving platter, arranging them always with the stems pointing up. (Bear in mind that the stems are not merely decorative. They have an excellent flavor and they are to be eaten along with the rest of the artichoke.) Reserve the oil and juices from the pot and pour them over the artichokes just before serving. They should be served either lukewarm or at room temperature. The ideal temperature at which to serve them, if you can arrange it, is when they are no longer hot, but haven't quite completely cooled off.

NOTE

Try to prepare them the same day they are going to be eaten because, like most cooked greens, they lose part of their flavor when refrigerated.

MENU SUGGESTIONS

This is one of many vegetable dishes that Italians use primarily as an antipasto or even a first course, rather than a side dish. As an antipasto, it goes practically anywhere, preceding either a simple dish of spaghetti with tomato sauce or the elegant Fettuccine Tossed in Cream and Butter (page 123). As a first course it can lead to any roast, from beef to fowl.

BRAISED ARTICHOKES WITH MORTADELLA STUFFING

Carciofi ripieni di mortadella

For 4 persons

4 medium artichokes	1 egg
½ lemon	A small pinch of nutmeg
½ teaspoon finely chopped garlic	½ teaspoon salt
1 tablespoon chopped parsley	Freshly ground pepper, about 4 twists of the mill
½ cup chopped *mortadella*	2½ tablespoons fine dry bread crumbs
⅓ cup freshly grated Parmesan cheese	⅓ cup olive oil

1. Clean and trim the artichokes exactly as directed in step 1 of Artichokes, Roman Style (page 326), leaving the stems *on*. (Remember to rub with lemon, squeezing juice over the cut parts.)

2. In a mixing bowl, combine the garlic, parsley, *mortadella*, Parmesan cheese, egg, nutmeg, salt, pepper, and 1½ tablespoons of the bread crumbs. Mix thoroughly and divide into 4 equal parts.

3. Stuff the artichokes with the *mortadella* mixture, sealing the tops with the remaining bread crumbs.

4. Choose a deep casserole that can later accommodate the artichokes standing. Put in all the olive oil and the artichokes, laying them on their sides. Turn on the heat to medium, and slowly brown the artichokes on all sides. When nicely browned, stand the artichokes with their stems pointing up, put in ⅓ cup of water, and cover the casserole, placing between the cover and the pot a double thickness of water-soaked paper towels. Turn the heat down to low and cook for about 30 minutes. Test the hearts with a fork. If easily pierced, the artichokes are done. (If they are still firm, and there is no liquid left in the pot, add 1 or 2 tablespoons of water as needed. And don't worry if the leaves next to the bottom of the pot stick and darken.) When

done, transfer the artichokes to a serving platter, pouring over them any juices left in the pot. Serve warm. Do not refrigerate or reheat.

MENU SUGGESTIONS

Follow the suggestions given for Artichokes, Roman Style (page 330).

CRISP-FRIED WHOLE ARTICHOKES

Carciofi alla giudia

There is a substantial tradition of native Jewish cooking in Italy, centered mainly on Ferrara in the north and Rome in the south. That of Rome goes back to the days of the Empire, which must make it, no doubt, the oldest Jewish cuisine in Europe. One of the dishes prized by both ancient and modern visitors to the ghetto is *carciofi alla giudia*. These are young Roman artichokes, trimmed of any hard leaves, flattened, and fried to a golden brown. The finished product is particularly beautiful, looking somewhat like an opened, dried chrysanthemum.

The frying is done in two stages. The artichokes are first fried at a lower temperature, to give the heat time to cook them thoroughly. They are then transferred to a pan with hotter oil, which is excited further by being sprinkled with cold water. This is what gives the leaves their crisp finish, while the heart remains moist and tender.

The best artichokes to use for this recipe are very young, tender artichokes.

For 6 persons

6 medium artichokes	Vegetable oil, enough to
½ lemon	come 1½ inches up
⅓ heaping teaspoon salt	the sides of both
Freshly ground pepper,	pans
6 twists of the mill	

1. Trim the artichokes exactly as directed in Step 1 of Artichokes, Roman Style (page 326), but now leaving only a short stump of a stem. Keep the inside rows of leaves progressively longer, giving the artichoke the look of a thick, fleshy rosebud. Make sure, however, to cut off all the tough part of each leaf, because no amount of cooking will make it edible, and remember to rub all the cut edges of the artichoke with lemon juice to keep them from discoloring.

2. Turn the artichokes bottoms up, gently spread their leaves outward, and press them against your work surface to flatten them as much as possible without cracking them. Turn them right side up and season them with salt and pepper.

3. Heat the oil in a deep skillet (preferably earthenware) over medium heat. When it is hot, add the artichokes, with their leaves facing down. Cook for about 5 to 6 minutes, then turn the artichokes, adjusting the heat to make sure they don't fry too rapidly. Turn them every few minutes as they cook, until their bottoms feel tender at the pricking of a fork. Times vary greatly, depending on the artichokes, but it may take about 15 minutes if they are very young.

4. When the artichokes are tender, turn them so their leaves face the bottom of the pan and press firmly on them with a wooden spoon to flatten them some more.

5. Meanwhile, heat the oil in another deep skillet over high heat. When it is very hot, transfer the artichokes from the other pan, with the leaves always facing down. After they have fried at high heat for about 5 minutes, turn them so that the leaves face up, dip your hand in cold water, and shake the water into the hot oil, keeping at a distance from the pan because the oil will splatter.

6. Transfer the artichokes to paper towels to drain. Serve them piping hot, with the leaves facing up.

MENU SUGGESTIONS

This can be not only a side dish but also a hot antipasto or even a first course in any meal whose second course is meat or fowl. It goes particularly well with Hothouse Lamb, Roman Style (page 271) and Sautéed Lamb Kidneys with White Wine (page 290).

FRIED ARTICHOKE WEDGES

Carciofini fritti

For 4 to 6 persons

3 medium artichokes or 1 ten-ounce package frozen artichoke hearts, thawed	Vegetable oil, sufficient to come ¾ inch up the side of the skillet
½ lemon	Salt
1 tablespoon lemon juice	
1 egg, lightly beaten, in a bowl	
1 cup fine, dry unflavored bread crumbs, spread on a dish or on waxed paper	

1. If you are using fresh artichokes, detach and discard the stems; then prepare as directed on page 335, but cutting them into smaller wedges (about ¾ inch thick at the broadest point) and remembering to rub with lemon as you cut to keep the artichoke from discoloring. Drop in boiling water containing the 1 tablespoon lemon juice. Cook for 5 to 7 minutes, or until tender but not too soft. Drain and set aside to cool. (If you are using frozen artichokes, simply pat dry when thoroughly thawed.)

2. Dip the artichoke wedges into the egg, letting the excess flow back into the dish, then roll in the bread crumbs. (The artichokes may be prepared up to and including this point as much as 3 or 4 hours ahead of time.)

3. Heat the oil in a skillet until a haze forms over it. Slip the artichokes into the skillet, frying them on one side until a golden crust forms, then turning them until a crust has formed on all sides.

4. Transfer to paper towels to drain; then add salt. Serve while still hot.

MENU SUGGESTIONS

Fried artichoke wedges are a perfect accompaniment for any fried meat such as Breaded Veal Cutlets, Milan Style

(260), Baby Lamb Chops Fried in Parmesan Cheese Batter (page 272), or Fried Breaded Calf's Liver (page 288). Like all fried vegetables, they fit beautifully into any type of *fritto misto*. They are also a good accompaniment for Pan-Broiled Steak with Marsala and Hot Pepper Sauce (page 228), Meat Loaf Braised in White Wine with Dried Wild Mushrooms (page 238), Pork Loin Braised in Milk (page 274), Sautéed Chicken Breast Fillets with Lemon and Parsley (page 303), or Stewed Rabbit with White Wine (page 309).

BRAISED ARTICHOKES AND PEAS

Carciofi e piselli stufati

For 6 persons

2 large or 3 or 4 medium-small artichokes	1 tablespoon chopped parsley
½ lemon	Salt
2 tablespoons chopped yellow onion	Freshly ground pepper, about 4 twists of the mill
3 tablespoons olive oil	
½ teaspoon finely chopped garlic	
2 pounds fresh peas (unshelled weight) or 1 ten-ounce package frozen peas, thawed	

1. For this recipe you need to cut the artichokes lengthwise into wedges about 1 inch thick at their widest point. It may be easier, therefore, to first trim away the hard outer leaves and the green tips as in Step 1 of Artichokes, Roman Style (page 326). Then cut the artichoke into wedges and from there proceed to remove the choke and the soft, white curling leaves directly above it. (You may discard the stems, if you are so inclined, but it would be a pity, because they have a tart, interesting flavor and can be quite tender. If you use the stems, cut away the green outer layers, leaving just the white inner core.) Remember as you prepare each artichoke to rub it with the lemon, squeezing juice over the cut portions, or it will discolor.

2. Put the chopped onion in a casserole with the olive oil and sauté over medium-high heat until translucent. Add the garlic and continue sautéing until it becomes lightly colored but not brown. Add the artichokes and ⅓ cup of water, cover, and cook over medium heat.

3. After 10 minutes add the shelled fresh peas, the chopped parsley, ½ teaspoon salt, pepper, and, if there is no more water in the pot, ¼ cup of warm water. Turn and mix the peas and artichokes. (If you are using frozen peas, add them only after the artichokes are almost completely tender, because they take only about 5 minutes to cook.) Cover and continue cooking over medium heat until the artichokes are tender all the way through. Test with a fork or, even better, taste, correcting for salt. (If there is too much water in the pot when the vegetables are cooked, uncover, raise the heat to high, and boil the water away rapidly.)

MENU SUGGESTIONS

Braised Artichokes and Peas is a perfect accompaniment to broiled and roasted meats, to roasted fowl, to sautéed veal *scaloppine*, and to Breaded Veal Cutlets, Milan Style (page 260). It does not go well with meats that are cooked in a cream- or milk-based sauce.

BRAISED ARTICHOKES AND LEEKS

Carciofi e porri stufati

For 6 persons

3 large artichokes or 5 or
    6 small ones
½ lemon
4 large leeks, about 1¾
    inches in diameter,
    or 6 smaller ones

¼ cup olive oil
Salt
Freshly ground pepper,
    about 4 twists of the
    mill

1. Prepare the artichokes as directed in Braised Artichokes and Peas (page 335), remembering to rub the lemon over the cut portion of each artichoke as you finish preparing it, or it will discolor.

2. Cut off the roots of the leeks, remove any leaves that are withered and discolored, and slice off a small part of the green tops. Slice the leeks into two lengthwise sections and wash thoroughly under cold running water.

3. Choose a casserole with a tight-fitting lid. Lay the leeks in the casserole, and add the oil and enough water to come 1 inch up the side of the pot. Cover and cook over moderate heat for 10 minutes. Add the artichoke sections, salt, pepper, and, if necessary, a little warm water. Continue cooking over moderate heat, turning the vegetables from time to time. The vegetables are cooked when they are tender. (Cooking times vary greatly according to the freshness and quality of the vegetable. The only way to tell is by piercing them with a fork or tasting a small piece. If they take long to cook, you will have to add a little warm water from time to time, but all the water must be absorbed by the time they finish cooking.)

MENU SUGGESTIONS

This dish is an ideal accompaniment to roasted meats and fowl, to Sautéed Chicken Breast Fillets with Lemon and Parsley (page 303), or Veal Scaloppine with Lemon Sauce (page 252) or with Marsala (page 251). Do not pair them with a second course carrying a cream or milk-based sauce.

BRAISED ARTICHOKES AND POTATOES

Carciofi e patate

For 4 to 6 persons

3 medium potatoes
    (about ¾ pound)
2 medium artichokes or
    3 or 4 small ones
½ lemon
⅓ cup coarsely chopped
    yellow onion

5 tablespoons olive oil
¼ teaspoon finely
    chopped garlic
Salt
Freshly ground pepper,
    about 4 twists of the
    mill
1 tablespoon chopped
    parsley

1. Peel the potatoes and wash in cold water. Cut into lengthwise wedges about ¾ inch thick at the broadest point.

2. Prepare the artichokes for cooking as directed in Braised Artichokes and Peas (page 335), remembering to rub the lemon over the cut portion of each artichoke as you finish preparing it, or it will discolor.

3. Choose a casserole just large enough for the artichokes and potatoes. Over medium heat sauté the onion in the olive oil until translucent. Do not let it color. Add the garlic and sauté until it colors lightly. Add the potatoes, artichokes, 1 teaspoon salt, pepper, and parsley and sauté long enough to turn everything two or three times.

4. Add ¼ cup of water, cover the pot, turn the heat down to medium low, and cook, turning the artichokes and potatoes from time to time, for about 40 minutes, or until the artichokes and potatoes are tender when pierced by a fork. (If, while they are still cooking, there is no liquid left in the pot, add 2 tablespoons of water as needed.) When done, taste and correct for salt. Serve warm.

MENU SUGGESTIONS

Follow those given for Braised Artichokes and Peas (page 335). In Italy you would use this as a side dish in a light evening meal, where the first course would not be pasta but a vegetable soup, or a rice-and-vegetable soup.

JERUSALEM ARTICHOKES

Topinambur

The Jerusalem artichoke is not an artichoke, nor has it ever seen Jerusalem. It is a tuber, the edible rootstock of a variety of the sunflower plant, native to Canada and the northern United States. Jerusalem is apparently a corruption of *girasole*, the Italian word for "sunflower." It is much prized in the Piedmont and Friuli regions of northern Italy, where it is called *topinambur*. It has an exquisite texture and a delicate flavor that faintly recalls that of artichoke hearts. It is delicious raw in salads (page 391), sautéed, or gratinéed. It is available usually from late fall through winter. If you find it at your market, buy one or two pounds of it, even though you might not be ready to cook it immediately. It easily keeps for a week or more in the refrigerator. It looks somewhat like ginger root, so be careful that what you are buying is Jerusalem artichoke. It is not easy to use up two pounds of ginger root, as I once found out to my dismay.

When buying Jerusalem artichokes, make sure they are as firm as possible, not spongy. Dig into one or two with your fingernail: if the color under the skin is pinkish, not the creamy white it should be, do not buy them. And peeling them will take half the time if you choose the least gnarled and twisted roots.

SAUTEED JERUSALEM ARTICHOKES

Topinambur trifolati

For 6 persons

1½ pounds Jerusalem artichokes	Freshly ground pepper, about 6 twists of the mill
¼ cup olive oil	
1 teaspoon finely chopped garlic	1 tablespoon finely chopped parsley
Salt	

1. Pare the artichokes with a potato peeler, or, if you don't object to the peel, scrub them thoroughly under cold running water with a stiff brush. Drop them into boiling salted water, the largest pieces first, the smallest last. As the water comes to a boil again, remove the artichokes and drain. Cut them into very thin slices, about ¼ inch thick. They should still be fairly hard.

2. In a skillet sauté the chopped garlic in the olive oil over medium heat. When the garlic has colored lightly, add the artichokes and stir. Add salt, the pepper, and the chopped parsley and stir again. Turn the artichokes a few times while cooking. They are done when quite tender at the pricking of a fork. Taste and correct for salt, and serve hot.

Sautéed Jerusalem artichokes are a natural accompaniment for all roasts of veal or chicken, and they make a fine side dish for broiled meat. Try them also with Little Veal Bundles with Anchovies and Cheese (page 256), Sautéed Breaded Veal Chops (page 258), Fried Calf's Brains (page 289), or Sautéed Chicken Breast Fillets with Lemon and Parsley (page 303).

GRATINÉED JERUSALEM ARTICHOKES

Topinambur gratinati

For 4 persons

1 pound Jerusalem artichokes	¼ cup freshly grated Parmesan cheese
Salt	2½ tablespoons butter
Freshly ground pepper, about 4 twists of the mill	

1. Preheat the oven to 400°.
2. Peel or scrub the artichokes as directed in the preceding recipe. Drop them in boiling salted water, holding back the smaller pieces a few moments. Cook until tender but firm at the pricking of a fork. (Jerusalem artichokes tend to go from very firm to almost mushy in a brief span of time, so watch them carefully.) When done, drain and allow to cool.
3. Cut the artichokes into slices ½ inch thick. Arrange them in a buttered bake-and-serve dish so that they slightly overlap. Add salt and pepper, sprinkle the grated cheese over them, dot with butter, and place in the uppermost part of the preheated oven. Bake until a nice golden crust forms. Allow to settle briefly before serving.

Gratinéed vegetables take easily to all roasts and broiled meats. They are also an excellent accompaniment to Pan-Broiled Steak with Marsala and Hot Pepper Sauce (page 228), Beef Braised in Red Wine Sauce (page 231). Sautéed

Veal Scaloppine with Lemon Sauce (page 252) or with Marsala (page 251). There is actually no dish which they cannot accompany gracefully, but to avoid monotony, try not to pair them with those already containing cheese.

ASPARAGUS

Asparagi

HOW TO PREPARE AND BOIL ASPARAGUS

To have good cooked asparagus, you must first buy good raw asparagus. The surest sign that asparagus is over the hill is an open, droopy tip. It should always be tightly closed and firm. The stalk should feel crisp and look moist. You can buy early asparagus, if you don't mind the price, but avoid it at the end of its season, in late June.

Preparation   Asparagus must be trimmed so as to make the entire spear edible. At the tip it is very tender, but it can be very tough at the base, with differing degrees of tenderness in between. The parts that must be eliminated are the very end and a thin layer of fibers surrounding the lower half of the spear.

Start by slicing off about 1 inch at the butt end. If, in cutting, you find the flesh hard, fibrous, and somewhat dry slice off more of the stalk until the exposed end is tender and moist. (If the asparagus is very young, it will not need to have much of the base sliced off. If it is older and drier you might have to cut as much as 1½ to 2 inches.) Now, using a sharp paring knife, trim away the tough, outer fibers. Start your cut at the base, going about ¹⁄₁₆ inch deep, and gradually tapering to nothing midway between the tip and the base. Remove any small leaves sprouting below the tip. Soak the trimmed asparagus in a basin of cold water for 10 minutes, then rinse in 2 or 3 fresh changes of cold water. It is now ready for cooking.

Cooking   In Italy we partially boil and partially steam asparagus in a special cooker. Inside the cooker there is a separate, perforated liner that holds the spears upright and lifts out to remove the asparagus when it is cooked. While the butt of the spear is under boiling water, the tip is cooked by the rising steam. This method compensates for the difference between the butt and the tip so that both are cooked to an even degree of tenderness. The Italian asparagus cooker is available in all good housewares shops and departments, and I heartily recommend it to you. You can, however, cook asparagus almost equally well, as the French have always done, in a fish poacher, or in a deep, oval pot large enough to hold the spears horizontally. Here are directions for both methods.

Asparagus Cooked in the Italian Asparagus Cooker

1. Make a bundle of the asparagus, tying it in two places, one above the butts, the other below the tips.

2. Put enough cold water in the cooker to come 2½ inches up the side of the pot. Add 1 teaspoon of salt. Put in the asparagus bundle, cover, and cook at a steady, moderate boil for 15 to 20 minutes. Test the base of the asparagus with a sharp-pronged fork. If it is easily pierced it is done.

3. Transfer the asparagus bundle to an oval platter and remove the ties. Prop the platter up about 1 inch at one end so that the liquid thrown off by the asparagus runs down to the opposite end. This liquid is to be discarded when the asparagus has been well drained.

Asparagus Cooked Without an Asparagus Cooker

1. Make a bundle of the asparagus exactly as in Step 1 above.

2. Bring at least 4 quarts of water to a boil in a fish poacher or in a deep oval pot large enough to contain the asparagus horizontally. Add 2 teaspoons of salt. Wait a moment for the water to return to a rapid boil, then put in the asparagus. Cook the asparagus at a steady, moderate boil, uncovered, for 15 to 20 minutes. After 15 minutes test the base of the asparagus with a sharp-pronged fork. It is done when easily pierced.

3. Hook one or two forks under the bundle's ties and transfer it to an oval platter. Remove the string, loosening the asparagus, and proceed to drain it of its liquid as in Step 3 above.

ASPARAGUS WITH PARMESAN CHEESE

Asparagi alla parmigiana

One of spring's most exquisite gifts to the Italian table is young asparagus, first boiled, then briefly baked with fragrant, grated aged Parmesan cheese. Of all the many dishes called *alla parmigiana* this is an authentic specialty of Parma, which does not keep it from being a great favorite all over Italy, or even in France, where, curiously, it is called *à la milanaise*.

For 4 persons

2 pounds asparagus	⅔ cup freshly grated
½ teaspoon salt	Parmesan cheese
	5 tablespoons butter

1. Preheat the oven to 450°.
2. Trim, peel, and boil the asparagus as directed on page 341.
3. Smear the bottom of a rectangular bake-and-serve dish with butter. Arrange the boiled asparagus in the dish side by side, in slightly overlapping rows, setting the tips of the spears in one row over the butt ends of the ones in the row ahead. (Never cover the tips.) Sprinkle each row with salt and grated cheese and dot with butter before lapping the next row over it.
4. Bake on the uppermost rack of the oven for about 15 minutes, until a light, golden crust forms. Allow to settle a few minutes before serving.

MENU SUGGESTIONS

This is often served as a first course. It goes well before Rolled Stuffed Breast of Veal (page 244), Veal Rolls in Tomato Sauce (page 255), Roast Spring Lamb with White Wine (page 268), Hothouse Lamb, Roman Style (page 271), or Roast Chicken with Rosemary (page 296). If you are using it as a first course, you can dispense with green vegetables later and serve instead Diced Pan-Roasted Potatoes (page 372).

ASPARAGUS WITH PARMESAN CHEESE AND FRIED EGGS

Asparagi alla parmigiana con uova fritte

Serving asparagus *alla parmigiana* with fried eggs is a succulent enrichment of an already delectable dish. It can no longer, in fact, be considered a side dish. It has all the substance of a full second course and should be employed as such.

For 4 persons

2 pounds asparagus	Freshly ground pepper,
8 eggs	about 8 twists of the
¼ cup butter	mill

1. Prepare the asparagus as directed in Asparagus with Parmesan Cheese (previous page).
2. After you remove the asparagus from the oven, fry the eggs in the butter.
3. Divide the asparagus into four equal parts and place on individual dishes. Slide two fried eggs over each portion of asparagus; then spoon the juices left in the baking dish over the asparagus and eggs. Grind pepper over the eggs and serve immediately.

NOTE
This dish, to be enjoyed, needs some abandonment of etiquette. Eat the asparagus with your fingers, holding it by the stem and swirling it in the eggs.

MENU SUGGESTIONS

Like a *frittata*, this can be the mainstay of a light but elegant lunch, preceded by a clear soup or Bresaola (page 44).

FRIED ASPARAGUS

Asparagi fritti

The sweet inner core under the crusty exterior of fried asparagus makes this one of the most delectable of all fried vegetables. Virtually no trimming is required because only the tips and the most tender part of the stalk are used.

For 4 persons

1 pound crisp, fresh
    asparagus
Vegetable oil, enough to
    come ½ inch up the
    side of the skillet
1 egg, well beaten, in a
    deep, oval dish

1 cup fine, dry
    unflavored bread
    crumbs, spread on a
    dish or on waxed
    paper
½ teaspoon salt

1. Snap off the bottoms of the stems of the asparagus, leaving a stalk about 4 to 5 inches long, including the tips. Remove all the tiny leaves below the tips and wash the asparagus thoroughly in cold water. Pat dry with a towel.
2. Heat the oil in a skillet over high heat. When the oil is very hot, dip the asparagus in the beaten egg, roll it in the bread crumbs, and slide it into the skillet, doing just a few stalks at a time so that they are not crowded in the pan. When the asparagus has formed a crust on one side, turn it. When it has formed a crust on the other side, transfer with a slotted spatula to paper towels to drain, and add ½ teaspoon salt. When all the asparagus is done, taste and correct for salt and serve immediately.

MENU SUGGESTIONS

See Fried Artichoke Wedges (page 334). Fried Asparagus is a particularly nice side dish for Beef Braised in Red Wine Sauce (page 231).

FAVA BEANS, ROMAN STYLE

Fave alla romana

Fava beans usually appear in the vegetable markets from the middle of April until the end of June. They are best at the very beginning of their season when they are young and sweet and very small. In Italy, when they are at their peak, they are often served raw. The pods are brought whole to the table, and everyone shells his own and eats the beans, dipping them in salt. When eaten raw, fava beans are usually served at the end of the meal, replacing fruit. The raw fava bean has an intriguing bittersweet taste that usually turns very mellow and sweet when cooked. The Romans claim to have the best fava beans. There the beans are cooked with pork jowl (*guanciale*), and you will find them listed in the menus as *fave al guanciale*. Since pork jowl, as the Romans know it, is hard to come by here, I use *pancetta*, which is a totally successful substitute and is easily available in all Italian food shops.

For 4 persons

3 pounds small, young
   fava beans
   (unshelled weight)
2 tablespoons olive oil
2 tablespoons finely
   chopped yellow
   onion
1 slice rolled *pancetta*, ½
   inch thick, cut into
   strips ¼ inch wide

½ teaspoon salt
Freshly ground pepper,
   3 or 4 twists of the
   mill

1. Shell the fava beans and wash in cold water.
2. Heat the oil in a casserole and sauté the onion until translucent. Add the *pancetta* and sauté 30 seconds more.
3. Add the fava beans, salt, and pepper, and stir, coating them well. Add ⅓ cup water and cover the pot.
4. Cook over low heat. If the beans are very young and fresh they will cook in 6 or 8 minutes. (If there is any water

left, uncover the pot and raise the heat until it has evaporated.) Serve immediately.

MENU SUGGESTIONS

Fave al guanciale makes a very tasty antipasto. An unconventional but happy pairing is with Bresaola (page 44). As a side dish it goes beautifully with roasts of lamb, especially Hothouse Lamb, Roman Style (page 271), and with Baby Lamb Chops Fried in Parmesan-Cheese Batter (page 272).

GREEN BEANS

Fagiolini verdi

Very fresh, properly cooked green beans, used either as salad or vegetable, are one of the finest pleasures of the table. When you can appreciate the virtues of a salad of crisp beans, seasoned with nothing more than salt, olive oil, and lemon juice, you have understood Italian eating at its best—simple, direct, and inexhaustibly good.

When buying green beans, the best ones to look for are the smallest, youngest beans. They should be vividly green and should break with a snap, revealing a moist, meaty interior with very tiny, undeveloped seeds. Vegetable markets, in their tireless efforts to frustrate good cooking, often lump together beans of assorted sizes. These are practically impossible to cook evenly. If you have a choice, buy beans that are uniform in size.

COOKING GREEN BEANS

All it takes to cook green beans properly is plenty of salted boiling water and a readiness to drain them the moment they are tender but still crisp.

1. Snap both ends off the beans, pulling away any possible strings. Soak the beans in a basin of cold water for a few minutes, then drain.

2. For 1 pound of beans, bring 4 quarts of water to a boil. Add 1½ tablespoons salt. After a moment, when the water is boiling rapidly again, drop in the green beans. Hold the heat at high until the water returns to a boil, then regulate it so that the beans cook at a moderate boil. Do not cover. Since cooking times vary, depending on the size and freshness of the beans (very young, fresh beans may cook in 6 or 7 minutes, while larger, older ones may take 10 or 12), start tasting them after 6 minutes and drain them the moment they are tender but firm and crisp to the bite.

Boiled green beans can be used for salad (see page 397) or in the following recipe, which requires further cooking.

SAUTÉED GREEN BEANS WITH BUTTER AND CHEESE

Fagiolini verdi al burro e formaggio

For 6 persons

1 pound fresh, crisp green beans	Salt, as required
¼ cup butter	
¼ cup freshly grated Parmesan cheese	

1. Prepare and cook the green beans as directed above, being certain to drain them when they are tender but still crisp.
2. Put the green beans in a skillet with the butter and lightly sauté over medium heat for 2 minutes. Add the grated cheese and stir. Taste and correct for salt. Stir once or twice more, transfer to a warm platter, and serve immediately.

MENU SUGGESTIONS

Follow those for Gratinéed Jerusalem Artichokes (page 340). These green beans go particularly nicely with veal dishes, especially Sautéed Breaded Veal Chops (page 258) or Breaded Veal Cutlets, Milan Style (page 260).

GREEN BEANS WITH PEPPERS AND TOMATOES

Fagiolini verdi con peperoni e pomodoro

For 4 to 6 persons

1 pound green beans
1 green pepper
3 tablespoons olive oil
1 medium yellow onion,
   cut into slices about
   ¼ inch thick

⅔ cup canned Italian
   tomatoes, coarsely
   chopped, with their
   juice
1½ teaspoons salt
Freshly ground pepper, 3
   or 4 twists of the
   mill

1. Snap off the ends of the green beans, pulling off any strings they may have. Wash in cold water and set aside.

2. Wash the green pepper in cold water, and, if you find the peel as disagreeable as I do, remove it with a potato peeler. Remove the core with all the seeds and slice the pepper into strips a little less than ½ inch wide. Set aside.

3. Heat the oil in a casserole and sauté the onion until translucent.

4. Add the strips of green pepper and the chopped tomatoes and cook over medium heat until the tomatoes separate from the oil and thicken into sauce, about 25 minutes.

5. Add the green beans, stir a few times until they are all well coated, and add ⅓ cup water, the salt, and the pepper. Cover and cook until tender, about 20 to 30 minutes, depending on the freshness and size of the green beans. Add 1 or 2 tablespoons of water from time to time if required. (If, however, at the end there is too much liquid in the pot, uncover, raise the heat to high, and boil it away quickly.) Taste and correct for salt.

NOTE
These green beans maintain their excellent flavor also when prepared ahead of time and warmed up.

MENU SUGGESTIONS

These beans are a tasty accompaniment for broiled or roasted meats and for veal cutlets and other veal dishes, as long as these are not sauced with cream or with tomato.

SAUTÉED BROCCOLI WITH GARLIC

Broccoli all'aglio

For 4 to 6 persons

1 bunch fresh broccoli (about 1½ pounds) Salt 2 teaspoons finely chopped garlic	¼ cup olive oil 2 tablespoons chopped parsley

1. Cut off the tough butt end of the broccoli stalks, about ½ inch. With a sharp paring knife, peel off all the dark-green skin on the stalks and stems. (The skin is thicker around the larger part of the stalk, so you will have to cut deeper there.) Split the larger stalks in two, or if extremely large, in four, without cutting off the florets. Rinse well in 3 or 4 changes of cold water.

2. Bring 4 quarts of water to a boil with 1 teaspoon of salt. Drop in the broccoli and boil slowly until the stalks can be pierced easily by a fork, about 7 to 10 minutes, depending on the freshness of the broccoli. Drain and set aside. (You can prepare the broccoli several hours ahead of time up to this point, but do not refrigerate, because refrigeration impairs the flavor.)

3. Choose a skillet large enough to accommodate all the broccoli without much overlapping. Sauté the garlic in the olive oil over medium heat. As soon as the garlic colors lightly, add the broccoli, about 2 teaspoons salt, and the chopped parsley and sauté lightly for about 2 to 3 minutes. Turn the broccoli two or three times while cooking. Serve hot.

MENU SUGGESTIONS

Follow those for Sautéed Jerusalem Artichokes (page 339). Broccoli also goes well with Beef Patties with Anchovies and Mozzarella (page 234) and Casserole-Roasted Lamb with Juniper Berries (page 269).

SAUTÉED BROCCOLI WITH BUTTER AND CHEESE

Broccoli al burro e formaggio

For 4 to 6 persons

1 bunch fresh broccoli	½ cup freshly grated
¼ cup butter	Parmesan cheese
1 teaspoon salt	

1. Peel, wash, boil, and drain the broccoli as directed on page 350.
2. In a skillet large enough to accommodate all the broccoli without much overlapping, melt the butter over medium heat. When the butter foam begins to subside, add the boiled, drained broccoli and the salt, and sauté lightly for about 2 to 3 minutes, gently turning the broccoli two or three times. Add the grated cheese, turn the broccoli one more time, and serve.

MENU SUGGESTIONS

Follow those for Gratinéed Jerusalem Artichokes (page 340).

NOTE

On many distressing occasions I have seen people eat the florets and leave the stalks on the plate. They are evidently under the impression that they are choosing the more delectable part. Actually, it is just the other way around.

CARROTS WITH PARMESAN CHEESE

Carote al burro e formaggio

For 6 persons

2 bunches carrots	¼ teaspoon sugar
5 tablespoons butter	3 tablespoons freshly
Salt to taste	grated Parmesan
	cheese

1. Peel the carrots and slice them into disks ⅜ inch thick. (The thin tapered ends can be cut a little thicker.) Put the carrots and butter in a skillet large enough to contain

the carrots in a single layer and add enough water to come ¼ inch up the side of the pan. (If you have too many carrots for your largest pan, divide them equally between two skillets, using 2½ tablespoons of butter per skillet.) Cook over medium heat, uncovered.

2. When the liquid in the skillet has evaporated, add the salt and sugar. Continue cooking, adding 2 or 3 tablespoons of warm water as required but not too much at one time. The object is to obtain carrots that are well browned, wrinkled, and concentrated in texture and taste, which will take about 1 to 1½ hours of watchful cooking, depending on the carrots. When they begin to reach the well-browned, wrinkled stage do not add any more water, because there must be no liquid left at the end. (If you have been using two pans, the carrots reduce so much in volume that halfway through cooking they can be consolidated into a single pan.)

3. When cooked, add the grated Parmesan, stir once or twice over heat, and then transfer to a warm platter and serve immediately.

NOTE

This is a time-consuming dish, although not a complicated one. You can prepare it entirely ahead of time, however, stopping short of adding the Parmesan. Add the Parmesan only after reheating the carrots. Carrots cooked this way become very condensed in flavor, as they lose all their liquid, and very satisfying in texture.

MENU SUGGESTIONS

These carrots are a good accompaniment for all roasts, for broiled meats, for all sautéed veal dishes, for game—in short, for nearly all meats or fowl except those sauced with tomato.

CAULIFLOWER

Cavolfiore

A head of cauliflower should be very hard, its leaves should be fresh, crisp, and unmarked, and its florets should be compact and as white as possible. If speckled or slightly discolored, don't buy it. Fresh cauliflower keeps very nicely in the refrigerator for several days.

HOW TO BOIL CAULIFLOWER

Remove all the leaves from a head of cauliflower and cut a cross at the root end. Bring 5 quarts of water to a boil. (The greater the quantity of water you use, the faster cauliflower cooks and the sweeter it tastes.) Add the cauliflower and cook at a moderate boil, uncovered, for about 30 minutes, or until it is tender at the pricking of a fork. Drain immediately when cooked.

Boiled cauliflower can be served lukewarm or at room temperature as salad (page 398), or it can gratinéed or fried.

CAULIFLOWER GRATINÉED WITH BUTTER AND CHEESE

Cavolfiore gratinato al burro e formaggio

For 6 to 8 persons

1 head cauliflower (2 to 2½ pounds)	2 teaspoons salt
¼ cup butter	⅔ cup freshly grated Parmesan cheese

1. Preheat the oven to 400°.
2. Boil the cauliflower as directed above, and when it has cooled detach the florets from the head. If they are rather large, divide them into two or three parts.
3. Choose a bake-and-serve dish large enough to hold the florets in a single layer. Smear the bottom with butter and arrange the florets so that they overlap slightly, like roof tiles. Sprinkle with salt and grated cheese and dot thickly with butter. Place on the uppermost rack of the preheated oven and bake for about 15 minutes, or until a light crust forms on top. Allow to settle a few moments before serving.

MENU SUGGESTIONS

Follow those for Gratinéed Jerusalem Artichokes (page 340).

FRIED CAULIFLOWER

Cavolfiore fritto

For 6 persons

1 head cauliflower (2 to 2½ pounds)	1 cup fine, dry unflavored bread crumbs, spread on a dish or on waxed paper
2 eggs, lightly beaten with 2 teaspoons salt, in a bowl	Vegetable oil, enough to come ½ inch up the side of the pan

1. Boil the cauliflower as directed on page 353. When it has cooled, detach the florets from the head and cut into wedges about 1 inch thick at the widest point.

2. Dip the florets in egg, letting the excess flow back into the bowl, then turn them in bread crumbs. (They can be prepared up to and including this point a few hours ahead of time.)

3. Heat the oil in the skillet over high heat. When it is very hot, slip in the floret wedges, no more at one time than will fit loosely in the pan. Fry to a nice golden crust on one side; then turn them. When both sides are done, transfer to paper towels to drain. Serve piping hot.

MENU SUGGESTIONS

Follow those for Fried Artichoke Wedges (page 334). Fried cauliflower is very nice also with Sautéed Chicken Livers with Sage (page 293), and Rolled Breast of Chicken Fillets Stuffed with Pork (page 304).

BRAISED AND GRATINÉED CELERY WITH PARMESAN CHEESE

Coste di sedano alla parmigiana

In this recipe, celery undergoes a nearly complete range of cooking procedures. It is first blanched, then briefly sautéed, braised in broth, and finished off in the oven. It is actually very much simpler than it sounds, and the result is a remarkably fine dish that is as elegant as it is delicious.

For 6 persons

2 large bunches crisp, fresh celery
3 tablespoons finely chopped yellow onion
3 tablespoons butter
¼ cup chopped *pancetta*, OR prosciutto, OR unsmoked ham
Salt

Freshly ground pepper, about 6 twists of the mill
2 cups Homemade Meat Broth (page 10) OR 1 cup canned beef broth mixed with 1 cup water
1 cup freshly grated Parmesan cheese

1. Trim the tops of the celery and detach all the stalks from the bunches. Lightly peel the stalks to remove most of the strings. Cut the stalks into lengths of about 3 inches. Drop into 2 to 3 quarts of rapidly boiling water, and 2 minutes after the water returns to a boil, drain and set aside.

2. Preheat the oven to 400°.

3. Put the onion in a saucepan with the butter and sauté over medium heat until translucent but not browned.

4. Add the *pancetta*, stir, and sauté for about 1 minute.

5. Add the well-drained celery, a light sprinkling of salt, and the pepper and sauté for 5 minutes, turning the celery from time to time.

6. Add the broth, cover the pan, and cook at a gentle simmer until the celery is tender at the pricking of a fork. (If, when the celery is nearly done, there is still much liquid in the pan, uncover, raise the heat, and finish cooking while the liquid evaporates.)

7. Arrange the cooked celery in a bake-and-serve dish with the inner sides of the stalks facing up. Spoon the sautéed onion and *pancetta* from the pan over the celery, then add the grated cheese. Place the dish on the uppermost rack of the preheated oven and bake for 6 to 8 minutes, or until the cheese has melted and formed a slight crust. Allow to settle for a few moments, then serve directly from the baking dish.

Follow those for Gratinéed Jerusalem Artichokes (page 340). This celery goes particularly well with Beef Braised in Red Wine Sauce (page 231), Rolled Stuffed Breast of Veal (page 244), and Rolled Breast of Chicken Fillets Stuffed with Pork (page 304).

CELERY AND POTATOES BRAISED IN OLIVE OIL

Sedano e patate all' olio

For 4 to 5 persons

5 medium potatoes, about 1¼ pounds	⅓ cup olive oil
1 large bunch celery	Salt
	2 tablespoons lemon juice

1. Peel the potatoes, wash them, and cut into halves.
2. Detach all the celery stalks. Since only the stalks are used in this recipe, remove the leafy end entirely, and set aside the white, inner heart for use in a salad. Snap off a small piece from the narrow end of each stalk and pull down to remove as much of the celery strings as possible. Cut the stalks into 3-inch lengths and wash thoroughly in cold water.
3. Put the celery, olive oil, and ½ teaspoon of salt in a casserole and add enough water to cover. Cover the casserole and cook over medium heat for 10 minutes. Add the halved potatoes, 1 teaspoon of salt, and the lemon juice. (If there is not enough liquid to cover the potatoes, add water.) Cover and cook for 25 minutes. Test both the celery and the potatoes for tenderness with a fork. (Sometimes the celery lags, while the potatoes are already tender. If this happens, transfer the potatoes to a warm, covered dish, cover the casserole, and continue cooking the celery until tender.)
4. When the celery and potatoes are done the only liquid left in the pot should be oil. If there is still some water left, uncover the pot, raise the heat, and quickly evaporate it. If the potatoes were removed, return them to the casserole after boiling away the water. Cover, turn down the heat to medium, and warm up the potatoes for about 2 minutes. Taste and correct for salt. Serve hot.

This is a good vegetable to choose when making up a meal without pasta. It is excellent with Open-Faced Italian Omelets (page 315–321), with Veal Rolls in Tomato Sauce (page 255), and with Fried Calf's Liver (page 288).

SWISS CHARD STALKS WITH PARMESAN CHEESE

Coste di biete alla parmigiana

For 4 persons

2 bunches mature Swiss chard, the ones with the broadest stalks Salt	¼ cup butter ⅔ cup freshly grated Parmesan cheese

1. Pull off all the leaves from the Swiss chard stalks. Do not discard the leaves; they make an excellent salad (page 399). Wash the stalks in cold water, trimming away any remaining leaves, and cut them in lengths of about 4 inches.

2. Drop in abundant boiling salted water and cook for approximately 30 minutes. (They should be tender but firm because they will undergo additional cooking in the oven.)

3. Preheat the oven to 400°.

4. Smear a rectangular bake-and-serve dish with butter. Arrange a layer of stalks on the bottom of the dish, laying them end to end. Trim them to fit if necessary. Sprinkle lightly with salt and grated Parmesan cheese and dot with butter. Place another layer of stalks over this, season as above, and continue building up layers until you've used up all the stalks. The top layer should be generously sprinkled with Parmesan and well dotted with butter.

5. Place the dish in the upper third of the preheated oven. Bake for 15 minutes, or until the top layer acquires a light, golden crust. This dish is at its most agreeable in texture and flavor when warm, but not too hot, so allow it to settle and cool a bit before bringing to the table.

Follow those for Gratinéed Jerusalem Artichokes (page 340).

EGGPLANT

Melanzane

Italian eggplants are very small, often just slightly larger than zucchini, whose shape they resemble. Similar eggplants are available here, but I have always found them rather sharp in flavor and do not recommend them. The most consistently good eggplant is the medium-sized one, weighing about 1½ pounds. The skin should be glossy, smooth, and intact. Avoid eggplants with skin that is opaque, discolored, or even slightly wrinkled. Fresh eggplants are resistant to the touch and compact, never spongy. They will keep in the refrigerator for 5 to 6 days.

The skin on American eggplant is quite tough, so it is best to peel it for any of the following recipes.

FRIED EGGPLANT

Melanzane fritte

Fried eggplant is the key ingredient in some very appealing Italian dishes, such as Eggplant, Parmesan Style (page 359) or Thin Spaghetti with Eggplant (page 94), and on its own it makes an excellent side dish. There are two points to remember in order to fry eggplant successfully:

- Before it can be cooked, eggplant must be drained of its excess moisture. This is done by salting it and letting it stand for 30 minutes.
- Eggplant must fry in an abundant quantity of very hot oil. When properly fried, it absorbs virtually none of the cooking fat. Never add oil to the pan while the eggplant is frying.

For 6 to 8 persons

2 to 3 medium eggplants (3 to 4½ pounds) Salt	Vegetable oil, enough to come 1 inch up the side of the pan

1. Peel the eggplants and cut them lengthwise in slices about ⅜ inch thick. Set the slices upright in a pasta colander and sprinkle the first layer of slices liberally with salt before setting another layer next to it. Put a soup dish under the collander to collect the drippings and let stand at least 30 minutes.

2. Add enough oil to a large skillet to come 1 inch up the side of the pan. Turn on the heat to high. Take as many slices of eggplant as you think will fit in one layer in the skillet and dry them well with paper towels. When the oil is hot (test it with the end of one of the slices: it should sizzle), slide in the eggplant. Fry to a nice golden brown on all sides, then transfer to a platter lined with paper towels to drain. Dry some more slices and continue frying until they are all done. (If you see that the eggplant is browning too rapidly, lower the heat.)

NOTE

Fried eggplant can be served hot or at room temperature.

MENU SUGGESTIONS

Combined with Oven-Browned Tomatoes (page 374), fried eggplant makes a marvelous accompaniment for Breaded Veal Cutlets, Milan Style (page 260).

EGGPLANT, PARMESAN STYLE

Melanzane alla parmigiana

For 4 persons

2 medium eggplants
  (about 3 pounds),
  sliced, drained of
  their moisture, and
  fried as directed in
  Fried Eggplant (page
  358)
2 cups canned Italian
  tomatoes, drained,
  seeds removed, and
  coarsely chopped

Salt
1 whole-milk mozzarella
  cheese, coarsely
  grated on the largest
  holes of the grater
4 to 5 tablespoons freshly
  grated Parmesan
  cheese
1½ teaspoons orégano
2½ tablespoons butter

1. Preheat the oven to 400°.
2. Line the bottom of a buttered bake-and-serve dish (10

inches square, or its rectangular equivalent) with a single layer of fried eggplant slices. Top this layer with chopped tomatoes. Add a pinch of salt, a generous sprinkling of grated mozzarella, a tablespoon of grated Parmesan cheese, and a pinch of orégano and cover with another layer of sliced eggplant. Continue building up layers of eggplant, tomatoes, and cheese until you've used up all the eggplant. The top layer should be eggplant. Sprinkle the remaining Parmesan cheese over it and dot with butter. Place in the upper third of the preheated oven.

3. After 20 minutes pull out the pan and, pressing with the back of a spoon, check to see if there is an excess amount of liquid. If there is, tip the pan and draw it off with the spoon. Return to the oven for another 15 minutes. Allow it to settle and partly cool off before serving. It should not be piping hot.

NOTE
It can be prepared entirely ahead of time, refrigerated when cool, and warmed up several days later. It will still be good, although not quite as fragrant as the day you prepared it.

MENU SUGGESTIONS

Eggplant *parmigiana* is too hearty to be just a side dish. It can be a light luncheon on its own followed by a mixed green salad or, in a fully organized meal, it can precede Breaded Veal Cutlet, Milan Style (page 260), Fried Baked Calf's Liver (page 288), or Baby Lamb Chops Fried in Parmesan Cheese Batter (page 272). It can also become a second course, preceded by Potato Gnocchi (page 185) with Genoese Basil Sauce for Pasta and Soup (page 132). Do not combine it with either heavily sauced or delicately flavored dishes. In restaurants it is often served at room temperature as a summer antipasto.

SAUTEED DICED EGGPLANT

Melanzane al funghetto

This eggplant is called *al funghetto*, "mushroom style," because it is sautéed with olive oil, garlic, and parsley. This is the same technique as that used in making *funghi trifolati*, or "truffled" mushrooms (page 365), which are called "truffled" for obscure reasons of their own. Some people also add anchovies and orégano. I do not.

For 4 to 6 persons

2 medium eggplants (about 3 pounds)	2 tablespoons finely chopped parsley
Salt	Freshly ground pepper, about 6 twists of the mill
1 teaspoon finely chopped garlic	
5 tablespoons olive oil	

1. Peel the eggplant and cut it into 1-inch cubes. Put it in a colander and sprinkle liberally with salt. Toss and turn the eggplant cubes so that there is some salt on all of them. Allow to stand for at least 30 minutes, draining the eggplant of as much of its excess liquid as possible. Remove from the colander and blot with a paper towel.

2. In a skillet, over medium heat, sauté the garlic, with 4 tablespoons of the olive oil, until it colors lightly. Add the eggplant pieces, turning them frequently. At first the eggplant will absorb all the oil. Don't panic—turn the pieces rapidly and keep shaking the pan. Add 1 more tablespoon of oil after 5 minutes. (You will not need any more oil because as the eggplant cooks the oil will reappear on the surface.) After 10 or 12 minutes, add the chopped parsley and stir it well. Add the pepper and continue cooking until the eggplant is tender but firm, about 30 minutes, give or take a few minutes, depending on the eggplant. Taste and correct for salt; then spoon into a warm platter and serve.

NOTE

You can prepare the dish entirely ahead of time and when cool refrigerate in its cooking juices, under plastic wrap. When reheating, put it in a skillet (no additional oil is required) and warm it slowly over medium-low heat.

MENU SUGGESTIONS

Follow those for Sautéed Jerusalem Artichokes (page 339). Eggplant is also a tasty accompaniment for Thin Pan-Broiled Steaks with Tomatoes and Olives (page 230) and Veal Scaloppine with Tomatoes (page 253).

FINOCCHIO

Finocchio is a sweet variety of fennel, also known as Florence fennel. Most people have seen it in Italian vegetable markets, some may have had it raw in salads in Italian restaurants, but few know what a fine vegetable it is for cooking. It is sweeter cooked than raw, losing most of its slight taste of anise. It has an interesting flavor, gentle and forward at the same time, and its texture is quite similar to that of celery.

There are two basic types of finocchio. One is squat and bulbous, the other is flat and elongated. The squat, bulbous one is crisper, sweeter, and less stringy and should be the only kind used for salads. For cooking, either variety will do, although the stocky one always gives better results. Finocchio is generally available from late fall through early spring.

SAUTÉED FINOCCHIO WITH
BUTTER AND CHEESE

Finocchi al burro e formaggio

For 4 persons

3 large finocchios or 4 to 5 small ones	Salt
5 tablespoons butter	3 tablespoons freshly grated Parmesan cheese

1. Cut away any wilted or bruised parts of the finocchio. Cut off and discard the tops and cut the bulbous lower parts into vertical slices no more than ½ inch thick. Wash thoroughly in cold water.

2. Put the sliced finocchio and the butter in a fairly broad saucepan, and add enough water barely to cover. Cook, uncovered, over medium heat. If there is too much finocchio for your pan, put in as much as it will hold, cover the pan, and cook for 5 to 8 minutes, or until the finocchio has wilted and come down in volume. Add the rest of the finocchio, mix well, cover the pan, and cook for 3 or 4 more minutes. Uncover the pan and cook, turning the finocchio from time to time, until it is tender at the pricking of a fork, from 25 to 40 minutes all

together. You may add as much as ⅓ cup of warm water if it is necessary, but at the end the finocchio must have absorbed all the liquid and should have a glossy pale-gold color. Before removing from the heat, add salt to taste and the grated cheese. Mix well and transfer to a warm platter. Serve while hot.

NOTE

When cooked, the tender parts of finocchio will be soft but the firm ones rather crunchy. Don't try to eliminate this natural and interesting contrast in texture by cooking until the finocchio is all soft.

MENU SUGGESTIONS

Follow those for Gratinéed Jerusalem Artichokes (page 340). This finocchio is quite lovely with Roast Pork with Bay Leaves (page 275) and Meat Loaf Braised in White Wine and Dried Wild Mushrooms (page 238).

FINOCCHIO BRAISED IN OLIVE OIL

Finocchi all' olio

For 4 persons

3 large finocchios or 4 to 5 small ones	⅓ cup olive oil Salt

Follow the recipe for Sautéed Finocchio with Butter and Cheese (page 362). The procedure is identical, step for step, except that olive oil is substituted for butter and the grated cheese is completely omitted. While the procedure is the same, the taste and texture are quite different when finocchio is braised in olive oil. It is perhaps somewhat less elegant than finocchio done in butter, but it is sweeter, with a smoother texture.

MENU SUGGESTIONS

Finocchio all' olio is a suitable accompaniment for zesty dishes such as Pan-Broiled Steak with Marsala and Hot Pepper Sauce (page 228), Thin Pan-Broiled Steaks with Tomatoes and Olives (page 231), and Veal Scaloppine with Tomatoes (page 253).

FRIED FINOCCHIO

Finocchi fritti

For 4 persons

3 finocchios	Vegetable oil, enough to
Salt	come at least ½
2 eggs, beaten lightly	inch up the side of
with ¼ teaspoon	the pan
salt, in a bowl	
1½ cups fine, dry	
unflavored bread	
crumbs, spread on a	
dish or on waxed	
paper	

1. Cut off the tops of the finocchios and trim away any bruised or discolored parts. Cut the finocchios lengthwise into slices about ⅜ inch thick. Wash thoroughly in several changes of cold water and drain.

2. Bring 3 quarts of water to a boil, add 1 teaspoon salt, then drop in the finocchio slices. First drop in the slices that are attached to part of the fleshy core, since these take a little longer to cook. After a minute or so drop in the others. Cook at a moderate boil until the core feels tender but firm at the pricking of a fork, about 6 to 10 minutes, depending on the finocchio. When done, drain and allow to cool.

3. Dip the cooled, parboiled finocchio slices in egg, then turn them in bread crumbs.

4. Heat the oil in the skillet over high heat. When the oil is quite hot, slip in as many finocchio slices as will fit loosely. Fry to a golden brown on one side, then on the other. Transfer to paper towels to drain. Taste and correct for salt.

MENU SUGGESTIONS

Follow those for Fried Artichoke Wedges (page 334). Fried finocchio is also particularly nice with Roast Spring Lamb with White Wine (page 268).

SAUTÉED MUSHROOMS WITH GARLIC AND PARSLEY

Funghi trifolati

Trifolare describes the classic Italian method of quickly sautéing sliced vegetables or meat in olive oil, garlic, and parsley. To these basic elements other flavors, such as anchovies or wine, are sometimes added. The term is derived from the word *trifola*, which in Lombardy and Piedmont means truffle. It is not exactly clear what the connection with truffles is, because there are no truffles in this dish. One explanation is that the ingredients are sliced thin, as one would slice truffles. Another is that anything cooked in this manner becomes so delicious it almost could be truffles.

For 6 persons

1½ pounds crisp white mushrooms	Salt
1½ teaspoons finely chopped garlic	Freshly ground pepper, 5 to 6 twists of the mill
½ cup olive oil	3 tablespoons finely chopped parsley

1. Slice off the ends of the mushroom stems. Wipe the mushrooms clean with a damp cloth. If there are still traces of soil, wash very rapidly in cold running water and dry thoroughly with a towel. Cut into lengthwise slices ¼ inch thick.

2. Choose a large, heavy skillet that can later accommodate the mushrooms without crowding, and sauté the garlic in the olive oil over medium-high heat until it colors lightly but does not brown. Turn the heat up to high and add the mushrooms. When the mushrooms have absorbed all the oil, turn the heat down to low, add salt and pepper, and shake the pan, stirring and tossing the mushrooms. As soon as the mushroom juices come to the surface, which happens very quickly, turn the heat up to high again and cook for 4 to 5 minutes, stirring frequently. (Do not overcook, because the texture and flavor of mushrooms are not improved by prolonged cooking.)

3. Taste and correct for salt. Add the chopped parsley, stir rapidly once or twice, and transfer to a warm platter.

NOTE
Serve immediately if intended as a side dish. If prepared ahead of time and allowed to cool to room temperature, this makes an excellent antipasto.

MENU SUGGESTIONS

Follow those for Sautéed Jerusalem Artichokes (page 339).

SAUTÉED MUSHROOMS WITH HEAVY CREAM

Funghi alla panna

For 6 persons

1½ pounds mushrooms	Salt
1½ tablespoons finely chopped shallots OR yellow onion	Freshly ground pepper, about 4 twists of the mill
2½ tablespoons butter	½ cup heavy cream
1½ tablespoons vegetable oil	

1. Slice off the ends of the mushroom stems. Wipe the mushrooms clean with a damp cloth. If there are still traces of soil, wash very rapidly in cold, running water, and dry thoroughly with a towel.

2. Cut the mushrooms into wedges, each section of which should be about ½ inch thick at the thickest point of the cap. (If the mushrooms are very small, cut them into halves or leave them whole.)

3. Choose a skillet large enough to hold the mushrooms later without crowding them. Over medium-high heat, sauté the chopped shallots in the butter and oil until pale gold in color. Raise the heat to high, and add the mushrooms. When the mushrooms have absorbed all the fat, turn the heat down to low. Add salt and pepper and stir-cook the mushrooms until their juices begin to come to the surface, in a few seconds. Raise the heat to high and cook for 3 to 4 minutes, shaking the pan and stirring the mushrooms frequently.

4. Add the heavy cream and cook for just 2 or 3 minutes longer, until part of the cream has been absorbed by the mushrooms and the rest has thickened slightly. Transfer the entire contents of the skillet to a warm platter and serve immediately.

MENU SUGGESTIONS

Possibly the most delicious way to serve these mushrooms is to mix them with Veal Stew with Sage and White Wine (page 262). Another lovely combination is with Sautéed Veal Chops with Sage and White Wine (page 261). Actually they will go beautifully with any veal dish, as long as they do not have to compete with a tart or tomatoey sauce.

SWEET AND SOUR ONIONS

Cipolline agrodolci

The secret of these delectably tart and sweet onions is not so much in the preparation, which is rapid and simple, as in the very long slow cooking. It takes 2 to 3 hours of patient simmering to bring them to their peak, but it is well worth while because this is one of the most successful dishes of vegetables you can serve.

Since vinegar varies in strength and acidity, adjust the dose in this recipe according to the vinegar you are accustomed to using.

For 6 persons

3 pounds small white onions of uniform size	2 teaspoons sugar
	¼ teaspoon salt
¼ cup butter	Freshly ground pepper, 3
2½ tablespoons vinegar	or 4 twists of the mill

1. In peeling the onions it can save you a great deal of time and tears if you first plunge them in boiling water for about 15 seconds. Remove just the outside skin and any dangling roots. Do not remove any of the onion layers, do not trim anything off the top, and leave the base of the root intact or

the onions will come apart during the long cooking. Cut a cross into the root end.

2. Choose a skillet or a shallow enameled cast-iron pan large enough to contain the onions in a single layer. Put in the onions, the butter, and enough water to come an inch up the side of the pan. Cook over medium heat, turning the onions frequently, adding a little bit of warm water from time to time as the liquid evaporates. After about 20 minutes, when the onions begin to soften, add the vinegar, sugar, salt, and pepper. Turn the onions again. Continue to cook slowly for 2 hours or more, turning the onions frequently. Add a tablespoon or two of warm water as it becomes necessary. They are done when they have turned a rich, dark golden brown all over and are easily pierced by a fork. Serve while hot.

NOTE

If prepared ahead of time they can be reheated slowly before serving.

MENU SUGGESTIONS

This dish is a perfect accompaniment to almost any meat and fowl and it is particularly splendid with roasts. Avoid pairing it with any dish that is sharp in flavor, such as a spicy *pizzaiola* tomato sauce.

SAUTÉED PEAS WITH PROSCIUTTO, FLORENTINE STYLE

Pisellini alla Fiorentina

In Florence, the peas one uses for this recipe are very tiny, freshly picked, early peas. They cook quite rapidly and are very sweet and tender. No other kind of peas really works as well, but, if you can't find very young fresh peas in the market, frozen tiny peas are to be preferred to mature, mealy fresh peas.

For 4 persons

2 cloves garlic, peeled
3 tablespoons olive oil
2 tablespoons prosciutto
  or *pancetta*, diced
  into ¼-inch cubes
2 pounds fresh, early
  peas (unshelled
  weight) OR 1 ten-
  ounce package
  frozen tiny peas,
  thawed

2 tablespoons finely
  chopped parsley
Salt
Freshly ground pepper, 4
  or 5 twists of the
  mill

1. Over medium-high heat sauté the garlic cloves in the olive oil until they have colored well.

2. Remove the garlic, add the diced prosciutto or *pancetta*, and sauté for less than a minute.

3. Add the peas, parsley, salt, and pepper, turn the heat down to medium, and cover the pan, adding 2 to 3 tablespoons of water only if you are using fresh peas. Cook until done, 5 minutes or less for frozen peas, 15 to 30 minutes for fresh, which vary enormously. The only way to tell is to taste. While tasting, correct for salt. Serve immediately.

MENU SUGGESTIONS

These peas go well with practically any meat or chicken course, which is fortunate because this is one of the tastiest of all Italian vegetable dishes. Try them with Braised Veal Shanks, Milan Style (page 246), Sautéed Breaded Veal Chops (page 258), Baby Lamb Chops Fried in Parmesan-Cheese Batter (page 272), or Sautéed Chicken Breast Fillets with Lemon and Parsley (page 303).

ITALIAN MASHED POTATOES WITH PARMESAN CHEESE

Purè di patate

There is something about potatoes that seems rarely to have stimulated Italian cooks to a very high pitch of creativity. Rice has had a similar perplexing effect on the French, whose *risotti* are so unsatisfactory. There are one or two nice things we do with potatoes, however. *Gnocchi* is the most famous of these. Another is this lucious purée of potatoes made with butter, milk, and a substantial amount of fresh Parmesan cheese.

For 4 persons

1 pound boiling potatoes	⅓ cup freshly grated
3 tablespoons butter	Parmesan cheese
½ cup milk	Salt to taste

1. Put the potatoes, unpeeled, in a large pot with enough water to cover them well. Cover the pot, bring to a moderate boil, and cook until tender. (Do not test the potatoes too often with your fork, or they will become waterlogged.) Drain, and peel while still hot.

2. Bring water in the lower portion of a double boiler to a very slow simmer. Cut up the butter and put it in the upper portion. Purée the potatoes through a food mill directly into the upper pan.

3. In a separate pan, bring the milk to the verge of boiling. Turn the heat off just as it is about to boil.

4. Start beating the potatoes with a whisk or a fork, adding 2 to 3 tablespoons of hot milk at a time. When you have added half the milk, beat in the grated cheese. When the cheese has been very well incorporated into the potatoes, resume adding the milk without ceasing to beat, except to rest your arm for an occasional few seconds. The potatoes should become a very soft, fluffy mass, a state that requires a great deal of beating and as much milk as the potatoes will absorb without becoming thin and runny. (Some potatoes absorb less milk than others, so you must judge the correct quantity of milk as you are beating, both by taste and thickness of the mass.) As you finish adding milk, taste and correct for salt. Serve piping hot.

NOTE

If necessary, you can prepare this up to 1 hour ahead of time. Just before serving, warm in the double boiler and beat in 2 or 3 tablespoons of very hot milk.

MENU SUGGESTIONS

The perfect marriage for this dish is with Sautéed Chicken Livers with Sage (page 293). Other congenial combinations are with Beef Braised in Red Wine Sauce (page 231), Rolled Stuffed Breast of Veal (page 244), Braised Veal Shanks, Trieste Style (page 249), and Sautéed Lamb Kidneys with White Wine (page 290). You will, of course, omit pasta from the same menu. Choose a light soup for the first course.

POTATO CROQUETTES WITH CRISP-FRIED NOODLES

Patate spinose

These tiny balls of mashed potatoes are fried with a coating of thin, crumbled noodles, which makes them look like large thistles. Not only is it an attractive dish, but also the creamy potato core and the crackly noodle surface offer an interesting and enjoyable contrast in textures.

For 4 to 6 persons

1 pound boiling potatoes, unpeeled
1 tablespoon butter
1 egg yolk
1 teaspoon salt
⅛ teaspoon nutmeg

1 cup *fedelini* OR *vermicelli* (hair-thin noodles), hand-crushed into fragments about ⅛ inch long
⅓ cup all-purpose flour
Vegetable oil, enough to come ¼ inch up the side of the skillet

1. Put the unpeeled potatoes in a saucepan with enough cold water to cover them. Cover the pan and cook at a moderate boil until tender. Drain. Peel while still hot and mash through a food mill or potato ricer into a bowl.
2. Swirl the butter into the potatoes. Add the egg yolk, mixing it in with a fork very rapidly, lest the heat of the potatoes cook it. Add the salt and nutmeg and mix thoroughly again.
3. Combine the crumbled noodles and flour in a dish.
4. Put the oil in a 10-inch skillet and heat over medium-high heat. Shape the puréed potatoes into 1-inch balls, roll

them in the noodles and flour, and slip them, a few at a time, depending on the size of the pan, into the hot oil. (Don't crowd them in the pan or they won't fry properly.) Fry, turning them on all sides, until a crisp, dark-golden crust has formed all around. Transfer with a slotted spoon to paper towels to drain. Serve hot.

MENU SUGGESTIONS

Follow the general indications for Italian Mashed Potatoes with Parmesan Cheese (page 369). These croquettes are also very nice with Pan-Broiled Steak with Marsala and Hot Pepper Sauce (page 228).

DICED PAN-ROASTED POTATOES

Dadini di patate arrosto

For 4 to 6 persons

1½ pounds boiling potatoes, not Idaho or other dry, mealy potatoes	5 tablespoons vegetable oil 2 tablespoons butter 2 teaspoons salt

1. Peel the potatoes, rinse in cold water, pat dry, and dice into ½-inch cubes.

2. Heat the oil and butter in a 12-inch heavy-bottomed or cast-iron skillet over medium-high heat. When the butter foam subsides, put in the potatoes and turn them until they are well coated with the cooking fat. Turn the heat down to medium and let the potatoes cook until a golden crust has formed on one side. Add the salt, turn them, and continue cooking and turning until every side has a nice crust. After 20 to 25 minutes, test them with a fork to see if they are tender. If not, turn the heat to low and cook until tender.

NOTE

These potatoes cannot be prepared ahead of time and reheated, but they stay crisp even when lukewarm. They are at their best, of course, piping hot.

These are an ideal accompaniment to any roast, of meat or fowl. They are almost equally well matched with most sautéed dishes. Do avoid potato soups or *gnocchi* as a first course if you are going to have potatoes later.

SAUTÉED SPINACH

Spinaci saltati

For 4 to 6 persons

1½ to 2 pounds fresh spinach OR 2 ten-ounce packages frozen whole-leaf spinach, thawed	Salt 2 cloves garlic, peeled ¼ cup olive oil

1. If you are using fresh spinach, discard any leaves that are not crisp and green. Snap off the hard, lower end of the stem on young spinach, remove the whole stem on more mature spinach. Soak it in a basin of cold water, dunking it with your hands several times. Lift out the spinach, being careful not to pick up any of the sand at the bottom of the basin. Change the water and repeat the operation. Continue washing in fresh changes of water until there is no more sand at the bottom of the basin.

Cook the spinach in a covered pan over medium heat with a pinch of salt and no more water than clings to the leaves after washing. It is done when tender, 10 minutes or more, depending on the spinach. Drain well but do not squeeze. (If you are using frozen spinach, simply cook the thawed spinach with a pinch of salt in a covered pan over medium heat for 1½ minutes; then drain.)

2. In a skillet, over medium-high heat, sauté the garlic cloves in the olive oil. When the garlic is well browned, remove it and add the drained, cooked spinach and about ½ teaspoon salt. Sauté for 2 minutes, turning the spinach frequently. Taste and correct for salt. Serve hot.

Follow those for Sautéed Jerusalem Artichokes (page 339). This sautéed spinach is also very good with Veal Scaloppine with Tomatoes (page 253) and Casserole-Roasted Lamb with Juniper Berries (page 269).

OVEN-BROWNED TOMATOES

Pomodori al forno

In this recipe all the wateriness of fresh tomatoes is drawn off through long, slow cooking. What remains is a savory, concentrated essence of tomato.

Don't let the quantity of oil alarm you. Nearly all of it gets left behind in the pan.

for 6 persons

9 ripe, medium tomatoes OR 6 large ones, such as the beefsteak variety	Salt to taste
	Freshly ground pepper, about 6 to 8 twists of the mill
3 tablespoons finely chopped parsley	6 tablespoons olive oil, or enough to come ¼ inch up the side of the baking dish
2 teaspoons finely chopped garlic	

1. Wash the tomatoes in cold water and slice them in half, across the width. If the variety of tomatoes you are using has a large amount of seeds, remove at least a part of them.

2. Preheat the oven to 325°.

3. Choose a flameproof baking dish large enough to accommodate all the tomato halves in a single layer. (You can crowd them in tightly, because later they will shrink considerably.) Arrange the tomatoes cut side up and sprinkle them with the parsley, garlic, salt, and pepper. Pour the olive oil over them until it comes ¼ inch up the side of the dish. Cook on top of the stove over medium-high heat until the tomatoes are tender, about 15 minutes, depending on the tomatoes.

4. When the tomato pulp is soft, baste with a little bit of oil, spooning it up from the bottom of the dish, and transfer the dish to the next-to-the-highest rack in the oven. From time to time baste the tomatoes with the oil in which they are cooking. Cook for about 1 hour, until the tomatoes have shrunk to a little more than half their original size. (The skins and the sides of the pan will be partly blackened, but don't worry—the tomatoes are not burned.) Transfer to a serving platter, using a slotted spatula, leaving all the cooking fat behind in the pan. Serve hot or at room temperature.

NOTE

These tomatoes can be prepared several days ahead of time. Since they must be reheated, they should be refrigerated with all or part of their cooking fat. When refrigerating, cover tightly with plastic wrap. To reheat, return to a 325° oven for 10 to 15 minutes, or until warm.

MENU SUGGESTIONS

This dish is a tasty accompaniment to roasts and to Mixed Boiled Meats (page 311). You would never use it, of course, next to any dish already sauced or flavored with tomato. Nor does it get along well with cream or milk sauces. Its perfect marriage is with Fried Eggplant (page 358), when both are at their peak, in midsummer, and the two make a sensational combination as a side dish with Breaded Veal Cutlets, Milan Style (page 260).

FRIED TOMATOES

Pomodori fritti

I have not yet found a vegetable that does not take well to frying, and among all fried vegetables none can surpass tomatoes. They reach that perfect combination of outer crispness and inner juiciness that is always the goal when frying vegetables.

The best tomatoes for frying are those that are firm and meaty, with few seeds and as little water as possible.

For 4 persons

2 or 3 large tomatoes
1 cup all-purpose flour,
     spread on a dish or
     on waxed paper
1 egg, lightly beaten with
     ½ teaspoon salt, in a
     soup dish or small
     bowl

1 cup fine, dry
     unflavored bread
     crumbs, spread on a
     dish or on waxed
     paper
Vegetable oil, enough to
     come 1 inch up the
     sides of the pan
Salt, if necessary

1. Wash the tomatoes and cut them horizontally into slices ½ inch thick, discarding the tops. Remove the seeds, but handle the tomatoes gently, without squeezing them.

2. Turn the tomato slices lightly in the flour, dip them in egg, then dredge them well in bread crumbs.

3. Heat the oil over high heat. When the oil is very hot, slip in the tomatoes. When a dark golden crust has formed on one side, turn them and do the other side. When both sides have a nice crust, transfer them to paper towels to drain. Taste a little piece and correct for salt if necessary. Serve piping hot.

MENU SUGGESTIONS

Follow those for Fried Artichoke Wedges (page 334).

ZUCCHINI

Zucchine

Zucchini is one of the great favorites among Italian vegetables, and its first appearance in the markets in early spring is an event eagerly looked forward to in Italy. Its very delicate taste is sometimes mistaken for blandness, which some try to cover up with seasonings. In Italian recipes, however, its fine, distinct flavor is carefully nurtured and emerges quite clearly, undisguised.

WHAT TO LOOK FOR WHEN BUYING ZUCCHINI

Recognizing quality in raw zucchini can make all the difference between a successful dish and a tasteless one. Good zucchini are never very large. Do not buy any that are much broader than 1½ inches or longer than 6 inches. Unless you are going to stuff them, small, skinny zucchini that are 1 inch or less in diameter are the most desirable. Look for bright color and glossy skin, and avoid zucchini whose skin is mottled or discolored. Zucchini should feel very firm in your hands. If it is flabby and bends easily it is not fresh. When cut, the flesh of good, young zucchini should be crisp and show very tiny seeds.

CLEANING ZUCCHINI

Soak zucchini in a basin of cold water for 10 minutes, then scrub thoroughly under cold running water until the skin feels clean and smooth. Sometimes no amount of washing and scrubbing will loosen imbedded soil. If the skin feels gritty after scrubbing, peel it lightly with a vegetable peeler. Cut off and discard both ends of the zucchini. They are now ready for the preparation of any recipe.

ZUCCHINI FRIED IN FLOUR-AND-WATER BATTER

Zucchine fritte con la pastella

Zucchini fried in *pastella* is crisp and light and absolutely irresistible. *Pastella* is a flour-and-water batter that produces a thin, crackly coating that stays perfectly bonded to the zucchini and keeps it from absorbing any of the frying fat.

If you like fried onion rings, but loathe, as I do, the thick spongy wrapping in which restaurants usually present them, try them at home with *pastella*. It will be a revelation.

For 4 to 6 persons

1 pound zucchini	**Salt**
⅓ cup all-purpose flour	
Vegetable oil, enough to come ¾ inch up the side of the pan	

1. Clean the zucchini as directed on page 377. Cut them into lengthwise slices about ⅛ inch thick.

2. Put 1 cup of water in a soup plate and gradually add the flour, sifting it through a sieve and constantly beating the mixture with a fork until all the flour has been added. The batter should have the consistency of sour cream.

3. Heat the oil in the skillet over high heat. When the oil is very hot dip the zucchini slices in the batter and slip only as many as will fit loosely into the skillet.

4. When a golden crust has formed on one side of the zucchini slices, turn them over. When both sides have a nice crust, transfer the zucchini to paper towels to drain and sprinkle with salt. Continue in the same way until all the slices are fried. Serve piping hot.

MENU SUGGESTIONS

Follow those for Fried Artichoke Wedges (page 334).

FRIED ZUCCHINI WITH VINEGAR

Zucchine fritte all' aceto

For 4 to 6 persons

1 pound zucchini	**2 cloves garlic, lightly**
Salt	**crushed with a**
Vegetable oil, enough to come ¼ inch up the side of the pan	**heavy knife handle and peeled**
1 cup all-purpose flour, spread on a dish or on waxed paper	**Freshly ground pepper, about 4 twists of the mill**
2 to 3 tablespoons good-quality wine vinegar, preferably imported French vinegar	

1. Clean the zucchini as directed on page 377. Cut them into sticks about ¼ inch thick. Sprinkle with the salt and set aside for 30 minutes.

2. When the 30 minutes have elapsed, the zucchini will have thrown off quite a bit of liquid. Drain them and pat them dry with a cloth or paper towels.

3. Heat the oil in a skillet over high heat. When the oil is quite hot, lightly dip the zucchini in flour and slip into the skillet. (Don't put too many in at one time. They should fit very loosely in the pan.) Turn them as they brown.

4. When the zucchini are a deep golden brown, transfer to a deep dish, using a slotted spoon. While they are still hot, sprinkle them with vinegar. You will hear them sizzle.

5. When all the zucchini are done, bury the garlic in their midst, and season with pepper. Serve at room temperature.

NOTE

After you've done these once, you can regulate the quantity of vinegar and garlic to suit your taste. I don't like any more than an intriguing suggestion of garlic, so I remove the cloves after about 5 minutes.

MENU SUGGESTIONS

In addition to being a superb accompaniment to meat, especially pork or sausages, these zucchini make an enticing antipasto. They are also a tasty side dish for a buffet.

SLICED ZUCCHINI WITH GARLIC AND TOMATO

Zucchine all'aglio e pomodoro

For 4 to 6 persons

1½ pounds zucchini
½ cup thinly sliced yellow onion
⅔ cup olive oil
1½ teaspoons coarsely chopped garlic
2 tablespoons chopped parsley

⅔ cup canned Italian tomatoes, coarsely chopped, with their juice
1 teaspoon salt
Freshly ground pepper, 4 to 6 twists of the mill
4 to 6 fresh basil leaves (optional)

1. Clean the zucchini as directed on page 377 and slice them into disks ⅜ inch thick.

2. Put the onion and oil in a flameproof bake-and-serve pan and sauté over medium heat until pale gold. Add the garlic and sauté until it colors lightly. Add the parsley, stir once or twice, then add the tomatoes and their juice. Cook at a steady simmer for 15 minutes.

3. Preheat the oven to 350°.

4. Add the sliced zucchini, salt, pepper, and basil. Cook until tender at the pricking of a fork, 20 minutes or more, depending on the age and freshness of the zucchini. (Do not overcook. The zucchini should be tender but firm.)

5. Transfer the pan to the uppermost level of the preheated oven for about 5 minutes, until the liquid the zucchini throws off while cooking has dried up. Serve immediately in the baking dish.

MENU SUGGESTIONS

Serve with any simple roast or with broiled meat. Avoid competition with a strong tomato or garlic presence.

BAKED STUFFED ZUCCHINI BOATS

Barchette di zucchine ripiene al forno

For 4 to 6 persons

8 to 10 young, very fresh, firm zucchini
Salt
2 tablespoons butter
1 tablespoon vegetable oil
1 tablespoon finely chopped yellow onion
3 or 4 slices unsmoked ham, chopped
Freshly ground pepper to taste

Béchamel Sauce (page 25), made with 1 cup milk, 1½ tablespoons all-purpose flour, 2 tablespoons butter, and salt
1 egg
3 to 4 tablespoons freshly grated Parmesan cheese
A tiny pinch of nutmeg (optional)
Fine, dry unflavored bread crumbs

1. Clean the zucchini as directed on page 377. Slice off the ends and cut the zucchini into lengths of about 2½ inches. With a vegetable corer or peeler scoop out the zucchini from end to end, being careful not to perforate the sides. The thinned-out wall of the zucchini should not be less than ¼ inch thick. Set aside the pulp extracted from the inside of the zucchini.

2. Cook the hollowed-out zucchini in abundant boiling water, to which 1 teaspoon of salt has been added. Cook only until half done, or until lightly resistant when pierced by a fork. Drain and set aside.

3. Heat 1 tablespoon of butter and all the oil in a skillet. Sauté the chopped onion and chopped ham, and then add half the zucchini pulp, roughly chopped. Add salt and pepper and cook over high heat until the pulp turns creamy and acquires a mellow golden color. Lift away from the skillet with a slotted spoon or spatula, leaving all the cooking fat behind, and set aside.

4. Preheat the oven to 400°.

5. Prepare a thick béchamel sauce using the quantities indicated above, remembering that to make a béchamel thicker you simply cook it longer. As soon as the béchamel is ready, add the cooked zucchini pulp and quickly stir in the egg, the freshly grated Parmesan, and the optional pinch of nutmeg. Mix well, then set aside.

6. Smear the bottom of a rectangular bake-and-serve dish with butter. Split the cooked zucchini in half lengthwise and line them up in the dish, hollowed side facing up. Salt lightly, and fill each half zucchini with the béchamel–zucchini-core mixture. Sprinkle with bread crumbs and dot lightly with butter. (If you wish, you can wait up to a few hours before baking, but you must finish cooking the zucchini the same day or they will lose freshness.)

7. Bake in the upper third of the preheated oven for about 20 minutes, or until a light golden crust forms. Do not serve immediately but allow to settle until no longer steaming hot.

MENU SUGGESTIONS

Although this has been suggested elsewhere in the book as an elegant side dish, it also makes an excellent first course. Serve before Beef Braised in Red Wine Sauce (page 231), any of the three lamb roasts on pages 268–272, Roast Pork with Bay Leaves (page 275), or Pan-Roasted Squab (page 308).

ZUCCHINI STUFFED WITH MEAT AND CHEESE

Zucchine con ripieno di carne e formaggio

For 4 to 6 persons

10 fresh, young zucchini
    about 1¼ to
    1½ inches in
    diameter
3 cups thinly sliced
    yellow onion
3 tablespoons vegetable
    oil
2 tablespoons chopped
    parsley
2 tablespoons tomato
    paste diluted with 1
    cup of water
3 tablespoons milk
⅔ slice firm white
    bread, crust
    removed

½ pound lean beef,
    chopped
1 egg
3 tablespoons freshly
    grated Parmesan
    cheese
1 tablespoon chopped
    prosciutto,
    mortadella, pancetta,
    OR unsmoked ham
Salt
Freshly ground pepper, 3
    or 4 twists of the
    mill

1. Clean the zucchini as directed on page 377. Slice off the ends and cut the zucchini into lengths of about 2½ inches. Hollow them out completely, removing the pulp with a vegetable corer or peeler, being careful not to perforate the sides. The thinned-out wall of the zucchini should not be less than ¼ inch thick. (You will not need the pulp in this recipe, but it would be a pity to throw it away because it makes a lovely *frittata* or an excellent *risotto*.)

2. Choose a covered skillet large enough to accommodate later all the zucchini in a single layer. Slowly cook the sliced onions in the oil until tender and considerably wilted.

3. Add the parsley, stirring it two or three times; then add the tomato paste diluted in water and cook slowly over low heat for about 15 minutes.

4. Warm the milk and mash the bread into it with a fork. Let cool.

5. In a mixing bowl put the chopped meat, the egg, the grated cheese, the bread mush, and the chopped prosciutto or its substitute. Mix thoroughly with your hands. Add 1 teaspoon salt and the pepper.

6. Stuff the mixture into the hollowed-out zucchini sections, making sure they are well stuffed but not pushing too hard, to avoid splitting the zucchini. Put the zucchini into the skillet, turn the heat to medium low, and cover. Cook until done, from 40 minutes to 1 hour, approximately, depending on the quality of the zucchini. (You can tell for sure only by testing the zucchini. When done it should be tender, but not too soft.) Look in on the zucchini from time to time and turn them.

7. If, when the zucchini is cooked, there is too much liquid in the skillet, uncover, raise the heat to high, and boil away the excess liquid for a minute or two, turning the zucchini once or twice. Taste for salt, transfer to a serving platter, allow the zucchini to settle for a minute or two, and serve.

NOTE

This is a dish that has nothing to gain from being served the moment it is cooked. On the contrary, it actually improves in texture and flavor upon being reheated a day or two later. Always serve it warm, but not steaming hot.

MENU SUGGESTIONS

This is always served as a second course. It can be preceded by such antipasti as *bresaola* (page 44), Fried Mortadella, Pancetta, and Cheese Tidbits (page 45), or mixed Italian cold cuts. For a first course serve Spaghetti with Genoese Basil Sauce for Pasta and Soup (page 132), Risotto with Parmesan Cheese (page 171), or Rice with Fresh Basil and Mozzarella Cheese (page 183). This also makes an appetizing and easy-to-handle hot buffet dish.

FRIED ZUCCHINI BLOSSOMS

Fiori di zucchine fritti

Zucchini blossoms are extremely perishable, and for that reason they are not very frequently brought to market in America. But they do appear from time to time, and, if you should happen to come across these luscious orange flowers, do try them. They make an attractive and delectable dish that is extremely simple to prepare. The method for cooking zucchini blossoms is identical to that for Fried Zucchini in Flour-and-Water Batter (page 377).

For 4 to 6 persons

12 to 14 zucchini blossoms	The flour-and-water batter from page 377
Vegetable oil, enough to come ¾ inch up the sides of the skillet	Salt

1. Wash the blossoms rapidly under cold running water and dry them gently on paper towels. If the stems are very long, cut them down to 1 inch in length. Cut the base of the blossom on one side, and open the flower flat, without dividing it.

2. Heat the oil over high heat. When it is very hot, dip the blossoms quickly in and out of the batter and slip them into the skillet. When they are golden brown on one side, turn them and cook them to golden brown on the other side. Transfer to paper towels to drain, sprinkle with salt, and serve promptly while still hot.

MENU SUGGESTIONS

Follow those for Fried Artichoke Wedges (page 334).

AN ITALIAN BARBECUE: CHARCOAL-BROILED VEGETABLES

Verdura mista in gratticola

Americans have practically reinvented cooking over charcoal, but the uses to which all the marvelously practical barbecue equipment is put are incredibly few. Whenever our family goes barbecuing on a public campsite or picnic area, our grill topped with tomatoes, eggplant, peppers, onions, mushrooms, and zucchini is soon the object of ill-concealed wonderment as the only bright island in the midst of a brown atoll of hot dogs, hamburgers, and steaks.

Barbecuing vegetables is one of the most effective ways of concentrating their flavor. Charcoal-broiled peppers are all that peppers should be, and never are when done any other way. Zucchini turns out fresher-tasting than the most skillfully fried zucchini and is just as crisp and juicy. Even indifferent tomatoes are returned by the fire to their ancestral tomato taste and become nearly as full flavored as the vine-ripened tomatoes of San Marzano.

Doing vegetables need not interfere with the unquestioned pleasure of charcoal-broiled steak. Cook the vegetables in the first flush of the fire. When they are done, the fire is ready for broiling steak or whatever else you are having. With a full load of vegetables, calculate about 25 to 40 percent more coal than you would use ordinarily for steaks or hamburgers alone.

For 4 persons

1 large flat Spanish onion	Olive oil
2 sweet green or red peppers	Crushed peppercorns
2 large, firm, ripe tomatoes	1 teaspoon chopped parsley (optional)
1 medium eggplant	⅛ teaspoon chopped garlic (optional)
Salt	½ teaspoon fine, dry unflavored bread crumbs (optional)
2 medium fresh, young, firm, glossy zucchini	
¼ pound very fresh and crisp mushrooms	

1. Remove the outer, crackly skin of the onion, but do not cut off the point or the root. Divide it in half horizontally.

2. Wash the peppers in cold water and leave whole.

3. Wash the tomatoes in cold water and divide in two horizontally.

4. Wash the eggplant in cold water, then cut in half lengthwise. Without piercing the skin, make shallow cross-hatched cuts, spaced about 1 inch apart, in the eggplant flesh. Sprinkle liberally with salt and stand the halves on end in a colander for at least 15 minutes to let the bitter juices drain away.

5. Wash the zucchini thoroughly in cold water. Cut off the ends; then cut the zucchini into lengthwise slices about ⅜ inch thick.

6. Wipe the mushrooms clean with a damp cloth. Unless

they are very small, detach the caps from the stems. You are now ready to light the fire.

7. When the highest flames have died down, place the onion on the grill, cut side down. Place the peppers on the grill as well, laying them on one side. After 4 or 5 minutes check the peppers. The skin toward the fire should be charred. When it is, turn another side of the peppers toward the fire, at the same time drawing them closer together to make room for the tomatoes and eggplant (see Step 10 below). Continue turning the peppers, eventually standing them on end, until all the skin is charred. Remove them from the grill and peel them while they are as hot as you can handle. Cut them into 2-inch strips, discard the seeds, put the cut-up peppers in a bowl, and add at least 3 tablespoons of olive oil plus large pinches of salt and cracked peppercorns. Toss and set aside.

8. While the peppers are still cooking, check the onion. When the side facing the fire is charred, turn it over with a spatula, taking care not to separate the rings. Season each onion half with 1 tablespoon of olive oil and ½ teaspoon of salt. Move to the edge of the grill, making sure there is some burning charcoal underneath.

9. When the onion is done, in about 15 to 20 minutes, it should be well charred on both sides. Scrape away part of the blackened surface and cut each half in 4 parts. Add it to the bowl of peppers, tossing it with another pinch of salt and cracked pepper. (The onion will be quite crunchy, which makes a nice contrast with the peppers, but it will also be very sweet, with no trace of sharpness.)

10. When you first turn the peppers (see Step 7 above), make room for the tomatoes and eggplant. Place the tomatoes, cut side down, on the grill. Check them after a few minutes, and if the flesh is partly charred, turn them. Season each half with ½ teaspoon of olive oil, a small pinch of salt, and the optional parsley, garlic, and bread crumbs and cook until they have shrunk by half and the skin is blackened.

11. Shake off any liquid from the eggplant. Pour 1 tablespoon of olive oil over each half and place it on the grill with the cut side facing the fire. Allow it to reach a deep brown color, but don't let it char, which would make it bitter. Turn the eggplant over and season each half with

another tablespoon of olive oil. From time to time as it cooks, pour ½ teaspoon of oil in between the cuts. The eggplant is done when it is creamy tender. Do not cook it beyond this point or it will become bitter.

12. When the eggplant is nearly done, put the zucchini slices on the grill. As soon as they have browned on one side turn them over and cook until done, 5 to 8 minutes. Remove to a shallow bowl and season with a large pinch of salt, pepper, and about ½ tablespoon of oil.

13. When you turn the zucchini over, put the mushrooms on the grill. These cook very quickly, about 1 minute to a side, including the stems. Add them to the bowl of zucchini and season the same way.

NOTE

It is unfortunate that the length of this recipe makes it appear so forbidding. It is actually about as simple to execute as grilled hamburgers and hot dogs. The whole secret lies in mastering the sequence in which the vegetables are put on the grill. Aside from that, there is very little to do except watch them. The fire does nearly all the work. The entire process should take about 35 minutes.

SALADS

Le Insalate

There are two basically different dishes that appear in an Italian meal, both of which are called salads.

One contains cold cooked fish, meat, or chicken, and occasionally rice, mixed with either raw or cooked vegetables. Although it is called a salad, it is usually served as an antipasto, a first course, or even a second course but rarely, if ever, as the salad course. A choice group of these salads appears later in this chapter.

The true salad course is something else entirely, with a special and fixed role. It is served invariably after the second course, signaling the approaching end of the meal. It releases the palate from the spell of the cook's inventions, and leads it to sensations of freshness and purity, to a rediscovery of food in its natural and artless state.

In this kind of salad, vegetables and greens are used raw or boiled, alone or mixed. Its composition changes with the seasons. There are always some greens available throughout the year, but in fall and winter salads raw finocchio and artichokes are frequently dominant. Boiled asparagus and green beans appear in the spring, followed by new potatoes. Then there are tart and nutty wild field greens, and in the warmer months zucchini, both raw and cooked, and tomatoes.

ITALIAN DRESSING

There is absolutely nothing mysterious about the dressing for an Italian salad. The ingredients are salt, olive oil, and wine vinegar. Pepper is optional, and lemon juice is occasionally substituted for vinegar.

Italians would find any discussion of something called "salad dressing" very puzzling. Although the term could be translated, it would have little currency. For Italians, salad dressing is not an element separate from the salad; it is not added on to the greens as you might add a sauce to pasta. Dressing is a process rather than an object, a verb rather than a noun. It is the act that transforms greens and vegetables into salad.

There are many old folk sayings that illustrate this. According to one of them, to make a good salad you need four persons: a judicious one with the salt, a prodigal one with the oil, a stingy one with the vinegar, and a patient one to mix it. You do not need to know very much more than that to make a proper Italian salad. There is no way to give precise proportions of salt, oil, and vinegar. It takes less oil to dress green beans than an equivalent amount of lettuce. Asparagus and potatoes take more vinegar, tomatoes and cucumber more salt. Other factors that vary are the fruitiness and density of the oil, the acidity and bouquet of the vinegar, and even the character of the salt. The only foolproof method is to taste and correct the salad before serving it.

Do not begin to dress the salad until it is quite dry. Water dilutes the flavor of the dressing. You can use a special wire basket to shake the greens dry, if you like. My own method is to wrap the greens in a towel, gather the corners of the towel in one hand, and give it a few vigorous jerks over the sink.

Seasonings and oil and vinegar are never mixed in advance. They are poured directly on the salad in the following order:

First: Sprinkle the salt. Do not overdo it. You can add more salt later if necessary.

Second: Add the oil. There should be enough oil to coat the salad greens or vegetables and give them a surface gloss, but not so much as to form a pool at the bottom of the bowl, which would make the salad soggy.

Third: Add the vinegar. This is the hardest ingredient to judge. A few drops too much will ruin a salad. There must be just a hint of tartness, enough to be noticed but not so much as to grab your attention.

Toss the salad thoroughly and repeatedly, taking care not to bruise and blacken delicate greens such as field lettuce. Taste and correct for oil, salt, or vinegar. Serve immediately. Never allow salad to sit and steep in its seasonings.

From time to time you can add other seasonings to sharpen the flavor of the salad and to avoid monotony. Shredded fresh basil leaves or chopped parsley go very well into an Italian salad. They are particularly nice with tomatoes and cucumbers.

For zest you can add chopped shallots or thinly sliced onion. After the onion is sliced very thin it should be soaked in two or more changes of cold water for at least ½ hour before putting it in the salad. This helps to sweeten it.

To add the heartiness of garlic to a salad rub a small piece of bread with a lightly crushed garlic clove. Discard the garlic and add the bread to the salad. After the salad has been seasoned, dressed, and thoroughly tossed, remove and discard the bread.

Note on oil and vinegar: To call any oil that is not pure olive oil salad oil is a contradiction in terms. Tasteless vegetable oils merely grease the greens. The flavor of the olive oil is absolutely indispensable to a good salad, and the denser and fruitier the olive oil is the better.

The choice of vinegar is also very important. It should be wine vinegar, preferably red, with all the characteristics of good wine: strength, flavor, and a well-developed bouquet. A fine vinegar should not be spiked with tarragon or other herbs, any more than you would make a fruit-flavored "pop" wine out of good Burgundy. Most familiar brands of vinegar, unfortunately, do not measure up to these standards. However, most specialty food shops, and many of the better supermarkets, do stock good French wine vinegar. It can be ordered by mail from many department stores, such as Bloomingdale's in New York. It is certainly not cheap, but a little goes a long way, and it will make all the difference in the world to your salads.

JERUSALEM ARTICHOKE AND SPINACH SALAD

Insalata di spinaci e topinambur

For 4 persons

½ pound Jerusalem
  artichokes
½ pound very young,
  crisp spinach
Salt and freshly ground
  pepper, a liberal
  quantity, to taste

Olive oil
Red wine vinegar,
  preferably imported
  French vinegar

1. Soak the artichokes for a few minutes in cold water, then scrub them thoroughly under running water or peel them, if you object to the hard bite of the peel. Cut into the thinnest possible slices, and put into a salad bowl.

2. Detach the stems from the spinach, pulling them off, in one motion, together with the thin central stalk on the underside of the leaves. Wash the spinach in a basin of cold water, changing water frequently until it shows no more trace of soil. Drain, shaking off as much water as possible from the leaves. Wrap the spinach in a dry cloth and give it a few sharp, brusque jerks to drive away any remaining moisture. Tear the leaves in two or three parts and add to the salad bowl.

3. When ready to serve, toss with salt, pepper, enough olive oil to coat, and just a dash of vinegar.

SHREDDED CARROT SALAD

Insalata di carote

No salad takes so little to prepare as this excellent carrot salad. Its tart, gently bracing taste is particularly welcome after a hearty, robust meal.

For 4 persons

5 to 6 medium carrots	6 tablespoons olive oil
1 teaspoon salt	1 tablespoon lemon juice

1. Peel and wash the carrots, and grate them on the largest holes of the grater.
2. When ready to serve, add the salt, olive oil, and lemon juice. Toss thoroughly and serve immediately.

FINOCCHIO SALAD

Finocchio in insalata

When finocchio is eaten alone as it is here, neither vinegar nor lemon is used in the dressing.

For 3 or 4 persons, depending on the size of the finocchio

1 medium squat, bulbous finocchio	Olive oil
Salt	Freshly ground pepper

1. Cut off the tops of the finocchio and remove any bruised, discolored, or wilted outside stalk.
2. Cut off about ⅛ inch or less from the base; then cut the finocchio horizontally into the thinnest possible slices (The slices will be in the form of rings, some half, some whole.)

3. Wash the finocchio slices thoroughly in cold water, then dry them well in a towel. Toss in a salad bowl with salt, an abundant quantity of oil, and a liberal grinding of pepper.

MENU SUGGESTIONS

A salad of finocchio is ideal after any substantial meat dish and is especially appropriate after roast pork.

MIXED SALAD

Insalata mista

Everyone makes mixed salads, but the Italian ones seem to have an equilibrium and a freshness that many others lack. This is because even the most wildly assorted salad is never a catchall. It is assembled with an intuitive but nonetheless precise feeling for the correct proportions of greens and vegetables. There is never the monotony of too much green pepper, carrot, artichoke, celery. There is just enough, so that what is missing from one mouthful of salad is suddenly and delightfully present in the next.

The ingredients for the salad given below can be found, all at one time, at only certain moments of the year. When one or more is not available, substitute for it, in approximately equal proportions, whatever is currently in season.

Prepare all the greens and vegetables in any order you like, and add them to the salad bowl as they are ready. Save the tomatoes for last, however, or they may get crushed and watery. Note that arugola, listed below, is known in Italian as *ruchetta* or *rucola*. Its true English equivalent is "rockets." "Arugola" is 100 percent Italian-American.

For 6 persons

2 small carrots, OR 1
    large one
1 finocchio, of the squat,
    bulbous variety
½ medium green pepper
1 celery heart
½ head curly chicory,
    Boston lettuce, OR
    escarole, OR 1 head
    Bibb lettuce
½ small bunch lamb's
    tongues or field
    lettuce
½ small bunch arugola

1 medium artichoke
½ lemon
3 or 4 scallions, thinly
    sliced, OR ½ red
    Bermuda onion,
    sliced and presoaked
    as directed on page
    390
1 large OR 2 small
    tomatoes
Salt
Olive oil
Red wine vinegar,
    preferably imported
    French vinegar

1. Wash and peel the carrots, and shred them on the largest holes of the grater.

2. Trim the finocchio and slice it into thin rings, as directed on page 362. Wash thoroughly and dry well in a towel.

3. Remove the inner pulp and seeds from the pepper. Peel with a sharp vegetable peeler and cut into very thin strips.

4. Strip the celery heart of any leaves, then slice it crosswise into narrow rings, about ¼ inch thick.

5. If you are using curly chicory or escarole, discard all the outer, dark green leaves. Detach all the leaves from the head and tear them by hand into small, bite-sized pieces. Let them soak in one or two changes of cold water in a basin for 15 to 20 minutes, or until the water shows no trace of soil. Drain and dry thoroughly in a towel or a salad basket. If you are using Bibb lettuce, handle it very gently because it bruises easily and discolors.

6. Trim away the stems of the lamb's tongues and arugola, tear the larger leaves in two or more pieces, and soak, drain, and dry as directed above for lettuce.

7. Discard the artichoke stem, and trim the artichoke as directed for Artichokes, Roman Style (page 326), trimming a little more off the top than you would ordinarily to make

sure only the tenderest part goes into the salad and remembering to rub the cut parts with juice from the half lemon. Cut the trimmed artichoke lengthwise into the thinnest slices you can.

8. Add the presoaked onion slices.

9. Cut the tomatoes into small chunks or narrow wedges, removing some of the seeds if there is an excess.

10. When ready to serve, sprinkle liberally with salt and add enough oil to coat all the ingredients well and a dash of vinegar. Toss thoroughly but not roughly, and serve immediately.

NOTE

Other raw vegetables you can use are red cabbage, Savoy cabbage, or regular cabbage. Cabbage should be finely shredded. Add white or small red radishes, thinly sliced. Substitute cucumber for carrot. (Never have the two at one time; somehow they are not compatible.) Also, young zucchini may be used raw. They should be thoroughly scrubbed and washed or even lightly peeled, and cut into matchsticks.

BREAD AND VEGETABLE SALAD WITH ANCHOVIES

Panzanella

This salad was originally the poor man's dinner in parts of Tuscany and Rome. In the traditional version, two- or three-day-old bread is soaked in water, squeezed, and added to the salad in amounts proportioned to one's hunger. This procedure is quite successful with good, solid Tuscan country bread. I do not find it very appealing, however, when made with supermarket bread. I much prefer this version, however decadent it may be, in which the waterlogged bread is replaced by crisp squares of bread fried in olive oil.

For 4 persons

½ clove garlic, peeled
    and chopped
4 flat anchovy fillets
1 tablespoon capers
½ teaspoon salt
5 tablespoons olive oil
1 tablespoon red wine
    vinegar
¼ sweet green, yellow,
    or red pepper,
    cored, seeded, and
    diced
½ recipe Fried Bread
    Squares for Soup
    (page 84), but fried
    in olive oil rather

than vegetable oil
Freshly ground pepper,
    5 to 6 twists of the
    mill
½ cucumber, peeled and
    diced into ½-inch
    cubes
1 medium, firm, meaty
    tomato, preferably
    peeled, and cut into
    ½-inch chunks
½ red Bermuda onion,
    thinly sliced and
    soaked as directed
    on page 390

1. Mash the garlic, anchovies, and capers to a pulp in a mortar or in a bowl. Put into a salad bowl.

2. Add the salt, olive oil, vinegar, and sweet pepper and blend thoroughly with a fork.

3. Add the fried bread squares, pepper, cucumber, tomato, and onion and toss thoroughly. Taste and correct for seasoning and chill for 30 minutes before serving.

MENU SUGGESTIONS

Although this can be served on occasion after the second course, it is more suitable as an antipasto or a first course in a fresh and tasty summer meal.

ASPARAGUS SALAD

Insalata di asparagi

When asparagus is at the peak of its flavor, one of the favorite ways of eating it in Italy is as salad. No other way of preparing it brings one so close to the essential asparagus taste. The very finest asparagus should be chosen, because it will confront the palate thinly clothed in a light dressing of oil and vinegar. It is never mixed with any other salad vegetables.

For 4 to 6 persons

2 pounds asparagus	3 tablespoons red wine
Salt and freshly ground	vinegar
pepper to taste	(approximately),
⅓ cup olive oil	depending on taste
	and the vinegar

1. Peel and boil the asparagus as directed on page 341. When the asparagus is done it should be spread on a platter, leaving one end of the platter free. Prop up the end under the asparagus. After about 30 minutes some liquid will have collected at the other end of the platter. Discard it and rearrange the asparagus on the platter.
2. Add salt and pepper to taste. Season liberally with olive oil, and add the vinegar, taking into account the fact that asparagus requires a great deal of vinegar. Tip the platter in several directions so that the seasoning is evenly distributed. Serve either lukewarm or at room temperature, but never chilled.

NOTE

An alternative to seasoning the asparagus in the platter is to provide everyone with the seasonings mixed in individual shallow bowls, into which they will dip the asparagus.

GREEN BEAN SALAD

Fagiolini verdi in insalata

For 4 persons

1 pound green beans	Olive oil
Salt	Lemon juice

1. Trim, wash, and boil the beans as directed on page 347.
2. Put the beans in a salad bowl and add salt to taste. Add enough olive oil to give all the beans a thin glossy

coating. Add lemon juice to taste. (The salad should be just slightly, not aggressively, tart.) Toss well and serve immediately.

NOTE

Boiled green beans may be served slightly lukewarm or at room temperature, but never chilled.

MENU SUGGESTIONS

This salad may be served after any second course of meat fowl, or fish.

BOILED CAULIFLOWER SALAD

Cavolfiore lesso in insalata

For 6 to 8 persons

1 head cauliflower (about 2 pounds)	Olive oil
Salt to taste	Red wine vinegar, preferably imported French vinegar

1. Boil the cauliflower as directed on page 353.
2. Before the cauliflower cools, detach the florets from the head, dividing all but the smallest ones into two or three parts.
3. Put the florets into a salad bowl and season very liberally with salt, oil, and vinegar. Taste and correct for all three. (Cauliflower takes a great deal of seasoning.) Toss the florets carefully so as not to mash them and serve either lukewarm or at room temperature.

NOTE

If you cannot use the whole head for salad, season only what you need and refrigerate the rest. It can be made into gratinéed cauliflower (page 353), or fried (page 354) a day or two later.

MENU SUGGESTIONS

Cauliflower salad can follow any meat dish, but preferably not those that include tomato.

BOILED SWISS-CHARD SALAD

Insalata di biete cotte

Cooked Swiss chard leaves make a lovely, sweet salad that is particularly nice after pork or lamb. If the chard is mature and has large, white stalks, these can be utilized in Swiss Chard Stalks with Parmesan Cheese (page 357).

For 4 to 6 persons

2 bunches young Swiss chard or the leaves of 3 large bunches of mature Swiss chard	Olive oil
	1 or more tablespoons lemon juice
Salt	

1. If you are using young chard, detach the stems. If you are using mature chard, pull the leaves from the stalks, discarding any wilted or discolored leaves. Wash in a basin of cold water, changing the water frequently until it shows no trace of soil.

2. Put the chard in a pan with whatever water clings to the leaves. Add 1 teaspoon salt, cover, and cook over medium heat until tender, about 15 to 18 minutes from the time the liquid starts to bubble.

3. Drain in a pasta colander and gently press some of the water out of the chard with the back of a fork. Place in a salad bowl.

4. Serve cool (not refrigerated) or lukewarm, seasoning with salt, oil, and lemon only when ready to serve.

ZUCCHINI SALAD

Insalata di zucchine

An excellent demonstration that zucchini has a fine and distinctive flavor of its own is this salad of boiled zucchini. For a successful salad, it is absolutely essential that you choose young, fresh, firm zucchini. See the recommendations on buying zucchini on page 391.

For 6 persons

6 small to medium zucchini	2 tablespoons chopped parsley
3 large cloves garlic, lightly crushed with a heavy knife handle and peeled	Freshly ground pepper, about 8 twists of the mill
½ cup olive oil	Salt to taste
2 to 3 tablespoons red wine vinegar, preferably imported French vinegar	

1. Clean the zucchini as directed on page 377.
2. Bring 4 to 5 quarts of water to a boil, then drop in the zucchini. Cook at a moderate boil until tender but not soft and easily pierced by a fork—about 30 minutes, more or less, depending on the zucchini, from the time the water returns to a boil.
3. When done, drain, cut off the ends, and cut, lengthwise, into halves.
4. While it is still hot, rub the zucchini flesh with the crushed garlic cloves. Arrange the zucchini, flesh side up, in a single layer on a platter. Prop up the platter at one end so that while the zucchini cools any excess liquid will gather at the other end. Do not refrigerate.
5. When the zucchini are cool, discard the liquid from the platter and season with oil, vinegar, parsley, and pepper, adding salt only when just ready to serve, to prevent the zucchini from continuing to throw off liquid.

MIXED COOKED VEGETABLE SALAD

Insalatone

The sequence of steps indicated below is more or less arbitrary. Actually, all the ingredients can be prepared contemporaneously. This salad is at its most agreeable when its components are still slightly lukewarm. If you must prepare any part of it ahead of time, keep it at room temperature, do not refrigerate.

For 4 to 6 persons

3 medium boiling potatoes	Salt
5 medium yellow onions	Olive oil
2 medium sweet green, yellow, or red peppers	Red wine vinegar, preferably imported French vinegar
6 ounces green beans	Freshly ground pepper
1 8¼-ounce can small whole beets, drained	

1. Preheat oven to 400°.

2. Boil the potatoes with their skins on, until tender. Cooking time varies greatly with size and type of potato. Peel while hot, and cut into ¼-inch slices. Put into a salad bowl.

3. Put the onions, with their skins on, on a baking sheet, then into the upper third of the oven. Cook until they are tender all the way to the center at the pricking of a fork. Skin them, cut them each into three or four sections, and add to the salad bowl.

4. Broil and peel the peppers exactly as directed in Peppers and Anchovies (page 34). When peeled, cut the peppers into strips 1 inch wide, removing all the seeds and pulpy core. Add to the salad bowl.

5. Cook the beans until tender but firm, as directed on page 347. Drain and add to the salad bowl.

6. Cut the drained canned beets into halves if they are very tiny, into quarters if they are larger. Add to the bowl.

7. Add the seasonings, being liberal with the oil and pepper and stingy with the vinegar. Taste and correct for salt. Serve immediately.

MENU SUGGESTIONS

This salad is the ideal accompaniment to all broiled meats, and it can be served at the same time as the second course, in place of vegetables. It also goes well with fish, either broiled or poached. It can even stand on its own as a light summer meal, adding to it if you wish hard-boiled eggs, anchovy fillets, or tuna.

TUNA AND BEAN SALAD

Insalata di tonno e fagioli

Although this famous salad has been given often enough before in Italian cook books, it is included here because no survey of Italian salads can fail to take notice of it. Moreover, while most of the English versions suggest scallions, in this recipe we follow the traditional Tuscan use of red onion. It is a small difference but a significant one, because the crunchiness of onion is a delightful and essential relief for the creaminess of beans and the tenderness of tuna.

For 4 persons

1 cup dried white kidney beans, Great Northern beans, or other white beans OR 1 twenty-ounce can precooked similar beans

½ Bermuda onion, thinly sliced and soaked in water for 1 hour (see page 390)

Salt to taste

1 seven-ounce can Italian tuna OR other tuna packed in oil, drained

⅓ cup olive oil

2 teaspoons red wine vinegar, or more, according to taste and the strength of the vinegar

Freshly ground black pepper to taste (optional)

1. If using uncooked beans, cook them as directed on page 74. Drain.

2. Put them, or the drained canned beans, into a salad bowl. Add the onion and season with salt to taste. Add the tuna, breaking it into large flakes with a fork. Add oil, vinegar, and the optional pepper. Toss thoroughly and serve.

MENU SUGGESTIONS

This makes a very agreeable second course for a summer meal. It can be preceded by Cold Vegetable Soup with Rice,

Milan Style (page 65), Spaghetti with Tomato Sauce with Marjoram and Cheese (page 91), Spaghetti with Genoese Basil Sauce for Pasta and Soup (page 132), or Thin Spaghetti with Fresh Basil and Tomato Sauce (page 92). It can also be part of mixed antipasti for any meal with a rustic flavor, and is an excellent dish to add to a buffet.

SHRIMP AND VEGETABLE SALAD

Insalata russa con gamberi

This salad is beautiful to look at, absolutely delicious, and very simple to execute. It does take time and patience to get the ingredients cleaned, boiled, and diced, but it can all be prepared and completed well in advance, whenever you are not pressed for time.

For 6 persons

1 pound medium
    shrimps, unpeeled
1 tablespoon red wine
    vinegar
¼ pound green beans
2 medium potatoes
2 medium carrots
⅓ ten-ounce package
    frozen peas, thawed
6 small canned red
    beets, drained and
    dried on paper
    towels

2 tablespoons gherkins in
    vinegar, preferably
    French *cornichons*,
    cut up
2 tablespoons capers, the
    smaller the better
3 tablespoons olive oil
2 teaspoons red wine
    vinegar, preferably
    imported French
    vinegar
Salt
2½ cups Mayonnaise
    (page 23)

1. Wash the shrimps. Put them, whole and unpeeled, in boiling salted water. Add the tablespoon of vinegar to the water and cook for 4 minutes. Allow the shrimps to cool; then shell and devein them and set aside.
2. Snap the ends off the green beans, pulling away any possible strings. Rinse them and drop them into rapidly boiling salted water. Taste them early and drain them as

soon as they are tender but still firm, in as little as 8 minutes if they are very young and fresh.

3. Rinse the potatoes and boil them with the peel on. When they are easily pierced with a sharp fork, drain them and peel them while they are still hot.

4. Scrape or peel the carrots clean and drop them in boiling salted water. Do not overcook. Drain when tender and set aside.

5. Drop the frozen peas into boiling salted water and cook very briefly, not more than a minute or a minute and a half. Drain and set aside.

6. When the vegetables have cooled, set aside a very small quantity of each (potatoes excepted), which you will need later for garnishing, and cut up the rest as follows: the green beans into pieces ⅜ inch long; the potatoes, carrots, and beets diced into ⅜-inch cubes. The peas, of course, stay whole. Cut up the capers also if these are not the very tiny ones. Put all the ingredients, including the cut-up gherkins or *cornichons*, in a mixing bowl.

7. Set aside half the shrimps. Cut up the rest and mix with the vegetables. Season with the olive oil, wine vinegar, and ½ teaspoon salt. Add 1 cup of the mayonnaise and mix thoroughly. Taste for salt and correct.

8. Turn the mixture over onto a serving platter. Shape it into a shallow, flat-topped, oval mound pressing with a rubber spatula to make sure the surface is smooth and uniform. Now spread the remaining mayonnaise over the entire surface of the mound. Use the spatula to make it as smooth and even as possible. Indentations or deep pockets will spoil the effect.

9. Now decorate the mound. Here is one way of doing it. Place a thin carrot disk on the center of the mound. Put a pea in the center of the carrot. Make a rosette of shrimps around the carrot, placing the shrimps on their side, nestling one around the other. Over the rest of the flat surface scatter flowers made using carrots for the center button, beets for the petals, green beans for the stems. Emboss the sides of the mound with the remaining shrimps, heads and tails imbedded in the salad, backs arching away. There are limitless ways in which you can use shrimps and vegetables to decorate this salad. Use your imagination! Caution: if you are preparing this many hours or a day in advance decorate

with beets at the last moment before serving. Their color has a tendency to run.

NOTE
This dish should be refrigerated at least 30 minutes before serving.

MENU SUGGESTIONS

This is a wonderfully cool dish for a summer day, splendid for a buffet, and a magnificent antipasto for an important meal.

When it is used as an antipasto, it can be followed by Fettuccine with White Clam Sauce (page 128), Trenette with Potatoes and Pesto (page 135) (omitting the potatoes), or Risotto with Clams (page 182). The second course should be a beautiful Fish Broiled the Adriatic Way (page 214) or Baked Striped Bass and Shellfish Sealed in Foil (page 201), substituting red snapper for the striped bass. It can also be handled as a second course. Precede it with Baked Oysters with Oil and Parsley (page 29), Broiled Mussels and Clams on the Half Shell (page 31), and/or Fettuccine with White Clam Sauce (page 128). Alone, it is an exquisite midnight snack with champagne, followed by A Bowl of Macerated Fresh Fruit (page 435). It is worth staying up for.

HERB-FLAVORED SEAFOOD SALAD

Insalata di mare

This may well be the most popular cold seafood dish in Italy. Every region has its own version, each slightly differing in ingredients and seasonings. The one thing they all have in common, and the most notable characteristic of this dish, is the delectable juxtaposition of the varied textures of such crustaceans as shrimps, *scampi*, and *cannocchie* and such mollusks as clams, mussels, scallops, squid, and octopus. You can try making your own combinations, as long as they result in a variety of delicate tastes and interesting textures.

For 6 persons

½ pound medium
  shrimps, preferably
  the very tiny
  shrimps from Maine
  or the Pacific, if
  available
7 tablespoons vinegar
Salt
2 medium carrots,
  peeled and washed
2 stalks celery, washed
2 medium yellow onions,
  peeled
½ pound squid, cleaned
  as directed on page
  219
1 pound octopus
  tentacles, peeled
  like the squid
¼ pound sea scallops
1 dozen mussels, cleaned
  as directed on page
  53
1 dozen littleneck clams,

the tiniest you can
  find, washed and
  scrubbed as directed
  on page 50
6 black Greek olives,
  pitted and quartered
6 green olives, pitted
  and quartered
⅓ cup broiled sweet red
  pepper (page 34),
  cut into strips ½
  inch wide
¼ cup lemon juice
½ cup olive oil
Freshly ground pepper,
  about 6 twists of the
  mill
1 good-sized clove garlic,
  lightly crushed with
  a knife handle and
  peeled
¼ teaspoon dried
  marjoram or ½
  teaspoon fresh

1. Wash the shrimps in cold water, but don't shell them. Bring 2 quarts of water with 2 tablespoons of vinegar and 1 teaspoon of salt to a boil. Drop the shrimps into the boiling water and cook for 2 minutes after the water returns to a boil. (Very tiny shrimps may take 1½ minutes or less, depending on size.) Drain. When cool, peel and devein the shrimps and cut into rounds ½ inch thick. If very, very tiny, leave whole. Set aside.

2. Using two separate pots, put 3 cups of water, 2 tablespoons of vinegar, 1 teaspoon of salt, 1 carrot, 1 celery stalk, and 1 onion in each pot. Bring to a boil. Add the squid and their tentacles to one pot and the octopus tentacles to the other, and cover. Cook at a slow, steady boil, testing the squid with a knife or sharp-pronged fork for tenderness after 20 minutes. Drain when tender, and when cool cut into strips ⅜ inch wide and 1½ inches long. Test the octopus tentacles for tenderness after 40 minutes.

Drain when tender, and when cool cut into disks ⅜ inch thick. Set aside.

3. Rinse the scallops in cold water. Bring 2 cups of water, with 1 tablespoon of vinegar and ½ teaspoon of salt, to a boil. Add the scallops and cook for 2 minutes after the water returns to a boil. Drain, and when cool cut into ½-inch cubes. Set aside.

4. In separate covered pans, heat the mussels and clams over high heat until their shells open. Detach the mussels from their shells and set aside. Detach the clams from their shells and rinse them one by one in their juice to remove any possible sand.

5. Combine all the seafood in a mixing bowl. Add the quartered olives, the red pepper, the lemon juice, and the olive oil and mix thoroughly. Taste and correct for salt, and add pepper, the crushed garlic clove, and the marjoram. Toss and mix all the ingredients thoroughly. Allow to rest for at least 2 hours, and retrieve the garlic before serving.

NOTE

You can prepare this salad many hours ahead of time, if you like, but it is best if it is not refrigerated. If you absolutely must refrigerate it, cover it tightly with plastic wrap. Remove from the refrigerator well in advance of serving so that it has time to come to room temperature.

MENU SUGGESTIONS

Its fragrance and cool, fresh taste make this an ideal summer dish. It can be served as antipasto for a multicourse fish dinner, or as a first course in a simpler dinner followed by Fish Broiled the Adriatic Way (page 214), Red Snapper with Sautéed Mushrooms (page 206), or Pan-Roasted Mackerel with Rosemary and Garlic (page 205).

RICE AND CHICKEN SALAD

Insalata di riso con pollo

Cold boiled rice and cheese are the basic ingredients of a number of salads that are very popular in Italy, particularly in the summer. They can be varied with the addition of cold chicken, shrimp, lobster, finely diced cold boiled beef or veal, or cold, diced hot dogs, which in Italy are called *wurstel*. These salads are never served after the second course, but are offered as an antipasto, a first course, or as the basis of a light hot-weather lunch.

For 4 to 6 persons

1 tablespoon salt
1 cup raw rice

DRESSING:

1 teaspoon Dijon OR
    German mustard
½ teaspoon salt
2 teaspoons red wine
    vinegar
6 tablespoons olive oil

½ cup finely diced Swiss
    cheese
¼ cup black olives,
    pitted and diced
2 tablespoons green
    olives, pitted and
    diced
¼ cup sweet red, yellow,
    or green pepper,
    seeded, cored, and
    diced

3 tablespoons diced sour
    gherkins, preferably
    French *cornichons*
1 whole breast of a
    young chicken,
    boiled and diced
    into ½-inch cubes

1. Bring 2 quarts of water to a boil. Add the 1 tablespoon salt; then drop in the rice. When the water returns to a boil, adjust the heat so that it simmers gently. Stir the rice, cover, and cook for 10 to 12 minutes or more, until *al dente*, firm to the bite.

2. Drain the rice, rinse in cold water, and drain thoroughly once more.

3. Put the mustard, 1 teaspoon salt, and vinegar into a salad bowl. Blend well with a fork, then add the oil, incorporating it into the mixture.

4. Add the drained rice and toss with the dressing.

5. Add the remaining ingredients, mix thoroughly, and serve cool, but not refrigerator cold.

THE CHEESE COURSE

Il Formaggio

Salad, cheese, and fruit, in that order, are the three courses that gradually cleanse the palate of the taste of cooking and bring an Italian meal to a natural close.

The simple, universal combination of cheese and good crusty bread is beyond discussion. But here are a few other ways in which cheese is served at an Italian table.

Parmesan

There is no more magnificent table cheese than a piece of aged, genuine *parmigiano-reggiano*, when it has not been allowed to dry out and it is a glistening, pale-straw color. It is frequently combined with the fruit course and eaten together with peeled ripe pears, or with grapes.

Gorgonzola

When it is soft, ripe, and mild, gorgonzola is one of the world's loveliest blue cheeses. Italians sometimes mash it into a paste with some sweet butter, or simply spread butter on the accompanying bread. (This is one of the rare occasions when Italians have bread and butter during a meal.) When gorgonzola is not overripe, it develops extraordinary flavor and texture if it is wrapped in aluminum foil and sent into a 250° oven for 2 to 3 minutes before serving.

Provola affumicata

This is smoked mozzarella, and looks exactly like any other mozzarella, except that it has a tanned skin. Remove the skin, slice the cheese into thin strips, and serve with good olive oil and a liberal amount of freshly ground pepper.

Cheese and olive oil

The combination of cheese and olive oil, as above, is a favorite one for both mild and pungent cheeses. A soft, white, full-flavored cheese called Robiola is mashed through the largest holes of a food mill, and the resulting strands are soaked in olive oil for a day or more. It can be refrigerated, but must be served at room temperature. There is no Robiola available here, but the same treatment is very effective with Taleggio or Fontina. I have found it to be astonishingly successful with Boursault cheese.

DESSERTS
AND FRUIT

I Dolci e la Frutta

Italians take their sweets and their apéritifs away from the dining table, at a pastry shop or café. Drinks, except for wine and liqueurs, do not belong on an Italian table, and desserts but rarely.

When the palate has traveled the peaks and valleys of an Italian meal with its first courses, second courses, side dishes, salads, and cheese, all it needs is the pause and refreshment of some fresh fruit. Of course there are circumstances in which a dessert does appear. These are almost always special occasions, either a religious holiday or a family celebration, such as a wedding. But these sweets, save those from Sicily, are, both in substance and appearance, modest, earthbound creations.

Italy does indeed produce some of the most luscious and beautiful desserts in Europe, as it has for centuries. But this is the work of pastry cooks. It is rarely done even in restaurant kitchens, and practically never at home.

Elaborate desserts do not have a significant part in Italian cooking or in the design of an Italian meal. For that reason there is no notice taken of them in this chapter. What you will find instead are some very plain but excellent traditional

411

cakes and puddings, coffee and fruit ices, and a very good coffee ice cream. There is also a simple home version of that delicious Tuscan specialty *zuccotto*, and what is probably the most elegant dessert in the home repertory, the chestnut-and-cream Monte Bianco.

In addition to desserts, there are two recipes for fresh fruit. In my opinion, these are the ones that take the cake, if that is the correct expression.

A RICE CAKE AND TWO PUDDINGS

Here are three traditional desserts based on such modest staples as rice, semolina, and bread. The rice cake is the most famous one of the three. It is a specialty of Bologna, where it was customary to serve it only at Easter, with lively rivalry among those families that claimed to have the most delicious cake. The recipe given here is an authentically venerable one, belonging to Bolognese friends, who have had it in their family for generations.

None of the three desserts is a very glamorous creation. Their virtue is in their nostalgic, homespun flavor, their plain, straightforward goodness that seldom palls or cloys.

RICE CAKE

Torta di riso

For 6 to 8 persons

1 quart milk
¼ teaspoon salt
2 or 3 strips of lemon
    peel, yellow part
    only
1¼ cups of granulated
    sugar
⅓ cup raw rice,
    preferably Italian
    Arborio rice
4 eggs plus 1 yolk
½ cup almonds, skinned,

toasted, and
chopped as directed
on page 432
⅓ cup candied citron or,
if not available,
candied lemon peel,
coarsely chopped
2 tablespoons rum
Butter
Fine, dry unflavored
    bread crumbs

1. Put the milk, salt, lemon peel, and sugar in a medium-sized saucepan and bring to a boil.

2. As the milk comes to a boil, add the rice and mix with a wooden spoon. Cook, uncovered, at the lowest possible simmer for 2¾ hours, stirring occasionally. The mixture should become a dense, pale-brown mush, into which much of the lemon peel will have been absorbed, but remove any large, visible pieces. Set aside and allow to cool.

3. Preheat the oven to 350°.

4. Beat the 4 whole eggs and the egg yolk in a large bowl until the yolks and whites are blended. Beat in the rice-and-milk mush a spoonful at a time. Add the chopped toasted almonds, the candied fruit, and the rum. Mix all the ingredients thoroughly.

5. Smear butter generously on the bottom and sides of a rectangular 6-cup cake pan and then sprinkle with bread crumbs, shaking off excess crumbs. Pour the mixture from the bowl into the pan and bake in the middle level of the preheated oven for 1 hour.

6. Remove the cake from the oven and let it cool to lukewarm. Put a platter over the pan, turn the pan over on the platter, give it a few vigorous taps, and lift it away. Serve the cake at least 24 hours after making it.

NOTE
This cake keeps improving for several days after it is made.
Do not refrigerate if you are using it the next day.

GLAZED SEMOLINA PUDDING

Budino di semolino caramellato

For 6 to 8 persons

½ cup plus ⅔ cup
    granulated sugar
Generous ⅓ cup small
    seedless raisins
2 cups milk
¼ teaspoon salt
⅓ cup semolina

1 tablespoon butter
1 tablespoon rum
¼ cup mixed candied
    fruit, chopped into
    ¼-inch pieces
Grated peel of 1 orange
All-purpose flour
2 eggs

1. Choose a 6-cup metal mold. (A simple cylindrical shape
is the easiest to work with.) Put the ½ cup sugar and 2
tablespoons water in the mold and bring to a boil over
medium heat. Do not stir, but tilt the mold forward and
backward from time to time until the syrup turns a light-
brown color. Remove from heat immediately and tip the
mold in all directions to give it an even coating of caramel.
Keep turning until the caramel congeals, then set aside.
2. Put the raisins in a bowl with enough lukewarm water
to cover and soak for at least 15 minutes.
3. Preheat the oven to 350°.
4. While the raisins are soaking, put the milk and salt
in a saucepan over low heat. When the milk is just about
to come to a boil, add all the semolina in a thin stream,
stirring rapidly with a wooden spoon. Continue cooking,
without ceasing to stir, until the semolina has thickened
sufficiently to come away from the sides of the pan as you
stir. Turn off the heat, but continue stirring for another 30
seconds to make sure the semolina won't stick.
5. Add the ⅔ cup sugar and stir, then add the butter
and rum and stir. Add the candied fruit and grated orange
peel, stirring them evenly into the mixture.
6. Drain the raisins and dry with a cloth. Put them in a
sieve and sprinkle them with flour while shaking the sieve.

When the raisins are lightly floured, mix them with the other ingredients in the pan.

7. Add the eggs, beating them very rapidly into the semolina mixture. Pour the mixture into the caramelized mold and bake in the middle level of the preheated oven for 40 minutes. Remove from the oven and cool.

8. When the pudding is cold, refrigerate for 10 minutes to give it extra firmness. To unmold, first very briefly warm the bottom and sides of the mold over low heat to loosen the caramel, then place a dish over the mold, turn the two upside down, and give the mold a few sharp taps and downward jerks. It should lift away easily.

GLAZED BREAD PUDDING

Budino di pane caramellato

For 6 to 8 persons

½ plus ⅓ cup granulated
    sugar
2½ cups roughly cut-up
    stale, lightly toasted,
    crustless, good-
    quality white bread
¼ cup butter
2 cups milk

½ cup small seedless
    raisins
All-purpose flour
¼ cup pine nuts
3 egg yolks
2 egg whites
¼ cup rum

1. Caramelize an 8-cup rectangular cake pan as directed in Step 1 of Glazed Semolina Pudding (opposite page), using the ½ cup granulated sugar.

2. Put the bread and the butter in a large mixing bowl.

3. Heat the milk, and as soon as it comes to a boil pour it over the bread and butter. Let the bread soak without mixing, and allow to cool.

4. Put the raisins in a bowl with enough warm water to cover and soak for at least 15 minutes.

5. Preheat the oven to 375°.

6. When the bread is cool, beat it with a whisk or a fork until it is an even, soft mass.

7. Drain the raisins, and squeeze them dry in a cloth. Put them in a sieve and dust them with flour while lightly shaking the sieve. Add them to the bowl with the bread mass.

8. Add the ⅓ cup sugar, pine nuts, and egg yolks to the bowl and mix all the ingredients thoroughly.

9. Beat the egg whites until they form stiff peaks, then fold them gently into the mixture in the bowl.

10. Pour the contents of the bowl into the caramelized pan and place it in the middle level of the preheated oven. After 1 hour turn the heat down to 300° and bake for 15 more minutes.

11. While the pudding is still warm, pierce it in several places with a toothpick, and gradually pour 2 tablespoons of the rum over it. When the rum has been absorbed, place a platter on the pan, turn the pan over on the platter, give it a few sharp downward jerks, and lift it away. Pierce the top of the pudding in several places with a toothpick and pour the rest of the rum over it.

NOTE

Plan to serve the pudding the day after you make it. It improves in texture and flavor as it rests. You can refrigerate it for several days, but always take it out sufficiently ahead of time to serve it at room temperature.

CRUMBLY CAKE

Torta Sbricciolona

For 6 persons

1⅓ cups all-purpose flour	2 egg yolks
⅔ cup cornmeal	¼ pound butter, softened to room temperature
⅝ cup granulated sugar	
Grated peel of 1 lemon	
4 ounces almonds, skinned and dried as directed on page 421 and ground to powder in a blender	1 tablespoon confectioners' sugar

1. Preheat the oven to 375°.

2. In a bowl mix the flour, the cornmeal, the granulated sugar, the grated lemon peel, and the powdered almonds. Add the two egg yolks and work the mixture with your hands

until it breaks up into little crumbly pellets. Add the softened butter, working it in with your fingers until it is completely incorporated into the mixture. (At first it may seem improbable that all the ingredients can ever be combined, but after mixing for a few minutes, you'll find that they do hang together, although forming a very crumbly dough.)

3. Smear the bottom of a 10-inch round baking pan with butter. Crumble the mixture through your fingers and into the pan until it is all uniformly distributed. Sprinkle the top with confectioners' sugar and place in the upper third of the preheated oven for about 40 minutes.

NOTE

This cake has a very crusty and crumbly consistency, which is part of its charm, but if you prefer to have it available in neat serving portions you can cut it into sections before it cools completely and hardens. It keeps beautifully for several days after baking.

This is an ideal cake to take with a glass of chilled dessert wine or in the afternoon with tea or coffee.

SWEET PASTRY FRITTERS

Chiacchiere della nonna

The dough for these fritters is cut into ribbons, then twisted into bows and fried in lard. For the sake of those who are put off by lard I've tried frying them in every other fat, but they do not really come off as well. There is nothing terribly subtle about them, but they are very nice to have at the end of a hearty, homey meal or at any time of the afternoon or evening with friends over a glass of *vin santo* or other dessert wine.

For 4 to 6 persons

1⅔ cups all-purpose
    flour
Lard
1 tablespoon granulated
    sugar
1 egg

2 tablespoons white wine
¼ teaspoon salt
Confectioners' sugar

1. Combine the flour, ¼ cup lard, 1 tablespoon sugar, the egg, wine, and salt and knead into a smooth, soft dough. Put the dough in a bowl, cover, and allow to rest at least 15 minutes.

2. Roll out the dough with a rolling pin to a thickness of ⅛ inch, then cut into ribbons about 5 inches long and ½ inch wide. Twist into simple bowlike shapes.

3. In a skillet, over high heat, melt enough lard to come 1 inch up the sides of the pan. When it is quite hot, add the pastry bows. (Do not put in any more at one time than will fit loosely in the skillet.) When they are a nice, deep gold on one side, turn them over. When both sides are done, transfer to paper towels to drain, and sprinkle liberally with confectioners' sugar. They may be served hot or cold.

NOTE

If kept in a dry place, they maintain their crispness for several days.

APPLE FRITTERS

Frittelle di mele renette

For 4 persons

3 apples, any firm, sweet eating variety	⅔ cup all-purpose flour
¼ cup granulated sugar	Vegetable oil, enough to come ½ inch up the side of the skillet
2 tablespoons rum	
1 lemon peel, grated	Confectioners' sugar

1. Peel the apples, core them, and cut them into slices ⅜ inch thick. (The slices should look like miniature cartwheels, each with a hole in the middle.)

2. Put ¼ cup sugar, the rum, and lemon peel into a bowl and add the apple slices. Let the apples macerate for at least 1 hour.

3. Make a batter of the flour and 1 cup water, according to the directions in Step 2 of Zucchini Fried in Flour-and-Water Batter (page 377).

4. Pour enough oil into a skillet to come at least ½ inch up the side of the pan. Turn the heat on high.

5. Pat the apple slices dry with paper towels. Dip them in the batter, and when the oil is very hot slip them into

the skillet. (Do not put in any more at one time than will fit loosely in the skillet.) When they are golden brown on one side, turn them. When both sides are nicely browned, transfer the fritters to paper towels to drain. Sprinkle with confectioners' sugar. Serve hot.

RUM-AND-COFFEE-FLAVORED CHOCOLATE LAYER CAKE

Il Diplomatico

The marvelous thing about this dessert is that it requires no baking, and you can put in a little less rum or a little more chocolate, add or subtract an egg, and you'll still come up with a successful and delicious cake. It is practically foolproof. In its easygoing approach and its knack for transforming simple ingredients and procedures into a most enjoyable concoction, it is quintessentially Italian. It will, however, lose character if you use the blander American coffee instead of Italian espresso.

For 6 to 8 persons

4 eggs

1 teaspoon granulated sugar

THE RUM MIXTURE (to be repeated as often as necesary using the same proportions):

5 tablespoons rum
1¼ cups strong espresso coffee (see How to Make Italian Coffee, page 437)

5 teaspoons granulated sugar
5 tablespoons water

1 sixteen-ounce pound cake

6 ounces semisweet chocolate drops OR chopped-up squares

THE FROSTING:

4 ounces semisweet chocolate drops OR chopped-up squares
1 teaspoon butter

Whipped cream and maraschino cherries OR walnuts for garnish

1. Preheat the oven to 250°.

2. Separate the eggs and beat the yolks together with 1 teaspoon of the sugar until the yolks turn pale yellow.

3. Line a 9-inch baking pan or any equivalent container with buttered waxed paper, extending it up the sides and above the rim. Combine the rum, coffee, 5 teaspoons sugar, and 5 tablespoons water in a soup dish. Cut the pound cake into slices ¼ inch thick. Soak each slice in the rum-and-coffee mixture and place it on the bottom and along the sides of the baking pan, until it is completely lined with rum-soaked pound cake. (You've got to be quick about dipping the slices in and out of the mixture before they get too soggy to handle.) If you run out of rum mixture, prepare more, following the same proportions.

4. In a small saucepan, melt the chocolate in the oven. (I have found this the easiest and least problem-fraught method of melting chocolate, especially when using chocolate drops. If you have another method you are happy with, by all means use it.) Mix the melted chocolate into the beaten egg yolks. Whip the egg whites until they form stiff peaks. First combine 1 tablespoon of the beaten egg whites with the egg yolks and chocolate, mixing normally, then add the rest of the egg whites, folding them with care into the mixture.

5. Spoon the entire mixture over the rum-soaked pound cake in the pan. Cover the mixture with more slices of pound cake dipped in the rum-and-coffee soak. (Don't worry about how the cake looks at this point. What you are looking at is the bottom, and the rest will be completely covered by frosting.) Refrigerate overnight.

6. The following day turn the pan over on a flat serving platter, holding your thumbs on the protruding waxed paper. The pan should lift away easily, leaving the paper-covered cake on the platter. Carefully peel off the waxed paper. The cake is now ready for the frosting.

7. The customary frosting for *il diplomatico* is chocolate. In a preheated 250° oven, melt 4 ounces of chocolate in a small saucepan together with 1 teaspoon of butter. Cover the entire exposed surface of the cake with the melted chocolate. Refrigerate for an hour or less until the choclate hardens. Decorate with curls of whipped cream topped with maraschino cherries and/or walnuts. Since you can prepare

il diplomatico a week or ten days ahead of time, add the whipped-cream decorations just before serving.

NOTE

For a lighter texture and more delicate taste you can substitute whipped cream for the chocolate frosting. Whip 1½ cups very cold heavy cream together with 2 teaspoons of granulated sugar until it is stiff. Cover the entire exposed surface of the cake with cream. Decorate with candied fruit arranged in simple patterns. Cream is always best when freshly whipped, but, if necessary, it can be refrigerated for one or two days.

ZUCCOTTO

Zuccotto is a dome-shaped Florentine specialty inspired, it is said, by the cupola of Florence's Duomo. Whether that is true or not, I don't know, but it is a fact that almost anything hemispherical seems to remind Florentines of Brunelleschi's ever-present dome. Zuccotto used to be found only in Florentine cafés and pastry shops, but it is now produced and distributed all over Italy. It requires no baking or any special confectionary skills, yet it is an extremely presentable and successful dessert.

For 6 persons

2 ounces shelled, unskinned almonds	2 tablespoons maraschino liqueur
2 ounces shelled whole filberts OR hazelnuts	2 tablespoons Cointreau
1 ten- to twelve-ounce pound cake	5 ounces semisweet chocolate drops
3 tablespoons Cognac or other grape brandy	2 cups very cold heavy whipping cream
	¾ cup confectioners' sugar

1. Preheat the oven to 400°.
2. Drop the almonds into boiling water and boil for 20 seconds. Drain. With your fingertips, squeeze the almonds

out of their skins. Place the peeled almonds on a baking sheet and put in the oven to dry for about 2 minutes. Remove from the oven and chop them roughly. Set aside.

3. Place the filberts on a baking sheet and put in the oven for 5 minutes. Remove them from the oven and rub off as much of their skin as you can with a rough, dry towel. (Don't worry if it doesn't all rub off.) Chop roughly and set aside.

4. Reset the oven thermostat to 250°.

5. Choose a 1½-quart, perfectly round-bottomed hemispherical bowl, and line it with a layer of damp cheesecloth.

6. Cut the pound cake in slices ⅜ inch thick. Cut each slice on the diagonal, making of it two triangular sections. There will be crust on two sides of the triangle. Moisten each section with a sprinkling of the cordials and place it against the inside of the bowl, its narrowest end at the bottom, until the inside of the bowl is completely lined with moistened sections of pound cake. Where one side of the section has crust on it, have it meet the crustless side of the section next to it, because when the dessert is unmolded the thin lines of crust running down the sides should form a sunburst pattern. Make sure that the entire inside surface of the bowl is entirely lined with cake. If there are any gaps, fill them in with small pieces of moistened cake. (Don't worry about the appearance of the dessert. A little irregularity is part of its charm.)

7. Split or coarsely chop 3 ounces of the chocolate drops. Then, in a chilled mixing bowl, whip the cold heavy cream together with the powdered sugar until it is stiff. Mix into it the chopped almonds, filberts, and chocolate drops. Divide the mixture into two equal parts. Set aside one half and spoon the other half into the cake-lined bowl, spreading it evenly over the entire cake surface. This should leave a still unfilled cavity in the center of the bowl.

8. Melt the remaining 2 ounces of chocolate drops in a small pan in the 250° oven. Fold the melted chocolate into the remaining half of the whipped-cream mixture. Spoon it into the bowl until the cavity is completely filled. Even off the top of the bowl, cutting off any protruding pieces of cake. Cut some more ⅜-inch slices of pound cake, moisten them with the remaining cordials, and use them to seal

off the top of the bowl. Trim the edges until they are perfectly round. Cover the bowl with plastic wrap and refrigerate overnight, or up to 1 or 2 days.

9. Cover the bowl with a flat serving dish and turn it upside down. Lift off the bowl and carefully remove the cheesecloth. Serve cold.

PURÉED CHESTNUT AND CHOCOLATE MOUND

Monte Bianco

This is an especially lovely winter dessert. The mound of puréed chestnuts and chocolate topped with whipped cream is supposed to recall Monte Bianco, a mountain in the Italian Alps whose upper slopes are always snow clad. It can be decorated in many charming ways, using those paper or balsa-wood figures of skiers, Santas, and firs that are readily found in party-supply shops. It cannot be prepared too long in advance because the chestnuts turn tart in taste. It can certainly be prepared in the morning for the evening, however.

For 6 persons

1 pound fresh chestnuts
Milk, enough to cover
A tiny pinch of salt
6 ounces semisweet
    chocolate drops OR
    chopped-up squares

¼ cup rum
2 cups very cold heavy
    whipping cream
2 teaspoons granulated
    sugar

1. Wash the chestnuts in cold water. Chestnuts have a flat side and a round bellying side. Being careful not to cut into the chestnut meat itself, make a horizontal cut in each chestnut starting on one end of the flat side, coming across the entire width of the round side and terminating just past the other edge of the flat side; the cut should not go all the way around and meet. (This method loosens both the shell and the inside skin while the chestnuts boil and makes peeling them a fast and simple task.)

2. Place the chestnuts in a pot with abundant cold water, cover, bring to a boil, and cook for 25 minutes. Peel the chestnuts while still very warm, pulling them out of the hot water a few at a time, and making sure to remove both the outer shell and the wrinkled inner skin.

3. Preheat the oven to 250°.

4. Put the peeled chestnuts in a saucepan with just enough milk to cover, and a pinch of salt. Boil slowly, uncovered, for 15 minutes more or less until the milk is entirely absorbed. The chestnuts should be tender but not mushy.

5. Put the chocolate drops or chopped-up chocolate squares in a small saucepan and place in the 250° oven until melted.

6. Purée the chestnuts through a food mill into a bowl and mix with the melted chocolate and the rum. Pass this mixture through the mill again, using the largest holes available, letting it drop directly onto a round serving platter. Start dropping it close to the dish with a circular movement, beginning at the edge of the dish, and as it piles up gradually move upward and toward the center. You should end up with a cone-shaped mound. Do not pat it or attempt to shape it.

7. Whip the cream with the sugar. Use half the whipped cream to cover the top of your mound, coming about two-thirds of the way down. It should have the natural look of a partially snow-covered mountain, so do not strive for smoothness and regularity, but let the cream come down the mound at random in peaks and hollows. When serving the dessert, bring the remaining half of the whipped cream to the table for anyone who would like to have a bit more "snow" on his portion.

COLD CHOCOLATE FOAM

Spuma di cioccolata

For 6 persons

6 ounces semisweeet
    chocolate drops
2 teaspoons granulated
    sugar
4 eggs, separated
¼ cup strong espresso
    coffee (see How to
    Make Italian Coffee,
    page 437)

2 tablespoons rum
⅔ cup very cold heavy
    whipping cream

1. In a 250° oven, melt the chocolate in a small saucepan.
2. Add 2 teaspoons of sugar to the egg yolks and beat with a whisk or the electric mixer until they become pale yellow. By hand mix in the melted chocolate, the coffee, and the rum.
3. Whip the cream in a cold bowl until it is stiff, then fold it into the chocolate-and-egg-yolk mixture.
4. Whip the egg whites until they form stiff peaks, then fold into the mixture. When all the ingredients have been gently but well combined by hand, spoon the mixture into glass or crystal goblets, custard cups, or any other suitable and attractive serving container. Refrigerate overnight. (This dessert can be prepared even 3 or 4 days ahead of time, but after 24 hours it tends to wrinkle and lose some of its creaminess.)

NOTE
Don't exceed the recommended amounts of rum and coffee, or you may find a liquid deposit at the bottom of the dessert.

ZABAIONE

Zabaglione

Zabaione must not cook over direct heat. It is necessary to have a double boiler. Since it is desirable that the upper part have a heavy bottom, you might use an enameled cast-iron saucepan or other heavy ware and hold it over water simmering in any other kind of pot. Be sure to choose a large enough pot—the mixture increases greatly in volume as you beat.

For 6 persons

4 egg yolks	½ cup dry Marsala
¼ cup granulated sugar	

1. Put the egg yolks and the sugar in your heavy-bottomed pot and whip them with a wire whisk (or an electric mixer) until they are pale yellow and creamy.

2. In a slightly larger second pot, bring water to the brink of a simmer, not a boil.

3. Place the pot with the whipped-up egg yolks over the second pot. Add the Marsala and continue beating. The mixture, which will begin to foam, and then swell into a light, soft mass, is ready when it forms soft mounds.

4. Spoon it into goblets, cups, or champagne glasses and serve immediately.

FRIED SWEET CREAM

Crema fritta

This cream requires substantially more flour than would a regular custard cream, otherwise it would not be firm enough for frying. In order for the flour to become evenly and smoothly blended, the cream must cook very slowly over very low heat, and you will have to stir virtually without interruption the entire time it is cooking. It takes patience, but it is not very hard work, and part of the time you can let your mind run on other thoughts while you are doing it. It is best to prepare it in the morning for the evening, or even a day ahead of time.

For 6 persons

3 eggs
⅓ cup granulated sugar
½ cup all-purpose flour
2 cups milk
2 small strips lemon
  peel, yellow part
  only

1 cup fine, dry
  unflavored bread
  crumbs, spread on a
  dish or on waxed
  paper
Vegetable oil, enough to
  come 1 inch up the
  side of the skillet

1. Off the heat, in the upper part of a double boiler, beat 2 of the eggs together with the sugar until the eggs are well blended and the sugar almost completely dissolved.

2. Still off heat, add the flour to the eggs 1 tablespoon at a time, mixing thoroughly, until the eggs have absorbed all the flour.

3. While you are doing this, bring the milk to the edge of a boil in another pan. When the eggs and flour have been thoroughly mixed, add the hot milk very gradually, about ¼ cup at a time, beating it into the mixture. When all the milk has been well blended with the eggs and flour, add the lemon peel.

4. Unite the two parts of the double boiler and put it over very low heat. The water in the lower half must come to only the gentlest of simmers. Begin to stir, slowly but steadily. Fifteen minutes after the water in the lower pan has started to simmer, you may raise the heat slightly. Continue cooking and stirring for about 25 minutes more. When done, the cream should be thick and smooth and have no taste of flour.

5. Pour the cream onto a slightly moistened large platter, spreading it to a thickness of about 1 inch, and let it cool completely. (If you are going to use it the following day, refrigerate it, when cool, under plastic wrap.)

6. When the cream is cold, cut it into diamond-shaped pieces about 2 inches long. Beat the remaining egg lightly in a soup dish or small bowl. Dredge the pieces in bread crumbs; then dip them in egg; then dredge them in bread crumbs again.

7. Heat the oil in the skillet over high heat. When the oil is very hot, slide in the pieces of cream. Fry them until a dark, golden crust forms on one side; then turn them and

do the other side. When there is a nice crust all around, transfer them to paper towels to drain. Serve piping hot.

Aside from its role in Mixed Fried Meat, Vegetables, Cheese, Cream, and Fruit (page 322), fried cream is an excellent accompaniment for many single meat courses. Serve it somewhat as you might a potato croquette. It goes beautifully with Sautéed Breaded Veal Chops (page 258) or Breaded Veal Cutlets, Milan Style (page 260), Fried Breaded Calf's Liver (page 288), of Baby Lamb Chops Fried in Parmesan Cheese Batter (page 272). It is also, of course, a delectable hot dessert after any meal.

VANILLA ICE CREAM WITH MACAROONS

Gelato agli amaretti

For this preparation you should use imported Italian macaroons. They are packed two to a wrapper, and that is why the quantities given below are for double macaroons. If you cannot find Italian macaroons where you live, you can order them from the specialty food shops of many large-city department stores. They keep crisp almost indefinitely.

For 4 persons

8 double macaroons, ground

5 tablespoons strong espresso coffee (see How to Make Italian Coffee, page 437)

1 tablespoon ground dry espresso coffee, powdered in a blender

1 pint vanilla ice cream

2 double macaroons soaked in 1 tablespoon rum for garnish

1. Mix the ground macaroons with the brewed coffee until the macaroons are thoroughly moistened. Mix in the coffee powder.

2. Line a small dome-shaped bowl with lightly buttered waxed paper. Spread a little less than half the ice cream

along the sides and bottom of the bowl. Spread the macaroon mixture over the ice cream, then cover with the rest of the ice cream. Place in the freezer for at least 4 hours before serving.

3. To serve, turn the bowl over on a plate, lift away the bowl, and gently remove the waxed paper. Garnish, pressing the four parts of the rum-soaked macaroons into the sides of the ice cream. When cut into 4 portions, there should be a macaroon to each portion.

VANILLA ICE CREAM WITH POWDERED COFFEE AND SCOTCH

Gelato spazzacamino

This is not just window dressing for plain ice cream. It is a combination of unexpected textures and flavors that act upon each other with extraordinary success. Everyone must have a favorite way of serving ice cream. This one is mine.

The doubly roasted taste of espresso coffee is essential here. Grind regular espresso coffee in the blender at high speed until it is a fine powder. You can make a substantial quantity at one time and keep it in a tightly closed jar.

For 1 person

2 scoops vanilla ice cream	1 tablespoon Scotch whisky
2 teaspoons ground dry espresso coffee, powdered in a blender	

Spoon the ice cream into individual shallow bowls, sprinkle 2 teaspoons of coffee powder over each serving, and over it pour the whisky.

NOTE
The quantities of coffee and whisky given are suggestions. Regulate them according to taste.

ESPRESSO COFFEE ICE CREAM WITH HOT CHOCOLATE SAUCE

Gelato di caffè con la cioccolata calda

For 6 persons

4 egg yolks	1 cup heavy cream
⅔ cup granulated sugar	
1½ cups espresso coffee, made using milk in place of water (see How to Make Italian Coffee, page 437)	

THE CHOCOLATE SAUCE:

⅔ cup heavy cream	4 teaspoons granulated
2 tablespoons cocoa	sugar

1. Beat the egg yolks and sugar until they become a pale-yellow cream.

2. Combine the coffee and heavy cream and mix into the beaten egg yolks until uniformly blended. Warm the mixture in a saucepan over low heat, stirring constantly until it swells to nearly twice its original volume.

3. Pour into freezer trays without the ice-cube grids. When cool, stir thoroughly and place in the freezer for at least 5 hours. Stir every 30 to 40 minutes.

4. Just before serving, prepare the sauce by combining the heavy cream, cocoa, and sugar in a small saucepan and stirring it over low heat for about 6 minutes, or until it becomes a smooth, thick cream.

5. Spoon the ice cream, which should be quite firm but not rock hard, from the freezer trays into individual bowls. Pour the hot sauce over each serving and serve immediately.

COFFEE ICE WITH WHIPPED CREAM

Granita di caffè con panna

A *granita* is a dessert ice made of very fine-grained frozen crystals of coffee or fruit syrup. By far the most popular *granita* in Italy is *granita di caffè*, coffee ice. It is usually taken at a café after lunch, and, as you sit outdoors on a steamy afternoon watching life flow by, you let the *granita* melt between tongue and palate, spoonful by spoonful, until the inside of your mouth feels like an ice cavern dense with coffee flavor.

It should go without saying that you use only Italian espresso coffee to make *granita di caffè*.

For 6 to 8 persons

2 cups espresso coffee (see How to Make Italian Coffee, page 437)

2 tablespoons sugar, or more to taste

Freshly whipped cream, made with 1 cup heavy cream and 2 teaspoons sugar (optional)

1. Put all the coffee in a pitcher and dissolve the sugar in it while it is still hot. Taste and correct for sweetness. Do not make it very sweet because sugar weakens its flavor.

2. Remove the ice-cube grids from two freezer trays and pour the coffee into the trays. When the coffee is cold, put the trays in the freezer and set a timer at 15 minutes.

3. When the timer rings, remove the trays from the freezer and stir the contents to break up the ice crystals. (Ice forms first at the sides of the tray. It is important that you break this up thoroughly each time before it becomes solid.) Return to the freezer, and set the timer again for 15 minutes. When the timer rings repeat the operation and reset the timer for 10 minutes. The next time set the timer for 8 minutes, and continue to stir the coffee every 8 minutes for the next 3 hours. If you are not ready to serve the *granita* immediately, continue stirring every 8 minutes until just

before serving. Serve in a glass, goblet, or crystal bowl, topped with whipped cream, if desired.

NOTE

By exactly the same procedure, you can make orange ice (*granita di arancia*), using 2 cups freshly squeezed orange juice and 1 tablespoon granulated sugar, and lemon ice (*granita di limone*), using ½ cup freshly squeezed lemon juice, 1½ cups water, and ¼ cup granulated sugar.

CARAMELIZED ALMOND CANDY

Croccante

Croccante is the same thing as French praline, except that it is usually less sweet. It is an excellent candy, so very much better than commercial brittle. Crushed or powdered it is marvelous in desserts or as topping for ice cream. In an airtight jar or tightly wrapped in aluminum foil it keeps almost indefinitely.

Yield: About 2½ cups, if crushed or powdered

6 ounces (about 1½ cups) shelled, unskinned almonds	1 heaping cup granulated sugar A potato, peeled

1. Preheat the oven to 450°.
2. Drop the almonds in boiling water. Twenty seconds after the water returns to a boil, drain the almonds. Squeeze the almonds out of their skins with your fingers and spread them on a baking sheet. Toast them in the preheated oven for 6 minutes, until they are a light brown. (Make sure they don't burn.) If you prefer to do them under the broiler, watch them closely—it will take only a few seconds. Chop the toasted almonds until the slivers are half the size of a grain of rice.
3. Put the sugar and ¼ cup water in a small, preferably thin-bottomed pan. Melt the sugar over medium-high heat, without stirring but tilting the pan occasionally. When the melted sugar becomes a light golden color, add the chopped almonds and stir constantly until the almonds

turn a deep tawny gold. Pour out *immediately* on a greased sheet of aluminum foil. Cut the potato in half and use the flat side to spread out the hot mixture to a thickness of ⅛ inch.

4. If you want to use it as candy, cut it into 2-inch diamond shapes before it cools. When cool, lift off and wrap each piece tightly in aluminum foil. Store in a dry cupboard, where it will keep indefinitely. (For use in desserts, it can be ground coarsely in a mortar or pulverized in a blender when it has cooled. Store in an airtight jar. Do not refrigerate.)

FRESH FRUIT WHIPS

Frullati di frutta

These are not served in Italy after meals, but they are a refreshing and nourishing accompaniment to a light summer snack. Italians, who, as a rule, eat nothing for breakfast, will sometimes have a *frullato* in the middle of the morning to tide them over until lunch. If you are traveling in Italy with the children and are enjoying an afternoon Campari at a sidewalk café, this is a nice refreshment to order for them. If they are very young children, you can ask the waiter to omit the liqueur.

For 2 persons

⅔ cup milk
1 banana or a
    comparable quantity
    of fresh
    strawberries,
    peaches, apricots,
    etc. (see note below)

1½ teaspoons sugar
3 tablespoons crushed ice
2 tablespoons maraschino
    liqueur

Whip all the ingredients in the blender at high speed until the ice has completely dissolved. Serve immediately.

NOTE
All the fruit except the banana must be washed in cold water, and all except berries must be peeled. Peaches and apricots, of course, must be pitted.

MACERATED ORANGE SLICES

Arance tagliate

Among all the ways in which a meal can be brought to a happy close, there is none, I think, that surpasses a dish of sliced oranges. Their bright, joyous color is an instant promise of refreshment, which they maintain by loosening from our taste buds the thick traces of the preceding courses, leaving nothing but happy memories and a fragrantly clean palate.

For 4 persons

6 eating oranges, such as navel, temple, or tange-orange
Grated peel of 1 medium lemon

5 tablespoons granulated sugar
Juice of ½ medium lemon

1. Peel just four of the oranges, using a very sharp knife. Take care to remove all the white spongy pulp and also as much as possible of the thin skin beneath.

2. Cut the oranges horizontally into thin slices about ⅜ inch thick. Pick out any seeds. Put the slices into a shallow serving bowl or deep platter and then grate the lemon peel into the bowl. (Avoid grating the white pulp beneath the peel.) Add the sugar. Squeeze the other two oranges and add their juice to the bowl. Add the lemon juice. Turn the orange slices over a few times, being careful not to break them up. Cover the bowl with a dish and refrigerate for at least 4 hours, or even overnight. Serve chilled, turning the slices once or twice in the macerating liquid just before serving.

NOTE
You may add more sugar if you like the oranges much sweeter. Some people add 2 or 3 tablespoons of maraschino or Curaçao just before serving. I do not because I find it interferes with the fragrance of the lemon peel. Try it both ways, if you like, and decide for yourself.

PINEAPPLE SLICES WITH MARASCHINO

Ananas al maraschino

It isn't without some embarrassment that I include this recipe for what is little more than pineapple slices out of a can. It is quite popular with many Italian restaurants, and before coming to this country I was certain that it was commonly served by all Americans. Pineapple is certainly not Italian; in Italy it is, in fact, very expensive canned and prohibitive fresh. When I first started serving it here, however, I discovered that people were startled by this version. It doesn't really have any pretensions, but if you like pineapple you might want to try this simple Italian approach.

For 1 person

2 slices canned
    pineapple, with 2
    tablespoons of their
    syrup
1 maraschino cherry

1 tablespoon maraschino
    liqueur, or more to
    taste

Put 2 slices of pineapple in an individual dish or saucer. Place the cherry in the center, in the hole. Add 2 tablespoons of the syrup from the can, and 1 tablespoon of maraschino liqueur. Refrigerate for 2 hours or more. Serve chilled.

A BOWL OF MACERATED FRESH FRUIT

Macedonia di frutta

The name *macedonia* is borrowed from a region in southern Europe that includes parts of Yugoslavia, Bulgaria, and Greece. It is an area known for the mixture of races that populates it, and its name is well taken for this dish, whose success depends upon the variety of its components.

The indispensable ingredients are apples, pears, bananas, and orange and lemon juice. To these you should add a generous sampling of seasonal fruits, choosing them for the diversity of their colors, fragrances, and textures. In Italy, when *macedonia* is made in summer, we always add peaches. Italian peaches are silken in texture and immensely fragrant. I have never found comparable peaches here, but there is a thoroughly acceptable substitute in ripe mango. If it is locally available, I strongly recommend your using it.

For 8 persons or more

1½ cups freshly
  squeezed orange
  juice
Grated peel of 1 medium
  lemon, yellow part
  only
2 to 3 tablespoons freshly
  squeezed lemon
  juice, or to taste
2 apples
2 pears
2 bananas

1½ pounds of assorted
  other fruit, such as
  cherries, apricots,
  nectarines, plums,
  peaches, grapes,
  mango, cantaloupe,
  honeydew melon
6 tablespoons to ½ cup
  granulated sugar,
  according to taste
½ cup maraschino
  liqueur (optional)

1. In a large serving bowl (a tureen or punch bowl) put the orange juice, the grated lemon peel, and the lemon juice.

2. If you are using grapes, wash them and detach them from the clusters. Add seedless grapes whole to the bowl. Cut the other varities in half and remove the seeds before adding them to the bowl. The cherries, too, must be pitted before they are put in.

3. All the other fruit must also be washed, then peeled, cored or pitted, and cut into ½-inch cubes. Add each fruit to the bowl as you cut it, so that the juice in the bowl will keep it from discoloring. (Remember, do not put in any unpeeled fruit, except for grapes, cherries, and berries.)

4. When all the fruit is in the bowl, add the sugar and the optional maraschino. Mix thoroughly. Cover the bowl with a dish and refrigerate for at least 4 hours or even overnight. Serve chilled, mixing three or four times before serving.

NOTE

For full flavor and fragrance, fruit should be ripe. Don't use any overripe fruit, however, or it will become mushy. It is better not to use strawberries for the same reason. If you really want strawberries in the dish, add them just 30 minutes before serving.

HOW TO MAKE ITALIAN COFFEE

Italian coffee has so many admirers throughout the world that it does not need additional appreciation from these pages. Aside from its merits as a drink, however, it is by far the best coffee to use in any dessert in which coffee is an ingredient, and for Italian desserts in particular it has absolutely no substitute.

Making Italian coffee at home is incredibly easy and quick. All you need is double-roasted espresso coffee and an Italian coffeepot. All Italian coffeepots, whatever their special design might be, share the same working principle. Water is heated to a boil in one chamber of the pot, then filtered through the ground coffee and collected in a second, serving chamber.

The traditional coffeepot, which may or may not have been invented in Naples, is known in Italy nonetheless as *la napoletana*. Neapolitans, in fact, consider themselves supreme custodians of the secret of good coffee, and, without any doubt, no one in Italy makes better coffee.

HOW TO MAKE COFFEE WITH THE *NAPOLETANA*

1. Fill the bottom half of the pot, the one *without* the spout, with cold water up to the tiny escape hole near the top.
2. Insert the metal filter for the coffee. Fill with coffee until

The Napoletana

The Moka

it forms a mound, but do not tamp the coffee down. Always fill the filter to capacity.

3. Tightly screw on the top of the filter.

4. Place the empty half of the pot, with the spout pointing *downward*, over the filter, and snap the pot shut, pushing upper and lower halves together.

5. Place the pot over medium heat exactly as you assembled it, with the spout on top, pointing downward.

6. When you see steam leaking out of the escape hole on the side, turn the pot over and turn off the heat. The spout should now be at the bottom, pointing upward. It will take

several minutes for all the water to filter through into the bottom chamber.

NOTE
Some Neapolitans do not assemble the pot in advance. First they boil the water in the lower half of the pot, then they insert the coffee filter, attach the other half of the pot, and turn the pot over. Their explanation is that, by assembling the pot in advance, the heat of the water before it reaches a boil dissipates some of the coffee's flavor.

HOW TO MAKE COFFEE WITH THE *MOKA*

There is another, more modern type of pot that works faster and also makes first-rate coffee. In Italy it is known as *la moka*.

1. Fill the bottom chamber of the pot with cold water up to the small, round safety valve.
2. Put in the coffee filter and fill exactly as with the *napoletana*, up to capacity, forming a mound, but without pressing the coffee down.
3. Screw on the top of the filter.
4. Screw the upper half of the pot on tightly and place over medium heat. (In this system, hot water is drawn up through the filter and into the upper chamber, so that there is no turning over to do.) For best results, keep the lid open.
5. When the coffee begins to emerge, lower the heat to a minimum. (By reducing the speed at which the water seeps through the coffee, you concentrate the flavor.) When the chamber is nearly filled, close the lid. When you hear the coffee sputtering, it is all done. Turn off the heat.

NOTE
Italian coffee should never be reheated.

AFTERTHOUGHTS

What people do with food is an act that reveals how they construe the world. It is no coincidence that the same country that produced the Confucian system of ethical conduct imposes on the ingredients of its cooking a rigid discipline of cut and shape. The work of art that is a Japanese meal is a natural legacy of the only society where aesthetics, at one time, entirely governed life. And the achievement of classic French cuisine, its logic, the marvelous subtlety of its discoveries, could have occurred only in the country of Descartes and Proust.

The world of Italians is not a phenomenon that needs to be subdued, reshaped, arranged in logical patterns. It is not a challenge to be won. It is there simply to be enjoyed, mostly on its own terms. What we find in the cooking of Italy is a serene relationship between man and the sources of his existence, a long-established intimacy between the human and natural orders, a harmonious fusion of man's skills and nature's gifts. The Italian comes to his table with the same open heart with which a child falls into his mother's arms, with the same easy feeling of being in the right place.

The essential quality of Italian food can be defined as fidelity to its ingredients, to their taste, color, shape, and freshness. In the Italian kitchen, ingredients are not treated as promising but untutored elements that need to be corrected through long and intricate manipulation and refined by the ultimate polish of a sauce. The methods of Italian cooking are not intended to improve an ingredient's character, but rather to allow it as much free and natural development as the tasteful balance of a dish will permit. The taste of Italian cooking is discreetly measured but frank. Flavors are present and undisguised, but never overbearing. Pastas are never swamped by sauce. Portions are never so swollen in size as to tax our capacity for enjoyment.

Because Italian cooking simply does not come off without

440

raw materials of the freshest and choicest quality, it is sometimes the most costly of the world's cuisines to produce. But it is probably the one whose satisfactions are the most accessible to the home cook. Although a few of the recipes require a little practice and some manual dexterity, there is not a single dish in this book that is beyond the competence of any moderately alert person. Italian cooking techniques are disciplined by tradition, but they allow an individual approach to food that is spontaneous, immediate, and uncomplicated. Italian cooking does not lend itself well to the regimentation of professional chefs. When Aristotle said that a work of art should imitate the motions of the mind and not an external arrangement of facts, he was anticipating a definition of the art of the Italian home cook. In Italy the source of the very best Italian food is the home kitchen. There is no reason why this should not be equally true here.

And so this book comes to a close. And with it, a long year's work, the exasperating and sometimes almost intolerable task of fixing the fluid intuitions of half a lifetime of cooking within the step-by-step frames of a recipe. Although frequently I felt like a gymnast forced to retrace his twists and somersaults in slow motion, I wrote, tasted, rewrote each recipe until it was as clear and reliable as I was able to make it. I hope they will work as well in your kitchen as they have in mine. I cannot expect from anyone a total conversion to Italian cooking, but if even a few of these dishes together with their proper placement within an Italian meal become a natural part of your life at table, I shall feel handsomely rewarded for my efforts.

INDEX

About the Author

Marcella Hazan was born in the fishing village of Cesenatico, Italy, and now divides her time between New York and Rome with her husband, author and wine critic, Victor Hazan. After a first career as a scientist, she started giving cooking lessons and has become America's premier teacher of Italian cuisine. She has toured widely, taught on the West Coast, and two years ago established a summer school for Americans in Bologna. She is also the author of MORE CLASSIC ITALIAN COOKING, and is currently at work on a new collection of recipes.